DAUGHTER OF THE CROCODILE

Duncan Sprott was born in 1952. He is the author of *1784, The Clopton Hercules, Our Lady of the Potatoes* and *The House of the Eagle: Book One of the Ptolemies Quartet*. He lives in Ireland.

DAUGHTER
OF THE CROCODILE

BOOK TWO
OF THE PTOLEMIES QUARTET

———

DUNCAN SPROTT

faber and faber

First published in 2006
by Faber and Faber Limited
3 Queen Square London WC1N 3AU
This paperback edition first published in 2007

Designed by Humphrey Stone
Typeset by Alex Lazarou, Surbiton, Surrey
Printed in England by Mackays of Chatham, plc

A CIP record for this book
is available from the British Library

ISBN 978-0-571-22623-8

2 4 6 8 10 9 7 5 3 1

I show you a son as an enemy,
A brother as a foe,
A man killing his father.

The Prophecies of Neferti

The learned scribes made not unto themselves pyramids
of bronze. Books of instruction became their pyramids, and
the reed pen was their child. The surface of the stone
was their woman.

Papyrus Chester Beatty IV

I show you the land in calamity; the weak-armed now
possesses an arm, and men salute one who used to do the saluting.
I show you the lowermost uppermost . . .
The poor man will achieve wealth, while the great lady
will beg to exist.

The Prophecies of Neferti

Contents

Main Characters

Ptolemies

PTOLEMY PHILADELPHOS (Sister-Loving) called MIKROS – son of PTOLEMY SOTER; married to ARSINOË ALPHA; then to his sister, ARSINOË BETA

PTOLEMY EUERGETES (Benefactor) – son of PTOLEMY PHILADELPHOS and ARSINOË ALPHA; married to BERENIKE BETA

PTOLEMY PHILOPATOR (Father-Loving) – son of PTOLEMY EUERGETES and BERENIKE BETA; married to his sister ARSINOË GAMMA

PTOLEMY EPIPHANES (God Made Manifest) – son of PTOLEMY PHILOPATOR and ARSINOË GAMMA

PTOLEMAIOS (of Telmessos) – son of ARSINOË BETA and LYSIMAKHOS of Thrace

Others

ARSINOË ALPHA – daughter of LYSIMAKHOS of Thrace; wife of PTOLEMY MIKROS

ARSINOË BETA – daughter of PTOLEMY SOTER and BERENIKE ALPHA; also called ARSINOË PHILADELPHOS

ARSINOË GAMMA – daughter of PTOLEMY EUERGETES and BERENIKE BETA; wife of her brother PTOLEMY PHILOPATOR

BERENIKE BETA – daughter of MAGAS of Kyrene and APAMA of Syria; married first to Demetrios Kalos of Macedon; then to PTOLEMY EUERGETES

BERENIKE MIKRA – daughter of PTOLEMY EUERGETES and BERENIKE BETA

BERENIKE SYRA – daughter of PTOLEMY PHILADELPHOS and ARSINOË ALPHA; wife of Antiokhos Theos of Syria

LYSIMAKHOS – son of PTOLEMY PHILADELPHOS and ARSINOË ALPHA; called Uncle Lysimakhos

ESKEDI – son of OLD ANEMHOR; High Priest; married to NEFERRENPET

PADIBASTET – son of ESKEDI; High Priest; married to NEFERSOBEK

ANEMHOR (II) – called Young Anemhor; High Priest; married to HERANKH
DJEDHOR – High Priest of Ptah; son of Young Anemhor
HOREMAKHET – High Priest of Ptah; son of Young Anemhor; married to
  NEFERTITI
HORIMHOTEP – younger son of Young Anemhor
PASHERENPTAH – son of Horemakhet and NEFERTITI

Chronology

All dates are approximate

Alexandria

Old Harbour

Prevailing wind

Port of Pirates

ISLAND OF PHAROS

Temple of Isis

Diamond Rock

Pharos Rock

Submerged rocks

Pharos Lighthouse

Breakwater

Reefs

GREAT HARBOUR

ANTIRHODOS

Small Harbour

Island Palace

Private Royal Harbour

Palace

Temple of Isis Lokhias

Cape Lokhias

Poseidonion

Arsenal

Theatre

ROYAL QUARTER

Tomb of Alexander

STREET OF THE TOMB

JEWISH QUARTER

Eastern Nekropolis

Hippodrome

Helios or Sun Gate

to Kanopos

Canal

City Wall

City Wall

to Kanopos & River Nile

KANOPIC QUARTER

Lake Harbour

LAKE MAREOTIS

Pancion or Park of Pan

Agora

Library

KANOPIC STREET

Gymnasion

Timonion

Admiralty Port

Naval Dockyards

Mouseion or Museum

Heptastadion

Temple of Isis

PORT OF EUNOSTOS

Kibotos Harbour

Selene or Moon Gate

RHAKOTIS

City Wall

Sarapieion

Stadion

Ship Canal

City Wall

Western Nekropolis

7 Stadia =
1400yds =1.28 kms

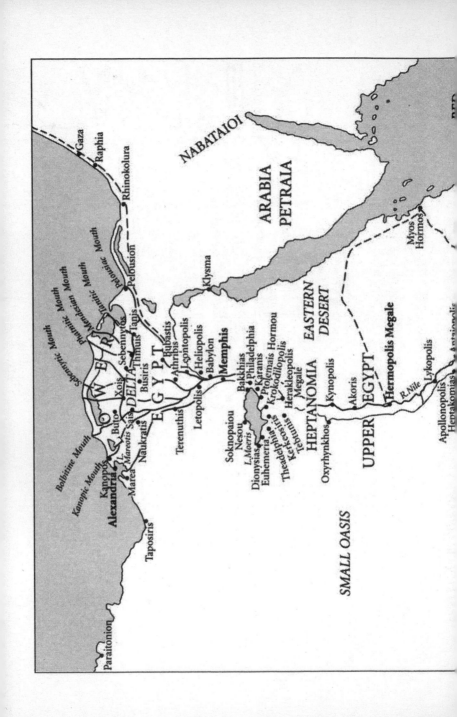

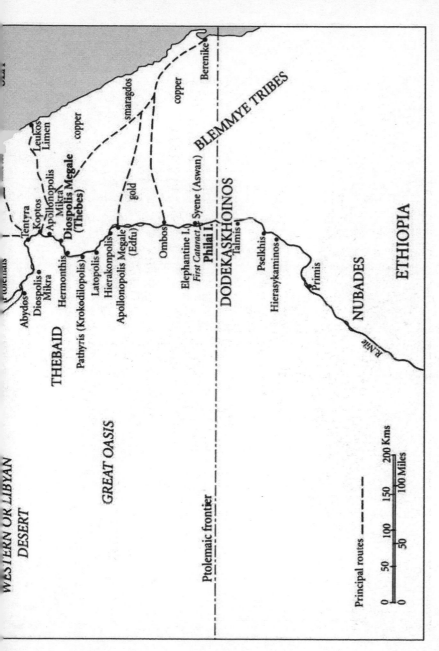

WESTERN OR LIBYAN DESERT

GREAT OASIS

THEBAID

Abydos
Diospolis Mikra
Hermonthis
Pathyris (Krokodilopolis)
Latopolis
Hierakonpolis
Apollonopolis Megale (Edfu)
Ombos
Elephantine I.
First Cataract
Syene (Aswan)
Philai I.

Tentyra
Koptos
Apollonopolis Mikra
Diospolis Megale (Thebes)

Leukos Limen

copper

smaragdos

copper

gold

Berenike

BLEMMYE TRIBES

DODEKASKHOINOS

Talmis

Pselkhis

Hierasykaminos

Primis

NUBADES

ETHIOPIA

R. Nile

Egypt

Ptolemaic frontier

Principal routes ----

0   50   100   150   200 Kms
0   50   100 Miles

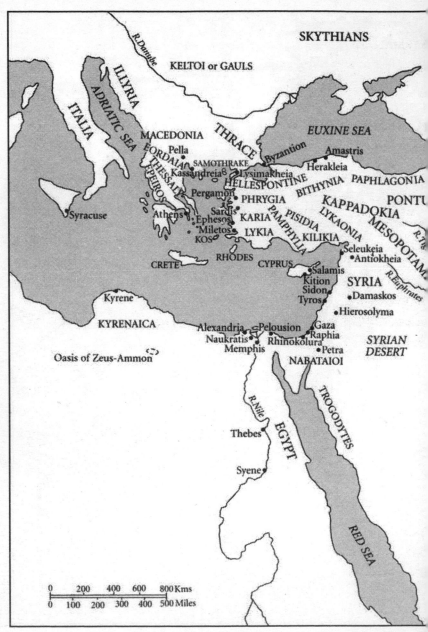

Alexander's Empire

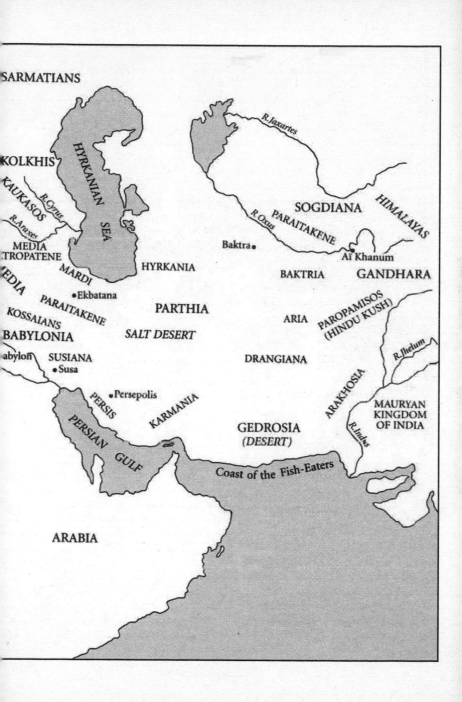

Greek Pharaohs of Egypt

THE HELLENISTIC PERIOD

332–30 BC

Macedonians

ALEXANDER (III) the Great	332–323
PHILIPPOS (III) ARRHIDAIOS	323–316
ALEXANDROS (IV)	316–304

Ptolemies

PTOLEMY (I) SOTER (Saviour)	304–284
PTOLEMY (II) PHILADELPHOS (Sister-Lover)	285–246
PTOLEMY (III) EUERGETES (Benefactor)	246–221
PTOLEMY (IV) PHILOPATOR (Father-Loving)	221–205
PTOLEMY (V) EPIPHANES (God Made Manifest)	205–180
PTOLEMY (VI) PHILOMETOR (Mother-Loving)	180–164; 163–145
PTOLEMY (VII) NEOS PHILOPATOR (New, Father-Loving)	145
PTOLEMY (VIII) EUERGETES (II) 'PHYSKON' (Fat Belly)	170–163; 145–116
PTOLEMY (IX) SOTER (II) 'LATHYROS' (Chickpea)	116–110
	109–107
	88–81
PTOLEMY (X) ALEXANDROS (I) (Mother-Slayer)	110–109
	107–88
PTOLEMY (XI) ALEXANDROS (II) (Stepmother-Lover)	80
PTOLEMY (XII) NEOS DIONYSOS 'AULETES' (Flute-Player)	80–58; 55–51
BERENIKE (IV) (Put-to-Death-by-Her-Own-Father)	58–55
KLEOPATRA (VII) THEA PHILOPATOR (Goddess)	51–30
PTOLEMY (XIII) (The One Drowned in the River)	51–47
PTOLEMY (XIV) (The One Poisoned by His Own Sister)	47–43
PTOLEMY (XV) KAISARION (Little Caesar)	44–30

THE HOUSE OF PTOLEMY

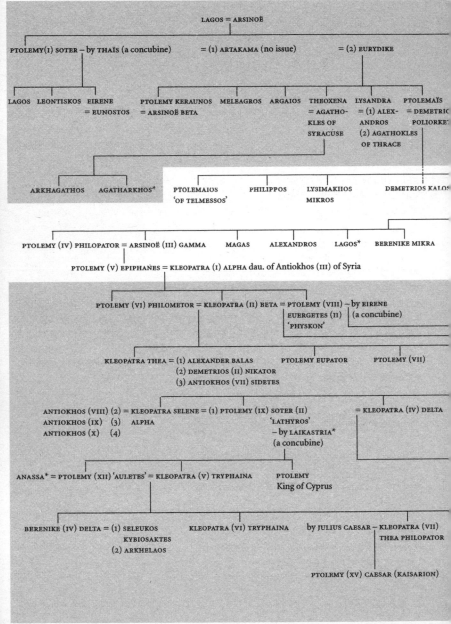

* = hypothetical name.

Note: *Daughter of the Crocodile* comprises the stories of those appearing between the shaded areas.

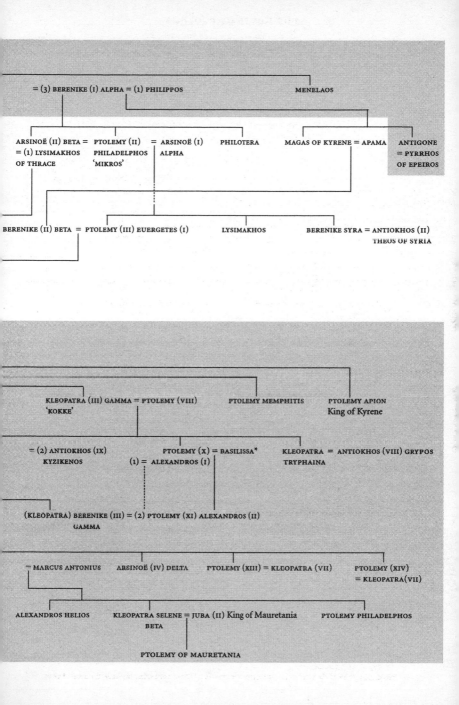

= (3) BERENIKE (I) ALPHA = (1) PHILIPPOS   MENELAOS

ARSINOË (II) BETA =   PTOLEMY (II) = ARSINOË (I)   PHILOTERA   MAGAS OF KYRENE = APAMA   ANTIGONE
= (1) LYSIMAKHOS   PHILADELPHOS   ALPHA   = PYRRHOS
OF THRACE   'MIKROS'   OF EPEIROS

BERENIKE (II) BETA = PTOLEMY (III) EUERGETES (I)   LYSIMAKHOS   BERENIKE SYRA = ANTIOKHOS (II)
                                                                                          THEOS OF SYRIA

KLEOPATRA (III) GAMMA = PTOLEMY (VIII)   PTOLEMY MEMPHITIS   PTOLEMY APION
'KOKKE'   King of Kyrene

= (2) ANTIOKHOS (IX)   PTOLEMY (X) = BASILISSA*   KLEOPATRA = ANTIOKHOS (VIII) GRYPOS
KYZIKENOS   (1) = ALEXANDROS (I)   TRYPHAINA

(KLEOPATRA) BERENIKE (III) = (2) PTOLEMY (XI) ALEXANDROS (II)
GAMMA

= MARCUS ANTONIUS   ARSINOË (IV) DELTA   PTOLEMY (XIII) = KLEOPATRA (VII)   PTOLEMY (XIV)
                                                                              = KLEOPATRA (VII)

ALEXANDROS HELIOS   KLEOPATRA SELENE = JUBA (II) King of Mauretania   PTOLEMY PHILADELPHOS
                     BETA

                     PTOLEMY OF MAURETANIA

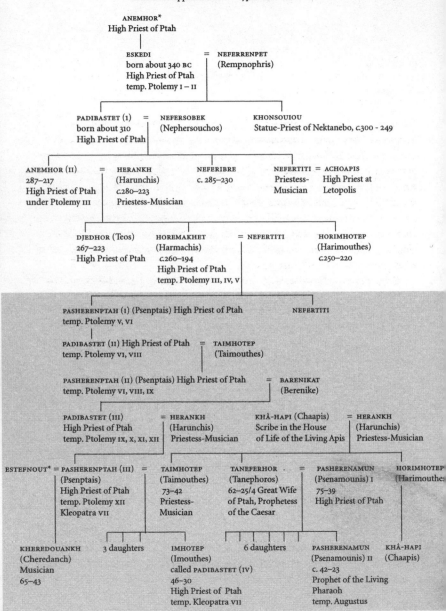

HIGH PRIESTS OF MEMPHIS

(*Greek names appear in parentheses*)
All dates are approximate. * = hypothetical name.

ANEMHOR*
High Priest of Ptah

ESKEDI = NEFERRENPET
born about 340 BC (Rempnophris)
High Priest of Ptah
temp. Ptolemy I – II

PADIBASTET (1) = NEFERSOBEK   KHONSOUIOU
born about 310   (Nephersouchos)   Statue-Priest of Nektanebo, c.300 - 249
High Priest of Ptah

ANEMHOR (II) = HERANKH   NEFERIBRE   NEFERTITI = ACHOAPIS
287–217   (Harunchis)   c. 285–230   Priestess-   High Priest at
High Priest of Ptah c.280–223   Musician   Letopolis
under Ptolemy III Priestess-Musician

DJEDHOR (Teos)   HOREMAKHET   = NEFERTITI   HORIMHOTEP
267–223   (Harmachis)   (Harimouthes)
High Priest of Ptah c.260–194   c.250–220
                 High Priest of Ptah
                 temp. Ptolemy III, IV, V

PASHERENPTAH (I) (Psenptais) High Priest of Ptah   NEFERTITI
temp. Ptolemy V, VI

PADIBASTET (II) High Priest of Ptah   = TAIMHOTEP
temp. Ptolemy VI, VIII   (Taimouthes)

PASHERENPTAH (II) (Psenptais) High Priest of Ptah   = BARENIKAT
temp. Ptolemy VI, VIII, IX   (Berenike)

PADIBASTET (III)   = HERANKH   KHÂ-HAPI (Chaapis)   = HERANKH
High Priest of Ptah   (Harunchis)   Scribe in the House   (Harunchis)
temp. Ptolemy IX, X, XI, XII Priestess-Musician of Life of the Living Apis Priestess-Musician

ESTEPNOUT* = PASHERENPTAH (III) = TAIMHOTEP   TANEFERHOR = PASHERENAMUN   HORIMHOTEP
             (Psenptais)   (Taimouthes)   (Tanephoros) (Psenamounis) I (Harimouthe
             High Priest of Ptah 73–42   62–25/4 Great Wife 75–39
             temp. Ptolemy XII   Priestess-   of Ptah, Prophetess High Priest of Ptah
             Kleopatra VII   Musician   of the Caesar

KHEREDOUANKH   3 daughters   IMHOTEP   6 daughters   PASHERENAMUN   KHÂ-HAPI
(Cheredanch)   (Imouthes)   (Psenamounis) II (Chaapis)
Musician   called PADIBASTET (IV)   c. 42–23
65–43   46–30   Prophet of the Living
                             High Priest of Ptah   Pharaoh
                             temp. Kleopatra VII   temp. Augustus

Note: High Priests in *Daughter of the Crocodile* are above the shaded area.

Prologue

Greetings, Stranger. So you are once again upon the road into Egypt. It is good, very good, until the sweat pours into your eyes, and your donkey is overtaken by the storm of sand. You are blinded by sand, suffocated in the whirling yellow fog. For sure, you despair. Oho, Stranger, but this is Egypt, where you must often have sand in your eyes and see darkness by day. You think you will see darkness for all time, but, you know, the sandstorm will pass. Nothing in the world lasts for ever, except the old gods of Egypt. Aye, the gods, for they are still watching and listening, still waiting for your offerings: one hundred of onions, one hundred of geese, one hundred of beer. Believe, Stranger: the gods have not ceased to exist, they have merely been forgotten.

If you look into the yellow fog, you will see the figure of a man beside the road, holding out his hand, asking for money. He wears the dog-mask of Anubis, the divine dog who is Pharaoh of the Underworld. He will not bite you. Anubis is your friend, your guide. You could breathe easy, Stranger, if you had not the sand up the nostril. Do not pass by without hearing him, without a greeting. For that figure upon the road is myself.

In the desert you may see not only what is, but also what is not. The sands will become a lake of water. Your eyes are sure to play tricks. Even the gods may play tricks with you, shifting their shape. Even I who am speaking to you, Stranger, can shift my shape. When I take off the Dog Face mask, who am I? Not a dog, not a bird, for sure, not even a man. I am not Thoth, the ibis, the god of learning. I am his wife, his sister. I am SESHAT, the Writer. I am the goddess of History, the Lady of Hieroglyphs. I have written this book with my own fingers.

You do not know me, but I know you, Stranger, from of old. You will not believe it, but I know you, for I know everybody. I was there at your birth amid blood and screaming, for I am present at every birth. I have been keeping count of the days of your life for you ever since. Take a deep breath. Breathe in, Stranger. Breathe out. Deeper, breathe deep. You should know that I am the goddess who allows you to go on breathing. You are in my power every moment of your life. You have forgotten me, but I have not forgotten you. I am the goddess that forgets nothing. I am the Chronologer and the Chronographer, the one who has fixed the day upon which your breathing must stop, the day of all days that terrifies you to think of it because you do not know what lies beyond; because you fear there is nothing but nothingness after this life of yours, nothing but the dark. But you are wrong about that, for what you think is the end is just the beginning. Anubis the jackal is waiting for you, waiting to be your Guide in the Afterlife, wagging the tail. All the gods are waiting for you. You may even sail with us in the Night-barque of Ra, if your heart is light enough in the Balance. Try to think as the Egyptian thinks: look upon death as no more terrible than moving house, no more to be dreaded than putting on a fresh suit of clothes. Keep your heart light, light as the feather.

We shall begin well, Wise One, if you will call me by my proper name: not to speak of SESH-at, if you please, but sesh-AT. Repeat after me: sesh-AT, sesh-AT, sesh-AT. And you should mind yourself, Stranger, for I can see everything you are doing.

I can see you sitting with my book unrolled upon your knee, lost in your thoughts of today, your dreams of tomorrow. Forget your todays and your tomorrows for a while, Stranger. For the goddess of History only one thing matters: Yesterday. Why not let Seshat take you back there? Why not let her lead you by the hand? Oho! Oho, Stranger, the Lady of Hieroglyphs will not allow you to resist her. Sure, you are busy, you have your duties – measuring the fields, building the house, milking your goats – but Seshat says to you, stop trying to escape. You may find profit in reading her history of the House of Ptolemy, mortals such as yourself, who became gods in their own lifetime.

Do not quit reading so soon, Stranger, for the goddess who remembers everything has much to tell you. First, though, you must let her tell you about herself.

I am Seshat (sesh-AT), mighty Sister of Thoth, the Ibis, the Lord of all Learning. I am also his wife, the Wife of the Ibis, the Wife of the Baboon, but my book is not about him, my book is about me, SESHAT, the Ancient One, who has been writing since the very beginning. I am the Lady of the House of Books, the Mistress of Literature. I am the goddess that Time forgot, but you should know that I am tired of being forgotten. Picture me in your heart, Stranger, wearing my dress of leopard spots that stand for the starry sky, my skin-tight leopardskin. Since the beginning of Time I wore the headdress like a flower with seven petals, like a star, with a pair of upside-down cow's horns on top of it.

In my right hand I hold a reed pen, and my black and red ink cakes. In my left hand I hold the palm-wood stick upon which I have carved a notch to mark the passing of every year ever since years began, for I am the Lady of Years. The palm-stick ends with a tadpole – the hieroglyph that stands for one hundred thousand – and the hieroglyph for Infinity, for I myself am Infinity, and I shall go on carving the notches until the years come to a stop. I am the ageless one, the Changeless One, old but young, living for ever, like Pharaoh himself.

I used to count the King's jubilees. I used to record his offspring, for I am the goddess of Fate, that gives to every Pharaoh his span of life. As Controller of the Foreigners in Egypt I kept a special count of Ptolemy. For two thousand years I have put off writing down his bloody history, but now it is time. Happy the King who has his deeds recorded by my fingers, for I am Mousa to the Greeks, the Muse of History. I am the Egyptian Klio. I am Seshat, who is Eternity, the one who has charge of Time. I am still here, Stranger, still counting the days.

Mistress of the Builders is my other name, for I am the inventor of Architecture, the Lady of Plans. I love to build. I love also to write, of course, fitting one weighty word next to another word. Words, as good as blocks of stone, that will last for all time. I stack the words upon the page like sun-dried bricks. I pile the books one upon another to make a mighty monument for my brother THOTH, the Library of the Gods. I am the Mistress of the House of Books, and I say that although a well-built temple is a wonderful thing, a book is even better.

Thoth the baboon perches upon the shoulder of every scribe, helping him to write, but Seshat's picture is painted on the right-hand side of his writing-palette. No scribe can write one word without the aid of Thoth, but he also reveres Seshat, the goddess of Arithmetic, the one who counts the words.

Thanks to the lady in the leopardskin, this scribe is just about ready to begin. I think we may let him start writing now. We shall be pleased to take possession of his life and soul until he is done. He will carry the burden of this bloody story, day and night, for years. Divine dictation, Spotous, she says to me, Tell them how Arsinoë Beta flew back to Alexandria in Egypt like some homing vulture, thirsting after another woman's blood. (Call her name ar-SIN-oh-ee, Wise One, or ar-ZIN-oh-ay.) Make them hear her terrible harsh shout, like the wind howling in the desert. Make them feel the blowtorch of her tongue. Make their eyes fly across the page, faster than greyhounds, swifter than light. Tell them how Arsinoë Beta turned herself into a goddess, and saved Egypt, and how a one-time dog-boy nearly destroyed it.

xxvii

PART ONE

Sister-Lover
Ptolemy Philadelphos

1.1

Lady of Dread

About Year Four of the Pharaoh called Ptolemy Philadelphos, or Mikros (call him *MEE-krahss*, Stranger), Arsinoë Beta, his elder sister, sailed home to Egypt from Samothrake, with her once golden-yellow hair turned grey by the horrors that happened there, and her life in ruins, ruins. When she stepped off that ship, Arsinoe Beta had been gone from Alexandria twenty years and was about thirty-six years old. She still wore the white *peplos* spattered with her children's blood, in order to gain her brother's sympathy. Soon she would change not only her dress but also herself. She thought, *I shall be like Isis. I can assume any shape or form I choose. There is nothing that Arsinoë Beta cannot do. I shall be Laughter-Loving Aphrodite.*

Aye, now she even forces herself to smile, something she was never famous for in the past. She smiles like the crocodile, whom the Egyptians call Hot Mouth, and Face of Fear. Sure, this woman's mouth is hot. Her tongue can burn a man's ears off. Sure, she is beautiful, but arouse her anger and her face is fearful to behold, like the Gorgon Medusa, enough to turn a man to stone. She is very like the crocodile who floats silent in the River pretending to be a tree trunk: soon she will thrash about in the water, like Sobek, like the god of death himself. And the first man she will swallow up is Ptolemy Mikros, the twenty-nine-year-old Pharaoh, her younger brother.

Stranger, it is her purpose to *marry* him.

If the thought of a sister married to her own brother offends you, Wise One, shut this book forthwith and put it down, for there is much more of that kind of thing to follow. Seshat urges you to set aside all your thoughts of propriety. This is ancient times, when any thing might happen. Stranger, it is bizarre beyond any thing you ever read in your life.

When Arsinoë Beta stepped off that ship in the Harbour of Eunostos, the Harbour of Happy Returns, nobody remembered who she was; nobody believed that this scarecrow of a woman could be the Great Royal Sister, and the harbour master threw her in chains, for the crime of claiming a false identity. But when she screamed and raved, demanding to be taken to his Majesty, they took her to the palace where the officials told her to stand in line and wait, like everybody else, and hold her tongue. To stop that woman talking, it was next-to-impossible, but she did keep quiet, she did wait, and it was like the stillness before the earthquake.

As she walked through the monumental bronze doors of her brother's great white marble palace she was surprised first by the greenery that had sprung up – giant palm trees, exotic climbing plants – in the vastness of the marble-columned entrance hall, that had been quite bare in the time of her father. She was surprised to see pools of running water, spurting fountains, and exotic birds in golden cages. She was astonished to see that the slaves now wore not rough serge but golden tunics, and that her brother's women sat there in her father's house, brazen, his concubines in golden dresses, fanning themselves with ostrich-feather fans, laughing. Soon she would put a stop to their laughter.

The golden audience chamber looked to her much the same as before – the Corinthian columns, the mosaic floors with sea-gods and monsters of the deep, the furniture of solid gold or gilded wood, the walls painted with scenes from Homer. The black-and-white-striped rugs, the monkeys and Egyptian cats inside the house, everything was the same. Everywhere was the glitter of gold, the babble of foreign tongues, the smoke of burning incense, and the ceaseless buzz of the flies, angry, like herself.

She saw first of all the happy domestic scene – the Pharaoh Ptolemy Mikros and his beautiful wife sitting upon thrones of gold, wearing the fixed half-smile of living gods. The people of Egypt queued up, patient, before them, and Mikros listened, or did not listen, to their petitions. Her younger sister Philotera sat there too, the pure one, smiling, plying her needle. These were the only members of the family left living: all the rest, his brothers and half-brothers, his illegitimate half-cousins, Mikros had murdered them.

Arsinoë Beta's eagle eye fixed firm upon the Queen, her smiling sister-in-law and stepdaughter, her best enemy. Aye, the other Arsinoë, called Alpha, the one in the vulture headdress, the ostrich-feather-and-cow's-horn head-dress, and the golden shoes embroidered with cobras and vultures. She would not smile for much longer. When Arsinoë Alpha looked up she had no difficulty identifying the stranger: she stood up like she had seen a ghost, clapped her hands to her mouth and fled, shrieking. Every Greek courtier bearing papyri, every Egyptian official with his reed pen raised to write down orders from his Majesty, every black-faced slave of the fan and palace dwarf pulling a leopard on a golden leash, they all turned the head to look at the woman in the blood-splashed *peplos*, her grey hair very like a bird's nest, her eyes wild, like a madwoman's eyes, the woman in chains of iron, wondering who she was. Aye, and Mikros should have kept the chains on her, for she was thinking the wicked thought that Arsinoë Alpha, the Great Royal Wife, the Queen of Upper and Lower Egypt, the Mistress of Happiness, was one more relative to be gotten rid of.

The Dioiketes, or Vizier, led the sister forward, and told her, rough, to wait, to have patience, like everybody else. She stood there wearing her face of thunder, raging within at the humiliation, taking stock, thinking.

She saw her younger brother grown up to man's estate, twice as tall as when she saw him last, broad of chest, powerful in the thigh, a bit heavy from too much feasting, dressed in the *chendjyt*, or white linen kilt of Pharaoh, and the Double Crown of the Two Lands, red and white, the Lady of Spells and the Lady of Dread — names that might more fittingly have been applied to herself. She saw the Egyptians bowing down to him, kissing the mosaic floor at his feet. She saw the great ostrich-feather fan, worked by black slaves from the Land of Punt, that did not keep his Majesty cool. She saw the sweat trickle down his forehead and smelled the rank armpit smell that did battle with the rose powder, for that Egypt was too hot for him. He was still red of face, his fair skin scorched by the sun, and she could still divine what he was thinking – that though he loved to be Pharaoh he also hated it. She stared at the great jewelled Eye of Horus necklace that hung about his neck, thinking, *He is the Horus, the Living Image of the Falcon.* She saw the stern face of Pharaoh, sure, but she also saw her useless younger brother, the lazy boy whose delight was not work but pleasure, the soft one.

She saw also Eskedi, High Priest of Memphis, calm, grave, dressed in his leopard-spot mantle as before, standing at her brother's elbow, translating the petitioners' words for his Majesty, flicking the golden fly-whisk back and forth. *Why*, she thought, *does he not tell my brother who has come? He knows who I am.* For yes, this was her wise friend, the High Priest of Ptah, now bent with age, his face wrinkled like the walnut shell, and she could tell that Mikros did not listen to a word he said about property disputes and complaints about taxes, but dreamed of other things – no doubt of roast flamingo flesh, of succulent Syrian dates, of his succulent women. Arsinoë Beta had her spies' reports. She knew what her brother did and did not do. She had not come back to Egypt without the most careful making ready. Aye, she had planned her homecoming like a military campaign – in which hers was the victory.

Arsinoë Beta saw also Mikros's infant children, playing with a lion cub on the steps beside their father's throne: the four-year-old Ptolemy, who would be called Euergetes (Wise One, call his name *yoo-ER-ger-teez*), Lysimakhos, his three-year-old brother (*lie-SIM-ak-koss*), and Berenike (*ber-en-EYE-kee* or *ber-en-EE-kay*), the one who would be called Syra, just two years old. Aye, the children of her enemy, Arsinoë Alpha: three hot Greek children pretending to be Egyptians, with the head shaved close but for the Horus sidelock, fidgeting with the golden talismans on their wrists, the talismans that should protect them from the evil worked by people such as herself.

Eskedi did know who the madwoman was, and in his heart he saw a vision of blood, a pool of Greek blood spreading across the palace floor, and the thought made his heart beat faster than was safe for an old man's health.

Now Arsinoë Alpha ran back into the audience chamber, without her vulture crown, her pristine *peplos* all awry, her face streaked with tears, the Queen of Egypt, running – an unheard of thing – and she gathered up her children, hurried them to a place of safety, away from the evil eye of their aunt.

At last Ptolemy Mikros turned his head to look, and the fixed half-smile of Pharaoh fell upon this haggard woman. *There is something familiar,* he thought, *about her.* And then the stubble prickled upon the back of his neck. Arsinoë Beta stepped forward, barefoot, having thrown overboard her shoes, with her feet made to look bloody. She stared deep into the eyes of Pharaoh, holding his glance, doing a thing that no respectable Greek woman should ever do, trying to stare him out, just as she had done when they were children in this same palace years ago.

Nobody in all Egypt looked into the fierce eyes of Pharaoh without terror, but Arsinoë Beta was not terrified. Her eyes locked with his, glittering half for anger, half for amusement. She did not hold the hand up to her face so that she should not be burned up by the terrible glance of Ra, by the Son of the Sun. She did not throw herself upon her knees before his Majesty and kiss the floor. She knew her brother far too well to be afraid. No, it was rather her glance that would burn up *him*.

Who is this woman? Mikros asked the Dioiketes, angry, but before the man could open the mouth she spoke up herself: *Hail to thee, Horus,* she said, sarcastic. *Hail to thee, mighty King, Bull, Subduer of Bulls. We are Arsinoë, your sister. Perhaps you do not remember us.*

I did not know thee, he murmured, standing up slow, shocked, unsmiling, from his chair of gold, shaken by the look of her. He made signs for her chains to be removed, a chair to be fetched, the petitioners to be sent away. But he did not love the sister so much that he threw his arms about her neck and kissed her eyes. He did not touch her flesh, did not even take her by the hand, but sat down again, feeling faint. She had been sixteen years old when he saw her last. Now she had the marks of age and care upon her, and the scars from clawing the cheeks in mourning. His heart went out to her, just a little, when he remembered what she had been, the beautiful sister. *She is thinner than the jackal of the desert,* he thought, *and the light in her eyes is strange, strange, and there is an odd, half-crazed look, that was not there before.* Aye, he remembered her only too well.

We are glad to see thee safe home, he said, not sure whether he meant it. For no Greek woman was supposed to return to her father's house once she had been married off, and was as good as dead, to be forgotten about, but here she was, like a ghost come home to haunt him. He fingered the crocodile teeth that he wore on his upper right arm, strung upon a rope of gold, wondering whatever he was to do with her. He touched the golden *phallos* talisman that hung round his neck for luck, thinking of beautiful Stratonike, first of his concubines. No, the thought that his own sister might end up in his bed did not so much as enter his heart. Of course not. But Arsinoë Beta, even at first sight of her brother, thought of nothing else.

Aye, already she was hot to marry him, murmuring even so soon the words of the most powerful magic spells, that would make him lust after her scrawny body. She saw him, sure enough, stroke the solid gold talisman against the evil eye, his talisman against all malice, and she knew what were his thoughts; that he was afraid of her, afraid, and that her homecoming troubled him no end. Aye, Strong Bull shifted about upon his golden throne, uneasy in her presence, as she willed him to desire her flesh, willed him to take her into his bed, willed him to be her fresh husband. He felt the curious fluttering in his heart, as if he had been struck through upon the spot by the darts of Eros.

You should know, Brother, she said, *that fresh incense under the arms may be an effective deodorant,* but what she was thinking was quite different. *Let me be a magnet,* she thought, *let him be attracted to me like iron.*

For sure, he scowled at her, then, knowing they must quarrel, just like they quarrelled when they were children, and in his heart he had the sinking feeling that comes upon a man when some horse he was fond of has been killed. No, he was sure, it could not be the darts of Eros. By no means.

Mikros's first thought was to send his sister straight back to Samothrake. But no. He did not send her away. He had to hear what she said, must listen to her story. And yes, although she looked different, she was the same as she had always been: for she began to boss him and tell him what he should do, and make demands, just as she had done when he was only eight years old.

Brother, she said, *I have come home for good. I shall need some place to sleep, some rooms for myself. For the time being I think I must retire to the women's quarters with your wife and children.* And she did so, smiling, smiling like Arsinoë Alpha had never seen her smile before. And Mikros, he knew what his sister had done: that she had brought about the murder of his wife's brother, and yet he did not stop her from moving in to live beside her.

And why was it? It was because as soon as she put on fresh clothes she put on a fresh face. She smiled and made herself pleasant, as if she was quite different from how she had been before, so that Mikros thought the old Arsinoë had changed for the better. Aye, all the while she behaved toward Arsinoë Alpha as if they were the best of friends, not bitterest enemies, keeping up a torrent of pleasant conversations and happy memories of their shared past in Thrace, false words, false memories. She would start telling some amusing but totally fictitious story, about made-up people, saying, for example, *Do you remember what the General Andronikos said about the Keltoi?* But Arsinoë Alpha would shake her head, and remembered, of course, nothing, so that every time Arsinoë Beta was able to say, *Brother, your wife has forgotten,* or, *Brother, I do believe your wife is losing her memory.*

And so she began straight away to make Arsinoë Alpha look mad for not remembering a word of the past.

Arsinoë Alpha was terrified to be in the same room with Arsinoë Beta. Her voice trembled when she spoke. When she stood up she felt faint. When she sat down she felt sick. Arsinoë Alpha changed upon the instant from one who laughed and smiled into one who frowned and wept. And Arsinoë Beta, indeed, that had frowned and been disagreeable, now changed into one who smiled and smiled. Sometimes she even managed to make herself laugh.

Brother, Arsinoë Beta said, *I shall need guards for my door . . .*

Brother, she said, *I shall need a dozen waiting-women . . .*

Brother, she said, *Alexandria feels so cold, I shall need a brazier. And you must send the Milk of Magnesia, for my bellyache . . .*

Mikros gave her everything she asked for, without complaint.

Mikros knew of the sister's aged husband killed upon the field of battle, of the sacrilegious marriage to her own half-brother, Ptolemy Keraunos, and of his well-deserved death, fighting the Gauls in the waste lands north of Thrace. Mikros had his spies, was not ill-informed about foreign affairs. He knew well enough about the death of Agathokles of Thrace, the dreadful thing she had done to him: how she had murdered her own stepson in cold blood. But it was all in the past, and Mikros had nothing to do with the past. He had wiped it out. Mikros lived in the present, for the pleasure of the passing moment. Seshat weeps to write it, but for this king yesterday was just as meaningless as tomorrow.

8

Mikros's thoughts were in any case occupied with other matters. He had his women of the night to think of, and his war with Syria. He lived one day at a time, in an everlasting present. Tomorrow, he believed, would take care of itself. As it happened, he was wrong about that: his sister would take care of tomorrow.

Even on her first day back in Egypt, Arsinoë Beta began to pick up the delicate clipped half-moons that were the parings of Arsinoë Alpha's finger nails. She gathered up the stray hairs from her pillow, long dark hairs. When Arsinoë Alpha washed her teeth and spat into the golden bowl, Arsinoë Beta would come along afterwards to scoop up her spittle into a jar, and hide it away, for later use. Such things were her secret weapons, the ingredients for her magic spells. Aye, to be rid of her she would use every weapon at her disposal: natural, unnatural and supernatural.

Aye, and horrible too, for she also said, *Brother, where have all the crocodiles gone? We must have some crocodiles in the palace. Have his Excellency send up half a dozen from Memphis, would you?*

And then she sent for a couple of snakes from Mikros's Beast Garden, and walked about with them draped round her neck. Olympias, the mother of Alexander, had done the same. It was not quite normal behaviour for the Greeks, and Arsinoë Beta had never shown much liking for snakes in Thrace. By no means. She adorned herself with snakes now only because she knew Mikros would be unsettled by it, to show who was the boss: not him, but her.

For sure, Mikros was used to seeing the *Agathos Daimon*, the lucky tame house snake of Alexandria, wherever he went, but he shuddered to see his sister handling serpents inside his palace, and Arsinoë Beta saw him shudder. It was all done so as to make stronger her hold over him. Aye, and they were like the reflection of herself: poison.

The sister, bathed and given clothes and shoes, and cosmetics for the face, used up her brother's day making demands, endless demands: for dogs and slaves of her own, for a handsome allowance, for horses, chariots, bodyguards, and with talking, catching up with twenty years of not having set eyes upon the city of Alexandria, hearing all about the Pharos, or Lighthouse, and the death of their father, and what was happening up-River, in Upper Egypt.

We shall also need, she said, quite casual and offhand, *a food-taster.* And when the man was chosen and sent for, and did his work, Mikros watched her pick at her food. She ate seven snails only, snails, against the bellyache, then pushed the gold plate away. Unknown to her brother, this new, different, smiling Arsinoë Beta now sprinkled arsenic over her food, much as any other person might make use of salt, thinking to build up her resistance to poison, against the day when she might be the victim of a murder attempt. When Mikros had agreed to all her demands, she sat with him, telling her story – blood, murder, massacre, escape – but all the time making herself out to be the injured party, and all the time planning what to do, thinking, *Must move quick, like the snake to strike.*

I shall do my best to help you, Mikros said. *I shall find you a fresh husband,* he said, although just then he could not think of any king to whom this whippet-thin and rather manly sister might prove pleasing. He thought, *No man of sense will want to take this monster of a woman to wife.*

We are grateful to you, Brother, she said, *for your kind words.* But her voice was harsh, as if she had thoughts of her own upon the subject of a fresh marriage. And Mikros thought, *I do not know this sister; she is a stranger unto me.* And yet at the same time he knew her only too well. When at length she retired to bed, he breathed the sigh of relief.

Arsinoë Beta kissed Arsinoë Alpha goodnight with kind and affectionate words, and it was all so very unlike her former behaviour that Arsinoë Alpha wondered wherever her nastiness had gone to. Still trembling, she dragged heavy chests across the floor of her bedchamber and rammed them against the door. Then she lay in her bed listening to the pounding of her heart, thinking that Arsinoë Beta must, at any moment, break through the door and attack her with a knife. Aye, she slept not for the racing of her thoughts, for sheer terror that she found herself sleeping in the next-door apartments to the woman who had murdered her brother.

Hardly had Mikros closed his eyes that night than Arsinoë Beta burst into his private chamber wearing her night clothes, shouting and screaming, quite hysterical, *Somebody has tried to poison us, Brother. Somebody has put arsenic in our sleeping draught.*

And she made her brother climb out of his bed of gold to see for himself the body of her food-taster, sprawled on the floor, a dead man. She made Mikros wake up everybody in the palace in the small hours, so as to find out who had done this terrible thing. But no man knew one word about that crime, for the very good reason that Arsinoë Beta had put the poison in her sleeping draught herself.

It is a great mystery, is it not, Brother? Arsinoë Beta said. *But I have my suspicions. I think I know who is the poisoner. I think you will find that the guilty one is Arsinoë Alpha.*

Mikros snorted, as if he thought the idea impossible. But when he was allowed to go back to bed, he dreamed that his bedclothes were on fire, and he woke himself up with his shouting. He sent for Eskedi at dawn to ask this great oneiroscopist, *What does it mean, such a fearful dream?*

Eskedi told Mikros most of the truth. *For the Egyptians, Megaleios,* he said, *it is bad: it means driving away your wife.*

1.2

Snake Poison

Arsinoë Beta slept sound enough after the attempted poisoning – apart from the usual interruptions of her ghosts – but she was awake before dawn, the hour that is best for working magic, to light her brazier. No, she did not need this article for warming her hands. By no means. It was for working her magic. That morning, the first dawn of her return to Egypt, she scratched some letters in red ink upon a piece of papyrus, and they were the secret name of Arsinoë Alpha. She whispered the words of power and threw the papyrus into the flames. Whatever is done to the name is done to the person named. Just as the letters burned, so Arsinoë Alpha would break. The word is the deed: to say the word is to make it happen. But Arsinoë Beta would be broken too.

Mikros knew his sister was a trouble-maker, that she was sure to boss him, just as she had done when they were children. Now there was poison, on her very first night back in Egypt, like a warning to him of how his life might change with the sister living at home again. Why did he not send her away at once? Why did this high Prince, who could have any thing he wanted in the world, not send his sister straight back to Samothrake by the next swift ship?

Seshat has forgotten nothing. Seshat will tell.

Stranger, Arsinoë Beta had known this King as a helpless child. She had been as much as her brother's nurse. She had carried him about the palace in her arms day after day for years. She had cleaned up his filth and overseen his bath. Mikros had been like her living doll. Now it was her wicked thought to play with him some more.

Really, if Mikros had had any sense he would have thrown the sister into his prison and left her there. But no, he did not do that. He took pity on her because she was homeless, because she had lost her husband, her sons, her kingdom, her title of Queen of Thrace – everything; and because she was his sister. Mikros still jumped when she snapped her fingers: he had not forgotten her terrible bad temper over the slightest thing, and yet he still half loved her, just as he had half loved her when he was a boy of five years old, because in spite of being so ill-tempered, she was the only member of his family that took any notice of him. He was not the heir just then. His fate, in those days, was to be murdered himself.

If Mikros did not send Arsinoë Beta away it was because, in the beginning, as he said, *All strangers and beggars are from Zeus.* He ordered the famous hospitality of the Greeks that must be shown to every visitor. He thought, *Perhaps I shall send her away later.* But in the end it was because his elder sister had a certain hold over him, almost as if she had bewitched him. It was because she had the answer to his every question, the solution to all the things that he found most difficult about being Pharaoh. Aye, in the end it was because he needed her excellent and most excellent cleverness.

In the morning Arsinoë Beta went to her brother and said, *We are feeling a little unwell after our shock during the night. We shall need a doctor to wait upon us, a Greek doctor.*

Mikros removed the red and white striped headcloth of Pharaoh and scratched the scalp, thinking. *Herophilos of Khalkedon is your man,* he said, *the very first of doctors . . .*

Aye, Herophilos was the best, but he was famous for dissecting live monkeys. Rumour said that he also dissected human victims, the prisoners in Mikros's gaol, with Mikros's full permission, while they still lived.

We shall not meet your Herophilos, she said. *We have heard he stinks of death. You must think again, Brother.*

Khrysippos is a very good man, Mikros said. *He attends her Majesty. Or his colleague Amyntas. These are worthy medical men, who know all about women's troubles. Courtiers and common people alike swear by their wonderful abilities.*

Khrysippos and Amyntas were duly presented. For sure, these Greek doctors inspired confidence. They had the long beards of wise men. They had great knowledge of drugs and charms.

These are the gentlemen who attended Arsinoë Alpha in childbed, Mikros said, *and saved her life three times. Is it not so, Khrysippos?*

Khrysippos bowed the head, smiling.

Arsinoë Beta smiled. Mikros smiled.

They also saved my own life, Mikros said, *when I was suffering from the hot and cold fever. For sure, there is no cure for the ague, but Khrysippos and Amyntas knew what must be done, and what must not. A man may die of the marsh fever if he neglects to take proper care of himself.*

Arsinoë Beta smiled fit to bust her jaw.

Sister, Mikros said, *I promise you, these are men you may trust, physicians of the highest honour.*

But Arsinoë Beta thought, *Trust not a friend. A king may trust nobody, nor a queen neither.*

Later that day she sent for Khrysippos and Amyntas, the court physicians, to ask about her health, when Khrysippos said to her, *We have sworn our oath, of course, Madam, the oath of Hippokrates . . . .*

Whatever I see or hear . . . Amyntas added, *which ought not to be revealed. I will keep secret and tell to nobody.*

You will be quite safe, Madam, Khrysippos said, *in our hands . . .*

Aye, quite safe, possibly, but Arsinoë Beta was already scheming. From the very beginning she found these perfect doctors less than perfect, and while continuing to smile, she complained of their carelessness, of their daily mistakes, and of their failure to make her belly better. Amyntas and Khrysippos had received the Gold of Praise for saving the lives of Mikros and Arsinoë Alpha. Unfortunately, Mikros would not save their lives in return.

At almost the very start of his reign, Ptolemy Mikros took what was quite the worst decision regarding the sister: he made her welcome. Her homecoming was bad in many ways for Mikros, but in some ways it was also good: she would save her brother, if not the whole dynasty of Ptolemy.

To speak true, it was as if Arsinoë Beta the serpent had sloughed her skin and made herself into something new. Like being reborn; like being a fresh person altogether, twice as poisonous as before.

1.3

Erotikos

Ptolemy Mikros, sitting upon his throne of gold and ebony and ivory, this Greek Pharaoh, this Macedonian who had never in his life looked upon the hills of Macedon, was not a foolish man. He was an honourable and right-thinking king. He had achieved what the Greeks called *ataraxia*, balance of the soul, so that nothing disturbed him. You should not expect this Ptolemaios to live up to his name and be warlike. He was a scholar, a man of peace: that was why he had been named as his father's heir. His thoughts were balanced, scholarly thoughts. His temper was calm.

Mikros, as Pharaoh, had five Egyptian titles. His Horus name was The Strong Youth. His Two Ladies name was Whose Might is Great. He was meant to be a powerful monarch, but he preferred to let his advisers think of war. He was keener on geography than strategy, more interested in zoology than tactics.

His Golden Horus name was Who His Father Has Raised to the Throne. He had been sitting on that throne of his for just four years, but he was already tired of thinking about the pig tax, the salt tax, the oil tax, the date and fig tax, the flax tax. He was bored by having to worry about how to keep the Egyptians living up-River, beyond Thebes, quiet, and happy.

His throne name was Who is Made Strong Through the Ka of Ra, Beloved of Amun. He tried to be strong, but his strength was nothing compared with that of his sister, nothing. The sister would wear the *krepides*, or soldier's boots, more often than her brother.

Mikros was, for sure, much more interested in pleasure than duty. He enjoyed eating roast pig stuffed with thrushes, and flamingo cooked in a seafood sauce. He liked to gorge on baked fishes. He loved to tip the fine wines of Mareotis down his throat and be a little drunken. He had everything he wanted. There was nothing that he could think of to ask for that he did not already have, except perhaps the lightening of the burden of the kingship; except, perhaps, the end of the unending war, the war that interfered with his pleasures. But war and government happened to be two things that, by chance, his sister could help him with.

By day he dreamed of his concubines, for above all other things his great delight was women, his many women, dozens of them, who passed the day wearing nothing but a lotus flower, a necklace, a bracelet, with nothing better to do than look out of their windows for the chariot of his Majesty beating up Kanopic Street in a cloud of dust, on his way to shower them with gold.

You might think, Stranger, how could such a man not be happy? Mikros was happy enough, just then, but for most of the day, day after day, he had to think about the threat of invasion, the difficulties of the corn supply, the uncertainty over the Flood of the River, and always, always, the petitions of his subjects, their petty quarrels, their tiresome complaints. Only when he was with his women could he forget the burden of the kingship.

Mikros delights in many things, losing himself in his books, Aristotle's *History of Animals*, Theophrastos his *History of Plants*, the *Histories* of Herodotos of Halikarnassos. But the furrow of anxiety soon reappears on this King's brow. He is less of a stranger in Egypt than his father was, but he is a stranger nonetheless. He is a Greek, a Macedonian, and he must never forget it. At the same time, though, he must try to be an Egyptian King, even though he cannot so much as write his own name in the hieroglyphs. He must wear his Egyptian costume, and the Pharaoh's jewelled collar when Eskedi tells him to, and he must wear his Greek tunic, his Greek *khlamys* or cloak, when the Dioiketes tells him to. Whatever clothes he wears, he must stir up the displeasure of somebody. Sometimes, when the night is very hot, and he is alone with his wife, he forgets *ataraxia*, balance, and shouts about his impossible position.

Arsinoë Alpha does not know what to do when Mikros is angry. She wrings her jewelled hands and weeps. She hides her face under the bedsheet, and says nothing. A great king has nobody to speak his private thoughts to apart from his wife, nobody. But this wife offers no word of comfort, has no suggestions about what he might do. She is the perfect Greek wife, her head always inclined, her eyes always downcast. She must not look her husband in the face, even when he is in bed with her. She has been brought up to be unseen, unheard, next to invisible. When Mikros rages he often falls ill with a pain in the head. He groans, longing for Macedon, a place where he has, to be sure, never set his sandal, but where he thinks he might live happy with his goats, untroubled by the threat of war, revolts, uprisings and bloody murder.

Mikros does not ignore his beautiful and most beautiful wife, Arsinoë Alpha, but she knows nothing about siege-engines, torsion-catapults, or drilling the phalanx. She does not know how to outmanoeuvre an enemy at sea, or how to undermine a city by tunnelling, any more than her husband does. She knows nothing of men's business: her delight is the needle, spinning wool, kneading dough to make bread, cooking honey-cakes, and caring for her children.

It just so happens, though, that Arsinoë Beta is possessed of the exact same skills that her brother lacks. She can do mathematics and geometry just about as well as Euklid – who was once her tutor. She can spot a mistake in a tax return better than her brother's Minister of Finance. She knows how to wage war, how to govern a great kingdom. Aye, her thoughts are very like a man's thoughts, as if she is only one part woman but nine parts man.

The family of Ptolemy Mikros was happy enough until Arsinoë Beta flew back to Egypt like the vulture, bent upon making trouble, and Arsinoë Beta is perched, waiting now, waiting, like the vulture that roosts in a tree beside the field of battle, thinking about the feast of blood and guts that is a dead body – the dead body of Arsinoë Alpha.

Always it is easier for Ptolemy Mikros to do nothing. Always it is easier to have himself carried aloft in the *skollopendra*, the litter named after the millipede, upon the shoulders of twenty men, than to go to the trouble of walking. He is Pharaoh, a god in his own lifetime. He has himself carried even to the women's quarters, to greet his wife. When she is troubled by the heat, or too tired to receive him, he is carried through the city to the house of Stratonike, or Didyme, or Myrtion, or Kleino, or Mnesis, or Potheine, or Bilistikhe, to satisfy his craving for *aphrodisia*. He has other women, too many to name. They call this king *erotikos*, for he is amorous, even more amorous than his father. Ptolemy Mikros is the great master of the art of love.

Preoccupied with his duties and his pleasures, Mikros really did not notice the electric storm that was brewing between the two Arsinoës. He was too busy with the business of Pharaoh, too busy with his dozens of concubines, too busy with his Syrian War, to see that his sister was simply dying to kill his wife.

At the coronation Eskedi had said to him, *Thou art the rudder of the entire land, the land sails in accordance with thy command,* but it was as if the man who steered Egypt just then was wearing a blindfold, with his ship heading for the roaring white waters of the Cataract that make a man deaf upon the instant, for he saw nothing amiss. Just then, the ship of Ptolemy Mikros looked as if it might crash into the rocks.

1.4

Laughing

In the palace of this great monarch there was a good deal of noise – the chatter of monkeys, the squawk of caged birds, the twang of musicians' harps, the trumpet sounding the hour, the hubbub of petitioners, the crash of the sea upon the beach – but above it all rose the shrill laughter of Sotades of Maroneia, Mikros's Cretan jest-maker, making jokes about the attempted poisoning of the sister. Aye, Sotades retched, and threw himself on the floor, writhing, acting out the cruel death of the sister's food-taster. Sotades' laughter echoed round the vast marble-columned halls from sun-up to sundown, but it was accompanied now by the sound of Arsinoë Beta shouting at him. She had a special dislike for this inoffensive old man, who had first been employed by Ptolemy Soter to make his wife Eurydike laugh, and to try to make his daughter Ptolemaïs smile during her thirteen-year betrothal, when no woman in Egypt was more miserable. Mikros loved Sotades; Arsinoë Beta hated him. *Sotades is the past*, she said, *an old man full of old jests.* Arsinoë Beta did not like jests, but treated every last thing with the greatest seriousness. Nor did she like anything old. She did not like to think of her terrible yesterdays, but lived in the present moment, following the philosophy of the Kyrenaic School, her father's philosophy. Mikros thought just the same, and it was the first thing this brother and sister had in common. Arsinoë Beta thought, *I am today, modern times, the glorious future. There is no place for yesterday here.*

Sotades, however, still made Mikros burst into great peals of laughter. When the burden of the kingship weighed heavy upon his soul, Sotades would always cheer Mikros up. The jest-maker was in high favour because he made his Majesty feel that his caged and golden life was not bad but good. Perhaps the only person in Alexandria who did not love Sotades was Arsinoë Beta, and she would be responsible for his fall from favour, his terrible fall, for being unable to see the funny side of a harmless joke. Men said it would be easier to teach the Sphinx to sing than to stop Sotades laughing. For the time being not even Arsinoë Beta could silence him. But it was not his fate to laugh much longer, and though, for sure, he would die laughing, his end would not be amusing.

The end of Arsinoë Alpha would not be amusing either. For always Arsinoë Beta suspects that her amiable stepdaughter is planning her revenge for the death of her brother Agathokles *(uh-GATH-oh-kleez)*. Out of the corner of her eye she still sees the shabby grey figure of his handsome ghost following her. She thinks she sees hatred in the glance of Arsinoë Alpha, whose eyes are glossy, like black olives, the same as Agathokles' eyes, and all the time Arsinoë Alpha speaks in her brother's voice, with the same Thracian accent: she sounds like Agathokles, looks like Agathokles, and it makes Arsinoë Beta hate her all the more, and yet she goes on smiling at her, smiling, as if there is nothing wrong whatever.

But there was plenty wrong. Arsinoë Beta drove her new chariot out to the Agora the day after her return, and bought herself a falcon in a papyrus cage. *So that I may honour the Horus*, she said. She drove herself also that day to pay her respects to the dead – or living – Alexander, who still lay in the tomb at the intersection of Kanopic Street with the Street of the Soma, or Body. She ordered the golden coffin lid shifted by the guards so that she might look upon his face, and she helped herself to a fistful of hair from the dead man's head.

When she got home she took one of Arsinoë Alpha's hairs and one of the hairs from the head of the dead man, and tied them together. Next she tied the knotted hair to the leg of her falcon, took him in her hands and opened the window. Then she let him fly away, watched him soar into the blue vault of the heavens; watched him until he was nothing but a black speck: magic, guaranteed to make Arsinoë Alpha go mad.

For most of her life Arsinoë Beta had been famous for nastiness, whereas Arsinoë Alpha was famous for sweetness. Now Arsinoë Beta, who used to frown, smiled and even laughed. It would not take her long to unhinge Arsinoë Alpha. Even to share living quarters with Arsinoë Beta was enough to derange her. Magic might help her along the road to madness, but she would go there anyway, soon enough. Now the once-smiling Arsinoë Alpha frowned. Soon she would have cause to weep; soon she would be made to go completely crazy.

1.5

Razor-Tongue

Arsinoë Beta smiled now, but she was really not much given to laughing. Her purpose was far too serious for laughter. She had always been clever, and the latest instance of her cleverness was the arrival of a merchant ship from Amorgos, the easternmost island of the Kyklades – an event ordinary enough, save for the fact that the ship captain refused to unload his cargo without Arsinoë Beta standing by.

She came down quick from the Palace – by no means too grand to walk upon her own feet – almost ran, because this was her own ship, sailed on her orders from Kassandreia to Amorgos on the day her sons were killed. Even in the midst of murder and massacre, she had had the sense to order her personal fortune to be hurried to safety. No king or queen alive did anything less, of course: it was the standing orders for what to do in a crisis such as enemy attack, or everything falling apart in an earthquake. Nobody ever suggested that Ex-Queen Arsinoë Beta was poor at the end of her twenty years in Thrace. By no means. She had lost two sons, a husband and a kingdom, but she was still possessed of fabulous riches in her own right.

*

Nor had she lost all her heirs: she had one son left alive, and now that she had found a safe haven she sent a messenger across the Great Sea, into Illyria, where her son had taken refuge. Aye, she sent even so far as the court of Monounios, the barbarian chieftain, to fetch her son into Egypt – that Prince Ptolemaios of Thrace who would be known for the rest of history as Ptolemaios of Telmessos.

This Ptolemaios now took ship for Alexandria, thinking to offer his mother his support, but also in order to make the acquaintance of his Uncle Mikros, and perhaps benefit from his patronage.

When Ptolemaios walked into her chamber some time later, his mother fell upon his neck with tears. She did not wholly lack human feelings. By no means. She told him the story of the murder of his two brothers, and he hung his head to hear it. For a few difficult months he had been King of Macedon, until he was thrown out. He had known what it was to enjoy the power of a king. He had had the experience – disastrous though it was – of his war against the *Keltoi*, or Gauls. He knew what was success and what was failure. And he knew well enough how to murder a man.

Arsinoë Beta said to him, rather dry and cold, *It may be that it is your fate to be King here in Egypt instead of your Uncle Mikros. I am sure that you will be happy to do whatever I ask of you.*

Ptolemaios said, *Mother, whoever you may wish a dead man, I shall not be doing your murdering for you a second time.*

But really, it was no man that she had in mind to be dead, but a woman. She thought to have Ptolemaios her son dispose of Arsinoë Alpha, who happened also to be his half-sister. If Arsinoë Alpha's two sons could be killed off, the only male Ptolemy left would be her own son, and they would have to make him the Pharaoh. Arsinoë Beta was not so foolish as to get blood upon her own hands and live with the bloodguilt for ever, the angry ghost, and risk being found out in her crime. She had ghosts enough to handle already.

What young man in the world, she said to her son, *would not give all his teeth to be Pharaoh of Egypt if just three murders stood in his road?*

But though she beat Ptolemaios with the razor that was her tongue, she could not make him go back on his word. He would not do a murder.

Arsinoë Beta smiled. *We shall find some other way, then,* she said, *some other man to do our will, some other man who would like to be Pharaoh.* But for all her threats, for all the poisonous and scornful words she spat at this son, calling him coward, and traitor, and worse things, she did not change his heart.

Mikros eyed this other Ptolemaios warily, suspicious of the strapping young man with black hair and dark eyes, who said almost nothing, who had not the yellow hair of a true Ptolemy, and who was taller than himself, and he wondered why he was so keen to enlist in his uncle's army and fight for Egypt. He worried about how Ptolemaios might occupy himself in his spare time; whether he might not be thinking about helping his uncle to eat poison, or to fall down some marble staircase.

Perhaps, he thought, *this Ptolemaios will try to push us off our throne. Perhaps he wants to be King of Egypt himself.* He could not think that Ptolemaios did not know that the normal family custom was to murder every male relative in sight. *What can my nephew's thoughts be,* Mikros thought, *if they are not thoughts of violence? Perhaps it is Arsinoë Beta's wicked idea that she might make this Ptolemaios the Pharaoh in her brother's place, and rule Egypt through her son, make him do whatever she tells him.*

And, of course, how can it not have been so? This woman is poison made flesh. She lives by poison, is pure poison.

Aye, Mikros sensed it. He said to her, quite plain, *I already have my heir, Ptolemy Euergetes. You should know, Sister, that I will not take that son of Lysimakhos for my heir.*

Arsinoë Beta wore her face of surprise, as though she had never dreamed of asking for him to do such a thing.

You are so suspicious, Brother, she exclaimed. *How could you think such a thought?*

I know what you did to Agathokles of Thrace, Mikros said. *And you should know that if you lay a finger on my wife or children to harm them, you will be a dead woman yourself. Swear to me now, Sister, that you will not touch them.*

Arsinoë Beta made, of course, the face of How-Could-You-Think-of-Making-Me-Swear?

Swear it, Sister, Mikros said, *or leave Alexandria by the next ship, never to return here so long as I live.*

She stamped the foot, frowning. She let out a torrent of filthy abuse, fishwife language. But then she paused. *Very well, Brother,* she said, smiling. *I swear, but I know just what you did to our Uncle Menelaos, and to our half-brothers, Meleagros and Argaios, innocent young men, guilty of no crime. You cannot tell me that your hands are clean. Do you not feel guilty, Brother? For sure, you have done plenty of murders yourself.*

Mikros, unable to think of a suitable answer, turned on his heel and left her. But she called him back.

In your turn, she said, *you must swear that you will do no harm to me, or to my son Ptolemaios, but protect us while we are under your roof.*

Mikros had to swear. But no, he did not trust the sister, and he was right not to. She was a woman utterly ruthless, quite lacking in scruples, urgent to have what she wanted – the power in Egypt for herself, and never mind who must die in order for her to get it.

Aye, but the sister made her brother think that another was the one guilty of wanting to harm him. She told him straight: *It is not myself you should worry about, it is that wife of yours, who had poison by her in Thrace from a very young age, and was pleased to make use of it wherever she could. I have to tell you that I was most surprised when I heard you were willing to take that poisonous woman to wife.*

And so, yes, Mikros began to be suspicious of Arsinoë Alpha instead of his sister.

Ptolemaios of Telmessos stayed in Egypt, for the moment. Sometimes he spoke with Arsinoë Alpha of Thrace, his half-sister, about the end of Lysimakhos their father, or about the lobsters of the Hellespont that were so good to eat, but Arsinoë Alpha was already in a decline.

His mother said to him often, *You may be sure that if you will not do away with your Uncle Mikros he will, before long, be pleased to do away with you instead . . .*

But Ptolemaios's heart was strong to do what was right. Mikros, for his part, still felt the pangs of guilt over the other family members he had sent early down to Hades, and he was warier still of arousing his sister's anger by getting rid of her son. Mikros continued to eye Ptolemaios with unease. At length, nervous of the threat to his security, he sent him away to Telmessos, in Lydia, to be the governor there, and to get rid of him.

You should not doubt it, Stranger: Arsinoë Beta could just as easily murder her own brother as marry him.

1.6

Dolls of Wax

But no, maybe Arsinoë Beta would not have to do another murder. She would find it quite easy to remove Arsinoë Alpha from court without killing her, without the use of knives, simply by her will-power, by words alone. She thought of it as a challenge, like some game among the scholars of the Mouseion.

About this time Arsinoë Beta asked for flour to be delivered to her apartments, though she was not known for her skill at cooking. Really she was not much interested in eating, except eating poison. No, she had other uses for flour besides baking bread.

She also began to make daily sacrifice of a cock to Asklepios son of Apollo, the god of Health, for her bellyache grew worse now, or she made believe it did. She drank less than the grasshopper. She might have expected trouble in the guts.

She sent for Khrysippos and Amyntas four and five times a day. The doctors, most concerned to restore her health, gave her their best of remedies, but she tipped half the dose down the throat of one of her dogs, kept for the purpose, to see whether he might puke up or drop dead upon the spot. It was the standard practice: no king or queen of this time could afford to trust anybody, least of all the physicians, who had the easiest access to poison. Her dogs never did puke up or die, though, because Khrysippos and Amyntas were men of the highest honour, who had sworn the usual oath: *I shall give no poison to any man or woman, even if they ask me for it . . .*

Even so, Arsinoë Beta began to say, quite loud, in her brother's hearing, *Really, a queen should trust nobody. I am not sure that I trust these doctors.*

She went through the motions of trusting the gods. She dedicated silver entrails, coiled up lengths of golden intestines. She sacrificed oxen to Asklepios, and to Hygeia his daughter, and to Panacea, the divinities in charge of medicine. She carried the strip of papyrus to stick down her throat and make her vomit, which was the only way she could find relief from what she said was her terrible indigestion.

Mikros believed not a word of her nonsense. He would say to Khrysippos and Amyntas, *There is nothing wrong with her . . . she makes herself sick up her food so as to stay thin.* Or *She never eats a proper meal.* Or *A good plate of flamingo and turnips would cure her.* Or *She has the bellyache because she is hungry.*

The doctors did their best for her, but they were more concerned just then about the health of Arsinoë Alpha.

Aye, for Arsinoë Alpha was now to be heard wailing by night, and it was the thought that her brother's ghost went unavenged, and her fear of Arsinoë Beta lay behind it. Her behaviour became strange also by day: she began to go about smashing earthenware pots on to the mosaic floor, and held conversations with herself at the top of her voice, conversations about unnatural death.

Arsinoë Beta was kind, sympathetic, affectionate to her sister-in-law and stepdaughter. She sent Khrysippos and Amyntas to talk with her, urging them, *Surely you can find some cure for her Majesty's trouble. The poor woman needs expert help. You should give her the hellebore, hellebore will help with madness.*

Aye, but what Arsinoë Beta said and what she thought were two different things. She thought of the hair of the murdered man and the hair of Arsinoë Alpha tied to the legs of the falcon, and in her heart she saw, as it were, the soul of Arsinoë Alpha hauled up into the sky, screaming, unable to get down again. Her magic was working.

Arsinoë Alpha barely slept by night. By day she wandered about the palace, haggard, tearful, talking to herself, spitting on the ground and swearing by Zeus and Pan and all the gods, like one of the hired soldiers, like a woman possessed of demons. She fell down and bruised herself on the marble steps. She stopped painting her face, was careless of her dress, neglectful of her appearance.

About the same time Arsinoë Beta began to take a great deal of trouble over how she looked. She had new clothes made, dyed her grey hair yellow, and made herself look more like the Great Royal Daughter of Pharaoh that she was.

She went to Mikros now, and said, *Really, Brother, I think you will have to send your wife away to the Asklepieion at Kos in search of a proper cure.*

Mikros looked at her hard. Sure, he had begun to have some doubts about his wife's sanity. Sure, he had begun to think, *Indeed, she is very sick.* But he also thought, *What if she were the victim of magic? What if my sister has bewitched my wife?*

What, indeed. What if she had bewitched both of them?

Better to keep her here, Sister, he said, *close by us, where we may help her: the best of medical help is to be found here in Alexandria.*

The sister rolled her eyes. *Kos is best,* she began. But Mikros cut her off.

Remember, Sister, he said, *what Thales of Miletos said: Do not beautify your face but be beautiful in your behaviour. Remember you have sworn not to harm my wife or children.*

She struck him upon the cheek for saying it, and they hurled abuse at each other, then, calling each other *Pig* and *Hippopotamus* and *Kakos* and worse things, as if they sought to outdo each other in shouting, like big children.

Now that Lysimakhos of Thrace, the father of Arsinoë Alpha, was dead, there was no longer any pressing diplomatic reason for Ptolemy Mikros to keep her as his wife. The Thracian Alliance, Mikros's sole reason for marrying Arsinoë Alpha, was no longer valid. He had, really, no thought to divorce her, but the situation was not much different than in any other Greek house: the wife was for the ploughing of legitimate children, and for running the house-hold; it was the concubines who gave a man pleasure.

But when the wailing started, Mikros stopped going to Arsinoë Alpha after dark altogether. He had never spoken with her very much. Now he spoke with her not at all.

At Alexandria Arsinoë Alpha had played the Greek Queen, wearing the white *peplos*, the golden tiara and necklaces, the exquisite brooches with golden flowers and bees of gold nestling among them. When she sailed up-River to Memphis she had worn the vulture headdress, the red dress of a god-dess, and rattled the bronze *seistron* in the Temple of Ptah. She had smiled ever the vague, distant smile of the Lady of the Two Lands. Her twice-life-size statue as Isis in pink granite stood in front of the newly finished Pharos. She quite left Arsinoë Beta in the shadows for jewels and finery. In Egypt Arsinoë Beta was merely the daughter of the late Pharaoh, no more than a princess, and she liked it not. But now that Arsinoë Alpha wailed by night, Arsinoë Beta said to Mikros, *Brother, the heat up-River will not improve your wife's health. Perhaps it will please you to take your sister with you instead?* And so Arsinoë Beta travelled to Memphis with her brother, and his wife was left behind.

Arsinoë Alpha had always been pretty quiet. She had never spoken at length to her husband upon any matter. Now, however, she began to make a great deal of noise, throwing pots out of her windows, and she got for herself a strange wild laugh, so that Arsinoë Beta said to Mikros, *Brother, it would be better for Arsinoë Alpha to stay in the gynaikeion. It looks so bad for her Majesty to be heard shouting like a madwoman.*

Mikros agreed for his wife to be confined to the *gynaikeion* with her wait-ing-women. And then, a while after, he allowed Arsinoë Beta to have her own quarters, elsewhere, out of earshot of the nightly wailing, and, as it happened, rather nearer to his own apartments. Mikros sent the doctors to his wife, sure, but he did not go near her himself. By no means. He thought, *She is sick. She must have done something to anger the gods. And he got for himself fresh talismans against evil spirits.*

As for Arsinoë Beta, she thought, *It is our magic working upon her soul.* And in the privacy of her new private chamber she laughed much the same kind of mad laugh as Arsinoë Alpha.

Mikros, preoccupied with his war, with his duty, let matters go on as they were. He sent medical help. He urged the doctors to seek a cure, and he made generous offerings to Asklepios for the restoration of his wife's health. He sent night and morning to ask after her condition. *If the gods wish it,* he thought, *she will recover; if not, she will not.* For Mikros all was in the hands of the gods, all was a matter of waiting. But Arsinoë Beta could not sit by and do nothing. She had wasted half her lifetime waiting in Thrace. She felt she must take every action as soon as she thought of it, for her days upon earth were running out.

One night she fashioned a doll out of wax, and pushed a handful of Arsinoë Alpha's dark hair into the navel. She stuffed a scrap of papyrus into the back of it. The hair would transfer the essence of the person it belonged to into the doll. Whatever rites Arsinoë Beta performed over it would affect the owner of the hair. She chanted. She whispered. She murmured the words of power that must sever Arsinoë Alpha from her husband. And then she threw the wax image into her brazier so that it melted away to nothing, hissing in the flames. There was no cure for one against whom such magic was worked. She was bound by the spell, bound to die.

In the meantime, while the sister waited for her magic to take its most dramatic effect, what did she do all day? Not tapestry, for sure. No, she made herself useful to her brother. She told him her thoughts about the proper level of taxes. She suggested wonderful improvements to the fiscal system. She wanted to know about the royal banks and the royal granaries. She discussed the camel post and the harbour regulations. She went out of her way to talk with him about Egypt's agricultural problems, such as watering the fields. She urged him to pay for the repair of dykes and canals, and to implement the famous Screw of Archimedes for getting the water out of the River. Already she helped him to carry the burden of government.

Above all she talked to him about his war with Syria, the forever war, saying, *If I was you I should fetch up some more elephants from the south country, to be elephants of war . . . If I was you I should dredge the bottom of the Canal of Nekho, and strengthen your border forts in the east.* Aye, she told him not only what he must do today, but also what he should plan to do tomorrow, always thinking ahead, always calculating.

For sure, Arsinoë Beta was just as keen as her father and brother to live for the present moment, but she also thought of the future. She knew all about what had been happening in Egypt during her absence, had kept pace with affairs at home. Aye, the truth was that she knew just as much about Egypt as her brother did, maybe more. Mikros was grateful to the sister for taking an interest. He thought, *My wife knows none of these things. My wife is no help to me.* At the same time, though, he was uneasy, because having the sister's help must be a temporary thing. Always she urged haste, saying, *I must deal with your war soon, before I go away again, before I set off to marry my fresh husband.* And thus she made Mikros think the thought that he would be worse off without her.

Sensible of his sister's uncertain position, Mikros did send ambassadors to his neighbours to ask what princes were available to be husbands, saying he needs must get her off his hands.

She is a charming and capable woman, he wrote, *who will make any king a most excellent wife. She is skilled in military matters and foreign affairs . . . She is quite out of the ordinary run of women.*

What he wrote was true. The sister did not lack good looks. She even had the ability to make herself perfectly charming. But every Greek-speaking king had heard, by now, of Arsinoë Beta's terrible reputation: it was common knowledge that she had murdered Handsome Agathokles of Thrace; that she had milked Lysimakhos, her aged husband, of his last obol; that she was as thin as the whippet, and as poisonous as a nest of serpents.

There was the further problem that Arsinoë Beta was a used wife, a second-hand wife, and that any fresh marriage would be her third marriage, for though the Greeks liked to say *The third time is the lucky time,* they also said *The third-time wife is no better than a whore,* and it was always the occasion for much sniggering.

None of Mikros's friends wanted to take on the challenge of Arsinoë Beta, whatever wonderful political skills she might possess. They thought she would be just about as much trouble as Helen of Troy. No suitor called upon Ptolemy Mikros to ask for the hand of his sister in marriage, then, not one, so that it looked like he would be stuck with her living at home with him for ever – which, of course, was just what Arsinoë Beta wanted.

Every morning she would come to talk with her brother, about ships of war, siege-engines, the balance of payments, the spice trade, everything under the sun, but above all, about elephants of war, that were a king's greatest weapon. When she did not sit beside him, he would look round and miss her. Of course he had his Dioiketes, his vizier, his Hypodioiketes, or under-vizier, his Eklogistes, or minister of finance, his Epistolographos, or private secretary, his Hypomnematographos, or writer of memoranda, his ministers for foreign affairs, and war, and so forth, very many worthy advisers – but Arsinoë Beta already showed herself better than all of them put together. When she was not at Mikros's side, helping him, he began to send messengers to ask for her thoughts, because she had upwards of twenty years' experience of government, whereas he had only four.

Aye, the greatest lesson Arsinoë Beta had learned from her mother was: *Make your husband need you, make the man utterly incapable of living without you.* She was in no hurry to reply to his messages. She did not go running to his side. It was her pleasure to keep him waiting. *Soon,* she thought, *he will be unable to take any decision without me. Soon I shall force him to marry me.*

When even Arsinoë Beta wearied of talking about war, she might lecture Mikros about Zeus, king of the gods, and his wife Hera, who also happened to be his elder sister. And why was it? Because she wanted to sow the seeds of a particular thought in her brother's heart – that a brother–sister marriage was no wickedness, but a perfectly natural thing, really the most natural and lovely thing in the world.

Mikros lay awake at night, worrying about what to do with his sick wife, what to do about his bossy sister, but he had never been much good at decision-making. It was Arsinoë Beta herself who, in the end, decided for him. On the hottest nights, when she could not sleep, she would amuse herself by sticking pins in a fresh doll of wax, dozens of pins in each one, until she had a long row of wax images of Arsinoë Alpha hidden under the floor of her bedchamber.

When Mikros did manage to sleep he dreamed that Arsinoë Alpha was creeping up on him as he slept, with an axe.

1.7

Black Feathers

Sotades overheard Arsinoë Beta telling her brother what to do, and what not to do, so many times, so insistent, so very harsh, and was amused to hear her berating her brother for his shortcomings. Sotades wrote a poem called *Amazon,* about a woman with great muscles of iron, who beat her brother with a heavy club. He recited his poem for every man in the palace to laugh at, because it already looked as if Mikros had to do just whatever his sister told him, as if the sister was the one with the power.

Aye, the Amazon, this sister who was in many ways so very like a man, moved pretty quick to increase her hold over her brother. She knew that what controlled Mikros was not fate, not the gods, not even his belly, but the intense power of Eros, that is stronger than geometry. *If I can make my brother love me,* she thought, *I might have total power over him.* But even more powerful than Eros is magic, and Arsinoë Beta was not quite so modern and sophisticated that she did not try out every filthy old Greek charm in order to eject Arsinoë Alpha from the palace, from Alexandria, from the land of the living.

For sure, this woman of power had no need to resort to murder.

She stuffed a dog's excrement in the post hole of Arsinoë Alpha's door, murmuring, *I sever Arsinoë Alpha from Ptolemy son of Ptolemy.*

She worked the spell called How to Separate a Woman from her Husband, whispering, *Send the fire of hatred to his heart and the flame to his place of sleeping, until he cast Arsinoë daughter of Lysimakhos out of his dwelling, she having hatred to his heart, and quarrel to his face.*

She sang, *Grant for them nagging and squabbling, fighting and quarrelling at all times, until they are separated, without agreeing again for ever.*

She thought, *I shall force the gods to help us.* But some days she thought otherwise: *While praying to the gods, one must also help oneself.*

One morning she went to Mikros and said, *Brother, your wife has ripped up our Odyssey of Homer.*

Too bad, Mikros said, *but it is not the only copy. Ask the scholars for another.*

Another time she said, *Your wife has smashed a marble bust of our father.*

Mikros sighed. *Arsinoë Alpha is sick,* he said, his thoughts elsewhere, with the concubines, with the imports from the island of Rhodes, the whereabouts of the army of Syria. *We must send in the doctors more often.*

Whatever Arsinoë Beta did, whatever fault she found with her brother's wife, Mikros would not hear a word against her. He did not see guile in any of her strange actions. Even when she set his bedchamber alight he said, quite calm, *It is but a symptom of her illness. I have heard that a woman may suffer from the melancholia after the birth of a child. That is all that is wrong with her. She will soon recover. Khrysippos and Amyntas will be sure to find a cure.*

But when the Dioiketes hauled Arsinoë Alpha before Mikros, screaming and in chains, accused of a terrible crime, and he heard what the trouble was about, Mikros was forced to think different. He hid his face in his cloak, groaned and wept. He could not believe that his amiable wife had anything to do with magic spells, let alone the spell called How to Procure the Death of your Husband.

Arsinoë Beta was, by chance, on hand to read the papyrus aloud to him, exclaiming for amazement as she did so.

Listen, Brother, she said, eager, so eager, *to what has been found in your wife's possession – it is a recipe designed to send you down to Hades . . . It says, Kill the hen, and catch her blood in a vessel, for it is the blood that attracts spirits . . . It says, Find an egg laid by a hen with black feathers only. Upon the egg write a magic square with the hen's blood . . . It says, Burn some incense, hold the egg over the fumes written-side downwards. Now hide the egg in a tomb, for the tomb is the haunt of spirits . . .*

Oh, it is terrible, terrible, she exclaimed. Then she turned to the Dioiketes.

Tell his Majesty, she said, *what you have found . . .*

A dead chicken has been found in the Queen's chamber, the Dioiketes said, *a black chicken, and a bowl of blood.*

It is nothing to do with me at all, Arsinoë Alpha shrieked. *If anybody put it there, it was your sister, your evil sister.*

Arsinoë Beta ignored the outburst. She said to the Dioiketes, *And now please to tell his Majesty what was found in the doctors' apartments.* And the Dioiketes said, *We found, Megaleios, a papyrus with the same recipe written upon it in the possession of Khrysippos and Amyntas.*

Arsinoë Beta said, *The first person to suspect of guilt in such a case is always the doctor, who may so very easily get his hands upon every kind of herb and poison, every kind of magic charm.*

Aye, even Khrysippos and Amyntas, whose diligence and skill had saved the lives of both Mikros and Arsinoë Alpha, even the doctors who had brought their three children into the world, were now arrested, bound like prisoners of war and dragged before Mikros to be questioned. Aye, and again Arsinoë Beta happened to be there to offer her advice, the great administrator of criminal justice in Thrace, who had twenty years' experience of sentencing offenders and extracting secrets from foreign spies.

You should squeeze them, Brother, Arsinoë Beta said, voice low, *to make them confess.*

Mikros felt sick to think of it, but he had the two physicians taken away to be stretched, when they swore they had done nothing against their Hippokratic oath, nothing wrong whatever. They were beaten next upon the palms of the hands and the soles of the feet. They would never walk again. Arsinoë Beta watched the beating, urging on the torturers, smiting her thigh with her hand, seeming not to notice that she bruised herself.

Khrysippos and Amyntas groaned and exclaimed, but they would say nothing against Arsinoë Alpha. They would say nothing but, *Whatever I have seen or heard . . . which ought . . . not to be . . . divulged, I will keep . . . secret and . . . tell to . . . nobody . . .*

For these two great criminals, however, it would not be a matter of never walking again but a matter of not breathing.

Mikros did not stand and look, knowing that he would puke to see it, his friends' slow murder at his sister's hands. He wept when he heard that Khrysippos and Amyntas had gone down to the House of Hades.

The rotting corpses of Khrysippos and Amyntas hung in the Agora for days. The crows pecked out their eyes and picked at their flesh until there was nothing left but bones, which were cast into the sea off Pharos island.

Friends of the King these doctors were, and yet, under the stern rule of his sister, he did not raise his voice to save them. Mikros let his friends die, because he thought the sister told the truth.

He railed against his sister in the privacy of his own apartments. But whatever she demanded in the way of punishment for his wife, Mikros stood firm.

Arsinoë Alpha is a sick woman, he said. *She needs help, not punishment.*

But why was it? If he punished the doctors, why would he not punish this traitor? Why would he not execute the wife who wished him dead? It was because he was a man of his word, famous for never having told an untruth in his lifetime. At his betrothal he had sworn his oath before the ambassadors of Lysimakhos, to take care of Arsinoë Alpha whatever happened. He had watched the wax figures melt in the fire. He had repeated the words, shuddering: *He who breaks this oath, let him melt away to nothing like these figures of wax. Let him and his children and grandchildren be liquefied. Let his fortune be melted down . . .*

When Arsinoë Beta insisted that his wife be given the same treatment as the doctors, he stood up to her. His voice shook when he thought of the melting wax, but he said, *My wife is the anointed Queen of Upper and Lower Egypt. Whatever she may have done, I absolutely refuse to have her put to death.*

But when the sister took Mikros to the *gynaikeion* and showed him the clothes press of her Majesty, hidden at the bottom, under his wife's dresses, he saw the stuffed doll that Arsinoë Beta had made, a representation of Mikros himself – for his own name was written upon it in what looked like blood. When she said, *Look at this, Brother – I fear it must be the work of your wife,* Mikros looked. He saw that the stuffed doll was stuck full of pins, dozens of bronze pins, and he believed the sister must be right.

Your wife wants you a dead man, Brother, Arsinoë Beta murmured. *You should act now, before it is too late.*

1.8

Egyptian Cuckoo

Arsinoë Alpha, brought before Mikros for further questioning, shrieked, *I will swear upon my daughter's eyes that I never plotted your death. I will swear upon my mother's tomb that I never wished you dead.*

Mikros could hardly bring himself to speak. His wife's good looks had vanished. She had clawed at her face. Her eyes were wild, her hair rumpled. Now it was Arsinoë Beta, wearing gold and jewels and fine white linen, who looked more like the Queen of Egypt.

Hear my words, Arsinoë Alpha said. *The plot of which you speak, it is nothing but the lies of Arsinoë Beta.* But she found her tongue too late. Ptolemy Mikros, blinded by the cleverness of his sister, no longer trusted his wife to tell him the truth.

No, Mikros's fixed thought now was that Arsinoë Alpha had, indeed, been trying to murder him, that she wished him dead and gone down to Hades. It was Arsinoë Beta that sowed the seeds of hatred for his wife in her brother's heart, just as she had sown hatred in the heart of Lysimakhos, her first husband, a terrible hatred for his own son. She was trying to do a second time just the same as she had done in Thrace.

Seshat asks the question: *What could Arsinoë Alpha hope to gain by killing her husband?* If Ptolemy Mikros were dead and gone, and Arsinoë Alpha took charge, who would be King of Egypt? Her young son, Ptolemy Euergetes, four years old, for whom, perhaps, she might have been Regent. Perhaps her thought was to take all the power of Mikros and rule as king herself. Such a thing was not unheard of in Egypt. But Arsinoë Alpha knew nothing of how to rule a kingdom, nothing of armies or fleets, nothing of how to wage a war. She hardly knew the names of her husband's ministers, let alone their faces. She was a woman of Thrace, with no friends in Egypt but her waiting-women. All her kin were dead, except Ptolemaios of Telmessos, and she could no more flee to Thrace if things went ill for her than fly to the Moon, because the court of Lysimakhos her father was finished, a thing of history. Arsinoë Alpha had no good reason to want her husband dead. It was in her interests to keep him alive for as long as she could.

Seshat swears: *If Arsinoë Alpha plotted at all, she plotted against Arsinoë Beta, not against the husband that she loved.*

Arsinoë Beta took to wearing the fur from a hyaena's forehead in order to avert the evil eye that Arsinoë Alpha had cast upon her. She made great use of the strip of papyrus that she stuck down her throat to make her vomit, saying, *We are sure somebody is trying to feed us poison again* . . . and then the noise of her retching would be heard, very like the rasping voice of the hyaena, who attracts his victims by mimicking the noise of a dog sicking up his guts. *We are sure some terrible magic is afoot,* she said.

Aye, but it was the terrible magic worked by herself, not that of anybody else. Arsinoë Alpha was innocent of magic, a completely innocent woman.

These were indeed the days of the hyaena, for the howling of her Majesty still came by night from the chamber in which she was locked, pending her husband's decision about what he would do with her, and it went on for several days and nights, because Mikros could not decide what was for the best.

At length he asked the opinion of the sister. *What to do? Whatever am I to do?* he said, spreading the hands. Without stopping to think for one moment she said, *A public stoning is the only punishment for plotting against the King.*

He gave her his Do-Not-Trust-You look. *We are not barbarians here,* he said quietly. *I will not give my wife such treatment. I will not hear of it.*

Arsinoë Beta said, *You must throw her into the River, then.*

But Mikros said, *I shall not drown the mother of the next Pharaoh. I bear her no ill will.*

She would have you dead, Arsinoë Beta said, *but you will not punish her?*

She is the mother of the next Pharaoh, Mikros said. *She shall be the Great White Cow That Dwells in Nekher.*

Arsinoë Beta scoffed, as if it were out of the question. She wanted to be the Great White Cow herself. *She has ordered up your death,* she said, *and you will let her son be king after you?*

I have no complaint against her, Mikros said.

You must send her away from here, Arsinoë Beta said, *for her own good. Kos is a healthy place with good doctors; the climate is good for cases of the black melancholia.*

Mikros was silent, watching the grey sea from his window, the palm trees bent double in the wind.

I cannot live under the same roof as a screaming madwoman, Arsinoë Beta said. *I live in fear of what your lovely wife will do next. Shall I be set on fire? Shall I be poisoned again? For I am sure, now, that it was she who tried to poison me the last time . . . I shall give you a choice, Brother, either Arsinoë Alpha must go, or I shall have to go myself.*

Mikros still said nothing. Arsinoë Beta stared at him, wearing her face of disgust, then she left him alone, thinking, *Let him decide himself, for once.*

It was about this time that her Majesty vanished from Alexandria, and was reported to be not up at Memphis either. Aye, Arsinoë Alpha disappeared, just as surely as Uncle Menelaos and Mikros's spare brothers and all the rest of his relatives had disappeared. Really, it was better not to ask too many questions about what had happened.

But yes, the truth was that Arsinoë Beta had ousted the Queen her step-daughter from Alexandria, much as a fledgeling cuckoo pushes a sparrow's young out of the nest that is rightfully theirs, and within one month of her return to Egypt. Some said it took Arsinoë Beta as long as six years to remove Arsinoë Alpha. Seshat believes them not. It had never taken Arsinoë Beta six years to get rid of an enemy. For her, it was oust or be ousted, kill or be killed, and as quick as she could. She moved like lightning, like the serpent.

Arsinoë Beta herself now lay awake by night, thinking, *Must move fast, must strike quick, now*. She thought of the advice of Berenike Alpha on how to catch a man, how to win a man's affections. She retired to bed with her face plastered with fish glue and oil of fenugreek, to remove the wrinkles. She cleared her complexion with swan's fat. She covered up the livid scratchlines of her mourning with white lead. She put a rosy colour upon her pale cheeks with crocodile dung. She made her eyebrows and eyelids dark with kohl, Egyptian eye-paint, designed to frighten off the flies, but arranged in the elongated paint stripe of the Egyptians, going far beyond what any Greek woman had done in Egypt before. She got hold of the hair dye made of canary egg yolks to make her hair more golden-yellow than before, like the goddesses' – like golden-haired Aphrodite, fair like the hair of Helen of Troy. She made herself look ten years younger. Even at Memphis the people waved and cheered her as Pharaoh's Daughter when she drove her chariot through the streets. She dressed in white linen, wearing the simple gold diadem of an Egyptian princess in her now brilliant yellow hair, and the golden serpent-bracelets snaked halfway up her arms – Egypt began to love her.

1.9

Foreign Affairs

Aye, as soon as the Queen had gone, Arsinoë Beta moved quick indeed. On the first morning after the departure of Arsinoë Alpha, she followed her brother into the meeting of his Council of War. She sat herself down at the great marble and gold table beside his Majesty, with his Dioiketes and ministers of state, and Eskedi, High Priest of Memphis, and she took charge of the meeting herself. She did not keep her mouth shut and listen, but stood up and spoke about Egypt and Macedon, and Greece, and Phrygia, and Kilikia, and Syria, as if she meant to take the control of foreign affairs into her own hands.

Indeed, in his heart, Ptolemy Mikros *wished she would*.

Soon, Egypt will be at war, she said, and she was right one million times.

Our quarrel with Antiokhos over Syria is of very long standing, she said, *going back to the peace signed after the Battle of Ipsos in Phrygia by our father, when all of Syria was given to Old Seleukos, but Ptolemy Soter held on to it even as far as the River Eleutheros in the north ... Even though these lands may not have been rightfully his, my father refused to give them up ... He made things worse by taking the cities which Old Seleukos claimed were his ...*

This time, she said, *the heart of our dispute is the coast of Phoenicia. Everybody wants this coast, because whoever controls it will lay his hands upon a limitless supply of ship timber – the best cedar wood – the best shipwrights, the best sailors in the world ...*

If we can get hold of Tyros and Sidon we shall control the markets at the end of the camel routes that come north from Arabia and Petra, and west from Babylon and Damaskos ... We also want control of the Aegean Sea. We must have command of the sea-passage through to the Black Sea ...

She smiled, folded her arms, then went on, fiercer.

But Antiokhos Soter of Syria wants all this for himself. That is why we are at war with Syria, and that is why we are going to defeat Antiokhos and grind his face in the sand.

Mikros's ministers were astonished to hear a woman talk so confident of men's affairs. Mikros said himself, *Applause for the sister, my friends. Applause. She will save Egypt.* And they did applaud. They banged their fists on the table. And she would save Egypt.

Eskedi was full of admiration. Not even Berenike Alpha, her mother, had been so fierce as this. Eskedi, who saw the future clearer than any other man, thought, *She will be good for Egypt, she will win this war. If we can keep her here.*

In the afternoon of that day, when Alexandria slept on account of the heat, Arsinoë Beta made Mikros forego his usual visit to the concubines and drive her in his chariot to the Mouseion and the Great Library, to show her what he had done since he became king, what was new in Alexandria.

We have been encouraging the scholars, he said. And he presented her to the Priest of the Muses, who was, of course, a Greek.

Mikros introduced – or reintroduced – the sister to his scholars, saying, *This is Herophilos, the great physician ... This is Zenodotos of Ephesos, who has charge of the Great Library, and is a noted scholar of Homer ...*

We aim to have every book in the world, Mikros said, *that is, the Greek world. The barbarians do not have books, do not know about reading. Nor will we have any Egyptian books in here.*

But the sister said, quite quiet, *You know, there are plenty of books among the barbarians: we shall get hold of them as well . . . If a man can read the books written by his enemies, he may learn how better to defeat them . . .*

Mikros introduced his sister to the scholars who wrote plays for his great theatre: such as Philitas of Korkyra, now working on his forty-second tragedy, one tragedy, as he said, for each of the forty-two *nomes*, or districts, of Egypt.

Meet Aristarkhos of Samos, the astronomer, he said, *meet Homeros of Byzantion . . . Meet Sosiphanes of Syracuse, who has written seventy-three tragedies.* And so on, until she had met all one hundred scholars.

But Arsinoë Beta said, *We have already seen enough tragedy to last a lifetime . . . I think we shall support the poets from now on . . .*

Mikros introduced his sister, then, to the poet whose verses could be read both backwards and forwards. She met the scholar who was engaged in rewriting the entire Odyssey of Homer without once using the letter *sigma.*

We think it is a great feat, Mikros said, *for just about every word in Greek ends in -os. To write Greek without any sigmas is quite a challenge . . .*

She met the poet-scholars who wrote verses in which the total of the letters taken as numbers added up to just the same total in every pair of lines. Mikros liked unusual things like this, exotic things. Everyday things bored him. *It is remarkable, is it not,* he said, *to be able to write in such a manner?*

Mikros presented the sister to the poets who had written verses about birds in the shape of birds, axes in the shape of axes, serpents in the shape of serpents. *It is clever, you know, very clever,* he said. *Not many men would think of doing that . . .*

Some men sneered at the Mouseion, calling it the Birdcage of the Muses, because what the scholars were best at was squawking and quarrelling; but the truth was otherwise. Arsinoë Beta said it herself, to anybody who cared to listen: *Our Mouseion is the beating heart of Alexandria, the Thinking-Shop, the Palace of Fresh Ideas. Our Mouseion will make the city glorious; it is the great glory of the House of Ptolemy.*

Mikros noticed that she called the Mouseion *ours*, as if she was part of it herself; as if she meant to take charge of that as well.

At the end of the afternoon Arsinoë Beta breathed a long sigh, and let her smile fade away. *Really, Brother,* she said, *your Mouseion is a wonder, but most of what is done there is of no use whatever. Tell me, Brother, if you would be so kind, what is the use of the Odyssey written without the letter sigma?*

Mikros opened the mouth, then closed it again. He spread the hands. *It is a fine thing,* he said, vaguely, *to turn the old into something new . . . is it not?*

Homer is wonderful, Arsinoë Beta said, *but almost every man in Alexandria knows his work off by heart. Why not ask the poets to write us something new? Why not let them tell the story of Jason and his Argonauts properly? That has never been done before. That would be much more interesting than regurgitating Homer . . .*

Mikros called Apollonios Rhodios, the poet, to him, for Arsinoë Beta to repeat her request. Upon the instant the poem called *Argonautika* was commissioned, and Apollonios Rhodios began writing within the hour.

The feeling roused in Mikros during Arsinoë Beta's inspection of the city was something like fear, for whatever he had built, or improved, whether it was the Lighthouse, or the Temple of Apollo, or the Macedonian-style landscaping of the palace gardens, the sister said, *We could have done this so much better . . . We would have built that in quite a different style . . .* finding fault with everything she saw, so that Mikros felt as if he could do nothing right.

Arsinoë Beta went on: *Your Mouseion is a fine thing, Brother, but what have you shown me today that will help Egypt win her wars? What has the Mouseion done to fill the treasury of Egypt with gold? How will the Mouseion provide a return upon your great investment of capital?*

As it happened, Mikros could answer that question, and he drove her to visit the workshops of Ktesibios, the noted engineer.

Ktesibios showed Arsinoë Beta his automatic torsion-catapult in action, firing a great bolt into the Harbour of Eunostos. He demonstrated his new machinery for scaling walls. He revealed the prototype of a machine that would squirt water, and put out fires. At last the sister showed some genuine interest. She questioned Ktesibios for some time, and it was not just polite remarks.

She made Mikros drive her to inspect the arsenal of weapons, then to the helmet manufactory, the siege-machine sheds, and the barracks, all the time telling him how he could do things better.

You must double the output of weapons, she said. *You must not allow the troops to sleep away the afternoon. You must keep up the war effort throughout all the hours of daylight.*

Wherever she went she said, *Egypt is at war with Syria. No man may rest until we have won our victory.*

As they sat down to eat their dinner – for she even presumed to feast with the men, as if she was a man herself – she asked her brother, *Have you heard what has happened at Damaskos?* But Mikros did not know, had not asked for the news from Syria that day. *They are desperate for your orders,* she said. *Are you quite sure you can spare the time for drinking this evening? Is there not still much work to be done?* And she made him send the messenger before he picked up his golden goblet.

All through that dinner, amid the roar of conversation and the laughter of the generals and admirals, Arsinoë Beta thought, *Like the serpent, move quick, strike like the snake. Take what you want, for he will never offer it to you.* At the end of the dinner, when the guests had departed, and Mikros still lay on his couch, too stuffed with roast peacock to move one fingerbreadth, she took hold of his hand to stroke it. Mikros cried out, indeed, as if he had been bitten.

Do not touch me, Sister, he screamed, *it is disgusting.* But she looked into his face and sparkled her eyes just as she used to do with Agathokles of Thrace, and she held on to his arm, gripping it with a man's grip, and stroked his hand some more. *To love your sister,* she said, *that is the proper Egyptian way.* Then she began to stroke his thigh. For sure, Mikros let out a noise then, halfway between a laugh and a scream, as if all the horrors of Hades were about to fall upon his head, but he also smelled the divine smell of her perfume, as if she were one of the goddesses herself. A strange feeling crept across his heart, like horror and delight all mixed up together, and she felt him shudder.

We should be pleased for you to kiss us, she said, *upon the lips . . .* And she affected not to notice the look upon his face. *A pharaoh without a wife,* she said, *is like a fish taken out of the water.*

Mikros opened his mouth and closed it without speaking, very like the fish, speechless with disgust. He had his concubines. He had not thought of taking a fresh wife, had not so much as dreamed of it.

Why not marry me, yourself, Brother, she said. *I should love to be Lady of the Two Lands . . . I could help you win your every battle . . .*

I beg you not to touch me, Sister, he said, but she kissed him all the same, so that he could not say more, and though he whimpered to find her tongue inside his mouth, she held on to him so that he could not escape, and he stopped trying to push her away. At the end of it, when she paused for breath, Mikros said, angry, *The gods saw that. You know very well, Sister, that intimacy with your own brother is a grotesque affront to the gods. I have no wish to be married to you, none whatever.*

Arsinoë Beta laughed in his face. *We are gods in our family,* she said, *and we may do just as we please. Have you forgot what our friend in Memphis said? Gods are immortal humans, humans are mortal gods. It is not such a big thing for a Greek to become a god. I think I shall enjoy being Isis, and Hera, and Aphrodite, and Hathor. I shall love being a goddess in my own lifetime.*

Can you imagine what our mother would have said? Mikros said, loud.

Our mother is dead and gone below to Hades, she said. *Her spirit sleeps easy. She knows nothing of what we do here upon earth.*

A man may not marry his sister, Mikros said, very slow. *It is an abomination, an abomination.*

We are all Egyptians now, Arsinoë Beta said, *and to the Egyptians a marriage between brother and sister is no wrong. Whatever are you afraid of, Brother? Why are you such a coward?*

I will never agree to it, he shouted.

But Arsinoë Beta knew better. She had seen the future in a bowl of water with oil floating on the surface. Her future glittered, and sparkled.

Never say never, she said. *I shall persuade you soon . . .*

And to help him be persuaded she went away to her private chamber and fashioned another doll, this time out of dough, flesh-coloured, and warm as flesh, and she stuck thirteen bronze needles into it: one and two in the eyes, so that he should see only Arsinoë Beta, three and four in the nostrils, so that he should smell only Arsinoë Beta, her divine perfume, five and six in the ears, so that he should hear no voice but hers, seven in the mouth so that his tongue should be hers, eight in the heart, nine in the navel, ten in the belly, eleven and twelve between the legs, and thirteen behind, so that his heart, his belly, his *rhombos*, even his *pehwit* should be under her command and control. Each time she drove in the needle she murmured, *I pierce the stomach of Ptolemy Mikros . . .* or *I pierce the heart . . .* and so on, *so that he may think of nobody but me, Arsinoë Beta.*

Magic was the only use Arsinoë Beta had for pins and needles, apart from the pins she used to plot the position of Egypt's army on the map of Syria. Aye, the mixing of dough for the doll was the closest she ever got to practising the arts of the kitchen. Dough, for sure, she never used it to make bread. Dough was for the dolls that would work the most powerful magic; the means of getting whatever she wanted.

Her brother was bound, literally spell-bound, she was sure of it.

1.10

Wall of Metal

The Greeks were quite useless at pronouncing Egyptian names, but Arsinoë Beta sat down and learned them from her slaves, so that she could speak with Eskedi not of Thebes, or Diospolis, but of *Waset,* not of Memphis but of Mennefer, or *Ineb-Hedj,* or the White Wall, and so acquire *kudos.* Eskedi praised her for taking the trouble to learn a little of his language. He was pleased when she asked after the health of his wife Neferrenpet, and his sons, Padibastet and Khonsouiou, junior priests, how they were getting along in the temple hierarchy, whether they suffered from the marsh fever, at what age they might be married. She knew from of old how to win over a man's heart, how to get a man to do whatever she wanted.

And what did Arsinoë Beta want from Eskedi? His support in the campaign to make her brother marry her. Not a difficult thing, as it happened, but a good thing all the same. Always she calculates, Stranger. She is almost as good as Seshat, goddess of Arithmetic, at calculating.

Whether it was the sister's fearsome spells, or just his common sense, now that Mikros found himself wifeless, he began to think that being married to the sister – if only to keep her from marrying somebody else – might not be such a bad thing. But at the same time as he began to give in to her, he had the terrible doubts that any Greek must have about breaking all the Greek rules. Some days he thought he believed in the power of the gods; other days he thought perhaps he did not. But now that he was about to indulge in behaviour that might arouse anger on Olympos, the terrible wrath of all the gods from Apollo to Zeus, he thought, *We must be careful, lest they take offence. Without a doubt, they will see marrying the sister as a dreadful instance of hubris, and we shall be punished.* Mikros wavered, thought better of the wicked marriage, thought he might bring Arsinoë Alpha back after all. Meanwhile, encouraged by the sister, he stepped up his making ready for war, and she was at his side all day, calm, wise, sensible, helping him, asking the most searching questions.

How much sinew will you take for the catapults? she asked.

Silence from the brother.

How many wagons for the baggage train? she asked.

Not one word came forth.

How long will it take the elephants to march to Gaza? she asked.

No answer.

And however many drachmas to pay fifty thousand men for three months?

How much wine do you need for the troops? she asked. *And how much water?*

Much water, he said at once, *and even more wine.*

And what about the soldiers' whores?

A lot, he said, quick. *The whores are the most important thing to take to a war.*

And so on. Always she asked such questions, and Mikros did not have many of the answers to hand. Nor, this time, did his officials. But Arsinoë Beta did know such things.

Really, Mikros, she said, *you should have gotten a grasp of these important matters by now. The only things you know about are the whores and the wine. You need help, more expert help than your pathetic advisers can offer. You need the help of your sister for a campaign of this size . . .*

For sure, Mikros knew it.

When his spies sent the intelligence that Anatolia had been invaded by the *Keltoi*, the Gauls, and that Antiokhos had marched right through Kilikia and Pamphylia, deep into Anatolia, as far west as the city of Sardis, to deal with them, leaving Syria virtually undefended, Arsinoë Beta urged Mikros to drive Egypt on to war and mobilize the troops as soon as he could.

Is not this the most wonderful chance of your lifetime? the sister said. *If you attack Antiokhos now, you cannot fail to beat him.*

Mikros gave her one dozen very good reasons why he should not invade Syria. Really, he preferred not to make war unless he had to, unless he was attacked first. He was truly not an aggressor. No man, they say, is so foolish as to desire war more than peace, and certainly no woman, but, just then, Arsinoë Beta kept saying, *I have a very great desire to do battle with Syria.*

She sat for hours talking to the Great Commander of the Army of the Two Lands about the evil desert of Sinai, that she had only heard tell of, or read about in books, so that she might advise Mikros of the best way to get himself across it.

She spoke to the Master of Horse about the number of beasts they needed. She asked for reports of the terrain from the fortress-commanders. Everywhere she helped Mikros, who, because of childhood illnesses, marsh fevers and suchlike, had himself avoided the full military training. He had

not the physical strength that other men had. He had never been very keen to
exercise himself naked in the *gymnasion*, that was every other boy's basic
training for war. Unlike the sister he was not war-mad.

Arsinoë Beta it was that made Mikros mint extra tetradrachms to pay the
troops, and call up half the donkeys out of Upper Egypt to carry the baggage.
She sent the surveyors on ahead to mend the road. She fixed up the water
depots in the desert, and made the fleet ready to sail alongside with fresh
water during the march through the dry country. She even recruited the
whores to keep the soldiers happy in a foreign land.

Arsinoë Beta took the lead, showed the way forward, but she was careful
not to undermine her brother's authority. She did not take more liberties
than was proper. Mikros was the supreme commander, who had the last
word; she was merely the one who offered advice.

She made sure her brother was surrounded all day by heralds bearing dispatches from Syria, and by ambassadors, and army intelligence men. She had
his spies and scouts queuing up to read him fresh reports of the situation –
her frowning brother. He hit his head with his fists for not knowing what to
do with his war that he did not want to fight, but every day the news was better: Antiokhos had left only one division of troops to guard the whole of Syria.

Arsinoë Beta made sure Mikros had no time to spare to visit his concubines
in the afternoon, and by nightfall he was too exhausted to do any thing but fall
into his golden bed and sleep. She made sure he was woken up in the night,
every night, by some urgent dispatch, true or false. Every morning she would
come along and sort out for him every last difficulty concerning the march –
the weapons, the wages, the horses, the elephants, the food and wine and, of
course, the whores, the hundreds of first-class Greek whores. Aye, every day the
sister came to pour light on what was, so far as Mikros was concerned, utter
darkness. He hated the thought of this war, hated it, but Arsinoë Beta loved it.

She also appeared to love her brother, and she would often make her voice
supple and murmur soft words into his ear such as, *Would you not be pleased
to marry me, Brother, in order to secure my services with regard to the military
for all time?*

Mikros, if preoccupied, would shake his head and say, *Leave us, Sister,
think only that the gods hear whatever words you speak.* At other times he
might storm from the chamber, scattering documents, screaming, *Leave us
alone, Sister, think not such filthy thoughts.*

And all the while, the day that they had named for Egypt to march off to
war loomed closer. When the sister did leave his side, Mikros began to wish
that she would come back.

*

While Mikros still refused to marry Arsinoë Beta, he found he did not know how to handle her, for she now became very difficult. *I think I shall withdraw my services as your military adviser,* she said. *I am tired of you saying you will not marry me. I think you are quite able to deal with foreign affairs by yourself.*

Mikros, haggard from lack of sleep, let his mouth drop open, for he knew in his heart that he was not; that he needed her help.

I cannot pass the rest of my life as a widow, she said. *I must take a fresh husband. I believe that Antiokhos of Syria will be glad of my military expertise in his forthcoming war – against yourself.*

Mikros pretended not to hear.

Antiokhos says he will be pleased to put away his present wife, she said, *and marry Arsinoë Beta instead . . .*

Mikros shouted at her, then, *Even to suggest it is treason. I shall have you put to death on the spot.* He roared for the guards to take her away.

Arsinoë Beta was not bothered. *Do not trouble the guards to come running,* she said. *I do not think you would dare to kill me, Brother,* she said, quite cool. *I am far too valuable to you. Whatever would you do without me?* Aye, and she waved his soldiers away with her jewelled hand, quite unruffled.

She could read Mikros's thoughts like reading a book. She knew what would happen in the end, just as Seshat knows. Aye, Arsinoë Beta was almost as good as the Lady of the House of Books. She knew he would not let her marry anybody else; she saw that he was weakening.

With the date for marching barely fourteen days off, she stood in the council chamber with him late one night, with the oil lamps flickering, surrounded by maps of Syria and Anatolia with bronze pins stuck in them to show where the troops of Antiokhos were, or were not, and she willed him to desire her body, willed herself to be like iron, for him to attract his body to hers like the loadstone.

I shall ask you once more, Brother, she said. *Will you not take me to wife?*

Mikros looked at the fishes on the mosaic, the sea-monsters, monsters just like his sister. He looked at the maps on the wall, then went back to scratching his name on a pile of papyri, lips drawn tight, angry.

Very well, she said, *you are on your own. You shall have no help from me now.* And she swept out of the chamber in a temper, slamming all the doors behind her so that he should think the worst, that he had lost his finest military adviser for good.

Aye, Arsinoë Beta stopped troubling herself with her brother's wars now. She went to talk to Ktesibios the Engineer – not about siege-machines, catapults, or flame-throwing engines, but about his new automatic *klepsydra,* or water-clock, a most accurate machine for keeping the time during peace-time.

Both Mikros and Arsinoë Beta loved the new *klepsydra* that dripped with such remarkable precision, keeping both the daylight hours and the hours of darkness, winter and summer, regardless of sunshine. *It will be of great use to the military,* Ktesibios said, *who must change guard at all hours of the night, when nobody knows what is the right time.* Ktesibios had cleverly adapted the outflow of the water from the *klepsydra* by a system of cogs and stopcocks so that the little man that pointed to the hour moved, bells were rung, puppets danced, birds chirped, and miniature trumpets were sounded. Arsinoë Beta declared Ktesibios a complete genius. She was so delighted that she kept his *klepsydra* in her own apartments, and she made sure that Ktesibios was kept fully occupied, so that Ptolemy Mikros could not have such a machine for himself but would have to wait.

Aye, Mikros would have to fight his war without her help. His stomach had that sinking feeling a man will get upon learning that his favourite dog has eaten poison.

He sat down with the generals and had to discuss with them himself the details of the moving off, the timing for the march south to Memphis, north to Pelousion, east into Syria. The generals declared their support for Arsinoë Beta's master plan. Aye, her bold campaign was too brilliant to cancel. The timing was right. The season of the year was right. Antiokhos was still thousands of stades away, at Sardis in Phrygia. Mikros would have to go ahead and fight without the sister's help. But it would be simple, he thought. There was no enemy to speak of. Syria could not fail to fall into the hands of King Ptolemy without him having to fight any battle whatever. All the same, Mikros had never undertaken a campaign of such size before, and he was ill-prepared for it. He had relied too heavy upon the sister.

1.11

Lion-Jaws

Throughout Mikros's final making ready for his Syrian triumph, Arsinoë Beta kept up a stubborn silence. She watched her brother muster his troops, let him do everything himself, watched what he did wrong. He stopped the archers' target practice early. He gathered not enough donkeys and mules for the baggage that must be taken. He let the troops sleep late and drink deep, just as he did himself. He did not even know the exact total number of baggage-handlers, grooms and hangers-on, and so could not work out the precise quantity of grain needed to feed them all. He spent more time seeing that the whores were properly looked after than to the requirements of the soldiers themselves: devoted more time to whores than to weapons. He showed more concern for soothsayers than his elephants of war.

Aye, and she watched him make regular sacrifice to Athena, goddess of War, as if he trusted more in the gods than in his own ability.

She watched him order up great quantities of *meat* to take with him, that would go bad in the heat of Syria, and cheese, that would stink, and attract the flies, wondering why his advisers did not stop such foolishness.

She watched every last detail, thinking how he did everything not so well as she could have done it herself, knowing that short of a miracle sent by the gods he must be defeated – if, indeed, it came to pitched battle. But she bit her lips and said nothing, no, not one word.

But perhaps a pitched battle can be arranged, she thought, smiling to herself.

She did not show her face at the Council of War now, nor in the audience hall, but sat in the *gynaikeion* all day. She even picked up the needle to begin some tapestry work, showing the face of Arsinoë Beta crowned with the walls of the city of Lysimakheia in Thrace.

Mikros affected not to care. He wrote her a message, saying, *I can handle this campaign. I have my generals and advisers. I have no need of your help, Sister . . . You should not trouble yourself to come near me; you can even marry my enemy if you like. Feel free to leave Egypt whenever you want. You are not a prisoner here. We shall do much better without your constant interfering.*

Arsinoë Beta did not quit Alexandria, of course. She had no intention of leaving. She made a show of sacrificing not to Athena for the war but to Asklepios, for her health. But throughout the day, every day, she received a steady procession of her scouts and spies, who told her whatever her brother did, what was his mood, what were his exact words – and in the frantic making ready he was too busy to keep track of what she was doing, having detailed his own spies to attend to more urgent matters.

Aye, for she had sent messengers on her own account, even unto Sardis in Phrygia, and Mikros knew nothing of it, suspected nothing.

At last Mikros gave the order to Dion, his general, and the great column of troops set off, marching out of Alexandria to the sound of drums and trumpets, kicking up the dust on the road to Memphis. But Mikros himself made ready only for driving as far as the house of his concubines. No, his Majesty did not ride with his men even so far as the Gate of the Sun.

Quite by chance Arsinoë Beta was not in the women's quarters just then, but returning in her chariot of war from waving off the troops herself, and she was riding in through the palace gates with her women when she happened to pass her brother in his chariot, riding out. Mikros was not wearing his armour, not going east but west, when Arsinoë Beta reined in her horses and stopped to speak, knowing very well where he was going.

Greetings, Brother, she said, showing all the teeth. *We trust you are in the best of health for marching to Syria.* It was the first time she had spoken with him in thirty days.

Mikros stared, hostile. She had let him down.

Then she said, *Are you not going to wear your armour for the great campaign? Are you not going to the war yourself, Brother?* And she watched him open his mouth to answer, but close it again without one word coming forth.

Your father tramped eleven thousand miles behind Alexander, she said, sarcastic. *Your father rode into battle ever so many times. What would he think of his fine son who skulks at home while the brave soldiers of Egypt ride out to meet the enemy without their King to lead them?*

Mikros said nothing, whacked his horses with the golden whip and drove at crashing-speed to the house of the concubines. Bald Stratonike did not speak to him of war, or of siege-machines, or of smashing his enemy to bits. Black Didyme did not, of course, speak of swords, or spears, or torsion-catapults, but Mikros suddenly could not stop thinking about these things. He passed the night wide awake, restless, feeling guilty. Before dawn he returned to the palace, shouting for his chariot of war, his escort of mounted troops, for the Dioiketes, and he put on the *khepresh* and the costume of Pharaoh, and followed the column south to Memphis. Mikros raged against the sister, all the way, lost his famous *ataraxia* altogether.

But it was the sister that made him go.

And he had to appoint her as Regent to look after Egypt in his absence. She was the best person for the job. She would acquit herself very well, sending out many letters, attending to all the business that her brother had neglected. Aye, and she sent another messenger, by sea, to Sardis in Phrygia.

So what happened? Mikros summoned the best of his warlike spirits. He caught up with his land army and marched the men into Koile-Syria, Hollow Syria, where Antiokhos was not; where there were no troops to oppose Mikros, no, not one battalion. The result was that Antiokhos had to fly out of Sardis to defend himself, and he swept back into Syria at the head of his army, force-marching infantry and cavalry, elephants, peltasts and hoplites towards Mikros, who had thought to take every city for himself and call Syria his own without a struggle, unopposed. Every man roared like a lunatic against Ptolemy and Egypt.

Mikros was appalled to see Antiokhos' tens of thousands of troops ahead of him. He had not expected Antiokhos to show his face. He had not thought to fight any battle in Syria at all. What had happened? Whatever had gone wrong with the sister's flawless plan?

Mikros kept himself cool enough, thinking of his *ataraxia,* calmness, balance. He did not drink to excess. He made the troops ready for battle in the proper Greek manner, as best he could. He had his generals. He was not alone, but he was supposed to be in charge. He made sacrifice to Ares, god of War. He made the proper offerings of white bread and cake to Montu, Lord of Thebes, the falcon-headed one, the Egyptian god of War, for a resounding victory. The Greek priests took omens from the sacrificial bull just before the clash, and they were not quite right, but Mikros, that day, must do battle, however bad the omens were, whether the gods were with him or not.

Even the goddess of History knows not where Mikros's battle was fought. This was one of those fights that has not even a name, because there was no word written down of it ever having been fought, and that was for very good reason. Mikros was on a horse somewhere in the thick of it, or in his chariot of electrum, directing operations, trying to copy the example of Alexander. How could he not have been? He was weighed down with protective gear, greaves, breastplate, the red-plumed helmet with the gaping lion-jaws, just like Alexander's helmet, but that was as far as the comparison with the great man went. Mikros had never made any great study of strategy or tactics. What he knew of phalanx warfare he had gotten from a book, Xenophon's *How to Be a General,* and he had not read that through to the end. No, land battle, he had very little idea about it.

There was blood, of course, much blood, and the usual howling, the usual blinding cloud of dust. Tens of thousands of men screamed for blood, for death, for Ptolemy and Victory, and the Syrian horse thundered across the battlefield, sweeping Ptolemy Mikros's men before them, knocking them down like toy soldiers. You will have to imagine for yourself, Stranger, the chaos, the snorting horses, the confused uproar, the stench of death, the rivers running red with blood. Seshat has not the precise details. What she does know is that everywhere he looked that day Mikros thought of some question to ask the sister, something to which he knew she would have a satisfactory answer. He badly missed her presence. She had deserted him in his hour of greatest need.

Mikros's heart stayed quiet, even so. He did not scream orders, but nodded the head, raised the arm, pointing, made signals. He was famous for this *ataraxia,* this calmness, this balance of his soul, but what a man in charge of a battle needs is the ability to lead from the front, to scream orders at the top of his voice, and inspire his men, to throw himself into the fray and not care if his face and hands are covered in another man's blood, let alone his own. He should not care even if he loses his life. But Mikros was not like that. He was a scholar, not a warrior, interested in animal behaviour, in his Beast Garden, in his Great Library, not in how the left wing of his cavalry should wheel in order to smash the right wing of the enemy horse. Mikros liked to keep his hands clean. He had a horror of blood. Far better, Stranger, not to tell you that Mikros did not quite know what he was doing. He was a great king, but he was not a great soldier.

Aye, Ptolemy Mikros fought and lost that battle, was routed, shamed, disgraced, and Dion lost the city of Damaskos. The troops had to retreat from Syria, or be made prisoners of war, sold into slavery, with the horror of the right-hand thumb cut off, that meant a man would never draw the bow or wield the sword again. Mikros got his armour dented, his tunic bloodied. He came home with his jaw ripped open, was lucky to escape with his life. Others, many others, did not.

When he rode into Memphis he found the sister waiting at the palace gates for him to give an account of himself. She was eager to listen now, quite willing to talk to him, at last, about his war, but with her tongue ready to thrash him all over again, just as he was, unshaven, with the mark of battle still upon him, even before he took his bath, following him into the palace, talking at him.

Welcome, Brother, welcome back, she said. *Thank the gods for preserving your life and sending you home with the joy of victory upon you.*

Mikros looked at her, looked, aghast, at the smile upon her face, the false fixed smile, her crazy glittering crocodile eyes.

Oh, she said, sarcastic. *Did you not win a mighty victory after all, then? By Zeus, not a defeat, Brother? Surely not defeat? How could it be so? Have the gods been unkind to you? Did you perhaps lack the best advice? Perhaps you should have taken notice of your big sister after all . . .*

Mikros slammed his golden fly-whisk into a table.

We lost, he said. *The gods have forsaken us.*

Do not say so, she said, putting a hand upon his right forearm, as if in sympathy, but he shook her off, furious. *Do not touch me,* he shouted. *Leave us,* he screamed, but she did not go, would not go. She was enjoying herself far too well.

Oh, she exclaimed, *such anger . . . whatever can have gone wrong?*

But Mikros did not want to tell her.

Give it mouth, she said. *Maybe we shall help you, after all.*

Mikros sat, holding his head, mopping up the tears with his cloak.

Before the battle, he sobbed, *we could get no favourable omen from the sacrifice . . . The liver had no lobe. Then Antiokhos appeared from nowhere. He was supposed to be in Phrygia. I blame the lord Sarapis for our troubles . . .*

The sister paced up and down, slapping her thigh, laughing a dry laugh at everything he said, as if she was delighted to hear of his defeat.

I believe that the gods' anger lay hard upon us, he said, thinking how much worse it would have been if he had married her. *Even the High Priest of Memphis said, Behold, we shall have a bad time. Did we forget some sacrifice? Have we overlooked some promise to the gods?*

Arsinoë Beta shook her head, dismayed. *The reason you lost your battle, Brother, was that your troops were ill-led. You let the men sit idle for too long; they have grown fat waiting for your war.*

Mikros's heart sank further, knowing what was to come.

Aristotle said that an army is like steel, she said. *It will lose its fine temper if it is kept always at peace. The ruler who does not teach the proper use of peace-time has only himself to blame if he is beaten. Peace-time should always be used to make ready for war.*

I did my best to . . . he began, but she cut him off.

I have heard, she said, *that you stood in your chariot and watched, that you never so much as lifted up your sword to fight. I have heard that you did nothing in that battle, nothing.*

Mikros put his hands over his ears and stopped listening, heard only her muffled voice shouting, *Failure . . . Failure . . . Failure . . .*

Listen to me, she said, angry, shaking him, *listen. The light-armed troops are like the hands, the cavalry are like the feet, the line of men at arms is like the chest and breastplate, and the general is like the head. As for you, Brother, you are supposed to be the eyes, the mouth, the breath of life . . . But what did you do? I have heard that you did not say a word, you did not breathe life into your soldiers, and that is why they were like dead men . . . You are supposed to do the thinking, Brother, but I have heard you did not even manage to shout the orders to your generals. You should have learned all this twenty years ago . . . You are like a man in a dream, Brother. You have been asleep all your life. When will you wake up? Wake up . . . Wake up . . . Wake up.*

Her voice grew ever louder, the words tumbling from her lips, on and on, until Mikros shouted, as, of course, she meant him to, *Why do you not take charge of the army yourself, if you are so completely wonderful? . . . Let us see whether a woman can do any better . . .*

She stopped her shouting, then.

Take charge? she said, breathing hard, unable to hide her delight.

Yes, he said, driving his bloody sword into a golden chest.

I may have a free hand, she said, *to do as I please with the Wall of Metal?*

Yes, he said, slashing at a lemon tree.

And Full Flame? she said. *The fleet also?*

Yes, yes, yes, he said, *so long as you win,* and he threw the lion's-jaw helmet, now lacking its red plumes, at her. She caught it, of course, and he watched her put it on, noticed again her crazy shining eyes, her lunatic smile.

Aye, and how good it felt to wear the helmet of the commander-in-chief. How good she felt, like the vulture puffing up her feathers at the thought of blood, like the snake rearing up to spit forth poison. How good it felt to be like Sakhmet, Lady of the Bright Red Linen, the lioness goddess of War herself.

I promise you, Brother, she said, *you will not regret this favour.*

And now that she had charge of war, of course, it meant that to keep her services he would have to take her to wife, even his own sister.

1.12

Elephants of War

Aye, Arsinoë Beta, this warlike and most warlike woman, now took both the land army and the fleet, all military matters entirely into her own capable hands. She spent days upon end speaking with her brother's admirals, Patroklos of Macedon, Kallikrates of Samos, Artemidoros of Perge. It was Arsinoë Beta who now sent the daily dispatches to the generals in the field, and took charge of every Council of War, while Mikros sat lost in thought, stroking the *phallos* talisman, thinking of his concubine of the day, answering every man's question with, *Ask the sister, ask the warlike one.*

Herself, she rose ever earlier, driving her chariot at dawn to the artillery sheds, the catapult factory, the armour workshops, to speak with the head men. She would say, *One hundred and fifty arrow-firing catapults is not enough . . . we need three hundred . . .* or, *You are doing well, only two hundred more siege-engines to build . . .* or, *Your helmets are the finest in the world.* She urged the men on, shouting, *Must work harder . . . twenty-five more stone-throwers by the end of the month of Khoiak . . . Must win this war, must win next time.*

Then she would visit the barracks, where Mikros seldom showed himself, where no respectable woman ever went before, to encourage the regular soldiers. She even made her tour of the vast camps of tents put up by the hired soldiers outside the city walls, ordering an extra ration of wine for every man, to mark the occasion. She walked through the camp wearing the lion's-jaw helmet, the purple cloak of the Great Commander of the Armies of Egypt. And because she took an interest in their well-being, the troops loved her.

She spoke often with Ktesibios, the artillery expert, not about water-clocks now, but about the torsion-catapult that was fired by horsehair springs; about the great machine called the *lithobolos*, that hurled stone shot up to three talents' weight high into the air. On Ktesibios' advice she ordered Phoenician engineers, expert artillery-men, to be brought to Egypt to maintain and adjust her machines of war, that could be just as temperamental as herself. She showered the Gold of Praise upon Ktesibios, and the great mechanician loved her, because she understood the fine art of artillery just as well as he did himself.

She had now the clever idea to set up a trading station on the Red Sea coast to make easier the import of elephants of war from the south country. She called this place Ptolemaïs of the Elephant Hunts, for great numbers of elephants were trapped hereabouts and sent north to Memphis to be trained for use in her next war.

The elephant is a great asset, she told Mikros. *He cannot gallop like a horse, but if he is well-treated he will obey orders and run. When he charges he may reach a speed of six hundred and eighty-four stades in one hour.*

It is good, Mikros said, thinking the elephants got much better treatment than he did himself.

Arsinoë Beta did, indeed, treat her elephants with kindness. She took them hay, green leaves, and coconuts. The elephant would take the coconut from her hand with his trunk, and break it open by pressing gently upon it with his front foot. When she gave them beer to drink they loved her, for an elephant kept in captivity has a great passion for liquor, sucking up the filthy *booza* of the natives twenty-four pints at a time. Aye, even the elephants loved her.

After one month in command, Arsinoë Beta had Ktesibios stage a great show on the waste ground west of Alexandria, on the edge of the desert. The sight of his hundreds of engines of war in action, the tumultuous noise, the wonder of giant rocks hurled into the air was awe-inspiring beyond anything seen since the time of Alexander. The targets, buildings of sun-dried brick, and stretches of imitation city wall, were blown up in the most satisfying manner.

Ktesibios showed off the latest version of his giant bellows-like machine that breathed fire at wooden breastworks, and laid on a remarkable hail of bolts, fire-balls and flaming arrows. Mikros sat beside Arsinoë Beta under a golden canopy, watching the flames, and was often moved to clap his hands together. *Every Syrian city will surrender to us on the spot,* he cried. *Rejoice, Sister, the Syrians will flee in terror when they see us coming.*

But Arsinoë Beta did not rejoice as if she had won her battle already. She snapped at her brother, *A machine cannot win a battle. Pharaoh is the man who wins a battle, if he has the ability to command . . . or a sister who will do his job for him.*

Ktesibios' most astonishing invention, however, was the fire-engine, worked by compressed air and a double-action pump that sprayed vast quantities of water. His proudest moment that day was not the sight of his flying fire-balls, nor his exploding houses, but the flaming walls of straw, extinguished upon the instant.

Afterwards Arsinoë Beta asked Ktesibios, *What machine shall you invent next? Perhaps the fresh chariot that has no need of horses?*

No, Megaleia, he said, laughing, *not yet . . . I am working on a different kind of machine – a hydraulic organ, to make music for his Majesty's festivals and military processions.*

Arsinoë Beta was pleased. *We look forward, Ktesibios,* she said, *to hearing you playing the Song of Victory on your organ.*

And she noted with satisfaction that the engineer had called her *Megaleia*, as if she was the Queen already.

The next time Egypt had to fight Antiokhos, Arsinoë Beta would be ready. She took note of the omens and auspicious days, but she based her decisions on more reliable things, such as her spies' and scouts' reports. She made her elephants rehearse their charge in Memphis, on the sandy plain south of the Temple of Ptah. She did her best to ensure that the hired soldiers did not desert, by binding them to her and to Egypt, promising a plot of land in the District of the Lake to every man if they won her a victory.

She put the infantry – four phalanxes of four thousand and ninety-six men, making up the Grand Phalanx of sixteen thousand three hundred and eighty-four men – through gruelling sessions of close-order drill, standing on the parade ground in the heat of the sun, screaming the orders herself. Aye, and the phalanx moved as one body, in perfect step with each other, and in perfect step with Arsinoë Beta, who sometimes condescended to march with them herself, in the front file, showing them how every last thing should be done – a woman leading the men. Always she wore the purple cloak, the helmet with the blood-red plumes, and all the time the bloodshed loomed closer.

1.13

Whiskers of the Cat

Arsinoë Beta watched the flight of birds with care, saying, *Whether such things are nonsense or not, no pious general would dream of fighting if the omens were unfavourable.*

There is no vegetation along the coast, she told Mikros, *so we shall take fodder from Memphis, or find it in Syria.*

She knew just how long it should take the troops to march from Memphis to Gaza. *We shall march thirteen miles each day,* she said, *and it will take ten days to go from Pelousion to Gaza, one month to reach the Syrian border.*

Meat will go rotten, she said. *The troops need grain, for biscuits, bread, and porridge, not meat. We shall save up the luxury of eating meat for the victory celebrations, for the great sacrifice when the battle is over.*

She knew just how far her elephants could march in one day – not very far – and she sent them on ahead, by ship, so that all was ready. *Timing is of the utmost importance,* she said. *If the timing is wrong, we shall have another misfortune to explain away.*

When the battle orders came, Arsinoë Beta had no thought of retiring to her chamber, and letting the generals do what they would, without her. No, she could not bear not to see her beloved troops in action. She would go with them, leading the way through the desert of Sinai. And when the fight was fought, she would watch the chaos from her chariot, signalling to her generals on the field, when to push forward, when to draw back, shouting orders and encouragement through a speaking-trumpet. But no, at the last moment the bellyache struck her down and she was too ill to travel. The generals must win the war without her. Mikros went. She made him go, and this time the victory was his.

Mikros won a minor success in Syria, a modest success. Seshat knows but little of it. A small victory, with not many dead, not many prisoners of war, not much booty. But the Seleukid was not defeated utterly. He would regain his strength and fight some more, and because of it Arsinoë Beta would allow no triumphant entry into Memphis, no great victory parade. *We shall wait*, she said, *until we are sure that we have brought about the end of all war, a peace that will last for the rest of time.* To Mikros she said, very plain, *To celebrate too soon would be to bring down the wrath of those wonderful gods upon our heads.*

Even so, she had her heart warm with joy, like metal glowing in the furnace.

Back in Memphis, Mikros embraced her, kissed her cheek, and the tears of gratitude fell from his eyes, while Arsinoë Beta stared straight ahead, smile fixed, thinking, suddenly, of other things than war and bellyache.

She retired to her private room, the room with the brazier that kept her hands warm in cold weather – and was, truly, for no other purpose; the room that had in it the ingredients for her stomach potions arranged in bottles round the walls, that is all, bottles that were really nothing whatever to do with working the most powerful magic in the world. She muttered, even so, the words of the wondrous spell of binding a lover:

I bind you, Ptolemy Mikros, by the tail of the snake, by the mouth of the croc-odile, by the horns of the ram, by the venom of the asp, by the whiskers of the cat, by the phallos of the god, that you may not be able to have aphrodisia with any woman but me alone, Arsinoë Beta.

Mikros, for his part, felt again the strange fluttering in his chest, like moths trapped in his tunic, trying to escape. *It is the arrows of Eros*, he thought, and it worried him. He woke in the dead hours, thinking of the sister, and his heart was still fluttering. Mikros knew what it meant: more trouble from Eros, the one who controlled him, his ruler, the wild boy.

But Mikros did not speak to his Greek ministers of personal things. A king must trust nobody, has no true friends, only sycophants and flatterers. That is why the kings of his time valued an able wife so very highly. The best kind of wife would support her husband, and be trusted with state secrets. That is what a king's wife was for, but Mikros did not have a wife. No, the only per-son Mikros could speak to from the heart was, by a strange paradox, a for-eigner, one who, in different circumstances, might have been his sworn enemy, but who had become his friend – the High Priest of Memphis.

Aye, when Eskedi next showed his face in Alexandria, Mikros ventured to ask about his private affairs. *Excellency,* he said, *my sister would have me for her husband. What would Egypt think of such a thing?*

Eskedi looked as if he did not know all about this matter already. His brown eyes shone. *Megaleios,* he said, smiling his mysterious half-smile, *you know that among the Egyptians it is no crime to marry the sister . . . The Pharaoh Seqenenre married his own sister,* he said. *So, too, did Ahmose, and the* first and fourth Tuthmosis, and the second Ramesses, and Merneptah, and also Siptah . . . Even the great god Osiris married his sister, Isis. Such a marriage should not be a trouble to his Majesty. Egypt will think it nothing out of the ordinary. The people will be in joy to hear the news.

But what will the Greeks say? Mikros said. What will the Macedonians think? It is really not the custom for a Greek to pleasure his own sister, let alone for the whole world to know about it.

Megaleios, Eskedi said, the gods of Egypt will not be offended if Ptolemy and Arsinoë follow the desire of their hearts.

Mikros glared at him. Even in the city where nothing was forbidden, no Greek had ever dared to marry his full sister. The Greeks in Egypt were careless of many of the old traditions, but they cared very much about incest, and Mikros knew it.

If I marry my sister, Mikros said, there will be a revolution among the Greeks.

Eskedi made the face of Surely-it-is-Not-Such-a-Great-Crime. Even your Zeus married his own sister, he said. Is it not so?

Mikros had to nod the head.

But what of the children of such a marriage? Mikros murmured. Will they not turn out to be monsters? What about the famous pig's tail children that result from this kind of union? Aye, that was half the trouble: his sister had been quite open about it, saying she must have a child by him; that she would not put up with half a marriage, but was expecting him to climb into her bed. His own sister.

But Eskedi said, The Pharaohs who were the offspring of brother and sister had no deformities. There has been no pig's tail to my knowledge, not in living memory, no, not ever. Really, Megaleios, you have nothing to worry about.

Mikros breathed hard, swung the arm, as if, unwarlike though he was, he might punch this High Priest.

In any case, Eskedi said, your sister is no longer young . . . You have already your son and heir. Perhaps she will have no child at all.

He looked into Mikros's troubled face.

It would be a goodly thing, he said, if the Pharaoh were to marry his sister.

Mikros stared at the mosaic of dolphins, shaking his head. The Greeks say, he said, slow, that if a man who has been married takes another wife, he is like a shipwrecked sailor who sets sail again upon the dreadful deep.

The thought of having his sister for his wife felt to him, indeed, more than ever like the dreadful deep, rough seas, shipwreck, all hands lost. And yet, at the same time as he did not want to marry the sister, he could not imagine her married to anybody but himself.

*

Arsinoë Beta could tell his mood from the soft look in his eyes. Her magic was working. That night she went to Mikros waving a letter from Antiokheia. She said, *I shall ask you one more time, Brother, one last and final time. If you will not be married to me, I shall marry myself to Antiokhos of Syria. I have his letter of proposal here in my hand. Are you sure you will not marry me, Ptolemaios Mikros? I shall not ask again.*

The Syrian marriage was lies, of course, all lies, but Mikros took the letter from her. It was faked, of course, but it looked genuine enough to him. He turned the papyrus over in his hands. He stared at the fishes trapped in the mosaic floor, just as he was trapped. He stared at the coffered ceiling of his golden prison. He stared at the sister. Her face was blank, but she was breathing silent prayers to all the goddesses she could think of: Aphrodite, Artemis, Bastet, Hathor, Isis, Nekhbet, Sakhmet . . .

Mikros looked away. *If I say no,* he thought, *I shall have to fight alone, and I shall lose my war. If I say no and she marries Antiokhos, I shall lose my war because I shall have to fight against the sister. I shall lose Egypt, lose the crowns. Antiokhos will be the Lord of the Two Lands. Arsinoë Beta will be Queen of Egypt whatever happens. Perhaps I should order the hemlock tipped down her throat now, while I watch, aye, let the poison chill her bones, congeal her blood, get rid of her at once. She is just as much a traitor as the other Arsinoë . . .* He was on the point of shouting for the bowl of hemlock – but no, he could not kill her. He needed her too much. He needed her warlike services too badly. *What would I do without her?* he thought. *What would I do if she went away?* He looked again at the floor, at the ships stranded in the mosaic as he would be stranded himself, without her. He thought of his golden life into which the sister had thrust herself. He needed her most desperately badly.

Very well, he said, *you can be Queen of Egypt, if that is what will please you.*

Arsinoë Beta did not lose control of herself for one moment. She went through the drama of falling upon his neck, squealing for delight, embracing him, all the time calculating, thinking what should be her next words. This time he did not struggle to be free of her but let her do what she would. His heart still fluttered, bound even by the whiskers of Bastet the cat goddess. And yes, to be held by Arsinoë Beta felt rather like being held in the embrace of some poisonous spider, in whose web he was caught, struggling. But at the same time it felt good, felt right, felt comfortable, for a creature as poisonous as his sister would be sure to win every battle.

1.14

Divine Honours

The contract for the marriage of Arsinoë Beta to Ptolemy Mikros her brother was drawn up by herself, and it was harsh, like herself, for she made him swear, had him write the words even in his own blood: *Nothing will be dearer to me than to protect you for the rest of your life, and if the fate of mankind befalls you, to see that you enjoy all divine honours.*

Take note, Stranger, she made him promise to turn her into a full goddess after her death.

Lay this to heart, the contract said, *nothing painful shall befall you. I shall take every care to see that you are untroubled.*

Take note of it, Stranger: there would be no question of doing away with her once he had gotten his hands upon her treasure. The marriage was not to be temporary, but for life. And he must allow her proper protection from her enemies, such as Arsinoë Alpha.

The contract laid down that Ptolemy should live with Arsinoë Beta *obeying her as a husband should obey his wife*, owning all his property in common with her.

Take special note, Stranger, that Mikros promised to obey her, and she did not promise to obey him in return. And her personal allowance would be generous, beyond any ordinary man's belief, fit for a goddess.

It would not be lawful for Ptolemy to bring in another wife besides Arsinoë Beta, nor to have children by any other woman but her, nor to run after handsome boys, for so long as she lived. She allowed him his concubines, but it would not be lawful for him to inhabit another residence over which she was not the mistress, nor to eject, insult, ill-treat, or abuse her, or to throw her out into the street. He would not dare.

They talked a little of how it might be, when they were husband and wife, what they should do, and the sister bullied Mikros a little, telling him, *You should be more Egyptian. You could do so much more for Egypt. The Egyptians would love you much better if you helped them.*

I am a Macedonian, Mikros said. *My habits of life are Greek habits. My thoughts are Greek thoughts. I should prefer to help the Greek scholars, in the Mouseion . . .*

Very well, she said, *do you help the Greeks. I shall help the Egyptians myself.* And she held him to what he said, made him do it, so that they divided everything up between them. Mikros would take care of the city of Alexandria, his great Greek Library, Greek learning, and Greek inventions, his beloved Beast Garden. The wife would manage war, finance, taxes, foreign affairs, Egyptian things – the affairs of state, which almost made Mikros weep for boredom, about which he knew little and cared less. In fact, Arsinoë Beta took responsibility for almost everything. It suited Mikros well enough. He would have been pleased to do nothing for the rest of his life. But no, she would never allow that.

While my limbs have power to move, I shall not let you sit idle, Brother, she said. *A king must think of his duty. I am not jealous of your concubines, not at all. I know all about the behaviour of stallions.*

She remembered Berenike Alpha telling her, *If you want to survive as a wife, you must learn to tolerate your husband's other women . . . Remember that the horse doctors recommend the stallion to cover the mare twice a day . . . Never forget that the stallion who is denied mares will go crazy.*

I shall take your women in hand myself, she told him, *just like the Egyptian queens of old. I shall be happy to run their households for you, and limit your spending on them.* And so she brought even his private affairs under her personal control.

Mikros did not complain. *Anything you say,* he said, *so long as Egypt wins her battles.*

He signed his *Ptolemaios* at the bottom of the papyrus in his own blood, glistening red. He had been brought up to believe that telling lies is a shameful thing in a monarch. He would keep his word, but she also made him swear in the time-honoured manner, upon a wax doll thrown into the fire.

May I melt like wax, he whispered after her, *if I break my word . . . May my fortune be liquefied if I break my promise . . . May my children bring forth monsters if I depart from the letter of the contract . . .*

Melt like wax, indeed. Her own dissolution was not far off. She would not survive much longer.

And yes, she knew just how close it was, her last day upon earth. She had asked the oracles, and they all said the same thing. She had barely three thousand days left in which to save Egypt and bring about the final defeat of Syria.

This marriage was Arsinoë Beta's first great triumph, for it would make the House of Ptolemy popular among the Egyptians for the rest of time – or so she thought. Arsinoë Beta took her third marriage most especially seriously.

1.15

Forbidden Fruit

Aye, it was good, all of this, good for Mikros, and good for Egypt, because the sister told him to his face what nobody else dared: that he should get a grip on himself and stop dreaming. In Alexandria they were saying that Ptolemy Mikros had conceived a violent passion for his own sister, and when the news was leaked out there was much talk – even in this place where nothing was forbidden – of him bringing down a curse upon the city because of it, for to marry your own sister was – to the Greeks – just about the worst thing a man could do.

But the thought of Mikros married to his own sister made Sotades of Maroneia shriek with laughter, louder than ever. His jokes about the forth-coming marriage were filthy, but they had the entire court bent double, weeping with mirth. Sotades found the idea of a brother–sister marriage hilarious, and he wrote many wondrous rude Greek verses in honour of this singular occasion. When he read his lines at the *Symposion* even in the hearing of Pharaoh, Mikros roared with laughter like everybody else. A jest-maker enjoys a certain licence. When Sotades criticized Bilistikhe of Argos, Mikros's favourite concubine, making fun of her melon-sized breasts, Mikros had laughed at that too. He liked much better to laugh than not to laugh. There was always a generous reward for any man who could make his Majesty's shoulders shake – men like the poet Philemon, who wrote ninety-seven comedies and died laughing at one of his own jokes. Mikros had often been happy, had often been quite cheerful, until the return of the sister.

Aye, Mikros had said to Sotades, years ago, *So long as you make me laugh, you can say what you like.* This great monarch even had the ability to laugh at himself.

But as Sotades heard every fresh whisper of the scandal, he wrote ever more outspoken poems about the sister:

> *Arsinoë Beta . . . first she murdered the Queen's brother . . .*
> *She stole the Queen's husband . . .*
> *She stole the Queen's jewels, she even stole her shoes . . .*

She was too old to have any more children herself...
So she stole the Queen's family, all her little ones...

The Alexandrians laughed with Sotades and condemned Mikros, in private, for tempting the gods to punish them all. Alexandria most certainly disapproved, every man murmuring that it must bring down the vengeance of the gods upon the city. But Arsinoë Beta heard nothing untoward.

Unchecked, Sotades grew bolder still. He wrote now his most famous obscene and wicked poem, called *Priapos*, after the Greek god of Fertility, and it was full of lines like this:

Thou piercest forbidden fruit with deadly sting...
Thou art thrusting thy prick into a hole unholy...
Thou art fucking an unholy hole...

Sotades was never sober. He had ever a jest or an obscenity in his mouth. He sat with the monkeys at Mikros's banquets because he was, as they said, nine parts monkey himself, and only one part human. Sotades thought his poem was rather good, and he grew so bold, or so foolish, as to recite it for the sister herself. Arsinoë Beta did not laugh, of course, but took the jesting words of Sotades very serious. She marched straight to her brother to shout at him about Sotades the blasphemer, the disgusting rhymer, the enemy of the monarchy.

When she asked, *How do you mean to punish him, Brother?* Mikros shrugged the shoulder, pursed the lips, spread the hands, opened the mouth — and shut it again.

He put his hands over his ears, but he could still hear her shouting, *Filthy ... Filthy ... Filthy ... Filthy ...*

Sotades is old, Mikros sighed. *He is a little mad, but he is quite harmless. He does not mean a word of what he says. He does not know what he is saying. You know how they say All Cretans Are Liars ... You should take no notice, Sister. It is just a harmless joke.*

He pleaded for the jest-maker whom he had known since he was a child, the little man who had never failed to make him howl with laughter. But Arsinoë Beta would not hear a word of it. *This is not a jest, it is not funny*, she screamed. *It is treason.* She passed the entire afternoon ranting about Sotades, and Mikros had to put up with her shouting, for she would not let him leave her side until he had decided how to punish the offender.

That evening, with Mikros still not having made his answer, but refusing to condemn his old friend, Arsinoë Beta said, *Never mind, Brother. Do not trouble yourself further*. And she took the matter into her own hands by sending the entire police force of Alexandria, the Belt-Wearers, to arrest Sotades for his unspeakable slander.

Admiral Patroklos had Sotades dragged away in chains, still laughing, and threw him into prison. Aye, the great prison of Alexandria that stood next to the sea, where the inmates were washed by the waves, forced to huddle upon a ledge, for fear of being drowned.

Later, they said, Sotades escaped, having a reputation as something of a trickster in such matters. A different story said he was released at a time of general amnesty, and fled to the town of Kaunos in Kilikia. Perhaps the truth was that Mikros set Sotades free himself, or allowed him to escape, out of pity. The sister did not quite take away all his power.

But Admiral Patroklos, who enjoyed the august title of Strategos Over the Islands of the Empire, was a particular favourite of Arsinoë Beta, and he showed no pity for her enemies. Patroklos pursued Sotades, and recaptured him. Aye, and just as the entire police force was detailed to arrest Sotades, so the entire fleet put to sea in order to attend his execution. When they were well out of the harbour, Sotades was hauled up on deck and Patroklos asked if he would be kind enough to step into a leaden box, to try it for size. Sotades jumped in, laughing, making monkey noises. Patroklos asked him to lie down, saying it was to let him see how it would feel to be a dead man, then he slammed the lid shut.

Inside the box Sotades went on making jests, and his muffled voice could still be heard as they banged in the nails and dragged the box on to the gunwale of the *trieres*. Sotades babbled away, keeping up his laughter to the end, screaming, *Every word I speak is untrue . . .* until they tipped the leaden box overboard, into the sparkling sea.

Men thought twice, after that, about criticizing the shameful marriage.

Thus passed Sotades of Maroneia, best of jesters, who invented the sotadean, a metre that allowed of great variations; who wrote more scatological poetry than any man before or since; Sotades the *kinaidos*, who left no wife and no posterity, just his godlike boys of sixteen or seventeen years, the dozens of olive-skinned boys made immortal by his immoral verse.

When Mikros asked, a day or two later, *What news of Sotades?*, thinking to hear the latest Greek silliness, and shouted for him to come at once, he at last heard what the sister had done. And no, she had not told him, and nobody else had dared to speak of it. He railed against her, shouting himself hoarse, quite against his philosophical principles, that said he should be upset by nothing whatever, and lost his famous balance. For sure, he screamed at Arsinoë Beta then, but she put her hands over her head, just as Mikros did himself, saying, *I have sand in my ears . . . Really, I cannot hear a word you are saying . . .*

Despite the black mood of her brother, despite her nightmare bellyache, Arsinoë Beta carried on smiling. With all opposition stifled, the making ready for her forbidden marriage went ahead as planned.

But nobody after that could make Mikros laugh quite how he had laughed before.

1.16

Dolphins

Knowing that rain was lucky for weddings, Arsinoë Beta made sure she was married at Alexandria in the winter time, when the sky is often elephant-coloured. With the help of Eskedi's magic, rain did fall on her wedding day, the wind roared in the palm trees in the palace gardens, and the grey-green sea crashed upon the beaches, smashed up all the fishing boats. For the Egyptians, however, rain is the manifestation of Seth, the most hostile of Egyptian gods. Rain is not a very auspicious sign in Egypt.

On the day that she became Queen of Egypt Arsinoë Beta wore the tight red silk dress proper for an Egyptian goddess, the blood-red dress of Sakhmet, the lioness-goddess of War, diaphanous stuff through which the thinness of her body was plain to see. She wore gold serpent rings on her fingers, gold serpent bracelets on her wrists and ankles, gold talismans on her arms, golden serpent earrings. She wore the jewelled vulture collar round her neck and the golden vulture headdress upon her head. Arsinoë Beta *shone,* and her crocodile teeth flashed throughout, smiling her terrible fierce smile.

At the Anakalypteria, or Festival of Unveiling, when the bride must take off her maiden veil, the bridegroom hardly troubled himself to look at her. She did not, in any case, count as maiden, was no longer a *parthenos.* Mikros knew what his sister looked like: little different from how she looked the day before; rather sulky when she forgot to smile, rather plain, in spite of the flatterers' talk about her fabulous beauty, and so thin that her ribs showed through the flesh, like greyhound ribs. *Really*, Mikros thought, *we like a woman to have a bit more meat on her bones*, and he lost himself dreaming of the beautiful and most beautiful Bilistikhe, of her breasts like melons, of her fleshy buttocks, and of the house of the concubines – that was now suffering under the harsh new management of the sister.

As a child Mikros the zoologist had, of course, given Arsinoë Beta presents at the new year, and on the anniversary of her birth – a papyrus cage full of song-thrushes, a black bird that spoke with human voice, a box of crickets. What would he give her now that she was to be his wife? Stranger, his wedding gift was a young crocodile, perhaps one cubit long, greenish, with black spots, and wicked laughing eyes. This wonderful beast had golden bracelets fixed to his forepaws, and he wore golden earrings, and had hundreds of glittering emeralds fastened upon his armoured hide.

She cried out when she saw it, of course, let out a great cry of horror, for it was the identical gift chosen by her half-brother for her second marriage, and the memory – Oh – Oh – of that terrible day in Kassandreia flashed into her thoughts: the baleful look of Ptolemy the Thunderbolt, her dying sons, the flying blood. She looked mustard at her brother, looked daggers, looked strychnine at him. *How*, she thought, *could Mikros have known? And what can he mean by it?* But Mikros did not know. The truth was that both the half-brother and the full brother gave her the most fitting gift – the mirror image of herself.

But at the same time as she cried out for horror, she cried out, of course, also for delight. Arsinoë Beta adored the crocodile, and she dragged her wedding gift about the palace on a golden leash for some time, until he grew rather too big for domestic comfort – when she sent him to join the sacred crocodiles up at Krokodilopolis, and replaced him with a fresh, and rather smaller model. From now on she had the crocodile with her always, an unusual house-pet, to be sure, and so very un-Greek, but at the same time, not entirely inappropriate. The jewelled crocodile, he was the beast of all beasts that was most like unto herself, glittering just the same as before, but with costlier precious stones. And she was still the same herself, still nasty, still dangerous, and more than ever likely to kill somebody.

On this day, Arsinoë Beta did everything according to the custom of the Greeks, for it was unlucky to do otherwise. Modern woman though she thought herself, she was not so foolish as to ignore tradition. Her wedding was like any other Greek wedding in that her waiting-women rubbed her flesh with ointments and anointed her drop by drop with all the perfumes of Syria. Mikros came to greet his sister properly dressed, Greek-fashion, in white clothes, crowned with crimson flowers, and dripping with myrrh, thinking still of the murder of his jest-maker, not quite managing to keep the smile upon his face. From the sister's point of view, Mikros was not, at least, an old man like Lysimakhos. He was still nervous of squashing cockroaches, nervous about snakes, but he would not, she thought, ill-treat his big sister. This time, she was sure, her wedding day would not end with a massacre.

In one matter, however, this marriage was unlike any other. Under normal circumstances a woman who marries a husband will increase the number of her relatives, adding her husband's father and mother to her family. In this marriage, though, there were no new relations to meet, for the two fathers and the two mothers of Ptolemy Mikros and Arsinoë Beta happened to be the same people, and, of course, both of them were dead. Aye, and just as well they were dead, Stranger, for had Ptolemy Soter and Berenike Alpha lived, they must have died of shame to see what their children had done that day to bring down the wrath of all the gods of Olympos upon their heads.

Further, any child of this brother-to-sister marriage would have not the usual four grandparents, but only two; not eight great-grandparents, but only four. If a brother marries his own sister, the number of their children's ancestors will be cut in two. There was a notable absence of grandparents in this marriage, and the Alexandrian Greeks absolutely did not like it.

Some of Mikros's courtiers whispered that Arsinoë Beta was past her time of burning desire; that she would make a chaste marriage with her brother, disabled as she so often was by the bellyache. As for offspring, they thought she would be content to look after her brother's children – Ptolemy Euergetes, Lysimakhos and Berenike – all still under the age of five.

Mikros's infant children did not run about, happy, at this wedding, like other children would have done, but were solemn-faced, looking about them for the lovely Arsinoë Alpha, asking every man, *Where is our Mémé?*

Arsinoë Beta, watching them, said to her brother in the middle of her wedding feast, not without a certain kindness, *When one mare has died, the mares that graze together will bring up the foals.* It was a good thing to promise to adopt her brother's children and bring them up as her own, a generous thought, spoiled only by the fact that their mother was not dead, but had been banished upon a false charge by herself.

No, those who thought Arsinoë Beta would make a chaste marriage were quite wrong. She had not stopped burning within, but very much wished to have some fresh sons. She had no intention of sleeping in any bed but the golden bed of the Pharaoh her brother, clasped in his royal embrace.

We shall be faithful as dolphins, she said to him, *faithful as two crows.* And she smiled at him a proper smile, not a fake smile, and Mikros could not but smile back, in spite of wondering what had he done, and how the gods of Greece would choose to punish him for breaking their unbreakable rules.

Aye, when she said to him, *The oracles give us promise of fair children,* Mikros said nothing. But to himself he murmured, *To Hades with your oracles, you have really upset the gods this time.*

Arsinoë Beta thought hardly at all about Mikros's concubines, who did not appear at the wedding. Really, she was not troubled that he would take his pleasure with other women besides herself. To have very many concubines was what was expected of a great king. Arsinoë Beta alone had the title and the splendour of a queen. But to puff herself up a little and set herself apart from Arsinoë Alpha, she took a new title for herself that day. *We are tired of being called Arsinoë Beta,* she said, *We shall be called Arsinoë Philadelphos, She Who Loves Her Brother, the Brother-Loving One.*

Mikros opened the mouth to protest, but he thought better of arguing, and so she was Arsinoë Philadelphos for the rest of her life – and, indeed, for the rest of time.

At the magnificent Greek wedding feast there were flamingo tongues, roast pigs stuffed with roast thrushes, roast ducks stuffed with roasted warblers, roast fowls, roast geese, roast quails, roast partridge, roast pigeons, roast hare, baked fishes. All these things were very good to eat, but even at her own wedding Arsinoë Beta would taste nothing but a few olives, thinking of her figure, and her bellyache. And of course, her usual cocktail of, by now, dozens of different poisons, each month a slightly bigger amount of each one, so as to increase her resistance to any attempt upon her life. Really, Arsinoë Beta never was much pleased by eating, except for her daily diet of arsenic, hemlock, strychnine, wolfbane . . .

They sang, of course, the Crow Song of the Greeks, for that the crow is the symbol of matrimonial love, and Arsinoë Beta herself stood on a table and sang the song called *Love Has Melted the Wax of Our Writing Tablet,* and she sat down to a tumult of clapping and cheering.

At the end of the feast the trumpet sounded, and the toast was drank to *Agathos Daimon*, the lucky tame house snake of Alexandria, and they raised the parting cup to Hermes, or Thoth, and it seemed that everything might now go well for the House of Ptolemy in Egypt.

But when the music of lyre and harp and flute started up, and the wedding dances began, Arsinoë Beta stood up, shaking her head, and refused to take part. *Dancing is for concubines,* she said. *Really, we have more pressing things to attend to.* And she went off, even in the middle of her own wedding feast, to send urgent dispatches to her generals at the Front, in Syria.

Eskedi also refused to dance, but the brother–sister marriage was nonetheless a great delight to him, for it was like a reflection in the mirror, a reminder that Isis and Osiris, husband and wife, were also brother and sister. Such things are not thought to be so terrible among the Egyptians. You should not forget, Stranger, that even Seshat is married to her own brother – to Thoth himself.

Alexandria would just have to get used to the profane marriage. The feast of one hundred roasted oxen helped to keep the people happy, and the free wine that flowed from every public fountain. Only Philotera stood up for decency now, saying, *Sister, your marriage is a crime against the gods of Hellas, they shall most surely punish you for it.*

But Arsinoë Beta was pleased to snap back at her, *Remember that we are gods in this House, and the gods ever did what they liked.* She shouted all manner of abuse, that only confirmed what Philotera thought, that the sister had taken leave of her senses.

In private many of the Greeks still muttered that the brother–sister marriage was unhellenic practice, not to be indulged in, for fear of upsetting the gods. For a Greek to marry his sister was behaviour of deepest dishonour, the very worst thing any man could do, so very bad that, when speaking of the most evil things, they always used to say, *It would be better to marry your own sister . . .*

In Egypt under Ptolemy Mikros, the Greeks found it wiser now to bite the tongue when they were moved to make that kind of remark.

Aye, every man in Alexandria knew what would happen: they would have a pig's tail child, and it would lead to the ruin of the House, and serve them right. Mikros knew it, Arsinoë Beta knew it, but they raced onward in their folly, the brother climbing into the sister's bed, heedless of the anger it must whip up on Mount Olympos.

To marry the sister, it was an unlucky thing for the Greeks. The tragic consequences of it were as certain as words carved upon a stone.

1.17

Lobsters

Ptolemy Mikros found that his *aphrodisia* with the sister was very like the mating of the crocodiles, inasmuch as she made use of her teeth, biting; and the nails of her fingers, for scratching; and her knees, for squeezing, and she was, of course, on top, in charge. And then it was like lobsters, for he took her from the rear. And then it was like camels, that take all day in their mating, and the groaning and bad temper was not dissimilar.

Mikros did not scratch and claw in return. By no means. He was not a man of violence. To be sure, he was exhausted by his sister, even though he was seven years younger, but exhilarated also. She had learned from Berenike her mother how to make use of all the tricks of a whore while playing the part of the wife. For sure, it was the secret of her success in Thrace. There was not much Arsinoë Beta did not know about the arts of Aphrodite.

True, she was very thin, but he did not, as it happened, find her body repellent unto him. She seemed to know what he would find pleasing. In their daily life she would often finish his sentences for him, and he hers, as if each knew what the other was going to say next. At times they would speak the same word at the same moment, and astonish each other, as if they even thought the same thoughts.

Mikros no longer thrust her from him in horror. He began to think that he might, after all, have done the right thing. He felt not bad but good about the *aphrodisia* with his sister.

In the morning he went so far as to send her a written message:

> *They drive me wild, thy rose-red lips . . .*
> *Thy soft breasts, glossy as poured cream . . .*

Arsinoë's heart swelled, but only for mirth. Proof, then, she thought, that her magic had worked. She sent back some nonsense of her own, but no, she did not love her brother. She loved only the ghost of dead Agathokles, the shadowy grey figure who followed her wherever she went. She told herself that she had had more than her fill of Eros. She had tried to steel that cold and hot heart of hers never to melt, never to fall in love again. So far she had succeeded.

You have Hera's eyes, Mikros wrote, *Athena's hands, the breasts of Aphrodite, blessed is the man who looks upon you, twice blessed is the man who hears your voice, a demigod the man who kisses your lips, a god who takes you for his wife.*

Well, Mikros was a god already – Zeus. Now Arsinoë Beta was Hera, wife of Zeus, very much of a wife, and – like Hera – often a complaining one.

So – he loved a little, perhaps, though he tried, of course, not to, for that to every Greek falling in love is next to madness; and she – she loved him not. But sometimes the two of them wavered, so that he did not love but hated her; so that she did not hate but loved him just a little. And so it will go on, as they fly headlong over the high cliff of their folly, playing at Zeus and Hera, aping the very gods of Greece, to the high offence of Mount Olympos. But they also play at being Isis and Osiris, and Arsinoë Beta often dresses herself up in the cow's-horn headdress of Hathor, Lady of the Sycamore, goddess of Love and Joy, who is the equal of Aphrodite, and it is a right and proper thing for the Queen of Egypt to do. She wears the eye-paint of an Egyptian queen every day. She is in high favour not only with the priests but with all the people of Egypt for doing these Egyptian things – which neither her mother nor Arsinoë Alpha had dared to do, for fear of upsetting the delicate balance of the two nations living in one land, Greek and Egyptian.

Sometimes, nevertheless, Mikros feels rather like the *trokhilos*, the little River-bird that the crocodile allows to creep inside her mouth so that he may pick her teeth. At any moment, he thinks, those great iron jaws might snap shut and crush him. Yes, of course he was wary of her. Of course he suspected her friendship was no more than *lukophilia*, wolf's friendship, utterly false. Many years ago he had sworn never to trust her in his life. And yet now, he was happy to let her help him rule his kingdom.

In the palace where she was now the mistress, Arsinoë Beta slipped her shining feet into the exquisite gold shoes of Arsinoë Alpha with the cobras and vultures embroidered upon the toes, and walked about. To step into Arsinoë Alpha's shoes did not feel uncomfortable in the slightest. She felt no guilt whatever. She wore her husband's gifts, the Egyptian necklace of golden cobras inlaid with blue glass paste. She wore the siren earrings of gold, with wings and claws, bird's tail, bird's legs and woman's body. She wore the serpent armlets of gold. The horrible sirens and the hateful snakes were a measure of his thanks for her having saved him from military disgrace, and perhaps, too, a measure of his hate, for the awful thing she had made him do. For the siren was herself, of course, the woman with claws, who had lured a man on to the rocks against his will. And the serpent was herself too, very like herself, ever with a mouthful of poison to spit forth, ever like to wrap herself round a man, even her own brother, and squeeze him to death.

The new husband, lazy or not, ordered a close watch kept upon his fresh wife. He might have affected indifference to what she did, but he made sure he knew where she was, made sure the spies told him of everything she did, just the same as she kept her watch on him. No, he had not forgotten his oath that he would never trust her in all his lifetime. However, she had now become *useful.* He simply could not live without her.

When the threat of war loomed yet again, Arsinoë Beta said, *Let Antiokhos do what he will, we shall not cancel the sailing up-River to show ourselves to the people.* And they set out upon their royal progress in the gilded barge with purple sails, and silver oars, and musicians with flutes and trumpets, and every Egyptian trapping such as ostrich-feather fans, golden thrones, palm trees, and perfume-burners, so that they travelled in a cloud of fragrant smoke, like gods indeed. The natives stood by the River to sing the song of welcoming the Pharaoh, and all looked to be well with the Two Lands. In the coming war Egypt was certain, now, to win the most magnificent victory.

They stopped at Mendes, in the Delta of the River, where they made lavish offerings to the Sacred Ram. They had heard that the women here had *aphrodisia* with the ram in public, a great honour, and were astonished to watch the performance. But when the High Priest of Mendes asked her Majesty whether she would be pleased to embrace the god in this fashion, Arsinoë Beta smiled sweet. *Excellency,* she said, *some other time, perhaps . . .* then spoke of the cold weather at Alexandria.

At Pithom, or Heroönpolis, in the eastern Delta, Mikros and Arsinoë Beta inaugurated the new Temple of Atum, the creator god. It was the sister who had speech with the High Priest of Heroönpolis – using Eskedi as her interpreter – about the plague of pink locusts, and the stubbornness of donkeys, while Mikros stood and looked at his feet, or stared at the screaming, wheeling flocks of lapwings, as if he were trying to divine his future from their crazy flight.

Arsinoë Beta spoke always first, said the word when they were ready to taste their food, when they would be pleased to retire for the night, and Mikros said next to nothing. Mikros already did nothing but smile the half-smile of Pharaoh and let his wife do the talking. Aye, and she talked till her tongue ached, as if she had been entered for talking in the Olympian Games.

When the sailing took them south of Memphis, they looked at the water-wheels in the District of the Lake, the whole of which was sacred to Sobek, the crocodile god, and saw in action the wonderful Screw of Archimedes, that was proving of the greatest use in watering the fields. When they sailed upon Lake Moeris, Mikros said to his wife, *There are twenty-two different kinds of fishes in this Lake.*

Arsinoë Beta stretched her eyes, as if she had never heard it before. After a while he said to her, *You are pleased, Sister, by the Lake?*

She flashed the teeth and sparkled the eye. *Indeed, Brother,* she said, *the Lake is beautiful.*

The Lake is yours, he said, *for the income of the fishing and the fowling.*

Arsinoë Beta gasped for surprise, though she knew very well the fishes had been the Queen's perquisite since time immemorial, for her pin-money, her unguents and personal adornment.

How much is the income thereof? she asked, as if she did not know already.

One silver talent a day, he said, and so it was, upon the instant: the entire annual income from the Lake poured into her Majesty's treasure-house.

And did she like fish better now that they paid for her trinkets? She did not. She loathed fishes as much as ever. She liked the *income.* Aye, she grabbed the income; she snatched everything for herself, very like the crocodile.

In Egypt the rich Arsinoë Beta got richer still, for that her brother-husband now bestowed upon her very many gifts, just as Lysimakhos, her first husband, had done. She still demanded rewards and payments for every last thing she did, granting and withholding her favours at will, much as she had withdrawn her military advice before the marriage, to make Mikros do what she wanted. Aye, and once again it was behaviour learned from her mother.

As for those who said Arsinoë Beta got no happiness from her third-time marriage, what with her husband running after his many concubines and ignoring her – they were wrong, quite wrong. She had now her heart's desire: power in her hands, and her brother in her bed. Sure, he slipped out from time to time to ride upon the back of beautiful Bilistikhe, or to bury his face in her perfect breasts, grunting with pleasure not unlike the Apis himself, but he did not ignore the new wife as he had sometimes been pleased to ignore the old one. Arsinoë Beta was a woman who would not be ignored.

Up-River this Queen was careful to make her generous offerings to the gods of Egypt. She singled out for special attention Sakhmet, Lady of the Bright Red Linen. Aye, the lady of the blood-soaked garments of her enemies, the lioness goddess of Memphis, the Powerful One, in whom she saw the reflection of her self. Sakhmet was the Daughter of Ra, the Eye of Ra. Her messengers sent plague. And yet she was called also Lady of Life, who breathed fire against the enemies of Pharaoh. This goddess was her Majesty's special delight.

She made also special devotions to Mut, the Vulture, first goddess of Thebes, one of the symbolic mothers of the Pharaoh. Mut, aye, yet another slim lady in a bright-red linen dress, patterned like the feathers of the vulture, who was so very like herself, the goddess that had control of war. War on its own, though, was not enough for Arsinoë Beta. Not many nights into her new marriage she said to her husband, *I have decided to be Aphrodite.*

Mikros stared at her, his face screwed up in puzzlement.

I am Aphrodite now, she said, *the great goddess, the goddess of Love.*

Mikros shrugged. He could have forbidden such presumption, but he knew that, if he did, he should know again the iron whip lash of her tongue. *You can be whoever you like,* he said, *so long as you win Egypt's battles.*

Do not doubt it, Brother, she said. *I am not only Isis and Hathor. I am also Tykhe, goddess of Good Luck, and Nike, goddess of Victory. There can be no question of failure. Our success is guaranteed.*

She made her brother put two eagles side by side on his coins, both of them standing on the thunderbolt, to show she was his equal. She put her own face beside her husband's on the coins of Egypt, drachmas, tetradrachms, and oktodrachms, just as she had done upon the coins of Ephesos and Thrace, and Mikros did not forbid that either.

Arsinoë Beta sat now enthroned in Egypt, adorned with every august costly stone, not unlike her jewelled crocodile, and for a while she led this sparkling creature into her Council of War upon a golden leash, like some beastly manifestation of herself, like Egypt personified, and her eyes glittered like the crocodile's eyes, just the same. Aye, and everybody in the palace knew that behind her smile there lay cruelty, nastiness, the urge to deliver death to her enemies, and perhaps even to some who thought they were her friends.

Now she even began to wear not just one snake upon her brow, like any other queen of Egypt, but two, as if she were twice as poisonous as any queen before her.

The three young children of Arsinoë Alpha – Ptolemy Euergetes, Lysimakhos and Berenike – were among those whom Arsinoë Beta was keen to make her particular friends, and they now saw a good deal of the smiling face of the aunt who had become their stepmother. She brought them sugared plums, and pyramidal honey-cakes, and leopard cubs, and crocodile eggs as gifts, things she thought must delight these children and make them love her. But Arsinoë Alpha's children did not love her. They wept for not being able to say *Goodnight* to their mother, the Mistress of Happiness, the Great of Love.

We are your mother now, Arsinoë Beta said, and she embraced her children with Greek embraces, the proper kisses upon both the cheeks, night and morning. She tried to tell them stories of her days in Thrace, about the miracle of ice and the mystery of snow, but these Egyptian children could not imagine such wonders and they would not listen to her. *You are not our Mémé,* Lysimakhos told her, *you are a liar.*

Call me Mother, she insisted, but they did not even want to speak to her. Some men say that very young children will not remember who is or is not their real mother, but these children did not forget the ever-loving Arsinoë Alpha.

You must call me Mother. Come now and embrace your Mother, she said, smiling, holding out her arms for them to come running to her poisonous embrace. But these children saw through her falseness. They would not run to her. By no means. They ran away, crying, *We hate you . . . .* They had already seen too much of her foul temper.

When Berenike Syra said to her brother Lysimakhos, in their stepmother's hearing, *I do not like her face,* Arsinoë Beta vowed to send them all away just as soon as she could. She had the power to conjure up ten thousand hired soldiers with one word from her iron lips, but she had not the power to make her brother's children love her. What is it the Greeks say? *Just as the land is more to be desired than the sea, so is a mother sweeter than a stepmother.*

Arsinoë Beta did find these infants useful to her in one respect, for the urine of children before their coming-of-age is good against the poison of the asp, whose pleasure is to spit venom into men's eyes. Always on the watch for whatever medicines would make life easier, she collected her stepchildren's urine in jars and kept it. For the asp, or Egyptian cobra, was no stranger to Alexandria, of course, but was fated to play a curious role in the drama of the House of Ptolemy.

As for the urine of Arsinoë Beta herself, it troubled the heart of Herophilos, her malodorous but very excellent new physician, for that noxious liquid was not clear in the morning as it should be, and it was a bad sign, very bad, meaning that she must die, and die soon.

If Arsinoë Beta could not make her brother's children obey her, she could control the court poet, Theokritos of Syracuse, from whom she commissioned a poem. Her orders were simple: *You must make our marriage seem wonderful to the Greeks.* And so Theokritos declared the royal incest a most beautiful thing, most divine and holy, an affair of the gods, after the example of Zeus and Hera, a marriage made in heaven.

He said the bride was *As lovely as Helen of Troy,* although she was thirty-seven years old, past the age at which most Greek women are grandmothers and settling into old age, if not into the grave. The Greeks did not guffaw when they heard it, but kept a straight face, for fear of reprisals such as burial at sea, or being cut open alive in one of Herophilos' brilliant anatomical experiments.

Some nights Mikros was woken by the sister snoring gently beside him in the golden bed, and when he thought of the other Arsinoë a tear would roll down his cheek for what he had lost – his beautiful wife, his favourite jester, two of his finest doctors, his freedom to do what he liked, even his affection for his children.

For yes, he had begun to take less notice of his own sons, the traitor's offspring. Arsinoë Beta had done very well her work of turning Mikros against his wife and children, his once perfectly happy family.

When he sent for Eskedi to ask the meaning of his wild dreams, and to tell him his troubles, the High Priest encouraged him, saying, *His Majesty should think not of what he has lost, but of what he has gained. He may have lost a wife, but he has found something much more valuable: security at home, peace abroad, and victory over his enemies. His Majesty's reign will be glorious because of the marriage to the sister.*

As it happened, Eskedi would also get what he wanted out of that unconventional marriage: an end to war, an end to uncertainty, and Egypt under strong government. Eskedi was beginning almost to love Arsinoë Beta for her most excellent fierceness. She was as much as Strong Bull herself.

1.18

Divine Breath of the Bull

Eskedi himself had not ignored his own children. He had not abandoned Padibastet and Khonsouiou to the tutor, but taught them the hieroglyphs himself. He had taught them to love the Egyptian gods. He had played the game of *senet* with them, to teach them fairness, and the shamefulness of cheating. He had taught them Greek, and how to treat the Greeks – with most careful politeness.

Padibastet and Khonsouiou had learned to sit cross-legged, papyrus scrolls spread out on their knees, balancing the water pot and cakes of red and black ink for writing. They had learned devotion to Thoth, god of scribes, repeating after their father, *A scribe does not go without; his scrolls are a boat upon the water.*

When they visited the Apis for the first time as junior priests, Eskedi said to them, *Sniff his divine breath, and you will gain the power to foretell the future. The care of Apis is just about your most important task in Egypt.*

He had taught them the art of prophesying by means of the sacred bull: how to forecast the rise of the Nile from the markings on his flanks; how to foretell tomorrow from what the Apis did today. He had long since made them learn by heart:

Apis is the protector of the King at his coronation. The King must always sacrifice to him, for the divine bull helps to guarantee the balance of creation.

He also was careful to teach them loyalty to his Majesty: *Adore the King, Ptolemy, living for ever, in your innermost parts,* he said. *His Majesty is*

Perception. *His eyes pierce through every being. He is Ra, by whose rays one sees. He illumines the Two Lands more than the Sun disk.*

The sons, of course, questioned it, as the young will question such things. Khonsouiou said to his father, *How may this Greek dog be Ra? Surely this filthy Macedonian is not Horus but Seth, the embodiment of Chaos.*

But Eskedi said, *Pharaoh cannot be filthy. Whatever his origins, the Greek is Pharaoh, and must be treated as Pharaoh. Otherwise the balance of the Two Lands will be overturned.*

He saw Khonsouiou's face fall, and said, *A Greek pharaoh will make the land green just the same, even more than a high flood. Even the Greek Pharaoh is Ka: his utterance is abundance.*

Khonsouiou opened his mouth to protest, but before he could say one more word, his father said, *Pharaoh is the one who builds for the gods. Prosperity means a year of monuments for Egypt. A high Nile and a good harvest will make his Majesty build for us. A new temple is his thank-offering to the gods . . . Pharaoh deserves respect for these great works. Do not be afraid to trust him.*

Eskedi took Padibastet into his confidence, teaching him everything the Great Chief of the Hammer should know. Padibastet knew what he must do, how to deal with the Greeks, why he must always support Ptolemy, whatever he did, and however much he might, in his secret secret thoughts, despise him.

You will serve the office of Pharaoh, Eskedi told him, *not the man who holds the office.*

Khonsouiou still resisted. *I should like to see an Egyptian pharaoh,* he said. *I think an Egyptian would do better than this foreigner. I should like to see the Egyptians rise up and fight him.*

But you see, Eskedi said, *there is nobody left who is worthy. There is no Egyptian left who might be Pharaoh instead of him. The Persians wiped out most of Egypt's nobility. The men of distinction that were left, they fled Egypt one hundred years ago. Only the family of the High Priest of Memphis would be suitable . . .*

Then you must rise up, Father, Khonsouiou said. *You should be the Pharaoh yourself.* And he threw himself upon the floor, bowing down, kissing his father's feet.

Stop, Khonsouiou, Eskedi said. *It is not the right time for this. How could Egypt fight the power of the Macedonian? If we did rebel, they would call upon their allies and crush Egypt. The priests must maintain order, and balance, must fight chaos. Revolution would mean chaos. Egypt must be kept calm. The best thing is to work with the Macedonian – who will fight Egypt's battles for her, and win. The one who praises his Majesty will be protected by his arm.*

He saw Khonsouiou roll his eyes, amazed to hear such words, but Eskedi was patient. He knew that his sons and grandsons would, at least, die in their own beds, of old age. The sons and grandsons of Ptolemy Mikros would not. All of Mikros's children would die violent deaths, aye, and six of his seven grandchildren the same.

So many times Eskedi murmured, *If we wait long enough we shall see them destroy themselves without the Egyptian having to lift one finger against them.*

1.19

Pig Tail

Mikros may have been inclined to laziness, but he was not completely incapable of asserting himself. He did his best to ensure that Arsinoë Beta worked no magic spell. Though she resisted with terrible screaming, he made her write the words again, in her own blood, *I swear that I shall do nothing to harm your children.*

In the end he made her adopt his children as her own, so that she should not murder them all. But these sulky, ungrateful spoiled infants were not what Arsinoë Beta wanted. *I must have another child, a child of my own,* she said. Aye, a child she could bring up nasty, like herself: a fresh son, who could be the next Pharaoh.

Sotades had screamed his forecast that Arsinoë Beta would lose no time in making her brother tie up the left-hand testicle and set to work, bouncing upon her skinny body. He had howled with laughter that she would soon be swigging the hawk dung in honey wine, and burning the incense made from brimstone, garlic and beaver's testicles, to speed up her getting a child by her brother. Sotades was not far wrong.

For his part, Ptolemy Mikros did not want any son of his sister to succeed him. He already had his son and heir. And yet, because the sister had so successfully turned him against them, he was not so sure, now, that he wanted any son of Arsinoë Alpha to succeed him either. He absolutely did not want to get a child upon his own sister. He forced himself to swallow daily a potion of herbs mixed with ox's urine, drank the divine piss of Apis himself, in order to guarantee him lifelong infertility.

Unfortunately, it did not have the desired effect.

*

What was the truth about this marriage? Some men swore by Zeus and Pan that Arsinoë Beta did bear her brother a son; others thought such a thing quite impossible, but Seshat says, *Why not? Why ever not?* She had been brought to bed of three healthy sons in Thrace. She was not so old that she could not produce a fourth. Seshat knows there was an extra child.

Arsinoë Beta thought, *How in the name of all the gods may I sit by and watch a son of the hated Arsinoë Alpha, the nephew of the murdered Agathokles of Thrace, be crowned Pharaoh when Mikros is dead? Surely, if Arsinoë Alpha's son succeeds Mikros, I shall be cast out. A Pharaoh who is Arsinoë Alpha's son must be our most bitter enemy.* She had seen already how these children loathed her. How much worse it would be when they grew up. *No,* she thought, *we must have a fresh son of our own who shall sit upon the throne instead, and to Hades with the traitor's offspring.*

Seshat cannot think that Arsinoë Beta did not try to have a son by her brother. Seshat swears that there was another son, delivered by Herophilos himself, who shouted his orders to the midwife from behind a curtain, amid the screeching of Arsinoë Beta, that was like fifty vultures.

The fresh Ptolemy slipped into the midwife's hands quite normal. He had the proper number of orifices. He did not have the club foot or the webbed fingers. He was perfectly normal, apart from the curled tail. Aye, the tail. About a palm's width long it was, covered with blond bristles, and it moved of its own accord.

Arsinoë Beta was delighted with her son, most amused by his little tail. To Mikros she laughed, *Does not Pharaoh himself walk about all day with the bull's tail swinging between his legs? Pharaoh is meant to have a tail, it is lucky, a sign, a mark of the gods' favour for the fresh Strong Bull.*

Aye, Strong Bull, for she had already talked Mikros into appointing him his successor, even while he kicked and kicked in the womb. *The youngest son is certainly the one to choose,* she said, *just as you were the youngest son yourself. The youngest son is always the best.*

Mikros paced up and down, angry like never before, saying, *But it is not a bull's tail, it is a pig's tail. It is proof of the gods' wrath, and we must cast him out.*

The sister would not have it. *No, Husband, no,* she said. *We must bring him up, and he must keep his lovely tail.* And when it was clear that she would rather die than have any other thing, Mikros was forced to agree. But regarding the tail, he also sent word to Herophilos, saying, *You had better fetch up your butcher's cleaver, and make haste.*

Ptolemy the Son they called this son, to distinguish him from Ptolemy the father, and Ptolemy the brother, and he was a normal son, once Herophilos (proving himself useful, at last, in the butchery department) had chopped the tail off. Aye, quite normal, apart from his pinkish eyes, and his hair, that was paler than straw, like the hair of an old man.

He will do well, Herophilos said, though with his colleagues in the Mouseion he made jests about trotters, and the child's incessant porcine grunting.

Disgraceful though it was to sire a pig's tail son, the father did not cast him out. By no means. Dreadful portent of the gods' anger though he knew it was, Mikros did bring him up, if only because Arsinoë Beta made herself so unpleasant, threatening to withdraw her services with regard to the war in Syria. For sure she screamed at Mikros when she saw the tail had gone. Aye, her tongue burned that day, singeing everything in her path like Sakhmet, Lady of Flame, indeed.

Perhaps it would have been better for these parents if they had exposed that pink-eyed, pale-haired boy, for he would grow up to cause his father much trouble, all of it forecast in his horoscope, all of it known to Eskedi, who went on smiling his half-smile, folding his hands under his leopardskin mantle, but kept quiet about the horrors that lay in the future. Aye, Eskedi said nothing, but he knew very well what the pig's tail meant: it was the mark not of the Horus but of Seth, the god of Chaos, who was incarnate in the pig.

Within one month of the birth Mikros made public the fact that Ptolemy the Son was his heir, over and above the two sons of the disgraced Arsinoë Alpha, the six-year-old Ptolemy Euergetes, and the five-year-old Lysimakhos. These boys were brought up ignorant of their claim to the throne, taught to think of the youngest son as the special one, as if to be born first meant nothing, nothing whatever. Arsinoë Beta led the way, and Mikros followed, treating Ptolemy the Son as the highly favoured one, like the only son he had. That is to say, he spoiled him, thinking of his glorious future. And Ptolemy the Son *was* spoiled.

But the Greek horoscopists pointed to the small ears and short fingers that every Greek knows are the signs of a short life, whispering to one another, *He will die young, in a foreign country. He will rebel against his own father.*

Among themselves, the wise men of the Mouseion shook their heads, muttering the words of Xenophon his *Memorabilia,* that those who break the rules regarding the strict ban on incest will be punished; that whatever good qualities they might possess themselves, their offspring will come to a bad end.

As for the mother of those three adopted and rejected children, she was told nothing of what went on in Alexandria. But Arsinoë Alpha lived. She had been cast out, for sure, but she had not been put to death.

1.20

Koptos

Up at Koptos, near the mines of *smaragdos*, hundreds of stades up-River, between Abydos and Thebes, Arsinoë Alpha had her mud-brick Residence, not unworthy of a queen. She had fasted and wept many days, but at length she said to herself, *Weeping will serve no useful purpose*, and found that she had a great hunger. Now she began to eat again: dates, sweets, honey-cakes – was always eating, eating, eating, and it went some way to comfort her in her distress. *Eating*, she said, *is the only pleasure I have left.*

Arsinoë Alpha was not a prisoner, but she seldom quit the chamber in which she sat, and her door was guarded day and night – for her own safety, as they told her. The eunuch guards came and went, but Arsinoë Alpha had orders not to set her sandal outside the city gates. She hoped to see her three young children again, but, Seshat knows, she would never look upon the kindly face of her husband until the day when she met him in the Afterlife.

She had some of her finery still, and her loom of acacia wood. But she did not wear the Eye of Horus necklace or the fabulous jewels of the Queen of Egypt. By no means. Arsinoë Beta now wore these things instead.

In the oven that was Koptos, Arsinoë Alpha dripped with perspiration When the hot season passed she would be troubled by the sand that flew up her nose, and settled in the folds of her raiment and every last crevice of her flesh.

Koptos was also the home of Min, the ithyphallic Egyptian god of fertility, who was equal to Pan of the Greeks. Min was called Great of Love, and the people of Koptos made offerings of lettuces to him, as the god who helped them perform the act of *aphrodisia* without ever growing tired. Arsinoë Alpha had no more use for love, no use for any god of fertility. She had lost her husband, her beloved, and was forbidden to take another. To be sure, it was Ptolemy Mikros who had more urgent need of lettuces.

A steward looked after her affairs – Senuu, a priest of the Egyptians. He was a Count and Prince of Egypt, Prophet of Isis, Prophet of Osiris, and Prophet of Horus. One time he had been Treasurer of the King. Senuu wrote many letters in Arsinoë Alpha's name, protesting her innocence, begging to be taken back as Great Royal Wife. She warned that any child Mikros had by the sister would be mad, misshapen, horribly deformed. She said it was bound to happen, it would be the punishment of the gods. *You should not dream of marrying that monstrous woman,* she said. But all Arsinoë Alpha's letters were intercepted by Arsinoë Beta and destroyed before Mikros saw them.

From Koptos started the caravan routes through the Arabian desert to the Red Sea, Sinai, the Land of Punt and the Spice Country, places that yielded incense, ivory, ebony, and leopardskins. Rumour said that Arsinoë Alpha was set to watch over this trade as she had once watched over the fleet of grain ships that sailed in her name up and down the River. She knew a little about spices and perfumes. Some said she had absolute authority in the Koptos district. She liked to think that if she made herself useful her husband might send for her to come home at least as far as Memphis, a place where, indeed, she had known some happiness.

Mikros provided this ex-queen with every goodly thing. She was a king's daughter, still his wife. He did not divorce her. So many times he said to Arsinoë Beta, *I am not a Tyrant. I do not wish the mother of my children dead, whatever she may have done.* At length Arsinoë Beta agreed with him. Yes, the traitor must stay alive. That way she would suffer more.

Senuu it was that built and beautified the shrine for Arsinoë Alpha, calling her, even after her banishment, The King's Wife, the Grand, Filling the Palace with her Beauties, Giving Repose to the Heart of Ptolemy. He raised statues of Arsinoë Alpha and Ptolemy Mikros side by side at Koptos, as if to show she was not disgraced. But he did not call her *Loving Her Brother.* He did not enclose her name in the *shenu,* or ring of rope, that showed she was Queen of Egypt, but Arsinoë Alpha did not go unhonoured.

It would have been no surprise if Arsinoë Alpha had turned to magic spells, and sought to take revenge for her shameful treatment. Nobody would have been surprised if she had lost her wits in the ferocious heat of Upper Egypt, but she recovered once she got away from Arsinoë Beta. She went back to being the amiable woman she had always been. She was not even angry, just very sad.

From time to time, when Arsinoë Alpha was full of black bile, melancholy mad, so that her health gave him cause for concern, Senuu might bring her a dose of calf's dung boiled down in wine, saying, *Her Majesty was lucky for her life to be spared* . . . He would bring his children to visit her. He might fetch her the gift of a pet goose. At length Senuu would be rewarded by the return of her Majesty's wan half-smile.

*

Mikros closed his heart to all of this, for from Koptos he received wild, mad letters from his banished wife, letters full of hate, threatening to kill him, page upon page full of unintelligible magic. She sent him wax dolls, representations of himself, stuck full of bronze nails. She sent parcels of rotten meat, crawling with maggots, dead birds, live scorpions, frightful things that made Mikros cry out, things that Arsinoë Beta made sure were delivered into his hands, for they were all her own work.

When Mikros showed her the letters and remarked upon the foul language, she would say, so earnest, *Brother, your wife is quite deranged ... How lucky you are not to have kept her here in Alexandria.*

Mikros looked hard at her, just then, wondering, wondering, but he said nothing. Whatever she had done, the sister had charge of his wars. He could not say or do anything that might make her abandon him.

Arsinoë Beta did her best to make Egypt forget about the disgraced queen. Now she was the Great Royal Wife herself, the Grand, Filling the Palace with her Beauties, Giving Repose to the Heart of Ptolemy – though, to be sure, she did not give that man's heart much repose, but bullied him until he did what she wanted. As for Loving Her Brother, it was all a make-believe. She hated so much, really, there was not much room left in her heart for anything else.

What of Mikros himself? What were his private private thoughts? Having banished his wife from court in order to please his sister, there were times when this Pharaoh, even sitting upon his throne of gold, found himself thinking that he had done completely the wrong thing. Mikros grew a little moody under the oppression of his sister's rule. He disliked her telling him what he might and might not do. On the one hand he needed her, was grateful for her wise advice. On the other hand, he dreamed of the day when he might have her led away in chains, or find an excuse to make her drink hemlock. Entire days would pass by during which he addressed not one word to his beloved sister-wife, for hating her so much. But no, she would never murder him. At least, she thought, not yet. Sure, she still dreamed of murder, but for the moment it was in her best interests to keep Mikros alive, while Ptolemy the Son grew up. She thought, *When he is old enough to kill his father, then, perhaps, we shall take over, and have everything done properly for a change.*

Indeed, Ptolemy the Son was growing up warlike enough, like a miniature centaur, rampaging about the palace, out of control, destroying whatever he could – uncannily like an exact copy of Ptolemy Keraunos. Not even the father could make Ptolemy the Son do what he did not want to do. Arsinoë Beta alone could handle him, but even she thought, *What kind of future can there be for a boy so wild as this?* All the same, it was all her own fault, for she encouraged him to be warlike like herself, not soft like his father. For what was going to happen, the parents had only themselves to blame, and, of course, fate. Sometimes it is good to blame fate, instead of blaming yourself.

Soon fate would catch up with Arsinoë Beta herself. Her days were running out. Nothing lasts for ever, only the gods of Egypt. Arsinoë Beta was pleased to believe she was Isis and Aphrodite, a living goddess, but she must pass away like any other mortal. It is Seshat, Lady of the House of Books, who will endure for ever. And, of course, the *temples*, that are under her special care.

1.21

Horn of Plenty

In the first few years of Mikros's reign, before the return of Arsinoë Beta, Eskedi had come often to King Ptolemy Mikros with plans for his Majesty to give money to the Egyptian temples. He might say, *It is the ancient custom for his Majesty to support the building. Would his Majesty like to make an offering for the Temple of Per-Hebet in the Delta, east of Sebennytos?*

Mikros would wear the half-smile of Pharaoh, but he always shook his head, saying, *Excellency, no funds to spare,* or, *First we must build up our Temple of Aphrodite.*

When Eskedi said, *The temple at Elephantine has fallen down,* Mikros spread his hands and murmured, *Bad indeed, but – so sorry, Excellency – nothing we can do, nothing.*

If the gods are not kept happy, Eskedi warned, *the River will not flood,* and he looked hard into Mikros's blue eyes, thinking that this man was becoming a master in the art of smiling the inscrutable smile of Pharoah. But Eskedi knew his thoughts well enough: that he would give nothing; that it was a waste of time even to ask him.

Your father built four temples only, Eskedi said. *Not much to show for forty-one years of being Pharaoh.*

My father built the city of Alexandria, Mikros said. *My father built the Pharos. We are all so proud of Ptolemy Soter's achievements.*

He watched Eskedi draw down the corners of the mouth. Alexandria was an alien, impure place, not an Egyptian city. And what use was the Pharos to the Egyptians? Eskedi showed anger. *If his Majesty does not build temples for Egypt, the gods will not be happy,* he said. *If the gods are not happy, the River will not rise. If the River does not rise, there will be no fertile ground, no crops, no harvest, nothing. Famine will follow hard upon it. If there is famine, there will be revolts, for a hungry people is an angry people. And what will Pharaoh do then? What will Pharaoh do?*

But showing temper made no difference. Whenever Eskedi came to him and said something like this, Mikros would push out the lower lip, as if he did not understand that every famine in Egypt was his fault; that Pharaoh alone is responsible for keeping the balance between order and chaos in the Two Lands.

Often Eskedi sailed his ship back to Memphis, thinking that Mikros was not the great king that Ptolemy Soter had hoped he would be, and that revolution could not be far off. Perhaps he would even lead the revolt himself.

No, Mikros handed over not one tetradrachm for the temples, not one hemiobol. Eskedi raised his voice, one time, saying, *Meanness is not a quality of Pharaoh.* But this gave Mikros the opportunity to say, quite calm, *We shall give nothing to the man who shouts at us.*

In the past, then, relations between palace and temple had been a little strained. But when Arsinoë Beta came back things were different. Aye, as usual, Eskedi set down before his Majesty the plaster model of the House of Horus at Isisopolis – a building begun by the late King Nektanebo – asking yet again for money to finish this fine temple of grey and red granite, four hundred paces round about, with its pylons and sacred lake. Mikros, as usual, pursed the lips and shook the head, but Arsinoë Beta walked round the model, exclaiming for delight. When Eskedi unrolled his designs for the carvings on the temple walls, with the barque of Isis, and Mikros offering incense to the goddess, and Arsinoë Beta behind him holding the Ankh and *seistron*, and wearing the Atef crown – the crown with the goat's horns and the triple ostrich-feathers flanked by serpents – accompanied by the gods of Egypt, all lavishly coloured and gilded, Mikros wore his face of Really-Cannot-Decide-About-This. But Arsinoë Beta said, upon the instant, *Excellency, it will be a great pleasure for us to help. You must begin building at once.* And the masons picked up their tools and started work the next day. Such was the power of Pharaoh: all that was needed was for him to say the word.

Now Arsinoë Beta said the word for him.

It is good to give, Brother, Arsinoë Beta said, when the High Priest had gone. *To build temples will stop the natives from rising up against us.*

Time after time she clapped her hands together and gave Eskedi permission to build whatever he asked for, so that his heart warmed still further to her Majesty.

Arsinoë Beta did not forget it was her duty to build for the Greeks as well, of course. She was ever aware of the debt she owed to the gods of Samothrake, the Kabeiri, for saving her life and allowing her to sail home safe to Egypt after her ordeal at Kassandreia. Now she fulfilled her vow to build a great Greek *propylon,* or entrance, for the temple on that island as a thank-offering to the gods for her escape. She raised a Ptolemaieion, or monumental gateway there. She raised more Corinthian columns than any queen before her, delighting so often to give mouth to those wondrous magic words, *My brother will pay,* and all in return for her taking charge of the interminable war.

She also ordered up an Arsinoeion, or great marble rotunda, for Samothrake, and it was dedicated by herself to the Great Gods, but paid for by the brother. She sailed there to perform the foundation ceremony, when there were great processions, magnificent sacrifices, and sumptuous feasts – at which she ate nothing.

The most wonderful thing about the Arsinoeion was the magnificent chryselephantine statue of Arsinoë Beta herself, gold and ivory, that towered inside, so tall that the top of her golden diadem scraped the roof. Her ivory face and arms were as white as they were in real life, and her body was just as thin, in the proper proportions, but her eyes, inlaid with precious stones, sparkled as if for delight at having erected the largest round building in the world.

The brother, watching the contents of his Treasury haemorrhage beyond his control, was not quite so pleased, but, really, it was not as if he could not afford it: there was no man richer than Ptolemy Mikros since Kroisos.

With such great works in progress men began to say that the marriage of Ptolemy Mikros to his sister began Egypt's fresh Age of Gold. They were not mistaken. Arsinoë Beta already had her face beside her brother's upon the coins, wearing the diadem and veil of a Greek queen. On the back side of them she now stamped the Horn of Amaltheia, the goat that suckled Zeus, which became, as it were, the personal badge of Arsinoë Beta, the miraculous Horn that promoted the fertility of the Two Lands, and poured forth gold and every goodly thing in an unstoppable flood. In Egypt, for sure, there was more gold than they knew what to do with, so that just about every item in the palace was of gold, gilded or gold-plated, right down to the taps on every black basalt bath. Mikros, however, did not always think of his sister's Horn of Plenty as pouring out a flood of riches. By no means. He knew many days when it seemed more like an unstoppable torrent of bad temper.

For the moment, though, the funds that might finance the very grandest of building projects were held back, to pay for the war. Arsinoë Beta never stopped talking about her war, planning for her war, building up the troops to peak fighting pitch for her war, although, for the moment, peace persisted. No man in his right mind goes to war because he loves a scrap – and no woman either, not even Arsinoë Beta. She would fight only when she had to, and she did not have to fight yet. Time, then, for Seshat to speak of the wonderful things that poured out of Alexandria during this Age of Gold. One of the very first of wonders was the medical researches of Herophilos, perhaps the greatest doctor of all time, apart, of course, from Imhotep, the Egyptian physician who was made a god, the equal of Asklepios.

Herophilos was very interested in the eyes, that the Greeks saw as the windows of the soul. His dissection identified the different parts of the eye – the cornea, the retina, the iris and the choroid coat – for the first time. A great boon. The posterior surface of the iris he compared to the skin of a grape. The retina he likened to a piled up fishing-net. Humble images, they will never be forgotten so long as the world endures.

He named the cavity in the fourth cerebral ventricle the *kalamos,* because it looked like the carved-out groove of an Alexandrian writing-pen. He named the styloid process *pharoid* because it was Lighthouse-shaped, like the great Pharos of Alexandria. He measured a certain part of the intestine and found it was equal to the length of twelve fingerbreadths, hence his name for it – *dodekadaktulos* or, Italian-style, the duodenum. Herophilos was the man who discovered the purpose of the liver, and that the arteries carry not air but blood; that the function of the heart is to pump blood through the arteries.

His interest in all medical matters is ceaseless, Mikros said to his sister, *his curiosity is without end. Soon he will find the cure for your dyspepsia . . .*

But she said, *I believe that I shall die of the bellyache first.*

Cadavers were still carried to Herophilos' house, as many as he wanted, without question. They said Mikros allowed him to have not only monkeys, criminals and prisoners of war, but even women, to cut them open while they still breathed, then sew them up again afterwards, in order to advance his new science of anatomy.

Why not let Herophilos peer at their guts? Mikros said. *It will reduce the crime rate if a man knows his belly will be sliced open for stealing a goose. And he might find some cure for the sister's dyspepsia . . .*

Herophilos was the first to give women's secret parts proper medical names instead of euphemisms. He showed great interest in woman, a creature no medical man had been allowed to approach with a scalpel before, and it was because Arsinoë Beta was his first of patients. His enlightened interest in woman was the direct result of her encouragement, even if she did sniff and say, *I can smell the smell of death again. Do not stand so close, O Herophilos.*

Every doctor must swear the Oath of Hippokrates, swear by Apollo, and Asklepios, and Hygeia, and Panacea, the divinities in charge of Medicine, never to administer poison, never to use the knife, never to breach any man's confidence. But Herophilos operated outside that oath, was a law unto himself. He made very great use of his sharp knife.

The heart and the brain he made his very close study, inventing a kind of portable *klepsydra*, with which to count the beats of pulse and heart. Herophilos agreed with the great Aristotle, who said that the pulse reflects the beating of the heart, but Herophilos was the first man to count the beats, the first to think of a man's pulse as *Steady, Quick,* or *Slow,* and the first to think that the pulse-rate meant something of significance, calling its beat *Bounding like the Antelope,* or *Crawling like Ants.*

Aye, Herophilos' most outrageous thoughts were about the human heart. He went so far as to tell Ptolemy Mikros, *The heart is not the seat of reason. If I remove half a man's brain while he is still alive and close up his head again, he may go on thinking, but if I remove half his heart, he is a dead man.*

Mikros raised the eyebrows, scratched his head, made faces. He did not know what to believe. Seshat, however, knows very well that a man's heart beats fast when he is excited, when he rides into battle, for example, or when he is boxing in the *gymnasion.* A man's brain does not beat fast under any circumstances. Seshat knows that Herophilos was wrong in this matter, wrong one million times. Mikros himself knew it. For sure, the part of Mikros that beat hard when he had a couple of concubines in bed with him was not his brain. The heart is the seat of reason so far as Egypt is concerned. It is your heart that will be weighed in the Balance, Stranger, not the useless grey stuff that lies between your two ears. Aye, it is what happens in your *heart* that is the more important, is it not so?

Herophilos was very often right, however. He said, *Health is the indispensable foundation of human happiness.* He said, *Without health wisdom cannot develop, skill cannot manifest itself, strength cannot compete in the struggle, wealth is pointless, and reason of no use whatever.*

Arsinoë Beta could not have been happy herself, in that case, for she had not her health. Herophilos' fame was already secure for all time, but his fortune lay in making Arsinoë Beta better. *Cure me,* she said to him, *make me well, and you can have half the gold in my treasure-house. If you were any good you would be able to cure my bellyache.* But Herophilos could not find the cure for her trouble. Neither could he, or any other man in Alexandria, find a cure for her terrible bad temper.

Perhaps the next greatest Alexandrian wonder after Herophilos was the poet Apollonios Rhodios, whom Mikros still encouraged, sending often to ask, *How goes the Argonautika?*

Apollonios was, indeed, still working at his long poem about Jason and the Argonauts, though he never strayed very far from Alexandria in writing it. For sure, the Argonauts had just as many dangerous and wonderful adventures as Odysseus, but Apollonios saw everything through Alexandrian eyes.

His Jason was the kind of hero who is very reluctant to move when action is called for, who cannot decide, but is much better at being told what to do; a man who never does anything for himself but always gets somebody else to do it for him.

His Medea, on the other hand, was a most dynamic and efficient woman, who – with a little supernatural help – had the power to stop even the stars in their tracks and halt the progress of the Moon. She had long golden hair, and thought nothing of committing murder in order to get what she wanted.

Who was Apollonios Rhodios thinking of when he wrote this famous poem? Surely his Jason and Medea, his Zeus and Hera, were portraits of Ptolemy Mikros and Arsinoë Beta. How could it not be so? And was not his disobedient Eros the very image of Ptolemy the Son? Love found a prominent place in Apollonios' writing, and that was an amusing irony in itself, because there was so little love lost between Mikros and his sister. Surely, the *Argonautika* was all a scholarly romp at the expense of royalty, full of Ptolemaic allusions and private jokes, for Alexandria was the world, and the world was Alexandria.

The first public reading of the work took up one entire day, during which the Mouseion scholars laughed up their sleeves, and snorted into their wine. Mikros himself laughed, but he had the sense not to tell his wife what caused his mirth, for fear of her throwing Apollonios into the sea in a leaden coffin for making a mockery of royalty.

The Mouseion rocked with suppressed laughter, but Arsinoë Beta did not see anything funny about the *Argonautika*. For sure, she *loved* it; she showered the highest honours upon Apollonios for his elegant hexameters, saying his poem was a triumph, that it would be remembered as long as the *Odyssey*, for all time. She was right, of course, for you may read the *Argonautika* in your own day, Stranger, but not, if you please, until you have finished reading the works of Seshat. But no, Arsinoë Beta, sitting in the front row of the Theatre with her husband, was so spellbound by that wonderful story that she did not realize she was the artist's model herself, both for Medea the witch-maiden *and* for the bossy wife of Zeus. She did not recognize her brother disguised as both Zeus and Jason.

The one courtier who did not laugh at the *Argonautika* was Kallimakhos, formerly Apollonios Rhodios' tutor, who knew very well the devious way his pupil's heart worked. There was much squawking in the Cage of Fowls when their Majesties had gone home, because Kallimakhos did not like what Apollonios Rhodios had done. He kept up a violent and bitter quarrel with him for years and years.

Mikros and his wife did much more, of course, than Seshat can possibly tell you about. But perhaps there is space and time to tell you that Arsinoë Beta urged Mikros to explore the incense route. She thought that if they could discover incense south of Egypt there need be no dependence upon Rhodes for trade in that most important item.

She urged Mikros to explore the Red Sea properly, both upon the west side and upon the east side. Mikros, thinking of fresh exotic beasts for his Beast Garden, sent Satyros, who was the first to sail right down the African coast, where Arsinoë Beta named the remotest town in the world after Philotera, the disapproving sister.

Ariston they sent to explore the coast of the Sinai peninsula, right round to the Nabataian Ailana, south of Petra, where he found gold country hitherto unknown, a gold-bearing river, and nuggets of gold. He held talks with the Nabataians, who had the reputation of pirates and raiders. He fixed up the export of horses and, of course, he carried off as much gold as his ships could carry.

This king and his fresh wife were not idle. By no means. They laboured from sun-up to sundown to make Alexandria and all Egypt glorious, and themselves richer than any other king and queen alive.

Far greater than either medical or literary or geographical wonders was the *Hydraulikon*, or water-organ, invented by Ktesibios. This astonishing musical machine had seven great pipes of different lengths fixed together in a row, like the *syrinx*, or pan-pipes – partly of bronze, and partly of reed. Music was made by forcing air into the pipes by the flow of water, and the sound that came forth was utterly wonderful and unique. Ktesibios had the letters of the *alpha beta* marked upon a keyboard, so that any man who had the wit to tap the finger upon the keys might play a tune upon it.

The only drawback to the Hydraulikon was its loudness: so loud was it that Ktesibios was forced to stopper his ears with papyrus plugs so as not to damage his eardrums. The Hydraulikon was used at the Stadion, for festivals and processions, and in the great Theatre of Dionysos, to terrify the audience when the ghosts came up from the Underworld. Such was the phenomenal noise blasted out that when Ktesibios played at Alexandria his organ could be heard – if the wind was not blowing in the wrong direction – even at Memphis, eight hundred stades away.

Mikros was delighted. *Surely*, Arsinoë Beta said, *we may use this as a weapon of war, with which to terrify our enemies . . .* and for a time Ktesibios made jests about an armoured Hydraulikon, for military use.

Death by music, he laughed. *It is Egypt's new secret weapon . . .*

But what did Arsinoë Beta herself do that was good for Egypt, for Alexandria, and for her brother now that she had gotten her way, and was the Lady of the Two Lands?

She believed that she had just two thousand one hundred and ninety days left to live. She consoled herself by planning her funeral procession, that would be the grandest thing Alexandria ever saw. But while she was dictating her last orders, thinking of her final appearance, she had the greatest idea of her life. It was during this five years' lull in the fighting over Syria that she thought of a grand procession followed by magnificent games, to be held every fifth year. It would mark the return of Arsinoë Beta to Alexandria. It would celebrate her military success in Syria, and her own personal triumph in becoming her brother's wife.

Mikros yawned aloud to hear of it. *I am not interested in athletic games,* he said. *Sports are a total waste of time. To stage such a procession would be a waste of money . . . And how can you think of holding such festivities when all the war-time economies are in force? I shall have nothing to do with it.*

It is the winter time, Brother, she said. *The troops stand idle. There can be no more fighting until beginning of the sailing season. Why should the people not enjoy themselves?*

Mikros shrugged, as usual, but it was because he sneered at her great idea that she became urgent to make her procession a mighty success. Made keener by his apathy, Arsinoë Beta took charge of everything, because the greatest purpose of the Great Pompe, as she called it, was to make the Greeks forget the scandal that their king had gotten himself married to his own sister; to make them see that the brother–sister marriage could give rise to marvellous things.

The Egyptians had their own festivals, so many that almost every other day seemed to be an excuse for a holiday: the Pompe would delight the

Greeks. It would be the grandest procession of all time, entirely Greek, by the Greeks and for the Greeks, as if to underline the Greekness of the Ptolemies, who had taken it upon themselves to wear Egyptian crowns. Perhaps it was not possible to make Alexandria a happy place for ever, but Arsinoë Beta boasted, *I swear that I shall make Alexandria happy, if only for one day, by honouring Dionysos, god of Wine, and letting the people drink themselves into a beastly stupor.*

When Mikros realized there would be drinking, he gave his royal approval at once, and he did manage to work up some enthusiasm, a month or two before. It was Mikros who made the Pompe into a grand procession of Dionysos the Laugher. Aye, Dionysos who was equal to Osiris, who was equal to Pharaoh, to Ptolemy Mikros himself. When Mikros realized that, he found he was very enthusiastic about the Pompe, which became the physical embodiment of his personal philosophy: to blot out the bad dream that was yesterday; to forget the looming nightmare that was tomorrow, but to enjoy the pleasure of the passing moment while you can, the pleasure of now. Drink! Dance! Be drunken now! Lest Hades, or Anubis, grab your hand during the night.

1.22

Pompe

They heard the wild uproar of the Pompe first, in the distance, the stupefying din of an invisible procession, a distant cacophony that slowly turned into the music of thousands of drums and trumpets, flutes and crashing cymbals, all playing different tunes at once. For Arsinoë Beta's procession was, indeed, to honour the god of Wine, the mad, drunken god, the god of Frenzy, the Son of Fire.

Aye, Dionysos the Laugher ruled over this procession, the great god in whose veins ran not blood but flames: Dionysos, followed by a crowd of drunken, dancing worshippers. Only Ptah can make Time run backwards, but Arsinoë Beta managed to make Time stop that day, for the Pompe stood for Time itself. The time of Dionysos's festival was Time out of Time, so that the ordinary man might forget himself and his troubles and the horror of the present moment. Alexandria went mad for the most delightful and the most frightful of Greek gods, the one who loves the sword, violence, and bloodshed. It should be no surprise to you, Stranger, that in the family that worshipped such a god, murder should be their favourite pastime, for the coming of Dionysos brings a divine madness.

For the moment even Ptolemy Mikros and Arsinoë Beta forgot their troubles, forgot the threat of poison and murder. Dionysos says put on the mask, be free, join the procession, be happy now, today. The Great Pompe was the wild procession of Dionysos writ large, very large indeed, very drunken, and very wonderful.

At dawn it began, and every man, woman and child in Alexandria either marched in the procession, or watched it pass by, and the first miracle was that though it was the winter time there was blue skies, no wind, no rain, and no shivering. The procession moved at snail's pace from the Hippodrome in the east, along Kanopic Street to the Stadion in the west. The Hydraulikon boomed the tunes that the Greeks sang at every banquet, the warlike marching songs, the songs of victory in battle, and all day Alexandria sang.

First
came Aglaïs
the famous trumpet-blower,
a woman of giant size,
upon whose head
was a golden wig,
and a tall
plume of white ostrich-feathers, that swayed
as she marched,
belly wobbling, wearing a dress of leopardskins,
Gluttony
made flesh,
who blew her trumpet, then, shrieking
with laughter, twirled her body round and round.
Behind her came
the Procession of Eosphoros,
the Morning Star, personified as
a gold-winged boy,
who held up a flaming torch
to stand for the light of the Star:
a naked boy,
painted gold
from head to foot, who
rode upon a great white

horse with a golden harness, and he was the infant
Ptolemy the Son,
the Spoilt One,
a boy made of gold, but whose fate it was to be
melted down before he was twenty.
Next,
the Procession of Dionysos,
led by forty Senior Satyrs
wearing purple cloaks, who held back the crowd.
Forty Junior Satyrs,
youths of the city,
came next, naked but for
leopardskin loincloths, with tails
and giant *phalloi* attached, carrying
flaming gilded torches.
Now
came the
Nikai, or Winged Victories,
gold-painted women dressed
in white tunics,
carrying incense-burners
six cubits tall, filled with myrrh and
frankincense to purify the atmosphere around the divine
Dionysos.
One
hundred and
twenty singing boys carried
frankincense, myrrh and saffron
– symbol of divine purity and majesty –
on golden plates,
and sprayed saffron mixed with water over the crowd.
Forty
naked Satyrs wearing
crowns of golden ivy,
bodies stained purple,
carried between them a giant gold
crown of vine and ivy leaves.
Next
Eniautos,
personification of

the Year, played by Arsinoë Alpha's son,
Lysimakhos, aged five,
in tragic costume
carrying a golden Horn of Plenty.
Then
Penteteris,
personification
of the five-year festival itself,
adorned with gold and jewels,
who was played by the ever disapproving Philotera.

Upon a long wagon dragged by one hundred and eighty slaves marshalled
by slave-drivers with leather whips sat a mechanical statue of Dionysos himself, ten cubits high, in purple gown and golden slippers, and crowned with
vine leaves, who stood up, poured a libation from a golden cup, and sat down
again, the excellent and most excellent work of Ktesibios the engineer.

Next,
a great wagon dragged by three hundred slaves,
devotees of Dionysos,
bore a gigantic wine press twenty-four cubits long,
fifteen cubits wide, overflowing with ripe grapes.
Sixty naked
Satyrs trampled the grapes
and sang the grape-pressing songs,
spraying grape juice into the air,
for the Alexandrians to catch in their mouths.
A
silver krater holding six hundred measures
of wine for the feasting was carried on a wagon dragged by
six hundred slaves.
Next came
the Treasure,
King Ptolemy Soter's
share of Alexander's eastern booty:
two giant silver cup stands,
ten great silver basins,
sixteen large silver *kraters*,
six silver cauldrons,
twenty-four silver measuring vases,

two silver wine presses,
a solid silver table twelve cubits long,
thirty more silver tables,
eight silver tripods,
twenty-six silver water pitchers,
sixteen silver amphoras,
one hundred and sixty silver wine coolers,
a golden wine press,
two golden bowls, two golden cups,
twenty-two golden wine coolers,
four large gold three-legged tables,
a jewel-encrusted chest,
ten gold water pitchers,
twenty-five gold trenchers,
followed by sixteen
hundred Greek boys,
wearing white tunics and ivy
wreaths, carrying
gold or silver pitchers,
gold or silver wine coolers, and singing the drinking songs.
Three
hundred and seventy Greek
boys dressed as Ganymedes,
or Cupbearers of Zeus, in nothing at all, carried gold
or silver wine jars, and handed out cups of wine.

Next, a wagon dragged by five hundred slaves bore the Cave of Hermes, shaded with ivy and yew. All along the route pigeons, ring-doves, turtle doves were released from it, their feet tied with ribbons so that the crowd might catch them. Two springs gushed from the cave, one of milk, one of wine. Inside the cave sat Hermes, holding his herald's golden staff, surrounded by Nymphs in golden crowns. The next wagon showed the Return of Dionysos from India, with a giant statue of the god, riding an elephant with golden trappings.

Six hundred men
dragged a great car with a gigantic
two-hundred-and-forty-thousand-pint
wineskin made of leopardskins
stitched together,

spraying wine in all directions.
Five
hundred small girls
marched behind with cymbals and castanets, wearing
purple tunics and golden girdles.
One hundred and twenty
Satyrs in silver or bronze
armour with giant gold *phalloi*.
Twenty-four
two-wheeled chariots,
each pulled by four elephants of war
made drunk on barley wine, so that they
should not run amuck and trample
the Alexandrians.

In the Stadion, the Pharaoh and his sister-wife sat upon a dais of gold and ebony under a purple awning. As the ninety-six elephants of war marched in front of King Ptolemy in the Stadion, they knelt down, raised the trunk and trumpeted before him.

Arsinoë Beta, blowing kisses to her elephants, said, *Do you know which animal has two hearts, Brother?*

Not I, by Zeus, he said.

The elephant, she said. *He has one heart for anger, one heart for gentleness. He has the ability to think double.*

Mikros made the face of never having heard such a thing in his life. He said, *You are like the elephant yourself, Sister. You have two hearts as well, but both of them are for anger.* Without removing the smile from the face, and without stopping their waving acknowledgement to the passing show, they exchanged the now customary words of vicious abuse. And so the elephants stood up, the procession moved on:

Sixty
chariots drawn by one hundred and twenty goats.
Twelve chariots drawn by twenty-four antelopes.
Seven chariots drawn by fourteen white oryxes.
Fifteen chariots drawn by thirty gnus.
Eight chariots drawn by sixteen ostriches.
Four chariots drawn by eight onagers.
Four chariots drawn by four horses each.
Six chariots drawn by twelve camels.

A small boy crowned with pine rode in each chariot;
beside each boy rode a small girl crowned
with ivy, armed with shield and lance.
Forty-five
camels carried
three hundred *minas*
of frankincense, three hundred
minas of myrrh, two hundred *minas*
of saffron, cassia, orris, cinnamon – a total of
five tons of spices.
Six hundred Ethiopian tribute-bearers
walked behind, each with
a great elephant tusk in his arms.
Sixty Ethiopians carried sixty *kraters*
full of pieces of gold and silver.
Two thousand huntsmen
with gilded hunting-spears led
two thousand four hundred hunting-dogs.
Forty-six white Indian Cows.
Fourteen leopards and sixteen cheetahs on golden leashes.
Four Persian Lynxes.
Three
leopard cubs carried by Nubian keepers.
One
Camelopard,
out of Upper Nubia, as
tall as three men, and famous for drinking
two hundred pints of cow's milk every day.
The
Two-Horned White
Rhinoceros of Ethiopia was the darling
of the Pompe, stamping in his cage of iron,
mounted upon a cart.
Last
in the animal
procession walked
the Rare White Bear from Thrace,
the wedding gift of King Lysimakhos on
his daughter's marriage to Ptolemy Mikros,
part of her dowry. Formerly the

property of Arsinoë Alpha, now he belonged to
Arsinoë Beta, her great delight.

Now
came gold
and ivory statues
of Alexander and Ptolemy Soter
wearing crowns of gold ivy,
flanked by statues of Arete, or
Excellence made flesh, and of Priapos, god of Fertility,
wearing crowns of golden ivy.
Now came a wagon
bearing a gigantic
mechanical
phallos of gold
fully one hundred and twenty cubits
long, and six cubits
round, decked with
golden ribbons,
its tip
glittering with silver, which
rose and fell,
(the *phallos*
is Dionysos, or
OSIRIS) and when
it rose to its highest point it
was made to ejaculate
papyrus stars
of silver
and gold high into
the air, which
floated down
and were caught
by the delighted
Alexandrians,
who said that
Ptolemy Mikros
– who was Osiris –
himself must have
been the model for it.

Next
twenty-four huge lions,
led by their trainers
upon golden leashes.
Golden statues of Ptolemy's allies were cheered.
Statues of Ptolemy's enemies dressed as prisoners of war, kneeling and
bound, were hissed.
Three hundred musicians
with gilded lyres, and golden crowns.
Two thousand identical black bulls
with gilded horns,
golden crowns and golden necklaces,
for even the dinner marched in the Pompe.
The bulls were the great feast for the
foreign ambassadors, and people of Alexandria, and two thousand two
hundred Greek priests led them on halters, the
victims
for the sacrifice.
Next,
the processions of Zeus
and all the gods of Greece,
and
the Procession of Alexander,
whose larger-than-life-size golden statue
stood upon a golden chariot drawn by four elephants,
flanked by Nike, goddess of Victory,
and Athena, goddess of Wisdom.
On and on it went:
seven
gilded palm trees
five cubits high;
one
forty-cubit gilded Thunderbolt;
one
pair of gilded eagles, fifteen cubits high,
standing for Ptolemy Mikros and Arsinoë Beta.
Sixty-four suits of solid gold armour.
A pure gold Horn of Plenty thirty cubits long.
And one thousand two hundred and twenty
cartloads of silver plate, gold and spices.

At the rear marched
fifty-seven thousand six hundred foot soldiers,
armed with the *sarissa,* or pike, of Macedon, ten abreast,
singing the songs of war,
in a column one hundred and fifty stades long, that stretched right round
the
city walls, followed by
twenty-three thousand two hundred horse.
As they entered the Stadion they
saluted King Ptolemy with
the battle cry, the blood-curdling
Alalalalai
and marched on.
At the tail end
of the procession came
golden statues of
Ptolemy Soter and Berenike Alpha
riding in golden chariots.
A golden statue of Ptolemy Mikros
dressed as a Macedonian king
rode in a golden chariot behind them.
A golden statue of Arsinoë Beta was
dressed as the Female Pharaoh, the
Female King of Upper and Lower Egypt,
wearing the double crown
of Egypt with the double *ouraios* serpent upon her
forehead.

At the very end
came the Procession
of the Evening Star,
Hesperos,
personified as a naked golden boy with golden wings,
riding the largest white horse ever seen,
and he held up a flaming torch to represent the light
of the Star.
The boy who came last, personating Hesperos, was
the seven-year-old Ptolemy Euergetes,
who had once been first.
As it happens, though, the Morning and

Evening Star were fated to change places once again.
By the time
the figure of Hesperos reached the Stadion
it was dusk, for Hesperos himself
hung low in the sky
over
Alexandria,
and
the Great Pompe
of
Arsinoë Beta
(and Ptolemy Mikros)
was
at an end

There was more, Stranger, very much more, but if Seshat wrote down everything that marched up Kanopic Street that day, the procession would fill
every page of her book. Every Greek sacrifice begins with a procession: the
Great Pompe was merely the procession to the sacrifice on a very large scale.
All was to honour the god, Dionysos, and to honour King Ptolemy. And so
after the procession came the feasting in honour of Dionysos, when the two
thousand two hundred black bulls went under the knife, bellowing, and the
blood flowed into the streets in a river, like a foretaste of the future of the
House of Ptolemy and the History of Alexandria. Aye, Stranger: blood, and
more blood.

The roasting of bulls began, upon two thousand two hundred fires, and
the smoke rose to the heavens to satisfy the gods, making contact possible
between the human world and the divine. The gods of Greece must have
been delighted, for the whole city stank of animal blood; the smell of burnt
beef and incense filled the air. Nothing in Excess was quite forgot. By the light
of the Pharos the city drank, gorged, danced, roared, until sunrise.

How many eaters, then, ate at that feast? A slaughtered bull will provide
portions for eight hundred people. Two thousand two hundred bulls would
feed one million, seven hundred and sixty thousand. Moderation in all
things, of course, but anything less than three helpings might not have
counted as a feast. If they all came back for the third time, the lucky time, as
the Greeks called it, then there might have been five hundred and sixty-six
thousand, six hundred and sixty-six diners. They would have queued all
night. That may also give you, Stranger, who are so curious to know such
things, the population of the illustrious and most illustrious city of

Alexandria at this time. It was not a small city. By no means. It was the greatest city upon earth, according to the Greeks, that is: the Egyptians liked to pretend that Alexandria did not exist.

Thirty days of Greek games and lavish entertainments followed the feast – for those who could move after everything in excess – to delight and honour Zeus, and Apollo, and Hermes, who is Thoth. Arsinoë Beta had organized every kind of race – foot-races, races in armour, chariot races, horse races, races with torches, and a Great Ostrich Race, in which she rode in person, and carried off the first prize. She laid on dramatic performances, in honour of Dionysos, patron of theatre, and because she loved the drama herself. She had arranged flute contests, singing contests, dancing contests, boxing and wrestling championships, but the greatest event was the pentathlon – consisting of a race, a jump, the diskos, the javelin, and the wrestling, one after the other. These Alexandrian Games made the Olympian Games look small, mean, provincial, and outdid them both in size and in magnificent prizes, in every respect, on purpose, to make Alexandria the envy of the Greek-speaking world. Truly, Stranger, nothing has been seen to match it in the world ever since.

Just as the dwellers beside the Cataracts of the Nile in Upper Egypt are said to be deaf because of the great roaring of the waters there, so the people of Alexandria became a little deaf, that day, from the very great noise of the Hydraulikon. Mikros showered Ktesibios with gold and honours for this great invention, so that the barber's son who had begun his life walking barefoot, now not only wore shoes, but rode in a very modern wicker carriage of his own design and manufacture. He might have received posthumous worship as a hero had he not been responsible for so much deafness.

If you are wondering why this machine is not heard in your own day, Wise One, the answer is simple – it was declared too loud for the ears of men, fit only for the gods. Aye, the wonderful Hydraulikon of Ktesibios the Engineer was loud enough to knock the very limpets off the rocks.

1.23

Calculating

Many men have said that Arsinoë Beta, as well as saving Egypt, made her own special contribution to its ruin, for somebody had to pay for all that golden extravagance, and the fabulous free dinner of wine and savoury meat.

What, then, was the cost of Alexandria's great display of hubris, feasting and beastly drunkenness for no better reason than to boast of Alexandria's wealth and honour the god of drunken orgies? Even Arsinoë Beta did not know. She had simply said, *My brother will pay.*

How much did it cost? Mikros asked, rather offhand, when the excitement was over, in the middle of stuffing cold pigeon into his mouth.

But Arsinoë Beta, surrounded by receipts, scraps of papyrus, butchers' accounts and wine merchants' bills, was still calculating.

One hundred talents? Mikros said, shovelling in olives.

Arsinoë Beta shook her lion's mane of golden hair. *Sometimes I think, Brother,* she said, *that you must be as stupid as a fish.*

Mikros's mouth hung open, very like to catch a fly.

Tell me, he said, *how much it cost.*

Her voice was a whisper: *Two thousand two hundred and thirty-nine talents, fifty minas, sixty drachmas and four obols exactly.*

Mikros struck his head with his fist. *I am ruined,* he wailed. *That is as much as three Lighthouses at eight hundred talents a time. You have thrown away the cost of an entire year of war in Syria. Whatever has become of your famous economy?*

Did you not love it? she asked. *Was it not wonderful? Was it not worth every last golden dodekadrachm?*

Mikros sat with his head in his hands, groaning.

Did you not have a happy day? she said. *Every pleasure has its price – you should know that well enough.*

Yes, he said, after a while, *it was grand.* He was not cast down for long. *Not to worry, Sister,* he said, *we have plenty of money left.*

They could, indeed, afford the Pompe, but the sobering thought was that because they had publicly announced that the Pompe would be a penteteric festival, they must repeat it just the same, *if not better,* every fifth year until the end of time. Some said it was this wise King and his lovely sister who were pleased to make Egypt bankrupt, not Mikros's dread grandson, Ptolemy Philopator, as yet unborn. But, in truth, it was not so. The figure commonly bandied about for Mikros's annual internal revenue was fourteen thousand eight hundred silver talents, and one million five hundred thousand *artabas* of wheat. Some have doubted the accuracy of the calculations, saying that six million *artabas* of wheat may be nearer the mark. Whatever the figure was, suffice to say that the royal granaries were stacked to the roof. As for the revenue in coin, it had the purchasing power of somewhere between five and seven hundred thousand man-years, so much coin that the Treasury could not hold it all. Complain though he did, Mikros was not exactly poor. He could have put up eighteen lighthouses every year with an income like that – if he had not the Syrian War to fight.

Seshat has devoted many pages to the Great Pompe, but she is not going to apologize. Goddesses do not apologize, Stranger – you should have realized that by now. Seshat has given you the whole of the Pompe, Stranger, almost, whether it pleases you or not: because it was one of the best things the Ptolemies ever did.

The Great Pompe was indeed worth every last dodekadrachm: it was a celebration of monarchy, designed on purpose to make the House of Ptolemy more *popular*. More important, the procession made Alexandria *like* Arsinoë Beta, and perhaps that was its true, hidden, secret purpose. The Alexandrians had been a little hostile to the sister upon her wicked marriage. They had scrawled rude Greek graffiti on the Palace walls and flung filth at her golden chariot. There was no hostility after the Pompe, none. Arsinoë Beta could do no wrong now, not then, nor ever after, living or dead.

Arsinoë Beta oversaw all, understood all. She was Egypt's steward, Egypt's divine housekeeper, and yet she had overspent. She was not a stupid woman. By no means. She had done all this on purpose, out of her hot and cold calculating personality – to make Egypt love her; to make ready the ground for Egypt to worship her as a goddess ever after. That, Stranger, is the whole truth of it.

By some miracle the Pompe did not arouse the wrath of the gods overnight because of its boastfulness about the Ptolemies, but it did send a clear signal to Antiokhos Soter in Syria that of all the kings in the Greek world Ptolemy Mikros had to be the wealthiest, and perhaps the most foolish. Hearing from his spies of Mikros's fabulous display of riches, Antiokhos' desire to take Egypt for himself became more urgent than ever.

A sure signal also flew up-River to the native Egyptians who must pay their taxes to Ptolemy Mikros. Because of his Syrian wars their taxes had gone up. The ordinary workmen of Egypt, farmers and peasants, were poor enough already. Their anger grew, and Eskedi, ever on the watch for signs of the punishment of hubris, knew what would happen. He said to Neferrenpet his wife, *It will not be long now. Upper Egypt will rise in revolt, then Lower Egypt, and it will be more than just throwing stones.*

1.24

Mistress of the Builders

Having spent so much money on the Great Pompe, did Arsinoë Beta try to be more economical? No, of course not, she spent all the more, as if she had only just gotten the taste for reckless extravagance. It was no accident that every statue of her had the Horn of Plenty tucked in the crook of her arm, and showed her faintly smiling. She controlled the strings of the purse, just as she still controlled the strings of the puppet that was her brother, making him do just whatever she wanted.

When Mikros tried to staunch the fresh haemorrhage from his treasury, he enjoyed the wintry storm of the sister's tongue, her squalls of sulking, the hurricane of her temper. When he said, *You should spend less, Sister* . . . she would scream at him, *I am a goddess, I shall do what I like* . . . And so it went on, until he gave in to her, sued for peace, and found he must hand over some golden gift to make up for his being difficult.

Arsinoë Beta argued, of course, that her expenses were necessary, that she had to support Eskedi in his temple building, in return for helping Mikros to survive as Pharaoh. Aye, for it was still a surer than sure thing that Mikros and Arsinoë Beta could not have lasted so long as thirty days in Egypt without Eskedi's help. Pharaoh and High Priest still had very great need of each other.

The threat of war returned with the start of the sailing season, and Arsinoë Beta's thoughts returned to the field of battle – if they had ever left it. With one eye upon winning her wars, she embarked upon a massive programme of public works. First she thought of the Canal of Nekho that had once joined up the River Nile to the Red Sea. Darius the Persian had reopened it long ago. Now it had silted up again and fallen into disuse. Arsinoë Beta made Mikros pay to have it dredged anew and made navigable once again. *The Canal will be very useful,* she said, *if our war cuts off the supply routes from the north.*

At Naukratis in the western Delta she restored the Temple of Aphrodite, and made generous gifts to the Hellenion, the temple to all the Greek gods, so that they did not feel neglected, but the first of works was her gigantic new pylon, or gate, for the Egyptian Temple of Amun and Thoth there.

Next she agreed to build the enclosure wall and massive outer gateway that would finish the sandstone Temple of Amun that stood half built at Hibis in the western desert, surrounded by palm groves.

She then talked her brother into finishing the Temple of Isis at Isisopolis, east of Sebennytos, in the Delta. Nektanebo, last of the native Egyptian pharaohs, began it, but Arsinoë Beta continued the work, fitting stone upon stone, for the goddess who was said to take an interest in stomach troubles. Mikros was even persuaded to repair the Temple of Per-Hebet.

She gave her most gracious permission for the building of a pylon in the enclosure wall of the Temple of Mut the Vulture at Thebes. She was most particularly devoted to the cult of the vulture goddess that sat upon her brow, and was the patroness of war, whose red dress she put on like a fresh tide of blood every morning.

Up on the desert plateau, opposite Memphis, she began the Anubieion, or Temple of Anubis the jackal. Mikros paid for all these things, but always, driving him forward, was the sister. Without that woman, and without Eskedi, that king might have done nothing for thirty-eight years but fuck his concubines.

Arsinoë Beta sent often to ask, *How goes the temple?* She sent regular gifts of bread, beer and onions for the builders. She did not skulk in the *gynaikeion* all day stuffing her mouth full of dates like Arsinoë Alpha. Seshat, patroness of architects and builders, smiles upon this queen for her great generosity to the gods. Seshat knows that what Arsinoë Beta built would last for all time.

Stranger, the future looked good just then for Ptolemy Mikros and his sister, in the midst of their Age of Gold, but trouble lay ahead, and the first sign of it was the revolt of Magas, Mikros's half-brother, in Libya.

1.25

Mud Bricks

Aye, upon the horizon was Magas, Berenike Alpha's son, the young man whom Ptolemy Soter had sent as Strategos, or Governor, to Kyrene thirty years before. What had become of Magas? For sure, he was still alive, now an old man of fifty. He had not long since married a wife, Apama, daughter of Ptolemy's great enemy, Antiokhos Soter of Syria – though he had no male heir. He had left the business of fathering a son rather late, was not in good health, and now he was angry.

When the sister read the spies' report she went to Mikros in some distress. *Our half-brother has allied himself to Antiokhos because of his Syrian marriage,* she said. *Magas is planning to attack Egypt so as to distract us while Antiokhos takes back his territories in Koile-Syria. We are about to be invaded, Brother.*

I do not believe it, Mikros said. *Magas would never dare to attack us. We are his only relatives.*

But as so often in this family, *relative* meant much the same as *sworn enemy.* Mikros worried, but he did not lose much sleep over the new threat. The sister was the one who worried about war. Aye, worried sick, literally, she began to stick bronze pins in wax images of Magas. But she thought also of the threat from Syria. It would need more than bronze pins to take care of Antiokhos. It was Year Six when she made Mikros ride into the desert with her, east of the Delta, to inspect the border fort of Heroönpolis, on the isthmus called Klysma, that you, Stranger, may have heard called Suez. Barely a month later she was back in the desert again, to encourage the weapons manufacturers in the border fort of Tjaru.

She rode out a third time that year in order to re-open the Canal of Nekho. Mikros went with her, complaining, because he liked much better to stay close to his concubines, but Arsinoë Beta would not let him say no to her. She, not Mikros, had examined the plans and surveyed the progress of the canal. She, not Mikros, had given the orders, hired the engineers and paid every man's wages. It was only fitting that the canal should be called the Canal of Arsinoë Philadelphos.

Mikros rode with the sister to Heroönpolis to check the defences yet again, but he acted like a man in a dream. Back home he had promise of a fresh concubine, guaranteed the coolest woman in Egypt, very good for the hottest nights. Aye, Mikros spent more time looking at the blue sea, marvelling at the pounding surf, than he did looking at the mud-brick walls of Heroönpolis. Arsinoë Beta was the real inspector.

Pay attention, Brother, she said. *One day you may have to handle these things on your own.*

Mikros shrugged, too tired to notice, too hot to care.

What do you think about the walls? she said.

Silence.

Brother, she said, *the walls should be ten cubits thick if they are to be undamaged by stone-shot fired by enemy catapults.*

Mikros, overpowered by the heat, and the will of the sister, pushed out the lower lip, but he said, *Sister, you know very well that Antiokhos is useless with artillery. We shall be quite safe. You are worrying yourself for nothing.* Mikros stayed calm, trying to enjoy the passing moments that contained nothing but flies, and sweat, and dust up the nose.

Arsinoë Beta it was that sent the urgent messages, spoke to the master of works, gave the order to strengthen the walls, ordered the building up of what was broken down. She, not the brother, ordered the millions of mud bricks to be hauled through the desert on donkey carts. It was the sister who loved to build, just as Seshat loves to build, not her brother.

But Mikros was right. She need not have troubled herself. The rumours of war were again unfounded. For sure, Magas's marriage had sealed the alliance between Kyrene and Antiokhos of Syria in opposition to Ptolemy. Trouble did lie ahead – there would always be trouble ahead – but in that year Eskedi reported to the palace, *The Flood of the Nile, father of gods, is twenty cubits, two palms, one fingerbreadth in height. The threat of famine is over for another year. It is an ample flood, a fine flood. Egypt will prosper. The gods are pleased with us.*

And why were the gods pleased? Because Arsinoë Beta had built temples for them. If Pharaoh – or his wife – builds for the gods, and makes the proper offerings, the gods will help them, all will go well. If he – or she – does not build, the gods will not help. It was a simple thing. Arsinoë Beta understood what made Egypt flourish, and under her strong rule Egypt did flourish.

1.26

Romans

Arsinoë Beta did not, of course, stop worrying about the war that must come. When she heard of the defeat of Pyrrhos of Epeiros his troops at the hands of Rome, a city of some size in Italia, she bit the nails of her fingers to the quick for worrying. Aye, for her greatest fear just then was the threat Rome presented to the order and balance of the Greek-speaking world, and the order and balance of Egypt.

What can we do to stop Rome turning herself into Egypt's best enemy? she asked her brother. *We still face the threat from the Kyrenaica. We still have Antiokhos threatening to creep down and take Koile-Syria from us. Egypt really does not need a third enemy.*

Mikros screwed up the eyes, scratched his shaven scalp. *You will think of something, Sister,* he said. *I have great faith in your divine abilities.*

What can we do to stop Rome treating Egypt like she treated Epeiros? she said. *Something out of the ordinary run of things is needed.*

Mikros made faces, trying to think of an answer.

We need firm friends, Brother, strong alliances, she said, *just as our father did. I think we must send our messenger, to see whether it will please Rome to be the friend of Egypt.* She shouted, *Call the Dioiketes. He must write a letter.*

Mikros wanted nothing to do with it. *Where will it all end?* he said. *What horrors do you think you will unleash now?*

But the sister said only, *Arsinoë knows best . . . the sister knows what she is doing.*

She suggested a formal exchange of ambassadors to talk about trade, and the corn supply, for Egypt was the granary of the world, and had an overplus of grain to sell. Her real purpose in suggesting the embassy, though, was to find some means of keeping the peace.

Aye, Arsinoë Beta made the opening move, and her ambassadors set sail, carrying with them warm greetings and generous gifts for the Senate and People of Rome. For the first time, then, Rome makes her appearance in the Annals of Egypt, and it was an uncertain moment, for even Arsinoë Beta did not quite know whether Rome was or was not her enemy, but trod cautious, like the cat upon hot sand, keeping hidden, for the moment, her sharp claws. But Seshat knows nothing of what happened at Rome. She has not so much as a scrap of burnt papyrus about that embassy, and never mind the precise date of it either.

Arsinoë Beta said to her brother, *Better good friends than good enemies. A mere exchange of ambassadors can do no harm.* Mikros had his doubts. He thought that to invite the Romans to Egypt was ill-advised. *It is like letting the wolf inside the house,* he said, *the wolf, who will eat up whatever he wants.* He awoke his sister's bad temper for saying it. Sure, she shouted at him, but Mikros was right. The House of Ptolemy would never be rid of the baleful shadow of Rome after this.

A few months later, in Year Ten, an embassy of three distinguished Roman senators arrived in Alexandria, led by their *Princeps Senatus*, Quintus Fabius Maximus Gurges, the man who had dedicated the first temple of Aphrodite, or Venus, at Rome, and who twice filled the august office of Consul of that city.

With him was Quintus Orgulnius Gallus, the man who had brought the serpent cult of Asklepios from Epidauros to Rome a few years previous, so that the sacred dogs and snakes might lick the wounds of the sick, and work miracles even in Italia.

The third man was Numerius Fabius Pictor, also sometime Consul of Rome, and the two Fabii were men who claimed descent from Herakles, as did the Ptolemies, so that, by chance, in a manner of speaking, the two parties were related.

Mikros and Arsinoë Beta greeted the Romans with the usual *dexiosis*, or Greek handshaking, when the Romans squeezed fit to crush Mikros's hand and brought tears to his eyes, though Arsinoë Beta gave back as good as she got. Mikros could not but stare at the Romans, who had their hair cut so short that they looked like slaves, and the skin drawn so tight over their cheeks that the bones showed through. He stared at the curious white blanket that was their daily dress, for this was, indeed, the first appearance of the toga in Egypt.

The Romans stretched their eyes to see the marble colonnades on Kanopic Street, dazzling white in the sun. They were amazed by the great Greek palace of King Ptolemy, all of shining white marble, for there was nothing at Rome to compare with it for splendour, neither in Greek mosaics nor Corinthian columns, nor in exquisite wall paintings of scenes from Homer, nor in pedimented porticoes, nor in statues of naked gods and athletes, nor in the vastness of echoing audience halls, nor in sumptuous chairs of ebony and ivory and gold, nor in zebra-skin counterpanes upon every bed, and golden sofas upholstered with leopard-spots. For Alexandria was, to be sure, not only more Greek than Greece, but also the doors to Africa.

The senators were amazed, sure, but they also disliked King Ptolemy's palace for its pointless extravagance and golden ostentation, and they thought the ordinary people on Kanopic Street looked poor, and hungry, and that Mikros himself looked very much overweight.

Mikros gave the Romans gifts, as a sign of good will – great golden cups and bowls – but he was surprised to find that Q. Fabius Maximus Gurges would accept nothing.

Sir, he said, *we are but ordinary citizens of Rome. Our mission is about trade. We did not expect to be treated like princes. We have no use for this golden gear.* And he made a point of offering the gifts to the *aerarium,* or State Treasury, of Rome, thereby getting himself a wonderful reputation for abstinence and incorruptibility.

Mikros wore the costume of Pharaoh, and made a point of flashing the teeth. Arsinoë Beta wore the vulture headdress, the cow's horns of Hathor, the ostrich-feathers of Maat, her cobra-and-vulture shoes, and the blood-red dress of a living goddess. She put on her Egyptian face paint, and the fabulous jewels of the Lady of the Two Lands. The Romans thought little of what they called her whore's display, and less still of her bright yellow hair that was dyed – indeed- the exact same colour as that of the common prostitutes at Rome. They thought much more of her spirit, though, for it was Arsinoë Beta who did all the talking. It was she who brought up the subject of an *Amicitia,* or Treaty of Everlasting Friendship, whereby Alexandria might send corn and perfumes, elephant tusks and leopard skins to Rome, and so get richer still by trading peacefully with Italia and all the broad lands of the barbarian that lay beyond. The Romans seemed pleased by the thought of it, nodding the head to everything she said.

The ambassadors were by no means ignorant of Greek ways, nor were they hostile to the gods of Greece. They had learned Greek in their school days, after a fashion, like all educated Romans, so that their conversations with Ptolemy and his sister were not awkward, but approached a certain ungrammatical fluency.

So far so good, but when Arsinoë Beta spoke of Alexander, Q. Fabius Maximus Gurges said, *Madam, we do not know who you are talking about.*

Surely you must know, she said, *of Alexander son of Philip, who conquered half the world. He was the greatest hero that ever lived, second only to Achilles. How can you not have heard of him?*

But he said, *No, Madam, I do not recall the name.*

Surely, she said, looking hard at Q. Fabius Maximus Gurges, *you have heard tell of Alexander of Macedon?*

But no, Q. Fabius Maximus Gurges shook his head from side to side, pretty slow; his eyes looked deadly nightshade, and his lips betrayed nothing that could be called a smile. Alexander was a Greek, not a Roman, and he knew nothing of non-Romans.

How can you know nothing of the great Alexander? she asked Q. Ogulnius Gallus. *Why, he was the founder of this very city.*

Q. Ogulnius Gallus stared at her, mouth set grim, eyes like weasel's eyes, but said nothing.

Arsinoë Beta stood up, angry, and said, *Well, then, follow me, if you please. Come now, quickly.* And she led the Romans on foot through the streets, almost running, so that Mikros, unaccustomed to the use of his legs, began to pant. The crowds parted easy enough in front of them, though the applause was polite only for the unsmiling foreigners from Rome – a place of which, in their turn, the Alexandrians had barely heard.

At the crossroads where Kanopic Street meets the Street of the Soma, or Body of Alexander, Arsinoë Beta made the Romans stoop and enter the stifling calm of the Tomb, where the lamps burned day and night before the living corpse of the greatest hero the world had ever known. She had the guards drag the lid off the golden *sarkophagos* and uncover the peaceful face, the still incorrupt flesh. And yes, Alexander was still fast asleep, did not look like a dead man at all.

Alexandros has slept now, she said, *seventeen thousand two hundred and fifty days and nights exactly.*

Out of the corner of her eye she saw the Romans exchange a smirk.

The people of Alexandria believe, she said, *that if the city is invaded, Alexander will wake up and save them.*

The ambassadors showed a lot of teeth, then, though you still could not call it smiling, and gave each other knowing looks, thinking the Greeks must be children if they believed such absurdities. Worse, the ambassadors foresaw the day when the Roman legionaries marched through the Gate of the Sun, military boots crunching in perfect step, right up Kanopic Street in their tens of thousands, unopposed, and took Alexandria and all Egypt for Rome. Aye, and then the smiles could not be wiped off the faces of Q. Fabius Maximus Gurges, N. Fabius Pictor, and Q. Orgulnius Gallus, and their cold laughter rang out in the sacred place, making Mikros exchange a worried glance with his sister.

The Romans affected to know nothing about Alexander of Macedon because Rome had had nothing to do with him, and because they had heard stories of his private life that did not much please them. They could not acknowledge the existence of a man who had been greater than any Roman, far more successful than any of themselves, and yet was nothing but a filthy *kinaidos*, who got his pleasure by taking not only eunuchs but even grown men into his bed.

The awkward moment passed, however, and the talks resumed. The ambassadors asked a great number of questions about ships of war, and merchantmen, and ship timber, and the export of wine, and the threat of pirates in the Great Sea. They interrogated Arsinoë Beta about the size of her corn harvest, and about the best route for the grain ships between Alexandria and Ostia, the port of Rome. There was no question to which her Majesty could not provide the perfect answer.

Arsinoë Beta talked much of war and the threat of war, because war was her specialty. She spoke of the hired-soldier markets of the Peloponnesos, and of the continuing threat of the *Keltoi,* or Gauls, from the North Lands, and of the obscure fog-bound islands that lay off the north coast of Gallia itself, which she knew of from questioning the sailors.

When the two parties did not talk of the *Amicitia,* they feasted on turtle broth, Nile perch, roast swan, smoked duck breasts in white wine, followed by the *argurotrophima,* or silver delight, that was guaranteed to melt in a man's mouth like snow, and the plates and cups and forks were of solid gold. The Romans made polite remarks about the food and wine, but their private thought was that Mikros's table was too lavish. They thought like the Spartans, that a little was better than much, and that to entertain with such luxury was mere showing off, bound to provoke the gods to hideous vengeance.

The sixth time King Ptolemy clapped the hands for his cooks to carry in upon their shoulders the great golden dish piled high with flamingo, decorated with the beaks and pink feathers all stuck back in the meat, and the birds' eyes staring out of it, Q. Orgulnius Gallus pushed his plate away in disgust, saying, *Sir, we should be satisfied with the plainest food – a little bread, a few black olives.*

As for Arsinoë Beta, who was, of course, present at the feast – a thing which in itself the Romans found very surprising – she ate little. Aye, the great Oracle of Zeus-Ammon in the Libyan desert had told her that she had but one thousand and ninety days left to live, and she was fearful that her days must be used up before she had finished making glorious the Two Lands, herself one of the immortals, and her fame proof against the deleterious effects of Time. She was urgent to find the road to peace, and an end to Egypt's troubles before Hades took her; before she had to leave Mikros to rule without her help. No, she hardly stopped talking about her wars, or her belly, for one moment. Talk, the Romans had never heard anything like it, so that the non-stop wagging tongue of Arsinoë Beta became, indeed, the talk of Rome.

Between talks and feasts Arsinoë Beta felt well enough to show the Romans the sights. They craned the neck to look at the giant bronze statue of Poseidon that reflected the sun from the top of the Pharos, higher than any building at Rome, and Arsinoë Beta herself stepped into the wicker basket with them and rode to the top upon the hydraulic mechanism, in order to point out the view of the city from the top.

Mikros made his excuses and kept his feet on the ground. Later he showed the Romans the Great Library, where he bragged, *We have four hundred thousand scrolls, one copy of every book in the world.*

The Romans raised the eyebrows, and murmured, *Mirabilissimus . . . Most impressive.*

In the adjoining building, the famous Mouseion, Mikros introduced the one hundred Greek scholars, and the senators passed a morning making polite conversations about Greek poetry, Greek drama, and Greek science. The visit ended with a performance by Ktesibios to demonstrate his famous Hydraulikon.

Too loud, the Romans screamed, hands pressed over their ears, so that Ktesibios thought once more about adapting the Hydraulikon for use in battle, and of the complete redundancy of such things as catapults and elephants of war.

Afterwards Q. Orgulnius Gallus said, *Sir, your Mouseion is a marvellous institution. We have nothing like this at Rome.*

When Arsinoë Beta, as Mistress of the Mint, showed the senators how they made their coins in Egypt, they could not hide their very great interest, for her silver drachmas looked far superior to any coin struck at Rome. She showed them how her tetradrachms and oktodrachms were cast, for she knew everything about dies and the different properties of bronze and copper and gold. She talked about unimaginable sums of money with great confidence, just like a man.

The Romans, who had come to Alexandria with little thought of anything but trade, and courtesies, took home with them – at Arsinoë Beta's insistence – half a dozen Egyptian moneyers, who taught the Romans how to mint the best of silver coins. The Egyptian moneyers left their mark in Italia, for the *cornucopia,* or Horn of Plenty, that now appeared upon the Roman coins was, of course, Arsinoë Beta's personal badge, and a subtle reminder that the splendid new Roman money was the result of superior Egyptian craftsmanship.

Mikros took the Romans to see his famous Beast Garden, that was full of exotic creatures that most men had only heard tell of, for although he kept many quite common animals he also had rarities such as the two-horned Ethiopian rhinoceros, the white bear from Thrace, the long-necked camelopard, and snakes as much as twelve or fourteen cubits in length, kept in iron mesh cages. Such wonders caused even the world-weary Romans' jaws to drop open for astonishment.

But what astonished the Romans far more than gigantic snakes was Arsinoë Beta herself, her furious loquacity, her phenomenal command of international affairs, and her detailed knowledge even of the city of Rome. They were specially impressed that this Greek woman could speak to them in their own language.

Were you ever at Rome, Madam? Q. Orgulnius Gallus asked, for he could not bring himself to call her *Megaleia.*

Numquam, Arsinoë smiled. She was the one exception among the Alexandrian Greeks, for she did not turn up the nose at the Latin language. The senators were amazed that this queen, this *woman,* appeared to have read and remembered everything they had read themselves, for she was able to fence with quotations in Latin, and to hold her own in the obscurest backwaters of

Roman philosophy – a subject for which Mikros himself cared little, apart, of course, from the Kyrenaic School. She was unlike any woman the senators had met at Rome or, indeed, heard of anywhere else. For a woman to be possessed of such learning was as much a miracle as the armoured hide of the Ethiopian rhinoceros – and, of course, Arsinoë Beta had that as well.

More than any other thing, these Romans were struck by the boldness of the woman who could say, *I am Aphrodite – not Aphrodite Pandemos, but Aphrodite Ourania, Aphrodite the Wife, the Heavenly One . . . I am Isis, Lady of Many Names, I am Hathor, Lady of the Turquoise.* For she conducted herself rather haughty, saying she was a living goddess and no one should contradict her. They thought it strange that, for all her learning, she seemed to have overlooked the words of Homer: *It would surely be most unseemly for a woman to compete with a goddess in elegance and good looks.*

Q. Fabius Maximus Gurges, the senator with the particular devotion to Aphrodite, was so angered by Arsinoë Beta's blasphemy that he had to bite the lips not to say what he thought of her. The senators spoke among themselves of her hubris, her outrageous presumption, when N. Fabius Pictor said, *I can only think that her end will be terrible because of it. The woman who brags about being a goddess can but tempt the gods to exact horrible punishment.*

When the Romans were done with looking at Alexandria, Mikros sent them up-River to look at the Pyramids, and the great Temple of Ptah at Memphis – or as much of it as the High Priest would allow them to see. The senators questioned Eskedi about the curious animal-headed gods of Egypt, and were impressed by his courtesy, by his charm, and by his surpassing wisdom. He pleased the Romans by offering them simple fare, and by saying, *A cup of water is enough to quench thirst . . . A mouthful of leeks will make the heart strong . . .* Aye, it seemed as if Eskedi took more account of *Nothing in Excess* than Ptolemy Mikros did himself.

Back in Alexandria, the final draft of the *Amicitia* was drawn up – what the Greeks called a *Philia*, a Friendship, or Alliance – by which these new political relations were made permanent and binding. Arsinoë Beta was, as it were, the powerful glue that held it all together, and it was not for the first time in her life. Without her, there would have been no embassy, no *Amicitia*, no peace with Rome, for the entire document was her own work.

The Romans insisted that the Alliance be concluded Roman style, with the sacrifice of a pig, and they made Mikros repeat after them the words of the oath, in Latin, saying, *Let him who breaks the alliance be killed like this pig. Let his throat be slit. Let him squeal. Let his blood fly out. Let his flesh be eaten of dogs. Let his children bring forth monsters.*

The sacrifice of a pig is not a pleasant spectacle, for that beast never did die quietly. The blood spurted in all directions, splashing the hem of Arsinoë Beta's white *peplos*, tearing open her soul's wounds and all her griefs afresh, making her think again of the death of Agathokles of Thrace, and the murder of her two sons at Kassandreia, so that her fixed smile gave place to her old look of horror. But she thought, *If we can have peace with Rome, it will be worth a few moments of bad memory. Peace is worth blood on the dress.* And her smile returned, then, for not only did she have absolute control over Egypt, she had also what is of far greater value, absolute control over herself.

Mikros now honoured the Romans by giving them crowns of oak leaves, made out of the thinnest gold, with golden bees hidden among the leaves, all of exquisite Alexandrian workmanship, which the Italians did not refuse, this time, for fear of endangering the success of their mission. But the next day they told him, *Sir, we cannot think of putting on crowns at any feast. We are but ordinary citizens of Rome, not royalty.* And they put the crowns on statues of Ptolemy and Arsinoë in the Agora instead.

At the last feast Mikros served up black bread, and cow cheese, and no *argurotrophima,* saying it served the Romans right, that had been rude about his food and spurned his gifts. And he gave them water to drink, instead of wine.

For these things the Romans were truly thankful.

When Mikros and Arsinoë Beta waved off the ambassadors from the private royal harbour it was with some relief that their ordeal was over, but this was how trade was begun between Alexandria and Rome. For all that, there was little contact between the two cities in the twenty-seven years that were left of Mikros's reign, because most of Rome's energy was used up in fighting Carthage. But if neither side had much occasion to call upon the *Amicitia*, it was not null and void; it was by no means empty words, but of the very first importance.

Aye, because of the *Amicitia*, Egypt had the great good fortune to remain neutral during the long-drawn-out war between Rome and Carthage – the First Punic War – that would last fully twenty-three years. Much good came out of Arsinoë Beta's friendship with Rome. Of course, the *Amicitia* was also the beginning of something bad, a different kind of trouble, as Mikros had sensed when the Romans began to laugh in the Tomb of Alexander. For though this was the first appearance of Romans in Egypt, it would not be the last.

Later that year came news of the plague at Babylon, when Ptolemy and Arsinoë Beta made generous offering to the gods, grateful that this evil had not fallen upon themselves. No, the catastrophe of the plague did not, just then, visit Egypt. But the plague of the dyspepsia now laid itself more heavily upon the frail body of Arsinoë Beta, as if her guts was slowly being eaten up from the inside.

1.27

Arkamani

Arsinoë Beta thrust the papyrus strip down her throat to make her puke, night and day. She retched like the hyaena and moaned like the camel, but she never stopped thinking about the defence of the Two Lands. She looked not only west, towards Rome, not only to the defences of Egypt upon the east side: she thought also about the south country, the Land of Punt, that some call Kush, or Nubia, or Ethiopia, where she knew there was much gold, and many elephants. She thought of Elephantine, Egypt's southern border, worrying whether the Two Lands were not in grave danger of attack from the south. She had to be safe on every side.

What can we do about the south? she asked Mikros, who cudgelled his head, as usual, while he waited for Arsinoë Beta to answer her own question.

I think we must send an expedition up-River, she said. *Yes, I think we must send Admiral Timosthenes to find out more about the Meroites.*

Good, Mikros said, mouth full of roast quail, his thoughts on the flesh of handsome women. *Let him sail this afternoon.*

Timosthenes of Rhodes was a geographer, who had explored the Coast of the Fish-Eaters and the coast of the Trogodytes, a good choice to lead an expedition up-River into the Land of Punt. His orders were to seek out the city called Meroë, where no Greek had ever set his boots, a place that was still a mystery to Alexandria, and which the native Egyptians spoke of with horror as nothing less than the Land of Ghosts.

Timosthenes sailed from Memphis with twenty *triereis* and ten transport ships. He took with him a great number of goodly gifts from King Ptolemy – beads, sweetmeats, glittering things, with which he hoped to bribe the King of Meroë into being Egypt's friend rather than her enemy.

He stopped at Thebes, to talk with the High Priest of Amun about the passage of the Cataracts. His Excellency was not unfriendly. He gave his best advice, where to find guides and interpreters, where to go, and where not. All along the banks of the River the natives waved the arm and showed the teeth. No stone was hurled. No Egyptian was beaten.

The Greeks were struck by the blackness of the Meroites, by their habitual stark nakedness, and by their barbaric welcome of drums and dancing, but they saw no sign of ghosts. Timosthenes held his talks about keeping the peace, and about trade, and when he suggested a treaty of friendship, Arkamani, the King of Meroë, agreed to it. But what could Timosthenes do to seal the peace and make it binding for all time? Arsinoë Beta had said she would not dream of marrying even Arsinoë Alpha's children into a family so very black of face or so very un-Greek in their manners as the royal house of Meroë. She had been very firm, telling Timosthenes, *A non-Greek marriage is out of the question. But you may find that an exchange of princes will prove acceptable.*

Perhaps, Timosthenes said, through his interpreter, *the King of Meroë's eldest son would be pleased to make the journey to Alexandria, in order to learn Greek. At the same time King Ptolemy's eldest son might be pleased to journey to Meroë, for a living proof, as it were, of the good intentions of both parties.*

Arsinoë Beta had put it rather different: *Like an exchange of hostages,* she said, *for a guarantee of good conduct.*

As it happens, the King of Meroë liked the idea of sending his son and heir into the north lands, and the boy himself, then perhaps thirteen years old, said he wanted to go. It was, then, a good beginning.

Timosthenes and the King of Meroë came to a friendly agreement about trade, and many fine trophies were carried off to Alexandria: leopards, monkeys, parrots, gazelles, for the Beast Garden; crocodile leather for shoes, hippopotamus hide for shields, ebony and ivory for furniture; elephants of war, black slaves for the palace, much gold in rough lumps, and every august costly stone. For Arsinoë Beta he secured the Meroites' promise of protection for her elephant-hunters and gold-miners. In return the King of Meroë was promised goods from Alexandria, such as wine, beer, scent, amphoras full of pickled fish, olives, or salt meat, Greek honey. Aye, he could have anything he cared to ask for except bows, arrows, swords, siege-machinery, spears – anything but the wherewithal to turn him into the enemy of his new friend.

The Egyptian border round about Elephantine had suffered much from the raids of the nomads in Lower Nubia – including the Meroites themselves. Timosthenes' expedition brought lasting peace in the south. Many elephants of war now travelled north to enlist in Arsinoë Beta's army. The most interesting trophy that Timosthenes carried off to Alexandria was the boy with very black skin and very white teeth, who was now obliged to cover up his nakedness by wearing the white tunic and felt sun-helmet of the Greeks, and to wear sandals for the first time in his life: the young Prince Arkamani of Meroë.

Meanwhile, the Ptolemy called Euergetes, now twelve or thirteen years old, was sent to live at Meroë, to learn how to trap elephants, and how to extract gold from the living rock. The moving force behind the swapping of princes was, of course, Arsinoë Beta. At the same time she sent the Prince Lysimakhos away to live with his mother at Koptos. Soon Arsinoë Beta hoped to achieve the betrothal and marriage of the little Princess Berenike as part of some great alliance to turn yet another of Egypt's best enemies into her best of friends. For the moment, however, she must stay at home. She was too young to go further than Memphis, where, fascinated by the sparkling water, she fell in love with the River, and where Eskedi told her, *The Nile issues from the sweat of the crocodile.*

Aye, Arsinoë Beta said to herself, *it will be a goodly thing to be rid of all the children of Arsinoë Alpha.* She had sworn not to harm them, but she had not sworn never to send them away. Yes, the sister had so successfully turned Mikros against his own sons that he minded saying *Farewell* to them not in the least. In fact he let them go without saying goodbye. He had another heir, Ptolemy the Son, who delighted him more, who was the youngest son, just as Mikros had been the youngest son himself. Ptolemy the Son, now perhaps six years old, was the only prince left at home in Alexandria, where he alone would enjoy Mikros's affection, as was only right for the boy who must grow up to be the next Son of the Sun.

Arsinoë Beta was not quite so thoroughly hostile to Arsinoë Alpha's children that she did not find the time to bring up the little Berenike tough, so that she would make a useful wife to some great Greek monarch. She was the only daughter Arsinoë Beta had, and she strove hard to mould this little girl in her own image. Berenike was soon riding a war horse. Then she learned how to fire arrows from a fast-moving chariot, how to hurl missiles at a target, how to manage a battle and a siege. In short, she grew up to be quite like her stepmother – even acquiring something of her furious ill temper.

When Arkamani heard Arsinoë Beta snapping at her slaves and officials, snapping even at his Majesty, he was reminded of the fierceness of the crocodile, and of the Meroites' respect for that beast. To Arkamani she seemed not unlike those Meroites who had the power to call the crocodile out of the water. She was fierce like the members of the Nubian tribe who had the crocodile for their emblem, and could make him come when he was called, and march up and down at the word of command. *Nya Nyanga* was what they called the members of this tribe, Daughters of the Crocodile, for it was as if they were possessed by the crocodile spirit, as if they had been hatched from the crocodile egg. *Nya Nyanga*, Daughter of the Crocodile, was how Arkamani came to think of the Queen: her snapping jaw and glittering eyes almost made him love her.

Arsinoë Beta already had her peace with Rome. Now she had also peace in the south. Magas of Kyrene, her half-brother, was supposed to keep the peace in the west, and although the rumours still came about his disloyalty, he did not, for the moment, attack. The Great Sea protected Arsinoë Beta from trouble on the north side, and her daily blood sacrifice of a bull and twelve lambs to Apollo seemed to keep all the gods happy. The last serious threat to her peace was from the east, from Syria and the House of Seleukos – from Antiokhos Soter, still the great enemy of Egypt.

How may we achieve peace with Syria? Arsinoë Beta asked Mikros, sighing, as if she thought he knew the answer. *We really must try to marry off little Berenike to the King of Syria*, she said. *If we could do that, we might keep the peace with the Seleukids for ever.*

But all Mikros had to say on the matter just then was this: *Sister, you know that Antiokhos Soter already has a wife. Little Berenike is too young to be married to anybody. You said yourself that even if a betrothal could be agreed, Antiokhos is hot to pursue his war until he wins a glorious victory. If Antiokhos was interested in talking about peace we should have had peace years ago.*

Perhaps we shall one day be able to marry little Berenike to Antiokhos' son, Arsinoë Beta said, thinking aloud. *We must have peace,* she said. *Peace is far less trouble than war.* But at the same time, she dreamed of just one magnificent battle before she went down among the dead ones herself, just one glorious victory that would make her name live for ever. She had been raised to see war as her work, not motherhood; pitched battle with sword and spear, not tapestry, not the needle. Arsinoë Beta lived to fight. She was, truly, as much as Sakhmet the lioness, the Lady in the Bright Red Linen, who breathes flames upon her enemies. *It is a fine thing,* she said to her brother, *for the troops to do what they have been trained to do. An army should never be allowed to stand idle for very long. I think I shall go to war with Syria soon. The gods abhor idleness.* Indeed, she was urgent now to breathe flames. She must win her victory before it was too late. Aye, for just then Arsinoë Beta's greatest battle was with her belly, her interminable bellyache, which was the one battle she would not win, never.

1.28

Dyspepsia

In Year Thirteen Arsinoë Beta reached the great age of forty-five. By Egyptian standards she was an old woman, but she had studied the book called *How to Make the Old Young*. Defeat was a word she had no use for, except with regard to the enemies of Egypt. She had long since gone to war against Time itself, dyeing her turned-grey-overnight hair the golden yellow of a goddess. Now she attacked the lines in her face afresh with oil of fenugreek. She preserved the fairness of her complexion with lion's fat and rose oil, and made liberal use of miraculous potions such the Elixir of Aphrodite.

Her health, however, she could not fix up so easy, for she was often racked by grinding pains in the guts, and the pains were growing worse. She would pass whole days giving orders from her golden bed, fanned by black slaves with ostrich-feather fans, surrounded by anxious officials clutching papyri, dispatches from abroad – officials who sometimes found themselves trembling for fear of arousing her Majesty's displeasure. The doctors were seldom far from her chamber, bringing some new filthy medicine to be swallowed. They trembled too, for fear of being accused of trying to poison her. Her only condition was that they taste, in her presence, whatever they wanted her to tip down her throat. A Queen of Egypt may trust nobody, not even her own brother. Especially not her brother.

Crocodiles crept about the mosaic floor. Snakes twined and untwined themselves about her neck and arms. The dog-faced baboon that is Thoth, the great chronologer, perched on the foot of her bed, eating dates. Arsinoë Beta was, indeed, no ordinary woman. She was Isis, Hathor, Sakhmet, Aphrodite, Hera, a living goddess, the most powerful woman in Africa; the richest woman in the world, the Female Pharaoh indeed, running Egypt almost single-handed from her sickbed, propped up on her purple pillows. Her brother came and went, sometimes holding Ptolemy the Son by the hand – so that he should not smash up his mother's gilded chamber, anger the baboons, strangle the cats, or annoy the crocodiles even unto biting. For Ptolemy the Son was, in truth, already just about as wild a boy as Eros.

Mikros himself wandered about the sister's great bedchamber, looking out of her windows at the swell of the grey-green sea.

How go the finances? he asked.

Never been better, she said, *though your war will be costly. We shall have to practise the strictest economy with those concubines of yours.*

I will get rid of my women, he said, *when you get rid of your snakes and crocodiles.*

Aye, both things were impossibilities.

Spend nothing, she shouted. *I shall dismiss those painted women.*

Thus they bandied words, quarrelling a little. Thus they kept going from day to day, year to year.

Mikros did not do nothing – the sister would not allow that. In the morning he might sit in the Mouseion with the scholars, listening to them argue about how to measure the circumference of the earth. Sometimes he sat with Apollonios Rhodios, now Director of the Great Library, hearing about the latest unputdownable acquisitions, about the charms of cataloguing, the delights of classification. Sometimes Mikros could not stifle his yawns. Often he sat by himself, reading – Thukydides, perhaps – making scholarly notes in the margins of the papyrus with his own hand, or thinking ornithological thoughts about the identification of the Stymphalian Birds, or the authenticity of the list of the ships in the *Iliad*. He seldom appeared on his own parade ground to review the troops. He did not sail out with the fleet. Such things were his wife's business. Mostly he sat, and because he sat he grew stout in the belly. At noon, because of too much wine for his breakfast, he might fall asleep in his gilded chair. He was an old man of thirty-eight.

But in the afternoons, when to sleep might have been excusable because of the furious heat, and Arsinoë Beta went on working, Mikros was wide awake. He would wave away the officials who brought papyri from the sister with *Must sign the name* or *Must read every word* written on the label in her snaky hand, and drive the electrum chariot and four white horses fast up Kanopic Street to visit his concubine of the moment.

Arsinoë Beta, whose spies still told her everything the brother did, turned her blind eye to it. She understood the ways of men, that Mikros was set in his habits, would never change. She carried on ruling Egypt without him, knowing very well that she had just seven hundred and thirty days left in which to defeat Syria and make a peace that would last for ever and always – after which Mikros must rule alone, subject to whatever the fates might throw at him. *Must hurry,* she said to herself, *must work faster.* She worked against the *klepsydra,* counting down the days. Very often she sat up in her bed, working through the night, when the doctors begged her to send the officials away, to sleep, or at least try to rest, but she would not hear of it.

We may not sleep, she said, *until we have stamped upon the face of Antiokhos with our heel; we may not rest until we have signed our peace with Syria.* Many times she worked until dawn, drinking hourly the *astonos potos,* the Greek potion guaranteed to chase away sighs, saying, *In any case, the bellyache will not let us sleep.*

She ordered thousands more hired soldiers from the Peloponnesos for her land army. Working with Admiral Kallikrates she created a navy of one dozen very large ships of war, eighty medium-size ships, and one hundred and seventy-five small ships. Her total naval personnel numbered near to fifty thousand men, and one woman: the Great High Admiral of Egypt, who was herself.

Arsinoë Beta's fleet was a fine sight, riding at anchor in the Great Harbour of Alexandria, with all oars raised, ready to put to sea. The fleet represented perfection. Her only fear was that Mikros would wreck her good work when she was gone, for a fleet, however great, is only so good as its commander. For the moment Full Flame was safe in the hands of Kallikrates.

Black-and-white-striped horses hauled her chariot wherever she went – inspecting the troops, giving orders to the commanders of the army – and she wore now not the Atef Crown but the *khepresh,* that should by rights only be worn by Pharaoh. She was the Gracious One, the Lover of the West Wind, the ever-smiling Mistress of Happiness, Arsinoë Thea Philadelphos, Goddess, The One Who Loves Her Brother. But in truth she loved Mikros not. She loved Sakhmet, Lady of the Bright Red Linen, goddess of War, more. Aye, and now that the greatest moment of this goddess of war was at hand she ordered up a suit of armour for herself, not of bronze or gold but of crocodile hide.

1.29

The Crocodile Suit

Word came now from Arsinoë Beta's scouts beyond Gaza that Antiokhos Soter really was marching through Koile-Syria with his fifty thousand foot, edging into the territories that had been snatched from him by Old Ptolemy, in order to take back what was his by right. The great battle must be fought now, or Antiokhos would sweep into the south and take Egypt for his own possession. Antiokhos clapped his hands together and roared with laughter to think of it, but in Alexandria things looked black, for the news came again from the spies in the west that Magas was making himself ready to attack, and would invade Egypt just when Antiokhos tried to take Koile-Syria. Magas was reported to be on the road, backed up by half the nomads in Libya. If true, it was grim news, because Mikros and Arsinoë Beta must fight a war on two fronts at the same time.

Sure, we can handle it, Arsinoë Beta told her council of generals. *We shall prevail, come what may, but even a goddess in her own lifetime cannot be in two places at once.*

She sent for Eskedi, and ordered the state magic to be worked against Syria, when his Excellency set to work smashing pots, burning papyrus boats, and chanting over wax effigies of Antiokhos thrown into the flames of his brazier.

In the palace Arsinoë Beta began to shout with fresh urgency. Ministers who walked were now screamed at: *Run, run, Egypt is at war, facing invasion east and west, you must make haste.* Her eyes shone to think of it, her heart beat high, and really it was nothing to do with her shaky health, but the exhilaration of having the Two Lands at last upon a war footing. *Double war*, she thought, *that is the reason for the two snakes on our brow. Twice as powerful, twice as poisonous.*

Magas of Kyrene had kept up his friendship with Egypt for more than thirty years, happy to co-operate with Ptolemy Soter, his stepfather, and Ptolemy Mikros, his stepbrother. But now he broke off diplomatic relations, declared an end to trust, and sent his ambassadors into Syria, saying, *We do not like what we hear about Arsinoë Beta in Egypt. We do not like her messages that come full of orders, telling us what to do.*

Magas had heard the stories of Arsinoë Beta's handling of affairs in Thrace, how she had murdered her stepson, how she stripped her aged husband of his wealth. Magas liked still less what he heard of her ousting Arsinoë Alpha and marrying her own brother.

So many times the news of Magas's invasion had been false, and the troops sent out against him had found nothing moving in the desert west of Alexandria but snakes and lizards, that, for once, Arsinoë Beta ignored the rumour for a while, and concentrated her vulture gaze upon the border with Syria. This time, however, the rumour happened to be true. Magas had mobilized his troops and was on the road. He took the city of Paraitonion for himself and came within three days' march of the Gate of the Moon without the alarm being sounded. The word of his actual appearance upon the horizon took Egypt by surprise, with Mikros in the exact wrong place to fight him off. Aye, for Arsinoë Beta herself was still confined to bed, and Mikros was eight hundred stades away, in Memphis.

When Arsinoë Beta's agents told her of the forthcoming revolt she had hired, by means of Antigonos, her recruiting officer, a legion of four thousand soldiers, *Keltoi,* or Gauls, savage young warriors who fought naked, with their yellow hair greased into spikes and their muscled bodies painted blue. She boasted of her Gaulish legion as a most useful possession, for these were the men who wore the torc, or collar of gold, about the neck, than whom there were no more savage fighters anywhere in the world. At least, she boasted until they were found plotting to turn against her and seize Egypt for themselves, when she unleashed her venom, through the agency of her brother.

So what happened? It was the season of the Inundation, with the River rising fast, and Mikros himself managed to lure the Gauls on to a deserted island in the Nile. They had with them their swords and shields and trumpets, but even the longest and sharpest sword is no defence against Sobek, the Policeman of the River. Even the most savage-sounding trumpet will not change the heart of the Face of Fear once he has decided to attack. For Hapi, god of the Nile, was now pleased to flood this island with water, so that the unfaithful Gauls were either drowned or eaten by the crocodiles.

Eskedi smiled to hear it: Sobek was once again the saviour of Egypt.

Ptolemy Mikros was there, supposed to be giving the orders, but Seshat believes that he did nothing but stand in his chariot under a silken parasol, a mere onlooker. Always he had been good at doing nothing. But this was the sole action that the poet Theokritos could think of as a heroic feat of arms in which this king was personally involved in all his lifetime. True or false, only now that the Gauls had been dealt with could Mikros ride north to beat Magas back.

Alexandria had never been invaded by any foreign force since its foundation sixty years previous. The sleeping corpse of Alexander, like a lucky talisman, had kept the city safe. But Mikros now had to put on greaves, breastplate, helmet – gear that had seldom adorned this king's body before – and take up arms against his enemy. Alexander did prove lucky, however, for Mikros, red in the face and streaming with sweat, was hardly ten stades out of the Gate of the Moon at the head of his army when he met the messenger carrying news that the Marmarica Libyans, or nomads of the desert, had taken advantage of Magas's absence to rise in revolt against him, and that Magas had been forced to go home to deal with them – instead of attacking Alexandria.

Mikros held up the arm and gave the signal to about turn, and his cavalry and infantry poured back into the city, singing the Song of Victory. For the Greeks the best kind of victory is the bloodless victory, with no lives lost, won without so much as drawing the sword. Mikros sang louder than any of them. Mere words cannot describe the relief of his sister.

In due time Arsinoë Beta sent her messengers to Magas in Kyrene. *We appeal to you upon our beloved mother's eyes,* she wrote, *leave Egypt alone, and you may keep possession of Kyrene for your lifetime . . . Dare to march against Egypt a second time, and we shall be pleased to grind you to a powder, and take your kingdom from you by force.*

Magas gave his word. He disliked war, fighting, unpleasantness. Arsinoë Beta's terms were not unreasonable. These three – Mikros, Magas, Arsinoë Beta – shared the same mother. For them to go to war, it would not be pleasing to their mother's ghost. Relations would be a little difficult between Egypt and Kyrene for the next twenty years, but Magas was now bringing up the daughter whose fate it would be, many years later, to heal the rift for good – the famous Berenike Beta.

A sort of uneasy peace, then, was agreed between Kyrene and Alexandria – made easier by Great Sand Sea that lay between them – but it still looked likely that Antiokhos would attack Egypt from the east without delay. Arsinoë Beta was forced to take drastic measures to check what the scouts told her would be a massive invasion by both land and sea. She was wonderful to behold, in her element now, the goddess of war made flesh, and that iron heart of hers beat like crazy, while her belly, quite forgotten, troubled her hardly at all.

Let it begin, then, she said. *Make ready the fleet for sailing. Mobilize the land army. Call up every veteran to Memphis. We cannot wait to wipe the House of Seleukos off the face of the earth.*

From her sickbed she fired questions at the men who had the best knowledge of desert warfare. She ordered the sappers, surveyors, carpenters, wheelwrights, and transport officers to march east, and set up the advance camp – fortified, Macedonian-style, with the usual ditch and palisade. She directed water depots to be set up in the sere, parched desert of Sinai. She had the siege-machines loaded on to the ships, saying, *Far easier than trying to drag them through the sand.* Every man shouldered his knapsack, and the column of troops marched out of Memphis, singing, to the wild applause of those who were left behind.

There were sixty-five thousand foot, and six thousand horse, spaced out for the marching so that the front and rear men were one hundred and fifty stades apart, and the tail of the column entered the camp five hours after the head. Aye, and the march followed the coast, keeping to the wet sand, lest the men sink into the shifting dunes, and the fleet sailed alongside, with fresh water, just as in the time of Alexander. Arsinoë Beta force-marched the men for eleven days between Pelousion and Gaza, in order to conserve rations. Her troops almost *ran* to Syria.

Let Antiokhos do what he will, she cried. *We shall skin him alive.*

And then she climbed out of her golden bed. She waved aside the dwarfs who brought the *peplos,* the vulture headdress, the Atef Crown. She screamed at the slaves who brought her jewels to take them away again.

Bring me my crocodile armour, she said, smiling her best reptilian smile, *and make it snappy.* It was perhaps the first jest she had made in all her lifetime.

First, she had the waiting-women fasten the crocodile greaves on her shins. Second, the crocodile forearm-guards. Third, the crocodile neck-protector and shoulder-pads. Fourth, the crocodile breastplate decorated with gold, that glittered in the half-light of dawn. Fifth, the crocodile *krepides,* or soldier's lace-up boots. Sixth and last she put on not the lion's-jaw helmet with the red plumes, but the new helmet, her crocodile-leather helmet, studded with *smaragdoi,* emeralds, that had the grinning jaws of Sobek gaping open above her brow like the jaws of war.

Aye, her most drastic measure was to send herself into battle as supreme commander. She walked rather awkward under the weight of all that leather, like the crocodile himself: slow, and deliberate. And like the crocodile she would have what she wanted: her enemy chewed up, smashed to bits in her terrible jaws. This time the bellyache would not stop her.

Now she gave the order, *Make ready the white horses. We shall ride into battle ourself, and show Mikros of what metal his sister is made.*

And then she sent for Ptolemy the Son, saying, *Plato said that children should see war . . . we shall take Ptolemy the Son with us, and his tutor also, as part of the lessons in strategy and tactics.* She did not send for Ptolemy Euergetes or Lysimakhos, the traitor's children, to go with her. By no means. These boys were as much as her enemies. It was Ptolemy the Son who saw this war, so that he started his violent career early, at just six years old. When Berenike begged to be allowed to go as well, the little girl of seven or eight years, whom she was training up to be just as fierce as herself, Arsinoë Beta allowed it. *Girls should see war too,* Arsinoë said. *The experience may be useful to her some day . . .* Berenike was not too young to break pots with her enemy's name scratched on them, not too young to sink model ships with *Antiokhos* written on the side. Even Berenike did what she could for her stepmother's war.

Arsinoë Beta sent her ambassadors to the pirates who operated in the Great Sea, with gold to bribe them into co-operating with her, so much gold that they could not refuse to help her in the daring raid that meant advancing upon Syria from the seaward side, in the pitch dark, and descending at the same moment upon every coastal city of Syria at once, from Seleukeia-in-Pieria in the far north to Gaza in the south.

Arsinoë Beta was with the fleet, Full Flame, on board her flagship, with her admirals, directing the operation herself. Once before, as a girl of eight or nine years old, she had known the thrill of sea-battle. Now she found again that her spine tingled for excitement. And once again, she found herself with her head hung over the side of the ship, obliged to sick up her guts in the middle of giving some order.

Aye, she sent her fleet to attack all the weak points on the Phoenician coast on the same day, at the same hour, just before sun-up, so that it was impossible for Antiokhos to defend any place properly. Her oared galleys darted back and forth, oars rising and falling like the wings of some giant sea-gull, firing bolts and rocks from siege-machines mounted upon the decks. And when they were done with bombarding the shore from the sea, they dragged the ships on to the beaches, and fought their way inland.

Arsinoë Beta revelled in the whistle of missiles, crying, *The Fates will bestow victory upon us, Nike is watching you. Onward . . . Onward . . .*

Eskedi stood at her side, working his most powerful magic. *The serpent upon her Majesty's brow is a living flame,* he said, *that will burn her enemies to a cinder.* Eskedi identified himself with the *ouraios* serpent. He became strong enough to cut off heads. *The magician,* he said, *is the master of fire, the master of eternity. He will be as much as Ra in the eastern sky, as much as Osiris in the world below. He will win her Majesty's battle for her.* He sank the enemy ships by magic, just as if they were in a tub of water back in Memphis.

Arsinoë Beta set Syria on fire from end to end. Aye, Askalon, Ake, Tyros, Sidon, Berytos, Byblos, Tripolis, Arados, Laodikeia, Seleukeia-in-Pieria – every city on the Syrian seaboard, every seaport, fell into her hands. The coast was black with smoke, every city was on fire, and the sands of Syria were a sea of blood. Arsinoë Beta's heart beat faster to hear the news, relayed by signal from port to port, ship to ship, to her in the south; her heart was like the hammer for joy, and her bellyache had vanished.

She screamed her prayers to Nike, goddess of Victory, and she was as much as Nike herself, in the smoke of battle, like a beautiful apparition, and the sight of her urged the men forward. Some swore they saw Nike's wings upon her back.

By rights the great land battle should follow just here, Stranger, if Seshat had to hand the details of it. The two armies must have lined up opposite one another, dead still in the heat of afternoon, the hottest hour of the hottest day of the hottest season, the campaigning season. Exactly where it was, Stranger, Seshat does not know. All that can be said is that the armies of Egypt faced the armies of Syria somewhere in Syria.

Whatever the details, the battle would have been much the same as any other. The trumpets sounded. The terrible battle cry, the Macedonian *Alalalalai*, started up, screamed by both sides, for both Egypt and Syria were Macedonian at bottom, of the same nation. Their fathers had fought with Alexander and conquered half the world. Now they were pitched against each other, no longer friends but enemies. They clawed each other's flesh. They slit each other's throats, tore out each other's guts, made the blood flow, made a flood of blood. The elephants, you may be sure, acquitted themselves with honour, trumpeting, charging, trampling. The troops helped themselves to the armour of the enemy dead, swords and shields, to be hung up in the portico of the Greek temples, as thank-offerings to the gods for a great victory. Whatever valuables they could lay their hands on, they kept for themselves.

That is what every battle was like. There is nothing more to say except that Antiokhos' main attack was foiled. His land army was driven back, and the victory was Arsinoë Beta's, and the cheering of the troops, and the way they chanted *Beta – Beta – Beta – Beta* was pleasing to her ear, most pleasing.

Amid the shouts of victory, however, the word was shouted that Antiokhos had raised a fresh phalanx of sixteen thousand troops in Babylon; that he had gotten himself twenty fresh elephants of war out of Baktria; that he had already marched them almost as far as Gaza. Antiokhos was not going to accept defeat, but pressed on south, marching ever southward, and it was his grand purpose to storm Memphis and raze that most magnificent and ancient of cities to the ground. The land army of Mikros and Arsinoë Beta was forced to retreat before him, hurrying back to defend Egypt's borders. Now, however, at Eskedi's brilliant suggestion, they breached all the dykes in the eastern Delta so that the whole of the Pelousion district lay under a great lake of water, and the Syrian troops could not march through it. Without that High Priest of Ptah, that very great high priest, Egypt would have been lost.

Arsinoë Beta screamed her orders throughout the day from her chariot, from her horse, from a tower on the back of her best of elephants. Her face was from time to time screwed up in agony with her belly. Wherever she rode Ptolemy the Son rode with her, as part of his training to be warlike, far more warlike than his father, and the Son loved it. He shouted for Egypt and for Victory, for Nike and Tykhe together, goddesses of the golden wings, goddesses of Victory and Good Luck, both of whom were made flesh in his mother. Berenike did the same – shouting from the tower on the back of her stepmother's elephant, screaming as she rode in front of her stepmother on her horse, firing half-size arrows, playing her part in the defeat of Egypt's enemy.

Mikros did not, of course, shout or scream, but quietly gave his orders for thousands more troops to be sent down-River to Memphis. He talked with the generals, asking questions, encouraging. He visited the wounded. He kept his famous balance, but by night he dreamed lurid dreams in which Antiokhos burst into his bedchamber and set the bedsheets on fire.

Eskedi told him his dream meant Egypt's defeat, and that offerings to the gods was what was needed, substantial offerings earmarked for temple repairs, fresh statues of every god, and geese and loaves by the thousand for Montu, god of War.

Mikros promised to do whatever Eskedi asked – when the battle was over – but in the heat of the moment he did not forget the gods of Hellas, muttering, *It may be that Ares is the god who will save us,* and he ordered the sacrifice of a dozen black bulls. Then a second dozen.

As if in answer to Mikros's prayers, an extraordinary thing now happened, a miracle even, for Antiokhos found he was short of the tens of thousands of heavy bronze tetradrachms that he needed to pay his troops, and an urgent dispatch reached him as he approached Pelousion, saying that his entire force of foot soldiers at Babylon had sat down and refused to budge until he paid their wages, and that they were on the point of leaving his service for some other commander – perhaps even for Mikros himself. Then came a second messenger to tell Antiokhos that great numbers of his men had been struck down by plague; that Babylon choked under the black smoke of many funeral pyres, and was loud with lamentation.

Antiokhos could not, in such circumstances, go on, but was forced to abandon his plans to conquer Egypt. Up and down Syria his troops emerged from the gates of every city with their hands above their heads, burning incense as a sign of surrender. Antiokhos himself retreated north in a black melancholy.

Whose work was this lucky result? To whom must the glory in the First Syrian War be given? To Arsinoë Beta, to the sister, of course. Had she taken steps to infect the water supply at Babylon? Had she herself sent the messages to Antiokhos to tell him of the mutiny of his own troops? Some laughed that it was so. Arsinoë Beta herself was happy to let men believe it might be true. She smiled the half-smile and said nothing. Mikros himself had always been cautious in military matters. Boldness was his sister's attribute. Victory belonged to the sister, the wonderful and most wonderful sister.

Arsinoë Beta let herself rejoice, at last. *A victory is a victory,* she said, *whether or not the enemy is dead at the end of it.* She ordered triple wages for one month, and triple triple rations of wine for every man, and then cancelled it, saying, *No, let every man drink as much as he likes; let them drink just as much as they can; her Majesty will pay.*

Egypt went mad for delight. Mikros had kept control of Koile-Syria and Phoenicia, and the people made festival. Arsinoë Beta ordered the sacrifice of one hundred black bulls to Nike, goddess of Victory, and Alexandria gorged on roast meat and was drunk for days and nights without remembering. Herself, she still drank hardly one mouthful of water, ate no more than a handful of olives, but her heart swelled for pride, and she slept not by night for the thrill of victory was upon her.

Under the terms of the peace, Egypt was to keep the cities of Damaskos and Arados, and Antiokhos was left with no port to call his own along the entire Phoenician coastline. His fleet of oared galleys Arsinoë Beta kept for herself.

The Court Poet, Theokritos, made much of Mikros's triumph in a poem too long for Seshat to quote. Theokritos praised his Majesty, but where he sang that Ptolemy Mikros was braver than Achilles, really, it was nothing but flattery. If anybody was brave it was the sister. All this military success was hers, but she let Mikros take the credit for it.

Back at the palace, she asked him, *What may be my reward for winning my brother's Syrian wars for him? Even the best of poems is not much return for winning you a mighty victory and peace with Syria for ever and ever.*

Mikros thought for a while, said nothing.

Really, Brother, there is nothing I want so much as this, she said, *that you make your solemn promise, that you swear to me: After your death you shall enjoy the worship of all Egypt, and be a goddess, with your golden statue in every temple, Greek and Egyptian.*

She knew that she must die soon. Her demand was simple: total immortality.

Very well, Mikros said, *I swear.* To make the sister a full goddess would not cost him anything. And forasmuch as a queen may trust no one, she made him write it in his own blood.

For sure, Mikros obeyed. He was not ungrateful, just then.

As for the poet Kallimakhos, he sang: *Ptolemy Mikros will rule the whole world from the rising to the setting of the sun.* It was a charming thought, but if it ever came true, it would be through the efforts of his sister.

Proof, though, Mikros thought, that in the wicked marriage to the Sister he did absolutely what was right. He had no regrets now. He had almost forgotten about Arsinoë Alpha, her amiable character. Toughness and victory were far better. Truly, Stranger, without this Queen, Egypt would have perished. The sister's homecoming was like a gift from Zeus.

1.30

Evil Spirits

Like all gifts from the gods, however, that gift could just as easily be taken away again. And indeed, soon, very soon, Arsinoë Beta must perish herself. But what was wrong with her? Some said that, long before this, while doing her best to poison Handsome Agathokles, she had vowed that nobody should ever be able to do the same to her.

The rumour still flew about, saying that it was her habit to swallow a regular dose of poison, each day a little more than the day before; a cocktail of lethal poisons in order to survive a murder attempt. So that, whereas for ordinary mortals to eat poison was to die, Arsinoë Beta ate poison to live – at least, until the normal course of her earthly life was run. Such was the curious logic under which she existed: since she lived on poison, she would survive by poison.

Some men believed that her constant stomach aches and almost daily vomitings were nothing but symptoms of her slow self-murder, but the Greeks are scornful of self-murder as cowardice, and Arsinoë Beta was no coward. You might think that she had little enough to live for, having long since lost what she valued most – her two sons murdered at Kassandreia, her only surviving son sent away to govern Telmessos. And now even her great last hope, Ptolemy the Son, growing up to be the spitting image of Ptolemy the Thunderbolt, mad as a satyr, guaranteed by his fate to turn out for the worst. As for love, she had killed the only man she ever loved for the crime of not loving her in return.

What, then, made her go on working? Her very great love of the Two Lands, her very great desire to have control, her very great need to make the House of Ptolemy glorious and herself one of the immortals. She drove her body like some tireless siege-machine, day and night, as if she had vowed to test it to the limit of her endurance, until the very sinews snapped.

Others said that the rumours of poison were nonsense: that she was sick in her body, and that the search for the cure went on. More than once

Herophilos whispered to Mikros, *There is no cure in the Greek world that we have not tried. It rests in the hands of the gods alone whether she must die or live.*

Arsinoë Beta did not much like Egyptian medicine, for, as she said, the Egyptian remedies were all donkey dung and camel piss, and because she thought Greek medicine worked better. But not all the Greek gods of health together – not Asklepios, nor Hygeia nor Panacea – nor all the best Greek doctors, even the great Herophilos, had managed to cure her. Now she sent even unto Eskedi at Memphis, offering her body for a living experiment, agreeing to try whatever Egyptian medicine he cared to suggest, even the vulture guts and donkey dung, if he wished it, but always excepting, of course, the horror of going under the surgeon's knife.

Eskedi came to Alexandria in person, and when he stepped into her Majesty's chamber he startled her, for he wore the mask of the lioness herself. He *was* Sakhmet, and he circled the Queen's bed, growling and chanting. He burned incense before her. He addressed with sternness the evil spirit that had taken up his dwelling in her belly, and caused her so much pain. He ordered the evil spirit to leave her body, saying, *Thou hast no power of thy own . . .*

All that day this great sorcerer whistled, clicked his tongue, and mimicked the chirping of birds, but his noises made no difference to her Majesty's belly. The bad spirits liked the worn-out body of this poisonous queen far too well to leave it.

At the seventh hour Eskedi took off his mask and said, *Even Horus and Ra suffered from the dyspepsia . . . Every disease has a hidden cause, which may be the result of hostile forces, or the evil wishes of an enemy . . . Perhaps her Majesty has angered one of the gods . . .*

Arsinoë Beta stared at her golden ceiling.

Perhaps her Majesty has made a dead relative jealous . . .

No answer.

Perhaps some ghost has been troubling her?

The lips of Arsinoë Beta was as if stitched up, but her body trembled.

The magician's task, Eskedi said, *is to root out evil from his patient's body . . . I shall challenge the illness.* He put the mask on again and began to roar like the lioness herself: *Begone! Come out! Thou shalt be ill at ease in the part of the body where thou wishest to live . . . The tongue shall be a serpent and bite thee . . . The anus shall disgust thee with its stink . . . The teeth shall grind thee up . . . Begone! Come out! O poison, fall to earth, leave this poor woman's body.*

Shuddering so bad that her bedstead rattled, Arsinoë Beta heard a noise like the wind rushing in the palm trees on Cape Zephyrion, though she felt no draught. She heard a noise like water falling, like the roar of the Cataract above Elephantine. The magician told her to shade her eyes, lest the sun's light should dazzle her, and she put an arm across her face, against the light that must defeat her darkness.

Eskedi growled, roared, chanted, singing out the demons. Arsinoë Beta lost all sense of time, fell into a kind of dream in which she heard the screaming wind and the thundering water, and entered an even deeper darkness. Four times the great man made direct contact with her Majesty's demons, making them swear through her lips, and her body never stopped its frightful shuddering. Four times the demons resisted him, speaking with her Majesty's tongue. Four times this great master of magic made a demon come forth from her Majesty's mouth in a puff of black smoke, but many more refused to quit. At length, even this great magician gave up the attempt to cast them out, threw open the window shutter, brought her out of the trance, and withdrew.

Arsinoë Beta opened her eyes. She heard no noise now but the thumping of her heart, and in the distance the victory parade coming up Kanopic Street with drums and trumpets, and the crowd chanting her name in time with her heartbeat: *Beta – Beta – Beta – Beta – Beta . . .*

Now Mikros put his head round the door and pushed it open, grinning. He wore the Double Crown, the Horus collar, the *chendjyt* kilt of Pharaoh. In his hand he carried the crook and flail. *Time to show the face, Sister,* he said, *time to wave the arm.* And Arsinoë Beta put on the vulture headdress, the crown with the ram's horns and the solar disk, and the heavy jewelled vulture necklaces of the Mistress of the Two Lands. She shuffled to the Window of Appearances. Aye, every man, woman and child in the city stood below, roaring her name – *Beta – Beta – Beta – Beta* – waving the arms above the head, dancing for joy, and they would not let her go, but kept shouting for her to wave again.

Arsinoë Beta should have known what caused her bellyache: the demons sent by Arsinoë Alpha, her spells of binding and destroying; the dying curse of Agathokles of Thrace, his terrible ghost; the magic of her half-brother, Ptolemy the Thunderbolt, the most powerful magic known to man. All these years she had been troubled by terrors of the night, ghosts, wild dreams, strange noises in the inner ear. Even when she did sleep, the slightest noise would wake her up again.

The Greeks like to speak of the Golden Mean, saying that both too much and too little must be avoided, so that even too much health is dangerous. They say that a woman should sometimes try to be ill, should welcome her illness, because to have too much good health, too much good luck, will tempt the gods to vengeance. An excess of health must be reduced, much as the wise ship captain must throw overboard his excess cargo in a storm. But Arsinoë Beta's good health had abandoned her long ago.

The Greek thought is that health is the greatest gift of the gods. Frightening it is, to be sure, when the gods take that most precious gift back again. An innocent woman sleeps in peace, protected by magic. It is the guilty ones that sleep not. For them the night time is full of misery. Eskedi could protect himself, declaring that he was the master of the universe. He contemplated Ra. He could see the light face to face. But Arsinoë Beta saw only darkness. She had only her ghosts, her demons, for company, and the darkness grew deeper about her.

Soon enough, Eskedi thought, she must sleep the iron sleep herself, and her brother feared the same: Mikros half *hoped* it.

That night, when Arsinoë Beta finally slept, she dreamed the tumultuous dream in which the crocodile had his *aphrodisia* with her, thrashing about with her body in the Nile, his jaws agape and grinning, dripping with water, his eyes glistening as he banged at her body with his armoured *phallos*. Aye, even Sobek, Guide of the Dead in the Afterlife, came to her now, and – Oh – Oh – Oh – she liked it not at all, but woke in the greatest distress, wailing. Her heart banged like one hundred metal hammers.

Mikros came to her, after several urgent messages, and found her sitting up in bed, with the tears running down her face.

Whatever can be wrong? he said. *We have won a mighty victory . . . You should be happy.*

We have dreamed the most terrible dream, she sobbed.

Mikros sent for Eskedi, who was still in the city, and, of course, this man knew just what the crocodile dream meant. *Sobek,* he said, drawing Mikros aside, *is the friend of the dead, who will open the eyes of the dead. Sobek will be the dragoman, or divine guide, of her Majesty upon the highways and byways of the Afterlife. To dream of aphrodisia with the crocodile means that the dreamer must die.*

To Arsinoë Beta he said only, *It means that Sobek is with you, Megaleia. He is Ra, he is Helios, the creator of the world. He is good to the dead, but he is just as good to the living. To dream of him is most auspicious.*

For the night terrors he prescribed the right front foot of a chameleon to be tied to her left arm with a strip of hyaena skin, and then he left her, saying to Mikros, *Profound regrets, Megaleios, her Majesty's case seems to be hopeless.*

Arsinoë Beta herself groaned, *The bellyache is killing me . . . I am dying of heartburn . . . I shall not live to see another sunrise . . .*

When dawn broke, however, she was still breathing.

1.31

Beloved of the Ram

No, Arsinoë Beta did not fly to the stars quite so quick as Mikros feared, and hoped, she must. She soldiered on, turning the army of Egypt into a Wall of Iron, like herself; turning the Fleet of Egypt into a Scorching Torch, like herself; ensuring that her peace would last for ever.

Arsinoë Beta did not die. It was Philotera who died, the virtuous and most virtuous sister, about whose existence, Stranger, Seshat believes you have forgotten.

Never strong, at the age of thirty-nine she took sick of a fever and was found stiff in her bed one morning, sleeping so well that nobody could wake her.

The waiting-women shook her body upside down. They threw cold water over her face and tipped hot urine up her nose. They shouted in her ears. Then came the silence of disbelief. When Arsinoë Beta hobbled into the chamber she took one look and said, *Philotera is dead,* and she was the first to tear her garments to shreds and smear Nile mud all over her face and arms, though she had no strength left for further wailing. She had loved that sister, after her fashion. Now she gave the order for the palace slaves to gather sticks for the funeral bonfire of this high princess, King's Daughter and King's Sister, for that she had asked to be burned up upon the beaches, according to Greek custom. *Some Egyptian ways are good enough,* she had said, *but a Greek funeral is the best funeral.*

At his elder sister's prompting, Mikros announced details of Philotera's worship as a goddess. Her cult flourished, at first. Her waiting-women led the procession with her gilded statue up Kanopic Street to the Temple of Sarapis for her annual festival. In the Temple of Ptah at Memphis the eyes of Philotera's statue, inlaid with precious stones, shone in the gloom. Even Philotera, who died unmarried, without posterity, would not be forgotten. Her name would live.

But with the remembering, the forgetting began. Philotera had disapproved of the brother–sister marriage, had never stopped saying *Filthy . . . disgusting . . . filthy filthy filthy . . .* whenever her siblings were within earshot. Her name would not live for very long.

No, the one they would remember for all time was Arsinoë Beta, who was the equal of Isis, the leader of the Muses. They flattered her in Alexandria, this great female general, saying she was the Tenth Muse, and her chief of flatterers was the Admiral Kallikrates. Arsinoë the Muse knew both how to lie and how to reveal the truth. In the singing contest between the False Muses and the True, the False Muses were defeated and turned into birds. When the False Muses sang, the sky grew dark, and nobody listened. When the True Muses sang, everything stood still, even the sky, the stars, the sea, the rivers. Aye, the task of the Muses – daughters of Zeus and Mnemosyne, or Memory – was to blot out the memory of misfortunes, to offer some relief from the burden of cares, for the Muses have no cares. Arsinoë Beta, as a daughter of Zeus, was a Muse herself. But she never did quite blot out the memory of her own misfortunes. The burden of trouble still weighed upon her spirits.

In what were her last months, did this woman who had endured so much trouble in her private life enjoy one single pleasure? Yes, as a matter of fact, she did, for she thought, *Our brother has his women, why should not Arsinoë Beta have her man?* For, truly, Mikros never went near his sister now for the ploughing.

Who, then, was the lucky man that enjoyed the last hot gusts of Arsinoë Beta's passion? Kallikrates of Samos, of course, her handsome Admiral of the Fleet, Full Flame, her favourite. This man had dedicated a shrine to Anubis and Isis on her Majesty's behalf. Now he also put up, at his own expense, a small Greek temple to the divine Arsinoë Aphrodite on the road to Kanopos, at Cape Zephyrion. This bleak spot was named for the violent west wind that roars in the palm trees there in winter, on the seashore east of Alexandria, where the breakers crash furious upon the beach. In this temple the divine Arsinoë Aphrodite guaranteed a fair voyage and the calming of the roughest seas to all who made their prayers and offerings to her, thanks to the loyalty of Kallikrates.

Arsinoë Beta had always spent many hours with her handsome admiral, talking about battle at sea, flaming bolt-throwers, and the business of ram-ming the enemy. To talk of battle made her forget, for a time, the ghost of Handsome Agathokles, the ghost of her half-brother, Ptolemy Keraunos, the ghosts of her two dead sons, the ghost of Philotera. To talk of Egypt's brand new secret weapon, the miraculous bomb of tow and granulated frankin-cense, made her forget, for the moment, her bellyache. Kallikrates was the one man in Egypt who knew as much about war as she did. In his turn, Kallikrates admired her ferocity, her fearlessness, qualities wholly unsuitable in a girl, but utterly wonderful in a queen who had total charge of war. He loved this queen for being so very like a man. And Arsinoë Beta loved this admiral for being so like the mirror of herself. The great Aristotle wrote that it is quite inappropriate to give a female character either manliness or cleverness, but Arsinoë Beta is no invention of Seshat, no made-up character from the drama. However inappropriate it may have been, this woman was both manly and clever.

Kallikrates was her final flame, Full Flame himself. And what did Kallikrates think of that? He was happy enough, though to speak true, he had not much choice in the matter. An admiral must obey orders. As Arsinoë Beta said, *We expect the nauarkhos to do his duty,* and she wore him out, just as she had worn Mikros out. She had not made herself Aphrodite, goddess of *aphrodisia,* for nothing.

The learned Aristotle also happened to believe that goat's milk is the best of all milk. When goat's milk, best for invalids, improved her belly a little, Arsinoë Beta made her very special devotions to the Ram of Mendes. Aye, she made a point, now, of sacrificing to the beast with the iron stomach, the one who can eat even thistles without ill effect, in the hope that she might acquire the same qualities.

She also paid for the rebuilding of the temple of the ram-god, the billy-goat who was Lord of Djedet and symbol of fertility, whom the Greeks looked upon with special favour as the equal of Pan. About this time the Sacred Ram died, when he was mummified and given a golden face-mask and hoofs of gold, and the most lavish funeral rites, almost as elaborate as those of the Apis of Memphis. She sailed to Mendes with Mikros to install the fresh ram, when there were great celebrations, feasts and processions, for this was the Great Ram himself, the one the women of Egypt sacrificed to when they wanted to have children. They called Mikros himself Son of the Great Living Goat of Mendes, who was the earthly embodiment of the god, the Ba, or Living Image, of Osiris. The great goat also happened to be a loyal associate of Dionysos, for that he liked to eat vine-shoots.

Just as the virility of the Apis bull was strengthened when the women lifted up their skirts to show him their secret parts, so, too, the Goat of Mendes was made stronger by having his *aphrodisia* with a woman. The High Priest of Mendes said to her Majesty, *No greater honour could be paid to the Ram than for the wife of Pharaoh to present herself for the mounting.* For sure, the last time she had been offered this exquisite pleasure she had made her best excuses, horrified by the idea. But now, no, she had nothing to lose. She must die soon, whatever happened. Arsinoë Beta stepped into the festival tent, lifted up the red dress of the goddess of War and got herself fucked by the Great He-Goat, the lord Banebdjedet.

In the tumult of bleating she came eyeball to eyeball with the great god, was fixed by his staring, glassy eyes. Then, almost too quick for her to realize what was happening, his beard was on the back of her neck, and she smelled the sweetness of the god's breath. Attendants took the dancing hoofs of this god in hand, and held his horns, so that she was not battered and butted; so that the lord Banebdjedet flew. If you want to know the truth, Stranger, it was violent, but it was also wonderful. For sure, it made her forget the bellyache.

You should not doubt the truth of it, Stranger. Remember that Seshat is the goddess of History. How else do you suppose Arsinoë Beta might have gotten her title *Beloved of the Goat?* Believe, Stranger, if you please. You are in pagan times, when anything might happen, times when nothing that any woman might imagine to do was forbidden her, not even marrying her own brother, not even *aphrodisia* with goats. Your own day, Stranger, will be very dull by comparison.

For the few months that Arsinoë Beta survived this furious assault upon her person there was a fresh glitter in her eye, a curious shining. Sometimes she would be heard to murmur, *Like being fucked by Pan . . . Like being fucked by the god.*

But then the bellyache kicked in again and it felt indeed like the end of the world, the very end of the road for the Mistress of Happiness.

The last of all the belly remedies Herophilos suggested was the boiled crow, said to be useful in the treatment of indigestion. *Oh, why not?* she said. *Why not serve it up at once? I will be pleased to make trial of any thing you care to mention.*

Pharaoh's cook brought her the boiled crow before sunset, marinated in sweet wine and smothered in honey to hide the taste, arranged on a plate of gold like some great delicacy, decorated with the black feathers stuck in the black meat.

Arsinoë Beta sat eating it, she ate all of it, for sure, and her doctors and cooks watched her Majesty eat – for that, in itself, was something of a wonder. But crow's flesh is tough, greasy, disgusting, like eating a filthy old shoe, and there is no hiding the taste. When the borborygmi began, she fled. Aye, and she retched all that night. The boiled crow had no other discernible effect upon her health.

1.32

Vulture Feet

On the one hand Mikros was weary of the sister's bossiness, her tireless domination. On the other hand he was grateful for her help. Worried for the sister's well-being, or perhaps thinking to hurry her on to Hades, he spoke to Herophilos about her medical troubles. *You know, Herophilos,* he said, *you are the greatest doctor in Egypt since Imhotep, the greatest doctor in the world. You have even opened the throat of the nightingale to find out how she makes her song. Would you not now be pleased to open the sister's belly to see where her problem lies? Please to make yourself ready. Our sister seems to be in dire need of your surgical skills. I think the time has come to operate.*

For sure, Herophilos was willing enough, and he came the next day at sunrise with his surgical tools made freshly sharp, ready to open the belly of her Majesty and rearrange her disordered guts. But when his procession of white-clad assistants made their dramatic entry into her chamber – for Herophilos was accompanied by his team of one dozen slaves bearing strong ropes to tie her down, and by his one dozen muscular Greek assistants who would hold her body still while she went under the knife – and made to tip strong liquor down her throat in order to dull the pain, she realized at once what was planned, and she began to shout all manner of filth at this good doctor, and ran about the room, throwing down the golden furniture and hurling every golden object, so that he should not catch hold of her, aye, punching him, kicking him, and screaming abuse.

Mikros, standing in a corner, called to her, *It is for your own good, Sister. We have decided to help you. The operation will be for the best. You should calm yourself and submit to the investigation.*

But no, she would not have it. She screamed abuse at her brother for sending in the surgeon. *He shall not cut me up,* she howled. *He is nothing but a butcher. He may keep his filthy knives to himself – I am not one of his wretched monkeys.*

Really, her screaming was so far beyond madness that, at length, the great man was obliged to admit defeat, and withdrew, shaking his head.

*

Asked one time to describe the complete doctor, Herophilos said, *He is the man who can distinguish what is possible from what is not*. And the truth of it was that even the greatest doctor in the world did not know what was wrong with her Majesty. Even though she was a goddess in her own lifetime, she was in truth, and of course, no different from any other mortal in that she must die. She was dying, and she knew it: according to her best calculations she had fourteen days left to live. She lay propped up in her golden bed, eyes shut, cheeks sunk, face covered with ten thousand lines, breathing loud, and irregular. A snake coiled and uncoiled himself in her arms. Her brother came on the hour, when the trumpeter on the *klepsydra* blew, to see whether, by chance, she was dead, or to speed her on her way with a few rude words if she were not.

Do not worry, Sister, he said. *Do not let death weigh upon your thoughts.*

She opened the eyes, stared through him, unblinking.

I have left orders for the biggest funeral Alexandria ever saw, she said. *Never mind the cost. Take it from my treasure-house.*

You want to burn? he said, fitting a breast-shaped cheesecake into his mouth, *Or be stuffed?* She threw her pillow at him and the room was a storm of pigeon feathers.

Answer the question, he said, laughing. *What are your last wishes?*

Stuff, she said, angry, picking feathers from her mouth. Then this hard woman, who had never in her life showed fear of anything, let the tears slide down her face.

I am afraid, Brother, she said.

Afraid of what, Sister? he said, affecting concern.

Afraid of the judgement, she said. *Afraid of the Lake of Fire, afraid of the Forty-Two Demons, afraid of the black dog, afraid of dying, afraid of Eurynomos.*

Mikros made the face of Well-I-Am-Not-Unafraid-Myself, but truly, such fears were nothing to the man who knows he is immortal.

The crocodile god may fight Eurynomos off for you, Mikros said, rather vague, the geography of the Afterlife really not his specialty. But yes, all the Greeks feared Eurynomos, the demon whose skin is blue-black, the colour of the flies that land upon the butcher's meat; whose delight is to feed upon the flesh of corpses. For these Greeks had not the quiet confidence in the Afterlife that the Egyptians have, but were terrified of death. Even Arsinoë Beta, the iron one, feared the unknown.

They said of her, *The biggest vulture with the strongest beak rules the roost.* She had worn the vulture headdress, had been very like the vulture herself, Nekhbet, Lady of the Sky. Was she not her brother's Minister for War, a woman who might almost peck a man's eyes out while he lived? Like the vulture, she had been the Mistress of Death. But now the stink of death hung in her nostrils, and it was not the stink of Herophilos but herself, rotting within. Aye, the doctors drew Mikros's attention to the green urine that signifies diseased bowels, for that her urine trickled now a bright malachite green, the colour of the fields that surround the precinct of Ptah at Memphis, and it had a wondrous reptilian odour, like the urine of those who have not long since gorged upon asparagus.

Crocodile piss, Mikros said, disgusted, catching the whiff of it as the Dwarf of the Queen's Body carried the golden bowl past him in the corridor, held at arm's length.

On the day the urine of this Queen trickled red, Herophilos murmured about diseased blood, saying, *She has endured well beyond what was fated by the gods.*

Thinking that the end was close, Mikros sat with his sister to comfort her.

Do not worry, he said. *Anubis will take you by the hand . . .* He took her hand himself, feeling for the pulse at her wrist, that ran beneath the skin, like ants, and it made him think of the passing of his father, thirteen years previous, except that the sister's hand was not fleshy but thin, like the gnarled foot of some great bird.

Vulture feet, he thought. But the pulse of Arsinoë Beta beat strong, and it looked to Mikros as if this woman of iron would be just like the crocodile, difficult to kill: a long time dying.

1.33

Dog-Breath

The day of the full moon in the month of Pachon in Year Fifteen of Ptolemy Mikros, when the heat was insufferable even at Alexandria, was the day that Arsinoë Beta had counted down to be her last day among the living, the seventh day of the seventh month of her forty-sixth year. The paradox was that she felt better, if a little hot. She was surrounded, as usual, by ministers, ambassadors, officials, doctors, courtiers, waiting-women, scribes, fan-bearers of the right or left hand, still running Egypt even from her deathbed, still knocking back one thaumaturgic drug after another, washed down with a mouthful of Milk of Magnesia. Ptolemy the Son sat on the end of her bed, eating olives, spitting out the pips at his mother's cats. Her monkeys chattered on the window ledge, eating grapes. Her crocodiles still crept about the mosaic floor. She had the snakes in her bed still, letting them slide about her neck and arms. Wondrous strange, you will be thinking, Wise One, but every man there was used to her Majesty's most excellent strangeness. At this court strangeness had become normality – and so it would be in the future, stranger and stranger than ever.

Arsinoë Beta looked more hollow in the cheeks than before, ancient as the Sibyl, and thin as one of her own snakes, but she felt good. She had no pain in the belly just now, no gurgling in the guts, no untoward symptoms whatever. She was seized, then, with a desire to walk up and down. *Out,* she cried, waving the crowd away. She could not think that she was about to depart this life.

She stood up, unsteady, for it was the first time her feet had touched the mosaic in thirty days. She stumbled to her windows, looking west, across the Great Harbour, towards the Heptastadion that was the thought of Alexander, and the towering Pharos that was her father's triumph over Time. She stared down Kanopic Street, jammed as usual with carts and chariots, horses, donkeys and camels, crowded with Greeks and Egyptians going about their business. If everything was ordered for the best, as Mikros liked to say, it was because the sister had made it so.

At the seventh hour, still untroubled by her belly, she thought it might amuse her to call up one or two gods and question them about the day of her death, for at the seventh hour one may ask any question one likes and be given a satisfactory answer.

She walked into her private chamber, the one lined with jars marked *Snake's Eggs, Bat's Blood, Vulture Feathers* . . . ingredients for every kind of marvellous magic spell. She lit her brazier and melted the wax in a bronze pan. She kneaded the herbs. She scrambled the lizard. She fried the brains of a black ram. This was Arsinoë-Medea, the witch-maiden of Apollonios Rhodios, who had the power to stop the stars in their tracks and halt the Moon's progress across the heavens.

She threw a hyaena's heart, sizzling, into the brazier, and the stink of it was – Oh – Oh – insupportable, but the proper thing to do if you want to speak with the gods.

She looked at the instructions in the book of words, and read: *Not to be used without due care . . . The god will raise up those who do not protect themselves and let them fall from on high . . . Do not play with the rites or you will attract an angry spirit.*

She chanted the invocation, chanted again. Nothing happened.

She must force the god to come in and answer her question. She thought then of the Egyptian practice of procuring a vision by smearing strychnine upon the eyes. She took down the jar from the shelf, curious. She took off the lid, dipped the finger, smeared the stuff.

Nothing? she said. *Is nobody there?*

In the absence of any priest to ask her whether she would speak with a dead man's soul or with a god, she held the dialogue with herself, whispering the words of power.

With Anubis, she said. *Let the dog show his face.*

As the black shadow fell across the wall in the lamplight, she felt some mighty thing descend upon her head, a blow of very great weight. The chamber grew dark, her eyes grew dim, her knees gave way beneath her, and she looked into the black eyes of the Great God, Pharaoh of the Underworld, Lord of the Desert, awesome, terrifying, and yet gentle. She heard his growling, and the thump of his tail upon the door frame and was not afraid.

The black dog padded into her chamber, Anubis, black as a man of Nubia, and he took her roughly by the arm, as a god might manhandle one who does not quite believe in him, and led her out of the room, and his dog's skin was hot, smooth, black, and his dog-eyes were edged with gold, and she felt his dog-breath, hot, and smelled the smell of him, not like the wet-dog smell of any other dog, but sweet, like the perfume of the gods, and she felt the wet nose of Anubis upon the back of her neck, nudging her forward.

Upon the floral mosaic lay the body of Arsinoë Beta, and she had the answer to her question, and the smile was fixed upon her face.

Many men have called Arsinoë Beta a wicked woman, but Seshat raises her up. Seshat, who forgets nothing, inscribes Arsinoë Beta's name for millions and millions of years. Seshat records the fantastic and most fantastic deeds of Arsinoë Beta, the mighty Builder, for all eternity.

1.34

The Field of Rushes

According to the Egyptian priests Arsinoë Beta, belly eaten of worms, or whatever it may have been, flew to the sky to join the company of Ra. The Greeks, on the other hand, swore she was snatched away to heaven by the

Dioskouroi, Kastor and Polydeukes, sons of Zeus, the Heavenly Twins whose cult she had brought to Alexandria from Samothrake herself.

However she flew skywards, the wonderful thing for Mikros was that she had gone: the Olympian gabbling of the sister was silenced, and for those who had suffered by living too close to her it was something of a relief. The paradox was that where the Palace feared this woman whose evil temper raged like the storm of sand from the desert, the people of the city loved her. She was beautiful, generous, good to the gods, they said: she was Isis, Aphrodite, a true goddess, to whom they were almost panting to offer heart-felt worship.

Did Ptolemy Mikros weep for hours upon end, inconsolable, for the loss of the lovely Arsinoë Beta, the Mistress of Happiness, Fair of Face, She Who Delights the Heart of His Majesty, the Sister That He Loved? Some said so but, really, it was just another jest. No, of course he did not weep. He could not stop grinning. He could not keep his feet still for wanting to dance for joy. The face of Pharaoh was dry, dry but for the sweat that trickled down his brow in the summer heat. Tears, he shed them not. He might pretend that he mourned her loss, but what man that had suffered under the iron rule of such a sister could do anything but rejoice that she had gone?

The first order Mikros gave after the death of the sister was to the Dioiketes: *Be so kind as to remove from my house, upon the instant, every crocodile and every snake.* And her late Majesty's reptiles were taken to the Beast Garden, never to return.

So often Mikros had murmured, *To bury a woman is better than to marry her.* So many times he had whispered, *The man who bemoans the death of his wife . . . he is a fool, a fool, who does not appreciate his good luck.* Now he might say such things aloud, without fear of her scourging tongue. Aye, Mikros thought much the same as any other Greek husband, that the proper place for a woman, after her work in the marriage-bed was done, was in the necropolis.

But what would Mikros do with his dead sister? For a family that was neither wholly Greek (or Macedonian) nor yet wholly Egyptian either, this was the great problem of problems. How to bury the dead one without annoying either the Greeks or the Egyptians? What to do? What to do? When the Dioiketes sent to ask, Mikros did not know, said he was thinking about it. Eskedi, knowing what he was very like to order, did not hesitate to warn him of the consequences: *If you burn her Majesty on the pyre after the manner of the Greeks, her Ka – her double, or vital force – will be quite destroyed, her shadow will be ruined for ever. To lose the body by burning up is a calamity. If the corpse is destroyed, there can be no life for her Ka in the Field of Rushes.*

Really, Mikros could not shift the grin off his face.

Please to think, Megaleios, Eskedi begged, *of preserving her Majesty's flesh by embalming. Not to think of destroying her in the flames. Not to wipe out the name and power of the sister in the Afterlife.*

But Mikros did not want the sister to have power even after she was dead. He wanted rather badly to bring her dreadful power to a stop. He paced the fishy mosaic of his apartments, frowning. If he burned her up, she would be dead for ever, and he would be rid of her shadow, but if he bandaged her, he must meet her again in the Afterlife of the Egyptians, and endure the clang of her iron tongue, unhappy ever after.

I have no desire to meet the sister again, he said. *I do not wish to walk hand in hand with her through the Field of Rushes for the rest of time. I do not want to be bossed by her for all eternity.*

And so he told Eskedi, *We are Greeks here, she must have the Greek Rites.*

He saw the look of horror on Eskedi's face as he turned to go, but his heart was firm. *Burn her up,* he said to the Dioiketes, and the slaves began gathering the sticks of palm and acacia for the fire that would fry his sister like a side of Greek bacon.

Mikros was not wholly without mercy. He shoved not the usual two obols between her teeth, but one of his own gold dekadrachms, so that she might at least pay the ferryman of the Styx her boatfare, and give the wretched man a proper tip; so that she might at least reach her destination, even if it was not quite where she wanted to end up.

In later times men would dare to say there was no record of one single good deed upon the part of this Queen, but they were wrong, wrong one million times. She did very many goodly things, much that was very excellent for Egypt.

Truly, Megaleios, Eskedi said to Mikros, *the Sister was among the greatest administrators that ever lived, one of the cleverest women in the history of the Two Lands.*

Eskedi did not excuse her iron hardness. *A ruler must be hard,* he said. *Egypt needed ever a strong ruler. Soft is bad. Hard is good.*

For the Greeks a female murderer is a dreadful thing, but Arsinoë Beta's murders were nothing compared with what Alexander or Philip of Macedon did. By no means. Eskedi had loved her for her firmness, for her devotion to Egypt, for her generous offerings to the gods, for her constant kind attention to the requirements of Ptah of the Beautiful Face. Mikros might not have missed her, but Egypt missed her very much. For Egypt, the passing of Arsinoë Beta thirty years before her time was a very great calamity.

Eskedi wept for Arsinoë Beta dead, but even Eskedi, when he spoke of the late queen, would sometimes murmur, *Wisdom of Ani: a woman is like very deep water, her current is not known.*

If the solemn funeral of Arsinoë Beta looked rather like the Great Pompe, Stranger, it was partly because she had planned and ordered it to be so, and partly because her brother was too lazy to think of doing it any different.

The procession began at dusk, with flaming torches, and went on till dawn and the Pharos was left unlit for the first time, as a mark of respect. The fat lady of the Pompe wore black, and her towering ostrich-feathers was black. She twirled not at all but walked in a straight line. Dionysos and laughter were left behind. The five thousand horses were black, and the fifty-seven thousand black-clad foot soldiers marched the slow march to the gloomy drubbing of drums and the braying of solemn trumpets. There was no wine and no drunkenness (until afterwards).

The body of the beautiful Arsinoë Beta lay upon a wagon pulled by twelve of her black-and-white horses, whose stripes make a man dizzy to look at them, with black ostrich-plumes on their heads. Her funeral car was piled high with sixteen thousand seven hundred and forty-two white roses, one rose for every prickly day of her life. The mighty hydraulic organ of Ktesibios boomed its most mournful music throughout, so that no man could have slept even if he wanted to – but everybody stood on Kanopic Street to see the last journey of this very great Queen.

She was brought to her funeral pyre on the beach just before sunrise, when the procession ended. To put it simply, Alexandria blubbed for Arsinoë Beta. If you would only believe her, Stranger, Seshat would write down that the streets flowed with tears. It was almost the truth.

Dry-eyed Mikros lit the bonfire, and Arsinoë Beta's mortal remains hissed and crackled, eaten up in the usual wall of flames. The family and the courtiers, who knew her true character, stood looking out to sea, shifting their feet about in the sand for embarrassment, because it felt good to say: *Fare thee well, Arsinoë Beta, even in the House of Hades.* If they wept it was because the smoke got into their eyes and made them water. No man in his senses could have called it tears.

Of Mikros's sons, her adopted children, Ptolemy Euergetes, aged about fifteen, was still away at Meroë. Lysimakhos, perhaps thirteen years old, still lived up-River at Koptos. Only Ptolemy the Son was left at home to see the frying, and there was no tear upon the cheek of this warlike boy either. Ptolemaios of Telmessos, away in Lykia governing his own territories, was equally unmoved to hear the news. No, the family mourning for her Majesty was quite dry.

The Prince Arkamani was there, however, though he stood at the back of the crowd. Blackface Arkamani, in the dark, dressed in black, was just about invisible till he showed the teeth, but a tear fell down his face for his fierce patron, the woman who had been neither fierce nor unkind to him; the one he thought of as *Nya Nyanga*.

As soon as the smoke billowed, Ptolemy Mikros felt the first stabs of guilt. By burning her up he had rendered the sister a dead woman for ever and always, denying her entry to the Afterlife of the Egyptians, where he himself must pass his own millions of years. She would not now be Arsinoë the Ever-Living, could not be.

At the *perideipnon*, or funeral banquet, the dead woman was supposed to preside as hostess. Mikros wore garlands of flowers and delivered the eulogy, short, but full of nothing but praise, for the Greeks do not dare to speak ill of the dead. He stared at the chair set in the tomb for the sister, stared at its emptiness. *How, in any case*, the modern scientist in him thought, *could a dead woman be present anyway? She is dead and gone, gone for good.* He drained his golden cup of wine very many times. When he looked up again he saw a shadowy grey figure sitting in the chair, the skull with eyeless sockets and grinning teeth, her hair mangled once more, and she glared, as if to accuse him of burning her up when she had wanted the bandages.

Aye, how could she fail to haunt him? She had died too soon, and must hang about the world of the living until the natural span of her life was used up. Suddenly every hoopoe flitting about Mikros's palace gardens seemed to have the face of Arsinoë Beta, her long beak of a nose, the same beady eye and startled look. Her ghost fluttered about Mikros in his dreams; its bat-like squeaking kept him sleepless, like the proverbial donkey in the thornbush.

Mikros sighed. He could not undo the burning up. *Perhaps,* he thought, *I shall feel less bad if I follow, after all, the minute instructions of her Will. Truly, I did not realize quite how much Alexandria loved her.* For sure, Alexandria loved Arsinoë Beta almost to madness.

1.35

Beloved of the Crocodile

Aye, the dead sister's very great popularity took Mikros quite by surprise. Suddenly, he could not do too much to honour her and keep fresh her memory. He minted gold coins that showed her solemn bug-eyed face. He founded the great Alexandrian festival called the Arsinoeia, at which her solid gold statue was hauled up Kanopic Street on the shoulders of strong men. He raised a golden statue of her astride a bronze ostrich, to mark her famous victory in the ostrich race. He put up an altar to the divinised sister in the Agora and slew upon it countless horned beasts for her blood sacrifice – blood to keep happy her ghost.

He laid the foundations of a giant Greek temple with multiple Corinthian columns for the worship of Arsinoë the Gracious, Lover of the West Wind – the famous Arsinoeion. It overlooked the Great Harbour, and had the statue of herself reclining upon one elbow in the triangle of the pediment, surrounded by the Muses, for as Isis she was the first of the Muses, goddess of the sea, and patroness of sailors. Aye, and he had a seventy-two cubit high obelisk floated down-River from Heliopolis and dragged through the streets ofAlexandria by hundreds of slaves to stand in front of it, an Egyptian obelisk, tipped with gold that flashed in the sunlight for the sister of the Sun that was himself.

He built an Arsinoeion also at Memphis, within the precinct of his mud-brick palace, and he had a golden statue of Philotera housed there as well, so that his two sisters were worshipped under one roof – at least, until such time as Philotera's statue could be pushed into the shadows.

Arsinoë Beta was not alone in death, not short of a husband, for Eskedi made her the Great Wife of Ptah, and set up her golden statue even in the Temple of Ptah, at Memphis. Such was Eskedi's esteem for the sister that he put in his humble request to be made the first Priest, or Scribe, of Arsinoë Beta, and of Philotera as well.

Then the *prostagma* went forth from Mikros and Eskedi together that Arsinoë Beta was to be a temple-sharing goddess, her statue to stand beside the chief god in every temple, so that she was adored daily throughout Upper and Lower Egypt. It was the most unheard of thing, the most tremendous honour that could be paid her.

She was made a goddess even at Thebes, where the Thebans – never great friends of any King Ptolemy – let her wear the ram's horns of Ammon behind her ears, like Alexander, and gave her the august title Daughter of Amun.

The high priests even gave Arsinoë Beta a throne name of her own: Who is United in the Heart of Truth, Beloved of the Gods. The only queens to be so honoured before her were Hatshepsut and Tauseret, aeons ago, and they had ruled as kings.

Such exalted honours could never have been granted without the support of Eskedi. None of these almost unheard of things would have been done without every high priest in Egypt held this foreign queen in the very highest regard.

While Arsinoë Beta lived, Mikros had jested to his friends that one day he would fetch the largest magnet in Egypt and prove that she was not made of human flesh at all, but iron. Now he had the bright idea to put up an iron statue of the sister in the Arsinoeion at Alexandria. He applied his scientific knowledge, boasting that if a large enough magnet could be found, the statue would be sure to hover above the floor as a perpetual reminder of her metallic nature – and, of course, because the feet of a real goddess simply should not touch the ground.

It was just a jest, the famous irony of the Greeks, but the kind of thing that amused the Alexandrians, and so Mikros instructed Timokhares, his architect, to begin the work.

For all his enthusiasm to reward the sister, though, Mikros never finished building the Arsinoeion. Was his heart perhaps not in this project? Perhaps he could not justify the expense of such a gigantic building? Was the old Mikros re-emerging, who found it easier to do nothing? Or was it simply the case, after all, that he did not love the sister as much as they said he did?

No, Wise One, Mikros seemed keener now to adore his lovely concubines than his horrible sister. He said to the Dioiketes, *Bilistikhe is seven times more beautiful than Arsinoë Beta, let us make Bilistikhe Aphrodite instead.* And so it was. Bilistikhe found favour now, and Mikros made her the Eponymous Kanephoros of Arsinoë Beta as well, so that his concubine carried the basket in the annual procession in memory of his dead wife.

Better a live whore, he laughed, *than a dead sister.*

What will the Greeks think? the Dioiketes asked.

I do not care, Mikros said. *I am Zeus. I am Poseidon. I am Helios. I am Ra. I shall do what I like.*

He dedicated ornate golden shrines to the beloved Bilistikhe Aphrodite all over Alexandria, and the blood of bulls was spilled to honour his best of concubines as a goddess in her own lifetime. Then he put up statues of her in every Greek temple in Egypt in a sanctuary of her own. And had not Eskedi refused to allow such blasphemy, Mikros would have had the statues of this whore put up in every Egyptian temple as well.

Sure, Mikros suffered terrible pangs of guilt about the sister's Greek Afterlife, her everlasting sojourn down below, in Hades. *But she will enjoy meeting the members of the family who have gone ahead of her,* he thought. *Every new arrival in Hades receives a warm welcome from the long-established dead.* He wondered, for a moment or two, who, then, must greet her. Then he let out a shriek of mirth. *Why,* he laughed, *Agathokles of Thrace, the man she loved, the man she murdered. Bleeding Agathokles will greet his stepmother first in Hades.*

Mikros's shoulders shook to think of it. Tears of mirth poured down his cheeks. And yes, he thought, she would still be suffering from the bellyache, still asking for the Milk of Magnesia in the cellars of the earth, by the camel load. He found it a comfort to think that he would not find the sister slamming doors and throwing crockery in the Field of Rushes, where he would pass the Afterlife himself.

He had his best idea while he was attending to Pnephoros, the crocodile god, whose new temple-house he built within a court at Theadelphia, in the District of the Lake. Aye, it was when he saw the crocodile-god himself, his Living Image, strapped to a stretcher, with his smiling jaws wired up, carried in procession by the priests at his annual feast, that Mikros thought, *Surely, if her Ka assumes the form of any beast apart from the human-headed bird, it must be the crocodile.*

At Krokodilopolis, near the Lake, Ptolemy Mikros agreed to replace the old mud-brick Temple of Sobek with a brand new limestone building, inside a mud-brick enclosure wall. Up at Krokodilopolis the sister had delighted to stroke the god's nose. She had loved to send bracelets and anklets of gold, an hundred of geese, an hundred of pigs, an hundred of wine, for her crocodiles in the Sacred Lake there.

How may we best remember the sister in death? he asked himself. *How may we make the memory of her last in the District of Krokodilopolis?*

And then he smacked the thigh, for he had the answer. How fitting it would be to have the sister assimilated to the crocodile-god.

He murmured his private thoughts to Eskedi, the man who must approve the full Egyptian apotheosis of the sister: *She sent away my wife. She stole my wife's children and called them for her own, then did her best to turn me against them. She was so very like the crocodile. It is a small thing, but it is enough.*

He sent out the *prostagma* that the town of Krokodilopolis was to be called by the name of *Arsinoë*. Yes, and the entire District of the Lake, that had been the Krokodilopolite Nome, he renamed the *Arsinoite nome*, and made his sister the local goddess, so that she would stand smiling in the shrine of the crocodile god for ever. When people spoke her name they would think of his sister, her glittering eye, her snapping teeth, her false smile, her evil temper, and see the crocodile.

In this charming manner Mikros had his revenge; thus he expressed his undying hatred, disguised as undying love. In this delightful way he expressed his mixed feelings for his departed wife: his love and hate, his gratitude and loathing. It was at once an act of the greatest homage and the greatest contempt.

Eskedi approved, of course. The heart of Nefersobek his wife – whose name, you may remember, meant *Beautiful is the Crocodile* – was in joy. The Egyptians do not look upon Sobek with loathing, as Mikros did, but love him. Mikros had done exactly the right thing.

At Eskedi's suggestion he piled ever more Egyptian titles upon the dead sister, even giving her a Horus name and a birth name, as if she had been the King herself.

He called her Daughter of Geb, the earth god.

And Daughter of the Bull.

And the Great Generosity, the Greatly Favoured One.

And Image of Isis.

And Beloved of Hathor the Golden, Beloved of Atum.

He commissioned a triple statue for the Sarapieion of Alexandria, with Amun in the middle, Mikros on his right hand, Arsinoë Beta on his left, and Eskedi put words into the mouth of Amun, making him say to the dead queen: *I will make you a goddess at the head of the gods upon earth . . . I give you the breath of life that comes forth from my nose to give life to your Ba, to rejuvenate your body for ever.* Fine words, that made up, perhaps, for the fact that Mikros had wiped out her Ba for all time.

Why, though, did Mikros obey the sister's wishes to the letter, when it would have been so easy for him to ignore them? Stranger, she had so planned it that her curse must fall upon him if he departed from her orders in one iota. She had poured out the libation of undiluted wine upon the ground. She had spoken her solemn, chilling words while Mikros watched, open mouthed. His spine tingled to remember the spurting blood of lambs, her clawlike *dexiosis*, the harsh words as she made him swear to be true to her memory; not to play her false; her cackling vulture laugh.

In these times men truly believed in the overwhelming power of a curse. The sister was Isis, Great of Magic, and he was too afraid not to follow her orders. He might have laughed at first, but he was *more* afraid of her dead than living. He was quite capable of shedding tears of terror upon her tomb. All was done so that she should not harm him after she was dead, to keep happy her ghost.

He dreamed of her as Aphrodite Ourania, the Heavenly One, sailing through the night sky, riding not upon a great swan, as she should have been, but upon the back of a giant ostrich, with Ptolemy the Son perched in front of her. Often he woke up in a sweat, troubled by that wayward son of his. Mikros worried about that boy more than any other thing, just then, because he also dreamed of Ptolemy the Son hurtling towards him with knives fixed to the wheels of his chariot, trying to slice his father up.

1.36

Misfortune

Yes, indeed, Ptolemy the Son, the only son Mikros had left at home, was growing up angry and violent. He liked to strangle fowls with his bare hands. He was fond of torturing the palace cats, behaviour that would cause riot and revolution if ever the Egyptians got to hear of it. He was, even at nine years old, very like a boy with a demon. What would Mikros do with this lad? Some thought he should disown him, and said so. Others wagered that Mikros would do just what his sister ordered.

It was a simple thing, really: Mikros was a man of his word, and he had given his word. The sister had made him promise. When the Dioiketes came with a fresh report of Ptolemy the Son's bad behaviour, Mikros would not listen. When he questioned the wisdom of the succession, Mikros said only, *One must put up with the son that is born.*

At ten years old the Son began to race chariots, younger than was wise, because it is not easy for a mere boy to keep such a vehicle under control during twelve laps of the racing-track. Perhaps it was Mikros's fault, the indulgent father, who found it hard to say no to his only son, the son that he loved, but let him have whatever he wanted. The day came, of course, when, carved up by more skilful drivers, the Son flew right out of his speeding chariot and landed on his head in the dust, causing uproar in the Hippodrome. His injuries were nothing serious, but many thought this accident made him behave strange. Others said he was strange before the crash, pointing to his pinkish eyes, his pale hair, and the fact that his parents were full brother and sister. The incestuous marriage explained everything, they said: it was the wrath of the gods beginning to take effect.

The young Ptolemy the Son never stopped spinning the sword, throwing it up in the air and catching it. He was pleased to whistle aloud in the Greek sacrifice, where the law required total silence. Often, above the bellowing of the victim, came the laughter of the boy who must be Pharaoh.

Whenever the Son came to Memphis, Eskedi thought him more than ever the identical replica of his half-uncle, the war-mad Ptolemy Keraunos. The Macedonians could hardly complain of that, for to be warlike was what every Macedonian boy was meant to be, but already the Son went too far in violence.

On one solemn occasion he snatched the Blue Crown of War off Mikros's head and hurled it like the *diskos* into the air. Mikros screamed at him, but there was no beating, no proper punishment. The damage was done, though: the Son had thrown the crown away, and it was a bad omen.

What do the Greeks say? *A ruler must learn through being ruled. It is not possible to command without first learning to obey.* But Ptolemy the Son did not learn either how to be ruled or how to obey. Some said that it was not only the tail of this boy that was pig. The pig would indeed be butchered, but not yet. Before the day of blood must come the trouble. And yes, even though Pharaoh can do no wrong, the father was to blame. The mother, who had at least tried to keep him in order, was gone. Ptolemy the Son ran wild, and he was just like Mikros in that he said, even so young, *I shall do what I like.* He had even learned this from his father.

Apollonios Rhodios, the tutor of this rebellious pupil, had to tie his legs together so that he did not run away. Apollonios said of him only, *Wicked parents beget wicked offspring; the apple will fall under the apple tree.* But he did not dare to say such things to his Majesty.

Eskedi gave Mikros sound enough advice: *A boy's ears are to be found upon his back; he will hear if you beat him.* But King Ptolemy would not hear of beating the boy who was Harpokrates, the Young Horus, and so the Son went on doing what he pleased. Like father, like son, as they say.

Ptolemy the Son heard from Apollonios Rhodios the wise words of Kleobulos of Lindos: *A man should respect his father.* But he yawned to hear them. Sons often turn out unlike their fathers, but a son who is waiting to be Pharaoh, you might think he would look upon the old man with a little affection, help him along in his old age. Not a bit of it. The Son had already sworn never to help his father do any thing, except, perhaps, help him to die. Something had gone very badly wrong with this boy's upbringing. Perhaps it was the mother who was to blame, the mother, aye, who had done her best to make her son be like herself. The mother, indeed, who had brought up the son to despise his father, and taught him that he might, when he grew up, very easily take the throne from Mikros just as soon as he pleased; that there was no point in waiting for the old man to die. *Take what you want,* she had said, very dry. *You should make yourself like the snake, and strike quick.*

The odd thing is that, in spite of the trouble, Ptolemy the Son did not lose his place in his father's affections. He was the only son Mikros had left at home. As the heir to the throne, he wore the Horus sidelock of the Crown Prince, and had the rest of his head shaved, and he hated it. Up at Memphis he was the shadow at Mikros's side in every Egyptian ritual, and he hated it, hated the ritual baths in the Sacred Lake, hated the Egyptian costume he must wear. *A real man does not wear necklaces of precious stones,* he said. *I am a Macedonian. When I am king I shall fill this land up with Macedonians, and kick the Egyptians out of it, every one of them, and put their temples to the torch.*

Eskedi watched the Son throwing his sword and saw the same dark look that he had seen in Ptolemy Keraunos's eye, the same mad look, and he was troubled by it. Eskedi murmured even to his wife, *He is like the fool who will not hear; there is nobody who can do anything with him. He regards knowledge as ignorance and what is beautiful as something harmful. Men are angry with him every day.*

Ptolemy the Son scarce knew the number of his own fingers. He was not going to be clever like his mother. He would be like the mad dog that is chained up, who spends all day angry, barking at nothing.

Arkamani still lived in Mikros's palace, but he did not, as it were, bark at anything. The Macedonians garbled his name, calling him Ergamenes. Led by Ptolemy the Son, they mocked him for being different, for his thick lips and fuzzy hair, and called him Blackface. They laughed at him for being so very like the monkeys. Arkamani learned his Greek shivering in Alexandria, but he did not hate either the Greeks or their language. He was grateful to Ptolemy Mikros, his patron. Arkamani and Mikros, Meroë and Egypt, they were the best of friends.

Eskedi taught Arkamani the hieroglyphics and something of the wisdom of the Egyptians. In his turn Arkamani taught Mikros himself about Meroë.

Is it true, Mikros asked him, *that there are tribes lacking the upper lip, tribes without the tongue?*

Cut off by our enemies, Arkamani murmured.

And tribes that do not know about fire? Mikros asked.

No need of fire, Arkamani said, *in such a hot place.*

Even tribes, Mikros said, *that may speak only by nodding the head and waving the hands?*

Only because no foreigner can understand, Arkamani said.

Aye, the truth was that the Greeks did not understand this foreigner, and what they did not understand, they made fun of. The only education Arkamani was not given at Alexandria was military education. He was not allowed to pick up a sword. He was not even allowed to wrestle. He would be a scholar, lest he should learn how to rebel.

Arkamani raced chariots against Ptolemy the Son, who often won, and it may be true that his opponents let him win, because of who he was. Arkamani did not come first, not ever, but he was not bitter. *There are more important things than winning a race,* he said to Eskedi, *such as food for the people of Ethiopia; such as medicine for my people at Meroë* . . . but he had the sense not to say such things to Ptolemy the Son.

Eskedi saw the truth of it: that Arkamani would have made the better Pharaoh, but it was more than his life was worth to say so. But Mikros did not see the truth. He had a fresh outbreak of war to occupy his thoughts.

Two years after the sister's death Mikros was faced with fighting his first war without her help, the war called after Khremonides, one of the foremost politicians at Athens, who led the revolt of Greece against Macedonia. If you want to know the details, Stranger, it was all to do with the old cities of Greece, headed by Athens and Sparta, which had formed an anti-Macedonian League and were trying to get back the freedom that had been taken away from them one hundred years before.

The war began with Khremonides and Athens throwing off the rule of Macedon, when Khremonides' hopes of victory rested in getting Mikros to support him, for the Egyptian fleet had total mastery of the Great Sea. Mikros agreed to send his ships to Greece, because it was what his sister would have done, and he sent Admiral Patroklos to command it. Khremonides, however, had not done such a clever thing as he thought he had, because Egypt was already not the great sea-power she had been when Arsinoë Beta was alive.

In this war Mikros faced the formidable Antigonos called Gonatas, or Kneecap, a son of Demetrios Poliorketes. Antigonos invaded Athens and held up the Spartans at the Isthmus, while Patroklos kept the fleet riding at anchor off the coast of Attica – and did nothing.

Afterwards, Patroklos made his best excuses, saying that he had none but native Egyptians, famous bad sailors, but the rumour said that Patroklos refused to attack Macedon because he was a Macedonian himself – and that his loyalties lay with Macedon, not with Egypt.

Mikros had joined the Anti-Macedonian League, following the last wishes of Arsinoë Beta, who had left her orders telling him what to do if war broke out. But things had changed since her death, and her advice did not fit the complex troubles he was now faced with. He did not much want to sail to Greece himself. He preferred, as ever, to stay at home with his concubines.

So what did Mikros do? In the past he might have asked an oracle, but the sister had urged him, *You must be bold in matters of war.* Always she had said, *You must not rely on nonsense like omens and the flight of birds. Think for yourself. Never be afraid to attack.*

Mikros liked time to think things through. *Decisions* were so troublesome to him that he often ended up doing nothing. To suspend judgement was, in fact, part of his philosophy. And he did nothing now, except follow the sister's policy, as before.

The sister had been pretty good at thinking ahead, pretty smart at guessing which fleet would move where, and when. But Mikros could only make sense of his fleet when the ships were in front of him, riding at anchor. It was the same with the army: he could not see what should be done unless the men stood still. Once they started to move, and the battle was hot, and the boots kicked up the dust, he was soon confused. He could never keep a track of the cavalry, for the horses moved too quick. The truth was that he could only think of one thing at a time, and most of the time, in any case, he was thinking about *aphrodisia.*

Where war was involved this King was like a man with two left hands. He was *erotikos* – amorous – not *warlike.* Mikros and his late sister, they had complemented one another perfectly. But now – he had lost her.

Such were the problems of Ptolemy Mikros. He was not a fool. He was even a great king, for that he knew what were his shortcomings: that he was no good at organizing a war, absolutely no good.

Just then Mikros was more interested in the progress of Eudoxos of Knidos, who had built an observatory at Alexandria for watching the stars, and was the first to teach the Greeks something of the motion of the planets. Mikros had been pleased to join the astronomers, and learn about the mysteries of the heavens. He had been heard to say, *It is worth the stiff neck from looking upwards, if a man can see the red planet* . . .

Mikros was interested in the stars. Star were meaningful, important. War was nothing but pointless bloodshed, a waste of a man's energy, a waste of money. His generals and admirals were quite capable of running a war without him. Mikros hardly took any notice of the Khremonidaian War. But the result of it was that Kneecap got back Macedonia and crushed Epeiros, leaving Athens under siege. Athens, bombarded with flaming missiles, surrendered, the Alliance lost the war, and Mikros's fleet was thrashed by Agathostratos of Rhodes: half his great oared galleys were sunk, half his sailors drowned, and Kneecap was laughing at him, the king who could not win a battle.

The result of the defeat was that Khremonides himself fled to Alexandria, where he and his idle brother Glaukon entered Mikros's service, and Khremonides took personal command of the defeated fleet, what was left of it.

Mikros did not refuse to employ Khremonides after the failure of the war that bore his name. He was still in Ptolemy's service, still an admiral, eighteen years afterwards.

Why did he let Khremonides enter his service?

Mikros said, *For some reason the gods would not allow Khremonides a victory. The misfortune was not Khremonides' fault.* Khremonides was his friend. It was because he liked Khremonides. Really, Mikros had not a clue how to handle military personnel. In Alexandria they began to say: *Ptolemy Mikros does not know how to make war . . . he only knows how to make love.*

Throughout this war Ptolemy the Son, now perhaps thirteen years old, was co-ruler with his father. Mikros sent him off with Berenike, his older half-sister, to see the war of Khremonides, and learn about battle at sea, but they passed the time on board a *trieres* watching Patroklos do nothing, and although Berenike loyally insisted that Patroklos was a fine admiral, Ptolemy the Son thought he was just as useless as Mikros.

The eldest boy, Ptolemy Euergetes, now maybe seventeen years old, did not see that war, or any other war, for he was still in exile at Meroë. He had not been brought up with any expectations that he might succeed his father. Euergetes spent his days on horseback, chasing elephants, catching them with a noose round the hind leg, or by digging a pit on the path to their watering-hole. Or he might hunt giant snakes, for his father's Beast Garden. He was perfectly content.

The Nubian horoscopists told Euergetes over and over again that he would be Pharaoh after his father, but he did not so much as dream of going home to Egypt. He had no great wish to be a king. He had gotten used to the terrible heat of the south country. He did not hate his father for sending him away. By no means. But for the time being he stayed where he was: the out-of-favour son of Arsinoë Alpha, who could do nothing right, whereas Ptolemy the Son, however badly he behaved, in Mikros's eyes seemed perfect.

As for Berenike, the one that would be called Syra, she was fifteen years old, still living at home in Alexandria. Her breasts had outgrown the required three fingerbreadths in height that meant she was old enough to marry a husband, but she was not betrothed to any man. No, for Mikros was saving her up, against the day when he might make use of her to seal his peace with Syria.

In Year Twenty Mikros sent Ptolemy the Son, the co-ruler, the favoured one, to perform the dedication ceremonies for the new Temple at Mendes on his behalf. It was Eskedi's idea to give this boy some responsibility, to make him more mature. He said to Mikros, *An Egyptian prince does not do nothing but should make himself useful.* He thought also to train up the next pharaoh to think more of duty than pleasure.

So how did the Son fare at Mendes? Not too well, Stranger, for he refused to have his hair cut or the feathers shaved off. He declined to plunge his body into the Sacred Lake for the purification, saying it was filthy, full of pigeon shit. He laughed aloud and screamed like the vulture during the ritual. He refused to honour the stinking goat, the one-time Beloved of his mother, with offerings and sacrifice. Everything he did was a defilement of the sacred place. It was all as Eskedi had forecast.

Did his Majesty show anger when he heard of it? No, he did not. Did he have sharp words with that wayward son? No, of course not. He did nothing, said not a word. To Eskedi he said only, *This is but boyish mischief. He will behave himself when he grows up.* The Son was Harpokrates, the Young Horus. His fate was to be Pharaoh, Strong Bull, a living god, the one who could do no wrong. Mikros would not hear one word against that son, but was like a man besotted.

Eskedi, however, saw the boy's future in his heart. He knew that Ptolemy the Son was next in line not for the throne but for an early death; that he had barely five years left to live, and that his death, like his life, would be violent.

Ptolemy the Son had been no more than a lad when Arsinoë Beta died. But had she not taught him a very great deal? In her last days she had found the time to give him the last of her wise advice, showing him the road upon which he must go – the road of unpleasantness, poison and sudden death – teaching him her old maxim: *Too much niceness is the way to destruction.* She also told him, *You should not be afraid to kill in order to have what you want.*

You will be a god. The gods may do just what they please.

Arsinoë Beta had given up all hope of Ptolemaios of Telmessos taking the crowns of Egypt. Mikros had sworn never to let a son of Lysimakhos of Thrace succeed him. Ptolemy the Son was the sister's last great hope for the heirs of her own body to rule Egypt. And Ptolemy the Son behaved just like his mother's son, full of fire and rage, full of a furious desire for power and riches. He was born sulky, born rebellious, just like Ptolemy Keraunos, angry even at having to wear the *chendjyt* kilt. So often it pleased him to refuse to do as Mikros asked. Now it amused him further to thrust the point of his sword under the Pharaoh's chin and see him tremble. The first time the Son did this, he stopped when Mikros asked him to stop. But when he waved the sword, laughing, under Mikros's chin the tenth time, and did not stop when he was told, and could not contain his hysterical laughter, and calmed himself only when Mikros screamed for the guards to drag him away, something had to be done.

But what could Mikros do? He could not deprive the Son of the co-rulership, for there was no one else to give it to. He had sent his other sons out of Alexandria, never to return. Beating the Young Horus, he would not do it. Mikros took the decision, then, at last, to send Ptolemy the Son out of Egypt altogether for a while.

The Son would not like it, of course. He would not like it at all. Mikros knew there would be an ugly meeting, in which the Son would shout, refuse to go, offer violence, and behave just like his mother. No, Mikros did not tell the Son he was banished until he arrived in Miletos. Only when the ship tipped him out on the quay was the Son told to stay there and obey orders; that if he tried to enter Egypt without his father's say-so he would be arrested and imprisoned. His father's letter said, *All this is for your own good. You remain the heir to Egypt, but you shall not return here until you have learned some Greek manners.*

It was the good people of Miletos, then, who witnessed the tantrum of kicking, shouting, screaming, and swearing by the gods, instead of his father.

Four years passed, during which the anger of the Son boiled up. Aye, anger, for Miletos was the back of beyond, a place full of rough hired soldiers, Gauls and Thracians, and the Son liked Alexandria better. These years in Miletos were meant to civilize the Son, to make him see the mirror of himself, the rough ones, and want to change his ways. Unfortunately Miletos would have quite the wrong effect upon him, quite the opposite effect. The Son did not acquire civilized manners at all, but was moved to throw in his lot with the barbarians.

1.37

Radiant Heat

If the children of Ptolemy Mikros fared not so well, the family of Eskedi flourished. Not many years after the passing of Arsinoë Beta, Young Anemhor, Eskedi's grandson, the elder son of Padibastet, now twenty years of age and a junior priest in the Temple of Ptah, began to gather many offices. Padibastet said to him, *Now that you are thriving, you should set up your own household, you should think of taking a wife.*

Anemhor first saw Herankh as she was drawing water from the River. He spoke to her as she stood by the stall of the Apis, waiting for an oracle.

The first words he said to her were, *Your lips are like the lotus bud. Your arms are like the curving boughs of the young sycamore tree,* when Herankh's shy smile made his heart leap like the oryx, and swell for love. His dreams were full of her lips, full of her breasts, that were like the ripe fruit of the strawberry tree, and of her voice, that was soft, like the Sweet Breath of the North Wind.

Take note, Wise One, that unlike the family of Ptolemy, in the House of the High Priest of Memphis the sons do not marry the woman of their father's choice, but choose for themselves; and that although you yourself think that to marry the sister is the common Egyptian custom, in this house they did not do this at all, not once in twelve hundred years. And why not? As Eskedi said, *Fresh blood is good. To marry the sister is not forbidden, but neither shall we encourage it. To marry the sister may be good for the gods, but it is not so very good for mankind.*

He had seen enough deformed calves to know that inbreeding brings trouble, nothing but trouble.

When Herankh married Young Anemhor she was made a priestess in the Temple of Sakhmet, the lioness goddess, who is the Wife of Ptah. The great delight of Herankh was to play the *seistron*, and to make music to please the god. She also made music for her husband, like all Egyptian women. She did not learn to read and write the hieroglyphs. She had enough to do making bread and beer, helping Nefersobek and Neferrenpet run the household of the High Priest. For sure, she did not undergo the basic weapons training, like the daughters of the Ptolemies. She was not urged to be tough, violent, angry. Nor was any other woman of the Egyptians.

Young Anemhor was the great scribe in the High Priest's family, and his rise in the temple hierarchy came fast, for he was made Royal Scribe for Financial Matters in the Temple of Osiris-Apis, then Scribe of Arsinoë Philadelphos. Ptolemy Mikros was pleased to find a place for Eskedi's grandson. Truly, his promotion was nothing to do with his grandfather being High Priest of Memphis, nothing whatever. Young Anemhor was among the wisest, among the most deserving.

Padibastet already spoke of his son in the words of the Instruction of Ptahhotep:

> *The wise man is known by his wisdom.*
> *The great man is known by his good deeds.*
> *His heart matches his tongue,*
> *His lips are straight when he speaks.*

Of all his offices in the temple Young Anemhor loved best the care of the Apis. And did he give the Sacred Bull one hundred times more attention than he gave the cult of Arsinoë Philadelphos? Did he think that a native Egyptian would make a better pharaoh than Ptolemy? Was he not sympathetic to the priests of Thebes who wanted to get rid of the Greeks and have an Egyptian pharaoh again? Anemhor did not speak of such things. His loyalty to King Ptolemy was absolute. He had no thought to stir up rebellion. His life's work was to preserve Maat, the proper order of things in Egypt, and to keep back the forces of chaos.

Herankh showed her affection for Anemhor by rubbing noses with him, so that he said, *When I kiss her I am drunk without a beer.* Soon her belly began to swell, and she awaited the birth of her first child in fear of Seth, god of confusion and disorder, who governed, among other things, the misfortunes of pregnant women. Herankh need not have worried. She was guarded by many other gods.

All children are welcome to the Egyptians, who do not cast out their daughters like so many of the Greeks, but a man is always delighted to have a son to carry on his family line. A son will look after his father when he is old and infirm, just as the father looked after the son in his infancy, when he was helpless. A son will bury his father when the day comes for him to go to the Beautiful West.

Herankh's son was called Djedhor. His entire life would be dedicated to the service of Ptah, the great god. To serve Ptah of the Beautiful Face, the creator of the world, was the heart's desire of everybody in that family.

*

Young Anemhor's lifetime would be marked by great violence in the Greek world, when war followed quick upon war. In the clash that was called the First Punic War, Rome was pitched against Carthage, when the Carthaginians sent messengers begging Mikros to help them. They said they remembered the generosity of Mikros's father to the island of Rhodes in her hour of need, and that now the Carthaginians would be glad of whatever relief he could spare, but they specially needed money for siege-engines, catapults, bolt-throwers; money to build more modern ships of war.

Mikros sent word back to Carthage, saying, *Both parties in this dispute are our friends. We have long since given our promise to stay neutral in any war.* He was relieved not to be involved. Once again the sister's work was shown to be wonderful. She deserved her titles and divine worship, and he stepped up the blood sacrifice for her scowling ghost.

Soon after, Mikros named Apollonios as his Dioiketes, but please not to confuse him, Stranger, with Apollonios Rhodios, who was the Director of the Library. The fresh Apollonios was a merchant and landowner, with many ships at his disposal, who imported goods from Syria and Anatolia. Now he took charge of Egypt's performance in war, and must try to fill the sister's place, step into her shoes of fire. The name most often upon the lips of Mikros at this time was not Bilistikhe, or Didyme, but Apollonios. Regardless of the hour of the day or night, Apollonios had to come at once. Often he had to run.

In Year Twenty-Five of Ptolemy Mikros, when Eskedi was eighty years old, and growing frail, Nefertiti his granddaughter was married to Akhoapis. It was a good match for the husband was Scribe of the Gods of the Temples of Memphis. He was Master of the Secrets of Rostau, Who Enters into the Sacred Place. He was Purifier in the Secret Chamber. He was Master of Secrets of the Temple of Ptah. But his first office was High Priest of Letopolis.

Not long after this a second son was born to Young Anemhor and Herankh. They called his name Horemakhet, or *Horus Who is in the Horizon*, which happened to be the name of the Great Sphinx of Memphis. Horemakhet's horoscope said he must be High Priest of Memphis for as long as forty-three years. It was his fate to live through the reigns of three Ptolemies, and be the greatest Egyptian in the Two Lands. He would live sixty-six years, seven months, and seven days exactly.

They did not bandage any child in that family, and the house was filled with the laughter of happy children. The father said, *There will be plenty of time for the bandaging later.* How different from the family of King Ptolemy, where the house was so very often full of quarrelling, and where the son and heir – even at sixteen years old – hated his father enough to want to kill him.

Time passed, so much time that soon, even in the house of the High Priest of Memphis, somebody must die. Eskedi was stick-thin and the wisest man in Egypt, but by night he complained of the cold in his fingers, and of cold feet. He knew just what was the length of his life as laid down by the gods, and that his days were running out, but the thought of it did not trouble him, for he had lived a life of virtue. Death, for him, was more like moving house. He even looked forward to it, for he must meet the gods he had served all his life. His deepest wish was to be buried close to the tombs of the Apis bulls, across the River, up on the desert edge, above Memphis. He had built his Mansion of Millions of Years there himself. His new house was ready and waiting for him.

Neferrenpet sat with Eskedi in his last hours. She had been his wife for thirty years. She had been the Great Musician of Ptah, the most accomplished musician of Sakhmet the lioness. *Ancient One*, she called herself now, smiling, for her face was wrinkled like the face of the tortoise. On the very last of Eskedi's twenty-nine thousand five hundred and sixty-five days there was no struggle. The old man lay quiet in his bed, waiting for Anubis, the god who would lead him away to the Field of Rushes. When he saw the black dog he smiled his half-smile, and closed his eyes.

His last words were, *May the floodwaters never fail to come . . .*

Padibastet placed the embalmed and bandaged body of his father inside two massive wooden coffins. Eskedi's face was painted on the outer coffin, his youthful face that had long since been covered with wrinkles. That youthfulness would be restored in the Afterlife, and his great brown painted eyes shone, and the half-smile was still upon his lips, serene in death, sailing in the night-barque with the gods. Now he was a god himself, an Osiris, the Osiris Eskedi, with the golden skin and curled beard of a divine being, young for all eternity.

Padibastet did not place the usual papyrus scroll with the chapters of the Book of the Dead written upon it that the ordinary dead man needs, his indispensable Guidebook to the Afterlife, for Eskedi was no ordinary man. He knew those vital chapters off by heart. He knew the map of the Afterlife just as well as he knew the back streets of Memphis. No, Padibastet gave his father a much better thing, for he put into his coffin six blank scrolls of papyrus – each of them ninety cubits long, more than five hundred cubits of papyrus altogether – with his reed pens and cakes of red and black ink, so that Eskedi might be a scribe in the Afterlife; so that he might go on writing for ever.

Last of all Padibastet put in the coffin the *hypokephalos*, a disk of linen coated with plaster, decorated with four baboons worshipping the Sun, and inscribed with hieroglyphs. The moment when Padibastet slid this object under his father's head was magic, for it caused a glowing halo of flame and heat to surge through his father's body. Always Eskedi had shivered in the chill damp winters of Alexandria. The *hypokephalos* would keep him warm in the Afterlife, where it could be just as cold as it was by night in Memphis. Padibastet saw the shining for himself, just as his father had promised. He felt the heat spreading, and he closed the lid upon the golden face.

The Ka – or soul – of a dead man may sometimes be seen as a bird darting among the palm trees near his tomb. The Ka may also take on the outward form of some other object, such as a lotus flower – symbol of immortality – or a serpent, or many other things. Eskedi's Ka surely took the form of the ibis, the bird that is Thoth, for Eskedi was Thoth in all things, wisdom made flesh.

Padibastet was fifty years old when his father died, old himself by Egyptian standards. He was already Prophet of the Temple of Ramesses at Memphis, and Master of Secrets of the Temple of Ptah, and Overseer of the Mysteries in the Lake, and Prophet of Horus the Falcon, and Prophet of Arsinoë Beta, and Prophet of Isis, and Prophet of the Living Apis, and a Count and Prince of Egypt. Now he was made first of all the priests of Egypt.

Pharaoh himself came to Memphis to anoint the hands of Padibastet to his office. When Ptolemy Mikros stepped off his golden barge Padibastet was there to greet him, wearing pure white linen, and the leopard-spot mantle. He bowed down and kissed the ground seven times before Pharaoh, and the people of Memphis, gathered there in their thousands, did the same. Mikros pushed the two gold rings on to Padibastet's fingers, and placed in his hands the staff of electrum. *Thou art hereby made High Priest of the god Ptah,* he said. *His treasuries and granaries are under thy command. Thou art chief of his temple; all his servants are under thy authority.*

Modest though his personal habits were, Padibastet now took charge of a great household – his head steward, his chamberlain, his staff of scribes, guards, gardeners, cooks, bakers, butchers, messengers and sailors – hundreds of servants, more than any man after Pharaoh.

Padibastet knew the secret name of the god. He knew how to change the order of things, and make time run backwards, if he wanted to, but he wished to change nothing. In Egypt change was bad, staying the same was good.

Padibastet was not meant to make the world tilt. He must not upset the delicate balance of the Two Lands but keep the balance, fighting back the forces of chaos. For sure, he had prospered, but the rolls of fat upon the belly that many high priests had, he did not have. He ate little. He drank wine seldom. His soul sat light upon his body, very like the feather, just as it should.

For this great but humble priest, almost as important as being First Prophet of Ptah was to inherit the office of Scribe of the Rations of the Cow in the Temple of Memphis, the Divine Cow, who was Mother of the Apis, and become the Prophet of the Living Apis himself. Always, when he was in Memphis, he fed the Divine Cow and her now very great calf with his own hand. Eskedi had loved the Apis and his mother so much that he kept his offices till the day he died. Padibastet his son loved the Apis even more than his father did.

1.38

Bloody Tears

The years passed and Arsinoë Beta had been ten years a jar of ashes upon a ledge in the Tomb of Alexander. Mikros had survived four thousand days without his sister's wise advice, sound judgement, sweet smile and filthy filthy temper. Every man had murmured on her death, *What will he do without her?* How, indeed, had he survived without the irreplaceable one?

Sure, he had Apollonios the Dioiketes, and his military advisers, his men who sounded as if they knew all about war, ships, the olive-oil trade, and the proper level of the pig tax – all the things Mikros did not want to think about. His advisers were good enough, but they were neither so fierce, nor so forceful, nor so sure of their every move as the Great Generosity. All his financial advisers put together were not half so good as the sister.

Mikros suffered, then, four thousand restless nights of not quite knowing what was for the best in foreign affairs, but somehow muddling through, somehow hanging on to his kingdom. His subjects, Greeks and Egyptians alike, complained about the severity of his rule, but he had learned severity from the sister. Some men murmured that Alexandria was not quite such a friendly place as it was under his father, nor Egypt neither. It was Padibastet, who foresaw the drift of things, foresaw the revolution, and he warned Mikros of the future, full of trouble.

How may we avoid these troubles? Mikros asked. But Padibastet gave the same answer as his father before him: *Only one way, Megaleios, you must build bigger temples, you must make bigger offerings to the gods.* But Mikros had learned his lesson now: he did whatever the High Priest wanted. Padibastet knew best, just as Arsinoë Beta had known best. The troubles at home would not, in fact, come in Mikros's lifetime. First came the distraction of war, so that in the excitement of repelling her enemies Egypt quite forgot about revolution.

When the golden statue of Arsinoë Beta in her temple at Cape Zephyrion was reported to have moved, spoken, sweated, and then to have *wept*, Mikros drove his chariot there to see it with his own eyes, and the court followed, chariots and horses thundering up the Kanopos road after him.

How could she make her statue weep? Mikros muttered all the way. *She is no more a goddess than the boats in the harbour.*

Mikros ran – an unheard of thing – up the temple steps and strode into the sanctuary alone, angry at having his sleep disturbed, and the courtiers waited outside, as if holding the breath. Ah, how his heart was encouraged to see the sister's face once more, faintly smiling, Egyptian-style, with the Atef Crown upon her head, complete with snakes, and with the Horn of Plenty tucked in the crook of her left arm. He might just as well have put up a statue of Sobek himself.

He peered into her golden eyes. He tapped her copper eyelashes with a finger, pinched her inlaid silver nipples, rapped his knuckles on her infuriating smile. It was just a statue, perfectly dry. He made as if to go, but on the threshold turned back to take one last look. Now he saw beads of moisture on the sister's golden brow. In her right eye there welled up what looked like a drop of dew. He stared, horrified, as the dewdrop rolled down her golden cheek and dripped on to her golden breast, for it was red. Arsinoë Beta was weeping tears of blood.

Mikros was shaken. The fourth time he went back to check that he had not been tricked, it was about an hour after dawn, and he stood before the statue, listening. There was no sound but the chirping of the birds, and the waves washing on to the beach. Then he heard the voice of the sister say, *Get your armour on, Brother . . . We are at war with Syria . . .*

From the temple steps Mikros shouted, *Sharpen your swords . . . we are being invaded,* and the silence of the courtiers gave way to uproar.

The news that the troops at Babylon were on the move came within the month.

Mikros, seldom ready for any thing, was not ready for a fresh war. This time, to make things worse, he must fight without the sister's magnificent generalship, without her magnificent bad temper, and every oracle promised him eight years of disorder, two thousand nine hundred and twenty days of bloodshed.

Mikros had breathed easy for too long, far too easy, ever since he heard that his great enemy, Antiokhos Soter was dead. Hearing that the new King of Syria, though a young man, was weak, Mikros had stopped thinking about war altogether. Now he must act, because the weakling had gotten himself muscles.

This mighty Pharaoh turned his fury, then, towards a new enemy, the second King Antiokhos, called *Theos*, or God. He was twenty-six years of age, not weak at all, but full of fire, burning to lay his hands upon the valuable territories of southern Syria, Palestine and Phoenicia, wilfully stolen from him by Egypt. Mikros was not so young, forty-nine years old. He would be fifty-six before peace broke out. Eight years of uncertainty would turn him into an aged man. Mikros was the weak one, just then. It was not a full-scale Syrian invasion, however, but the folly of his own son at Ephesos that began this fresh war, the Second Syrian War, as they called it. Aye, for the idiot Ptolemy the Son, barely nineteen years old, now announced his intention to take up arms even against his own father, thinking to topple him from his throne and make himself King of Egypt in his place.

1.39

The Revolt at Ephesos

Ptolemy the Son was supposed to undergo the Macedonian-style military training at Miletos. He had a tutor to teach him the art and science of state-craft, the theory and practice of government, and it was but a making ready for ruling Egypt when his father died. To make his stay at Miletos seem less like banishment he had been given charge of the garrison, even though he was young, and a generous allowance of gold tetradrachms. He had his advisers to make sure he did what was right. He would not, Mikros thought, have too tough a time of it in Miletos. But the truth was that the Son rebelled from the start. He beat up his tutor, and managed to fall in with Timarkhos (*tim-ARK-ohss*), an Aetolian, from western Greece, who was one of the leaders of hired soldiers in Ionia. The tutor soon fled, saying it would be easier to teach the Sphinx to dance than Ptolemy the Son the Greek irregular verbs.

Timarkhos the Aetolian, the roughest of rough men, perhaps forty years of age, had pitched his camp of leather tents outside the walls of Miletos, from where he sent gifts of fine chariots and fast horses to Ptolemy the Son, and turned this unruly prince into his friend. Timarkhos told the Son stories of his life as a hired soldier – of his wars and massacres; of the delight and pleasure of killing. They drank a great deal of the powerful wine of Miletos, undiluted, when Ptolemy the Son took Timarkhos into his confidence. *I hate my father,* he said. *I loathe the way he sends me his orders, telling me what I must do, what I must not, demanding always a report of my every movement from his spies.*

You could bribe the spies, lad, Timarkhos said. *You could make them write your father He is Doing Well. Your money will keep his spies quiet.*

The Son grinned like a fool.

You could be King of Egypt as soon as you like, lad, Timarkhos told him, *with the help of a man like Timarkhos.*

The Son could not stop laughing. The thought was already in his heart.

You could be King of Egypt tomorrow, lad, Timarkhos said, *if you attached yourself to my leadership. I too should be pleased to see the King of Egypt a dead man.*

Ptolemy the Son had found in Timarkhos the Aetolian, then, a man who thought the same as himself. And so these two began to plot the murder of his Majesty.

Ptolemy the Son passed his days in the camp of the hired soldiers, where Timarkhos taught him advanced swordcraft and siegecraft, catapult science and marksmanship with the bow, advanced throat-slitting and disembowelment, and he was a rather more willing pupil than before. Timarkhos improved his technique until he was an Olympian pip-spitter. Timarkhos became this boy's hero, as much as Hektor or Lysander.

By night Timarkhos took the Son to the house of whores, showed him what was to be done, and what was not. He made sure the Son knew about olive oil, and the sling, and to ask for the *periplix* or the *amphiplix*, the serpent coils, all the things that delight a man the most. Timarkhos took this boy drinking and whoring, whoring and drinking, and fixed him up with a woman of his own, the beautiful Eirene. Timarkhos could not put a foot wrong. Ptolemy the Son put his whole trust in this criminal, aye, and it was like the blind man who relied on the lunatic to hold his hand, and walked with him over a cliff.

You might wonder, Stranger, what Mikros's officers were doing all this time, why they did not take the Son in hand, but he was the garrison commander himself, in charge of them, not the other way about, and he did much as he liked – as if he was Pharaoh already. He got away with it because he *would* be Pharaoh, because Mikros's command was slack, and because he gave his comrades double rations of wine, and warned them not to tell his father what he did.

No, Mikros did not hear that the Son lived the same rough life as his hired soldiers. The Son had gotten for himself all the iron hardness of his mother, eager for the great adventure that was rebellion against his father. And had not Arsinoë Beta suggested it herself? Had she not told him he would make a far better king than his miserable father? He bribed the officers who were going home to Egypt not to complain of him. The officers took his money, for sure, because this boy would be the next Pharaoh, and they thought of what kind of treatment he might deal them then if they betrayed him now. And so Mikros heard nothing of the trouble that the Son was cooking up in Ionia, no, not one word.

When a report from Miletos did, at last, reach Mikros's ears it troubled him so much that he had the Son moved to Ephesos, his main army base, among different company, with more to occupy his time in the way of keeping the peace. The Son was not pleased to be sent to Ephesos, the city built upon a swamp, where he was bitten by flies, but Timarkhos and the hired soldiers followed him, setting up their tents outside the city walls, as before. Discipline was just as slack among the troops at Ephesos. They never saw the Pharaoh's face. Why should they bother to obey him? Mikros did not know the half of what went on in his army. Nobody in Ionia took much notice of King Ptolemy's orders. And so the Son found it a simple matter to bribe the officers there as well, and carry on doing what he liked.

Padibastet, however, spoke with a traveller from Ionia and got wind of what was like to happen. He said to his Majesty, *Behold, they say he goes forth to follow at the heels of this Timarkhos, having cast off allegiance to his Majesty. He tarries with him like one of his vassals. He is hot in his desire to destroy his father.*

Mikros frowned. *I do not believe it,* he said. *It is not possible. It must be lies.*

Mikros only dealt with trouble when it happened, not before it happened. He thought of his philosophical principles, the Kyrenaic School, of the words of Aristippos: *Concern with the future causes nothing but anxiety and should therefore be avoided.* Above all, Mikros must keep his heart free from anxiety. And so he did nothing about the Son. He carried on eating flamingo and visiting the concubines, as before. Often he attended to nothing but his *aphrodisia*, just like his son and heir.

And Padibastet? What could Padibastet do, without the sanction of Pharaoh? He waited for the news to come, knowing very well what it would be. The gods had plans of their own for the House of Ptolemy. Padibastet waited, patient. It was a mistake to interfere with the will of the gods.

The Son spent his twentieth birthday drinking wine with Timarkhos, nine bowls, ten bowls, eleven bowls, dreaming of his violent rule over Egypt.

I am urgent to be Pharaoh of Egypt, the Son said. When I am Pharaoh I shall make you, Timarkhos, Great Chief of the Army. You shall have rich farmlands of your own in the District of the Lake. And Eirene, best of whores, shall be Queen of Egypt, the Mistress of Happiness.

Timarkhos drank a toast to the future, roaring drunk; all Ephesos was drunk under the governorship of Ptolemy the Son. Every man did what he liked, dreaming of a golden future when the Son was King of Egypt. As commander of the garrison that held Ephesos, the gateway to Asia, the one-time city of Arsinoë Beta, Ptolemy the Son had the money and authority to hire thousands of extra soldiers if he needed them to deal with some emergency, and that is what he did. He hired the half-wild half-mad men of Thrace, Greek-speakers, but barbarians nonetheless, who had no very good reason to be friends of King Ptolemy – or, in fact, friends of his son. For sure, the Son still had his advisers, for that he was young, and lacked military experience, but he said, *I do not like to be told what to do.* And he bribed his advisers to leave him alone so that he might lie in bed all day with Eirene, or sit up drinking all night with Timarkhos – behaving, in fact, just like his father.

At Ephesos Ptolemy the Son had his comforts. He had no reason for complaint. No young man in the world had a future more promising than his, but Ptolemy the Son was still dissatisfied. Why did he not wait? He was still the heir. He would have his kingdom in the end. Why should he want to rise up against his father? Seshat has not the answer, except to say that he had his mother's impatience to have a thing done today rather than tomorrow. For the rest, this boy must have been mad, for only madness accounts for what he did next.

Aye, for Ptolemy the Son now threw off all pretence of loyalty to Ptolemy the father and set himself up in opposition to him. He sent his messenger to Alexandria to declare war even on the Pharaoh of Egypt, saying, *We shall treat you as our enemy. Resist us and you shall be a dead man.*

This boy thought he could take on the entire armed forces of Egypt – sixty thousand foot, five thousand horse, one hundred and fifty ships of war – and win. Impossible, you might think. But the Son knew that his father was weak, indecisive, barely able to walk; that he had no interest in war; that he passed every afternoon in the arms of his concubines. He knew, or thought he knew, how easy it would be to murder him and take his power. Ptolemy the Son thought he would very soon be Strong Bull, Mighty Ruler himself, far mightier than the Sister-Loving One.

With Timarkhos's help the Son poisoned his own military commanders, or cut them up with the sword, and put his Thracians in their place. All the hired soldiers now attached themselves to the revolt and swore allegiance to Timarkhos and Ptolemy the Son instead of Ptolemy Mikros. It was Timarkhos, however, who proclaimed himself Tyrant of Miletos, Timarkhos who invaded the island of Samos, Mikros's major naval base – that was the mooring place for the Egyptian fleet in the Aegean Sea because of its magnificent harbour – and helped himself to Mikros's dozens of oared galleys. Ptolemy the Son had not the supreme command in this rebellion, but let Timarkhos take charge of it.

This time Mikros had to believe what he was told, and the shouting from behind the closed doors of his council chamber went on for half a morning. Stung into action, he had the word published regarding Ptolemy the Son: *Speak of him as one who is dead. Mention his name no more.* Upon the instant he deprived this boy of the co-rulership, saying to Padibastet, *Strike out his name wherever it is found. We shall have nothing more to do with him.*

But when Mikros spoke, his voice cracked, as if he might weep.

The revolt at Ephesos escalated, meanwhile, with Timarkhos winning successes and gaining confidence by the day. He was Tyrant of Samos and Miletos. Soon he would be Pharaoh of Egypt himself, and Ptolemy the Son, just as dispensable, just as worthless as his father, would be dead. Timarkhos laughed to think of it, and encouraged his co-revolutionist to drink as much as he could, and to lie in bed just as late as he pleased.

Back in Alexandria Mikros found himself heirless, fretting lest he should die during the night without having resolved the problem of the succession. There was only one thing he could do: he must bring back his eldest son from Ethiopia, his half-forgotten son. Aye, he named Ptolemy Euergetes as his heir for the second time, and ordered his return from Meroë.

At the same time he sent Arkamani back to his father, speaking fluent Greek, laden with gifts, a friend of Egypt, or so it seemed.

We pray to the gods, Mikros murmured as he watched him board the ship, *that our treaty of peace with Meroë will be upheld by Greek philosophy . . .*

But Arkamani had been on the receiving end of far too many insults by this time to be thinking of peace. He was already studying the philosophy of war.

When Ptolemy Euergetes walked into his father's palace, forty days later, he was perhaps twenty-five years old. He had been out of Egypt so many years, and his face was so darkened by the southern sun, that Mikros knew him only by his yellow hair.

I am Tryphon, he said, and he threw himself upon his belly before his Majesty, who raised him up and embraced him in tears.

You are my only son, he said, *for that other I count no son of mine.*

Euergetes had fared well in the South Country, very well. A boy who has gotten used to crawling head first into the den of snakes fourteen cubits in length and pulled these monsters out of their holes by the tail will never be afraid of anything again in his life.

But there it is: Ptolemy Euergetes was the heir to Egypt once more, and there was the most extraordinary change about. The almost forgotten son was restored to favour, and the favoured son, who thought to kill his father, lost everything he had been promised, threw it all away. Soon that idiot would lose even his life.

Meanwhile, on the island of Samos, Timarkhos and Ptolemy the Son had cut the throat of Mikros's general, and all the senior officers stationed there had perished with him. Aye, they planned to murder every last supporter of Mikros, until there was no man left to fight for Egypt. But just here the calculations of these two adventurers began to go wrong, for one morning the hundred warships of Antiokhos Theos of Syria appeared on the horizon, supported by the fleet of Rhodes. Before dawn, while Ptolemy the Son was still lying in bed with Eirene, and while Timarkhos slept off his usual nine bowls of wine, Antiokhos' troops waded quietly ashore in the half-dark, and stabbed to death the dozing guards and every hired soldier in sight. Antiokhos' men had the city of Ephesos under their control before breakfast, when they set about the customary orgy of looting and burning.

Ptolemy the Son had never taken much thought for the welfare of his hired soldiers. He had not been generous with their wages. He had not made himself agreeable by ordering the triple ration of wine on days of festival. He had no experience of high command in time of crisis, nor of handling hired soldiers on a battle footing. Nor did Timarkhos, in the end, inspire any confidence, for how could a mere captain of hired soldiers hope to take on the Pharaoh of Egypt and win? Timarkhos looked like a man who must be beaten. Ptolemy the Son looked weak and inexperienced. The hired soldiers changed sides upon the spot, much as usual, and swore everlasting allegiance to Antiokhos Theos instead.

The Son, woken by the smoke and crackling of his house burning down, ran barefoot through the colonnaded streets with Eirene, dressed in nothing but his breechcloth, finding it convenient, now, to put his trust in the gods and claim sanctuary in the great Temple of Artemis, where no god-fearing man would dare to commit a murder. Artemis was the moon goddess of the Greeks, whom they called Lady of Wild Things, and she was supposed to be the patroness of young lovers such as these two. But really, Ptolemy the Son had never bothered to honour Artemis, or any other deity. The gods would give him what he deserved: rough treatment.

The Thracians, no longer his friends, ran after him with drawn swords. Aye, the clatter of soldiers' boots followed the Son and Eirene as they dodged into dark corners, and hid in doorways, panting for breath. For sure, they reached the famous Temple of Artemis of the Ephesians, but hired soldiers do not worry about the sanctity of temples. Before Ptolemy the Son could reach the doors he was run through, with much squealing. As the lifeblood poured out of him those pinkish eyes bulged in his face. He clutched at his belly as the guts tumbled out at his feet and he was a dead man. One of the grinning Thracians hacked off his head and held it up by the long pale hair, dripping blood.

Eirene clung to the temple door, sobbing prayers to Maiden Artemis, claiming her protection, and shrieking, *Let me live, let me live, I have done nothing wrong, nothing to deserve death, I am a Thracian just like yourselves.* She might have saved her last breath, however, for the splash of red soon raced across her white garments, and her blood poured out on to the marble steps.

So much for heartfelt prayers; so much for the patroness of young lovers. Proof, you see, Stranger, that you cannot undo the thread of your life; you may not change your destiny. It was the fate of Ptolemy the Son to die young, die violent, not to be saved at the last moment by prayers to the moon goddess of the Greeks, who was, in truth, ever cold and disdainful. You would be better advised to put your trust in the moon gods of Egypt, Stranger, in THOTH, and in Khonsu, who is called Traveller, like yourself, not in the false gods of Greece.

Timarkhos the Aetolian laughed to hear of the death of Ptolemy the Son, but it was not his fate to survive him by very many days. His name does not feature in the pages of History again. Of his end Seshat knows nothing, except to suppose that it was bloody. The people of Ephesos and Miletos moved quick to hail Antiokhos Theos as their Saviour – in fact it was on that day that he came to be called *Theos*, God, because the Ephesians now pressed this august title upon him. They had not benefited from the brief rule of Ptolemy the Son and his rough friend. The Son could spit an olive-pip further than any other man in Ephesos. That was about all there was to be said for him.

When the news of this upheaval reached Ptolemy Mikros in Egypt he slammed doors and smashed vases for an hour or two. To behave in such a manner will go some way to make an angry man feel better. But from his private chamber there came also the sound of a man weeping. Mikros had loved Ptolemy the Son, in spite of his multiple faults, and it is one of the very few instances of genuine affection in the House of Ptolemy. Mostly these Macedonians hated each other's guts. But the Son had been Harpokrates, the Infant Horus. He had been the Strong Bull in waiting, the great hope of Arsinoë Beta. All a waste of time. All a waste of energy. The other son, the son of the traitor, would not fill the gap that was left in Mikros's heart. Not then, not ever.

Thus, at any rate, the cities of Ephesos – or Arsinoeia – sometime the personal property of this boy's mother – and Miletos, became enemy territory so far as Egypt was concerned. And that was how the Second Syrian War, against Antiokhos Theos, began.

1.40

The Taste of Fingers

Aye, Stranger, a man's death is the will of the gods. Even the defeat of a man's fleet may be the will of the gods. The will of the goddess Seshat, Lady of the House of Books, is that you, Stranger, should go on reading her divine words.

In Syria itself Mikros's armies fought a campaign round about Year Twenty-Six of which Seshat is meant to know nothing. You might suspect, Wise One, that if even Seshat knows nothing of it, Mikros did not quite come out of it covered in glory. He rode into the desert to fight, not because he wanted to, but because it was what the sister would have demanded. Syria is not a cool place in the summer months that make up the campaigning season. The biting flies made their feast upon his Majesty's flesh. The water supply dried up. Everything that could go wrong did go wrong, and that was before Mikros got anywhere near the field of battle. Forget the roar of war,

Wise One, forget the trampled dead, the circling vultures, the rhythmic clash of sword on shield before, and the quiet weeping after; forget the sickening stench of rotting flesh. Far better that Seshat should pass over the humiliating defeat of Ptolemy Mikros in silence.

Three years of uncertainty and minor engagements went by, and then matters came to a head in the sea-battle of Ephesos, an historical occurrence of which, one more time, Seshat is not meant to speak. Warned that the Rhodian fleet was heading for the Ionian coast, and that he must do battle, Mikros summoned his most warlike spirit and when he told the council of war, *We shall make Rhodes taste the taste of our fingers,* the generals banged the fist and roared approval, for Mikros was sounding warlike, at last. He gave the order to make ready the fleet for sailing, under Admiral Patroklos. When all the gear was loaded and the crews were on board, the trumpeter blew for silence, the ship captains said the customary prayers to Poseidon, and poured offerings of wine into the sea from gold and silver cups.

Mikros ordered the proper Greek sacrifice to Poseidon – a black bull with gilded horns – the women screamed the ritual scream, the blood gushed forth on to the beach, and the great head hung limp. But when the bull's belly was ripped open the Greek priest could find no good omen. For all the old man's frantic searching among the tangle of pink guts he could but spread his bloody hands, shake his head and look at the ground for dismay. The god was not with Mikros and Egypt, but had withheld his favour.

Mikros ordered a second black bull his throat slit, but still no good omen came forth. Alexander, to be sure, would have faked a good omen, so that he could do what he wanted, without the hindrance of the gods, but Mikros was not Alexander, nor much interested in Alexander either, and the memory of how the great man had gotten over such minor difficulties was fading fast.

After the third black bull hit the sandy beach, Mikros heard the angry voice of the sister inside his head, saying, *While appealing to the gods, one must also help oneself.* Mikros muttered something about the gods being in any case of little account, then he said, *Let us set sail anyway,* and he gave the order for the trumpet to sound, and the fleet to move off.

The men were uneasy, but the word of Pharaoh is law, and so the oars of his one hundred and fifty swift ships of war were raised over the water, the humming of the oarsmen started up, that helped them row in time, and one by one the ships dodged the Hogsback Rock and the Diamond, the reefs that are the sharp teeth of the harbour mouth at Alexandria, and raced each other across the sparkling sea to Ionia. The dolphins, creatures held sacred by the Greeks, raced alongside, and it seemed like a good omen at last.

But Poseidon ever was a cantankerous god.

Up-River, at Memphis, Padibastet lit the brazier in the Temple of Ptah. He chanted the spells that bind the enemies of Egypt, worked the best of the state magic that is guaranteed to destroy every foe. He floated seven papyrus ships of war in a tub of water: ships with *Antiokhos* written upon the side in red ink. Padibastet set fire to the ships, hurled rocks and sank them, screaming words of power. Just as the model ships burned and sank, so the real ships of Antiokhos must burn and sink, and his sailors must drown.

Padibastet had told Mikros, *Antiokhos, to slaughter is his joy, but it will go well with you,* but Padibastet was wrong. He might have been sinking Egyptian ships of war for all the good his magic did.

When Mikros's fleet met Antiokhos Theos' ships off Ephesos a few days later, a terrible, unmentionable, defeat took place, and the dead bodies were washed up on the beaches for days afterwards, faces torn by the fish.

So what went wrong? For sure, Patroklos had loaded every ship with the incendiary bomb made of pitch, sulphur, tow, pine sawdust and granulated frankincense, the great invention of Aineias the Tactician. For sure, he had packed the right ingredients into the sacks. For sure, he had given the ship captains fire to light the fuses. But a rough sea during the night made the sacks wet so that only one bomb went off, its flame fell short of the target and fizzed in the water, useless.

For sure, Patroklos checked that Ktesibios' engines of war were in full working order, with Phoenician engineers in charge, men fully qualified to fire them, but the rats chewed through the ropes during the night, so that he could not fire even one machine.

They said Mikros lost this sea-battle because he lacked the wisdom and guidance of Arsinoë Beta, and that, perhaps, was the real reason, the best excuse. The sister was dead, and he had not been able to find a minister of war who was her equal.

Mikros went through the motions, demanding an explanation. He railed against the gods of Greece and Egypt together for letting him down. He raged against himself for letting the sister die. He swore at the sister's ghost for leaving him to fight on his own. Whatever was the reason for this disaster, Ptolemy ordered the Sea-Battle of Ephesos to be left out of the annals, to be as if it had never been. This engagement was not a defeat, nor even a misfortune: it never took place.

At least trouble abroad was not matched by trouble at home, for in that year the rise of the River measured ten cubits, six palms, and two fingerbreadths. *The Flood is sufficient,* Eskedi told him. *Egypt will not starve. The threat of rebellion is over for another year.*

The peace with Meroë held up, in spite of Ptolemy Euergetes and Arkamani being no longer hostages in each other's territory. But the war with Syria went on, on and on, five, six, seven years of war. Mikros suffered further disastrous losses in the Aegean Sea about which Seshat is allowed to say not one word. At Alexandria the naval dockyards were kept busy, repairing, rebuilding, refitting the old, or building new ships of war to replace what was sunk without trace or smashed beyond recognition.

There was much trouble about the coast of Anatolia, a region of white beaches, fine for landing ships, where the Seleukids held the hinterland, the mountainous interior, and the Ptolemies the seaboard and all the ports. Mikros retained some kind of vague agreement with the pirates who had once been helpful to his wife in battle. Sure, the pirates said, they were still willing to offer him a little help. They won a few skirmishes at sea, set on fire a few Syrian ships, then their support dwindled away. Antiokhos Theos proved to be better organized, better equipped, and to have better naval advisers. The gods gave him victory after victory in Kilikia and Pamphylia, letting him win back territories lost during the First Syrian War. Aye, Mikros lost control of all this fertile plainland, and all the prosperous cities with good harbours where he liked to park his fleet. Worse still, he lost the lands bordering on the Gulf of Adalia, that produced one of his favourite wines. Mikros pretended not to know, but spread the rumour that he was doing well in his war, that the gods did nothing but smile upon the Macedonians in Egypt.

He slept as easy as a man can sleep who has been defeated in battle, who has lost the help of his more warlike sister, and whose beloved son and heir has betrayed him and been murdered by barbarians, his body left in the sun for the dogs' and birds' feasting. Mikros dreamed that Egypt was being invaded from all directions, heard the tumult of battle, saw his sister's ghoulish face, glowering under the crocodile helmet, and woke himself up night after night shouting for her ghost to come back and help him. But Seshat says: *No ghost ever won a battle.* Mikros was alone indeed.

1.41

The Feast of the Tail

A year later, when Mikros's fleet put out to sea in battle order, still under Admiral Patroklos, he tripled the recommended sacrifice to Poseidon, and took great care to wait for the right omens before sailing. He made waterproof the incendiary bombs. He kept the rats out of the ropes that strung the engines of war. Nothing could go wrong. Mikros wore the *khepresh* and managed to restore the permanent half-smile of the Lord of the Two Lands to his lips, confident of a naval triumph. He even sailed with the fleet himself, to take personal charge.

Kallinike, he shouted to the fleet just before the casting off, showing all the teeth, punching the air with his fist.

Kallinike, the sailors and oarsmen roared back at him – *Beautiful Victory.*

Alas, it would not be so.

The waters off Kos were calm, clear, blue, full of fishes when Mikros's fleet arrived. From the swift ships they could see sandy beaches, goats in the fields, shepherds with their flocks. But on the day of the clash the wind whipped up a rough sea. Had Mikros been any use himself he might have given the order to hold to. In the normal run of things, if weather conditions were not perfect for a fair fight the battle would be cancelled. But Mikros did not give the order, and his one hundred and fifty superb oared galleys began to take on water.

Mikros believed that an admiral should take decisions for himself. But even an admiral expects some leadership, and Patroklos looked to Mikros to signal what was to be done. He would do exactly what Mikros wanted, but Mikros had the last word, Mikros was meant to decide the strategy. But Mikros was waiting for Patroklos to take the lead.

Afterwards Mikros remembered the hail of flaming bolts, the phenomenal thwack of the giant catapults fired from the decks, the great blow as his flagship was rammed and splintered. He remembered thrashing about in the sea, going under, being fished out by Patroklos himself. Fires burned upon the water. Through the drifting smoke the Egyptian fleet was difficult to make out: three out of four ships of war had broken up.

So what went wrong this time? Arsinoë Beta's great strength had been training. In the past she made the galleys row out on calm days to rehearse manoeuvres. But because there was no Arsinoë Beta to give the order, the ships lay idle in the ship-sheds, and the oarsmen sat in the wine shops day after day, drinking. Truly, Mikros was more worried about keeping his women ready for active service than the need to keep his fleet fit for war.

Padibastet, of course, could find only one explanation for what happened. *Montu is angry with you, Megaleios,* he said. *The god of War must be kept happy if his Majesty is to win his battles. It is the gods of Egypt who will help him win.* Aye, it was easier to blame the gods than to blame human failure, especially if the human failure happened to be the Pharaoh himself.

But this time Mikros dismissed Padibastet, saying, *We have spent more than enough on your pathetic gods.* In the Council of War Mikros shouted at his admirals. He hurled fruit, golden plates, golden cups, anything that came to hand, screaming abuse. But behaving like Arsinoë Beta did not make much difference. Mikros was not Arsinoë Beta and never would be, thank the gods for that.

To Padibastet the next best way of making the gods look with favour upon this Pharaoh who would not build seemed to be to let him celebrate his jubilee, for it happened that the misfortune at Kos took place in the thirtieth year after he became co-ruler. The purpose of the jubilee is to make the old king young again, and the timing was perfect, for Mikros, at fifty-four years old, was beginning to look old indeed.

The festival that the Greeks called *Triakonteteris*, and the Egyptians *Heb Sed*, or Feast of the Tail, marked the anniversary of this king putting on the bull's tail for the first time thirty years previous. Padibastet was in charge of the ceremonial, and he told Mikros about the ceremony of running before Min, the fertility god, whom the Greeks thought of as Pan.

His Majesty's divine power, Padibastet said, *has been weakened by the hard life of earthly beings. Now it shall be made new. Pharaoh shall be made young again.*

Mikros wore his face of Do-Not-Think-It-Possible, but he agreed to do what must be done, this time. It was not in his nature to rage against a man so mild-mannered as Padibastet. He had regained his balance. He even begged forgiveness for his ill temper, something the fabulous sister never did.

By tradition the Sed Festival was held at Memphis on the first day of the first month of the Season of Emergence, when the Flood of the River begins to go down, and the fertile land reappears. Mikros was carried in the *skollopendra* from his palace to the place of the Sed Festival, by the necropolis of Memphis, at the spot that you, Stranger, may have heard called Saqqara. Mikros co-operated in every matter. He put on the ceremonial white cloak. He mounted the steps of the dais and sat down under the richly decorated canopy. He allowed Padibastet to crown him anew with the Red Crown of Upper Egypt, the Lady of Dread, then with the White Crown of Lower Egypt, the Lady of Spells. He sat patient through hours of prayer and chanting in the ferocious heat, all in a tongue of which he understood nothing more than his own name. The gods and goddesses of Egypt bestowed upon him renewed power. In return, despite previous reluctance, he promised them manifold offerings of bread and fowls, beer and onions, and endless worship. He even managed to keep the half-smile upon his face throughout.

But when Padibastet told him he must actually run a race, upon his own feet, against the Apis bull, Mikros made the face of Absolutely-Will-Not-Do-It. He was too hot to run. He had barely walked in thirty years, let alone run a race.

The race is the most important part of the festival, Padibastet explained, *when Pharaoh runs, wrestles, jumps and dances. When the Apis runs with him, his Majesty will be made young.*

Mikros made the face of We-Think-It-Is-Ridiculous. He sat still, refused even to stand up. His smile had disappeared.

Padibastet said, *The priests of Egypt beg his Majesty not to displease the gods.*

Let a younger man run for us, Mikros said, glowering.

His Majesty must run, in person, Padibastet said, *for the making young to be successful.* He pleaded with Mikros, before the assembled priests of Memphis and all Egypt, thousands of them, to do what every Pharaoh in his position must do. But Mikros sat with his arms folded, unsmiling. Sweat coursed down his cheeks.

In the end, though, it was always easier to agree with Padibastet than to resist him. At length Mikros stood up, unsteady, almost a stranger to the use of his own legs. He walked down the steps of the dais, to the starting line, and then, by some miracle, he did run, very slow, arms pumping the air, puffing, pouring with sweat. The heart banged in his breast. The flesh of his jaws flapped up and down. His belly wobbled. He panted like a dog, and Apis was persuaded to run alongside him, the placid bull, led on a tether by Padibastet's grandsons – Djedhor, now aged fourteen, and Horemakhet his brother, now aged eight. Apis ran slow, drooling from the mouth, just as reluctant as his Majesty. Apis bellowed, his great tongue lolled, his eyes showed fear. There was no winner in this race, which was as it should be, for the Apis and his Majesty were equals, but the old king was made young by it, magically made young.

Mikros returned to his palace reborn, with a youthful body. In himself he felt no different, apart from the aching of his legs. In the bronze mirror his face looked the same as before, if not older. *Made young, it is nonsense,* he said to himself. *How could it possibly be true?* He still badly needed a renewal of his failing powers, and Antiokhos Theos of Syria knew it, for he was already sweeping south into Koile-Syria with a mighty army, eager to smash Mikros with the final blow.

1.42

Blank Pages

Exactly what happened in Syria? Mikros undertook a campaign there in the spring or summer of Year Twenty-Six. And beyond that? Stranger, Seshat must explain away four years of mysterious silence, and you know very well what that means: four years of inconclusive war, if not four years of humiliating defeats. Seshat says that if Mikros's one hundred elephants, his phalanx of sixty thousand foot, and his five thousand horse had ground the myriad forces of Antiokhos Theos into the dust – we should know about it. If there had been a great victory it would have had a name, would it not? And there would be some word of the triumphal celebrations, some trace of the temples put up to commemorate it, and some record – inscriptions in honour of Montu, Lord of Thebes, and Ares of the Greeks, the gods of War who had sponsored the slaughter.

But no, there is nothing but silence, a profound silence, that makes Seshat think of the beat of vulture wings in the gathering dusk, and the squawk of gorging crows, and the distant cries of orphaned children. Seshat sees night falling over a battlefield carpeted with the Egyptian dead, and the sand blood-soaked, littered with bronze debris, the mangled armour of Mikros's troops, and the twisted bodies of the dead. Let the wind blow the sand drifting over this unfortunate picture. Let us cover it up, forget that it ever happened. That is what they would have wanted. Turn the page, Stranger. Let us think of pleasanter matters.

On the other hand, maybe Seshat should try to fill up the blank pages of History. That, after all, is what Seshat is meant to do. She owes it to Ptolemy Mikros and Egypt to do so. These four years contained this great Pharaoh's last battles, the last glorious military campaign of this very great monarch. He was not quite the inactive ruler that his sister made him out to be. He did many other things that Seshat has not the space to mention. Half of his story, after all, is lost. Seshat has just the bare bones of it, which she must flesh out as well as she can. At the best of times, Stranger, all the goddess of History has to go on is a few fragments.

Aye, should we not rather imagine Mikros riding out, the old king, for the last time, at the head of the right number of troops, having waited for the right omens, having gotten himself organized for the first and last time – as if to prove that he was not the useless commander his sister thought him, by no means, but one of the very greatest kings of his line? He had his reasonably competent military advisers. He had also two mighty fine sons: the perfectly able Ptolemy Euergetes, now aged somewhere between twenty-seven and thirty-one years, in the prime of his life and at the height of his military abilities; and Lysimakhos, Strategos of Koptos, the capable governor, the very excellent general. These young men, whom Mikros had willed himself to forget about for twenty years and more, were his first generals. Mikros was not alone. Of course not.

Ptolemy Euergetes, the heir, comes now to the fore. He is Strong Bull in waiting. He is Harpokrates, the Young Horus, the one who rides on the back of the crocodile, and he has the power of all the gods of Greece and Egypt behind him. Of course. Euergetes was in charge, astride his white horse with the leopardskin saddlecloth. He wore the lion's-jaw helmet with the red plumes. He was as much as Alexander himself.

Aye, Mikros saw the face of his enemy now, the young Antiokhos Theos, through a haze of sweat, through the yellow fog of kicked-up dust, amid the uproar of battle that was like the duck rising from Lake Mareotis, surprised by hunters at dawn, and Antiokhos Theos, covered in blood, looked like a man who would be defeated. Mikros would not have fought in person. He was an old man clinging to the rail of his chariot, a tired old man wearing the *khepresh,* assisted by all the magic of the gods of Egypt, for sure, trembling with emotion, watching from a distance the glorious victory won for him by his sons.

But what of his daughter? Where was Berenike? Was she with her father in the chariot, looking on? Or did she ride with the horse herself, waving her sword, screaming murder to the Syrian? For this is important. Seshat is quite sure this young woman was present on the field of battle. Even as a child she had been taken to see the war; the family custom was for even the girls to wield the sword and fight alongside the men. Berenike had been trained to fight. If she cut down even one of Antiokhos Theos's warriors with her terrible sword, she would have been the enemy of Syria for ever more. Aye, and it was just so. She rode out every time to fight the Syrian, *Just as good as a son,* as Arsinoë Beta had so very often told her, and it would be her undoing.

Euergetes was the one who shouted to encourage the troops before the battle. Euergetes gave the order to advance, urged on the elephants of war, screaming for Egypt and Victory, leading from the front, not fearful of getting blood on his face. Euergetes led the five thousand horse; Lysimakhos commanded the phalanx of tens of thousands. One battle is much the same as another, Stranger. The elephants lumber forward, trumpeting. The phalanx roars murder. The horses scream. The blood flies out. The chariots are smashed. Men writhe on the ground, wailing. Then the vultures rise and fall. Then comes the darkness, what the Greeks call the sleep of bronze.

Euergetes, covered in blood, galloped his horse after Antiokhos Theos, held the knife to his throat, captured him and spared his life. Would that, for Berenike's sake, he had killed him then and there. But no, Euergetes was a man of compassion, a man with normal human feelings, a merciful man, and he spared the life of Antiokhos Theos, his first enemy.

It was Euergetes that dealt Syria such a blow that Antiokhos was forced to the negotiating table, to talk of peace. If this was no triumph for Egypt, because the losses were so great, it was no disaster either, for although Antiokhos Theos fought with the entire military force of Babylon and the East behind him, he did not succeed in prising the coveted territory of Koile-Syria from the grasp of Egypt.

However it happened, it was by some rather more effective magic of the gods than running races with a bull that later in the year, the thirtieth year of his reign, Ptolemy Mikros came to an agreement with Antiokhos Theos about peace, bringing to an end his seven or eight years' war with Syria.

Mikros was desperate for an end to this war, so desperate that he stopped thinking about whether what he did was right. For this brilliant diplomat now gave voice to the clever idea that had been in his heart for many years: to offer Antiokhos Theos the hand of his daughter in marriage. Aye, the lovely warlike Berenike mentioned above, battle hardened and fully trained in the arts of war and diplomacy, aged now about twenty-seven years, he offered in marriage so as to make the peace binding, and Antiokhos, by some fluke of fate, agreed to it. Euergetes was not asked for his thoughts. Perhaps he might have married this sister himself, after the example of his father. But no, Mikros had a different, and better, plan. Euergetes was lined up to be married to a different Berenike, Berenike of Kyrene. It was the most wonderful piece of cleverness, whereby Mikros would achieve peace both east and west, with Syria and Kyrene together — by the simple ruse of two brilliant diplomatic marriages.

The terms of the treaty stated that the border between Egypt and Syria should be fixed at the Eleutheros River, north of Tripolis. The war with Syria was declared to be over, and the peace was to last until Mikros and Antiokhos were dead men, but would be renewable by their heirs, and it seemed a fine thing, at the moment of the signing. As for Koile-Syria, Mikros said, *To Hades* with Koile-Syria. Let Antiokhos have it if he wants it so badly. If the loss of Koile-Syria is the price of peace, let it be so, let him keep it. Koile-Syria never brought me any thing but trouble.

Berenike herself did say to her father, I do not want to be a Seleukid, Pappos. I have no desire to live in Syria. I have no wish to marry my father's old enemy. But Mikros screwed up his face, saying. My ears are full of grit . . . and made believe he could not hear a word she said.

1.43

Berenike Phernophoros

Yes, Stranger, it was to put an end to his Second Syrian War that Ptolemy Mikros dreamed up a peace treaty that would be sealed for ever by the marriage of Antiokhos Theos to his daughter, Berenike, who got to be called Syra because of it.

Aye, King Ptolemy was pleased to send his only daughter into a foreign land, rich in lions and bears and panthers, to dwell among murderers. The Seleukids, they were little better than beasts themselves, very like to claw the daughter of their much-loathed enemy to pieces. Seshat asks, How could Mikros let himself do it? But the answer is simple: he would have done almost any thing to have an end of that war. It was nothing for a great king of this time to marry his daughter to a complete madman in return for even a temporary cessation of hostilities. Sometimes all would turn out for the best with such a marriage, sometimes not. Everything was in the gift of the gods.

Berenike had been brought up very tough indeed. In this last battle she had proved herself able to drive a chariot just as well as a man – and much better than that late great charioteer, Ptolemy the Son. She had shown herself as warlike as Arsinoë Beta, wielding her sword and spear in this battle just gone by. At home she had demonstrated her skills with the javelin and diskos, and it was all the good work of Arsinoë Beta. Berenike Syra was a proud daughter of the House of Ptolemy, wondrous warlike, a credit to her father.

In the spring of Year Thirty-Three Mikros rode part of the way with his daughter to Syria. With them travelled her vast dowry in Nubian slaves, fast horses, fine linen, household goods of solid gold, incense, myrrh, and a small mountain of spices. There were countless sacks of gold tetradrachms, all with the bulging eyes of Ptolemy Mikros and Arsinoë Beta, the Brother-and-

Sister-Loving Gods, staring out of them, but the most important part of the dowry was the vast tracts of land in Koile-Syria and Palestine that changed hands with her. So very great was this dowry that Berenike got herself a nickname from it. She was Pharaoh's Daughter, the rich rich rich Berenike *Phernophoros,* the Dowry-Bearer.

The Syrian marriage was a fine marriage, marred by one thing only: the fact that Antiokhos Theos already had himself a wife, his surpassing beautiful cousin Laodike (*lay-oh-DEE-kay*), a granddaughter of Seleukos Nikator, King of Syria – though some said she was Antiokhos' full sister. Antiokhos Theos even had his heirs already, two sons aged nineteen and fourteen years, who were hot to have his throne and kingdom when he was dead, but in order to get his hands on the lost territories of Koile-Syria Antiokhos agreed to the foolishness of naming the son of Berenike Syra – when she had a son, if she had a son – as his heir instead.

It could be, Stranger, that even in the beginning Mikros was the victim of a trick on the part of Antiokhos Theos. If so, Mikros utterly failed to see it, but plunged blindly onward, like the man in the sandstorm. Ptolemy Mikros must indeed have been one of the stupidest men in the history of the world, both before and since, for he failed to foresee the dreadful things that were bound to follow. He had dreamed up Berenike's Syrian marriage, but he was a man who famously lived for the day only. *The future,* he always said, *will take care of itself.* Had he paused for just one of his precious passing moments to think about the future, he might easily have guessed what must happen in Syria.

All the same, Mikros had made it plain to Berenike why she must go: *Your marriage means peace,* he told her, *but it also means trade, for we need cedars of Lebanon to build our ships; we need Syrian bitumen, myrrh, balm and frankincense for our rituals of mummification. We have urgent need of Syrian dates, Syrian figs, Syrian wine for the palace kitchens.*

Without Syrian goods, life in Egypt would be very dull for Mikros and his concubines. He did not feel guilty for sending Berenike Syra away. It did not trouble his heart that he had sacrificed his daughter in return for an uninterrupted supply of luxury groceries. He smiled to think that the future King of all Asia would be his own grandson. He believed he had created a masterpiece of diplomacy worthy of Arsinoë Beta.

At Pelousion his Majesty told Berenike Syra for the last time that she was beautiful. He wished the traitor's daughter all the blessings of Tykhe, goddess of Good Luck. He embraced her like an ordinary father, as if he had real affection for her. It did not occur to him that Antiokhos' promise regarding the alliance might be false; that he was only interested in getting his filthy hands on his lost territories.

Write to us, he said. *Do not just disappear for ever* . . . but Berenike did disappear, and it would be for ever. She rode her camel into the storm of sand, and her face would not be seen in Egypt again. She would write many letters, but as it turned out, her father would ignore most of them.

The last thing she said to Mikros was, *Do not worry, Pappos, I shall have no trouble in Syria. You know that I can look after myself.*

Mikros did not worry. He was rather relieved to see the back of Arsinoë Alpha's daughter, whose face reminded him of his first wife, the one he had banished, the one he had loved.

Berenike was entrusted to the care of Apollonios, to deliver her to Antiokhos Theos somewhere north of Sidon. Three of her waiting-women rode with her, Gellosyne, Panariste, and Mania, and also Aristarkhos, first of doctors. The official reason for his going into Syria was to look after Berenike's health, to taste her food for poison, and if ever she found herself in any kind of danger, to fetch her safe back home to Egypt. But the underlying reason for his going was to keep her alive, and to make sure that she brought forth the son who would keep the peace with Syria in force for ever.

Aristarkhos would not save the life of this high princess, though. On the contrary, he would help her to lose it. No man may interfere with the workings of fate, and the horoscope forecast for Berenike Syra was that she must come to a most unfortunate end.

Aye, indeed, as Padibastet murmured to his sons, *What is it the ordinary people say? We would rather marry our daughter to the crocodile than to a Syrian.*

Exactly right, Stranger.

Berenike Syra entered the city of Antiokheia-upon-the-Orontes, the royal capital of the Seleukids, with the famous dowry strapped to the backs of one thousand racing-camels. The Antiokheians hissed her for the daughter of their great enemy, but the hissing was drowned out by Syrian drums and trumpets. Antiokheia made merry, for the time being, and no man that saw her magnificent procession emerge from the desert ever forgot it.

It will be no surprise to you, Stranger, to learn that Berenike Syra, a daughter of the House of Ptolemy, was not quite as other women. For a start she refused to drink anything in Syria but water drawn out of the River Nile, so that the procession of camels trotting between Antiokheia and Alexandria was never-ending.

Berenike Syra's water may have been meant for the ritual ablutions of Isis, the great goddess. Or it may have been an aid to fertility, for Berenike Syra, at twenty-seven years, was a bit old to be getting her first child. To drink the Nile, of course, also means that the drinker will be sure to return to Egypt. Seshat thinks it more likely that Berenike Syra exported the River Nile to Syria because she loved Egypt and longed to go back there. But she would not go back. The horoscopists could not foresee anything good about the Syrian marriage, and their grim forecast was that this beautiful bride would only go home to Egypt as dust and ashes in one of her own water jars.

Mikros would have shrugged the shoulder to hear of it. His peace was more important. He could not cancel a peace treaty on account of some horoscopists' nonsense.

So what happened in Syria? The agreement was for Antiokhos to throw out his then wife, the beautiful Laodike, whom he loved (but who can hardly have loved him back, for it would soon be her pleasure to murder him), in favour of Berenike Syra, whom he had never seen before in his life, *except as his enemy in battle*, and did not love, and her vast baggage of gold and silver, her *paraphernalia*, that some said was not her dowry but merely the indemnities for the war with Syria, the greatest bribe ever paid in the history of the Greeks.

Berenike duly settled down to be the wife of the King whose name was God, and who made her call him God, and she became an instant Goddess: much good it would do her. She heard everywhere the babble of Aramaic, and was pleased to have brought her own waiting-women. The Syrians, even in her husband's palace, spat upon the floor when she showed her face, and called her *Enemy*, and worse things. Even in the palace they whispered behind her back, so that she felt as if the Second Syrian War was not over, but that she had ridden into the eye of battle. Well, she was quite right.

The new goddess often sat at her window in the sumptuous palace of Antiokhos, surrounded by her golden goods, watching the flight of the crows, and she knew that the way they circled meant bad luck. She looked out at the mountains of Syria, and swigged the potions mixed by Aristarkhos that would speed up the birth of the son who should be King of Syria and All Asia, and guarantee the peace with Egypt for all time, and the thought of it was some comfort to her.

In the letters that Mikros sent with Berenike's water, he said always, *I make obeisance for you before Hermes. I pray for you in the presence of the lord Sarapis every day.* An ordinary man, however, might have given greater voice to his concern for the well-being of a loved one in a dangerous place, but there was not much love lost in that family. For the most part they thought only of themselves. Perhaps only Euergetes and Lysimakhos really cared what became of their sister.

Any man of sense could have foreseen the outcome of this crazy marriage. The greatest mystery was how Ptolemy Mikros himself, the supposedly loving father, utterly failed to realize what must happen. Aye, the truth of it was that he had sent Berenike Syra away to her death, married her off in enemy territory, among hostile strangers, who would be pleased to kill her.

1.44

Roast Thrushes

What, then, did Ptolemy Mikros do in Alexandria now that he had achieved his famous peace, apart from stuff his face with pickled mullet, and roast thrushes, and wolf down breast-shaped cheesecakes, and wear out the road to the house of Bilistikhe, his divine concubine? He relaxed, of course, enjoying the respite from the forever war, now over and done with forever. He made permanent festival, with endless feasting and drinking, music and dancing, instead of endless war, and he thought about Berenike Syra almost not at all. Out of sight, out of his thoughts, Berenike Syra was yesterday's girl. Mikros's girl of today, the passing moment, was the one who mattered, and she was Bilistikhe, who was the new Aphrodite.

In the year following Berenike Syra's departure for Syria, he chose Bilistikhe, first of concubines, to be the *Kanephoros*, or Bearer of the Golden Basket of Alexander and the *Theoi Adelphoi*, or Brother-and-Sister Gods, that was the highest honour for any woman in the city. Later that year he chose a young man called Ptolemy Andromakhou to be Priest of Alexander, and the rumour was that he was Bilistikhe's son by Ptolemy Mikros. If true, his Majesty had given his illegitimate son one of the highest-ranking offices in Alexandria. To some it looked as if Mikros might make Ptolemy Andromakhou his heir instead of Ptolemy Euergetes – as if he still thought that even the son of a common concubine would make a better king than the son of the disgraced Arsinoë Alpha, who was, at least, of royal blood.

At Athens the *Kanephoroi*, or Basket Bearers, who walked in the Panathenaic procession were required to be spotless virgins of untarnished reputation. Bilistikhe was hardly a spotless virgin, but nobody in Alexandria worried about that. Alexandria was the wonderful and most wonderful city where they boasted *Nothing Is Forbidden . . . Here You Can Do What You Want*. Marry your sister? No problem. Fritter your money away upon absurd processions? Splendid. Paint half the population gold from head to foot? Delightful. Be drunk out of your head thirty days in a row? Nobody minded. Have yourself a different concubine for every day of the month? Paradise. It was the heart's desire of every Macedonian, every Greek, to be as free as this, and live like Ptolemy did. They loved him for daring to defy the gods of Hellas, for daring to cast aside all the petty rules of the old-fashioned, out-dated gods of Olympos.

The divine Bilistikhe Aphrodite joined the procession, wearing little more than gold and jewels, still the most beautiful woman in Alexandria, almost. She was no longer young, but she had survived. She had her own residence within the palace grounds, her own white horses to pull her wicker carriage. The Alexandrians threw not stones but rose petals at her as she drove up Kanopic Street, smiling and waving. Had she not fared most excellently well? Perhaps Mikros would make her his wife and queen, they said. But on the matter of crowns, the lips of King Ptolemy was as if sewn up with strong thread. *No more wives,* he thought, *we have had enough of marriage.*

What, then, did the Alexandrians think of the cult of Mikros's parents, Ptolemy Soter and Berenike Alpha, the cult of his dead wife, Arsinoë Beta, the cult of his mistress as Aphrodite? Did they truly approve of these mortals who played at gods and goddesses? Or did they see all this as terrible hubris? Stranger, Alexandria had one extra day's holiday in honour of the procession of the deified Alexander, a second day for the procession of the gods who were the parents of the King, a third day for the procession of the divine Arsinoë Beta, and a fourth for Bilistikhe Aphrodite. The Alexandrians never murmured. The thousands of hired soldiers were not bothered that Mikros wanted to be a god. So long as he paid their wages, so long as he gave his war dead proper Greek funeral rites, so long as he ordered the triple ration of wine at every festival, this king might get away with doing pretty much what he liked.

Sure, the mood of the people of Alexandria was fickle. They were excitable Greeks, most of them, easily moved to tears, but just as easily moved to hideous and bestial violence, as you will see, Stranger, if you will be so kind as to keep reading, under this king's unfortunate and most unfortunate grandson. If Mikros put a foot wrong, things would have been very different – but for the moment, Mikros's precious passing moment, these were the most glorious years of the Ptolemies, and the Alexandrians smiled upon their king. Mikros could do no wrong. Alexandria even forgave him his misfortunes on the battlefield, blaming the gods, not their wonderful ruler.

Ptolemy Mikros was by no means unpopular. The good people of Alexandria were delighted to worship his late wife and sister. Soon they would be worshipping Mikros as a god as well. You would think, Stranger, that Ptolemy Mikros might have been happy in such an enviable position, having gotten for himself peace both at home and abroad, and more wealth than any other man upon earth, but it was not so. He stuffed his face with slices of cold octopus, chaffinches and lobsters, roast cranes and roast quails, and all those edible luxuries from Syria, but none of this made him a happy man. His unhappiness was that of the man who has everything. The delight of anticipation that the ordinary man enjoys did not exist for Mikros. For a king such as this, every day was like the best day of any other man's life. A man would get bored with that kind of luxury after thirty years. Sure, he had his sons, but having gone twenty years without seeing their father's face, they were strangers unto him, and the truth was that he was suspicious of them. The son that Mikros truly loved was dead. The wife that he had truly loved – he had been turned against her. The concubines did not bring him happiness, only never-ending *aphrodisia*. No, all the riches in the world had bought this man neither happiness nor affection, and the word of his unhappiness spread even as far as India.

1.45

Buddha

Some twenty years after Arsinoë Beta was ferried over the Styx, about Year Thirty-Five of Ptolemy Mikros, three Buddhist monks walked through the Gate of the Sun, sent by King Asoka of India, who had decided at his Third Council of Buddhists at Pataliputra to seek converts to Buddhism.

Asoka had heard that Tulamaya, King of Egypt, was unhappy, that he was tired of living. Perhaps, Asoka thought, Tulamaya might be pleased to hear about the Buddha, who promised the weary pessimist eternal forgetfulness, and so find happiness. Thus the mission. Seshat, of course, cannot approve of eternal forgetfulness. Seshat approves only of eternal remembering. Seshat is She Who Forgets Nothing. But she has not the Buddhists' names. Let them be called Prathama, Dvitiiya, Tritiiya, First, Second, Third, for a man with no name has no existence in the Afterlife.

The Buddhists presented their compliments at the palace and Mikros made them welcome, for even the Greeks who neglected their own gods still stuck to the belief that every stranger comes from Zeus. Mikros offered them the obligatory Greek hospitality, food and drink, and a place to sleep, and said he would be pleased to hear what they had to say.

His first surprise was that the Buddhists refused not only meat but even wine.

Mikros stared at the ambassadors, three small monks in dusty robes that might once have been red. Each man had his palms together, bowing to him. Each man smiled broad, showing all the teeth, eyes sparkling for happiness like nothing Mikros had ever seen before. He stared at their shaven heads, their rough sticks, their battered sandals, the small wooden bowl for begging. They were not so different from the priests of Egypt, but for the scarlet parrot perched on their leader's shoulder.

Have you no baggage? Mikros asked.

Prathama shook his head, showing all the teeth, sparkling the eyes. *None whatever,* he said, *but the psittakos. We hear of Tulamaya interest in wild animal. We bring Tulamaya gift of psittakos.*

How came you here? Mikros asked, thinking to water their beasts, but Dvitiiya pointed to their feet.

On the hoof, he said, smiling, *from India, across the land.*

Mikros wore his face of great surprise. He thought of living without horses, chariots, slaves, weapons, books. Such a way of life seemed impossible.

How can a man be happy, he thought, *who has nothing but one robe and one bowl?* He stared at their callused feet, their lined faces. He thought of the hardship of their journey. How could such men stand before him smiling?

Is there any thing that you wish for? he said.

Nothing, Prathama said, *except you hear our message.*

Really, the smiles did not leave the Buddhists' faces for one moment.

We bring gift of happiness, Dvitiiya said.

We come, Tritiiya said, *tell Tulamaya about Buddha.*

What is Buddha? Mikros said.

Buddha is great teacher, Prathama said, *teach peace, teach kindness to all living creature.*

Mikros the peacemaker said, *Peace is good, kindness to animals is good.* But he thought, *What have they to be so happy about?*

Tell us about King Asoka, he said.

Asoka is great Buddhist king of India, Dvitiiya said. And he spoke of Pataliputra, Asoka's capital, with its five hundred and seventy towers and sixty-four gates, and of his palace with its gilded pillars decorated with golden vines and silver birds, his beautiful park with fish ponds, his golden vessels four cubits across, and how when Asoka showed himself in public he rode upon an elephant with jewelled trappings.

When Dvitiiya spoke of Asoka's bodyguard of Amazons, fierce, muscular female archers, Mikros saw in his heart the face of the sister, and his attention wandered, but when they mentioned Asoka's hundreds of concubines, he sat up and listened.

Tell me more about your Asoka, Mikros said. *He sounds like a man after my own heart, a king who loves luxury.*

In his youth, Prathama said, *Asoka was great warrior. Defeated the Kalingans. One hundred and fifty thousand men deported; one hundred thousand men killed. Many died in this war.*

Ptolemy wore his face of shock. *War is wicked,* he said.

Asoka full of sorrow, Dvitiiya said, *wonder how to seek forgiveness. Wanted to live with no violence. What he do? He stop riding to war. He refuse hunt wild animal any more. He give up eating meat. He like teaching of Buddha so much he become Buddhist.*

Mikros wore his face of very great surprise.

All good man should live like Asoka, Dvitiiya said. *Even Tulamaya might follow way of Buddha, do what Asoka did.*

Mikros wore his face of mild disapproval. Although he loved peace, he knew the rest of the Greek world would never give up going to war. He smiled to think of putting the torch to his great arsenal of siege-machines and bolt-throwers, of melting down every sword in Egypt. He laughed to think that he might give up eating flamingo steaks.

So much laughing, Dvitiiya thought, *maybe he not so unhappy after all.*

We should be quite unable to do such things in Egypt, Mikros said. In his heart he saw the sister's face again. Aye, and the shade of Arsinoë Beta was grim.

To give up war would be like making eunuchs of our entire army, he said. *Egypt would be wide open to every invader.*

He saw the Buddhists' faces fall.

War is wicked, Mikros said, rather quiet, and then, rather loud, *but necessary.*

The Buddhists looked as if they could hardly believe their ears.

Mikros let the Buddhists tell him about the three great rules that a man must follow if he wants to go to heaven – self-restraint, charity, conscientiousness. Yes, he thought he had charity, although he liked also to keep most of what he had for himself. He had not much self-restraint regarding concubines. He did not always worry about his duty.

Wonderful is to have nothing, Tritiiya said, *wonderful is to spend no money.*

But Mikros's delight was great expense, and having too much of everything. He was devoted to extraordinary and excessive excess, and luxury without limits. *Do what you like* and *Eat and drink as much as you can* were his watchwords.

King must never keep subject waiting, Prathama said. *King must hear all urgent call at once. King's happiness is in happiness of his subject. Whatever please King himself – not good.*

But Mikros thought, *What is must?* He thought that what pleased himself was very good. He did not like to be told what to do. He saw again the crocodile-face of Arsinoë Beta.

Can we give you nothing? he said.

Little bread, Prathama said, smiling, *little water. We no need rich food of king.*

The Buddhists strove hard but Mikros would not give up his pleasures. He would never stop eating meat. They would find it easier to convert the Sphinx than to change the heart of Tulamaya.

When they presented themselves a fourth morning in succession, Mikros said, *Our half-brother Magas of Kyrene would love to hear what you have to say.* He offered to give the Buddhists camels, horses, a donkey.

Prefer the foot, Tritiiya said, and so the Buddhists walked up Kanopic Street, out of the Moon Gate, and along the coast road. Their smiles never faded.

Mikros might love peace, but the Alexandrians were more interested in violence. They liked to eat flesh more than any other thing, apart, perhaps, from fishes. In the rituals of Dionysos the Greeks loved to rip up the sacrificial beasts, tear them limb from limb and eat the flesh raw. How could the king of such a people become a Buddhist?

The Indian Embassy was, indeed, the great chance of Ptolemy Mikros to change himself and be happy, but he already had the temples of Greece and Egypt to cope with. As he said to Apollonios, *Really, Dioiketes, we have no room for a third parcel of gods.*

The words of the Buddhists, then, fell upon deaf ears. Mikros did send Dionysos, his envoy, to the court of Pataliputra in the lifetime of King Asoka, but he was sent because Mikros wanted Indian mahouts and trainers for his elephants of war, not because he sought further information about the Buddha.

The Buddhists brought nothing with them to Egypt, and they left nothing behind but the *psittakos*, a bird they had trained to screech *Dharma –*

Dharma – Dharma. But Dharma was a word that Ptolemy Mikros chose not to hear. He had grown tired of listening to the Buddhists, and when he tired of their screeeching parrot, he sent it away. When the people living round about the Beast Garden also grew tired of the parrot's screeching, he fetched up on a plate for the beast-keeper's dinner.

Mikros remembered, for a few days, some words of the first Buddhist monk: *If trouble comes inside family, must not blame others, must look at own heart, must follow right path*. But he could see no discord in his family.

He thought of the second Buddhist monk, who said, *Family is where hearts meet. If they love each other, the house is beautiful, like garden full of flower. If they quarrel, is like storm knock flower down . . .*

Mikros did not think his family was like a violent storm. It was not long before he forgot about the Buddhists and their wise words, and went back to being unhappy, as before.

So much for Dharma. So much for the Buddha in Egypt.

Asoka did not send a second mission to the Ptolemies, but left them to their barbarity – making war against their neighbours, killing each other, killing every animal in sight, and eating the flesh, day after day, with the blood and meat gravy trickling down their chins. In Alexandria the daily sacrifice went on as before, with the blood spurting from the slit throats of many bulls. The Alexandrian love of violence continued also. Soon the blood would drip even upon the exquisite mosaic floors of Ptolemy's wonderful white marble palace, a spreading pool of the Ptolemies' own blood.

1.46

Greek Miracles

Not long after the Buddhist Embassy seventy-two Hebrew Scholars, sent from Hierosolyma, sat down on Pharos island to translate the scriptures of the Hebrews into Greek. This great work was undertaken because the Hebrews living in Alexandria now spoke Greek so very well that they had forgotten their Hebrew, and were having trouble reading the scriptures in their own language.

The Hebrews had prospered in Alexandria. They had the ear of his Majesty, and they boasted that it was King Ptolemy who requested the translation to be made, so that he might read the Hebrew scriptures for himself.

They bragged that he had made a donation towards the translators' expenses – papyrus, ink, beer, bread and onions – while they laboured over the five books from *Genesis*, or Beginning, to *Arithmoi*, or Numbers.

When all seventy-two scholars threw down their reed pens on the seventy-second day, at the exact same moment, and it turned out that all seventy-two versions were identical, word for word the same, a mighty victory for Yahweh, god of the Hebrews, was declared, and excited shouts of *Miracle* were heard all over the city.

When Mikros was told what the shouting was about he was suspicious. *Oho,* he said, *we rather think somebody must have cheated,* and the royal shoulders began to shake. It was just a story, not, perhaps, to be taken literally. The truth, as always, was somewhat different. Mikros at least did not forbid the work.

Some men questioned even the fact of the translation being undertaken upon Pharos island, for the sensibilities of the Hebrews had been so upset by the sight of naked Greek statues all over Alexandria that an entire quarter of the city had been given over to them to live in, and declared a zone free of Greek nudity. The reason for it was that the Greek liking for naked statues broke Number Two of the Ten Commandments of the Hebrews, that forbade any kind of carved image, and the nakedness offended them still further, so that wherever the Hebrews walked they must either avert the eyes, or find some route about the city where there were no statues – which was difficult, because Alexander, the Ptolemies, and all the gods and goddesses of Greece stood on every street, displaying their divine nakedness for all Alexandria to delight in. No Greek thought the worse of it, of course not, because it was all part of Do What You Like. The Greeks are not ashamed of nakedness, not afraid of the human body, but delight in looking upon the divine beauty of man, that was the best thing the gods of Greece ever created.

So that, surely, the Hebrews would never have gone near Pharos island, which bristled with graven images, Greek and Egyptian, including half-naked statues of the wondrous priapic Amun, and the ithyphallic and most ithyphallic Min of Koptos. Even the place of the translation had to be an untruth or, at least, a mistake. That, at any rate, was the story of the Seventy-Two Scholars, whose famous translation was called the Septuagint, or Seventy (not the Seventy-Two). It was yet another great thing that came out of Alexandria in the golden age of Ptolemy Mikros.

The Hebrews presented a copy of this masterpiece of Greek prose to his Majesty, of course, for the Great Library, and Mikros promised to read it. Some months later, the High Priest of the Hebrews asked him, *How goes the reading, Megaleios?*

Excellency, Mikros said, trying to keep the smile on his face, *we could not put down your book for wanting to know what happened in the end.*

What was the truth, though? He did not get beyond *Methuselah lived nine hundred and sixty years . . .* when he threw down the famous Septuagint, saying, *The Hebrews must be liars. Nobody but a god could live as long as that.*

Some days Mikros felt just about as old as Methuselah himself.

Mikros liked to read, though, as a rule. Reading did not involve making decisions. But when Apollonios Rhodios told him of the splendid recent acquisition that was one million lines of *The Book of Zoroaster*, he did not wear the usual Pharaoh's smile, but said he was tired of reading.

Even his concubines were growing old. Now even his beloved Stratonike fell sick, and was buried by Mikros himself in the grandest of Greek tombs on the sea shore at Eleusis, east of Alexandria, where it had sometimes pleased him to drive with her in his chariot.

Whom did he squeeze now? Not Aphrodite Bilistikhe, whose divine flesh was shrivelled upon her bones, whose breasts sagged, whose smiling mouth showed none but blackened teeth. No, he did not take himself to visit his concubines quite so often: only once a day now, but sat many hours alone in his private chamber staring at the furious grey-green sea.

This King had everything riches could give him; he had nothing left in the world to wish for. But his mouth was fixed, now, with the corners turned down, as if life had lost all interest for him. He was even losing interest in breast-shaped cheesecakes. The Greek poets still compared him to a circling comet that shoots forth flames. *He is a young bull,* they said, *ready with his horns, irresistible.* But Mikros the comet no longer left a trail of sparks behind him. His fires seemed to be dying down.

But still, he did not totally lose his grip on affairs. For five, six, seven long years, he never failed to send the River water to Berenike Syra in Syria, even if he did not take much notice of what she wrote in her letters.

1.47

Antiokhos the God

Things did not look so bad for Berenike Syra in the beginning. Her palace at Antiokheia-upon-the-Orontes was a well-appointed modern residence, with Corinthian columns, beautiful mosaics of satyrs and sea-gods on the floor, and every home comfort in the way of roasted larks, stuffed pigeons, gold plates, eunuch slaves, and so forth. Antiokhos Theos her husband was not very old, just thirty-four years of age upon his marriage, with dark, curled hair, and olive skin, and eyes like blackcurrants. Berenike did not completely dislike her father's new friend, in spite of his having slaughtered her countrymen by the thousand. Antiokhos was not unpleasant to her, but she soon found that he liked to drink a great deal of wine, and that when he drank he did not behave himself very like a god.

Antiokhos drank his wine undiluted, of course, but he did not not stop at two or three bowls, which might have been Moderation. By no means. Even at the start of Berenike's marriage he was drinking eight or nine, and a nine-bowl man is proverbial among the Greeks for the kind of violence that involves throwing the chairs about, not far short of madness.

The first time Berenike's dispatch of water was delivered to Antiokheia, Antiokhos the God showed his temper, shouting, *What is the use of water? Why does not your father send us wine?*

Berenike Syra was not the shy, retiring kind of Greek wife who did not dare to look her husband in the face. She stared Antiokhos Theos in the eye and spoke to him straight, telling him she thought he drank more than was good for a man, that he might benefit from drinking a little water himself. *You know very well that the Greeks say Water is Best . . .* she said. And of course Antiokhos Theos did not like it. No god likes to be ordered about. Nor was he going to start drinking water, and perhaps this added to the trouble that was piling up for Berenike Syra from the moment she set her golden sandal in enemy territory, for she gave as good as she got. And Antiokhos did not like that either. A god expects to be worshipped, not shouted at by his wife.

In her letters to her father Berenike Syra made believe that nothing was amiss, writing only, *The heat is unbearable . . . I am melting . . . I long for the cool winter of Alexandria . . .*

Berenike Syra sensed that there would be trouble, though, and the beginning of it was the day when she found out that Antiokhos had let go his hold on power to two men from Cyprus, twin brothers, who ruled him in the most unpleasant manner. Themison was a handsome Macedonian of phenomenal strength, who entered himself for the public games calling himself a born-again Herakles. Aristos his brother was his exact lookalike, a man with muscles like iron. Between them they had won every prize for boxing, wrestling and the *pankration* in all Syria. Antiokhos was so besotted with Themison in particular that he had even let him become the object of public worship.

Berenike was puzzled when she saw the two Cypriots disappear into her husband's bedchamber and heard the bolts drawn across the door. She could not avoid hearing the shouts and groans that filled the palace, and she was astonished, for it sounded as if they were smashing up all the furniture, doing she could not imagine what it might be. And then she met her husband emerging from this violent meeting, his body bruised, black and blue, his nose streaming with blood, picking a smashed tooth from his jaw, but with his eyes shining, as if he had just enjoyed the very greatest of pleasures.

Berenike Syra did not complain to her father about her husband's violence. She could shrug the shoulder just as well as Mikros. She complained only of the bed bugs, the sand that blew in her eyes, and the clouds of biting insects. In return her father sent her a golden fly-whisk.

Things were not so terrible just then for Berenike Syra: she had her pick of the fabulous crown jewels of Syria; she enjoyed every imaginable luxury in the way of leopardskin carpets, chairs of ebony and ivory and gold, well-sprung chariots, and the fastest horses in the world. Some days she would drive out to Daphne in the cool of the morning – where she would amuse herself by shooting arrows into whatever wild beast she passed upon the road.

Berenike Syra's River water was delivered regular, once a month, when she might write to her father, saying, *The winter is cold . . . I long for sunny Memphis.* But just then she had no serious grounds for complaint. She came almost to enjoy being a queen and a goddess in her own lifetime. She almost grew used to her husband's strange recreations. She turned the blind eye to Themison and Aristos, who treated her with the proper respect – for she made it plain what she was capable of by knocking Aristarkhos her physician to the ground in front of the whole court. And that may have been how she turned Aristarkhos, the man who was meant to be her friend, into her enemy – by making him look weaker than a woman.

Antiokhos Theos did, at least, do his duty in the bedchamber with Berenike Syra, because her belly soon began to swell up like a pumpkin. So long as he did not offer violence to her, she felt able to carry on as his wife, and make believe there was nothing wrong, for the sake of her father's precious peace. In due course Aristarkhos delivered her of a strapping prince, who was on the day of his birth declared the heir to his father's throne – in accordance with the peace treaty. Antiokhos, sober for once, spoke several kind words to his wife, and played, for a while, at being the proud father. He had his son tattooed upon the thigh with the anchor that was the secret mark of the House of Seleukos, to distinguish him from children of less exalted rank, and to make sure that if he was swapped for some other child, or kidnapped, in that period when all babies look the same, before he found a face and an identity of his own, they would not lose him.

As it happened, though, Berenike Syra's son never did find an identity of his own, for he would not live much beyond his fourth birthday. His name, unsurprisingly, was Antiokhos, but he would not be remembered so much for how he lived as for how he died.

All might yet be well. Berenike Syra had brought forth an heir. The forecasts of the oracle of Apollo at Daphne did not make her future sound altogether hopeless. But the birth of her son was what caused Berenike Syra's troubles to grow rapidly worse. All might have turned out for the best but for the existence of her divine husband's discarded wife, Laodike, and her two rejected sons, who became the bitter enemies of Berenike Syra and her child overnight.

When he married Berenike Syra, Antiokhos Theos had sworn his oath to put away his first wife. He had given Ptolemy Mikros his promise to keep her at a distance, at Sardis, in Phrygia, thousands of stades away, while Berenike Syra was to live and reign in at Antiokheia, in Syria. But while foreign policy bound Antiokhos to the lovely Berenike Syra, his heart bound him to the still more lovely Laodike, who, as it happened, had never complained of his drinking deep, nor of his worship of the muscular catamites from Cyprus, nor of his addiction to spectacular domestic violence. By the fourth year of her marriage Berenike Syra very often found herself sitting alone in Antiokheia, and her spies told her that her husband was on the other side of the Tauros Mountains, in bed with his banished ex-wife.

Most Greek wives, of course, expected nothing less. Such treatment was the standard treatment: the wife lived in the half-dark of the women's quarters, and was lucky if she received nothing worse than pretty good contempt. Berenike Syra, however, was Pharaoh's Daughter, the rich rich rich Queen Berenike, and she thought she deserved better than to be completely ignored.

When Antiokhos Theos offered sacrifice upon the altar of Themison the Herakles, the strong man would flex his muscles of iron, and the King would hug him, kiss him upon the lips and eyes and stick his tongue down the man's throat. In return Themison squeezed Antiokhos until the bones of his back creaked. When Berenike witnessed this revolting performance she was more than a little worried. When Antiokhos staged an extravagant procession through the streets of Antiokheia to honour this Herakles, Berenike became alarmed, and she noticed for the first time the howling of wolves in the snow.

When Mania, her waiting-woman, showed her one of Antiokhos' newly minted gold oktodrachms that featured his Herakles lying on a couch with a lion skin draped about his body, holding a Scythian bow and club in his arms, she sent Aristarkhos her physician straight to Egypt by fast racing-camel, with a letter asking her father to fetch her home forthwith, for that her husband's wonderful strong man seemed to mean more to him than she did. She wrote, *Surely, the Queen's face might be expected to make its appearance upon the coins of Syria before the face of her husband's wrestling partner.*

But Mikros wrote back to say no, he would not fetch Berenike Syra home, because for a man to take his daughter back after she had been married off was an admission of failure for a girl, and an indelible mark of shame for her father. It was one of those things that every Greek regards as Absolutely Never To Be Done, because such a girl would never marry again, but be a burden to her father for the rest of his days.

Berenike had to stay in Syria, then, and she had to put up with the humiliation of having not the first but the fourth place in her husband's affections – after Themison the Herakles, after Aristos his brother, and after Laodike, his beautiful and most beautiful first wife, all of whose lips Antiokhos Theos seemed to like kissing better than her own.

When Berenike Syra heard that it had pleased her husband to found a fresh city in Phrygia and call it Themisonion after his favourite, she began to fear for her safety. She sent Aristarkhos off to Egypt with another letter to her father. She wrote, *We urge his Majesty to fetch us home to Egypt, for that not only has King Antiokhos not been pleased to name one single city after ourself, but there is not so much as one street in Antiokheia-upon-the-Orontes that bears our name ... Moreover, we believe that Antiokhos is now living at Sardis as husband and wife with Laodike, the wife he is supposed to have given up.*

But Mikros wrote back to say no, once again, he absolutely could not fetch her back home to Egypt. His peace with Syria was still in place. To bring Berenike Syra home would be as good as declaring an end to the Great Syrian Alliance, as good as announcing the resumption of his everlasting war. He wrote, *You must stay where you are. You are yourself the wonderful permanent glue that holds our glorious peace together.*

And so Berenike Syra had to stay where she was, glued to the spot, unable to unstick herself, very like some unfortunate Egyptian fly caught in a great Syrian fly-trap. The camel-trains carried on trotting through the desert, exporting the River Nile to Syria for Berenike Syra to drink and bathe in. The camels did not return along the military road from Syria carrying nothing. By no means. They were laden with Syrian wine, Syrian dates, Syrian figs, Syrian sweetmeats, and even great blocks of snow packed in straw, direct from the mountains of Syria, for cooling Mikros's wine. From time to time Gellosyne and Panariste, Berenike Syra's waiting-women, were moved to say to each other, *King Ptolemy seems to care more for his belly than his daughter.*

1.48

Gout

The sixtieth birthday of Ptolemy Mikros was celebrated throughout Egypt with public feasting, and dancing in the streets. This king had passed most of his life either eating, or clasped in the arms of his very many concubines. And why not? Why should a man pass his life without pleasure? But if he wished to live a long life, he should, perhaps, have lived it different. Mikros was not exactly a thin king, and in these days he breathed so hard in his *aphrodisia* that the women thought he must die of it. He had worn himself out with everything in excess. Now he began to fall into hypochondria, imagining himself ill when he was well, well when he was ill.

The dwarf slaves of the Pharaoh's body brought the mirror of burnished bronze that made him look thinner than he really was, and it was in spite of the custom that forbids a Greek man to look in a mirror lest it should bring bad luck – because the mirror is for women, for whores, and for softness, not for a hard man like Strong Bull.

But Ptolemy Mikros was soft. He had been young and soft. Now he was old and soft, and he had, as it were, outlived his reason, for he began to hold forth about living for ever, boasting that he alone had discovered the secret of immortality.

Sure, Padibastet had promised him that Pharaoh does not die, but lives for all time, for millions of millions of years, as one of the imperishable stars. But the Greek quack doctors had told him other things, had sold him elixirs that promised no death for Ptolemy Mikros even on this earth.

Arsinoë Philadelphos, the sensible wife, would have shouted at him, *Get a grip upon yourself, Brother, you were made mortal just like other men,* but that sensible and most sensible wife was dead.

Herophilos would have told him straight, *Nonsense, Megaleios, it is all nonsense.* But by this time even Herophilos had moved his dwelling-place to the necropolis east of the city, and set up his butcher's shop in the Afterlife.

Mikros was the Pharaoh, a living god. He would fly to the sky upon the whirlwind, in the dust storm, upon the wings of Thoth. He would himself become a star. But to be Pharaoh of Egypt for ever, and never die the death of a human? The physicians thought him a little deranged for thinking it, although they had planted his weird ideas themselves. It was left to Erasistratos, the new royal doctor, to humour him, feeding him ambrosia and nectar, divine foodstuffs that gave his body the power to resist time and defy death. Mikros was aged beyond his years. He had exercised his body too little and feasted too much. *One day he will just lie down,* Erasistratos thought, *like an overburdened camel, and never get up again.* Even the palace dwarfs whispered, *He will die soon,* and began to steal his golden trinkets, just as their parents had stolen those of his father.

When Mikros felt the first of the terrible shooting pains in his right foot, he murmured, *There will be a tempest . . .* and ordered the usual safeguards – the battening down of shutters, the proper mooring of the ships in the harbour, the ban on sleeping on the roofs. But the tempest did not come, and the pain in his foot passed. Some weeks later, he woke up with the shooting pain in his left foot, and sent for the great doctor once again. Erasistratos drew attention to the redness, the slight swelling of the lower legs and said to him, *Majesty, it is the gout.*

Mikros indulged himself in the luxury of an oath. *By Herakles . . .*

An attack of the gout is not serious, Erasistratos said, *but it is a warning that a man must re-order his way of life. His Majesty must avoid worry. He must take regular exercise. He must avoid taking a chill.*

But Mikros could not stop worrying about his kingdom. He could not, at his age, take up strenuous exercise. He often caught cold in the damp winters at Alexandria and fled to the drier atmosphere of Memphis. And he disliked the man who said *Must.* He shouted even at Erasistratos, *Nobody tells Pharaoh what to do.*

Erasistratos did not approve of drastic measures. He did not believe that bloodletting was of any use. He continued his investigations, urging Mikros to eat roast dog and drink cabbage water. He anointed his Majesty's feet with ants cooked in henna oil, figs, grapes and potentilla pounded in wine. But roast pigeon never did disappear from the royal table. Mikros could not stop gorging on roast flamingo. Every third day he stuffed his face with the pair of boiled ox-feet, a dish synonymous with heavy gluttony. None of the great Greek gout cures made the slightest difference, because Mikros was too old and too stubborn to change from excess to moderation.

*

When he was at Memphis, recovering from a specially vicious attack of the gout, Mikros looked out of his window and watched a party of Egyptians eating their simple luncheon of bread and onions on the River bank, laughing and enjoying themselves with their families. With a deep sigh he said, *If only I could be like them* . . ..

Mikros wanted to be ordinary, like other men, just as his father had wanted to be ordinary. He wished that he had the secret of how to be happy. And yet, only five years before, he had sent away the Buddhists, who had offered him that very thing. Some days he prayed to Hades to take him, prayed to be dead. Perhaps his rich and idle life, after all, had been more pleasant than was good for him.

Padibastet sympathized. *Pharaoh should not worry so much* . . . he said. *Even Pharaoh has the right to enjoy himself.* And he told him about Snofru, the Pharaoh who was bored with life, whose Vizier suggested that he launch his barge on the River, and take on board the most beautiful women in Memphis.

King Snofru called for twenty oars of ebony, Padibastet said, *and twenty beautiful girls with perfect breasts to row his barge. As Snofru watched the women rowing, he found that he forgot his sadness.*

Mikros's old, lined face brightened. Perhaps he would give his heart up to jollity one last time. He called up twenty young concubines, Greek and Egyptian, and had himself floated up-River in the royal barge. The concubines made music with their harps and sang songs to soothe the heart of Pharaoh, just like the ladies of Snofru. But Mikros's heart felt like a burnt-out torch. He was not delighted. He was not made happy. No, Mikros's famous half-smile would not now return; jollity had gone for good.

Tired of everything he did, Mikros became suddenly urgent to hand over the reins of government to his heir, to Ptolemy Euergetes. To Padibastet he said, *I have been Pharaoh for thirty-seven years. Let Egypt see a strong man upon the throne now. Let me retire, just as my father did.* And so it was agreed. Ptolemy Soter had gone back to marching in the phalanx with the troops, gone back to being a private soldier. Mikros did nothing so energetic. He wanted to do nothing, nothing but eat and drink.

The business of being Pharaoh had always interfered with his pleasures, the pleasures that no longer brought him pleasure. According to the custom father and son would keep up the appearance of ruling together, but really Mikros had had enough of being king. He had done well to hold up as long as he did. Any man would have staggered under the burden, but Euergetes took the duties of king upon his own shoulders and stood firm: the new Strong Bull.

As the winter rains lashed Alexandria, Mikros might be overheard murmuring the words of one of Theokritos' drinking songs, *One moment I am a god, the next a ghost, sunstruck or sunk in gloom*, and it was as if the words applied to himself. He thought of the Sibyl, the ancient woman who asked for eternal life but forgot to ask for eternal youthfulness, and he knew a fresh kind of despair.

Padibastet came to him more often now, to make him ready for flying to the sky, saying, *May you be a god, may you always be a god.*

Mikros would reply, *This name of mine shall live for ever. Eternity has been granted unto me. I shall not die, I have no end.*

But Ptolemy Mikros did not die, not yet. Even the aged Apis bull must be dragged to the necropolis before Mikros could fly to the stars.

1.49

The Gates of Oblivion

Aye, in Year Thirty-Five of Ptolemy Mikros, even the majesty of the Apis bull, Calf of the Cow Ta-Renenutet the First, rolled over, dead, and flew up to heaven. The great oracle of Memphis was no more. This Apis died young, in the eighth year of his age, fifteen years sooner than he should have done, and it looked to Padibastet like a sign of some great misfortune about to happen, such as the death of the king himself, whose fate was inextricably linked to that of the sacred bull.

Padibastet made the usual application to his Majesty for a loan to defray the colossal expenses of embalming this great beast. Mikros sent one hundred talents, less than the cost of a lighthouse, not so much as his lavish penteteric junketing. It was not as if there was no money in his treasury. By no means. His gold-house still overflowed like the sister's Horn of Plenty. Mikros had so much gold that he did not know what to do with it. *But what is the use of gold,* he thought, *if a man has neither youth nor health?*

The High Priest's family – Padibastet, Nefersobek, Young Anemhor and Herankh, Neferibre and Nefertiti – were head on knee for the Apis whom they loved. All Memphis followed his funeral procession, and saw the opening of the great bronze Gates of Oblivion and Lamentation, through which only the dead Apis was allowed to pass. His long horns, shining with gold leaf, stuck up above the bandages, with the gilded sun-disk and double plumes of ostrich-feathers fixed between them. Every citizen of Memphis followed Apis with dancing and music across the River and along the sacred way to the desert plateau, to the House of Rest of the Apis, the catacombs of the Sarapieion, that were called the Greater Vaults, where he was lowered into a gigantic *sarkophagos* of black granite. Every man had shaved his head in mourning. Every woman beat the breast, and piled the black mud of the River upon her head.

Padibastet, as old as Pharaoh, but looking half as young, led the procession, walking slow in his leopardskin, but while the other priests danced, leaped, shouted, sang, to celebrate the renewal of the Apis, his second birth in the Afterlife, Padibastet's face was grave, and streaked with tears. Mikros, carried in the *skollopendra,* his face ran with water, sweat and tears together, though he was not sure whether the tears were for the Apis or for himself.

Now began the hunt for the fresh bull-calf with the twenty-nine identifying marks on his body that stood for the stars, and showed when the Nile would rise in flood; the marks that proved him to be the divine calf, born of a virgin cow upon which a flash of lightning had fallen, in order to cause his birth.

Padibastet had learned from his father the art of forecasting the future by means of this bull. Handed down from father to son also, through upwards of forty-eight generations, was the precise science – or magic – that would help him find the new Apis – divining first the district, then the town or village, then enabling him to concentrate his thoughts and walk straight to the exact back yard in which he would find the timid calf with great black liquid eyes, unsteady on his feet, who was the Living Image of Ptah of the Beautiful Face, the creator of the world. Then the miracle would be declared, the dancing would begin, and the fresh Apis would board the gilded barge and sail on the River to Memphis, to be installed.

The science of finding the Apis was all very well, all very precise, but Padibastet could not find the right calf: the all-black calf with a square patch of white upon his forehead, a white eagle-shaped patch upon his back, a scarab beetle shape upon his tongue, and a white crescent-shape upon his right flank. He began to think that the fresh Apis would never reveal himself, had not been born, did not exist. He had scoured the ritual-books. His sons and their assistants had searched every last dried-up field in all the forty-two *nomes* of Upper and Lower Egypt, without success, and it was a disaster for the Two Lands, because the Apis was just about the most important thing in the kingdom, after Pharaoh. Padibastet did not want to think what it might mean if the new Apis did not show himself, if the Living Image of Ptah were not reborn at all. As he took to his bed, exhausted, he whispered, *It can only mean ruin for Egypt. The Two Lands will be destroyed utterly* . . .

Mikros poured with sweat on the day of the funeral of the Apis, but Padibastet complained of the cold, just like his father, and it was the height of the hot season. Every man in the palace thought Mikros looked so sick he must die, but it was Padibastet, not Mikros, who did not get out of his bed. The passing of the old Apis had grieved his heart. The hunt for the new Apis had worn him out. He would say nothing to anybody but, *Disease is in my bones.*

Nefersobek his wife called in the prophet of Sakhmet, the man who knew more about medicine than any other man in Memphis, apart from Padibastet himself. He prodded Padibastet's taut stomach, pressed the flesh behind his ears, peered into his bloodshot eyes.

To Nefersobek he said quietly, *It is Death that has penetrated his mouth and taken up its abode in his belly.*

In his sleep that night Padibastet flew to the stars himself, and in the morning the wailing spread across the city for the death of the great man. No word of Seshat can describe Nefersobek's sadness. Her flood of tears was no make believe. But at the same time as she wailed, she was happy, for the Egyptians do not think of death as a disaster. In the judgement, Anubis and Thoth would surely find Padibastet's heart as light as the Feather of Maat, the Feather of Truth. He was in the company of the gods, sailing through the heavens in the barque of Ra.

Anemhor slaughtered the ox for his father, and held for him the banquet in the tomb, his House of Eternity. The mourners feasted upon steaks, sauces, roast goose, beer, wine, every fine fruit. Neferibre and Nefertiti spoke of their father with affection, saying, *His name shall not perish eternally.*

Akhoapis, the son-in-law, thought rather of the succession, asking, *Who will be the new Great Chief of the Hammer?*

It is the custom, Nefersobek said, *for a man's eldest son, to succeed him in his office, but not a right.* They saw Anemhor looking at the ground, embarrassed, as if he knew what would happen regarding the succession. Young Anemhor was the man who best knew how to forecast the future, who could read people's hearts as other men might read a book, and he knew that Akhoapis had a strong desire to be Great Chief of the Hammer himself.

But Anemhor was the man of whom they said, *He loves good, he hates evil,* and *Even before the mouth speaks, he knows what you will say.* Anemhor, forty-three years old, was the man Euergetes the Regent chose to be High Priest of Ptah, and Director of the Prophets of All the Gods and Goddesses of Upper and Lower Egypt.

Herankh, Anemhor's wife, and his three sons, Djedhor, Horemakhet, and Horimhotep rejoiced. Their Uncle Neferibre was not jealous. Even Akhoapis offered Anemhor his best wishes and shook his hands. There were no *murders* on the installation of a new High Priest of Ptah. Nobody would die because a man had gotten a new job. The Egyptians were not full of hatred like the Ptolemies, but full of affection.

The first and most urgent task of Young Anemhor was to find the fresh Apis bull, which he did, by looking in the one place his father had not thought of looking: in Memphis itself, hardly two stades from where the old Apis died, in his own cattle-yards. The bull-calf he found here had all twenty-nine distinguishing marks, and there was no question of Young Anemhor having cheated by putting the marks on his coat himself with white paint so as to get himself out of the most serious crisis in Egypt in one hundred years. By no means. This calf was the real, true, divine calf, and Memphis went wild when the one hundred white-robed priests led him in procession, with his mother, the Divine Cow, to his stall. Aye, the fresh Apis, the one who had the answer to every man's question; who had the power to solve every man's problems.

In the first days Young Anemhor watched the new Apis prance from the left-hand stall into the right-hand stall, and back again. He watched him lick his right-hand nostril with his great grey tongue. He watched him blinking and unblinking, lying down and rolling over upon his back. He listened to the music of Apis grunting or bellowing. He took the omens from his excrements. All of these things Young Anemhor knew how to interpret, good or bad, lucky or unlucky for Egypt. He was the complete master of forecasting the future by means of Apis, the State Oracle of Egypt. Anemhor spent days on end staring at the bull, observing his behaviour, working out how best to advise the Macedonians about their endless difficulties.

Anemhor it was that took the first official oracle of the new bull-calf. He burned fresh incense on the altar. He filled the lamps there with oil and lit them. He placed his mouth close to the soft black ear of the god, and asked that most important question: *How many more years left for this King Ptolemy?*

Then he covered his ears up with his hands and walked out of Apis's dwelling-house, into the sunlight, until he was beyond the great mud-brick outer wall of the Temple of Ptah, among the palm trees, looking on to the sandy plain where the young scribes liked to kick a pig's bladder up and down. Whatever was the first words Anemhor heard when he took his hands from his ears, that would be the answer to his question.

At the moment when Anemhor took his hands down they happened to shout the score in their game, but there was no score, so they shouted: *None. None.*

Mikros was carried aloft in the *skollopendra* to install Young Anemhor in his august office, but he hardly noticed this new High Priest in his leopard-spot mantle. His thoughts were still of death, for it seemed as if everybody around him was dying, as if everybody was fated to die except himself. Just then, far from longing to live for ever, Mikros thought he might be very pleased to die.

Suddenly, living for the pleasure of the passing moment made no sense to him, for every moment was full of pain, and brought him no pleasure whatsoever. There were many passing moments when he wished that the eternal moment did not exist. So bad was his gloominess that he asked even for the instruction in the geography of the Afterlife. Aye, and Anemhor had to sit with him hour upon hour, making the passing moments seem longer than ever before.

In his innermost thoughts the Pharaoh imagined Thoth himself as an ibis-headed man, reed pen poised, ready to write down the judgement. He saw the Feather of Maat, the Feather of Truth, in the scales, and his own heart weighed against it. He saw the Baboon of Thoth perched on top of the Balance, chattering. He saw the flaming portals of the Afterlife, and his own lifetime ran quick before his eyes, like sand falling through a man's fingers.

Mikros repeated the words of the Negative Confession of the Dead, after the High Priest: *I have not done iniquity . . . I have not uttered falsehood . . . I have not uttered evil words . . . I have not been a man of anger . . .* He could not think that he had done any wrong thing.

He asked after Arsinoë Alpha, and Anemhor assured him, *She lives yet, Megaleios, she is in the best of health,* but Mikros did not ask to see her. By no means. The traitor must stay where she was. Arsinoë Beta's poisonous work of turning her brother against his wife was permanent and irreversible magic.

When Euergetes appeared Mikros wagged the finger at him, and said, very slow, very clear, as if in the possession of all his faculties, *On no account let Berenike Syra come back to Egypt. If she comes home, it will mean the renewal of bitter war with Syria.* But Euergetes reminded his father that he had himself achieved a stop to all war: *War is an impossibility, Pappos,* he said. *We are all friends in the Greek world now.*

Mikros still believed that it was true.

Anemhor told him that Berenike Syra was the mother of a son who should be King of All Asia, and Mikros's heart was in joy to hear it. He might now, perhaps, die happy, as happy as a man could be who had the gout in all his limbs at once; who cried out even when the dwarfs of the body touched his arm. He lay awake throughout the hours of darkness, listening to the creatures of the night scuttling about his gilded bedchamber, longing to be dead.

Now the concubines moved into his chamber with their harps and flutes, lyres and cymbals, so that Mikros might have his comforts closer: Bilistikhe, Didyme, Potheine, Mnesis, Myrto, Kleino, Glauke . . . among others. All grey hair and raddled flesh now, they settled down like a flock of vultures to wait for the end. His women dressed in white, bent in the back, but still dripping with jewels. They quarrelled, of course, about the order of their sitting down, about who should have the head for whispering her messages for the dead into his ears, about everything under the sun.

Mikros heard and did not hear, listened and did not listen.

Our last wish, he murmured, *is that you would all . . . just . . . go away.*

But the concubines did not go, would not, even when Ptolemy Euergetes told them to.

You are not the Pharaoh yet, Bilistikhe Aphrodite told him. *We shall not obey you until tomorrow . . .*

Didyme took his Majesty's wrist, and felt his pulse beat strong, like soldier ants beneath the skin, like steady marching. *Did not the man's father live to eighty-three?* she murmured. *He will recover, he has many years left to live.*

Young Anemhor, that knew everything, knew better. He stood by the bed of this Pharaoh, saying, *Anubis will take your arm . . . A stairway is set for you so that you may ascend upon it to the sky . . .* and the music almost drowned his words.

Mikros had asked for the music. He had read the Complete Works of Philetairos, the comic poet, who said that only those Greeks who died to the sound of music would be allowed to enjoy the pleasures of *aphrodisia* in the Afterlife. All the rest must carry the leaky jar, and try to fill it up with water for all eternity. Sure, Philetairos had been jesting, but Mikros took him serious. He did not want to fill the leaky jar for ever. Nor, though, did he fully trust the Egyptian version of the Afterlife. He wanted the best of both worlds, in case the Egyptians were wrong and the Greeks right. *Nobody has been down there – up there – and come back to tell the tale,* he said. *No man can be sure what lies ahead.*

Even so, Young Anemhor carried on speaking the words of comfort that the High Priest of Ptah must speak, above the noise of the King's music, for to send Pharaoh on his way to eternity properly equipped was his most important task, the sole reason for his existence.

Equip me, then, Mikros said, *to have aphrodisia for millions and millions of years, that is the only thing that matters . . .*

Young Anemhor promised to fix the talisman to his Majesty's right arm when he was dead, the talisman that guaranteed eternal *aphrodisia* in the Afterlife, and his deep voice droned on:

A dead man will wear white linen garments and sandals . . . He will sit by a lake in the Field of Rushes . . .. He will journey by water, in a boat rowed by the mariners of Ra . . . He will eat figs and grapes with the gods . . . He will live upon the Bread of Eternity and the Beer of Everlastingness . . .

Mikros thought only that such simple fare in the Afterlife would not suit him, that it sounded too much like Moderation.

Will there be no flamingo tongues and stuffed thrushes in the Afterlife? he murmured.

Young Anemhor shook his head, smiling not unlike Pharaoh himself.

What about our favourites, sow's matrix and boiled pig's trotters? Will they be on the menu in the Field of Peace? Mikros said.

Eternal bread that never goes mouldy, Majesty, Anemhor said, *eternal beer that never sours . . .*

Really, Excellency, Mikros murmured, *I think we shall be rather bored by an eternal diet of nothing but bread and beer.*

Then there was a small earthquake among the Egyptian cotton sheets that brought the music to a stop, the royal arms thrashed about, and Mikros sat up and said, quite loud and clear, *Excellency, do you mean to tell me there is no wine in the Afterlife?*

But before the High Priest could answer, the death rattle caught his throat, the last breath was gone out of his lungs, and he fell back on the pillows, making the feathers fly up. His mouth gaped. His eyes stared. There was a moment of shocked silence, and then the concubines started up the dreadful Greek caterwauling that meant the man was dead.

1.50

Imperishable Star

Now that Mikros had gone the Macedonians called him Philadelphos, giving him in death the title of the sister, and they became the *Theoi Philadelphoi*, the Brother-and-Sister-Loving Gods. It was the greatest honour, or, as some saw it, the final humiliation.

The Egyptian embalmers thrust the long wire up the dead King's nostril, rotating it to break down the grey matter that filled his skull into a liquid, much as his late Queen might have whisked up some noxious lizard potion. You will be worried about his brains, Stranger, but you have forgotten that a man thinks with his heart, not with his brain. It was Philadelphos's heart that beat double quick when he was excited by his women. His brain never beat fast under any circumstances, would be useless to him in the Afterlife. Aye, they hooked Philadelphos's brains out through the nose and fed the gloop to the dogs.

The embalmers made the usual incision in the stomach wall and hauled his bloody guts out through the slit. They peeled off the soles of his feet, that had not often trodden the mire of earth because he had been carried aloft, and replaced them with golden sandals. They prayed to the gods to grant milk to the Osiris Ptolemy that he might bathe his feet in it in the Afterlife. They steeped his body seventy days in a bath of dry natron, then filled up the chest and pelvic cavities with tar. Empty corners they stuffed with sawdust mixed with black mud of the River. His testicles they removed, filling the scrotum up with sawdust.

Now they gilded this great Pharaoh in death, giving him golden fingers, golden toes, golden eye-lids, golden lips, golden hands, and golden feet. Then, finding there was plenty of gold to be had, they gilded all the bits inbetween, so that he was all gold. They even gave him an artificial *phallos* of gold, laughing that his own member looked worn down by overuse; that he would need a new machine for ploughing if he were to have *aphrodisia* for all eternity, so that this star was imperishable even in his most vital organ.

His fingernails they tied on with string. They gave him onions for eyes, onions, that stand for eternal life, and with their strong stink prompt a dead man to breathe again. They placed the scarab beetle upon his chest and it bore the words that would urge his heart not to rise up as a witness against him in the next world. Now they crossed his arms over his chest, and bandaged him with four thousand cubits of best linen bandage soaked in cedar resin, eighty cubits of which alone disappeared up his nose. They hid among the bandages the one hundred and thirty-four talismans that would guard and protect him for millions of millions of years.

Between his knees they stuffed the papyrus that had written upon it Chapter Forty-Five of *The Book of Coming Forth by Day*, the words a man must know if his flesh is not to decay or fall to pieces in the Afterlife.

On the outside of his mummy case, they made his face of gold, flesh of the gods, and inlaid the eyebrows with blue glass. They gave him eyes of bronze, irises and pupils of obsidian, set in white stone. They gave this King in death the fat cheeks he had in life, and set his mouth in the serene half-smile of Pharaoh that he had hardly worn in five years.

Young Anemhor, who spoke the words of the ritual, said, *May your heart be glad and may your feet dance.* He did not give this king the *hypokephalos* to keep him warm. By no means. Too hot all his life, if he could not be ice-cold in Alexandria, it would delight his heart to be ice-cold in the Afterlife. But Anemhor did tie to the right arm of this most amorous of dead men the purple bead of amethyst, and he recited over it the spell that would enable Philadelphos to have *aphrodisia* for ever after, night and day throughout millions and millions of years. That would make his heart glad. For sure, they did not call this king *erotikos* for nothing.

Unhellenic practices though it was, Ptolemy Euergetes buried his father with full pharaonic honours, after the tradition of the Egyptians, if only so that he should not endure all over again the terrible and most terrible bad temper of Arsinoë Beta in the Afterlife of the Greeks.

Seshat said to his Ka: *I give to thee millions of years and life and prosperity, I inscribe years for thee as a million.*

Seshat said: *I establish thy name as King for ever in the writing of my own fingers. Thy years are as the years of Ra.*

In Philadelphos's funeral procession, wailing, beating their exposed breasts, ripping up the cheeks with the fingernails, tearing out their hair by the handful, walked his painted ladies, dressed in black. Sure, Philadelphos's whores had plenty to grieve about: their golden world was unravelling before their eyes, finished. The cascade of wealth that had poured down upon their heads now dried up overnight. They wept, indeed, for what use is it to a whore to have the title of goddess, and the votive offerings of an entire city, if she has at the end of it not one drachma with which to buy kohl to paint her eyes, not one obol for a loaf of bread?

Such is the fate of whores; such was the fate even of the divinized Aphrodite-Bilistikhe, whose statue on Kanopic Street was now pulled down, smashed up, and whose identification with the goddess was declared null and void by Ptolemy Euergetes in his first act as king, for causing high offence to the gods of Greece and Egypt together.

Perhaps the only man in Egypt who was relieved to hear of the passing of Ptolemy Philadelphos was Timokhares, hapless architect of the famous iron statue of Arsinoë Beta that had been twenty-four years in the making. Arsinoë Beta's iron eyes stared ahead, as they should, unblinking for ever, but she did not speak, weep, sweat, or utter one word about war, or anything else. A goddess was supposed to float above the ground, but however Timokhares fixed up the magnetic roof he could not make Arsinoë Beta hover even one fingerbreadth above the Arsinoeion floor.

Privately, Timokhares knew that his statue would never hover, but he was afraid to say so, lest his royal patronage be at an end. He had played for time, thinking up endless fresh reasons why the statue could not be finished. The Arsinoeion, then, stood permanently open to the sky, the rain collected in puddles and the pigeons shat all over the sanctuary.

Timokhares had done his best. He spread wide the net in his quest for ever larger pieces of magnetic stone in order to finish the largest magnetic roof in the history of the world. The iron statue of Arsinoë Beta would have been a cult statue, providing comfort to pilgrims. She would have worked miracles, and effected cures for any and every ailment, but most especially for chronic indigestion, bellyache, colic, griping, and stoppage of the guts. But no, it was not to be, for Euergetes cancelled the contract for the magnetic statue as a waste of money.

When Timokhares the Architect was told of it he kissed his wife and children and walked across the Heptastadion, very slow. He climbed the stairs to the third and topmost storey of the Pharos, even slower, and when he could climb no higher he stepped off the parapet. He had failed to make the statue of the late Queen hover, but he succeeded in becoming the first architect since Daidalos to fly.

Now, then, the third Ptolemy, called Euergetes, or Benefactor, made himself ready to arise as a beneficent king over all the earth. There was no night of hurried footsteps, no urgent running boots of soldiers, no night of bloody murder, for he refused to put to death his brother Lysimakhos, whom he loved, or any other member of his family.

I cannot kill my own brother, he said. *We have had enough murder in this family already. Let there be an end to violence under my own roof.*

Ptolemy Euergetes was just then in the thirty-ninth year of his age. He had long since been betrothed to the high Princess Berenike Beta of Kyrene, but he had not yet taken her to wife, for tradition allowed Pharaoh to marry only when he was crowned, so that his heir was born in the purple. And perhaps it was just as well, because the horoscopists forecast that his sure fate was *to be murdered by his own son.*

The murderous – or unmurderous – son Seshat shall treat of later. First, Stranger, you must hear of the murderous wife, Berenike Beta (*ber-en-EYE-kee* or *ber-en-EE-kay*), news of whose skill in the butchery department flew ahead of her as her five hundred racing-camels laden with gold loped through the sand towards Alexandria, saying she had done a murder when she was just fourteen years old; saying that the new Queen of Egypt was going to be just as terrible as the one before.

PART TWO
Husband-Slayer Berenike Beta

2.1

Amazon

You will remember, Stranger, that the Kyrenaica lies due west of Egypt, upon the north coast of Africa, and that Magas, son of Berenike Alpha, third wife of the first Ptolemy, was the ruler of it. Magas had been Strategos, or Governor, then King of Kyrene, for fifty years together, with charge over a vast kingdom of mountains and fertile plains, fine orchards, and cornfields that stretched down to the sea, producing three harvests every year. Kyrene was famous for fine-bred horses, for chariots and chariot-racing, for truffles and fair women.

Magas had been lucky. If his mother had not been Great Royal Wife of Pharaoh, the fortunes of Magas might not have turned out quite so marvellous. Had he stayed in Egypt he would have been a dead man on the day Philadelphos came to the throne, murdered, like all Philadelphos's other male relatives. Magas's rule had been just. He was always careful to do what was right in the eyes of the gods of Greece that had shown him such favour.

This king had been loyal to Egypt, sure, but his loyalty did not long survive the incestuous marriage of Philadelphos and Arsinoë Beta. Magas's own marriage was a clever piece of diplomacy, for his wife was the Princess Apama, daughter of Antiokhos Soter, King of Syria, who was now Magas's ally. What concerns Seshat now is not Magas's foreign affairs, which you know about already, but his domestic arrangements.

Apama, was, of course, a Macedonian by origin herself, though she had also some Persian blood. She had borne Magas one child only, a daughter, and, for whatever reason, was not like to have more. This daughter was called Berenike, after her illustrious grandmother, and in the absence of any sons Magas taught her every possible manly accomplishment, saying that she would have to be King of Kyrene herself.

Now do not be confused, Stranger, do not muddle these lovely ladies up: to distinguish her from her grandmother, Berenike Alpha, Seshat must call this girl Berenike Second, or Berenike Beta.

Magas worried about this daughter, even so, for however hard she made herself, a woman ruling alone would not bring stability to Africa. She would need a strong man to support her, and the most troublesome question was:

Whom should she marry? Aye, what man in the world would be strong enough?

The most suitable youth was her half cousin, Ptolemy Euergetes, the heir to the throne of Egypt. When the time seemed right, Magas sent word to Philadelphos, saying, *Peace is better than war. Friendship is better than fighting.* He was not much impressed with his fresh ally, Antiokhos Theos, who was reported to be drunken, and violent. He still thought Egypt was the best of all possible allies, and so he suggested that an end of coldness might be brought about by a marriage, and he hinted that Berenike Beta's dowry would be nothing less than the whole of the Kyrenaica.

How could Philadelphos refuse?

Magas, keen to do what was right in the eyes of the gods, sent his ambassadors into the sands of Libya to ask the opinion of Zeus-Ammon about his daughter's future, but though the Oracle said, *She shall know violence and die violent,* it also said, *She shall be a queen twice over, she shall be the mother of kings.*

Apama had her own thoughts about the Egyptian marriage, namely, that she did not like it, because she had thought to control the Kyrenaica herself when Magas stopped breathing, but if Berenike married Ptolemy Euergetes, Apama would be unlikely to get any power for herself. She wanted Berenike to have a husband who could be controlled by Apama. She waited to see what would happen. Magas was old and sick; he must die soon. She knew that her violent elder brother, Antiokhos Theos of Syria, wanted to use Kyrene as his military base so that he could invade Egypt not only from the Syrian side, but also from the west. She knew that in spite of Syria's famous peace with Egypt, her brother still desired more than anything else to take Egypt for his own possession.

Magas, at any rate, betrothed his daughter to Ptolemy Euergetes – now returned from Meroë. But because the heir to Egypt, by custom, did not marry until he became king, there must follow an indefinite delay, while Philadelphos grew old, and while Berenike Beta grew up, and the delay was just as well because she cannot, at her betrothal, have been much more than four years old.

As a gesture of good will, Ptolemy Philadelphos sent Magas two pair of rare Nubian ibex, and Magas sent back two pair of the famous white horses of Kyrene, and the betrothal was sealed and binding, when their ambassadors met in the desert halfway between Alexandria and Kyrene to swear the usual oath, *If we fail to honour the agreement, may our descendants bring forth monsters.* All that was needed now was for Philadelphos to die, and for Euergetes and Berenike Beta to stay alive.

*

Berenike Beta passed the age of eight, and the spies sent reports to Alexandria of her warlike progress. They said she was put upon the back of a horse at a young age, and had hardly come down off it ever since; that her great delight was fast chariots. She was quite fearless, even jumping her horse through hoops of flame. Aye, Magas trained her up to be hard, to steel her body for battle like the Amazons. From her daily exercise this little girl got herself a boy's muscles, biceps and triceps. She rode her horse astride, fast and furious, like the men. She galloped into the Libyan desert with her father's cavalry to hunt oryx and hyaena. The word was that Berenike Beta was just as good as a son and would make a very good king, so good that the jest among the troops was that she would soon be using the bronze razors, not only upon the face but also upon her chest.

When she was still quite young Magas taught her about horse husbandry and allowed her to be present at the covering of mares. He made her promise never to allow a stallion to mount his own mother, but to frown upon such things as unnatural, an affront to the gods. He also taught her to frown upon forbidden relations among humans, like all right-thinking Greeks, saying, *You must allow no nonsense with brother–sister marriages when you are Queen of Egypt.*

Magas showed Berenike the monsters that were born from inbreeding: two-headed lambs and blind calves. *There is a right way to do everything,* he said, *and the right way is the Greek way: the man with his wife, not the son with his mother, not the brother with his sister, no pretty boys, and no concubines.* Berenike grew up thinking strict moral thoughts, just the same as her father.

The Kyrenaica prospered under Magas's careful rule. The warlike Berenike Beta survived to celebrate her twelfth birthday, when she carried the basket in the great procession of Apollo. She sailed to Greece and raced chariots at the Nemean Games, and though it was not the proper thing for a woman, let alone a young girl, to crack the whip and drive her horses in person – only the Spartan women did such things – that is what Berenike did, and she won many prizes.

As the daughter flourished, the father declined, got sick of some mysterious African disease that made him so fat that he could walk only with difficulty. Some said the name of the disease was feasting.

Berenike Beta did not succumb to the marsh fever, the plague, the smallpox, or any other malady. She survived. She was the girl who must be Queen of Kyrene, if not Queen of Egypt, the girl whose fate it was to do a murder.

2.2

Howling

About Year Thirty-Five of Ptolemy Philadelphos, Magas died, and Queen Apama took control of Kyrene, as Regent for her daughter. Just how young Berenike was at her father's death nobody ever wrote it down, but Seshat, goddess of Arithmetic, finds it most likely that she was born in Year Twenty-One, which would make her just fourteen years old when the terrible events that were about to happen happened, hardly more than a little girl. Though she had been taught – unlike most Greek girls – to read and write, she was too young to manage waging war and negotiating peace. Such things needed mature judgement. She would need help, and Apama would help her until she was old enough to rule on her own. By which time Apama thought to have married her to some man who would do what she, Apama, wanted.

For Apama, of course, was a Seleukid, no less fierce than her daughter, and very keen to have her own way. Even so, she could not be called manly. Her concerns were women's things: jewels, tapestry, the weaving of purple cloth. *Aphrodisia* she had seen not much of in the palace of Magas, who, for whatever reason, took not much thought for squeezing his wife, but kept her much the same as any other Greek wife – more or less a prisoner in the *gynaikeion*. Apama stood at her windows and dreamed about the men she could see walking in the streets but could not have for herself. Most of the time, whatever Apama wanted, Magas refused to let her have it, and she found the ban on her pleasures very tiresome. Aye, she had some thoughts of her own about what she might do when her husband dropped dead.

So what happened? When Magas, upwards of seventy-one years old, breathed his last, Apama broke into peals of laughter, for she was free to do what she liked. She was a young woman, and she had found her aged husband's obesity disgusting. Aye, while the other women of Magas's household wailed, and beat the breast, and clawed the cheek till the blood flowed, Apama laughed, hysterical. The usual magnificent Greek funeral pyre was built upon the beach at Kyrene, and the corpse of fat Magas went up in flames, and the smoke blew into Berenike's eyes, but she would have wept anyway for the father whom she loved. Apama wept nothing but tears of mirth.

There was no ghost to speak of, for Magas had completed his full term of years. His spirit did not walk, but slept easy enough. So much for Magas of Kyrene. What concerns Seshat is his lucky – or unlucky – widow, the lovely Queen Apama, still in the flower of her perfect beauty, still young enough to attract a fresh husband. How would she behave herself? What would she do?

From the Egyptian point of view, Apama did absolutely the wrong thing, for on the day of her husband's funeral, as if drunk with her royal power, she sent ambassadors to Alexandria by fast racing-camel, saying, *We have made fresh arrangements regarding our daughter's marriage. The alliance between Egypt and Kyrene is cancelled. The betrothal is hereby broken off.*

It was as much as a declaration of war upon Egypt, as much as inviting Ptolemy Philadelphos to attack the Kyrenaica – but Apama had heard that Philadelphos was timid in matters of war, unlikely to fight unless she attacked him first. She was not afraid of Egypt.

Apama also sent ambassadors by swift-sailing *trieres* to the court of Antigonos Gonatas – Kneecap – at Pella, in Macedon, to invite a different prince to marry her daughter and be King at Kyrene. The lucky man was Kneecap's half-brother, Prince Demetrios Kalos (*dee-MEE-tree-ohss*), son of Demetrios Poliorketes, the late great Besieger of Cities, by his third wife, the famously unlucky Ptolemaïs, daughter of Ptolemy Soter. Apama had heard that Demetrios Kalos was handsome above every other man in Greece, if not the world, and that she would find it quite easy to make him do whatever she wanted. Apama urged Demetrios Kalos to leave for Africa at once.

2.3

Beautiful Demetrios

The Prince Demetrios was called Kalos from his astonishing good looks, for *Kalos* is the Greek word for Fair, Handsome, Beautiful. Athena had, indeed, invested this man with a more than human beauty. His hair was like the Sun, like a field of ripe wheat, a shock of golden curls. His limbs were like bronze, like the limbs of a Greek statue. He had the torso and muscles of an Olympian athlete. His teeth were like ivory, his eyes perfectly blue, like cornflowers. Suffice to say that he was handsome like no man seen before, or since.

Demetrios Kalos was just then about twenty-eight years of age, and pretty pleased with the course of his life so far. He thought he was lucky, because his horoscope forecast that he must die in the middle of *aphrodisia*, and he thought this meant he could not die in battle, but lived a charmed life, for to die in the arms of a woman was, to the Greek way of thinking, the best of deaths, the greatest blessing that the gods could send to any man. Demetrios had been an army commander in several battles. Like his father, this great warrior had not one scar upon his body, not a scratch. Now he thought himself luckier still. To be made King of the Kyrenaica seemed like a gift from Tykhe, goddess of Good Luck. He did not think, like the famous Polykrates, that he had more than his fair share of luck. He did not think that the gods might seek revenge upon him for being so very lucky. By no means. Demetrios Kalos had little time for the gods, but soon he would be a god himself. It would be a simple matter as King of Kyrene to announce his own divinity, arrange for his own worship. No king of his day did any less, except Magas. Aye, Magas alone, out of modesty, out of fear of divine punishment, had thought it prudent to remain a mortal.

The history of Demetrios Kalos was that after his father died, and his mother went crazy, he was taken to Pella, where he was brought up at the court of his grandfather, Antigonos Monophthalmos, One-Eye, the great enemy of Ptolemy Soter; and then, after One-Eye's death, by his successor, his own half-brother, Antigonos Kneecap.

Kneecap favoured the cult of Pan so highly that he put the image of this god – horns, goat's feet, pan-pipes – upon his coins. If Demetrios Kalos had taken any thought for the gods he would have known that it is wise to avoid stirring up Pan in the heat of noontide. But Demetrios Kalos was a modern prince, and thought himself above such nonsense. And although he was capable enough on a horse, wielding his sword against the enemies of Macedon, he was not specially famous for his wisdom off the field of battle. In fact, he was almost an identical copy of his father, in that he obeyed no rules except his own rules and held himself answerable to nobody. Aye, the godlike Demetrios Kalos had one rule only – *Do What You Like*.

But you should not make the mistake of thinking, Stranger, that he was some impetuous lad. He was a grown man in his prime, who had already married a wife, Olympias of Larissa, who was just as beautiful as her husband. He was even the father of a son – the Antigonos called Doson, who would grow up to be King of Macedon. But Demetrios could hardly take this wife and her child with him to Africa. Even he acknowledged that this was beyond the bounds of propriety. *So what did he do with them?* Stranger, he abandoned them to their fate, left them behind.

You may easily imagine how Olympias of Larissa felt when her husband told her he must sail away to Africa, leaving her to bring up a fatherless son. She must have clung to him, weeping. She must have begged him, in a flood of tears, not to leave her. Any woman would have done so. What, then, were his last words to her? Did he make his apologies, embrace her for the last time, murmuring, *A man must do what a man must do?* No, Stranger, he did not. Demetrios Kalos did not even bother to tell his wife that he was going. He did not stop long enough to say *Farewell.* He needs must go to Africa, and go at once. So much for this man's record as a faithful husband and devoted father.

Seshat can find no mention of Olympias of Larissa in the History of Macedon after this, either for good or ill. Seshat hears not one word of her remarriage. Perhaps she was delighted to be rid of Demetrios. Perhaps she lived much happier without him. On the other hand, perhaps she was not, and did not. Perhaps she went crazy herself. Perhaps she killed herself, for grief, and who could blame her?

Aye, Demetrios Kalos could not contain his laughter when he read Apama's letter. He borrowed a ship from Kneecap and sailed for Africa the same day. A few dozen of his friends made up the crew, went with him to be ministers, generals, and admirals. His friends might be trusted with his secret business, and run about with him in the *gymnasion,* and help him drink his wine after dinner, and help him to escape if things, by chance, happened to go wrong for him in Africa. Judge him not too harsh, Stranger. What young man would not have rushed out of Macedon by the next ship, with all sails raised, and row at ramming speed all the way to Kyrene if he was invited to be king of it? He would learn quick enough how to be a great monarch, how to make laws, how to condemn a man to death, how to declare war and broker peace. How could any young man turn down such an offer? Seshat thinks, Stranger, that in Demetrios Kalos's boots you might have done the same yourself.

But Seshat that knows all of the past also knows what lay in Demetrios Kalos's future. Seshat says, *Would that this most handsome of men had stayed at home in Greece. Would that this soldier of fortune had kept his place in the army of Macedon. Would that he never thought to set his foot in the shifting sands of Africa that would swallow him up.*

And did Demetrios Kalos know what was his fate? Had he sent to ask the famous Oracle of Apollo at Delphi what was his future? Of course not. He turned up the nose at oracles, soothsayers, divination from the flight of birds, the interpretation of dreams, as so much rubbish. He had faith only in Tykhe, goddess of Good Luck. He did not know what was going to happen to him.

But Seshat does know. Demetrios Kalos was not fated to equal Magas's record and rule Kyrene for fifty years. He would last barely fifty days.

2.4

The Darts of Eros

So often at the start of an ill-fated expedition everything will seem to be full of promise. When Demetrios' *trieres* docked in the great harbour of Apollonia, the sea-port of Kyrene, he leaped off it like a young god, and was struck by the African heat that felt very like a furnace. He set his soldier's boots upon the stone quay in a shower of rose petals, and he had little more to his name than his divine good looks, and the good luck talismans that he wore tied round his arms and neck, and that great black military cloak embroidered with the Sun and Moon, the Signs of the Zodiac and all the stars in heaven, that Ptolemaïs had sewed for his father, that had so often been soaked with her tears.

Perhaps Demetrios Kalos should have taken more thought for astrologers and soothsayers, though, for there were more tears due to his branch of the House of Ptolemy. Things had been bad enough for his mother, whose marriage lasted thirty days, but at least Ptolemaïs had lived: the fate of her son would be worse than that of a flayed cat.

Demetrios Kalos was welcomed by the ministers of Queen Berenike Beta, and he never stopped from sparkling his eyes and flashing his teeth for one moment as he rode with his friends towards the fairly illustrious city of Kyrene. Every woman he passed on the way fell in love with Demetrios Kalos on the spot. Every man marvelled at his unearthly beauty, and the word spread like the fire in a haystack that Apollo himself had landed at Apollonia, so that the country people dropped the plough and abandoned their beasts and ran across the fields to see him.

When Demetrios Kalos strode into the palace, all Corinthian columns and golden furniture – he found not the marriageable young woman he had expected, but a young girl with a flat chest and long yellow hair. And quite pronounced muscles in her upper arms. She sat on a chair of gold and ebony, eating dates and honey-cakes, fanned in the stifling heat by black slaves with ostrich-feather fans, and he saw that her feet did not touch the floor, and that her face was tanned by the sun, not white like the faces of other Greek girls.

The Greek rule said that a girl's breasts must be three fingerbreadths in height before she could marry a husband. Berenike Beta was not ripe for marriage. She was bronzed like a man, because she spent so much of her time in the saddle, or drilling with her troops, but very flat in the chest, and without the full rounded buttocks of a mature woman that Demetrios liked so much. She made Demetrios Kalos think of a parcel of cooked chicken, breastless chicken. She would need to grow a bit fatter before he would look at her with anything but disdain.

Like every other woman in Kyrene that day, however, the moment Berenike Beta saw Demetrios Kalos she was struck by the arrows of Eros and fell in love with him. Confused by her feelings, hot and cold all at once, and trembling, she managed to stammer a few words of welcome, then ran away to hide herself, leaving her visitor on his own, eyeing up the female slaves, wondering what he might do for a woman in Africa. But fate had lined up for him a fine woman, sure enough: Apama.

Where was Apama? At first she was busy resting from the unbearable heat, then she was busy making herself beautiful: painting her face with white lead, rouging her cheeks, plastering her eyes with kohl, brushing her long black hair, rubbing her body with the most costly perfumes of Syria, as if she was about to be married to Demetrios Kalos herself. She had heard the rumours of his impossible good looks. The most beautiful man in the world had just walked into her house. She was perfectly well aware that her daughter was far too young to be married to him. Apama had laid her plans quite carefully. She knew what she was doing, and she would make Demetrios Kalos wait before she appeared.

Unfortunately, the mother of Berenike Beta was where the trouble lay, for when Apama at last made her entrance, dressed in widow's black, and set eyes on the man, her heart jolted in her breast as if she might die of it. Aye, as the Greeks say, like a fierce wind Love shook her heart.

The beautiful Apama had, alas, been denied the pleasures that married women usually enjoyed. She was by nature hot in her flesh, just about ready to burst into flames at the best of times. Now and at last, she thought, she might indulge herself in a little passion. She did not run away to hide like her daughter, but tried to engage Demetrios Kalos in polite conversation. Magas had been old even before she married him, heavy, horrible in his bloated belly. Apama had never taken a young man like Demetrios Kalos into her bed before. She felt the heart bang in her breast as she asked the most beautiful man in the world, *Sit down beside us . . . Will you not drink a bowl of wine?*

Demetrios said little, but he was not obliged to say anything. Apama, never a woman to hold her tongue for very long, did the talking. She told him about the horses of Kyrene, the corn and apple harvest of Kyrene, the state of foreign affairs in Kyrene, the military strength of King Ptolemy – on and on, and the young Berenike Beta was nowhere to be seen. Demetrios drank a second bowl of wine, and a third, and Apama smiled broad, thinking herself lucky in her future son-in-law. But she could not stop staring him in the face – a thing that was unlucky, and highly dangerous, something no respectable Greek woman ever did. She stared into Demetrios Kalos's eyes, and he stared back at her. The Greeks say that the eyes are the windows of the soul; that the eye is the pathway for the wounds of love, the gate of entry for the disease of loving, and they say that the most intense moment of loving is when the lover's gaze falls upon the beloved for the first time.

Stranger, you would hardly believe it anywhere outside a made-up story, but the whole truth was that the mother and the daughter both fell in love with the same man on the same day, set on fire by Eros. But there was nobody to shake Apama and say *Beware, my friend, fan not the flame* . . . The flame of love was lit already, roaring up like a funeral bonfire, and there would be no putting it out.

The Greeks say *Love is Desire Doubled*. They also say *Love Doubled is Madness*. Apama already loved Demetrios Kalos like a madwoman. Her heart seemed to flutter, turning within her breast, like a hot bird. Aye, rather like a pigeon roasting upon a spit, captured, skewered, already burnt.

What does Euripides say? *Neither the sharp tongue of fire, nor the burning trail of the stars is more lethal than the dart of Aphrodite which speeds from the hands of Eros.* And so it was. Eros fired several more flaming darts that day, for Demetrios Kalos also fell a little in love, not with Berenike Beta, but with Apama, the woman who was meant to be his mother-in-law.

That evening Demetrios Kalos never stopped from fingering his talismans of good luck. He spoke hardly a word, but sat listening, half listening, to Apama's non-stop torrent of useful information. Demetrios Kalos had never needed to speak many words. All he ever had to do was smile and look handsome. A man as beautiful as this man has no troubles, no enemies. Every woman he met was ready to lift up her *peplos* for him. Every man wanted to be his best friend, if not play Ganymede to his Zeus. The only problem Demetrios Kalos ever had was fighting off the hundreds of men and women who craved his divine body for themselves.

No, Demetrios Kalos had not one personal enemy in all the Greek-speaking world. It was unfortunate, then, that he had come to Africa at all, for he was about to make the greatest enemy of his life.

Who, then, could be the enemy of Demetrios Kalos, the man without enemies?

Who could possibly dislike the man whom the whole world loved because he was the image of Apollo himself?

Stranger, it was Berenike Beta, the little girl who was due to be his wife, whose fate it was to do a murder, though she was only fourteen years old.

2.5

Divine Fire

On his first day in Africa Demetrios Kalos did little more than smile, drink too much wine and exclaim about the heat. When, in due course, he fell asleep in his chair, drunk, Apama had him carried to his bedchamber by her slaves, dark of skin and strong of arm, and she found it hard to stop herself from climbing into bed beside him. Herself, she lay awake for hours, thinking, *But I am the Queen of Kyrene. Why should I not do as I please? What does it matter?*

On the second day Demetrios Kalos smiled and drank too much, and was married to Queen Berenike Beta, because her mother said that even if the bride was too young for him, Demetrios Kalos must have what he had been promised – the kingship – lest he should change his heart and sail back to Macedon. It was also because just about the only thing Demetrios Kalos said was, *I hate to wait . . .* or *I do not like waiting* – whether it was waiting for his food, or his horses, or waiting for his wine to be fetched. Nor did he want to wait to be king, lest Apama changed her intentions and withdrew her offer. Having been promised power, he wanted to exercise it at once.

The king-making, then, was done literally overnight, and it was based not upon any noble words of Demetrios Kalos, nor upon his wise opinions and wonderful plans for his kingdom, for he had hardly said anything. If Demetrios Kalos had any thoughts about Kyrene, he kept them to himself. He had lived with the troops of Macedon, obeying orders. When he was not fighting some battle, he tried to keep up with his many women. When he was not having *aphrodisia* he liked to drink wine. When he had eaten and drunk he would sleep. Such was the simple life of Demetrios Kalos. He was made a king not because of how he behaved himself, but because Apama had heard reports of his amazing handsomeness; because both she and Berenike Beta wanted to feast their eyes upon his flawless flesh, because they loved to gaze upon his divine face, and it was all the most terrible mistake.

Apama thought, like all the Greeks, that a beautiful body means a beautiful spirit; there is nothing in the world higher than beauty, nothing in the world better than a handsome husband. Apama would not let this god slip through her fingers. By no means. She must keep him in Africa.

It was a sure thing, of course, that Demetrios Kalos did not mean to be told what to do by Apama or her daughter. He could have any woman he wanted, any woman in the world. A provincial city like Kyrene might suit him for today, but there would be other women, and perhaps other kingdoms, for Demetrios Kalos tomorrow. He already found Africa rather too hot for his comfort. Half a morning chasing ibex with the cavalry was enough to make his perfect skin blister and peel. He was a fair-skinned Macedonian, too proud of his golden hair to cover it up with the *kausia*, or sun-helmet, that any man of foresight would have worn in such searing heat. He was already thinking that he would not stay long in Kyrene, but that he could easily make himself king of some cooler place. Kyrene was indeed hot, but it would turn out far hotter for this man than he ever imagined.

Aye, Demetrios Kalos, then, a man nobody in Kyrene had known for more than a matter of hours, became King, upon the instant. Apama was satisfied with what Antigonos Gonatas had written her about his half-brother, his military prowess, his worthiness to be a ruler. Apama was herself in the very first days of having power in her hands. She was still, as it were, drunk with her new authority, ordering up great quantities of jewels and perfumes from Syria. Ever since the death of Magas she had walked about the palace giving orders, putting things to rights, dismissing Magas's old ministers and appointing her own men, and gorging on all the things Magas had forbidden her to eat, rather reckless, like a woman just released from prison. She did not think to wait a while to see what manner of man Demetrios Kalos really was. Aye, nobody in Africa knew the first thing about his character, except to suppose that because his face was fair his heart must be the same; that because he looked like a god he must behave like one.

But Seshat says the Greek gods always did behave badly towards their women.

When Demetrios Kalos was married to Berenike Beta, the royal diadem of a Macedonian king was tied round his head. The troops hoisted him on their shoulders and carried him round the palace courtyard, chanting his name, cheering and clapping, according to the Macedonian custom.

At the marriage feast the guests yelled and whistled to see Berenike do the war dances of Kyrenaica, the *men's* dances, for she had been brought up with the men, to be manly. She danced not only for Demetrios Kalos her husband, but also for her soldiers, whose applause was wild, for they loved this muscular Queen. But Demetrios was too busy staring at his mother-in-law to watch his wife dancing.

As for Apama, she danced the proper Syrian women's wedding dance, slow, at first, like the wind in the dunes, then furious like the sandstorm. She whirled on the spot right in front of Demetrios Kalos, clapping her hands. If the dances of Berenike Beta made the wedding guests go wild, her mother's performance sent them crazy. But the person Apama's dance had the greatest effect upon was Demetrios Kalos, who, whether because of the African heat, or the strong wine, or the violent music, was ready to leap on her.

Apama was firm about one thing regarding this marriage: she insisted that because of her daughter's age she must not be handed over to Demetrios Kalos for the ploughing of legitimate children, in case he should roll over in his sleep and squash her, or do some damage to her with his great *rhombos,* and it was agreed that he should wait to begin ploughing until her breasts were three fingerbreadths in height, like the proverbial two ripe apples of Macedon.

These precautions were all very sensible, and Berenike herself agreed to the delay, for that the three fingers was the Greek rule, and what her father would have wanted. But this arrangement left Demetrios Kalos without a woman to keep him happy in his bed, unless he took a concubine from the city. But Apama thought that if she let the whores get their hands on Demetrios Kalos she might never see him again, and the truth, of course, was that she wanted that divine body of his *for herself.* She thought, *To have aphrodisia with such a man must be very like sleeping with a god.*

She thought, *Yes, I shall keep Demetrios happy myself. When Berenike is old enough, I shall give him back to her, perhaps . . .*

So what happened? Because her daughter was too young for the ploughing, and went early to her bed, Apama entertained Demetrios Kalos, the new king, her son-in-law, herself, in her private apartments on his wedding night.

Instead of drinking with his Macedonian friends, he sat with Apama, who told him about the civil and criminal law of Kyrene, the finances of Kyrene, the pig tax of Kyrene, the lack of rain in Kyrene, the fine wines of Kyrene. And Berenike Beta, sound asleep, dreaming of fast horses and handsome husbands, knew nothing of what went on.

Demetrios Kalos began to seek out Queen Apama in the heat of midday, when the ostrich-feather fans had no effect, and even the palace slaves retired to darkened chambers to sleep until evening, when the heat was less over-powering. It was the hour when Berenike lay on her bed and read about the cleverness of Odysseus, so that she knew nothing of this either.

Apama asked what she could do to make Demetrios Kalos comfortable for the night – whether she might find him a woman, or a boy, or an animal of some kind, what would he prefer? Demetrios Kalos said he did not like boys, no, almost never. As for animals, well, he had not been brought up in the country to fuck nothing but the hens, but at Pella, city of beautiful women; and no, he had no time for any beast but his cousin Ptolemy of Egypt. He said he liked women very much. Best of all he liked a woman with olive skin, long glossy black hair, breasts like water melons, and great fleshy buttocks, a mature woman like Apama herself.

And so Demetrios Kalos began to let slip his tunic, because of the heat, and stretch himself out upon Apama's golden couch and take his mother-in-law in his arms to squeeze her. Aye, he even took off his good luck charms to kiss Apama, so that he wore nothing, nothing whatever, but it would have been better for him to have kept those charms *on*, for Tykhe was about to desert him.

It was noontide when Demetrios Kalos went to see Queen Apama, the time when the palace was quiet, and the slightest sound travelled a long distance. Noon was the most dangerous time of day to do what Demetrios did, for he ignored the old Greek warning against stirring up Pan in the siesta, and it was the biggest mistake he made in his lifetime.

2.6

Whispering

Demetrios Kalos began by kissing Apama, but he soon got into the habit of doing the other things men like to do, the secret things that belonged to her daughter. The sounds that echoed down the palace corridors during the long hot silence of afternoon were Apama's ecstatic panting, Demetrios Kalos his leonine grunting, and the extraordinary noise made by Apama's great gilded palm-wood bed, that was springy, the most modern kind of bed, its demented rhythmic creaking.

Apama was much about the same age as this young man. She did not think that letting her son-in-law ride upon her back and make her his whore would anger her daughter. And Demetrios Kalos did not stop to think that such behaviour might upset his wife. Love is blind, the Greeks say, and Demetrios and Apama were blinded by Eros indeed. They could think of nothing but their daily marathon of *aphrodisia*.

When Berenike Beta went to speak with her husband about what living quarters she might allot to him, or the number of bodyguards she could spare for his personal protection – but in fact with no other purpose than to stare into his perfect blue eyes and reassure herself that he was not a phantom – he did not want to listen. He had already taken what chambers he wanted and moved himself and his Macedonian friends into them, the men who made up his bodyguard.

When Berenike tried to talk to her husband about keeping the army happy by issuing the traditional extra ration of wine in honour of her marriage and his coronation, he did not stop smiling his devastating smile, but he shouted at her, *We shall speak with you when it pleases us.*

So soon as his third day in Kyrene, they said, Demetrios Kalos began to give Berenike Beta orders, as if he meant to keep her in her place, like any other Greek wife. *We shall start off,* he said, *how we mean to go on.* He would not be told by this little girl what he might and might not do. And all the time she was the Queen of the Kyrenaica, from whom he had gotten his hands on the title of King, and complete control of her vast kingdom.

One month of afternoons passed, and Beautiful Demetrios seemed more interested in exercising himself upon the body of the Queen Mother than in exercising in the *gymnasion*. He neglected the army he was meant to take charge of, complaining of sunburn, or the savage heat. When he did stir himself to ride out with the cavalry at dawn, they said he was overbearing, and that he affected to know more than his generals about war, whereas it was soon obvious that he knew less. And no, he never did order the triple triple ration of wine for every soldier. The troops, then, though they had been ready to love him for his handsome looks, did not love him for handsome behaviour. Seshat has said that soldiers care for nothing but the payment of their wages, but Berenike Beta's soldiers had been influenced by the strict morals of Magas. The whisper began to go round that their commander-in-chief was a man who was pleased to fuck not his wife but his mother-in-law. It did not exactly endear Demetrios Kalos to his men.

Much more than good looks is needed to win the hearts of an army. Even the most hardened of hired soldiers loved Berenike Beta, who looked after their well-being. It was the generals themselves, Berenike's friends, who first began to say aloud that Demetrios Kalos was unfit to be a king. Some of them said openly that he was idle, useless, proud, and must be thrown out.

And then somebody wrote Berenike an anonymous note telling her exactly what was going on between her husband and her mother.

2.7

Watching

For sure, Berenike Beta had heard the strange sounds that came from her mother's private apartments, and was curious to know what caused them. The next time she heard the rhythmic creaking she climbed over the roofs like a boy. Aye, she scrambled up the drain pipes and slid down over the roof tiles in order to reach the balcony from where she might see into her mother's chamber. She stood on her tiptoes and peered through the shutters to see – Oh – the naked Demetrios Kalos, glistening with sweat, straddling her mother, pumping away at her body like one of her father's stallions, getting a child upon his mother-in-law, doing with her mother what he was supposed to do only with Berenike herself.

Unnatural practices, Berenike thought, *unhellenic, unhealthy, disgusting, an offence before Apollo and all the gods.*

She did not know much about the arts of Aphrodite, but she knew what was allowed and what was not. Just as she disapproved of a stallion mounting his mother, so she knew she must thoroughly disapprove of a husband who mounted his mother-in-law.

What should she do? For sure, she knew that she could not do nothing. She told her friend the captain of the palace guard what she had seen. The next day she brought him to see how Demetrios Kalos occupied himself in the afternoon. In the next few days the captain of the palace guard brought the Nuktistrategos, the captain of the night watch, and the Nuktistrategos brought the Hypomnematographos, and so on, until all Berenike Beta's senior military men had seen the horror with their own eyes, the new husband trampling the bed of his wife's mother.

The days passed and the whispering spread, until every man knew what Demetrios Kalos was doing, and every man condemned it.

Berenike Beta lay sleepless by night, and it was not the amazing heat that kept her awake, for she was used to it, but the problem of what to do about Demetrios Kalos. *What would my father have done with him?* she thought. *He would have had the man torn apart in public.* No, Berenike Beta could not ignore this crime. Demetrios Kalos could not do what he did and go unpunished.

However Berenike chose to punish Demetrios Kalos, she felt it had to be within the law of her kingdom. She asked the Dioiketes, her friend, *What by chance may be the proper treatment for the husband who has aphrodisia with a woman who is not his wife?*

The Dioiketes knew what was going on, who Berenike was talking about. He did not try to talk her out of what she had to do. *A man caught in such an act may be delivered up for execution,* he said, *or he may be killed upon the spot, if you prefer.*

If only that man had never been born, she murmured, *or died unmarried.*

It is preferable, however, the Dioiketes said, *to avoid public dishonour. A wife might choose to deal with such a crime less harshly, by submitting the guilty party to a radishing.*

That man is good for nothing but looks, she said. *I shall drink his blood.*

2.8

Iron Heart

Demetrios Kalos showed no sign of leaving Apama alone. Often he passed the whole night lying in the Queen Mother's bed, careless of who knew he was there. He was a king now. He would make up his own laws as he went along, answerable to nobody. He had begun to enjoy his life in Kyrene. He was pleased to find that he always won the chariot race. He liked the Greek Theatre where he sat in the seat of honour, and the wide paved streets and shaded colonnades of his capital city that was more Greek than Greece. In the cool of the morning he would sometimes disport himself at the Greek baths, or make five or six circuits of the running-track in order to keep himself looking like a god. The regular grid plan of the streets, the Greek columns and temples, the regular blood sacrifice to Apollo, all this made him think of Macedon, of Pella, his homeland. Demetrios Kalos did not think ill of Kyrene any more. He was quite happy with how his new life was arranged.

But Berenike Beta could not be called happy. By no means. Her displeasure was fast turning into blazing anger. Upon the one hand she was delighted for

Demetrios Kalos to be her lawful husband, but she thought a husband should behave within the law. For sure, she loved him, this man who, in spite of giving her orders, made her feel faint whenever he smiled. Upon the other hand, this Macedonian marriage was not what she had wanted. She thought, *If Demetrios Kalos remains as our husband, we shall have to go to war with Egypt. But if our army has to fight under his generalship, we shall surely be beaten to a jelly.*

She thought of her father's dying wish, that Kyrene should be reunited with Egypt, and of his desire for lasting peace in Africa, not everlasting war. She thought that even though Prince Ptolemy Euergetes might not be quite so handsome as Demetrios Kalos, she might be better pleased by the Egyptian marriage after all. She questioned the Dioiketes, who told her, yes, it was as she had thought: Ptolemy Euergetes was what Demetrios Kalos was not – a *kalokagathos,* a perfect gentleman, a man of high honour. She liked the idea of reuniting Egypt and the Kyrenaica under one ruler. She also rather liked the idea of being an Egyptian goddess in her own lifetime.

In a moment of uncertainty she threw the dice to consult the Homer Oracle, but the oracle urged her on, saying: *Your heart should be of iron.*

Berenike spoke with her friend the captain of the palace guard and named the day of action. She had no doubts. What she had decided to do was the right thing in the eyes of the law, the proper Greek thing to do. She laid her plans with care. When the day came she sent her mother's waiting-women off to Taukheira to look for wild geese, and gave her mother's slaves and servants a day's holiday. Then this young girl carried on dealing with her royal business – sending ambassadors to Carthage and Rhodes, dispatching bread to the poor of Euhesperides, sentencing the criminals – all the business that Demetrios Kalos neglected in favour of being the furious jockey of his mother-in-law.

Berenike Beta paused in the middle of stamping her royal seal upon dozens of letters, and sent out the captain for stout ropes and a great fishing-net, and when her mother was in her bath, her tub of solid silver, she went to the chamber with him unobserved. Berenike tied the ropes about the lion's-paw feet of her mother's golden bed, tied them with her own hands, each rope with a noose or loop upon its end that could be drawn tight, and she hid the ropes under the bed, beneath the gold and purple counterpane. Apama would not notice. She was blind, blinded by Eros. She saw nothing but Beautiful Demetrios, his godlike body.

Comes the afternoon, the hour for resting with the shutters drawn against the brooding heat, when the head of Demetrios Kalos droops, and he sleeps off the wine he drinks with his luncheon, the excellent and most excellent wines of Libya; but before he sleeps he rides his mother-in-law. At this heavy hour, this dangerous, blazing hour, when even the flies quit their frantic buzzing, Demetrios Kalos has plenty of energy for his favourite kind of exercise. But this is just the time when great Pan sees everything a man does that is contrary to the will of the gods, and deals him his proper punishment.

Berenike Beta does not know what is weariness after luncheon, for she is not allowed to drink wine. It is the hour when she lies on her bed and reads how Odysseus, her hero, plunged the red-hot brand into the eye of the Kyklops; how he defeated his enemies by his most excellent cunning. But on this day she is too excited to read one word. She listens to the dripping of the *klepsydra*, her most modern water-clock, counting the regular drips. She stares at her dolls that are not women in dresses, but soldiers in Macedonian armour, men who do battle, like she does herself. Berenike Beta's work is the work of Ares, god of War, and now she must go to work. At last she lays down her book, her papyrus scroll.

Her mother's waiting-women have not returned from their excursion to Taukheira. The guards she has organized outside the door, guards who are her trusted friends, but no friends of her mother, or of Demetrios Kalos. The entire army of Kyrene she has ordered to be drawn up, silent, within the palace gates. Unknown to Demetrios Kalos, his Macedonian friends have already had their throats slit from ear to ear. The captain of the palace guard stands by with his sword made sharp, his men with him, silent in her mother's corridor, waiting. And one of them holds a giant radish.

Demetrios Kalos, of course, is in the middle of his horse race with Eros, riding fast. He has taken off his good luck talismans – the charm against unexpected sword wounds, the charm against bleeding to death, the charm against death by a thousand blows . . . He is careless of his safety, stark naked, unarmed and unaware, blinded by Eros himself, riding, riding faster and faster, and Tykhe has abandoned him.

Berenike Beta slides off her golden bed. She steps through the door leading to her mother's apartments, feels the mosaic cool beneath her bare feet. Her *peplos* is of pure white linen, but not for much longer. She sees her guards at the end of the passage. She raises her right hand, as if to say, *All is well, do, now, that deed of which we spoke.*

Outside her mother's door, Berenike holds her breath, listening. There is no sound but her mother's *Ohhhh– Ohhhh– Ohhhh– Ohhhh– Ohhhh–* her nightingale wailing, the ecstasy of her mother under the dead weight of

Demetrios Kalos, the King of Kyrene who is the husband of Berenike, the little girl, her lawful husband, and the urgent rhythm of the golden bed.

Berenike, her eyes shine with the suggestion of tears, but her mouth is set hard, frowning. Her heart hammers, and she remembers the captain's kindly words, *A woman's first murder is always the most difficult.*

2.9

Radishing

You will remember the treatise of Hippokrates, Stranger, *On Young Women,* in which he says that about the age of puberty a *parthenos* is specially liable to delusions, and that she may become murderous, or even think of killing herself. The stories of the Greeks often tell of young girls who make serious errors of judgement. It should be no surprise to you, Stranger, to hear what Berenike Beta did. She was a *parthenos* herself, just at the time of life when a woman is most capable of daring acts.

Remember to spare our mother . . . she whispers, and the captain of the guard nods the head, shows the teeth, raises a clenched fist, and his other hand is on the hilt of his sword.

Berenike pauses for a moment, having the last of her doubts, but no, her father would have ordered just the same. She must do what is right before the gods. Her heart turns over with the awfulness of what she is going to do. But then she hears her mother's shrill *Ahhh– Ahhh– Ahhh– Ahhh– Ahhh* and steels herself. She breathes the word that will put a stop to her mother's unlawful passion.

Ginestho, she whispers. *Let it be done.*

The guards scream the battle cry of Kyrene, and break down Apama's door, burst inside, fling open the shutters so the sunlight floods the room, and the great net flies over the guilty ones so they are trapped beneath. The ropes are pulled tight round their hands and feet, and Demetrios Kalos is on top thrashing about, and Apama is underneath, limbs writhing, held fast by Berenike's net and Demetrios Kalos twists and squirms, frantic to unloose his bonds.

There is no hurry, Berenike Beta says to the captain, quite without nervousness. *You may take your time.*

First they shave his head close with the bronze razors, very slow, that is the proper punishment for the man who likes to fuck his own mother-in-law.

Let him suffer, Berenike Beta says, *for his evil crime. Let him not enjoy the luxury of a speedy death.*

Real slow they shave his head, while Apama sobs, *Spare us, Daughter, do not put us to shame . . . We have done you no harm . . .* but Berenike Beta takes no notice.

When it is done, and Demetrios Kalos looks no better than a slave, the guards make much of sharpening their knives, until Berenike Beta says, *Let us carve him up, then,* and the blood flies at once out of his neck on to her white dress, making her squeal for surprise.

Aye, his blood shoots on to the white walls, splashes up on to the white-washed ceiling, spurts across the white linen of her mother's golden bed and into her mother's face. But no, her mother must not die, for the punishment for killing a mother is to pass the rest of your lifetime waited on by the Furies, the three women with snakes for hair. No, Apama must be let to live, and Berenike looks on, quite calm, as she rears up upon the mangled bed, naked, under the net, held by the ropes, dripping with her lover's blood, wailing, wailing.

Slice him up, then, Berenike Beta says. And so they take the sword and chequer his perfect muscled chest with cuts, like a bloody mosaic. His great thighs, perfect as a Greek statue, run with the river of his blood.

Ginestho, Berenike Beta screams, throwing the great radish to the captain of the guard, who catches it, and rams the vegetable between her husband's beautiful buttocks, kicking it home hard with his soldier's boot.

Ginestho, she screams, and in the flesh of Demetrios Kalos's beautiful back the eight-pointed star of Macedon glistens red. She screams again, takes a sword herself, and rams it home between her husband's bronzed buttocks, so that he screams a long scream. Berenike withdraws her sword in a fountain of blood. Time after time her sword thrusts in and out, and the blood pours out of him. There is blood dripping down the walls, blood on the floor, blood in her face and on her hands. Berenike stifles a sob. No, she had not known death would be like this.

Apama, soaked with blood, wails, *I beseech thee that I may not die.* But no, Berenike will not harm the breasts that gave her suck, nor the womb that bore her.

We must let my mother live, she cries, *let her suffer for what she has done.*

When Demetrios Kalos at last lies quite still, Berenike does what every Greek murderer must do. She closes the eyes, the most beautiful blue eyes in the world, with a forefinger, to stop her husband staring.

She chops off his necessity with her knife and stuffs it in his bloody mouth, as men in battle do to their beaten enemies, for the penalty for unlawful *aphrodisia* is emasculation.

She hacks off his beautiful feet and hands, his beautiful ears.

She strings these bloody extremities round the dead man's neck and under his armpits upon a string, as every murderer must.

With her right-hand forefinger she licks up the bright-red blood upon her tongue.

She licks up the blood a second time and spits it into his beautiful face. Three times she licks up the blood and spits out the pollution according to the Greek custom, so as to stop the terrible vengeance of a ghost with feet swift to pursue; to stop him following her ever after, to render his ghost powerless. Last she wipes her bloody sword upon the dead man's shaven head.

Just as in the *Odyssey* of Homer the gods came running to see Ares and Aphrodite caught in a trap, so now Berenike Beta punishes her mother by sending for her courtiers to see Apama naked and covered in blood, caught in the web of ropes and netting, shrieking, hysterical. The courtiers shriek back at her, shrieking with laughter.

But what is going on in Berenike Beta's heart? The hammering inside her flat breast has not stopped. She thinks this should be the end of her troubles, but the arrows of Eros, that she does not understand, are still stuck there, stuck fast, and Eros's arrows, that go in so quick, are not so easy pulled out. Only now that she has killed him does her love really take wing. She thinks her mother will suffer most, but she is quite wrong. She has killed the most beautiful man in the world and she will suffer more herself. Berenike Beta, brought up tough, does not weep. By no means. Her wound is upon the inside, a wound to the heart, and it will never heal.

She thinks her murder is over, but Seshat says a murder is never over. A murder echoes down the years, echoes. This was not the end of Berenike's horrors but the beginning.

2.10

Feasting

The body of Demetrios Kalos, what was left of it, the guards dragged away, threw out in the dust beyond the city walls, where the dogs and vultures made their feast upon his bloody flesh. Berenike Beta drove her chariot there every day to see that her orders were not disobeyed, for no one to sprinkle earth upon his corpse, no one to perform the funeral rites for him.

She thought she had seen the last of Demetrios Kalos, but now she began to see his shadow in the palace corridors. Now the tidal waves of guilt washed over her. She dreamed of the sea crashing on the shore at Apollonia, wave upon wave of blood, and herself sucked back by the bloody surf, drowning in the blood of Beautiful Demetrios. Berenike hardly knew what love was. Only now that she had destroyed the object of her love did she realize her mistake. No, her love for Demetrios Kalos did not die with him, but sprang to life, and started growing.

Brave Berenike Beta suddenly became fearful of the dark, seeing bloody Demetrios in her every dream. Aye, he lay on top of her, heavy, just as he had lain on top of her mother, tongue in her mouth, *rhombos* pumping in her secret place. She had rid herself of Beautiful Demetrios, for sure, but she had gotten his beautiful ghost for good.

Demetrios was not thirty years old at his death. The Greek thought is that the ghost of a man who dies before his time must walk for what is left of the natural term of his life. Aye, little Berenike Beta would be haunted forty years, upwards of fourteen thousand six hundred nights, until the day she died. She worked it out herself, wondered why she did not think of it before.

How vigorously she washes herself. How often she plunges her hands into water trying to make them clean, but no, she will never be clean of such a crime. The bloody stain of this murder lies not upon her flesh but on her soul.

Berenike Beta sent her ambassadors straight away to Egypt to say that her husband was a dead man, and that though she had been married, she was still a *parthenos*, and that the broken off betrothal might be renewed, if the Prince Ptolemy Euergetes were not already betrothed elsewhere, and if his Majesty were agreeable. Philadelphos did agree. He would agree to anything in return for peace. And so Berenike Beta settled down to wait for the old man to die, because Euergetes could not marry until he was Pharaoh.

She must have waited two, three, four years, for Philadelphos to fly to the stars. Meanwhile, she seems to have ruled Kyrene on her own, wearing the dark veil of mourning for her dead husband. Always she did what her father would have done, what was right before the gods of Greece.

But did she think about what would happen once Demetrios Kalos was gone? Perhaps not. Her old betrothal – to Ptolemy Euergetes – was made valid again, but while she waited for her fresh husband she struggled to keep a hold on her power as sole ruler of the Kyrenaica. Seshat must suppose that the friends of Demetrios Kalos were not so easily squashed; that Berenike Beta's own supporters suffered serious losses; that there was a battle for power when Demetrios Kalos died.

Seshat has heard tell of a republican party, that gained the upper hand, for the Kyrenians who were not such great lovers of Magas and monarchy invited two philosophers, Ekdelos and Demophanes, men of Megalopolis, a city in south-west Arcadia, to take charge of the state.

Some held that Ekdelos and Demophanes came to Kyrene *with* Demetrios Kalos. Others said the people of Kyrene took matters into their own hands and sent for them. However they got there, they championed their cause in a brilliant manner, and reformed the constitution, not unlike a brace of doctors brought in to attend a sick kingdom.

But Seshat really does not know how long these philosophers ruled in Kyrene.

Seshat really does not know what became of Berenike Beta under the republic.

Nor does she know how the republic, if there was a republic, ended. Seshat does not know, Stranger, does not know, does not know one word about it.

A different account holds that the city of Kyrene itself agreed to return to Ptolemaic rule, but that the other cities of Libya refused, and rebelled. Some say that Euergetes' armies had to go to war in order to reconquer western Kyrenaica, and that this operation took him as long as five years, and that all this happened before ever he succeeded to the throne of Egypt. At all events, Euergetes took fierce measures to punish the rebels. The city of Barke was deprived of its port, and had its name changed to Ptolemaïs. Taukheira was refounded under the name of Arsinoë. Euhesperides, conquered by Euergetes' hired soldiers, was replaced by a fresh city, built on the coast a short distance away, and renamed Berenike.

What was the truth of it? Did Berenike Beta collapse after her murder, fall seriously ill? Was it the truth that she could do nothing but weep for months together, toughness and boldness notwithstanding, for having destroyed the world's most beautiful man? She loved him, Stranger. She was the sorrowing widow.

There is only so much that even the goddess of History can tell you, Stranger. The rest is lost.

All the same, Berenike Beta's boldness won her the undying regard of her army. Every man was astonished by the courage and nobility of this *parthenos.* If she carried on being Queen of the Kyrenaica as before, it was without her mother's meddling. For sure, we hear no more of Queen Apama after this. No, not one word.

When Ptolemy Philadelphos died, Berenike Beta made herself ready for travelling to Egypt. Before she quit Kyrene she dedicated her earthenware dolls, her masculine dolls, hung them up in the Temple of Maiden Artemis, made generous sacrifice of jet-black bulls to Apollo, thus paying farewell to her somewhat unusual childhood.

She cast her golden dice one more time to ask the Homer Oracle what her future held. One-Five-Six she threw. She looked up the verse in the papyrus: *And the gateway is full of ghosts, and full also is the courtyard.* She might have guessed. Aye, soon there would be so many ghosts in the city of Alexandria that a man could not walk down the street at night for being jostled. The heart of Berenike, cold and stiff for horror at what she had done, sank a little further, if that were possible.

In the Kyrenaica they still repeat the old proverb: *Out of Libya comes always something new.* The new thing that came now out of Libya was Berenike Beta, the famous murderess. Through the swirling sandstorm she came, galloping up the military road that follows the coast. In the deserts of Africa, they say, ghosts will often meet the traveller and vanish in a moment. For sure, whenever Berenike Beta turned her head to look back, she saw a solitary figure trudging through the sand, hanging back behind the camel train, head down, battling against the wind, feet seeming not to touch the ground, and it was Demetrios Kalos, her beloved, whose home was neither with the living nor the dead, following her all the way to Egypt.

The news of Berenike Beta's murder flew ahead of her to Alexandria, where they said Demetrios Kalos got no more than he deserved. The jest-makers laughed that Berenike had given him the best of deaths, saying, *The most beautiful way to die is in the middle of aphrodisia.* It would not have done for the perfect body of such a man to grow old and wrinkled. By no means. Having died young, Demetrios Kalos would be the world's most beautiful man for ever.

PART THREE

Benefactor
Ptolemy Euergetes

3.1

Tryphon

Seshat returns, then, to Ptolemy Euergetes, son of Ptolemy Philadelphos and Arsinoë Alpha, in Alexandria, in Egypt. He is the third King Ptolemy, the one who must marry the murderess. For sure, he knew all about her adventures with the sword. He was not bothered to hear of it. On the contrary, he was proud of her. This was the kind of wife every pharaoh dreamed of: a wife who could look after herself was a very useful acquisition.

If Euergetes really was sent to Kyrene himself after the death of Demetrios Kalos, Seshat knows nothing more of it. If true, then Euergetes might have met his wife to be. He may have gotten to know her well, would have known what he was letting himself in for.

No crown prince of the Ptolemies ever married before he succeeded to the throne (apart from Philadelphos). Do you want to know why that was, Stranger? Life could be short in these times, and uncertain, and nowhere shorter or more uncertain than in a Greek – or Macedonian – royal family. Some mysterious foreign plague might wipe out an entire generation of Greek princes overnight. Sometimes the plague happened to be a sharp knife that found its way into a man's neck just beneath his ear. The heir might not survive to succeed his father. And they must secure the best of all possible foreign alliances by engineering the best marriage. Nobody could be sure who would win power on the death of the old king, when, according to custom, there would be a bloodbath of his Majesty's closest relatives. That is the real reason why there was no wedding before the coronation: they never knew which son would prevail. Pharaoh must make himself secure on his throne before he can begin to think of his domestic arrangements. And, of course, a son born too soon might be old enough to murder his own father and take the kingship from him.

Ptolemy Euergetes delayed his marriage, then, but he soon ended the thirty years schism between Egypt and Kyrene by marrying Berenike Beta. She was pretty plain, and most certainly not as other women, but Euergetes was not too much troubled. He did not marry his wife for her looks but to bring Kyrene back into the hands of the Ptolemies, and because she knew about royal power, and understood what it meant to be a monarch. She would help him carry the burden of ruling a turbulent kingdom.

Berenike made that husband of hers sing the Crow Song of the Greeks at his wedding, made him sing it twice. Euergetes did not object. He had doubled the size of his kingdom, protected his western border from invasion, and laid his hands upon the world's richest corn country. He thought of Egypt, where Famine was a constant threat, and of his cavalry, for in the stables of Kyrene were bred the world's finest horses. He slept easy in his bed, thinking himself blessed by the gods, little knowing what troubles lay only a few months into the future.

Only Anemhor saw into tomorrow, and Anemhor kept silence about what he saw: blood, and more blood. The Ptolemies lived one day at a time, in a perpetual present. They thought it was unlucky even to speak the word *Tomorrow*, for fear of tempting the gods to cancel tomorrow and carry them all off to Hades. Perhaps they were right to think thus. For the Ptolemies, tomorrow would always be bloody.

The new husband of Berenike Beta was kind enough, but, weighed down by affairs of state, he had gotten for himself already the distant manner of Pharaoh. He did not set Berenike Beta's heart on fire when she looked at him, and perhaps that was just as well. She had had enough of flames.

When Young Anemhor, the High Priest of Ptah, first came in his leopard-spot mantle to greet this queen, he said to her, *Wisdom Book of Ankhsheshonq: May the heart of the woman be like the heart of her husband that they may never quarrel.* He said, *May Ptah the Great give life, prosperity, health – a long lifetime and a great happy old age.* Berenike Beta smiled the half-smile of the Lady of the Two Lands for the first time, but Anemhor knew that old age was something neither the husband nor the wife would live to enjoy.

She had another visitor, of course, rather more regular than the High Priest of Ptah – the ghost of Demetrios Kalos, which followed her about, day after day. He came often to stand at the foot of her bed on the hottest afternoons, and then again in the night time, a mutilated Demetrios, naked and streaming with blood, even more beautiful dead than alive. The ghost made her tremble and cry out, at first, how could it not? She should have been capable of pretending that he was not there, of looking the other way, but mostly she looked; mostly she could not stop looking.

No, her love for the departed Demetrios Kalos did not grow any less fierce. When her husband came to her for the ploughing, and his face was close up to hers, she saw only the smiling face of Demetrios Kalos. At first she screamed a little, and bolted her door against her husband, asking for time, for a little time to compose herself. Euergetes understood, perhaps. He did not show anger. Berenike saw her dead husband walking the earth every day, but a woman who had won the chariot race at the Nemean Games should really have no fear of anything. Berenike began to recover her strength. When the ghost got too close for her comfort she would swear at him in the dialect of the Kyrenians, or give the word for her tame lion to step forward. She would soon have that ghost of hers pretty much under control.

On the other hand, she often smelled a smell that was not the fresh fish smell of the harbour of Alexandria, nor the rotten fruit smell of the Agora, nor a bad drains smell, nor the salt smell of the Great Sea, nor yet the smell of unwashed people. They say that a sweet smell is a feature of the gods, and it was now that she took a sudden interest in the perfume factory – but her interest in perfume was to smother the foul stench of the Harpies that hung about her because she had done a murder.

As he poured for her some Egyptian potion guaranteed to end her torments, the High Priest of Ptah said to her, *The Night-Demon will not bend over you.* But the Night-Demon did bend over her, night after night.

Berenike Beta had not quite known what she was doing when she killed her first husband, but she knew that what she had done was right. Her eyes were sad, with the sparkle gone out of them. She would sit staring at nothing, lost in her terrible history, stuck upon the day of the murder of Beautiful Demetrios. She would flinch when Ptolemy Euergetes touched her body. She washed her bloody hands over and over again.

Her Majesty must stop brooding, Anemhor told her. *She must throw herself into some work. She has not done wrong.*

Slowly, Berenike Beta got back her boldness. She tried to keep the half-smile on her face. But even the mosaicists failed to make a portrait of anything other than a plain round face with haunted eyes; the round, sad face of the woman who was in love with a ghost.

By this time Ptolemy Euergetes was perhaps thirty-nine years old, a seasoned warrior, an experienced general, quite different from his shrinking, scholarly father. He loved to hunt wild beasts. He knew more than any man in Egypt about elephants of war. Picture him, Stranger, on the back of a horse, galloping into the desert with his cavalry. His wife went with him. He got along quite well with that horse-mad woman. He even liked her.

What else does Euergetes like? He likes order. He likes facts. He likes to measure things. He likes efficiency, modern machines. Best of all he likes science, the precise sciences. He would like to organize a precise method for keeping track of the passage of time, a proper calendar, for it troubles him that in Egypt the harvest does not fall at harvest time, that the calendar does not synchronize with the seasons. He believes in progress, in making things better. He spends hour upon hour talking with the scholars of the Mouseion. He wants to know about the world, and to conquer it for Egypt. He is not just interested in women and eating, like his father.

Upon the day of his accession the new King Ptolemy assumed the fivefold titulary of the Egyptian monarch as his father and grandfather had done before him.

His Greek title, *Euergetes*, has already been useful, Stranger. Seshat hopes that you have not been confused uttterly by every male in this family having the same wonderful name of Ptolemaios, Warlike. *Euergetes* was the Greek equivalent of the Egyptian *Menches*, meaning Efficient, Beneficent, Excellent, which was what this King was. *Menches* happens to be also the title of Hapi, the Benefactor, the god of the Nile, the god who makes the River rise. Indeed, for the rising of the River the Pharaoh was held directly responsible, as Euergetes would soon find out. It also happened that Dionysos, with whom the king identified himself, was called The Universally Beneficent God. Euergetes, then, got for himself titles that were satisfactory both to Greeks and Egyptians, and it was all the excellent work of his Excellency, Anemhor, the wise man of Memphis.

Throughout his boyhood, however, Euergetes had been called *Tryphon* – a Greek name that means Soft-Living, Delicate One, Fastidious, Over-Indulgent in Goodly Things, Luxurious, as if this boy liked to eat more than was good for him; as if excess was his delight, and he was just like his father. But now Euergetes made a virtue of his name, and Tryphon came to mean also The Magnificent.

To be sure, Seshat has not a scrap of evidence for any luxurious habits of this Ptolemy, though you may assume that the lavishness of the court went on much the same as usual. No Ptolemy was ever moved to introduce Spartan ways in Alexandria. As for excessive love affairs Seshat hears not one word. There were none. Euergetes would be faithful to Berenike Beta his wife. To explain to you why that was, Stranger, is a simple thing. She was a muscular woman of unusual boldness. Wherever she went a lion padded behind her, sometimes on a golden leash, sometimes walking free. Never to be forgotten was the fact that she had done a murder. The husband of such a woman would not go out of his way to stir up her anger. But do not make the mistake of thinking he was soft like Philadelphos. Euergetes was just as capable as his grandfather, Lysimakhos of Thrace, of putting his arm down the lion's throat and ripping out its tongue, if attacked. And if the presence of a lion seems bizarre, at least Berenike Beta did not surround herself with snakes and crocodiles.

Euergetes heard the stories about his wife's intrepid murder, her unbending strictness. It was more than this man's life was worth even to think of keeping a concubine in the palace for his secret pleasure. There is no scandal to be written down about the love affairs of Ptolemy the Benefactor, Ptolemy the Magnificent. He had no mistresses. He was a most virtuous king, right-thinking, just like Magas of Kyrene and Berenike Beta herself. That is the official line.

There was only ever one rumour about Euergetes being involved with a woman who was not his wife. She was Oinanthe of Samos, his children's nurse. Perhaps the rumour of her involvement with his Majesty was somebody's jest, for Oinanthe was not the thinnest of women. Perhaps it was the truth. True or false, this Oinanthe was fated to play a significant part in the history of the House of Ptolemy. Seshat will deal with Horrible Oinanthe later. Try to control your impatience, Stranger, if you please.

3.2

Balance

To speak true, even Seshat, the goddess of History, does not know very much about Ptolemy Euergetes, but she will do her best. You should think of him, Stranger, as the most mysterious of the Ptolemies. He has strange fits of activity and idleness. He is notable both for his greatness and for his insignificance. Maybe it is the truth that his wife, Berenike Beta, the bold one, had the power, was the one who made him great. Maybe the truth is that Euergetes was just as magnificently lazy as his father, and that is why they called him *Tryphon*.

Lazy or not, it is not true that, as some men said, Ptolemy Euergetes did nothing for the first thirty-eight years of his life. He had trapped elephants in Trogodytica. He had spent years in Ethiopia, learning about the myrrh trade, the traffic in frankincense, dispatching elephants of war to Memphis. He had overseen the dispatch of gold from the South Country. He had written letters back and forth to Apollonios Rhodios, the Director of the Great Library, receiving from Alexandria parcels of Greek books. He did not lack either education or energy. He would be a strong king, Strong Bull, indeed, even if his queen was stronger.

*

Ptolemy Euergetes liked the look of Berenike Beta, and not only because her dowry was the entire kingdom of the Kyrenaica. She was round in the face, a little fat in the cheeks, a little plumper in the buttocks now, despite her vigorous manly pursuits – which, for sure, she kept up in Egypt, riding out most regular to exercise her horses. Like her father she loved to eat – roast meat, fowls, pigeon pies, but nothing in excess, of course – and how different she was from the late queen, Arsinoë Beta, who ate less than a bird. But how good it was for Egypt to have a queen again. Twenty years and more had passed without a Lady of the Two Lands.

The murderess smiled a little. Like her mother she was not afraid to stare her husband in the face, though her eyes seemed troubled, haunted. Your concern, Stranger, is for her heart, for her feelings. You want to know whether she loved or did not love. But the marriage of kings is about power, and this marriage was about Egypt getting back Kyrene, about Empire, not about Eros. Berenike Beta had already gotten her fingers burnt by Eros, aye, and her eyebrows singed. Some gave voice to the nonsense that Berenike Beta was greatly beloved by Euergetes, calling this marriage a happy marriage, as happy as a marriage can be in which the husband must share his house with a lion. She allowed this beast, they said, to lick her face with his tongue so as smooth away the wrinkles. He would share her table and eat from a plate, just like a human being. So they said. For sure, some held that this lion belonged to one of the other Berenikes, but Seshat swears it was this one, the boldest of the Berenikes. Among lions, mating is for life. Berenike Beta believed that among humans mating should be just the same.

Perhaps Euergetes and Berenike loved, perhaps they loved not. What does it matter? The important thing was that, before long, they would beget a fresh Ptolemy, an heir for Egypt. What mattered was the dynasty, the absence of war, the prosperity of the Two Lands, not love.

Berenike Beta made the best of her new life. The Greek poets, Homer and Pindar, say that married happiness is all about *homosophryne*, the union of hearts and minds. The happiest husband and wife in all the books of the Greeks were Odysseus and Penelope, and it was because they talked to each other, listened to what the other had to say. Euergetes and Berenike Beta were like that, Stranger, talking one to another, just like ordinary people. This wife did not keep up a frosty silence, or a barrage of insults all the time, like Arsinoë Beta. In part it was by reason of that lion of hers, over whom she had remarkable control. If Euergetes displeased her, she would direct the lion to go and wash her husband's face a little. Euergetes was more used to killing a lion than have him rip up meat at his own table. He came to listen for the click of lion's claws on the mosaic. Seshat says it again: *He was not soft, Stranger, like his father, but tough, warlike, skilled in the use of every modern weapon of war, just like his wife.*

Berenike Beta was Queen of Kyrene, queen of half Euergetes' kingdom. She would not let him neglect her country, but kept him up to the mark in respect of his royal duties there. Aye, and his duties were many, for he inherited from his father not only Egypt but Syria, Phoenicia, Cyprus, Lykia, Karia and the Kyklades. Nor would the burden grow any less, for he would make himself master of all the land within the Euphrates, Kilikia, Pamphylia, Ionia, the Hellespont, and Thrace as well. He would be the greatest conqueror of his family.

Euergetes got down to the business of being a monarch at once. He ordered the minting of his first coins, tetradrachms that showed him wearing a spiked or radiated crown, and looking much the same as his father and grandfather. He had the same short face, the same fat cheeks, not because he loved feasting but because this was how a king should look. He rode out with Berenike Beta and the cavalry every day, galloping around the shores of Lake Mareotis, or, when he was at Memphis, round the Pyramids, and deep into the desert. Unlike his father he did not neglect the military but took charge. Berenike Beta shared the burden, helped him. Anemhor was pleased by it, for the balance of Maat, or order, was maintained; the balance of the Two Lands. There would be no chaos under this great king. None.

The new Pharaoh was crowned by Anemhor, now perhaps forty years old. His sons, Djedhor, about twenty years old, a priest with important duties in the temple, and Horemakhet, about fifteen years old, and a junior priest, walked with him in the procession, his attendants, watching the ritual, remembering how things were done. If you yourself, Stranger, want to remember how the coronation was done, look at Thoth's account of it in the book before this book. In Egypt nothing changes very much. Every coronation was much the same, apart from the personages involved.

What was different this time was Anemhor's suggestion that Euergetes might be pleased to mark his coronation by building a Temple of Osiris at Kanopos, east of Alexandria. Euergetes was pleased, and the temple was begun at once. He agreed to complete the shrine of the Temple of Isis at Philai, begun by his father. For the Greeks he built a Temple of Sarapis at Kanopos, and the walls of it were fifty cubits square. These were the first of his great works, thank-offerings to the gods for their goodness.

One of Euergetes' first actions was to name as Librarian the famous Eratosthenes of Kyrene, who would stay in his post until the very end of the reign. Please to not confuse Eratosthenes with Erasistratos, Stranger. The former is the famous scholar, the latter the famous doctor. Eratosthenes was a very great man. In his great work, *Chronographiai,* he tried to fix the dates of every event since the beginning of time. Seshat says such a thing was impossible, beyond even the goddess of History, but Eratosthenes made a brave attempt. In Alexandria they called him *Pentathlos,* All-Rounder, for that he wrote not only geographies, a treatise upon comedy in twelve books, but also works on mathematics and astronomy. Eratosthenes was one of the first glories of Euergetes' reign.

See, then, Stranger: already the Benefactor did good things for Egypt. His reign was set to be no less glorious than that of his father. You should make the most of it, for the reign of his son would not be glorious. Euergetes was the last of the great Ptolemies. As for the others – it would be like the very best of Greek tragedies, bloody. Even under Euergetes the blood begins to trickle through the palace, under every door, edging across the mosaic, slowly turning every last colour to red. Onward, Stranger: let us wade together through the rising tide of blood.

3.3

Luck

Arsinoë Beta had to wait until she was dead for a Horus name. To Berenike Beta the high priests gave Egyptian titles at once, just like the Pharaoh. She had her Horus name – Daughter of the Ruler, Created By the Ruler, and a birth name – Berenike the Beneficent Goddess, Beloved of the Gods. She appeared at once upon the temple carvings as the companion of her husband, as a priestess enjoying equal rank, worshipping the gods of Egypt at her husband's side, and it was almost unheard of in the whole history of the Two Lands. She stood next to her husband even in the scene of the bestowal of power by Thoth, enjoying equal rights before the gods. Now she inherited even the title of her predecessor, Arsinoë Beta, The Female Pharaoh. She had doubled the size of Egypt's empire overnight. She even wore the ceremonial coat of Pharaoh. Seshat asks herself again, whether it was the truth that in this marriage Berenike Beta wore not only the Pharaoh's coat and crowns, but also, as it were, the *anaxurides,* even the trousers.

Quite early in his reign Euergetes was driving in his chariot with the Queen, both of them firing arrows at whatever wild beasts they passed, when they fell in with a young man – tall, powerfully built, with the flawless physique of a Greek god – running along the Kanopos road, in the middle of nowhere. Euergetes stopped his chariot, surprised he had run so far – thinking that he must be training himself up for the long distance race. Athenion the ambassador – who was among the courtiers travelling with him – said he knew this man, that he would make Euergetes smile, would be a good jestmaker. His Majesty asked the runner to climb up, to take a seat in his chariot, said they could give him a lift to Kanopos. But the runner said no, he must keep on running, must get himself properly fit, must win his race. Instead, Euergetes invited him to dinner, and that was how the runner got his feet through the doors of the palace, and it was the beginning of many things happening in Alexandria that should not have happened, terrible things.

The runner's name was Sosibios son of Dioskurides, an Alexandrian, and he was then about twenty years of age. Euergetes encouraged his athletic training, jested with him and enjoyed his company. He thought, much as Berenike Beta's unfortunate mother thought, that because Sosibios was handsome, and amusing, he must also be good. Euergetes became his patron, and paid for him to sail to Greece to run in the Olympian Games. He began at once to ask for Sosibios' opinion on everything that concerned Games in Alexandria.

Sosibios won his race at Olympia. He also won the men's wrestling at the Panathenaian Games. He won prizes for boxing at the Isthmian Games, and the Nemean Games, and there was no end to the rewards that were showered upon him. The island of Delos honoured him in a decree. Knidos put up a statue. He earned the admiration of the entire Greek-speaking world, was held in almost superhuman awe as an Olympian prize-winner, for such a victory was the most enviable piece of good luck that could fall upon any man. He was granted a parade on Kanopic Street in a hail of rose petals, free seats at the Theatre for life, and a free luncheon every day till he died. They said he ran so fast he was invisible; that he could make himself disappear. Sosibios thought he was certain to enjoy honours and blood sacrifice after his death, and receive worship as a hero.

As things turned out, he was wrong about that, wrong one million times.

From early manhood, all the same, Sosibios stood in high favour with Ptolemy Euergetes, and when he had completed his military service the King took him into the palace and asked his opinion not just about running and wrestling but upon every other matter. Soon he was travelling the world as a royal envoy, in a position of great responsibility, enjoying his Majesty's absolute trust, even though the wisdom of both the Greeks and Egyptians urged that a king should trust nobody.

What of Berenike Beta? You might think that these two great charioteers would have had something in common, something to talk about. So it was. They had some conversations about chariots, axles, whips, and horses. For sure, Berenike Beta encouraged Sosibios herself, in the beginning, but the more she saw of this young man the less she liked him. She thought Sosibios showed the teeth too much. She was told he had cheated in the wrestling. And she thought he made use of sharp practices in the Hippodrome, bending the rules in the chariot race to suit himself.

You shall hear more, Stranger, of this lucky, or unlucky, man. For now it must be enough to remember his ominous name. And no, Euergetes should not have trusted him. It would have been better for Egypt had Euergetes saved an arrow and shot Sosibios the moment he set eyes on him, for the truth was that Sosibios was not Euergetes' friend but his enemy.

It was also early in Euergetes' reign that Berenike Beta heard one morning the rattle of the dice-box and found her husband playing some game with his ministers at the same time as the Dioiketes read out to him the list of criminals for sentencing. According to what numbers he threw, Euergetes pardoned the man, or had him delivered up for execution. The punishment was determined by chance, regardless of whether the man was guilty or not, without thinking about his case.

> *Five – Cut off the nose and ears.*
> *Eight – Bind and scourge.*
> *Nine – To be crucified.*
> *Six – Let him live.*

Lives hung upon the fall of his Majesty's dice, but this was how the Greeks saw human fate in these times. They had begun to worship Tykhe, goddess of Luck, at the expense of all other divinities. What happened in a man's life seemed so often to bear not much relation to how many lambs he sacrificed to Apollo, or how many prayers he offered up to Zeus. A child was lucky if it survived the first year of its life, thrice lucky to live beyond the age of thirty. It seemed to many men as if the whole world was ruled by chance; as if some force outside themselves were throwing dice at random. Like a fickle god, Ptolemy Euergetes was amused to dice with men's lives himself.

But when Berenike Beta walked through the door and realized what her husband was doing, she snatched the list of names from the Dioiketes, shouting, *How could you do such a thing?* She threw the dice out of the window, and made Euergetes promise to change his behaviour.

Euergetes gave his word. He stopped dicing, and paid proper attention to each case. He took notice of this woman who had been educated to rule, for she knew all about government, how to handle armies, fleets, and foreign diplomacy. She did not keep quiet, but said what she thought. Quite often her husband was not allowed to say no to her. But there was no quarrelling. She had not the bad temper of Arsinoë Beta. She did not boss this king. The marriage was a perfect match, full of promise for the future, apart from the fact that Berenike Beta had some problems with letting her husband touch her. When his face came close up to hers, she would tremble, and cry out, for that she saw not her husband's face but the face of Demetrios Kalos. But Euergetes had little enough chance to touch his wife, for they had hardly gotten beyond the twenty days of coronation ceremonies before the messenger brought the news that the other Berenike, Berenike Syra, Euergetes' sister, now maybe thirty-four years old, was in grave danger, and Euergetes left Egypt for Syria.

As for Berenike Beta, Euergetes muttered some sharp words about her, just then. *Perhaps she will be pleased to open her door to us when we come back*, he said. *Perhaps a few nights on her own will make her appreciate her husband's attentions a little better.*

Indeed, this new married husband would keep away from his wife for five years.

3.4

Evil Eye

Ptolemy Euergetes began his reign by keeping up the dispatch of Nile water to his sister in Syria. He wrote letters, from time to time, to Berenike Syra, saying, *All your family in Egypt salutes you. If you are well, it is well . . . I myself am well . . .* The health of Berenike Syra was indeed sound, her child was thriving, but everything else now looked very far from satisfactory.

Several times she had written to her father saying that she was *polukammoros*, very miserable. *My enemies are edging closer,* she wrote, or, *I am very afraid of my husband's family.* Sometimes she wrote, *I believe they are trying to put poison in my food.* Philadelphos had not believed it possible, and ignored her complaints.

Now it was Euergetes that wrote back, a little more caring, perhaps, than his late father, saying, *The gods who live such easy lives themselves do not mean you to be so distressed.* He ended his letter with, *May the evil eye not touch you.* But even Euergetes was careful not to offer to fetch his sister back to Alexandria, because that would mean the end of the famous peace, the renewal of the bitter war.

Many times Panariste, Gellosyne and Mania, Berenike's waiting-women, sent for Arkhelaos, a dancer at the court of Antiokhos Theos, to try and make Berenike Syra laugh, but though he was the best of comic dancers, he did not manage even to make her smile. Berenike Syra had no reason for laughter. She had one wish only now: to get away from the Seleukids while she could. She longed for her old life in Alexandria. You might well ask, if she was so unhappy, why did she not flee? But it was because a woman, in these times, was like her husband's prisoner. And because she was a Ptolemy. She was torn between doing her duty – holding the peace in place – and running away. Aye, she was like a hostage for peace. If she left Antiokhos Theos it would mean bloody war. She was herself the glue that stopped the whole world from falling apart. And after all, her son was the heir to Syria. She had to stay where she was. Like glue, indeed, stuck fast.

Hardly two months into the reign of Ptolemy Euergetes the messenger came from Ephesos with news that Antiokhos Theos, Berenike Syra's husband, was dead, supposedly of natural causes. Perhaps this hardened drinker drank himself to death. Perhaps he would have died anyway in the summer time at a place like Ephesos, where a man may be carried off by fever, or almost bitten to death by the flies. His age was about forty years. His young son, Antiokhos, the child of Berenike Syra, was no more than four years old, but under the terms of the peace treaty he was the one who must be the fresh King of Syria. For Antiokhos Theos to die just then was the worst thing that could have happened, for Berenike Syra's son was too young to be king, and she would have to be the Regent for him. While her husband lived, she had not been in any very real danger. Now that he was dead, things were different.

A second messenger told Euergetes that Antiokhos Theos did not die of natural causes, but was poisoned by his first wife, Laodike – out of anger at being cast aside in favour of Berenike Syra, and because she wanted *her* son, Seleukos, not Berenike Syra's son, to inherit the kingdom.

A third messenger said Laodike murdered Antiokhos so that the succession of her own children should not be affected by his changeable moods – for some days he would be full of wild talk about letting Themison the Herakles, his favourite, have the throne after he was dead, but at other times he would still speak with affection of Berenike Syra's son as his heir, according to the terms of his treaty with Ptolemy Philadelphos. Perhaps the truth was that Laodike thought her husband had completely lost his wits, and took matters into her own hands while she had the chance. Whatever the reason, Antiokhos Theos was dead, and Laodike took his power for herself.

As soon as the man was dead, she kept quiet. She did not beat her breasts or do any of the extravagant things that Greek women always do when somebody dies. By no means. No ashes piled upon the head, no mud smeared on the face and arms, and no wailing. Then she sent for Artemon, the man who was her husband's identical lookalike, made him help her drag the corpse of Antiokhos into a closet. She dressed Artemon up in the royal nightshirt, and pushed him into her husband's golden bedstead.

She now called together the ministers and officials of the court, and had Artemon-Antiokhos make an announcement: *Our son Seleukos shall be the sole heir to our kingdom.* The fake Antiokhos not only looked like the king, but could mimic his drunken, slurred speech as well, and such was the clever way Laodike did all this that nobody had the slightest idea that Artemon was not who she said he was, or suspected Laodike herself of treachery of any kind.

Having sent away the courtiers, she made Artemon help her drag the real Antiokhos back into the golden bedstead, sent the fake Antiokhos on his way, and retired for the night.

At dawn she performed the drama of discovering that her husband had stopped breathing. Sobbing with fake grief she called in the doctors, and, really, acted the part of a bereaved wife most expertly. She set up the normal weeping and wailing for a dead man, beat her breasts, piled mud and filth upon her head and arms, and made believe that King Antiokhos Theos, the one that she loved, had passed away in his sleep. She clawed her cheeks. Her tears were real tears, until she was on her own, when they dried up just as suddenly as they had burst forth, together with the extravagant gestures.

The same day she proclaimed her own son, Seleukos, aged about nineteen years, King of Syria. This was the Seleukos called *Kallinikos*, or Gloriously Victorious.

Seleukos Kallinikos was, at least, nearly a grown man, just about capable of taking on the kingship, but Berenike's child was not. What Laodike absolutely could not allow was for Berenike Syra to be the Regent for her young son.

To be sure, Berenike Syra would make a very excellent ruler, for she had been brought up to know how to declare war and sue for peace, how to keep fifty thousand hired soldiers under control, and had ridden into battle, just like any other daughter of the House of Ptolemy, because the wife who would last the longest in a foreign land was she who would be useful to her husband.

Knowledge of the arts of statecraft and war was the best means for a royal wife to survive. Unfortunately, Berenike Syra had herself borne arms against the Syrian, and the people of Syria still looked upon her as their enemy.

Yes, indeed, she would struggle, a woman on her own, with a young child, in her fight against Seleukos and his mother, who had all the power of a mighty empire behind them, but she did fight. And indeed, the young Seleukos Kallinikos began his rule like every other king of his time – planning wholesale murder within his own family, and it was his mother, Laodike, that urged him on. *The first thing you must do,* she said, *if you want to keep your kingdom, is to put Berenike Syra and her son to death.*

Really, Seleukos Kallinikos did not need to be told twice.

The stories differ regarding what happened next. Some said Berenike Syra was taken prisoner by Laodike's party, and put under house arrrest. Her captors promised that she would not be harmed, that they did not mean to do her violence, and a guard from among the *Keltoi*, or Gauls, was set to keep a watch over her and stop her trying to escape. But that does sound all rather unlikely, much too friendly conduct for Laodike and the Seleukids to indulge in.

The more believable version says that when Berenike heard Laodike's men had been sent to murder her she fled – of her own accord – to the citadel of Daphne, near Antiokheia, barricaded herself inside and made ready for a long siege. She was still Queen of Syria. She had her hundreds of soldiers, her loyal bodyguards, her agents, messengers, scouts and spies. Whatever was the truth, it was now that, fearing for her life, she sent hysterical messages to Egypt either by fast racing-camel or swift-sailing *trieres*, or both, begging her brother to send help, for that her citadel was surrounded by her enemies and she could not hold out for ever.

There followed, of course, a delay, while Berenike Syra's letters were delivered, and while Euergetes' fleet made ready for sailing, and while he force-marched his land-army for thousands of stades, through the entire length of Syria, to Antiokheia. Meanwhile Berenike Syra was left waiting, waiting, sipping her River water and offering up prayers to Isis, Hathor, Apollo, Zeus, every divinity she could think of.

Berenike Syra did what she could. She had her own son, Prince Antiokhos, proclaimed king in Antiokheia. Though he was little more than a babe in arms, he wore round his head the royal diadem of Syria, his clothes were of royal purple, and the talismans that hung round his neck to ward off the evil eye were of solid gold. They would do him little good.

No, Berenike Syra did not, of course, sit by and do nothing. She was the daughter of Pharaoh. She sent what ships she had in the port of Seleukeia-in-Pieria into Kilikia to attack Laodike. Her troops took the city of Soloi and its citadel, and seized the local treasure from Aribazos, the Satrap. This man fled, running across the Tauros Mountains, where he was captured and put to death. His head was sent in a bag to Berenike Syra in Antiokheia, together with the fifteen hundred talents of gold that was the treasure of Soloi. The sight of her enemy's severed head never dismayed any daughter of Ptolemy. Berenike Syra was delighted. She took courage, and the heart of the Seleukid empire, around Seleukeia-in-Pieria and Antiokheia, stayed loyal to her.

In Syria itself Laodike had the greater number of troops, but the word was that Berenike Syra defended herself like a cornered tigress, claws out, snarling. She also had behind her the wrath of Egypt and the land-army and fleet of her brother, if only they would hurry. She prayed to the gods. She made sacrifice of a lamb to Apollo and had the Greek priests examine the entrails, holding the shoulder bone up to the light, but she could get no very good omen from it. As for the talisman that hung round her son's neck, it was next to useless. The evil eye had already fallen upon this boy and his unfortunate mother.

3.5

Asterization

Back in Egypt, Berenike Beta begged Euergetes to take her with him to rescue his sister. *We have much experience of war,* she said. *We shall be pleased to help you,* she said. *Did we not win the chariot race at Nemea?* To be sure, the legend was that she had ridden into battle herself and killed many enemies in Kyrene.

But Euergetes said only, *A woman's place is not on the field of battle. The wife should stay at home.*

When she brought in her lion and said, *Husband* . . . Euergetes raised his voice:

Seleukos Kallinikos, he said, *is your first cousin. You will not be coming to Syria.*

Perhaps, at the bottom of his heart, he thought that this daughter of Apama of Syria might prove treacherous; that she might side with his enemy.

Antiokhos Theos was, after all, Berenike Beta's uncle. In those days war was very much a family affair.

You will help us more, Euergetes said, *by looking after Egypt while we are away.* And he made her his Regent during his absence, leaving her Greek advisers and court officials. She would prove herself just as good as any man at administering the kingdom.

Berenike Beta cut off her long hair to help the war effort, to be twisted into ropes to fire the catapults, and in order to encourage the other women, but one great lock of hair she kept back for a different purpose. Instead of riding to Syria, she drove her chariot to Cape Zephyrion, to the Temple of Arsinoë-Aphrodite, where she hung up her hair and dedicated it to the golden goddess who had once wept blood to warn Egypt of war. *My hair is a pledge for victory,* she told Euergetes, *a pledge for your safe return from Syria.*

On the day Euergetes was due to leave Alexandria, every ship was in the water, the women were gathered on the quay to wave off the fleet, the oarsmen were already sitting on the benches, with the machinery of war loaded on board – when word came that Berenike Beta's hair had vanished from the temple. It was a great mystery, and such a bad sign that the crews refused to row, saying that in the past the lack of good omens had meant defeat. And so ships and men sat idle, ready to go, but unable to move off.

Find her Majesty's hair, Euergetes shouted through his speaking-trumpet, *find it. Make haste, any delay may cost the sister's life.*

The men dragged the ships on to the beaches, and the day was given up to searching for a hank of yellow hair. And though his Majesty raised the reward hourly for the return of the Lock of Berenike, nobody came forward to claim it. The sky darkened, the stars appeared, and the missing hair was still not found, but just then Konon of Samos, the mathematician and astronomer, stepped up and asked if he might speak with his Majesty.

Konon had spent half his life lying on his back on the roof of the Mouseion, observing the rising and setting of the stars, noting the comets, eclipses of the moon, and every kind of curious astronomical phenomenon. Nobody in Egypt knew more about the night sky than Konon – apart from the High Priest of Memphis.

Please to look up, Megaleios, Konon said, *look up at the stars.* And he took Euergetes to the Window of Appearances, pointing to the district of the sky that was near to the Great Bear.

Look, Megaleios, he said, pointing, *can you see a new constellation? The gods have snatched her Majesty's hair up to heaven, where it will shine for evermore. I believe that this is nothing short of the plokamos, or asterization, of Queen Berenike's hair.*

Euergetes let out a sigh of recognition, a sigh of relief. And he called his courtiers together, pointing up at the bunch of stars that the Romans would be pleased to call the *Coma Berenices*. You may have heard tell of it before, Stranger: it will still be there in your own day. The constellation is a pretty permanent fixture in the heavens.

Kallimakhos, the court poet, began to scribble on a scrap of papyrus. Before the court retired for the night, he read his new poem, *The Lock of Berenike,* making the hair, the stars, the poem, and himself famous for the rest of time. The applause for Konon, and for Berenike Beta, and for the court poet, was warm, and prolonged.

At dawn, the omens taken from the entrails of the black bull sacrificed to Poseidon being favourable, Euergetes embraced his wife, felt her flinch to see the face of her Demetrios, then stepped aboard his flagship.

The High Priest of Ptah bade farewell to King Ptolemy, saying, *The chiefs of all foreign lands are beneath thy sandals . . . Pharaoh, like a bull, will trample his enemies. He will charge the enemy ranks, fighting as a falcon pounces . . . The serpent upon his brow will fell his foes, casting her fiery breath in his enemy's face.* He also said, *Please to not forget, Megaleios, that if the Flood of the River is low, Pharaoh must return to Egypt at once.*

And so the fleet sailed for Syria, oars rising and falling like the wings of wooden vultures, to the sound of the drumbeat, and they raced each other across the sparkling sea, as usual, with the dolphins leaping alongside.

Seshat knows what you are thinking, Stranger: *Why should Ptolemy Euergetes care two obols about his crazy sister, who made him send water to her from a far country, requiring a ten-thousand-stade round trip every time?* You are think-ing Seshat has told you how the members of this family do not love each other. But you should know that Euergetes had gotten for himself in Ethiopia qualities that his relatives had not. Berenike Syra was the sister that he loved, the sister he might have married. His heart burned fierce. His feelings for her were not false. She was not just the excuse for fighting a war he would have fought anyway.

Meanwhile the army of Pharaoh, under the command of Lysimakhos, Euergetes' younger brother, his friend, had quit Memphis for Syria, marching out to Tjaru on the Roads of Horus, intent upon reducing Seleukos Kallinikos and Laodike his mother to a powder.

Berenike Beta settled down to run Upper and Lower Egypt. She burned incense before Sakhmet, Lady of the Blood-Red Linen, and kept up the daily sacrifice of a bull to Ares, for the success of the rescue. She did not forget

Montu, Lord of Tod, the Egyptian god of War, nor Horus the Falcon, nor the Apis bull, than whom, in Egypt, nothing is of greater importance after Pharaoh. She sent ambassadors, fresh weapons, and the fine wines of Mareotis to her husband. She saw to the minting of the coins that would pay his troops, and their swift dispatch. She took in hand the breeding of horses of war, so that her husband should not lack the means of winning his battles. She had charge of procuring elephants of war from the South Country, and she supervised their training herself, at Memphis, then sent them on to Syria by sea. She kept herself busy. She did not waste her time sitting in front of the loom. She had never had anything to do with tapestry, or sewing, or weaving, in all her lifetime. By no means. She did a man's work, was as good as a man, better, some said.

Did she fret when Euergetes was away in Syria? Did she want him to come back? No, she did not. She did not miss her husband's presence in her bed. By no means. The very sight of a bed still made her think of blood, and screaming. She had her attacks of panic in the dead hours of the night. But she was tough, tough like no other woman before her, apart from Arsinoë Beta. Slow, slow, she brought her raw feelings under control. Day by day she thought she saw a little less of the ghost of the man she had murdered. But she still saw nobody in her dreams but the beloved Demetrios Kalos.

3.6

Hot Snow

What was happening, then, in the meantime at Daphne? Berenike Syra sat under siege in her royal palace, trying to hold things together, taking omens from the flight and cries of birds, biting her nails, waiting. She still had with her the Gaulish guards, her fierce hired soldiers, but such men were famously fickle in their loyalties. In this exact spot the nymph Daphne, pursued by Apollo, was changed into a laurel tree. No such luck would befall Berenike Syra.

Laodike fought hard for what she wanted – the supreme power in Syria – but somehow she must lure Berenike Syra out of her refuge. Laodike was a clever woman. She had friends who were willing to help her cause, and yes, they helped her now, by bribing the Gauls to open the gates of Berenike's fastness to them. They captured the young prince's nurse, who went in and out of the citadel, frightened her with knives, then offered her more money than she had seen in her life, more than she could refuse. In the dead hours one night she pulled her cloak over her head and carried the Prince Antiokhos out of the nursery to change his small clothes. But then she kept on walking, down the staircase, through the courtyards, past the guards, out of the gates, with the child in her arms, and she did not come back.

In the morning, Berenike Syra picked up a child in the nursery that did not look like her child, and the screaming started. Frantic she tore off his night clothes, seeking the anchor tattoo upon his thigh, the token by which he might be identified. But this child had no tattoo. Berenike Syra shouted for the nurse, ran about the *gynaikeion* shouting, thinking the worst, but the nurse had gone.

If the Prince Antiokhos has been stolen, Megaleia, Aristarkhos the physician said, *it must be the work of Laodike.* Berenike was too overwrought to wonder why the physician smiled so.

Aye, Berenike Syra thought, it was the nurse, bribed by Laodike, who had taken her son away to kill him. Laodike had made a crafty move, thinking, rightly, that Berenike's motherly feelings would draw her out of the citadel and make her show herself. She was right: Berenike did come forth. The result of Laodike's stratagem was instant.

Take note of it, Stranger: Berenike Syra, a daughter of Ptolemy, tough as hippopotamus leather, but with motherly feelings nonetheless.

But what happened? Laodike spread the rumour among Berenike Syra's guards herself, saying that her son was being held hostage at a certain house near the Agora in the city of Antiokheia. Berenike was not such a prisoner, not so hopelessly trapped that she could not call for horses and ride out of her fortress if she wanted to. She put on her armour of bronze – greaves, breast-plate, and helmet. She grabbed weapons, harnessed her chariot and drove it herself, spear in hand. She was a daughter of Ptolemy, as good as a son, and her chariot hurtled out of the armoured gates, heading for the city. The three wait-ing-women went with her, hair flying in the wind, and Aristarkhos the physi-cian rode on horseback beside them. *I shall give you the directions,* he said. *I shall show your Majesty where the house is* ... It was just what Laodike wanted: for Berenike Syra to show her face. Now Laodike could launch her attack.

As soon as Berenike Syra reached the city gates, Gennaios – the chief mag-istrate, who supported Laodike – challenged her, and blocked the road with his guards. Berenike hurled a spear at him, he stepped smartly sideways, and the spear missed its target. Then this strong woman picked up a great stone from the road, flung it, hit Gennaios on the head so that he fell down, and she drove on, chariot careering up the street, fit to overturn.

Aristarkhos pointed out the alley, and a crowd of shouting, chanting Syrians gathered in front of the house where the Prince Antiokhos was supposed to be hidden. Some were hostile to Berenike Syra, others were her friends. But when Berenike Syra drew near, they fell back. Berenike waved a sword about her head. *I have come for my child,* she screamed. *Where is my son? Bring him out here.* She screamed for the door to be opened; her men broke it down, and swarmed inside.

Was the Prince Antiokhos, *King* Antiokhos, dead or alive? Was he even there? Nobody seemed to know. But the crowd now shouted in favour of Berenike, and the storm of public anger was so great that the magistrates must do something or have a riot on their hands. One of them carried a child out into the street, accompanied by all the pomp due to a king – trumpets, sunshade-bearers, armed guards. *Here is your son, Megaleia,* the man said, and Berenike Syra ran forward, of course, but in order to take the child in her arms she had to put down her weapons, and in doing that she exposed herself to danger. Laodike's men closed in. Berenike saw Themison the Herakles, and Aristos his brother, showing the teeth, eager to plunge the knife into the daughter of Syria's greatest enemy. Berenike Syra would fight, but she could not fight without letting go of her son, and her waiting-women had become separated from her: not so brave as their mistress, they cowered in a doorway and hid their faces.

The knives flashed, then, and despite her armour, and her brave efforts to defend herself with just one arm, Berenike Syra was wounded, first in the arms, then in the neck, then in the belly. Aye, she was cut to pieces in the public street, her blood poured out, and nobody moved to save her. She fought back, like the tigress indeed, but she could not prevail against a hostile crowd armed with knives and swords. She sank to her knees, her child was pulled from her arms and they sliced him up before her eyes, laughing. Aye, then Berenike Syra's attackers left her where she fell, and ran off.

The last thing she saw was the face of Aristarkhos, her physician, smiling down at her. *Farewell, Megaleia,* he said, *even in the house of Hades.*

Aye, Berenike Syra was led to trust the oath of her enemies that she would not be harmed, but it was her trusted physician, Aristarkhos, who had led her straight into their hands.

Panariste, Mania and Gellosyne managed to pull the body of the queen into the chariot and drove it, somehow, back to the citadel at Daphne, but by the time they arrived the fog had come down over her Majesty's beautiful eyes. Weeping, Panariste and Gellosyne hid the corpse in a clothes chest and dressed Mania up as the queen in her place. They smeared Mania with red paint, bandaged her fake wounds and put her in Berenike's bed – to make it look as if her Majesty was still alive. Then they showed Mania to the Gaulish captain, insisting that her Majesty was not dead, but recovering from her wounds. By a strange coincidence, then, these women did with the dead Berenike Syra just exactly what Laodike did with the dead Antiokhos Theos. Maybe the storytellers have played tricks upon us, Stranger. Maybe the story is false. Seshat offers it to the world in good faith. The goddess of History must use what materials she has to hand. The truth is often different to what you might think. Nobody disputes, however, that Berenike Syra died, and died violent.

These resourceful waiting-women now took hold of Berenike Syra's royal seal to send out further frantic messages in her name to King Ptolemy Euergetes. They dragged the heavy amphoras of Nile water into her apartments just as before, and Mania drank it. They took in her Majesty's food, and Mania ate it, keeping up the appearance of normality. They ordered the guards to stay at their posts, saying that her Majesty was not dead, no, not dead at all, but making good progress, sure to make a full recovery. Thus they thought to save their own skins, while waiting for his Majesty to rescue them. Meanwhile, the season being hot, the mangled corpse of Berenike Syra began to smell bad, and to attract great clouds of flies.

When Ptolemy Euergetes' ship dropped anchor at Seleukcia-in-Pieria, the port of Antiokheia, the Greek priests, city magistrates, officers and soldiers turned out to greet him. The streets leading to the harbour were garlanded with wreaths and full of cheering crowds. They did not hiss him for their enemy as they had hissed his sister. Even the Seleukid satraps and *strategoi* paid their respects: they knew Euergetes would have them cut to ribbons and burn the city to the ground if they gave him a hostile reception. The people of Seleukeia stayed loyal to Berenike Syra, thinking that the power of Ptolemy of Egypt would prove greater than that of the young Seleukos Kallinikos and his mother.

That evening Euergetes rode south to Daphne, thinking to visit his sister, to give her his protection and to talk with her about how best to overcome her present troubles. But he saw only the stinking horror of her bloody corpse, the face slashed with knife-cuts. Enough to make this tough king weep. And retch.

The death of Berenike Syra threw a great shadow over the soul of Ptolemy Euergetes. He wept and raged, saying, *We cannot afford to fight a long-drawn-out war with anybody,* but when Lysimakhos and the land-army arrived, they vowed that they would not go home to Egypt empty-handed but must avenge their sister's murder.

The storytellers agreed, at least, upon one thing: that Berenike Syra perished, together with her son. This was how the Third Syrian War began – the Laodikaian War, the War against Queen Laodike. And thus Ptolemy Philadelphos's famous everlasting peace with Syria, so recently secured, melted away after only five or six years, just about as permanent as snow in a bread oven.

3.7

Reptiles

Before this war men had spoken of Ptolemy Euergetes' peaceful disposition, still calling him Tryphon, and murmuring a little about how he always said, *Later, later* . . . letting the time for taking action slip by him, forgetting to make important decisions. Even his Dioiketes said, *I fear he looks like a delayer, just like his father.* This time, however, Euergetes was moved to act, beginning what would be a five-year campaign to punish Syria and her empire from end to end, and take it for himself.

You may well ask, Stranger, how this king who said he was so short of money managed to fight a five-year-long war in a far country. He complained that he could not afford this war, in spite of his father's annual income of fourteen thousand eight hundred talents of silver. But if Philadelphos's income had been great, his expenditure had been the same, reckless, towards the end, for an unhappy man will ever spend a great deal of money. How, indeed, Euergetes worried, could the war be financed? But he had the clever thought to set up a system of high sounding court titles – *King's Friend, First Friend* and *Companion of the King* – and he put the titles on sale.

Euergetes' titles were expensive, costing hundreds of talents. A court title was purely ceremonial, carrying no duties to speak of, but it gave to any man who could pay the price a prominent place at his Majesty's side, fanned by ostrich-feather fans, and seats at the front of the Theatre, and invitations to every royal banquet, and a privileged place under the royal canopy for viewing the Great Pompe, and unlimited access to his Majesty's ear – and so forth. For these reasons every man of substance wanted to be a King's Friend, and business was brisk. Euergetes got for himself, then, very quick, a loyal aristocracy, and thus he managed to finance a costly military campaign abroad, without having to raise taxes at home.

Euergetes rode about Seleukeia and Antiokheia on his horse, giving orders, shouting where he thought fit, and he brought these cities very quick under his complete command and control. Then he marched his land-army eastward on the desert road, deep into Syria, and Lysimakhos his brother, his friend, went with him. They marvelled to see the lizards fry as they crossed the highway in the midday sun. They were astonished by the heat that allowed a man to fry a goose egg upon a stone, but they kept on marching.

The word sent to Berenike Beta in Egypt was that her husband put down the Seleukid Empire as far as Babylon, and then kept going, into Mesopotamia, even as far as Seleukeia-on-the-Tigris. One year passed and Euergetes did not return to Egypt. Two years passed and Berenike Beta still ran Egypt virtually single-handed. She had her ghost under control, more or less. She most certainly had Egypt under control, at least, until the River began to cause troubles beyond even her power to deal with them.

It was Year Three of King Ptolemy Euergetes when Anemhor sent word to him in Syria, saying, *Lo, from Elephantine to Sebennytos, the Two Lands have fallen into rebellion against his Majesty. We do not know what may happen throughout the land. We urge his Majesty to come home as fast as possible.* Aye, it was the low Flood of the Nile that caused the trouble, for a low Flood meant poor crops, and poor crops meant famine, and famine meant anger, and unrest.

All this was explained to Euergetes, but he refused to turn back. *We have our wars to win,* he wrote. *We have a job to do out here, and shall not return until it is done.*

Instead he sent his brother Lysimakhos to help Berenike Beta manage internal affairs and to try to bring calm to Egypt. Lysimakhos did not take advantage of his brother's absence to snatch his kingdom. By no means. He remained loyal. He did his best to keep the Two Lands in order. But the next year Lysimakhos himself sent word to Euergetes that Egypt had suffered the misfortune of another very low Flood of the River; that the harvest was again poor, and the people, having little to eat, had risen in arms against their Greek masters.

The Egyptians began to attack Greeks living up-River, and the Greeks fought back, so that Anemhor said to his sons, *Do not walk the road without a stick in your hand.* He urged the temple scribes, *Do not walk alone at night.* He would not allow his daughters to walk outside the gardens of his residence even during the day.

As he barricaded the door of his bedchamber against the attacks of Greek soldiers, seeking what they could find even in the house of the High Priest of

Ptah at Memphis, Anemhor said to Herankh, *The god guards at night against the reptiles of the dark.*

Euergetes wrote to Lysimakhos: *Please to hold on, we have unfinished business to attend to at Babylon.* To Anemhor he wrote: *When we have conquered the east we shall return, not before.*

Egypt's conquest of the world, then, continued. In southern Anatolia Euergetes' forces took Kilikia. In the east he took the upper parts across the Euphrates River, Mesopotamia, Media, Paraitakene. Aye, and when he passed beyond the Euphrates they called him *Euphrates*. He had put down Babylonia, Susiana, Persis, and all the remaining territory as far as Baktria. They said he went even so far as India, and that he would have gone further still if he had not been urgently recalled to Egypt yet again to deal with fresh revolts. Otherwise he must surely have taken possession of the entire kingdom of Seleukos.

But Seshat asks, *What was the truth of it? Were not the victories of Euergetes exaggerated?* For some reports suggest that this king pitched his royal tent of purple and gold at Ekbatana and stayed there for the duration, refusing to travel one more stade. They said he sent word ahead with his messengers, and waited to see what would happen. The foreign ambassadors came, for sure, upon being informed that if they did not make haste to prostrate themselves before his Majesty he would shift himself much closer to them, setting fire to every house and field, burning all before him, just as Alexander had done.

Aye, the envoys from the dynasts of Parthia and Baktria and the region of the Hindu Kush came quick to do him homage, for in these remote parts the terrible memory of Alexander was not yet dead. They kissed the dust before his feet. They held the forearm across the eyes lest they should be burned up by the flame of the Son of the Sun, Ptolemy, Living for Ever, the Beloved of Ra.

Euergetes' success was quite sufficient to allow Seshat the Historian to speak of the Conquest of the East. But the enemy came to Euergetes rather than Euergetes going to the enemy. Reader, the truth of it was that King Ptolemy did not have to penetrate far into Persia to get what he wanted – the total surrender of every nation. Nor did he have to show his face in Sardis, where Seleukos Kallinikos and his mother still held together the remnants of an army, for they too, in the end, surrendered to his troops.

In Egypt it was understood that Euergetes carried all before him, fighting his way across Asia in battle after battle, winning spectacular victories, killing his thousands, his tens of thousands. The truth, as always, was rather different. Euergetes' progress was peaceful, not warlike. His army marched like a machine, regular, obeying the word of command upon the instant. In their youth these men had been trained under Arsinoë Beta, for her Pompe, to march as one. From time to time they amused themselves by performing the manoeuvre that Alexander had used to frighten the Balkan tribes, the fabulous display of precision marching and counter-marching, with the *sarissa* now up, now down, attracting onlookers, then rushing at them, to frighten them. Nobody was harmed in these displays, but the word of it spread ahead of the column of troops, what horror was coming.

Aye, the Seleukid garrisons on the road put up no resistance. They were made to surrender by words alone, were defeated by nothing more than the thought of slaughter. Euergetes achieved this miracle by sending messengers on ahead, to say that if the city in question did not surrender on the spot, he would level it with the ground, and put every man, woman and child inside it to the sword. It was an old trick, learned from reading his grandfather's *History of Alexander*. There was no pall of black smoke from one end of Asia to the other, no wailing, no lamentation, and, for the moment, no orgy of rape and pillage.

Euergetes the *kalokagathos* did not copy Alexander by burning every village. He did not play the part of the angry man who must destroy everything in sight.

Whatever city he marched to – Nineveh, Ktesiphon, Babylon, Susa, Ekbatana – the children walked out of the gates carrying the treasure, as a sign of surrender. Almost the entire Syrian Empire gave itself up to Euergetes without a fight, and it was because Seleukos Kallinikos and his mother looked too weak, just then, to put up the proper resistance.

Others said Euergetes marched no further east than Babylon, where he stayed put, enjoying the fleshpots, much as Alexander and his troops had done one hundred years before. Babylon was far enough, but Babylon was hardly India. Perhaps, after all, Euergetes did deserve that name of *Tryphon*.

Aye, this King was wonderful in his foreign achievements, almost as wonderful as Alexander himself, but he was neglecting Egypt.

In the fifth year of Euergetes' absence both Anemhor and Lysimakhos sent news of fresh troubles at home, saying that the Flood of the River was again low – as low as eight cubits, one palm and one fingerbreadth – and that things were worse in Egypt than any man could remember. It was not because Berenike Beta and Lysimakhos were no good at administration. By no means. It was a natural disaster, and the reaction of the Egyptians to it was always the same – to show violence. The *reason* for the failure of the Flood was the absence of Pharaoh.

Anemhor wrote to his Majesty, *Pharaoh is personally responsible for the failure of the Flood. The disaster has come upon us because Pharaoh has gone out of Egypt. We beseech his Majesty to return.*

Euergetes stayed where he was. He sent messengers home with his orders, what must be done: for the troops to squash the rebels; for grain to be sent from Syria and Phoenicia and Cyprus, at very great expense; but also for Lysimakhos to wield the stick. Euergetes' answer to the trouble was to use force. And he put up taxes in Egypt to pay for the campaign that had gone on longer than any man thought possible.

The uprisings did not die down, but still Euergetes refused to go home, saying only, *When we have had our fill of war . . . only when we have our victory. Our wife will not want to touch us, in any case. We have no good reason to hurry back to Egypt.*

When reports came of revolution even in Kyrene, it was bad, bad in the extreme, because Euergetes had taken to Syria almost the whole of Egypt's armed forces. Worse, the few thousand Macedonian troops that were left behind had lent their support to the native Egyptians who clamoured for a native pharaoh, and were stirring up hatred against Ptolemy in Upper Egypt.

Anemhor sent to his Majesty, saying, *Egypt has had enough of oppression. Wisdom of Ani: Observe the feast of the god and repeat its season. God is angry if you neglect it.*

Berenike added her voice, writing to him, *Egypt lacks a pharaoh, we beseech you to come home.* And then, *We have not see our husband's face for five years, not for one thousand eight hundred and twenty-five nights.*

Perhaps, now, Euergetes thought, *that wife of mine might be more willing to open her bedroom door.*

Now, at last, he did order the troops to march for Memphis, but first he appointed Antiokhos, one of his friends, to be governor of Kilikia and the west, and Xanthippos to govern the east, beyond the Euphrates. He rode home laden with booty: copper in vast quantities, swords, helmets, chariots, vases, panthers and lions, plundered goods without limit, and forty thousand talents of silver. Most remarkable, he carried off the two thousand five hundred sacred vessels and statues of gold that had been looted under Kambyses, during the Persian rule over Egypt, nearly three hundred years previous. These things Euergetes meant to give back to their rightful owners, the temples, in an act designed to make him popular. Now he earned that title of *Euergetes*, or Benefactor, becoming the King Who Brought Back the Gods.

Euergetes had gotten back the entire Phoenician coast for Egypt, and it meant ship timber more than he could use, the best shipwrights in the world, the best navigators in the Great Sea. He also regained Tyros and Sidon, so that Egypt controlled the ends of the great camel routes that came north from Petra, west from Babylonia and Damaskos. It meant spices for the palace kitchens, myrrh and incense for the temple rituals, more goodly things than Egypt knew what to do with them.

Such things made Euergetes smile more than the usual half-smile of the Lord of the Two Lands. Hardly an arrow had been fired, and it was as good as a conquest, achieved without fighting one battle. It was the greatest military triumph ever achieved by a Ptolemy, for the best kind of victory is a blood-less victory, in which the enemy surrenders without lifting up the sword.

His Majesty returned in peace to Egypt with his infantry and chariotry, all life, stability and dominion being with him. When Anemhor met him at the gates of Memphis he said, *Now that he rests in his palace of life and dominion like Ra in his horizon, the gods of Egypt hail him saying, Welcome, our beloved son, Ptolemy, the Son of Ra, Beloved of Amun, given life!*

Euergetes bowed the head in gratitude.

Peace is better than fighting, Anemhor said. *Very excellent is peace.*

As for Berenike Beta, she gave a good account of herself. She had not betrayed Egypt to the Seleukids. Lysimakhos and Anemhor together assured King Ptolemy that his wife's temporary regency had been blameless, that the revolts were not her fault.

Euergetes and Berenike Beta sailed up-River to show the people that Pharaoh had come back, and Egypt was returned to a state of calm by his delivering in person the stolen statues to the temples where they belonged.

Then this King spoke with his advisers.

What should we do, he asked Anemhor, *to please the Egyptians?*

Anemhor said what he thought: *God desires the good treatment of the poor more than respect for the noble. Every man who has a grievance, every man who thinks himself wronged – he wishes his voice to be heard.* He said, *His Majesty should hear the Egyptians. He must listen to his people.*

Euergetes sat in his audience chamber, meeting his subjects, hearing their complaints. He helped the Egyptian wherever he could.

When Ptolemy Euergetes had gone back home, the campaign in Syria went on without him. Seleukos Kallinikos sent his ships of war against the cities of Asia that had revolted against him, but lost them all in a sudden storm, as if the gods wished to take revenge upon him for the murder of Berenike Syra and her son. Tykhe left Seleukos nothing of all his mighty armament except his naked body and his life, and a few companions amid the wreckage of his fleet.

The outcome of the shipwreck was that the cities that had gone over to Ptolemy out of hatred for Seleukos had a sudden change of heart, as if the wreck of the fleet was his due punishment by the gods, and meant that they would punish him no more – and so they put themselves back under his command.

But why was it? When the news of the murder of Berenike Syra's son was published, the people's attitude changed about. There was nobody else in Syria now who could be king but Seleukos Kallinikos himself. As soon as Euergetes marched away to punish the rest of the Seleukid empire, the local rulers went back to supporting Seleukos. Ptolemy Euergetes was, after all, a foreigner, an Egyptian, their rightful enemy.

Thus Seleukos was, at length, able to make war upon Euergetes' forces, who defeated him in battle, though even Seshat does not know where it was fought. It looked to many men as if Seleukos had been born only for fortune to play with, receiving the power of a king only to have it taken away from him. And so he fled in fear to Antiokheia, not much better attended than he was after his shipwreck.

From Antiokheia Seleukos sent a letter to his young brother Antiokhos, begging for help, and he offered him all that part of Asia that lies beyond Mount Tauros as his reward. This Antiokhos, although he was only fourteen years old, was greedy for power, and jumped at the chance, rather like a robber. That was how he got for himself the surname of *Hierax* – Hawk, or Falcon – because of the way he snatched the possessions of others – not so much a human being, more a bird of prey.

Seleukos Kallinikos' counter-attack reached as far south as Damaskos and Orthosia on the coast of Phoenicia, which had been besieged by Ptolemy's forces. Seleukos Kallinikos delivered these cities. Then he tried to push further south, but in Year Eight of Ptolemy Euergetes, there occurred the disastrous and spectacular defeat of Seleukos Kallinikos somewhere in Palestine. Seshat knows nothing of it, neither the name of the battle nor the details. Some did say that Seleukos Kallinikos made a brave attempt to invade Egypt itself, but was speedily repulsed. Perhaps that was what this battle was.

Soon afterwards Ptolemy Euergetes signed a fresh everlasting peace treaty with Syria, when the Egyptian oracles and Greek horoscopists did their best to interpret the meaning of Everlasting. In this case the forecast was for as long as twenty years of peace. Lasting Peace was the towering achievement of this Pharaoh.

*

To mark the favourable outcome of the Third Syrian War, seals were made in the Greek style, showing the head of Berenike Beta. Now she was called *Thea Euergetis,* the Goddess Euergetes, and shown with her hair cut short, because it was hanging up among the stars. Euergetes minted gold and silver coins on which he wore the diadem made up of the sun's rays and the horns of Zeus-Ammon. This was Euergetes as Helios, the Sun-god, the equal of Ra. He was as much as Zeus-Ammon, or Amun of the Egyptians himself. He was Poseidon, lord of the sea. He was Hermes, or Thoth, great great great. Endless divine honours were showered upon him by the high priests for his victories. All of these things were good for Egypt, very good.

What, though, did all that success mean? Euergetes had triumphed over Syria and the Seleukids, for sure, but it all turned out to be a temporary triumph. He had plundered what he could carry home, but did he mean to keep those eastern territories for ever? Perhaps he did not.

I have no great desire to be king of the lands that belonged to Old Seleukos, he said to his wife. *How could I control India when I live in Egypt? An Egyptian government in the east would not last long. To govern those remote places would tie up thousands of our troops for ever.*

No, Euergetes was far more interested in the Anatolian coast, and the Phoenician coast, where his fleet took by force all these Seleukid territories from the sea side. To have lands in Thrace meant more to Euergetes than possessing Babylon and eastern Mesopotamia. He had got back Kilikia, Pamphylia, Ionia, Thrace and the Hellespont, rich Greek-speaking lands, where the people could at least understand what he said to them.

What do I want with barbarian territories? he said. *They are more trouble than they are worth.* Gradually, he would withdraw from the east. If you will be so kind as to look at the map of it, Stranger, you will see that Euergetes' empire now comprised the whole of the coastal lands of the eastern part of the Great Sea from Libya all the way round to Thrace – with only a few gaps, where Thrace bordered upon Macedonia. It meant that he had complete control of the eastern half of the Great Sea. He had guaranteed the military supremacy of Egypt for a further forty years.

What of Berenike Syra, who was the cause of the Second Syrian War? Did Euergetes bury her in foreign soil? Did he leave her behind? By no means. He performed the proper Greek funeral rites before ever he left Antiokheia, burning up his sister upon a great funeral pyre, and he gathered up her bones and ashes after. He had carried the remains of the sister with him even into Babylonia to remind him of his cause. And he carried her home with him too, in the same kind of earthenware jar as those in which his father had sent the water of the Nile to her in Syria, just as the horoscopists had promised.

The ashes of Berenike Syra, then, sat upon a shelf in the Tomb of Alexander, along with the remains of her ancestors. Euergetes poured out the funeral libations for the sister he had cherished, with his own hand. He made his prayers and offerings to all the gods, for peace, but especially to Sarapis. He prayed above all else just now for a son, an heir for Egypt, for the succession to be secure. This prayer, at least, the lord Sarapis was happy to answer, for with the end of the Laodikaian War, this Pharaoh now managed to climb into bed with his wife. Aye, Berenike Beta, less troubled by that ghost of hers, stopped bolting the door of her bedchamber against him. When the face of Demetrios Kalos came close up to hers now, she trembled not for fear, but for delight.

3.8

Spider-Web

When Ptolemy Euergetes returned home he found the expense of his war so very great that the mere selling of titles did not cover it. Every man who could afford to pay was already a King's Friend. Now his Majesty had to raise taxes, so that the burden fell very heavy upon the Egyptians, who received no advantage in return. Then he made matters worse by settling large numbers of prisoners of war upon farms in the District of the Lake, making them not slaves but royal tenants, with many privileges. The Egyptian farmers saw these immigrants being treated better than themselves, and they liked it not. Now they thought they would like to rid themselves of this foreign Pharaoh who put his swingeing taxes on oil, and dates, and grain, and flax; aye, upon every beast in the field, down to the very last pig.

Berenike Beta urged her husband not to raise but to lower the burden. *We have won a mighty triumph,* she said, *your people should be happy. You should try to make them smile. Let them pay less, reduce their taxes.*

Anemhor said the same: *His Majesty makes the Egyptians work too hard. They are worn out.* And he said, *A tired man is an angry man.*

Meanwhile, the unrest went on. Greeks were given bloody noses. Egyptians suffered broken arms and legs. Fist fights and savage beatings were reported every day. Even in Greek Alexandria there were riots about the price of bread. At Memphis the dwelling of the Greek Governor was set on fire. Though there was peace abroad, there looked to be no end to the war at home.

But Euergetes would not be told what to do. Angry himself, now, he did the opposite of what Berenike and Anemhor advised. He ordered more oppressive measures, stricter curfews, stiffer fines, fiercer sentences for violent offenders. He said the measures were temporary, but he left them in place for so long that the oppression began to look permanent. No man was allowed out of his house after the hours of darkness. Instead of reducing taxes he raised them higher still, so that Egypt howled with rage.

As the news worsened Euergetes would sit with his head in his hands for not knowing what to do. When the farmers marched on his palace at Memphis and spent the morning chanting under his Window of Appearances, Euergetes began to shout himself, and was all for sending in the army, to beat them with sticks.

Tell them Pharaoh will use the sword if they do not disperse, he cried, *then cut them down.*

Berenike Beta did not shout. She said, *A show of violence will not solve your problems. Violence will only make them hate you more. Listen to what they say. They would rather die than live under such severity. Instead of always raising the price of corn you could lower it, as we did in Kyrene.* For sure, she had learned how to do a murder, but she had also learned about mercy, about compassion. Her support for *Moderation in all things,* including taxes, derived from Magas her father.

And so Euergetes called in the Dioiketes and said, *Tell them the price of corn is cut in half.* The exercise of Pharaoh's power was as simple as that. The corn tax was reduced on the spot, for Pharaoh's word is law.The chanting of abuse gave way to the chanting of *Ptlumis, Ptlumis, Ptlumis,* the songs of victory wafted through the palace windows, and the crowd dispersed in peace.

Euergetes, encouraged by Berenike Beta, made his best efforts to feed Egypt, though the people's bellies still groaned. The next time the natives refused to pay their taxes, he cancelled them altogether, and imported ever more corn from Syria, Phoenicia, Cyprus, provinces now under his control.

Peace returned to Egypt, then, at length. There was no need, now, for Euergetes to make himself ready for battle. At the great feast to mark the end of all war, Euergetes hung up his shield, saying, *May spiders spin their delicate webs over our armour, and the cry of battle never be shouted here again.* His admirals and generals, the King's Friends, the Companions of the King, the First Friends, and the Silver Shields of his army all banged their drinking cups and cheered.

Before long Anemhor felt able to write to the High Priest of Amun at Thebes, *Once again our sons may walk along the road without having to carry the stout stick. We are tranquil here in Lower Egypt. Our cattle pasture in the papyrus marshes.*

3.9

Beer and Onions

When Anemhor next came to Pharaoh he was still solemn-faced, however. *His Majesty has taken and taken from Egypt,* he said. *Will he not now give something back to his people?* This time Ptolemy Euergetes listened with more care. To please the natives, he agreed to hold a pan-Egyptian festival on the day when the star of Isis rises, at the new year: an extra festival, an extra holiday, to keep Egypt happy. He ordered free bread, beer and onions to be distributed throughout the Two Lands, regardless of how much it cost the Treasury. At Anemhor's suggestion, he made offerings to the sacred animal necropolis at Memphis, for the upkeep of the ibises and baboons. He sent thousands of geese and fowls to the temples.

He ordered a new temple-house for Latopolis, many minor works for the temples at Thebes, and further additions to the full-size Temple of Min at Koptos, where his mother still lived, that other Arsinoë, Arsinoë Alpha, about whom Ptolemy Euergetes had almost forgotten.

Encouraged by this success, Anemhor suggested the foundation of a great new temple for Horus at Apollonopolis. *To mark his Majesty's great victories,* he said. *Let us make the proper thank-offering to Horus for his great goodness, Horus who helps us win the battles.*

Euergetes dismissed the idea out of hand, though. *No, no,* he said, *a great temple will be quite beyond our means.*

But Anemhor was surer of himself, now, having seen the troubles, and he did not stop asking. The next time he said, *It is the custom, Megaleios, it is what the god demands in return for granting you victory.*

Still Euergetes refused to help.

After the ninth application for funding Anemhor raised his voice and swept out of the audience chamber. But he came back a tenth time, with revised estimates for the project.

We cannot justify such expense, Ptolemy said. *Egypt cannot afford it. We think we are doing more than enough to help your temples already.*

They called this Ptolemy *Euergetes* – the Generous, the Benevolent, the Kind, and sometimes it was because these things were true; but sometimes it was because he gave, but did not give much. It was, in part, a sarcastic title. Euergetes had his moments of generosity, but he was still the great taxer.

The Peace, and Anemhor's persuasion, made Euergetes change – at length – his stubbornness about building. First, though, he looked to his Greek responsibilities, lest he should arouse even the anger of his own people. He finished the Greek-style Temple of Sarapis at Alexandria, for Philadelphos had not managed to do much more than throw up the artificial hill in the middle of Rhakotis. Euergetes built the quadrangle on top of the hill, and the inner colonnade, and the lecture halls, libraries and store-rooms round the edge, putting up Corinthian columns everywhere. The floors and walls were of marble, with gold, silver and bronze decorations. At the east end he raised a gigantic statue of Sarapis, adorned with ivory and gold, his outstretched arms almost touching the two side walls. In his left hand he held a sceptre; in his right, an image of Kerberos, the triple-headed hound of Hades. Aye, for Sarapis, dark blue of face, with jewelled eyes, who wore on his head not a crown but the tall basket that was the corn measure of Egypt, was the protector of Alexandria.

Euergetes made smooth the carriage road upon the north side and the south side. He made good the flight of two hundred steps that led to the great entrance portico of Greek columns with a great Greek pediment that had Sarapis reclining in it, like the entrance to the Parthenon at Athens, than which, as it happens, the Sarapieion was bigger, much bigger, and infinitely more grand. This was not the work of a king who was short of money.

For the inauguration of the Sarapieion, Euergetes rode with Berenike Beta right through the middle of the native quarter. No stone was hurled. No hand was raised in anger against their Majesties. There was really no need for the escort of hundreds of troops in full battle gear to ride with them.

Every day, before dawn, the great Temple of Sarapis was hallowed with fire, the sacred image of Isis was unveiled and exposed to the eyes of the faithful, dressed in its holy raiment, decked with vulture feathers and every august costly stone. The worshippers gazed in silence, hoping for miracles.

The priest of Sarapis, wearing his robe with seven-rayed stars, scarabs, and the crescent moon, performed the ritual three times daily, offering libations, sprinkling the faithful with cold water, full of the life-giving power of Osiris. There was sacred dancing and music, hymns sung to Isis four times daily, offerings of geese ... and so forth. Sarapis would be sure to help Egypt out of her troubles by bringing Greek and Egyptian together to worship one god. Sarapis might yet work the miracle of matching peace abroad with lasting peace at home. He did, at least, work now the miracle of getting Berenike Beta big with child.

3.10

Kicking Horus

Throughout her nine months of growing stouter down below, wherever Berenike Beta looked she saw ill omens: in the flight of birds, in the screech-ing of the storks, but especially in the ferocious kicking of the Infant Horus inside her swollen belly, for it felt like he was dancing even before he drew his first breath, and not dancing for joy either.

When the new Ptolemy was born, the Greek horoscopists noted that it was under an unlucky planet, and their forecast was just about the worst imaginable, so bad that no man dared to whisper it: that the son born to Ptolemy Euergetes and Berenike Beta was fated to murder his own father and mother.

Ptolemaios, they called this son, Ptolemy, for the father said, *How can we call him anything else?* And at once Euergetes set Egypt on the road to fresh disaster by naming him as the heir to the throne. Aye, having suffered such uncertainty in his own youth – first he had been the heir, then not the heir, then he was the heir again – he named this boy as his successor before he was one hour old, regardless of what his character might turn out to be, whether he was suitable to be king or not. Posterity would call this boy Philopator, Father-Loving. In spite of the fact that this title would not devolve upon him until he grew up, Seshat must call him Philopator from the beginning, or you will be in danger, Stranger, of getting all these Ptolemies confused.

Much as Achilles was bathed in the River Styx to make him invulnerable, so Berenike Beta, immune to all superstitious nonsense though she was herself, bathed this son in wine. Perhaps such a precaution did make him invulnerable to the assaults of others, but it would not make him proof against injuries inflicted by himself upon himself. To bathe the child in wine was a curious thing to do, a Greek thing, tantamount to dedicating the child to Dionysos. By chance, Philopator would, indeed, spend his adult life swimming in wine, wallowing in the worship of Dionysos, god of Wine, god of Frenzy, the mad god.

Berenike Beta gave Philopator every Greek talisman to protect him from bad luck, illness, the evil eye, and strung them across his chest upon a string. She laid him down to sleep upon an ass's skin. Very many infants in Egypt died before reaching their first birthday. The mother did what she could to keep this son of hers alive, but the horoscopists shook their heads, muttering dark words, *Better if he had never been born.*

For all that, Philopator would still be unlucky. And as it happened these few things were just about all Berenike Beta did for her son in his infancy. She did not put him to her breast, but let the nurse take care of him. Philopator was allowed to suck at a slave's breast, and some said he absorbed a slavish character with her milk. When he began to crawl, and then to walk, Berenike would speak to her son only to tell him what not to do, only to find fault, so that he grew up to think of her not with warmth and affection, but as the one who said *Do Not,* the one who disapproved.

No, this rather manly mother had very little time for babies, no interest in women's things. She had been brought up to be tough, to be as good and better than any man. She was more interested in her foals than her children. She had time for horses, for riding, for the army of Egypt, but she had no time to devote to childcare. She was The Female Pharaoh, the Great Lady of the Two Lands. The nurse was for looking after the children of a queen.

Aye, and Philopator's wet nurse was Oinanthe of Samos, the beautiful young woman with black hair and olive skin, who happened also to be the concubine of his father. Some were pleased to call her Horrible Oinanthe. Right or wrong, what is certain is that this woman was due to suffer a horrible death, a hideous violent death, but when she was young she was Lovely Oinanthe, who indulged and spoiled the child who must be Lord of the Two Lands. She did the same to his father.

Did Oinanthe bandage this prince? She did, yes, for Berenike let her do whatever she liked with him so long as she did not have to listen to his screaming – which was, of course, the result of the too-tight bandages, meant for making straight the limbs, after the time-honoured custom of the Greeks. Philopator, if not born sulky, grew up sulky, rebellious – showing, in fact, just the same family characteristics as Ptolemy Keraunos and Ptolemy the Son, but at least his legs were straight, good for dancing. His playmates were not the sons of his Majesty's First Friends, but Oinanthe's own children, who would grow up to be his enemies.

For, sure, Oinanthe could never have been a wet nurse without she had borne some children of her own. She had two children, in fact, dark as the shadows, dark as the crow. Who was their father? Nobody knows, Stranger, not even Seshat. Or nobody would say. He was Nobody indeed (unless, of course, he was Euergetes himself . . .). But Oinanthe's children were not fated to be nobodies. Agathokles of Samos and his sister Agathokleia would play a terrible part in the history of the House of Ptolemy. But just then, Oinanthe of Samos was young, barely seventeen years young, and her children were young – and the crisis they were due to bring upon Alexandria and all Egypt would be fully thirty years in the making.

Agathokles and Agathokleia were the foster brother and sister of Ptolemy Philopator. Oinanthe and her children were his real family. Euergetes and Berenike Beta were too busy with affairs of state to take much notice of him, except to correct and scold, and force him to do what he did not want to do. Aye, and they would pay a heavy price for it, the very heaviest price.

Ptolemy Philopator is often called the bad Ptolemy, Stranger, the one that came to no good. For the moment let it be enough for you to know that he was born, howled, crawled, stood up, and that before he knew his own name, a daughter was born to Berenike Beta, and called Berenike, after her mother, Berenike Mikra, so the one was not muddled up with the other.

It was Euergetes' bright idea for Ptolemy Philopator to marry this sister of his, after the custom of the Egyptians, and after the excellent example of Philadelphos and Arsinoë Beta. *It will keep the Egyptians happy,* he said, and from the start the father, at least, brought Philopator up to look upon his sister as the one who must be his wife. It would be good for the next Ptolemy to play Osiris to his sister's Isis: their son would be Horus indeed. The Alexandrian Greeks had gotten used to such enormity, but the ancient Greek horror of incest lived on in the heart of Berenike Beta, who shivered down the spine to hear her husband speak of it with such warmth.

She said, *We disapprove of incest. It is a filthy, disgusting thing.* She told her husband of the five-legged lambs she had seen in Kyrene, the result of much inbreeding. *We thoroughly disapprove,* she said, *of a brother marrying his sister. How can you think of planning such a monstrous thing?*

But Euergetes, busy flicking his fly-whisk of gold and *sappheiros*, affected not to hear her.

A brother–sister marriage, Berenike Beta went on, louder, *would be an atrocious insult to the gods in heaven. We completely disapprove of it.*

Euergetes whacked his fly-whisk into a gilded table. *To marry the sister,* he said, very loud, *is the custom in my family . . . By rights I should myself have been married to my sister, to Berenike Syra. In which case the poor woman might still have been alive today. I am the Pharaoh, and I will have no argument. The custom of marrying the sister is pleasing to the Egyptians.*

It sounded like his last word on the subject. Whether he had hated Arsinoë Beta or not, clearly he had listened too well to her urgings with regard to the purity of the blood royal. And so, yes, even Berenike Beta, this strong, warlike woman, felt she must keep quiet. She consoled herself with the thought that the shameful marriage could not take place for years and years; that there was no guarantee that either child would survive. *No,* she thought, *we do not need to stir up trouble in the matter of our children's marriages just yet. The marriage might not have to take place at all.* And so she let the matter rest.

Upon the birth of Ptolemy Philopator the High Priest of Ptah came with his best of best wishes and his gifts of gold, and he spoke of his pleasure at the birth of a new member of the family. Likewise, when Berenike Mikra was born. But this time he led the Pharaoh and his Queen out on to the terrace of the palace after dark and pointed to the heavens. *Look up, if you please, Megaleios,* he said. *Please to look up, Megaleia.*

The parents craned their necks, eyes searching the night sky, noting with satisfaction that her Majesty's hair was still hanging up, glittering, among the stars.

When a child is born, Anemhor said, *a new star appears.* And he pointed out the new star that was the star of Berenike Mikra, close by the constellation that was her mother's hair, snatched up by the gods, and he said, *This star is bright because it is the star of the new Princess of Egypt.*

Ptolemy and Berenike stared into the great blackness, scattered with one million million stars, and they thought of all the Greek children that the stars stood for, all the Egyptian children, and they smiled, thinking it a charming idea.

Anemhor did not speak of what happens to the stars on the death of children. *There will be time enough,* he thought, *to tell them what happens when a child dies.*

Euergetes was very keen for Berenike Mikra to be her brother's wife, to be useful to him, just as Berenike Beta was useful to himself. Because of it, he would bring her up to ride a horse, to drive a chariot, knowing how to handle fleets of ships, and armies of soldiers: she would have the same fierce upbringing that her mother had in Kyrene. Her mother approved, certainly, of all of that.

You are right, Husband, she said, thinking of Berenike Syra's fate. *Berenike Mikra must learn how to look after herself. She must be even better than poor Berenike Syra.* She would be just like her mother, a strong survivor, quite fearless.

The Greek horoscopists and soothsayers – ancient, bearded, unwashed – shuffled into his Majesty's audience hall and murmured, however, that the sixth day of the month was not a good day for a girl to be born on, and that, contrary to her parents' hopes, Berenike Mikra's life would be short. Euergetes shouted at them, sent them away without any payment.

The parents started Berenike Mikra young upon her road to fierceness, all the same, in the proud tradition of her female ancestors. Berenike Beta, that had not much time for children, managed to make herself love this daughter of hers when she was old enough to be lifted on to the back of a horse and she could teach her to ride. Aye, this little girl would be tough and bold, just like herself. Both the parents loved this sweet-natured daughter, and also, of course, they loved her because she was – with Ptolemy Philopator – the glorious future of the dynasty.

We shall do better without ill forecasts of the future, Euergetes said, and Berenike Beta agreed with him. They tried to be modern parents, ignoring the old Greek superstitions, and the nonsense of horoscopes – unscientific, useless trash, fit only for wild laughter. Euergetes preferred the exact sciences, not this fake science of zodiac signs, in which the planets were meant to rule a man's fate, instead of the gods. So often the horoscopists had been shown to be wrong, and ridiculous. As it happened, though, this time the horoscopists were right.

Ptolemy Philopator was taking his first steps, beginning to chase Agathokles and Agathokleia around the *gynaikeion*, and Berenike Mikra was beginning to crawl, when a third child landed between the feet of Berenike Beta, a second son, about whom the omens and horoscope forecasts that his parents refused to take any notice of were mixed. On the one hand he would be good, brave, strong, a fine soldier, but on the other hand, if Euergetes kept up the family tradition, it was his sure fate never to grow old. All sons after the firstborn son were fated to die on the same day as their father, and die violent. For the moment they wiped this thought out of their hearts, as if with a sponge, and tried to think of pleasanter things.

Let us not call him Ptolemy . . . Berenike Beta said, *We have enough Ptolemies in the family already . . . Let him be called Magas, after our beloved father.*

This time Berenike Beta, as not quite so often these days, had her way.

If the first son was destined to turn out for the bad, the second son would turn out much better, but such was the character of the father that, however many dozens of times Berenike Beta raised the subject in the next five, ten, fifteen years, he kept to his word about the succession, refusing to change his heart.

I have made my decision, he told his wife, *and I shall not go back on it. We shall not make the same mistake as our father in the matter of the heir. The eldest son shall be Pharaoh, the eldest.* He would refuse for twenty-three years to see sense and make the younger, better, son his heir.

And perhaps it was also in part because the horoscopists whom he so despised whispered in his ear that the fate of the fresh Magas was to be a *loutrodaiktos*, one slain in his bath, like Agamemnon. No, Euergetes refused to listen to them. He was Beneficent and Magnificent, perhaps, but stubborn, just like his father.

Right at the beginning of Ptolemy Philopator's life, then, the seeds of trouble were sown, and there would be trouble, not abroad, nor up-River either, this time, but within the palace, within the family. Aye, as sure as the Sun beat up every morning like an orange ball and was greeted by the chattering of the Apes of Ra, blood would be spilled.

In another year or so Berenike Beta gave birth to a third son, whom they called Alexandros. Unless some terrible accident, or some exotic African disease, did away with his two elder brothers, this boy would never be Pharaoh. It mattered not that he was not called Ptolemy. His only purpose in life was to be the spare son, lest any disaster should befall the others. He was a disposable prince, his mother thought, the son who would have to die, in order that the Pharaoh might live.

Two years later, there was born a fourth son whose name nobody could afterwards remember, and about whom just the same words apply as to the above Alexandros. He, too, must die. But Seshat says: *Let him be called Lagos, a good family name among the Ptolemies. Let him not be forgotten, even if his name is wrong. Without a name a man is damned for evermore.*

Quite early in the life of Ptolemy Philopator, Anemhor asked his Egyptian craftsmen in the Temple of Ptah to make a jewel, or cameo, out of sardonyx, that showed this prince emerging from a lotus flower. It was the finest Egyptian work, a gift for Pharaoh, and it showed the infant prince wearing the *pschent*, or Double Crown of Upper and Lower Egypt. The Horus lock of childhood curled round his ear. The first finger of his right hand pointed to his mouth. It was Ptolemy Philopator as Harpokrates, the Infant Horus. From the start Oinanthe brought up this son of the King pretty soft and comfortable. He was not made to do what he was told – except by his mother. Oinanthe did for him whatever he asked, got for him mechanical toys, leopard cubs, whistling birds – whatever he wanted, and Euergetes did just the same. Nobody said no to the boy who must be Pharaoh – except his mother.

If he did not wish to exert himself in the *gymnasion* in the heat of the sun, or practise the art of swordplay, he was not forced to. Every oracle forecast twenty long years of peace. Euergetes said Philopator might learn about weapons when he was older.

But of course, for a boy to grow up warlike, he must start young. In realizing that, Arsinoë Beta had done the right thing regarding Ptolemy the Son, but with disastrous results. Euergetes, thinking to avoid such an outcome with Philopator, fell into a different kind of error.

The trouble with Philopator was the opposite to what was the trouble with Ptolemy the Son, who had quit his childhood without learning how to obey orders. Ptolemy Philopator grew up with too much instruction. He was left with no hour of the day unoccupied, but he must sit with Eratosthenes learning about mathematics and geography, and every science under the sun. Euergetes made this boy's life so precise, so very ordered, that he was bound to rebel against order.

Magas, on the other hand, was trained from a young age to be a soldier, a general. His life would be spent either keeping his father's peace, or making his father's army ready for the next war: he might, at least, see something of the world beyond Egypt, until he had to die. Philopator's life would be nothing but petitions, dispatches, papyri, temple-building, nothing but ritual, and he would stay at home, because it was fatal – as Euergetes had discovered – for Pharaoh to leave Egypt. These two sons turned out, then, very unlike each another.

Ptolemy Euergetes liked to read the writings of Herodotos, whom some are pleased to call the Father of History, even though this happens to be one of the titles of Thoth. In the Histories of Herodotos his Majesty read: *How to Make Them Effeminate: first, forbid them to possess weapons of war; second, command them to wear tunics under their cloaks and buskins upon their feet; third, teach them lyre playing, singing and dancing. Then you will see them turn into women before your very eyes instead of men.*

These words were about subject peoples, of whom Herodotos wrote, *If you do these things you need not fear lest they revolt.* Euergetes smiled to read it. But he might just as well have been reading instructions How to Turn Your Son into a Daughter. Aye, because this was, in a manner of speaking, what was happening to Ptolemy Philopator.

Even his father thought, *How can a son who is given a wooden sword and leather shield refuse to play with them? How can such an unwarlike Ptolemy be good for Egypt?* But he thought better of it. *He will mature,* he thought. *He will change when he is a man. He will learn to love war.*

For sure Philopator would grow up to love weapons – the knife, in particular – but not quite in the way his father intended.

Aye, Ptolemy Philopator was the warlike one with no taste for war, none whatever, and little interest in doing what he was told. Euergetes knew what was the result of Ptolemy the Son never being given the beating he deserved by Philadelphos. He was pleased to hear the High Priest's suggestion: *A boy's ears are upon his back, he will hear when he is beaten.* When Philopator refused to obey the wrestling-master, his father beat him. When he refused to learn by heart the Pythian Odes of Pindar, or Gorgias's Funeral Oration, his father beat him. The rod is an important part of every Greek boy's upbringing – for what is the use of the lesson in grammar if he will not listen? What is the use of being told about strategy if the boy refuses to remember? Euergetes thought Philadelphos had been foolish not to beat Ptolemy the Son. He would not make that mistake himself. Philopator howled at first, but he was beaten so often that he began almost to enjoy the pain, the warm feeling, the delightful numbness that surged through his body when the rod struck his buttocks.

Those seeds of trouble began to sprout, then, and the future of Philopator was fixed for good the first time he saw the Galloi, the eunuchs of Kybele, the great Mother Goddess of Phrygia, in their yellow dresses, dancing down Kanopic Street in a frenzy, bashing their drums and cymbals, whipping themselves with leather straps, and drawing blood from their arms with razor-sharp flints. Yes, indeed, for Philopator was seized with a longing to do all of these things himself.

Euergetes warned his son, of course, as every Alexandrian father warned his son: *Have nothing to do with the half men. They are mad. They will chop your ballocks off . . .*

His mother warned him too, saying, *Keep away, the Galloi are dangerous.*

It would have been better for Philopator and for Egypt if Euergetes had banned the cult of Kybele altogether, and sent the Galloi packing, but Euergetes did not ban the followers of the Great Mother, because he was obliged to revere the Great Mother of all living things himself; because he believed in her greatness, her importance. You cannot abolish a goddess, Stranger. You do not forbid the worship of a goddess in whose efficacy you yourself have a profound and unshakeable faith.

But whatever his father and mother forbade him to go near, forbade him even to look at, Philopator needs must do the opposite. The cult of Kybele would be part of his rebellion against these well-meaning parents, these interfering parents, of his.

Ptolemy Philopator was born in blood, like every child, but he grew up to love the sight of blood, loving the colour of blood. He knew already the divine trembling that came over him when the bull's blood splashed in his face at the Greek sacrifice. He would bathe in blood. He would be showered with blood all his life. His end, like his beginning, would be bloody.

But Magas was quite different. He did not have his brother's strange obsession with bloodshed – except, perhaps, as part of his interest in war, and the wholesale slaughter of the enemies of Egypt. Magas liked to do things the right way, the Greek way, the good way, and in that he was very like his grandfather and namesake, the King of Kyrene. He was not interested in the un-Greek cult of Kybele. Somehow, every thing went wrong for Ptolemy Philopator, as if he had indeed been born under an unlucky planet. Everything went right for Magas – for the moment. He grew up well-balanced: warlike, but not too warlike. He would be a fine general of his father's troops. But under the old style of doing things he was unlikely to be a general for very long: the most likely thing to happen to Magas was that he would be murdered as soon as Philopator came to the throne, because he presented a threat to his brother's security – and his parents, of course, knew this perfectly well. Indeed, they must make sure it happened. For the younger sons to be put to death was the family tradition; it was how the heir survived – by murdering every one of his male relatives.

For sure, you should not suppose, Stranger, that the native Egyptian Pharaohs had done any different. They behaved just the same, even if History has kept quiet about it. Such was the way of the world in these violent times. But no, Euergetes had made his heart strong to change all that. There were no murders when he became king: there must be no murders when Philopator came to the throne either. He had raised his sons not to hate each other.

All the same, in her heart Berenike Beta believed more strongly than ever that Magas would make the better King of Egypt (and Kyrene), a far better king than Philopator. But her husband's word about the succession was as if carved in stone. In Berenike Beta's heart was fixed a desire to stick to the old ways. She thought to stop Philopator being king. She thought to keep on murdering. She thought she would murder not Magas but Philopator, and make quite certain that the best of her sons inherited the kingship. Aye, the seeds of a terrible tragedy were springing up fast, putting forth magnificent shoots, great sturdy branches.

3.11

Slave Children

Officially there never was the slightest rumour of Euergetes being anything but faithful to his muscular wife. He offered a shining example of husbandly virtue among the kings of the House of Ptolemy. There was not one squeak of a concubine, not one husky whisper of a handsome boy. But you need only look at his five year campaign in Syria to see the nonsense of all that: we know very well, Stranger, that Berenike Beta did not go with him into Syria. How could any man hold out for five years without any *aphrodisia*, all the time staying faithful to his wife back at home in Egypt? Of course Euergetes had his other women. Seshat records the truth: his comforter was the beautiful Oinanthe of Samos, the Great Royal Nurse, whose breasts were round, like great ripe apples, good for suckling infants. Perhaps she was even with Euergetes in Syria, with him in Babylon, with him at Ekbatana. Perhaps he picked her up in Kilikia, one of the soldiers' whores. History, Stranger, is a matter of joining up the fragments, of reading between the lines.

Like everything else, there were two sides to the stories about Oinanthe. On the one hand she was a slave-girl, from the gutter. On the other hand she was high-born, carried off by pirates and sold into slavery. True or false, it matters little. What matters is where Oinanthe ended up: in the palace, in the arms of Pharaoh, where she would do well, most excellently well, and where she would also cause the very gravest trouble. At first she played the flute for his Majesty, but she was also good on the trumpet, and a fine sambuca-player and drummer. She began, then, by soothing his ears. Soon she found herself giving suck to his children. Then she began to massage his back with her quick fingers, this Greek woman from Samos, whose beauty outshone that of Queen Berenike Beta, and one thing led to the next thing, until his Majesty found that Oinanthe was highly skilled in the arts of Aphrodite.

Oinanthe was Euergetes his great passion, they said. She did with this King things Berenike Beta never dreamed of doing, they said, things that only the whores did. Oinanthe was not haughty. She did not demand to be addressed always as *Megaleia*. She was not followed wherever she went by a lion. She was not haunted by the bleeding ghost of the most beautiful man in the world. Her spirits was not weighed down by the memory of bloody murder.

Her eyes were not sad, but sparkled, full of fun, full of mischief. Aye, mischief, there would be much of that. No, Oinanthe had not done a murder. Not yet.

Ptolemy Euergetes breathed easy. He had his peace. He had his five children, his heir to the throne, and three spares, lest Hades should take Philopator early. All seemed to be pretty well in the life of Ptolemy Euergetes, the Benefactor, the Magnificent, who sought out in the night time not the hard muscles and golden bed of his wife but the soft, ample flesh and pigeon's-feather mattress of Oinanthe of Samos.

Oinanthe, the wet nurse, the flute girl, the concubine of the King, had done wondrous well for herself, had she not? But what of her two young children, Agathokles and Agathokleia? What would become of them at the court of King Ptolemy? Oinanthe worried about their fate, but they had the best of beginnings, growing up under the same roof as royalty – Prince Ptolemy Philopator and his sister Princess Berenike Mikra, the ones who would be husband and wife, Prince Magas, Prince Alexandros, Prince Lagos – all of them playing at satyrs and maenads. It is a charming picture, all these children playing happily together, running about the palace without their clothes, for it was too hot to wear clothes; aye, naked, without even the talismans that ward off every evil spirit. They would have been better to keep those talismans on, for they were surrounded by evil.

It was Aristotle himself who said, *Children should have as little to do with slaves as possible, lest they become like slaves themselves.* Neither Euergetes nor Berenike Beta seem to have given a moment's thought to those words. No, they were too busy taking care of Egypt to take care of their children. Nobody in that palace thought to stop Ptolemy Philopator from playing with the children of Oinanthe. You might want to argue that Oinanthe was hardly a slave, her children not slave's children. You might wish to censure Seshat herself for arrogant thoughts, but read on, Reader, and you will see that Seshat is right, right one million times. She is the Lady of the House of Books, the Chronographer and Chronologer. Never forget it, Stranger.

At four and five and six years old Ptolemy Philopator, Berenike Mikra, Magas, Alexandros, Lagos, Agathokles and Agathokleia, playing and fighting together, were like one big happy family under the watchful eye of Oinanthe. But what they did in the future would be worse, much worse, than the harmless quarrelling of children.

Some men say that infants who suck at the same breast develop a closeness that will last all their lives. Perhaps that is why Ptolemy Philopator and Agathokles and Agathokleia of Samos were so close. In the beginning there was laughter, and high spirits. But they grew up much too close together.

When they were fully grown the laughter would stop, and the high spirits would end in tragedy, a Greek tragedy as dreadful as anything heard of in the world before or since.

Young though they were, Oinanthe's charming, handsome children did not, even at six or seven years old, do nothing. Doing nothing was for kings, for princes like Ptolemy Philopator. Agathokles and Agathokleia must work, in order to *survive*. Indeed, Agathokles of Samos began his working life very young, apprenticed to the man who throttled the stray dogs that wandered about the palace: old dogs, mad dogs, dogs that never stopped barking. From quite a young age he was Agathokles the dog-throttler, Agathokles the *strangler*.

Agathokles began young committing crimes against Anubis, the great god, the great dog, and you might like to think that, at the end of it all, Anubis had the sweetest revenge upon Agathokles for those youthful crimes. For sure, Agathokles wept, in the beginning, hating himself for what he must do, but he learned quick to stifle his tender feelings. He learned not to care about killing. This boy was not going to be soft like Ptolemy Philopator but hard, the hardest of the hard.

The smiling Oinanthe would say to him, *A handsome boy who can use his hands will always be useful to somebody. Such a boy might do anything. He will be sure to earn himself a pile of dekadrachms all his life.* She urged him onward, ever onward, in his strange career, urged him to love money, urged him to steal whatever he could, urged him to think that nothing was impossible.

And what of Agathokleia? While she waited for her breasts to grow to four or five fingerbreadths high, so that she might earn a good living with her beautiful body, and become, perhaps, even a king's concubine, she served her apprenticeship to the palace acrobats. She learned how to turn somersaults and walk a tightrope, how to leap from one galloping horse to another, how to swallow swords, how to charm snakes, how to juggle with firesticks. Then she learned the art of eating fire, and breathed great clouds of flame from her mouth. She learned how to keep her lips always wet with her saliva. She knew just when to breathe in, when to breathe out, when to hold her breath. She was careful never to inhale, never to panic. Very quick she picked up the art of blowing the best and most beautiful of flames.

All fire-eaters expect to burn themselves at some stage – that is the great hazard of their curious profession. Often Agathokleia suffered from heartburn. Many times, in the beginning, she swallowed the inflammable fluid by mistake and had to drink a gallon of milk. All her life she would belch up inflammable fumes. But a woman can get used to anything, almost. For the rest, she was so good that she never burnt her lips. She never burned so much as a finger. When she was still quite a young girl Agathokleia was declared to be the best fire-eater in all Egypt.

Agathokleia, that played with fire from her earliest childhood, was just as hard as her brother, if not harder.

Proud Oinanthe told her, *A girl with such skills will never be short of a rich man to throw money at her.* Oinanthe was right. Arsinoë Beta had been very *like* Sakhmet, the lioness, that breathes fire over her enemies. But little Agathokleia *literally* breathed fire. At the start she had no enemies to burn up. By no means. Alexandria loved Agathokleia just then. She would make her enemies later.

Remember these clever children's names, Stranger, if you please. Their history will send the shivers running up and down your spine. Every word is true, not *story* but *history*. That is why it is so awful. Agathokles and Agathokleia, that loved to play with fire and never get their fingers burnt, they were more like a couple of great moths, whose fate was to fly into the flame of an oil lamp and be consumed in the fire.

Seshat continues to count the days. Time flew like the falcon, fast. In the Great Pompe held in the year when Ptolemy Philopator was eight or nine years old, the usual procession held Alexandria as if bound by some magic spell from dawn to dusk. If you will be so kind as to turn back the page, Stranger, and cast your eye over Seshat's account of the first fabulous procession, you may remind yourself what the Pompe was like under Ptolemy Euergetes – that is to say, it was pretty much the same, but more wonderful, more extravagant; the excess of the Greeks was boundless, and the expense was more ruinous than ever. But the Ptolemies could not give up the Pompe even if they wanted to. By no means. To announce the end of the Pompe would be to invite uproar, riots, revolution, like asking for the end of the microcosm that was Alexandria.

Leading this Pompe was Oinanthe herself as the Great Fat Lady of Alexandria, blowing her golden trumpet, doing just exactly what Aglaïs did in the Great Pompe of Ptolemy Philadelphos. Oinanthe had grown fat. She had feasted very well, thanks to King Ptolemy, for years. She was the Great Royal Nurse (Retired) of the Infant Horus, but still the King's Great Concubine. Oinanthe screamed with laughter like the jackdaw. Her breasts had been in the mouth of the Horus one thousand days and she had almost anything she asked for because of it. On that day what she had asked for was a place for herself and her children in the great procession.

At the front of the Pompe was the procession of the Morning Star, Eosphoros, personified as a naked boy with golden wings, who held up a flaming torch to symbolize the light of the star, and he had a golden face and body, golden arms and legs, golden lips and golden buttocks. His golden hair was spiked like the points of the star that he personated, and he rode upon the back of a great white horse with golden trappings. This naked, golden boy was Agathokles of Samos, who had found favour for being handsome, and for being his mother's son.

On that day the young Ptolemy Philopator was struck by the arrows of Eros and fell a little in love with this golden boy after the charming custom of the Greeks. To be sure, Philopator would hardly know one day in all the rest of his life when he did not have Agathokles of Samos at his side, or in his bed, grinning. For sure, it was as if, that day, Agathokles of Samos got himself buttocks and *rhombos* not of gold paint but of solid gold, not temporary but permanent, for upon these two parts of his anatomy he would ride to power and phenomenal riches – and also to ruin.

In the middle of the same procession rode his sister, Agathokleia, dressed in golden robes as one of the *Nikai*, or winged Victories. She too was painted gold from head to foot and never stopped from smiling, for she sat on the back of a great white horse, and waved flaming torches about from dawn to dusk. And, for sure, it was as if the *bolba* and buttocks of this little girl was made of gold, for just the same words would apply to her as to her brother. Ptolemy Philopator fell now a little in love also with Agathokleia. She, too, would pass the most of her life in Philopator's bed, smiling, laughing, helping herself to everything that was his. But such things lay in the future. Just then, the only person Philopator truly cared for was his own sister, Berenike Mikra, the one who should be his wife, who sat beside him with their parents, in a golden chair, in the Stadion, watching the procession.

Euergetes thought it harmless enough to have these rough urchins ride in the Pompe, but the harm was done: Oinanthe's children had usurped the place of the royal children in the procession, and it was like a dreadful foreshadowing of the future. Because of it, the expectations of this golden family of slaves were raised a little above what was their proper station in life. Each time the part they took in the Pompe was bigger, so that Oinanthe began to think there might be no limit to the honours her children might enjoy. Government offices might fall their way when they grew up, she thought, or the satrapies of foreign lands, or perhaps they might even be royalty themselves. Oinanthe urged her children on, drove them forward, suggesting every kind of outrageous behaviour.

Really, Stranger, Oinanthe of Samos, screaming with laughter at the head of the Pompe of Ptolemy Euergetes, thought she had fallen upon the most tremendous good luck in Egypt. In point of fact, though, she was wrong. The

Greeks used to think that too much luck is not good for mortals, but is sure to tempt the gods to exact a terrible revenge. But the Alexandrians had stopped following so many of the old Greek ways. They had stopped honouring the gods of Olympos, for the most part, preferring to put their trust in Tykhe, goddess of Good Luck, and Dionysos, god of Wine. But Oinanthe had tempted the gods to punish her, and she would be punished.

Agathokles and Agathokleia: forget not their names, Stranger. These are the upstart golden children who will nearly break the House of Ptolemy. Already they have displaced the royal family from the procession. For Ptolemy Philopator, who might have been Eosphoros, was made to sit and watch with his parents, his brothers and sister, and he fidgeted, wanting to ride in the procession like his friends, a little jealous even of the ordinary boys who got to be junior satyrs. Philopator was the heir to all of the gold, but he did not, that day, get himself painted with gold paint. No, the costume he had to wear was nothing more exotic than the Greek-style white tunic, and the *kausia* or felt sun-helmet of Macedon, and he resented it.

Philopator sulked all that day. His face, even on his statues would always look like this, sulky, pouting, a little cruel. His face would always be a child's face, the face of a spoilt child.

For the most part, though, the family of Ptolemy Euergetes looked happy enough that day, apart, perhaps, from one or two stray ghosts. They would be happy for a while longer, but it was not their fate to be happy for ever. By no means. No, the real unhappiness comes later, relentless unhappiness, like the great grey-green waves that crash upon the beaches of Alexandria in winter, terrifying, unstoppable. But for the moment Alexandria is pretty calm, and Egypt is at peace both at home and abroad, peaceful for as much as eight thousand glorious days.

3.12

Dates

So very calm, indeed, were the Two Lands under the great peace of Ptolemy Euergetes that it seemed a good time for betrothals in the family of Anemhor. Horemakhet his son being just twenty years old, he made the agreement with his future father-in-law and was married to the beautiful Nefertiti, aged fifteen. She had long since made her prayers to Hathor the Golden, asking for what every Egyptian girl asked for: *Happiness, and a good husband*. Hathor was now pleased to grant her both of these requests. Aye, the High Priest's family was genuinely happy, so very different from the family of King Ptolemy.

Horemakhet murmured the words of the Egyptian wedding hymns into the ears of his wife, his beloved:

> *I have no fear of the depths*
> *No fear of the crocodile.*
> *The river is just like dry land to me.*
> *Love gives me strength,*
> *Love is my magic spell.*
> *I gaze on my heart's longing:*
> *She stands before me . . .*

Ptolemy Euergetes had never spoken such things to his wife. He did not speak to Berenike Beta of love. For the Greeks, love was madness, and did not what happened to Demetrios Kalos absolutely prove it? To fall in love was crazy, a thing to be avoided like the marsh fever. But the Egyptians think quite different: to love is what matters most; love is more important than anything else in the Two Lands – love of the gods, love of Pharaoh, love of husband for wife, wife for husband, parents for children. The Egyptian hates war, as if in truth the national character is to hate nobody. For sure, love is what matters most in Egypt.

Aye, love, and it was not long before Nefertiti brought into the world a son, whom they called Pasherenptah.

At the new year festival it was the custom for Pharaoh to give gifts to his high officials. This time Euergetes gave Anemhor, as High Priest, a scarab of gold, near to half a cubit long, inlaid with precious stones.

Horemakhet smiled, delighted. *It is a goodly thing that my father is the friend of his Majesty,* he said.

In his turn Anemhor gave to each member of his family a scarab beetle carved out of alabaster, small enough to fit in the palm of the hand, with *Good Luck* and *Happy New Year* carved on the bottom in the hieroglyphs. Anemhor's scarabs were of very fine workmanship but not of great value. He had great riches, great lands, as High Priest of Memphis, and gold in abundance in the form of bracelets and necklaces of office, but he had no desire to have as much gold as he could get, like the Greeks. An Egyptian priest has no need of rich things for himself but is content with little. Unlike the Greeks, he does not need gold to make him happy, but is happy already.

*

Though it may seem like only yesterday since the other Nefertiti, daughter of Padibastet, was married to the High Priest of Letopolis, the truth was that she had been gone from her father's house many years. She had borne her children, watched them grow up and enter the temple service themselves. Now Nefertiti was dead, leaving Akhoapis her husband grieving, head on knee. The members of this family did not look upon the idea of loving with horror, like the Greeks. But perhaps it is unfair of Seshat to write such things. It is not quite the whole truth, for in the palace of Ptolemy Euergetes and Berenike Beta love was not wholly missing.

Like all Greeks they loved their sons, though they tried not to make too much fuss of them. But Greek parents do not need to hold back love where a daughter is concerned. Berenike Mikra, their only daughter, received most of her parents' warm affection. They played chasing round the palace games and sang Greek songs together. They laughed and made jests. They kissed and hugged her. Of course they did. Just because they were King and Queen of Upper and Lower Egypt it did not mean that Euergetes and Berenike Beta ceased to be human – though of course they were gods too, living gods, and could be a little *remote*. They could be abrupt, even a little cruel, to Philopator, even though their cruelty was well-intentioned – for the father's beatings did not stop, and Berenike Beta did not stop saying *Stop doing that ridiculous dance* to her eldest son, or *Do not look at the half-men, you must look away*. But with Berenike Mikra they were most loving, quite natural, quite human, really most human.

When Ptolemy Euergetes announced that there would be a synod of all the priests of Egypt at Kanopos, Anemhor, High Priest of Ptah, sailed his great barge *Shining in Memphis* there. His three sons – Djedhor, Horemakhet and Horimhotep, all of them junior priests – sailed with him.

In the new Temple of Osiris at Kanopos, founded by Euergetes himself, that had been nearly ten years in the building but was almost finished, thousands of priests gathered from as far away as Philai. They sat on the ground in the great courtyard, dressed in their white linen robes. They would speak about many things, but the first thing to be discussed was the reform of the Egyptian calendar, which was in total disorder. Disorder troubled Euergetes, the lover of precision, and he thought to do Egypt a favour, by replacing the chaos of the dating system with a new and perfect Greek order.

Chaos, Euergetes said to Anemhor, *I know that is what Egypt detests.*

And so it was. Anemhor, in charge of the synod, proposed the simple change, saying, *The Egyptian year is six hours short, so that the calendar slips by ten days every forty years. Our friends from Macedon have shown us how to*

*alter the calendar so as to stop the winter festivals turning up in the summer
time, and so as to stop the summer festivals falling in midwinter.*

How bad things were with the dates in Egypt you can see from just one
example: under the old system the Egyptian harvest festival came at the time
of harvest just once in one thousand five hundred years. Seshat swears,
Stranger, it is the honest truth. Anemhor himself said, *It is time for change,
even in the land where nothing ever changes. I, for one, support the proposal.*

The fresh system was a perfect system. Euergetes' scholars promised that,
under the new Greek calendar, the harvest festival would coincide with the
harvest every year, for so long as there was a harvest to gather in and celebrate, for ever. The new calendar was guaranteed by the great Eratosthenes to
be correct and workable, but even Eratosthenes said it could not succeed
without the co-operation of the priests and scribes of Egypt, who must make
use of it every day. Aye, the only drawback was that the system was a Greek
system, dreamed up by the scholars of Euergetes' Mouseion, and because the
fresh idea was a Greek idea, the Egyptian scribes and priests hated it, said
they would not have it, and threw the proposal out.

To try and make the high priests agree to the reforms, Euergetes sailed in
his golden barge along the Kanopic Canal, and honoured the synod with his
royal presence. Berenike Beta and Berenike Mikra sailed with him. His
Majesty came to listen, and went away again several times. When he was
present the priests spoke Greek, were quite calm, and sounded as if they
might agree to the changes. As soon as he went away they spoke Egyptian,
disapproved of the reforms, and became very agitated.

One time the High Priest of Amun at Thebes stood up and said, *Egypt has no
need to change her calendar. It matters not at all if the harvest festival never falls at
the same time as the harvest: in Egypt everything should remain the same. We
Egyptians like things just how they are. The calendar was invented by Thoth himself. If Thoth made mistakes, they are divine mistakes. We do not want to be seen to
correct the gods. They will punish us for it. We hate the new calendar. We wish King
Ptolemy would stop interfering.* Then he raised his voice and said, *We should be
very pleased for this King to sail back to Rhakotis . . . In fact, Thebes would be very
pleased if Ptlumis sailed away to Macedon and never came back.* All the priests of
the south waved their papyrus agendas above their heads and cheered, while the
northern, Memphite, priests, sat quiet and looked uncomfortable.

When Euergetes came to Kanopos, and said he would stay there until the
priests agreed to alter the calendar, they felt they must agree to the reforms,
or they would never see their wives or their children again. Horemakhet was
particularly anxious about his wife, urgent to be back in Memphis with
Nefertiti and his young son.

The Egyptian calendar had twelve months of thirty days each, ending with five epagomenal, or intercalary days, which were the birthdays of Osiris, Isis, Horus, Seth and Nephthys. All the Greeks were proposing was to add one more day to the year, an extra epagomenal day, a day of festival – what will in your own time, Stranger, be called the leap-year day – every fourth year. When the synod at long last agreed to the change, there was applause, Euergetes showed the teeth, and there was rejoicing in the Mouseion.

The scribes now gave up using the old Egyptian Calendar in favour of the new Macedonian Calendar. At first they wrote down the Macedonian month only. But after just thirty days they began to write the Egyptian month after it as well, saying they were confused by the unpronounceable foreign names. When the order came from King Ptolemy in person, to encourage them, saying, *Please to Keep Using the New Calendar*, they ignored it. Aye, the scribes went back to using the old Egyptian system, and the time for sowing and for harvesting came and went, just as they had always done – all mixed up, all wrong.

The Egyptians would be pleased to ignore the leap-year day for two hundred and sixty-seven years exactly, when a new calendar was imposed upon Egypt by a man whose name Seshat cannot bring herself to mention, a man from Rome. And, without the priests of Egypt having been asked whether they liked it or no, they must obey his orders, or take the beating upon the soles of both feet.

3.13

Berenike Mikra

Berenike Mikra, being at the time of the Synod a little unwell, sailed back and forth with Euergetes on his royal barge to Kanopos, in search of a cure for her health. As her father said, *It will be a good opportunity for the Egyptians to get to know our family. Even if the Egyptian priests cannot quite bring themselves to love a Greek monarch, they might be able to love his beautiful daughter.*

The best thing that came out of the Synod of Kanopos was the great warmth of feeling that arose between Berenike Mikra and the Egyptian priests. Ptolemy was right: they were charmed by his young daughter. They practised their Greek on her, and made her smile with their gifts – Egyptian dolls of clay, with movable arms and legs fixed on with wires, by which they wanted to show the truth: that the Egyptians are a kind, friendly people.

When Berenike Mikra sailed home to Alexandria with her father the first time, they said to her, *Come back soon . . . Most of all we want to see you again in Kanopos . . .*

At the feast that marked the agreement on the calendar the High Priest of Ptah thanked Pharaoh for his generosity to the Egyptian temples. He praised his Majesty for his constant concern for the well-being of the Apis and all the other sacred animals, the falcons of Apollonopolis, the lions of Leontopolis, the crocodiles of Krokodilopolis, the sacred cats of Bubastis, the ibises of Hermopolis – and so on. At Anemhor's suggestion the priests granted to Euergetes and Berenike Beta the title of *Theoi Euergetai,* or the Benefactor Gods.

When Anemhor said, *King Ptolemy's generosity has been greater than any other Pharaoh we can think of since Ramesses . . . and it is all so that there might be peace in the Two Lands,* there was prolonged applause, even from the priests of Thebes.

When he said, *The Pharaoh is the father of his people, benevolent, watching over them like a shepherd over his flock,* the priests of Egypt – whatever their private thoughts – stood up and cheered him.

A shadow fell across these proceedings, though, when Berenike Mikra's health took a turn for the worse, and her father saw a dream in which he heard the words of the poet Menander: *She whom the gods love dies young.*

At first the royal doctors all said the same, *It is the usual fever, the usual derangement of the stomach, it will pass.* The parents were not greatly troubled, but they sent Berenike Mikra to spend the night in the Asklepieion, entrusting her to the care of the Greek god of Health, who was such a good doctor that he could even bring the dead back to life. However, to take any patient to the Asklepieion was a bad sign, for the sick only came here when every other remedy had been tried. Although Asklepios was a great god, he was also wise enough never to promise a cure for anything.

The sacred dogs of Asklepios trotted up to lick Berenike Mikra's hands and face, tails wagging, for the dog's tongue is a wonderful medicine. The sacred snakes of Asklepios were brought to lick her ears with their flickering tongues, and made her squeal with the tickling. She was not afraid. She had been brought up to fear nothing.

When Anemhor said that the best way to cure Berenike Mikra would be for her mother to eat a mouse, and have the bones put in a little canvas bag tied up with seven knots and hung round her daughter's neck as a talisman, Euergetes agreed to it, but Berenike Beta disapproved. *The Queen of Egypt and Kyrene,* she said, angry, *is not in the habit of eating mice.* And so Berenike Mikra continued much the same, very hot, and unable to eat anything.

*

As a last resort, Euergetes carried Berenike Mikra in his arms up the steps of the Sarapieion at Kanopos, founded by himself, and now almost complete, that was already a famous oracle and place of pilgrimage for the sick, and left her with the Greek priests to sleep the night, in hope of a miracle. But Anemhor was not so sure that Sarapis could cure anybody. *Has his Majesty forgotten already,* he wondered, *that this god is a false god, invented by his own grandfather?*

In the morning, when the restoration of Berenike Mikra's health should have been proclaimed with trumpets, the only thing to be declared was that she had passed away during the night, and all Kanopos wept, for she was just six years old.

After dark, Anemhor came to Pharaoh and said, *When your daughter was born, a new star appeared in the sky. After the death of the child to whom it belongs, that star will fall. That is what the falling stars are.*

Euergetes and Berenike Beta wept openly.

Look up, Majesties, he said. *Can you see the star that is Little Berenike, that falls upon the night of her passing?*

And yes, through their tears, they did see a star fall.

There are many stars, Majesties, Anemhor said. *There will be many new stars.*

And the parents had, then, their first thought of a new star, a fresh daughter, to replace the little star they had lost.

They left the body of Berenike Mikra behind in the Temple of Osiris at Kanopos at the special request of Anemhor, who begged them not to take her home to Alexandria, not to burn her up, but to bandage her after the Egyptian custom.

Even though Berenike Mikra was a daughter of Macedon, Greek-speaking, Euergetes let the Egyptians mummify her body and gild her face and feet. In her left hand they placed a bunch of red flowers. The inside of the coffin lid they painted blue like the sky, with gold stars like the falling star that was herself.

The funeral of Berenike Mikra was attended by all the high priests of Egypt in their leopardskin mantles, and all the prophets, those who enter the holy of holies for the robing of the gods, those who wear the hawk's wing, the sacred scribes and other priests, all of them, bald-headed, wearing white linen, in their thousands.

The priests sent to be buried with her a wooden crocodile with wagging tail, and a wooden hippopotamus with moving jaws, toys that would make Berenike Mikra laugh in the Afterlife of the Egyptians and prolong her delightful smile for millions and millions of years.

*

The Synod of Kanopos continuing, the High Priest of Memphis made a speech saying that the divinity of the King of Egypt was not something earned by his great deeds, as in the case of the *Basileus* of the Greeks, but a natural quality of the House of Ptolemy now that the family was a royal family, and the entire assembled priesthood of Upper and Lower Egypt drubbed their sandals in approval. When Anemhor said he would like to raise Berenike Mikra at once to the rank of a goddess in the Egyptian pantheon, just like Arsinoë Beta, the Synod approved of that as well.

Anemhor then suggested that since Berenike Mikra had gone over to the Eternal World much sooner than anybody had expected, while she was still a maiden, she might be granted the honour of a boat procession and a feast in all the temples of Egypt. It could take place, he said, in the month of Tybi that was the month of her passing, and a golden statue of her, inlaid with precious stones, might stand in the inner sanctuary of every temple, bearing the inscription *Berenike Mikra, Lady of the Virgins*. She would wear a headdress made of two ears of corn with an asp – or serpent – crown between them. The statue would be carried forth at every procession of the gods, and the bread given to the wives of the priests of Egypt at festival time could have a special shape, and be called *the Loaf of Berenike*.

The priests agreed to all of this, and then they voted for her to be assimilated with Tefnut, daughter of Ra. Aye, even Tefnut, goddess of the dew, the one with the head of a lioness, and it was very fitting for this fierce little girl.

No, the name of Berenike Mikra would not be forgotten.

Thus it came about that, as well as declaring Ptolemy and Berenike Beta to be an Egyptian god and goddess, the Synod of Kanopos also conferred divine honours upon their daughter. Little Berenike Mikra lost her life and missed her marriage to her brother, but ended up living for ever.

As for Anemhor and the other high priests, they hoped that by making Berenike Mikra a goddess they might bring the Greeks somewhat closer in line with the Egyptian way of thinking. Even Thebes was persuaded to approve.

These kind and, really, quite extraordinary gestures were a comfort to the distraught parents. Their public grief also did their reputation some good, for it showed that the Greeks did not entirely lack human feelings, but could weep real tears on occasion, just like anybody else, which until then some of the Egyptians had doubted.

All Alexandria was head upon knee for the dead princess, but the one who grieved most was Ptolemy Philopator, her eight-year-old brother. He had been very fond of the sister who should have played Isis to his Osiris, Hera to his Zeus. He had sobbed to see her cold, dead face. He insisted on being taken to Kanopos to pour with his own hand the libations of milk and honey and undiluted wine upon her tomb on the third, ninth and fortieth day after her passing, regardless of the fact that Greek rites were rather inappropriate.

As for Ptolemy Euergetes, in the midst of his weeping he said, *No man is now, or ever shall be, without his share of trouble.* Aye, Seshat knows, there was more trouble to come for him, much more trouble. As it happened, Berenike Mikra was the only one of Euergetes' children to die a natural death, of illness: the others would die unnatural, by violence.

3.14
Forgetting

After his own gods failed to save his daughter's life Ptolemy Euergetes asked Anemhor for Egyptian advice, what to do, how to make right what was wrong.

Anemhor urged him, *Try to be less Greek, Megaleios, less foreign. His Majesty is Pharaoh of Egypt. He should think more of pleasing the gods of Egypt. He must try to be more like an Egyptian. He should forget the gods of Greece, that have let him down so badly.*

Euergetes did not look the man in the eye, but watched the mosaic of hunters in the marshes, fowls, ducks, crocodiles.

His Majesty should not forget the Egyptians, Anemhor said. *He must maintain the balance of the Two Lands.*

The High Priest of Memphis made it plain to him. The Greek spies who kept an eye upon the trouble spots, who told what they saw of the Egyptians, what was their mood, what was going on up-River, said the same – warned that he should not be seen to do nothing.

Anemhor was no longer young, no longer in good health himself. The Synod of Kanopos had worn him out. In private he told his sons he was weary of his battle with King Ptolemy to make him build what any native pharaoh would have built without a word of complaint, as no more than the gods deserved for their great goodness to him. But then he was struck by personal tragedy himself, for Herankh, his wife, his beloved, flew to the sky.

Anemhor took the loss of the one he loved very hard. Herankh was old, fifty-seven years old, *seistron* player perfect of Sakhmet the great, the lioness goddess of Memphis. He missed her music-making. He missed her singing. Even six months after her passing, he would often be overcome by grief in the meetings of the Memphite priests. In the middle of the temple ritual he would forget the divine words, lost in thinking about his wife walking through the Afterlife hand in hand with Anubis, and be unable to go on. He decided to bring an end to his career as High Priest of Ptah, and devote the rest of his time on earth to the divine books. He told Euergetes, *I shall retire now, and make room for my son, if his Majesty will allow it.*

To his fellow priests he said, *My son Djedhor might be more successful than I at persuading King Ptolemy to build temples for Egypt.*

Young Anemhor was sixty-five years old when he renounced his duties. He kept just one temple office for himself, that of Scribe of the Rations of the Apis, the Sacred Bull, who was just about as dear to him as his wife.

Now Djedhor took over from his father as Great Chief of the Hammer, the one who must comfort King Ptolemy and Queen Berenike Beta for the loss of their daughter, and he did his best. But what of Ptolemy Philopator? Did he manage to forget Berenike Mikra? No, he did not.

When Berenike Beta found him still weeping, she snapped at him, saying, *Herakles never wept. Berenike Mikra was your sister. To think of marrying her is quite offensive to the gods on Olympos.* Aye, she was cold to her son, not warm. She did not offer him comfort in his grief. She did not clasp him to her breast and stroke his hair. She did not hold his hand, or tell him that she loved him, like an Egyptian mother would. The Egyptian does not think ill of tears, but Berenike Beta bottled up her own grief, thinking, indeed, *Herakles never wept.* The last vestiges of her motherly feelings she assuaged by galloping her horse very fast into the desert.

Philopator, seeing her go, murmured, *I hope she will never come back.*

Oinanthe of Samos was as much as the mother of Euergetes' sons. In the cool of the morning she would walk with them on the beach at Alexandria, followed by the customary guards, men armed as if for war. The younger boys would splash water, knock each other down in the sand, run laughing into the waves and swim like seals. Philopator did not do any of these things. He did not run. Never. When he tried to swim he swallowed water and sank like a rock. He had not smiled since the death of Berenike Mikra. He just thought of the dead sister and stared at his sandals.

Soon you will forget her, Oinanthe said, hugging him to her vast bosom, laughing. *Kick up your heels*, she said, *smile, you are the richest man in the world. Forget your sister, she has gone to Hades, the place of no return.*

But Philopator shouted, *I shall not forget. I shall never forget her.*

And the truth, surely, was that his sister was walking along the highways and byways of the Egyptian Afterlife, hand in hand with the crocodile. She was not down below, but had flown to the sky upon the wing of Thoth. She was Tefnut the little lioness, sailing through the sky in the barque of Ra.

For Ptolemy Philopator no woman would ever quite take the place of Berenike Mikra, who was meant to be his Queen, his Lady of the Two Lands, his Mistress of Happiness, She at Hearing Whose Voice the King Rejoices.

Some men always supposed that the loss of the sister was the reason for Philopator's heavy drinking, the explanation of his odd behaviour all through the rest of his life. Perhaps they were right. But some people will always seek causes for things. Philopator grew up the way he did because the gods had willed it. His fate was simply to be different from other boys, that is all.

And, for sure, he would be very different.

3.15

Dog-Throttler

Who, then, would Philopator fix upon to love instead of his sister? For he did love, even though love, to the Greeks, was madness. Aye, and they said Ptolemy Philopator was mad, though the best of his madness still lies ahead of us, in the future. Just then, his eye lit upon dark-haired, olive-skinned Agathokleia, so very unlike the fair Berenike Mikra, but much about the same age.

Perhaps he will love Agathokleia instead, Oinanthe thought.

For sure, he would love her. Fiery Agathokleia would be as much Philopator's great passion as her mother had been the great passion of Euergetes. But his eye lingered also upon dark-haired, black-eyed, olive-skinned Agathokles.

Maybe he will love Agathokles as well, Oinanthe thought. Her heart leaped up to think of it.

Aye, for sure, he would love both of them, love them with a crazy passion, and it was fortune beyond Oinanthe's wildest dreaming. Philopator was half in love with these palace urchins already, so very unlike the blue-eyed, fair-haired Ptolemies. They would have to fill the place of his dead sister.

Aye, Oinanthe prayed to the goddesses that Prince Ptolemy would love her children. She urged them on in their vicious career, told them to do everything they could to please him.

Even if he is ever so horrible to you, she told Agathokles, *you must be nice to him in return. Remember that he will be Pharaoh. One day you may have your revenge by wearing his crown upon your own head.* And even then, at nine years old, Agathokles' eyes widened to think of it.

While Philopator spent the days, day after day, with his tutors, undergoing the torture of learning by heart the Complete Works of Homer but, in very truth, proving rather good at it, Agathokles was employed strangling dogs and drowning puppies. He dived in the harbour, learned how to be slippery as the fishes, how to move quick as the eel, how to make himself next to invisible. He exercised in the *gymnasion* with his friend Magas, son of the King, turning his body into a living Greek statue. Philopator did not go there, not ever, and began to grow heavier. Philopator did not dive or swim, did not run, did not jump. He did nothing but read the *Iliad* and the *Odyssey*, losing himself in the unreal world of books, dreaming of what was not, the thrilling world of gods and heroes.

At ten years old Agathokles was promoted from dog-throttler to castrator of horses. At twelve years old he got into the Pompe again because of his mother's influence, and because he was more handsome than ever. At fourteen Euergetes took this lad into the palace to be his cupbearer, the naked boy who, according to Greek custom, carried round the wine at his Majesty's feasts, when he had his *rhombos* tickled, and his bottom squeezed by every man; aye, the boy whose pink rosebud, when every man was drunk, became their sport. Perhaps Agathokles was even the *eromenos* of Euergetes himself, to the delight of his proud mother. For sure, Agathokles was at the beck and call of every courtier, and you may suppose that, whether it was the Greek custom or not, he did not much enjoy himself.

What made up for his humiliation? The thought of the money, and the fact that he was allowed to play knucklebones with the heir to the throne. Perhaps it was the fact that the knucklebones were of gold, that even Philopator's chamber-pot was made of gold, and that he got to eat dates off a golden plate, that made Agathokles so keen to be the friend of this prince, and made him think of taking not just the knucklebones but all of Philopator's belongings for himself. Aye, it was Agathokles' great delight to be the friend of the boy who would be Pharaoh. Oinanthe his mother kept encouraging him, telling him how good it was to have this Prince for his friend, who would do whatever Agathokles told him to.

Aye, even at the age of thirteen or fourteen this lad was the squeeze of the King's Friends, who had power over his body, but in his turn Agathokles exerted power over another. A boy who is ill-used will often treat others the same as he has been treated himself.

If Agathokles said, *Ptolemy, lick my shoe,* Philopator would kneel and do as he was ordered.

If Agathokles said, *Be a dog,* Philopator would go down on all fours, barking.

If Agathokles said, *Lick my rosebud,* Philopator was happy to oblige, making Agathokles squeal for delight. And there were worse things, things that Seshat will not speak of.

Aye, Agathokles already had the future Pharaoh of Egypt completely under his thumb. Agathokles was as much as his hero.

Even so, what the horoscope of Agathokles of Samos said was that he must complete his life's journey *quickly.* He knew how to smile and to charm, how to sell his favours for a fistful of tetradrachms. He knew how to please a man by doing whatever he asked, how to take a man's money so that he never noticed it had gone. Nobler boys settled for a good horse or a hunting dog in return for granting their favours. Agathokles asked for gold, but got the horse and the dogs as well. He got himself a name for honesty at the same time as he lied and stole. He was the handsomest boy in Alexandria, but he learned a thief's tricks from his mother. Best of all, he knew how to get anything he wanted from Ptolemy Philopator. This was the beginning of the greed of Agathokles of Samos, then, that was fated to destroy him.

Meanwhile, Philopator having been made, at last, by many beatings, to do better at his lessons, Euergetes handed him over to a more illustrious tutor – Eratosthenes of Kyrene, who had come to Alexandria from Athens to be Director of the Mouseion and Head of the Library as the successor to Apollonios Rhodios.

Berenike Beta, at least, was well-disposed towards one of her countrymen tutoring her son. And was Eratosthenes paid eighty talents, the same fee that the great Strato of Lampsakos had for tutoring Ptolemy Philadelphos? Maybe he was. Whatever it cost, the education of Ptolemy Philopator was worth the sum. He would end up as good as the best Homeric scholars in the Mouseion. Homer became one of this prince's gods, with a temple to himself, second only to Agathokles of Samos.

They said Eratosthenes was as much as Aristotle in the breadth of his knowledge. He had written books of poetry, historical criticism, chronologies, philosophy, poetry, works on mathematics, a treatise on comedy, and an outrageous book on geography that said the world was not flat but round, and he taught not only the son many things, but also the father.

How can the world not be flat? Euergetes asked. *How can the world possibly be round?*

I could prove it to his Majesty, Eratosthenes said, *if he would give me a ship. I would show him that if a man sails west from the Pillars of Herakles, he may at length, if the gods preserve him, land his ship upon the shores of India . . .*

Euergetes looked as if he thought it highly unlikely. *We think this is nonsense, Eratosthenes,* he said, shaking the head.

All the seas in the world are joined to each other, Eratosthenes said. *I believe it is possible to sail right round Africa.*

Euergetes raised the eyebrows. *Well, we must send somebody,* he said, and he gave the word for the ships to be made ready at once.

Eratosthenes was just then thirty-five or forty years old. He would stay in Alexandria for twenty years, until Philopator was a grown man no longer in need of his teaching. But what effect did the tutor have on his awkward, sulky pupil? Did he make Philopator better, or worse?

Seshat swears it: *Eratosthenes was not the man who drove him to madness.* Eratosthenes was the one who appealed to the better side of his pupil's nature, the civilizing influence.

Seshat asks it: *What, then, happened in the boyhood of Ptolemy Philopator that left him urgent to murder his mother?* And, as some said, his father as well.

Was it not Berenike Beta herself, who loved so much to boss her son? Did she not goad Philopator, always making him do what he did not like?

Most Greek mothers leave their sons alone after the age of seven, to be brought up by the men, but Berenike Beta did not. She liked to know what was going on in Alexandria and all Egypt, and to be in control of it. She did not keep to the women's quarters, but walked about the palace seeing to whatever needed attention, just as she had walked about Kyrene as a young girl. She drove about the city in her chariot, putting everything to rights. She saw what the Pharaoh did not see. She was pleased to interfere. Why should she stop herself from trying to control how her sons behaved? Aye, especially her eldest son, upon whom so much depended. Berenike Beta wanted that imperfect son of hers to be perfect, like Magas her father and Magas her son were perfect. Either Philopator must make himself perfect, she thought, or he should not be Pharaoh at all.

You would think, Stranger that she would have found some way to change that boy's character, diverting his thoughts into more wholesome activities than dancing, such as throwing the javelin, or entering the chariot race. You would think she might have urged him to be bold and hard, like herself. But no, Philopator was not interested in exerting himself. Learning to ride a horse was as far as he would go. Really, the only physical exercise Philopator was amused by was dancing like the eunuchs. You might think his mother would have built him up instead of always knocking him down, but Berenike Beta was not like other mothers. She saw the ghost of Demetrios Kalos less often these days, but she was still a haunted woman, eating her heart out. She had still a very great anger with herself for having murdered the most beautiful man in the world, and she took out that anger on her less than perfect son, her not very handsome son.

No, neither the bossiest mother in the world, nor the best tutor in the world, nor all the money in the world would change Philopator's character, neither his slackness, nor his interest in dressing up in women's clothes, nor his desire to slice up his own body like the eunuch priests of Kybele – a desire which, strange to say, Agathokles of Samos did not share with him.

A man's character is fixed, from the start, is it not, written in his fate, as if upon a rock? The tragedy that was waiting to happen was all fixed up by the gods at his birth, and Berenike Beta could hope to change of it not one iota.

3.16

Beautiful Pylon

Formerly, Ptolemy Euergetes had three Berenikes in his life. He had now lost two of them – his only sister, and his only daughter. When his wife fell ill he worried that he might lose even the third Berenike, his excellent and most excellent wife, who did half his work for him, so that he had time for feasting, and drinking, always, of course, in moderation.

Have we done something to anger the gods of Egypt? he asked Djedhor. *What can we do to make up for it?*

Djedhor's answer, of course, was the usual answer.

How much has his Majesty built for the gods of Egypt? he said.

Euergetes said, *We built the Temple of Osiris at Kanopos. It is a fine temple. Was that not enough for them?*

Fine indeed, Djedhor said, *but his Majesty began that temple more than ten years ago. The gods require constant offerings, more regular offerings.*

Did we not put up a sandstone altar somewhere near Thebes? Euergetes said, though he had forgotten the name of the place.

Djedhor turned down the corners of the mouth. *The Pharaoh's first duty,* he said, *is to show his thanks to the divine rulers of the universe. One sandstone altar will hardly keep two thousand gods happy . . . His Majesty must build more, to show how grateful he is to the gods. How about a wall to enclose the Temple of Montu at Thebes to begin with? What about a fresh temple for Khnum?*

And so the battle of wills went on, the High Priest encouraging, the Pharaoh resisting.

Even Dositheos, his Greek Hypomnematographos, or chancellor, urged Euergetes to build for Egypt, saying, *Show them that a foreign king is just as good as a native.*

Very well, Euergetes said, at last, *let him have his wall at Thebes.* And so it was begun: built in a square, three hundred cubits long, three hundred cubits wide, a mud-brick wall of vast extent for Montu, Lord of Tod.

Then he built a small Temple for Pi-Khnum, the ram-headed god, near Latopolis, south of Thebes. Still Djedhor said the gods were not satisfied. This time he raised his voice, saying, *Khnum will hardly take any notice of such a small building.*

So Euergetes began putting up a sanctuary upon the south side of the great Temple of Montu, god of War, in his aspect of Falcon, that marked the northern boundary of Thebes.

The gods are pleased now? he asked Djedhor.

Djedhor pursed the lips. All he would say was, *Better, a little better.*

When Berenike Beta saw it she said, *We could have afforded a bigger sanctuary,* so that Euergetes was ashamed of his meanness.

He made his excuses, saying, *In time of peace we need not go out of our way to please the god of War.* But he did pay for a gigantic *propylon*, or gate, for the Temple of Montu at Thebes North, that would stand as tall as eight or nine men and last for evermore. (In your day, Stranger, they will call it Bab el-Abd, the Gate of the Slave, and you will find it at the place called Karnak, and every visitor will walk past without giving it so much as a glance, except yourself. Stand there, Stranger, and marvel. Remember Ptolemy Euergetes, the Benefactor, that paid the bill for it.)

It is good? Euergetes asked Djedhor. *It is pleasing unto you?*

It is very good, Djedhor said, *but in Egypt duality is so important, balance is so very necessary to please the gods. By rights we should build a second gate, on the other side of the enclosure of Amun-Ra . . .*

And so, upon the south-west side of the precinct of Amun, Euergetes agreed to put up an even bigger gate, as high as ten or twelve men, with a winged sun-disk cornice, and it was known as the Great Gate of Ptolemy Euergetes. Flanked by sphinxes, it was the largest *propylon* ever built in Egypt, and it stood opposite the entrance to the Temple of Khonsu. In the carvings Euergetes and Berenike Beta were shown receiving the symbols of perpetual reign from Khonsu the Falcon, the lunar god, the one who is the master of lifetime. They made offerings to Khonsu, the judge and healer, whom the Greeks worshipped here as the equal of Herakles. Here was Ptolemy making offerings to Osiris, Isis and Khonsu, and killing his enemies. On the upper frieze, the gods of Egypt were shown adoring the moon-disk, with the parents and forebears of his Majesty. The gate was to be the seat of justice, where oaths were sworn, and where the priestly judges gave judgement.

Does the new gate please his Excellency? Euergetes asked, when it was finished, and he had sailed up-River yet again for the inauguration. Amid the noise of trumpets and drums, and chanting priests, Djedhor said to him, *My heart is happy, his Majesty's gate is more beautiful than anything.*

That gate would also stand for ever – longer than the Kolossos of Rhodes, longer than the Pharos of Alexandria. Euergetes' gate will be standing in your own time, Stranger, the so-called Bab el-Amara, or Gate of the Moon. Seshat says it herself: *A wasted effort is building on the cheap. There is little point in putting up what will fall down.*

Philadelphos had been a great builder, eventually, but he had not, in truth, built very many temples. There was no truly splendid monument put up by Euergetes' father outside Alexandria. Euergetes would do better. He got the taste for building now, and – to the very great delight of Seshat, Lady of the Builders – found he did not want to stop.

He completed the Temple of Isis at Isisopolis in the Delta that had been begun by his father. He finished the Temple of Isis at Philai, which the High Priest of Isis told him would stand for two thousand years and more. Stranger, this temple will also stand for ever, if not in exactly the same place.

Near Elephantine, on the Nubian frontier, he began a small temple dedicated to Isis, with the usual many-pillared hall and towering pylons, in yellow sandstone. Everywhere there were carvings of Ptolemy Euergetes, the Benefactor, dressed as pharaoh.

In the doorway a carved Euergetes stood before Thoth the ibis. At his side was a carved Berenike Beta, the Great Royal Wife, The Female Pharaoh, who wore the same Double Crown as the King. No queen of Egypt had been shown like this since the days of the criminal Akhenaten and the beautiful Nefertiti one thousand years before. Even in the carvings that showed his Majesty slaying his enemies, Berenike Beta was there, sword raised, holding her enemy by the hair, in the act of cutting off his head. It was the warlike pose in which the Pharaoh was usually shown, not his wife. She was well pleased to see all these things: she had demanded them herself.

Seshat says it again: Berenike Beta was the one with the sword, and the pet lion. She even wore her husband's crowns and royal costume. Was not Berenike Beta the one who wielded power, the warlike and most warlike one? She did not keep quiet, did not shrink from giving voice to her thoughts, like other women. She had done her murder. She had proved her toughness. She was just as her father had meant her to be: just as good as a man, just as good as a king.

Euergetes sailed up-River, way beyond Thebes, for the foundation of this temple. With him sailed many scholars from the Mouseion, among them Eratosthenes the geographer, who walked about, asking questions. He was told of a very great curiosity hereabouts, the well into which the rays of the sun fell perpendicularly at noon on the day of the summer solstice, lighting up the water at the bottom, without leaving any shadow whatsoever. Eratosthenes knew at once that this was something of the first scientific importance, and he was eager to see it. The time of year being close to the summer solstice, he took donkeys, went to look at the well, and found that what was said about it was true. Because the sun's rays fell perpendicularly on that day Eratosthenes was able to calculate that Elephantine lay a little north of the Tropic of Cancer, and became surer in his belief that the world was not flat but round.

Euergetes the scientist, as keen as ever to prove the truth of his findings, sent men to measure the distance from Alexandria to Elephantine, and it was found to be one million two hundred thousand paces, or five thousand stades exactly. Fifty times that figure would give him the answer to what was the circumference of the earth.

At length Eratosthenes demonstrated his reasoning to his Majesty. *Megaleios*, he said, *there is no question of your ships falling off the edge of the world.*

And so it was. Eratosthenes' figure of two hundred and fifty thousand stades was generally agreed to be correct, as written in his treatise *On the Measurement of the Earth*, and would stand unchallenged for thousands of years. Not every man agreed with him, of course, nor every woman. Seshat, for one, *knows perfectly well* that the world is as flat as a honey-cake. Seshat would like to assure and reassure you, Stranger, that the world is flat, flat, flat. You should not be deceived by the trickery of these Greeks, these lovers of bizarre fiction. What was it that Seshat's brother-husband, Thoth, said? Aye, *There is no liar like a Greek liar.* The world is flat, Stranger, you may depend upon it. But the belief in its sphericity would persist for thousands of years.

Euergetes his temples would also last for thousands of years. His donations amounted to an enormous building programme. It was not meanness but the very greatest generosity. Seshat, Lady of the Builders, honours the name of Ptolemy Euergetes. She smiles for delight to think of his great works. To build temples for the gods, that is the whole purpose of Pharaoh.

3.17

Apollonopolis

After much pleading by Memphis, Euergetes agreed to finance even the great Temple of Horus at Apollonopolis in Upper Egypt, to replace the old temple that had fallen down in an earthquake. This would be the very greatest building work of his dynasty, a mighty fortress against Chaos.

Djedhor's heart bounded like the oryx to hear the news, and he forgot, in his excitement, the priestly rule about never to show all the teeth. *The people will rejoice when they see this magnificent temple,* he said. *The great gods are full of joy and satisfaction of heart. They will grant millions of years of satisfying life to his Majesty.*

In due course Euergetes sailed for Apollonopolis, amid great pomp, to perform the foundation ceremonies. Djedhor was at his side, smoothing every difficulty, acting as his interpreter and dragoman. Wherever they sailed Berenike Beta, her four sons and their tutors sailed also, dripping with sweat in the heat, still struggling along the royal road to geometry. Even Oinanthe and her children sailed with them. Even Sosibios went, gathering information about whatever might be taxed in Upper Egypt.

Philopator, catching sight of the remains of a giant barge listing in the River at Thebes, asked the High Priest what it was.

That is the barge of the Pharaoh Sesostris, Djedhor told him, *of cedar wood, two hundred and eighty cubits long. Once it was plated outside with gold, and inside with silver, so that it shone, like the barge of Ra himself.*

I shall build bigger, and better, Philopator said, *when I am Pharaoh.* And so the dream was born, to build the largest boat in the world, the dream of bigness.

Philopator marvelled to see so many snakes and crocodiles, so many palm trees, so many donkeys. Men would complain of his idleness, of the wasted opportunities in his life, but he would never neglect the Egyptian temples. He loved their strange atmosphere, their astonishing size. At a young age he learned what must be done to please the gods. Philopator loved Upper Egypt. He loved, indeed, all of Egypt. He was the great lover. In this respect his love was not misplaced.

Wherever Euergetes sailed his royal barge the people stood on the River bank, waving and smiling, singing the song of welcoming Pharaoh. The peace abroad seemed to be matched, at last, by peace at home. It looked to Djedhor as if Ptah of Memphis had worked some mighty miracle.

On the Seventh Day of Epeiph in Year Ten of his reign, at Apollonopolis, halfway between Thebes and Elephantine, Ptolemy Euergetes performed the ritual for Horus in the sanctuary of his new temple. After the hours of darkness Seshat herself, Mistress of the Builders, oversaw the staking out of the foundations in the sand. Helped by his Majesty she marked out the vast ground plan, stretching the cord between two poles. The placing of the four corners she fixed by the position of the stars, looking south to Orion, north to the Great Bear for orientation. Now Euergetes wrung the neck of the goose for the sacrifice with his own hands, and buried him in the foundations.

Next came the digging of the holes, when Euergetes stood back, arms folded, smiling his half-smile, expecting someone else to wield the spade. But the High Priest of Horus said to him, *With respect, Megaleios, nobody may carry out this labour but yourself.*

Euergetes took the golden spade in his hands. Really, this man hardly knew what a spade was for. He moulded with his own hand the four bricks of damp mud mixed with straw, to be the cornerstones of the temple, and filled the space around them with sand, in order to recreate the virgin soil on which every sacred building must be built.

While the priests of Horus chanted he lowered pottery, silver, gold, copper, iron, stone and faience into the holes, and golden plaques bearing the name of Ptolemy, and models of tools, and offerings to Horus the Falcon.

Seven days and nights were used up with rituals, prayers, incense, chanting.

Euergetes thought of the day when he might consecrate this new temple in person, striking upon the temple door twelve times with his stone mace. He looked forward to standing before the shrine of the god, eyeball to eyeball with the Falcon of Gold. He would be pleased to perform the morning ritual for the Horus who was himself.

But if he had really imagined to dedicate this House of Horus in person, he would be disappointed. He would not live to see this temple complete. Aye, Stranger, Seshat the Builder can tell you that the masons would still be levering one stone into place upon another stone, still beautifying the temple at Apollonopolis, in the time of the twelfth Ptolemy – three hundred and twenty thousand two hundred days later. Mark Seshat's words, Stranger: *Even one hundred and eighty years hence, a Ptolemy would still hold the office of Pharaoh.*

Excellency, Euergetes said, *even the Great Pharos took my father and grandfather only twenty years to build. Could not the builders work faster?*

A temple is different, Djedhor said. *A temple takes many many years. The hieroglyphs alone will take three men's lifetimes to carve, but they will never fade. His Majesty may be pleased to know that the House of Horus of Behdet at Apollonopolis will stand for ever – unlike the Pharos of his grandfather.*

Euergetes looked at him, mouth open. He had no idea that the greatest monument in Alexandria was doomed to fall. But Djedhor was right. Even the mighty Pharos would disappear, eventually, into the sea.

The consolation of his Majesty must lie in eternity, the High Priest of Horus said. *Never will his temple know destruction upon earth, eternally.*

And he was right, right one million times.

Stranger, you should know that the Temple of Horus at the place the men of your time will call Edfu still stands, with its roof and carvings almost intact. You may go there yourself and look upon the vastness of its walls. You may even be pleased to commit the sacrilege of standing inside the sanctuary, something that nobody but the King and his High Priest were allowed to do in antiquity. Go there, Traveller. Gaze upon the immortal work of King Ptolemy Euergetes. Speak the name of the man who paid for this mighty and most mighty temple, so that his Ka may live on in the Afterlife. And while you are about it, forget not Seshat, Patroness of Architects, Lady of the Builders, without whose kind attentions there would be nothing upon this spot but a sandy waste.

You see, Stranger, Djedhor was younger than Anemhor, better at making this Pharaoh think of doing his duty to the gods by being a builder. He also talked him into building at Panopolis another great temple, this time for Min, the ithyphallic and most ithyphallic one, the great god of fertility, whom the Greeks thought of as Pan. Euergetes put up the temple-house, and it balanced his Temple of Horus at Apollonopolis, one great temple on either side of Thebes, one temple to the north of it, one temple to the south of it, just as big. In the Two Lands *balance* is everything. It was probably Euergetes' son Philopator, the one who was so keen on bigness, that built the *pronaos* (Stranger, it is the columned hall of the temple, open at the front) that surpassed all other *pronaoi* in Egypt for size – with forty vast columns, and a huge stone slab of a roof – one hundred and sixty cubits wide, sixty cubits deep, and twenty cubits in height – but the main temple-house was the magnificent and most magnificent work of Ptolemy Euergetes. On the great double pylon was carved the usual giant images of Pharaoh smiting his enemies. Or, at least, Pharaoh's wife. But of this mighty Temple of Min at Panopolis, or Akhmim, however, not one stone will remain standing upon another in your own time, Stranger, no, not one stone.

3.18

Admirable Sosibios

Aye, even Sosibios saw the building at Apollonopolis inaugurated, Sosibios the runner. But he was not much interested in building up one stone upon another stone himself. He was keener on building up his own glory. The runner was now forty years old, and he had been a minister of the King for almost twenty years. As Priest of Alexander he marched at the head of the solemn procession to the Tomb on Alexander's birthday, and his deathday. On the anniversary of the founding of the illustrious and most illustrious city of Alexandria, it was Sosibios who had the honour to pour the libations of milk and honey and undiluted wine. He was also Priest of the Brother-and-Sister Gods, another office of the very highest dignity at Alexandria.

Sosibios had not forgotten the day when he he rode up Kanopic Street as a hero, with the crowd shouting *kallinike*, Beautiful Victory. Sosibios of the winged feet felt on that day as if he was indeed flying. Aye, he had a further taste of glory, another day of knowing the acclaim of the crowd, and he was urged on in his heart, dreaming of greatness, for he was now allowed the title of *paradoxos*, or Admirable, that was given to distinguished athletes, musicians, artists, and heroes of all kinds.

This hero of the Greek Games still had his athlete's physique, was still treated with awe, almost like a god. For Euergetes, this man's every word was perfection. Sosibios would save Egypt. But he would also do his best to destroy the House of Ptolemy.

And how was that? Try to control your impatience, Stranger. For the moment, let it be enough for you to know that Sosibios drove Agathokles of Samos onward in his evil career just as diligent as Oinanthe did. It was Sosibios that enabled Agathokles to rise in the world that was Alexandria. Without Sosibios smiling upon him, Agathokles might have been nothing more than a dog-boy, nothing more than the naked youth who filled his Majesty's cup with wine at the *Symposion*, nothing more than the Ganymede of Ptolemy Euergetes. Though, for sure, so soon as the dark bristles appeared on the chin of Agathokles, and the feathers began to sprout down below, he had to find himself a fresh occupation.

But fate had, indeed, far higher things in store for Agathokles than being a mere Ganymede. His future was already entangled with the person of Ptolemy Philopator, fatally entangled. You might think that Philopator would be the one who told Agathokles what to do, but it was very often the other way about. Imagine a spider's web, Stranger, with a fly caught in it. Think of Agathokles of Samos as the spider, pulling the gossamer threads tighter, controlling the position of the fly. Think of Ptolemy Philopator as the fly, the struggling victim, the one who would be killed.

3.19

Arsinoë Gamma

With the death of Berenike Mikra his Majesty was concerned that Ptolemy Philopator now had no sister who might be married to him. *What woman*, he asked Berenike Beta, *will my son and heir take to wife? We should betroth him young, and secure the best of all possible alliances.*

Berenike Beta kept her mouth shut, knowing her husband did not need her to answer, but was, as it were, merely thinking out loud.

With what kingdom should Egypt make alliance? Euergetes asked. *If Philopator marries a girl from outside the family, the pure blood of the Ptolemies will be diluted. Really, we cannot allow that to happen, can we?*

She looked at him in surprise. There was no female relative living whom he could have married in any case.

Yes, I think the only thing to do, Euergetes said, *is for you to have a fresh daughter, and let Philopator marry her instead.*

Berenike Beta sighed. If she had her way, Philopator would never be Pharaoh in any case. *Husband,* she said, *I have no wish to undergo the torment of childbed a fifth time. I thought I had heard the end of all that filthy talk about a brother marrying his sister. You know that I thoroughly disapprove of it. And what if the fresh child turns out to be another boy? What will you do then, Megaleios?*

This time it was Euergetes' turn to say nothing. But there were things a man might do to help on the birth of a girl: prayers to the gods, generous offerings, extra sacrifices of jet-black bulls. And, of course, tying the string round the right-hand testicle instead of the one on the left. That was what worked best.

It was rare enough for a Greek to pray for a daughter, but never was a daughter more longed for – at least, by her father – than this daughter.

Euergetes drank the potions, sacrificed the bulls, tied the string. By some luck of the gods he got what he asked for.

Unlucky to give a fresh child her dead sister's name, Husband, Berenike Beta murmured. *Let us call her Arsinoë. Perhaps she will be as great a queen as her immortal step-grandmother.*

And so it was. From the beginning they called this girl Arsinoë Gamma, the third Arsinoë.

The third time, Berenike Beta murmured, *is the lucky time . . .* hoping the fresh Arsinoë would be lucky, lucky enough to survive the derangement of the stomach that so often troubled the Greeks in Egypt, the kind of thing that had carried off Berenike Mikra. She prayed that the fresh daughter would be lucky enough to survive marriage to the rather strange Ptolemy Philopator, for her husband would have his way, and betrothed her before she was three days old – and he refused till the day he died to change his heart about that either.

Berenike Beta made many prayers to the gods, many prayers to Tykhe, but the truth was that Arsinoë Gamma would not have very good luck. She was not lucky to be betrothed to her elder brother. She would have no luck whatever. Her horoscope, that the parents had drawn up just out of curiosity, not out of any belief in its accuracy, just to see what might be round the corner, was neither good nor bad, saying only that she should not live long enough to see her twenty-ninth year. As for her end, even the Oracle of Zeus-Ammon would say nothing about it, save that it would involve fire.

Berenike Beta still did not put the child to the breast, but she took greater care of this daughter's health, making sure everything was done to avoid extremes of hot and cold. She said, *Arsinoë Gamma must not go the same way as Berenike Mikra.* She tied to her daughter's body every talisman that promised to protect her against agues and epidemics of marsh fever, death by snake bite or scorpion sting, death by diseases with spots, stomach troubles. *She shall be the Queen of Egypt, the Lady of the Two Lands, the greatest and happiest of queens,* her mother said. Aye, the fixed plan, however much Berenike Beta disapproved of it, was that as soon as her breasts were three fingerbreadths high, as soon as she was old enough to bear his child, Arsinoë Gamma would marry her brother, Philopator, the future Pharaoh, and keep the dynasty going.

All the same, Fate had made other plans for this girl. For a start Arsinoë Gamma did not have quite the same charm and sweetness as Berenike Mikra, and for a long time Philopator would not so much as look at her screaming purple face.

Aye, right from the very beginning the nine-year-old Ptolemy Philopator disliked the fresh sister. He was not pleased to think that he must marry this squawking lump of raw pigeon flesh.

Djedhor, the High Priest of Ptah, seeing his confusion, said to him, smiling, *You will be pleased by Arsinoë Gamma when she is older . . .*

But Philopator shook his head, and walked away from the High Priest in anger. *We hope she will die young,* he shouted, *like her sister.*

So much for brotherly and sisterly love. So much for affection. But this was how things would continue.

The only good thing in Arsinoë Gamma's horoscope was that she should be untroubled by ghosts. Unlike her mother, unlike so many of the women in her family, Arsinoë Gamma was not fated to do a murder. She would have something much worse than ghosts to put up with – her whole lifetime haunted by a husband who did not want her – and it would be just as good as a living death.

Berenike Beta dismissed the oracle report that said Arsinoë Gamma would never live to be old. *Really,* she said, *we have no time for absurd forecasts of the future.* Whatever her daughter's fate was, it lay years ahead. At least Arsinoë Gamma would *live* long enough to be a mother. Berenike Mikra had had to die.

Meanwhile, they all carried on existing in their everlasting present moment: Euergetes himself went on being Pharaoh, *Living for Ever,* measuring things, precise for ever. Berenike Beta went on riding her horses, encouraging the cavalry, and putting right what was wrong. Magas, her favourite son, was every day more warlike. The fresh daughter, Arsinoë Gamma, crawled, stood up, walked, ran. And Philopator went on growing, every day a little odder, like a plant running wild that nobody could hold back. Aye, for he copied even at nine years old the frenzied dancing of the priests of Kybele, the eunuchs, the stoneless ones – until his mother screamed at him: *Stop that absurd whirling. Stop.*

Aye, Berenike was hatching in her heart a fresh plan: for the new Arsinoë to marry not Philopator but Magas. Whatever Euergetes' demands about an end to violent acts, she must do another murder. Not her husband, this time, but her son. In fact, three of her sons must die.

3.20

Filthy Books

Up-River at Memphis Euergetes was an Egyptian king, wearing the Double Crown of the Two Lands, trying to think Egyptian thoughts, doing his best to remember the names of the Egyptian gods and comply with their endless demands. But at Alexandria he played the Greek ruler, thought Greek thoughts, and wore round his head the strip of white cloth that was the royal diadem of the Greeks.

So how did this great Greek king fill up his twenty years of peace apart from building for the gods? At first he barely knew what to do with his days for not having to think about foreign affairs, and the whereabouts of his sixty-thousand-strong army, but his thoughts turned, at length, towards the Mouseion, the Library, and to Greek scholarship – science, the latest inventions, marvellous modern machines.

Aye, during the peace the Mouseion flourished, for Euergetes visited the scholars often, and made generous donations for scientific research.

He spoke with Dositheos of Pelousion, the mathematician, who kept up the dialogue with the great Archimedes in Sicily. Day after day Dositheos wrote down his thoughts on weather signs; night after night he made careful observations about the time when the fixed stars made their appearance.

He spoke with Sphairos about Stoicism, though, really, none of the Ptolemies had much time for philosophers. Philosophy did not generate any income for the Treasury, for one thing, and for another, they had fixed in the beginning on following the Kyrenaic School, enjoying the sensation of the passing moment.

Euergetes also encouraged Antigonos of Karystos, who wrote a series of Books of Marvels. And Apollonios of Perge, the great mathematician and geometrist. And there was Philo of Byzantion, the brilliant mechanician, of course, who wrote on war-catapults, and siege operations, and automata, and a treatise on the Seven Wonders of the World, one of which – naturally – was the Pharos of Alexandria.

There was more of the same, Stranger, much more, but there are other books that you could read about the Mouseion, and Alexandrian scholarship. There is no other reliable book about Ptolemy but Seshat's book. Euergetes is

Seshat's first concern here. And building. And, of course, books. We must not forget to speak of Euergetes' passion for books, which was so great that he founded a second Library in the Sarapieion – the Greek counterpart of the Egyptian temple libraries, as if to show that the Greeks were just as good as the Egyptians. It is not true, Stranger, of course not, but it is what Euergetes thought, and if you are a Greek yourself, or a Hellenophile, it may please you to think the same. But Seshat says the Egyptians are more interesting, less violent, more reverent towards their gods. Moreover, their books are full of pictures.

This King, at any rate, collected very many books for his Great Library, and he did so in a singular way, for he ordered all scrolls unloaded at the Alexandria docks to be seized in the name of Ptolemy Euergetes, and he had hasty copies of them made by the most junior scribes. The Great Library kept the originals, and gave back the copies, so that the owners had to be content with words left out, lines that should be written once written twice, missing chapters, names spelled wrong, and, sometimes, utter illegibility. Unlike his stepmother, Euergetes did have a sense of humour. He thought this new way of building a library was rather amusing. Seshat smiles upon it herself, for even a library built by dishonesty is better than no library at all. The Mistress of the House of Books can only applaud such enterprise. Aye, this Pharaoh would do what he liked. If his wife knew of it, this time, she did not interfere to stop him.

Ptolemy Euergetes was gripped by the mania for collecting old books, and his next literary subterfuge involved asking to borrow from Athens the precious official texts of the greatest Greek dramatists: Aiskhylos, Sophokles and Euripides. Euergetes wrote a very charming, friendly letter to Athens saying that, by chance, he had taken the desire into his heart to correct the texts of these authors in his own Library by comparing them with the originals, side by side.

Will Athens allow Alexandria to borrow the original texts? he asked.

The Athenians were a long time answering that letter. They were very suspicious of this trickster. They said they could only agree to lend such valuable books if Euergetes paid a deposit of fifteen talents – an enormous sum of money – as a guarantee that he would return them intact. Euergetes promised, sure, to send them back undamaged, not with remarks scribbled in the margins, not with wine stains all over them, not chewed by the palace monkeys. By no means. He said he was very happy to hand over the deposit and swore by Zeus and Pan and all the gods to abide by the terms and conditions of the loan. Athens even consulted the Oracle of Delphi in order to find out the most auspicious month, the calmest days for sailing. At length, travelling under the kindly guidance of Zeus and, as it were, insured by the supreme sacrifice of a bull to the sea, the precious cargo turned up in the Harbour of Eunostos, the Harbour of Happy Returns.

Once Euergetes had these highly prized manuscripts in his own hands, his heart became urgent to keep them and forfeit the deposit. And so, yes, shameful though it is for the Lady of the House of Books to record such underhand behaviour, this noble King sent back the copies, suitably distressed, dog-eared and stained with boot polish to look old, like the originals.

Athens will never spot the difference, he said, laughing. And all the Mouseion scholars laughed with him. For sure, the Great Library under Ptolemy Euergetes was one of the very greatest glories of Alexandria.

An even greater glory was sent to Euergetes from abroad, as a generous gift from Sicily. The famous Archimedes had built a vast grain-carrier for Hieron of Syracuse, two hundred and fifty-five cubits long, the *Syrakosia*, with twin hulls that used up enough ship timber for sixty ordinary vessels, and required one thousand oarsmen to row it. It had a deck for sports, a garden deck, a marble swimming-bath, mosaic floors that told the complete story of the *Iliad*, and a twenty-thousand-gallon freshwater tank. There were giant catapults on board, designed by Archimedes himself, and cranes for dropping stones on to and grappling with enemy ships. And so on. But Hieron had overreached himself. His mammoth ship was too expensive to sail anywhere. Even if he could afford to sail it, the only harbour in the Great Sea big enough to accommodate it was Alexandria. So Hieron scratched out *Syrakosia* and painted *Alexandris* on the side of his monster vessel, filled it with eighteen hundred tons of Sicilian corn and every other goodly thing out of Sicily and sent it as a birthday gift to Ptolemy Euergetes, who was just then troubled by a shortfall in his grain harvest.

She is too big for a mere tyrant, Hieron wrote, *but she might suit a man who is a god in his own lifetime. Ptolemy Euergetes is the only man in the world who can afford the upkeep of such a vast ship.*

When Euergetes saw her, he said only, *Whatever am I supposed to do with that?* He was not going to sail off to war in the midst of a twenty year peace. Just once he tried to sail her up-River, when this wonderful vessel ran aground on a mudbank. *Alexandris* ended up in dry dock at Memphis, listing to starboard, where she would inspire the monster ship of the next King Ptolemy. For, indeed, young Philopator boasted again, *We can build bigger than that*, and he vowed to do it. *My ship will not run aground*, he said, *but will be useful.* Euergetes was pleased to hear him say it. *At last*, he said to Berenike Beta, *some sign of spirit in this lethargic boy. Perhaps the building of monster ships of war will make a man of him.*

Euergetes was not too bothered by his son's lack of warlike progress, but always Berenike Beta thought of her eldest son as little better than a monster himself. *A son who likes dancing,* she said to her husband, *is it not a curse sent by the gods, a great disgrace? Magas does not dance. He would make such a good King of Egypt.*

And again she screamed at Philopator, *Stop it, stop that dreadful spinning. Dancing is for kinaidoi.* But Philopator did not want to stop.

Euergetes reassured his wife, laughing, *Philopator will change. When he is a grown man his ways will be regular, his temper calmer. I promise you he will make a fine pharaoh.*

Euergetes chose to see only the good side of Philopator. He would not change his heart about the heir to the throne. By no means. But Berenike Beta saw both sides of Philopator, and the bad side of him bothered her very much. *I do not think a boy who likes to put on women's clothes is fit to be King of Egypt,* she said, quite firm.

Euergetes shrugged the shoulder. *It is not such a big thing,* he said. *You know very well that Dionysos himself is half man, half woman. Dionysos is Osiris. Osiris is Euergetes. I am even Dionysos myself. Philopator will be Dionysos. To wear women's dress is what Philopator is meant to do, in honour of the god of Wine. I cannot condemn such behaviour. I should be wearing women's dress myself...*

Berenike wore her face of thunder even so. *Unnatural,* she said, *shameful, disgusting... and utterly unhellenic...*

All the same, Euergetes did speak to the Admirable Sosibios, the wise Sosibios, about his son and heir.

He takes notice of you, Sosibios, he said. *He takes no notice of his parents.*

Sosibios bowed the head. *Always his Majesty flatters us,* he said.

We should be pleased for you to oversee our kingdom, Euergetes said, *when we fly to the sky, when we become one of the stars.*

Sosibios assured his Majesty that he would do what he could for the son who showed no enthusiasm for war, not the slightest interest in defending the borders of Egypt, but who must be Pharaoh even so, because he was the eldest son, and because his father had decreed it.

Sosibios said, *Nothing to worry about. He will do well. He is a fine fellow. He likes to read Homer. He wants to help the Egyptian people. He is pleased by the idea of building. He has many good qualities. He loves Egypt. What more can we ask for?*

In private Berenike Beta still muttered, *Magas would make a much better Pharaoh. Magas will be a much better army commander. Philopator will never understand war.*

Euergetes shouted her down, notwithstanding the presence of his wife's lion.

Surely, Berenike Beta said, trying her luck one more time, *we must make the best son the king, surely it is our duty to give Egypt the best of all possible rulers . . .*

Euergetes shouted again, *We passed most of our youth in banishment because of our father's foolishness. I am determined to uphold the custom that the firstborn son shall inherit. The firstborn son is Ptolemy Philopator.*

No, Euergetes would not change his heart. Stubbornness, that was perhaps the one serious flaw in the character of this otherwise perfect monarch.

Berenike Beta learned, at length, to hold her tongue about the succession, but she was making plans of her own. She vowed a silent vow to override her husband's wishes when the time came. *When my husband is dead*, she thought, *things will be quite different.*

Djedhor also had to learn to hold his tongue. He could see as well as Berenike what the future would be like if Philopator were to be King of Egypt: it would be a disaster from start to finish, total disaster.

Sosibios spoke his private thoughts only to the young Agathokles of Samos: *Better Sosibios on the throne of Egypt than all the sons of Ptolemy Euergetes put together,* he said. *And if not Sosibios, then maybe Agathokles.* And he put his hands under Agathokles' tunic and squeezed his buttocks. Agathokles of Samos laughed with him, dreaming of the impossible, and squeezed Sosibios back. Such, Stranger, were the curious practices of the Greeks.

3.21

Earthquake

In Year Nineteen of Euergetes disaster struck not Egypt but one of her neighbours, for a great wave came crashing upon the beaches of Alexandria in the middle of the night, smashed up all the boats in the harbours, and flooded the great ground-floor audience hall of the palace. Such violence of the sea could mean only one thing, and it was followed, not long afterwards, by the news that a sharp shock of an earthquake had demolished the famous Kolossos of Rhodes.

Aye, the most beautiful city in the world (after Alexandria) was in ruins, its impregnable walls reduced to rubble. The messenger that brought the news brought also the usual request for Ptolemy to help his friends in Rhodes, where they still burned incense and offered blood sacrifice at the shrine of his grandfather, Ptolemy Soter, and still held Egypt and the Royal House of Ptolemy in the very highest regard – despite having refused to support him in the late battle against Antigonos Kneecap.

Ptolemy Euergetes thought of the so-called earthquake-proof Kolossos and allowed himself to show the teeth, murmuring, *My father forecast the collapse of that statue* . . . He looked out of his Window of Appearances at the Pharos, the very great pride of the House of Ptolemy, that stood firm on its rock, and his smile broadened. Whatever the High Priest said, he did not believe that the Pharos *could* fall down.

Euergetes paced the mosaic. *We shall have to send something,* he said, *for old time's sake. We cannot have Rhodes reduced to dust, a prey to pirates, open to invasion. Rhodes must be restored.*

Dositheos the Hypomnematographos frowned to think of money squandered on the Rhodians, lascivious people, much given to hot drinks, who had failed so recently to support their Egyptian allies. *I hear that Seleukos Kallinikos has sent massive aid,* he said, *and ten great ships of war. Perhaps Egypt does not need to send anything* . . .

Write it down, Hypomnematographos, Euergetes said, very dry. *Forty thousand cubits of squared plane planking, to start with* . . . *Three thousand talents of bronze in coins for the repair of the Kolossos* . . . *One thousand more to restore the Ptolemaieion* . . .

Dositheos murmured, *Megaleios, Egypt cannot afford it* . . . *the Treasury will not allow* . . .

But Euergetes insisted, *We can afford it. We must afford it.*

And why? Because the rest of the world had now made friends with Rhodes; because this tiny island held the key place in trade, involving the whole of the Great Sea.

If Ptolemy quarrels with Rhodes, Euergetes said, *he will quarrel with all his neighbours. If trade with Rhodes comes to a standstill there will be no luxury goods in Alexandria, no spices, and no incense to burn before the gods. It has happened before, my friend.*

And so Euergetes sent these things to Rhodes, friend of Ptolemy or not, as a gesture of good will, murmuring, while Dositheos wrote:

> *Three hundred talents of silver* . . .
> *One million artabas of corn* . . .
> *Ship timber for ten triereis and ten pentereis* . . .
> *Three thousand pieces of sailcloth* . . .
> *Three thousand talents of copper for the repair of the Kolossos* . . .
> *One hundred builders and three hundred and fifty workmen* . . .

And so on . . . Seshat, Mistress of the Builders, is pleased to note the sending of the builders. Forget not, Stranger, that Euergetes was the Benefactor. He had not gotten that august and most august title for nothing.

Rhodes was, in due course, returned to its former glory. Everything that had fallen down was put back up as before – apart from the great bronze statue of Helios, the Sun-god, who was left lying on his face in the harbour. Helios had failed Rhodes. He had not been much of a protector against every evil. Aye, the Rhodians left the Kolossos where he fell, as a reminder that the gods do not always help man, however much money he wastes on incense and burnt offerings.

It was said that the Rhodians completely lost their faith in divinities on the night of the great earthquake, though some did say the disaster was all a divine punishment, for admitting foreigners to the Greek mysteries. Ever afterwards the Rhodians diverted their energies into more reliable channels – superstition, astrology, magic – and they kept a lookout, meanwhile, for new gods to replace the gods of Greece.

But what of Ptolemy Euergetes himself? What did he really think about the gods? What were his real thoughts? Stranger, he took care always to quote the wise words of Bias of Priene: *About the gods, say that they exist.* He paid lip service. He stood patient through all the proper prayers. He duly got his face splashed with blood at the Greek sacrifice. *If the gods keep only some of the people happy,* he said, *we must carry on worshipping them.*

And when Djedhor came to speak to him about the gods of Egypt, Euergetes listened more carefully than before. He sent the proper offerings to Memphis now: one hundred of geese, one hundred of beer, because above everything else in Egypt he must keep Djedhor smiling.

Making those great gifts to Rhodes was, as it happens, almost the last thing Euergetes did. As for Djedhor, he was not himself a very cheerful man at this time, for he lived under the dark cloud of illness, and there was nothing that even the gods of Egypt could do to help him.

3.22

Djedhor

In spite of his sickness Djedhor insisted on performing the morning ritual for Ptah, for nothing was more important in all Egypt; it was this ritual that kept the creator god happy. Djedhor had bathed himself in the cool waters of the Sacred Lake of Ptah at Memphis three times a day – at dawn, midday, and dusk – every day for twenty-eight years, ever since he had been made a junior priest at fifteen years old. That is to say, he had dipped his body in the waters no less than ten thousand two hundred and twenty times. Djedhor was indeed one of the purest of the pure.

But a man can bathe too much, do you not think, Stranger? A man can stand too long in cold water, day-dreaming of the great god, Ptah of the Beautiful Face. Even in the heat of Egypt it is not difficult to catch cold. Perhaps Djedhor had been over-zealous. He was sick, but he would not forego the purification. Nor would he deprive the god of his personal attentions so long as he could stand up. He should not have bathed, but he did bathe. He knew very well that he had arrived at the last day of his life. Even so, he would not neglect the gods.

Although his hands shook, Djedhor insisted on joining the procession. He walked through the double doors of his temple, at the end of the long line of priests, inhaling the sharp-sweet smell of the incense, chanting the hymns to Ptah for the last time. When they reached the sanctuary, Djedhor went in, closed the double doors behind him and was alone with the god.

Djedhor broke the clay seal of the shrine, fingers trembling, teeth chattering. He drew back the bolt and opened the gilded doors. He prostrated himself upon the floor in front of the shining golden face of the creator of the world, hardly able to get down there. He dressed the god in the usual manner – in white, to safeguard him against his enemies; in blue, to hide his face; in red, to protect him; in green, to ensure his bodily health. He laid before the god his breakfast of bread and beer, onions and pigeon flesh, hands shaking so violent that he spilled the beer. To end the ritual he dipped the little finger of his right hand into the ointment. Djedhor sneezed, then, and felt the dull ache inside his chest, the sharp pain there, as if a great weight were pressing upon his heart. His limbs felt heavy, heavier than they had felt in his whole lifetime. He touched the god upon the forehead with the ointment. Usually the god moved not at all, but now Djedhor saw him nod the head, and the golden lips of Ptah, Lord of Truth, spoke to him of the Afterlife, and he saw that all the great gods surrounded him: Thoth, Bastet, Osiris, Horus, Sobek . . . Then he saw Anubis the jackal. He knew what this was all about. It was time to begin his journey to the Field of Rushes. Aye, Anubis tapped him on the shoulder, growling gently, took him by the hand and led him away into the darkness, into the light.

Djedhor, had entered the sanctuary with the bell tied – as usual – to the rope round his waist. So long as those outside could hear the bell tinkling, it meant that Djedhor was moving about, that all was well with him. But now his brothers, Horemakhet and Horimhotep, pressed their ears to the bolted doors of the sanctuary, listening hard, because the bell had stopped tinkling, and it must mean that Djedhor was in trouble.

The silence in the sanctuary of Ptah continued, but the door could only be broken down after a two-days silence. Eventually the brothers smashed an axe into the door of cedar faced with bronze and gold. Through the gaping hole they saw Djedhor sprawled face down before the shrine, motionless, his robes and leopardskin mantle awry. Frantic, they hauled Djedhor out by the rope and turned him over. His mouth hung open. His eyes had stopped sparkling.

In Year Twenty-Three of Ptolemy Euergetes died Djedhor, High Priest of Memphis, aged forty-three years, with his old father still living. Ptolemy shook his head and said, *In peace sons bury their fathers, in war fathers bury their sons,* as if the natural order of things was turned upside down.

The father, Young Anemhor, grieved seventy days, then led the procession to the necropolis, on the high land, the desert plateau across the River, opposite Memphis.

When his Majesty asked Young Anemhor if he would not like to go back to being High Priest of Memphis, he said, *I am old, Megaleios, my memory is bad. I am happy in my retirement.* He lived in the house of his sons, and there was no anger between them. They looked after him, made him comfortable, gave him every goodly thing to eat, and asked his advice on every matter relating to the temple. Note, Stranger, that the Egyptians care for the old ones; their children love them. The sons in this family did not wish to *kill* their father. There was no hatred in this house, no quarrelling. How unlike the palace of Ptolemy, where there would never be any old ones to look after, *never*, because of murder and other violent death.

Since Djedhor had left no son to succeed him, the younger brother had to take his place. Horemakhet was made High Priest now, and though he had not thought to be raised to this high rank, for nobody had expected Djedhor to die so soon, he was ready. After all, it had been forecast at his birth. Aye, now Horemakhet, thirty-seven years old, was anointed as High Priest by Pharaoh, and given the rings of electrum. He would remain in office for the rest of Euergetes' reign.

The old father, Young Anemhor, would not be carried to the necropolis himself for seventeen years. He refused all honours and extra duties but one: Prophet of Arsinoë Philadelphos, out of his great devotion to her memory. It was nothing to do with the fact that this office was most lucrative. By no means. The money was nothing to do with it. He kept also the office of Scribe of the Rations of the Apis, the Sacred Bull, whom he loved almost as much as Ptah. Every day Anemhor walked with slow steps to the stall of this good god, the great forecaster of what was to come, gave him his food and burned incense before him. He whispered into his ears, and stroked his flank. Every day the Apis stared at Anemhor, unblinking, like the true god that he was, nodding the head or licking the nostril with his great grey tongue, inscrutable to the last, but perfectly comprehensible to one so expert as Anemhor.

How much longer, how many more years must Egypt suffer under foreign rule? Anemhor asked, as if he was not only weary of his old office but weary of the House of Ptolemy, worried for the future. He put his hands over his ears and stepped out of the stall into the light. He walked, unsteady on his feet, towards the sandy plain, edged with palm trees, where the young scribes were kicking the pig's bladder about, as usual. When he took his hands away from his ears he heard them shouting: *One hundred and ninety.*

3.23

Bloodsucker

Ptolemy Euergetes, now sixty years of age, also worried about what would happen to Egypt when he was dead. *Whatever will our son Philopator do to Egypt,* he asked Sosibios, *when he is Pharaoh?* For he still would not change his heart about who was the heir.

At first, Sosibios said, *he will do reckless things, but with a wise counsellor you may be sure that he will settle down.*

The wise counsellor was, of course, himself.

Euergetes was still uncertain. *We fear all will not go well with him,* he said.

Majesty, Sosibios said, *Philopator's ministers will take good care of Egypt . . .*

The first minister would also be himself.

Aye, Admirable Sosibios, this giant of a man, broad in the chest, bearded now, like Sarapis, calm of gaze, gentle of speech, and wise of counsel, he was a comfort to Euergetes in the last months of his life. All these years he had enjoyed his Majesty's absolute trust, and yet, beneath the veneer of loyalty, he was false, grasping, interested only in what he could get for himself. Berenike Beta sensed it, though, without proof, she had the sense to keep quiet about her fears. Her woman's intuition told her that Sosibios was not an honest man. But Euergetes, truly, suspected nothing amiss.

Sosibios had worn the purple robes of a hero ever since he was the victor in the men's wrestling at the Panathenaian Games. Now, as a man of wealth, he won chariot races at the Nemean and Isthmian Games in Greece, and he was the first Egyptian Greek to win this double victory, for which King Ptolemy showered him with ever greater honours and rewards, even giving him the Egyptian Order of the Golden Fly, that was meant only for valour in battle.

For the Greeks, the perfect body is an athlete's body. Perfect earthly beauty expresses perfect divine beauty. Sosibios was the goodliest Greek of his day. He still thought that, when the time came for him to go down to Hades, the Alexandrians would honour him with a hero's shrine. *Honour in one's lifetime is prized,* he thought, *but better still is an honoured name hereafter.*

It was not, however, the fate of Sosibios to have an honoured name hereafter. His name would be remembered, sure, but for all the wrong reasons.

Euergetes showered the Gold of Praise upon Sosibios time after time for his sporting successes: a golden tripod, four white horses of Kyrene, the golden chariot in which he had ridden during his victory procession, and his pick of the unmarried women in Alexandria. Sosibios was quite serious in his ambition to be a king. He thought himself better than any of the sons of his Majesty.

Euergetes thought Sosibios was the right man to be the first minister of his son. Philopator liked Sosibios well enough, who went out of his way to humour him, but only because to humour Philopator was a means of getting his hands on power. At the same time as being a hero, though, Sosibios also inspired much fear. Every man in Alexandria had seen Sosibios the wrestler break his opponents' fingers and walk away laughing, until he remembered that he was a minister of the King. Grown men trembled when they stood before this man, terrified of his harsh tongue, terrified of his power to make them disappear without trace. But Euergetes saw only the good side of this man, the Olympian athlete, the minister who collected so much tax that his treasury overflowed with gold. Really, Euergetes knew nothing of the bad side of Sosibios son of Dioskurides.

Euergetes seemed to have forgotten those wise words that a king should not trust even his closest ministers. He had perhaps forgotten that to be a king is to be a man without friends; that a king must trust nobody. His son Philopator would forget it too, for Philopator trusted Sosibios, and also Agathokles of Samos, who had become Sosibios' smiling henchman, the very man who handled the disappearances that his master ordered: disappearances of which Euergetes was quite unaware.

In the seventh Great Pompe of Ptolemy Euergetes, Sosibios had the honour to represent Eniautos, the personification of the Year. He carried the golden Horn of Plenty, one of the badges of the House of Ptolemy. His face, arms and legs, hands and feet were painted gold: Sosibios waved and showed the teeth, as if he knew what was to come in the year ahead, and the rest of Alexandria did not.

Horemakhet, the new High Priest of Memphis, sailed to Alexandria to watch this procession, which happened to be the last Pompe of Ptolemy Euergetes. He saw the gilded Sosibios, like a golden giant, and he thought of the Egyptian funeral ritual in which a dead man's face, fingers and toes were gilded, and sometimes, if the family could afford it, his entire body, so that in the Afterlife the dead one shone.

When he saw Agathokles of Samos, now twenty-four years old, gilded and shining from head to foot, standing on the back of an elephant, and that he wore nothing but a pair of hunting-boots and a crown of golden vine leaves, Horemakhet shook his head in disbelief. He thought, *Gold is the flesh of the gods. Gilding is for dead men. To gild the faces of the living is bad, bad in the extreme.* He thought of dead men walking. He thought of Sosibios and Agathokles as great golden flies themselves, blood-sucking flies, sucking the life-blood out of Egypt.

3.24

Golden Agathokles

Agathokles of Samos was too old by this time to personate Eosphoros. He was something bigger than a mere star. His chest was broad, deep, muscled like the chest of an athlete. His gilded flesh glittered in the sun. He was Dionysos, god of Wine, god of Frenzy, the laughing one. In this procession he rode an elephant, laughing himself, as if he, too, knew something that nobody else knew.

His sister Agathokleia, now by common consent just about the most beautiful woman in Alexandria, rode in this Pompe too, as Penteteris, the five-year festival personified. She was no longer the slender girl she had been, but in these times to be a little heavy was to be beautiful. Both Euergetes and Philopator liked heavy women. To eat and be fat was the fashion: to be thin was for the poor, for slaves.

Oinanthe had grown very heavy indeed during her twenty years' feasting, but she was still the Golden Painted Lady. Old Oinanthe led the Pompe once again, staggering, screaming with laughter, her great golden belly wobbling.

Every fifth step she paused to blow a long blast on her golden trumpet, when Alexandria roared approval. Between blasts she waved, leered, twirled, and Alexandria whistled, and threw flowers.

Horemakhet saw the future quite clear, just then: Oinanthe making her way up Kanopic Street with no happy applause, no cheering, no flowers, and the crowd roaring for her blood.

Oinanthe could not see into the future. She lived one day at a time, for the pleasure of the passing moment, like her masters, the Ptolemies. For the moment she went on laughing.

Her son Agathokles of Samos, throttler of dogs, and castrator of horses, the willing catamite of many men, laughed for many reasons, but the first reason was that he had Sosibios for his patron and the Prince Ptolemy Philopator for his closest friend. Of all the bodily charms of a young man there was none by which the Greeks were more enchanted than the eyes. Agathokles' eyes were like black olives, glittering, like black flames, and their dark fire had already scorched Ptolemy Philopator. Agathokles helped Sosibios in his office, carried messages to the torturers, messages to the Mouseion scholars, messages to and from his Majesty. Agathokles was most useful to Sosibios, most reliable, and he was well rewarded for his trouble.

Like the bee, Agathokles of Samos flitted from flower to flower, from man to man, offering his body to do things whereof Seshat cannot speak, and helping himself to whatever he could carry. Sometimes this great Greek bee would make use of his sting. With a man like Sosibios for a patron, a handsome young man like Agathokles might achieve almost anything he cared to think of. And what was he thinking of? Power. Riches. Women. And an end of having to kiss Ptolemy Philopator and every other man at court who cared to finger his golden rosebud. Soon, he thought, he would put a stop to having to work his golden tongue wherever a man told him to put it.

It would be many years before Agathokles had an end of all that. But the Morning Star that was Agathokles of Samos was rising in the world. Agathokles had soared like a shooting star, hurtling across the night sky, leaving a shimmering trail of golden sparks behind him. He was himself like one of the golden stars fired from the *phallos* of Osiris in the Pompe. Agathokles was almost the Sun himself, dazzling, burning, and Ptolemy Philopator was the darkness that he lit up. Aye, Stranger, you know that Philopator was supposed to be the Sun, and Agathokles the darkness: things had already gotten themselves the wrong way round. Ithyphallic Agathokles did not think that he could fall – he did not dream of the possibility. He lived for the day, and each new day was more lucrative than the day before. He thought that his golden days would go on for ever.

The naked Agathokles of Samos, whether he was running about shiny with oil or yellow with sand in the *gymnasion* with his friend Magas, or riding in the Pompe, gold from head to foot, or pouring out the wine at Euergetes' feast, or climbing into the bed of his friend Ptolemy Philopator, he was just about as good as Eros made flesh. And he would wreak just as much havoc.

Ptolemy Philopator, the crown prince, almost the last words his father spoke to him was the wisdom of Solon, Greek wisdom: *Do not make friends in haste, nor hurry to reject those you have made.* But Philopator hardly listened. He had never thought his father's advice very wise.

Horemakhet also delivered a warning: *Do not make of Agathokles One-Who-Draws-Nigh-to-Thee.* Philopator laughed at him. He had not made a friend of Agathokles of Samos in haste. *I have known Agathokles,* he said, *for as long as I can remember. I have no intention of sending him away.* Nor had Agathokles any thought of abandoning his royal friend. By no means. Philopator was Agathokles' income, his road to riches, and power.

What does Menander the Greek say? *We all, from time to time, turn from our drinking, from our pleasures of every day, and seek someone to share the heart's care of our life. Every man is sure he has found a marvellous treasure if he gains even the semblance of a friend.*

Philopator thought that in this Agathokles, this golden muscleboy, he had indeed found a marvellous treasure. He thought Agathokles better than all the gold in Egypt. Unfortunately, this marvellous, lifelong friend, was only the semblance of a friend, rather like the wolf who befriends the lamb he would like to eat for his dinner.

3.25

Feast of Flies

It was later in the year of this last Pompe, Year Twenty-Five, that Sosibios went to wake his Majesty one morning with the dispatches from Syria. This trusted minister walked past the guards as usual, entered the royal bedchamber without being searched, and thought something was wrong. The buzzing of flies, perhaps. The drip of some liquid on to the floor, perhaps.

Megaleios? he said, expecting his Majesty to stir in the bed.

No movement in the sheets. No groaning. No sound but the flies.

Megaleios, it is the hour . . . he began.

No answer. Still no movement, except something dripping that was not the *klepsydra.*

Sosibios took a step closer to the bed, walked round it. His Majesty snored not, neither did he twist in the sheets. The royal eyes were open. A fly walked across his lower lip, stepped inside the open mouth. There was no flicker of the pulse, no beating of the heart. Sosibios smiled to himself, turned, stood still, thinking, listening to the birds, the wind soughing in the palm trees, the monkeys' distant chattering, the waves washing on to the shore.

He was in the chamber quite long enough to murder his Majesty, but Seshat must not point the finger. By no means. Ptolemy Euergetes died of natural causes, not of poisoned food, not of strangling, not of being smothered with his own pillows. Sosibios was above suspicion, first of the King's ministers.

He turned the dwarfs of the bedchamber back from the door – dwarfs bearing linen, water, the breakfast of dough and honey – waved them away while he thought what to do.

His Majesty will sleep late, Sosibios said. Aye, later than ever before.

The hour was just after dawn, and Sosibios' first thought was of Magas and the two other brothers. Magas would be at the *gymnasion* already, exercising his body, the others, surely, still sleeping. And then he thought of Ptolemy Philopator, the man who should be Pharaoh, and allowed himself a momentary laugh, a derisory laugh.

Natural causes, they said, was the reason for Ptolemy Euergetes' death, but because he died sudden, and of a disease nobody knew what was its name, the Swift Rumour flew about saying the disease was murder, and the culprit was Ptolemy Philopator, his own son.

It is no slight matter, the Greeks muttered, *to kill a king.* Many of them called Philopator Guilty One, and Father-Killer, but it was easy to blame the weak one. To spread rumour might cover up for another, stronger man. It is rather late to open the case of one who died two thousand years ago, Stranger. Maybe Philopator was guilty. Maybe he was not. But what if Sosibios did this deed himself? Let us not think such a thought. It is not possible. Sosibios was the trusted one. Seshat inscribes the name of Ptolemy Euergetes eternally. She writes his name upon the leaves of the sacred persea tree. Whatever was the circumstances of his death, it is too late in the day to find out the truth.

You are not satisfied, Stranger? Do you think the goddess of History has failed you? Seshat laughs. Even Thoth, who boasted of knowing everything in the world, did not know the cause of Alexander's death. That is the great paradox, Stranger, is it not? That even the first of historians, even the god and goddess of History, the divine chronologer and chronographer, have not the solution to every mystery. But how could you have expected it to be otherwise? Thoth is he who listens, he who knows, he who heralds tomorrow, he who sees the future without ever being wrong. But he does not watch Babylon. Even the gods of writing cannot keep up with everything that happens in the world.

History is made up of fragments, like little bits of mosaic. *Tesserae*, the Romans would call them, small cubes with six faces, only one of which is coloured. Most of history presents one face only, but every story has its dark side, its shadow side, the minute details everybody has forgotten, that make you believe that you are being told the truth. There is always more to be discovered than meets the eye. Sometimes the bits of story fit together, make sense. Sometimes they do not. This time they do not. Euergetes died, and Philopator may, or may not, have murdered him. That is all that can be said. Let us move on, Stranger, to the next reign, in the hope of finding answers to other problems.

Aye, to Ptolemy Philopator himself, whose title meant *Father-Loving,* the son, the heir, the new Pharaoh, twenty-three years young, with all his wretched life before him.

Now the bad ones follow one upon another like a sky full of black clouds. Now the madness begins in earnest, and the blood. If you cannot abide the thought of blood, Stranger, you should quit reading right here, for now you must swim in it. Now you must go with Seshat into deeper darkness. But the darkness is not total: once or twice you may be pleased to arrange your lips into a smile. There is a little light, like sunshine streaming through the cracks in a wooden shutter. Onward, Stranger, onward. Seshat will hold your hand. The lady in the leopardskin dress will look after you.

Old man though he now was, Sosibios read the state of affairs in Alexandria very clear. Magas was the idol of the soldiers, and Philopator was not. Magas had gotten himself hard muscle where Philopator had sagging rolls of flab. Magas, his flesh was like polished bronze, from his regular exercise in the open air, whereas Philopator was white, like a girl, from skulking indoors reading Homer, hiding from the sun.

Sosibios would never control Magas, but he knew he could control Philopator. It was a simple choice, and in any case, just what Euergetes had planned. Magas was the man that must have the accident.

Magas was perhaps twenty-one or twenty-two years of age. He had no thought to usurp his brother's place. His father had brought his sons up not to hate each other. He was nothing but loyal to Philopator. And yet Magas, a young man of high spirits, beloved by his comrades, must die. He had to die not because of what he had done, but for fear of what he might do.

Sosibios sent for Ptolemy Philopator, and when he arrived Sosibios said, *His Majesty is dead.* Philopator looked at the body, stared, curious. He picked up the *nekhakha*, the golden crook, from beside the bed and poked his father's cheek with it. He prodded the dead man's face with the flail of gold and *sappheiros*. Philopator's own face was expressionless. He stood still, shrugged the shoulder, moved his lips about, twitched his wrists, yawned. He showed no sign of grief. He pushed over the table beside the bed so that it crashed on to the mosaic. Then he picked up the *khepresh* out of the mess and put it on, back to front, so that it came down over his eyes. He spun round once or twice, then stopped.

What is to be done? he said, at last.

You are the Pharaoh, Sosibios said, patient. *You know what you must do.*

Philopator looked at him, questioning.

His Majesty must get rid of his Uncle Lysimakhos, Sosibios said, *if his Majesty is to survive.* Aye, Uncle Lysimakhos, who had been let to live at the beginning of the previous reign, out of his brother's affection for him, would have to die this time. There would be no continuation of Euergetes' absurd policy of non-violence. There were murders to be done.

Philopator said nothing, crossed his eyes, put his hands over his ears, spun himself round upon his heel, very slow, lost himself in thought. *Our Uncle Lysimakhos, our friend,* he thought. *What wrong did he ever do us?*

The Prince Alexandros must be put to death also, Megaleios, Sosibios said.

Philopator was silent.

The Prince Magas and the Prince Lagos will also be a threat to his Majesty's safety, Sosibios said, *whatever your father may have thought.*

We have sand in our ears, Philopator said, *we cannot hear a word.*

He thought of the last words of his father: *Do not think of killing Magas and the others . . . we must have no more murder in this House. We are not barbarians. We shall not behave like barbarians.*

Three brothers, he thought, *the brothers that pushed us over on the beach. They never did any thing worse than that.* He did not really hate them much. The smiling ones. But he did not speak the word to stop Sosibios from doing what must be done.

Just as Seth killed his brother Osiris, Sosibios said, *his Majesty must kill the spare brothers, or lose his throne to whichever of them may prove the strongest.*

Silence. Philopator both did and did not want to do a murder.

This delaying could go on all day, Sosibios thought. He thought of a whole fresh reign full of such indecision.

We must act quick, Megaleios, Sosibios said, earnest.

Silence. Philopator spun on his heel again, thinking of his father dead. The father who beat him, who gave useless advice, who so seldom spoke to him but who had wanted him to be king nevertheless.

Silence means agreement, Sosibios thought, and so he sent for Theodotos the Aetolian, the Satrap of Koile-Syria, presently in Alexandria, and gave him his orders: to close the *gymnasion,* saying *Faulty boiler,* or whatever better reason he could think of. He gave Theodotos a message for Agathokles. And he gave orders that Berenike Beta should not be allowed to leave her apartments.

Think of it, Stranger, how dangerous Berenike Beta must have looked that day. If she managed to proclaim Magas king, she would have to kill Sosibios, and Philopator, and Alexandros and Lagos *that day, within the hour,* so that Magas might live, and reign, and be secure upon his throne.

Now, Stranger, you can see the lines drawn up for battle: Sosibios and Philopator against Magas and Berenike Beta – a battle between mother and son, brother and brother, Isis and Horus, Horus and Seth, as if everything that happened was just some weird upside down reflection of the stories of the gods. Had Berenike Beta taken more interest in the gods of Egypt, she might have been afraid, because Horus the son cut off the head of Isis his mother. Aye, now the Living Horus, the living falcon that was Philopator, would do battle with his mother, with the woman who was Isis, Great of Magic, and the falcon would try to peck her eyes out, screeching, screaming, dig his talons into her divine flesh. He must, indeed, become Horus the Falcon, that strikes in silence, without warning, with amazing swiftness.

Theodotos rode up Kanopic Street towards the *gymnasion,* slow, taking his time, thinking about Magas. He had liked Magas. Every man liked Magas. Once he turned his horse round and galloped back towards the palaces. Then he stopped, turned, went on. No, he must obey Sosibios' orders or be a dead man himself.

He found Magas running about the *gymnasion,* practising for the foot-race with his friends. Agathokles, friend of Magas, happened to be there, Agathokles, who had been brought up with Magas and the other princes, and took quite serious the business of running. Theodotos walked up to Agathokles, across the sand, spoke Sosibios' message in his ear. He sent the other runners away, on his Majesty's orders, saying, *Revolt in Kilikia, you are needed at the barracks.* But he left Magas and Agathokles to their running. Theodotos dismissed the guards, saying they were needed at the Mouseion. The bath attendants and rakers of sand, the guardians of clothes, the openers of doors, Theodotos dismissed them all, saying, *No athletics today, Egyptian festival.* And so there was nobody left in the great *gymnasion* but Theodotos, Magas, and Agathokles. Theodotos would hold the door himself. Agathokles would deal with matters inside.

Theodotos sat down to wait until Magas had finished running, until Agathokles could bring Magas into the bath house without making him suspicious. Aye, Agathokles, whom Magas trusted; whom he had known since his earliest infancy, Agathokles, his foster brother. Theodotos watched, having made sure, first, that the furnace for boiling the bathwater was roaring. For the sure thing was that after his exercise Magas would get in the bath.

As he came in, Magas said to Theodotos, *Where is everybody?*

Feast day of Fetket, butler of the gods, Theodotos said. *They have gone to the sacrifice . . .*

But in fact the sacrifice was at the *gymnasion.* It was the flies of Alexandria that had the free feast that day.

3.26

Hot Water

Magas leaped into a bath of scalding water without testing the temperature, and perished. That was the official story. The counter-story said Magas had scalding water poured over him, and that Theodotos took care of it, Theodotos, Satrap of Koile-Syria, who dealt with all the extra palace business that day, all the trouble. And there was trouble, for Magas did not die quietly, but screamed for help, so that his friends – who had left the *gymnasion* but stood outside, talking – ran to rescue him. It was Theodotos who stood outside the bolted bath-house door and fought them off, single-handed, and killed every one of them, barely escaping with his life, and he received no thanks for it. Theodotos was the man who made sure the order was carried out; who made quite certain that Magas was a dead man.

Who, then, was inside the steam room with the bolts drawn across the bronze door, pouring scalding water over Magas in his bathtub, holding his head under the water, squeezing his neck until he was dead? Agathokles of Samos did the dirty work. Agathokles the bath-boy, Agathokles the Ganymede, Magas's great friend.

Aye, Agathokles, the strong young man skilled in the use of the cleft stick that might hold a man's head under the water until the struggling stopped;

until the bubbles of his breath ceased to make even a ripple on the surface of the water.

Agathokles opened the bath-house door and walked out. He greeted Theodotos – who was panting, blood-stained, surrounded by dead bodies – with his usual friendly smile, not at all as if he had just drowned in his bath the man who should have been Pharaoh.

They always said of Agathokles of Samos, *A hungry dog will eat dirty puddings.* He was still the handsome gold-digging boy, entirely without scruples, who would do anything for money, whose charming smile and perfect manners meant that no man would suspect him of treachery. No, such a handsome youth could not be guilty of one murder, let alone four. Lagos, Alexandros, Uncle Lysimakhos, Magas, were all dead men that morning, so that Ptolemy Philopator might sit easy upon his throne; so that he might feel secure from every threat. Aye, but what was the whole truth? That Sosibios and Agathokles were a greater threat to Philopator than all those dead relatives put together. Sosibios and Agathokles should have been the dead ones that day but Sosibios and Agathokles lived, and laughed.

When Sosibios had the word from Theodotos that the relatives were dealt with, he sent for Berenike Beta, took her to see her husband's body. Berenike stared. She did not weep, did not howl. She did not laugh, hysterical, did not have the proper attack of grief and shrieking. She simply said, *Where is the Prince Magas? Send Magas to us, if you please.*

Sosibios had Philopator proclaimed King of Egypt, then. Aye, and the Silver Shields carried him round the courtyard of the palace upon their shoulders, cheering, chanting his name. Philopator struggled, afraid of falling, begged them to put him down.

For sure, Berenike Beta declared herself at once joint ruler, as if she thought her twenty-three year old son utterly incapable of ruling by himself, and perhaps she was right to think it. *We shall be most pleased to help you, my dear boy,* she said, amidst the cheering. That is to say, either she did not want him to rule alone, or she would not let him.

Philopator did not smile the smile of Pharaoh yet, but scowled at her.

Berenike Beta was still Queen of Kyrene in her own right, still The Female Pharaoh, The Female Horus. Even at hostile Thebes they called her simply The Ruler, and showed her wearing the ceremonial dress of the king. (Yes, Stranger, the mother dressed as a man; the son as a woman.) But Berenike Beta did not want to give up all these things to become the Great White Cow of Nekher. She wanted to keep her power, not give it away to somebody else. Sosibios she still suspected of wanting to snatch the kingship for himself.

And she was right to be suspicious. Sosibios had far too much power already.

And Philopator? What did Philopator think? Alone with Sosibios, talking of what must be done, and what must not, Philopator railed against his mother: *Why should I not rule by myself? Why can she not leave me alone?*

Sosibios spoke soothing words: *You shall rule by yourself, Megaleios.*

Why must my mother interfere? Philopator shouted.

She shall not interfere, Sosibios said. *We shall make sure she does not.*

Now that she could not rule through Euergetes, Berenike Beta thought she must rule and overrule Philopator instead, telling him what to do, keeping him in order, that son who had never in his life wanted to do what she told him. Sure, she called in the Egyptian embalmers to take care of the dead body, but for the rest of that morning she sent dispatches, talked with the High Priest of Memphis, urged on the building at Apollonopolis, as if Euergetes had not died at all. Berenike Beta's world did not come to a stop with her husband's death. She carried on with her business, as if the ruler of half the world was still sitting in the next room, still alive, not attracting every fly in Egypt.

She did not beat the breast or rub dust and ashes into her hair. She had long since steeled herself for this day. Aye, the day upon which she must murder three of her own sons, in order that Magas might be Pharaoh.

Berenike Beta sent once again for Magas to come to her. She sat thinking about what she must say to him. She would talk him into killing his brother, all his brothers, and taking the kingship for himself. Magas would refuse, of course. He would say, *I am not a murderer, not a brother-killer. My father did not wish it.* But no, she would persuade him. She would make him do it. For sure, a woman who has killed her own husband will not shrink from killing her own children.

She was not troubled by the thought of it. She had made herself ready for this day all her married life. They do not love, mostly, Stranger, in this family, but bottle up their feelings. They think they are gods, gods in their own lifetime. They are hardly human at all.

For sure, Berenike Beta moved quick that day, but she was old. Sosibios moved quicker. Magas's corpse was already floating in the bath-house drain, face down. *Drowned,* they said, when they found him, *burst pipe, faulty boiler.* Alexandros, Lagos, Uncle Lysimakhos, their bodies already lay in the sands beyond the city walls, on the waste ground beyond the western necropolis, where nobody but the shepherds went, and the crows pecked their eyes, and the tan-coloured Pharaoh dogs chewed up their flesh, wagging the tail.

3.27

The Bowl of Hemlock

In the Greek cult of Berenike Beta set up after her death by Ptolemy Philopator, she was called Benevolent Goddess. The truth of it was that Berenike Beta was not, and never had been, very benevolent towards her son and co-ruler, but found fault with everything he did.

She was not delighted to find Philopator unconscious from drinking too much wine. She was not pleased to meet him when he was dressed in women's clothes, women's jewellery, women's shoes, with his hair tied up with red ribbons, even if it was all part of the worship of Dionysos. As for Philopator's trying to dance like the eunuch priests, it left Berenike Beta speechless with fury to see it.

When she wagged the finger at him, saying, *Moderation in All Things, but especially moderation regarding the cult of Kybele* . . . Philopator had thrown a papyrus scroll at her.

When she said, *Do you think it seemly for the Pharaoh of Egypt to dress up in women's clothes?* Philopator had thrown a gold plate.

When Berenike did not stop criticizing he had thrown heavier things, an earthenware bowl, that made a more satisfying crash when it hit the floor at her feet, shattering on the mosaic. Berenike took no notice. Sometimes she would reach out a hand and catch whatever flew towards her and throw it back at Philopator. Unlike her son, she did not miss her target.

Berenike Beta was as much as fifty years old. Her hair was no longer golden yellow, but white. She was still round of face, round of body, still fond of eating. The liver spots had crept across the fleshy hands that carved up Demetrios Kalos, but she still drove the chariot fit to crash.

Berenike Beta was ever on the watch for poison, knives, murderers. But she was not so fast as Sosibios. This man of power would not put up with the old queen interfering. Sosibios the athlete had always been remarkable for speed. How fitting, Sosibios laughed to himself, how very fitting, that this murderess should herself be murdered. Sosibios, he moved quicker, like the Egyptian cobra, to strike.

*

But even Sosibios, a mere civil servant, however powerful he might be, was careful not to touch one hair on the head of a member of the royal house without the King authorized it. *Would you like to do the deed?* he asked Philopator, throwing him the knife. Philopator let it clatter at his feet, said nothing, moved the shoulders about inside his tunic, unsure. He opened his mouth to speak but the words did not come forth, as if some spell had locked his tongue.

Rumour said Philopator strangled his mother with her own insect curtains; that he attacked her in her bed, himself, much as she had attacked Demetrios Kalos, so that she died the same way as the man she had murdered, the mother's blood painting red the pure white tunic of the son.

Rumour said he hacked off her hands and feet and strung them round her neck upon a string; that he licked up her blood three times upon his tongue and spat it in her face.

Rumour said Berenike Beta's murderers were afraid of her courage, afraid that her famous boldness would foil their plot.

Rumour said that Philopator handed Berenike Beta over to Sosibios, to deal with her as he pleased, so that the bloodguilt for his mother's death did not fall upon himself. Aye, to Sosibios, who threw her into prison; who sent her poison; and that she went not screaming and fighting but drank it down without a fuss, as if she should have guessed what would happen to Egypt if Sosibios remained in power.

Rumour said Philopator was so weak he could not even stop the murder of his mother; that he cared nothing for the woman who gave him life – that he could not find it in himself to give her life in return.

Those who made up speeches to put in the mouths of the dying, the dead ones whose last words were lost, made her say to herself, *It is not painful for me . . . I have known so many troubles that I gain by death. What profits it me to live?* And so she drank down the bowl of hemlock, and the chill spread through her veins, congealing the blood.

For the murderess to be murdered herself, was it not the vengeance of the gods? Sosibios smiled to think that the first person to greet her in Hades would be Demetrios Kalos himself, the one she loved, the one she murdered. Berenike Beta thought of it too. Her last thought as she drained the bowl of hemlock was of Demetrios Kalos. Perhaps it was the poison chilling her blood that made her shiver, or perhaps it was the thought that she should soon meet Demetrios Kalos in the Afterlife, because to meet Demetrios Kalos again was the only thing left in the world that she wanted.

Some said that whatever kind of violent and unnatural death Berenike Beta got, she deserved it: that murder breeds murder, and her end was only to be expected.

3.28

Hysterics

When Sosibios showed him the body of his mother, dead, Ptolemy Philopator laughed for disbelief, and kept screaming with laughter, for that the palace and kingdom were his and his alone. Now that he was rid of his mother, he could do what he liked. He would spend the rest of his life laughing.

He sent for his band of musicians, who came running, playing wild barbaric music. He sent for his friends, the Galloi, the eunuch priests of Kybele, who danced through the palace courtyards, pounding their drums. He sent for the Geloiastai, or Laughter Makers, his drinking companions, who raced, shrieking with laughter, through the marble colonnades to Philopator's apartments.

He sent also for Agathokles of Samos and Agathokleia, who did not run or dance but walked slow, talking not of what had happened, for they had wiped it out of their hearts already, but of what they would do, laying their plans for a glorious future.

Let Ptolemy wait for his pleasure, Agathokles said. *If we are going to be King and Queen of Egypt, we had better start as we mean to go on,* and he stuck his tongue down his sister's throat, pushed her up against one of the great Corinthian columns and spent a long time kissing her. She did not push him away in disgust but returned her brother's kisses. Thus these servants began to ape the behaviour of royalty.

Ptolemy Philopator, King of Upper and Lower Egypt, called for his saffron yellow *peplos*, his gold-embroidered sandals, his diaphanous veil, his golden girdle studded with every august costly stone. He had Agathokles paint his face with white lead and rouge his cheeks for him and strap him into the *strophion* with the false bosoms. He had Agathokles smear his limbs with the liniment of ass's dung mixed with honey and sea salt that made his body supple for the dance.

Let us follow Dionysos, he screamed. *Let us dance with the Galloi . . . Let us honour Kybele the great goddess.*

There was nobody to tell him to stop, nobody to urge him to calm himself but his sister, Arsinoë Gamma, who was afraid to go near. Philopator was free, dressed as a woman, shining with desire and gleaming with unguents, dancing with the naked Agathokles of Samos. He leaped and spun himself in circles on the spot until he was in a trance. He was still spinning when the sun came up.

Philopator did not send for Sosibios that night, but Sosibios came to look, all the same, at the new Pharaoh, how he behaved himself now that he was Lord of the Two Lands. When he had seen enough, he walked slow through the marble corridors, back to his office, back to work, even though the hour was after midnight. He carried on turning over the letters from ambassadors, the palace accounts, the military despatches, papyri taken from the desk of her late Majesty. Aye, it was Sosibios who would run Egypt now, on his own, without interference from anybody. Sosibios knew how to handle revolts, riots, difficult neighbours. Above all, he knew how to handle Philopator, a difficult king – who must be left to follow his mad whims, his lunatic dancing.

To see the King of Egypt dressed as a woman did not bother Sosibios. By no means. Sosibios found his Majesty's odd behaviour most satisfactory, because it meant that Sosibios could take the command and control of the kingdom into his own hands. From the first day of the reign Sosibios sealed the seal of his Majesty to the bottom of the *prostagmata* himself, for Philopator's hands often trembled. He was most of the time too drunk, even at twenty-three years old, to write his own name.

Soon, Sosibios thought, *we shall kill Philopator too, and make Sosibios King of Egypt.*

But Agathokles was thinking, *Soon we shall kill Sosibios . . .*

3.29

The Furies

When Sosibios gave out the news of Berenike Beta's death there was the usual wailing of women, though it was nothing compared with the wailing for Arsinoë Beta. Philopator gave both his mother and father the proper decent Greek funeral – pyre on the beach, wall of flame, ashes in the Tomb of Alexander. Or the proper Egyptian mummification and bandaging, whichever it was. Seshat has never lied to you, Stranger. She does not know how their late Majesties were dealt with in death. But she can say for sure that

Philopator rebuilt the Tomb of Alexander, making it bigger – and maybe that was done so as to fit in the elaborate Egyptian *sarkophagoi* of his parents.

He did not shirk his duty regarding their funeral rites. He even honoured his mother's memory by appointing a special priestess, the *Athlophoros*, or Prize Bearer, of Berenike Euergetis. But how could he not be haunted by her? She had died twenty years too soon. The haunting of Philopator must last so long as the natural span of her life: for seven thousand three hundred nights. Nobody should be surprised to hear that this king was beset by terrors or that he slept ill by night.

The Greeks began to say, *Berenike lies foully slain by her nearest kinsman.* Whether the son did this deed with his own hand or not is of no consequence. *A mother-slayer must pay for his crime in Hades.* They say that to think of murder is just as bad as doing the murder. The man who had the thought of Berenike Beta's murder was Ptolemy Philopator. He was the man who could have stopped that crime, but he did not move a muscle to save his mother's life. He had wished her dead. He had laughed to see her cold, stiff face. Perhaps he would suffer for his crime in Hades, but for sure he would suffer for it also in this life, aye, like a man tormented, crazed with guilt. Already he saw out of the corner of his eye the women who would torment him for the rest of his lifetime, the women with bloodshot eyes, who had not hair upon their heads but dozens of squirming snakes.

3.30

Fragments

More than that, Stranger, Seshat really cannot tell you. Ptolemy Euergetes was not Alexander. He took no historian wherever he went to write down what he did. We know but little of his reign. These fragments will have to be enough.

PART FOUR

Father-Loving Ptolemy Philopator

4.1

Hippopotamus

Ptolemy Philopator, his mouth is small, pouting. His hair is yellow, curled, his nose upturned, his cheeks fleshy. Even the eyes of his statues seem to have a cruel look. He is the bad one, Stranger, the very bad one. Of Philopator they would say that he was the worst of all the Ptolemies, a useless king, unworthy, a bloodstained tyrant, guilty of hideous crimes. But during the twenty days of ritual and processions that made up his coronation, the High Priest of Ptah heaped the titles of Pharaoh upon him regardless:

Youthful Horus, The Strong One, Whom His Father Caused to be Manifested as King, Lord of the Asp-Crowns, Whose Strength is Great, Whose Heart is Pious to the Gods, Who is a Protector of Men, Superior to His Foes, Who Makes Egypt Happy, Who Gives Radiance to the Temples, Who Firmly Establishes the Laws Which Have Been Proclaimed by Thoth the Great Great Great, Lord of the Thirty Years' Feasts, even as Ptah the Great, a King like the Sun, Offspring of the Benefactor Gods, One Whom Ptah has Approved, to Whom the Sun has Given Victory, Living Image of Amen, Beloved of Isis, Living for Ever.

Enough titles, you will think, Stranger. But you should remember: it is the office of Pharaoh that is revered, not the man who holds it. Teaching of Merikare: *A king who possesses an entourage cannot act stupidly. He is wise from birth, and god will distinguish him above millions of men.* Ptolemy Philopator was the perfect god, the one who could do no wrong. Life! Prosperity! Health! to his Majesty.

The man who burns incense before the sacred bulls, and builds temples for Hathor and Maat, does not lack merit. Only the gods are perfect, and Pharaoh is the perfect god upon earth, *netjer nefer,* as the Egyptians call him. Whatever his private habits, he was the one who must avert the universal catastrophe that would happen if Maat were to be transgressed; he prevented the return of creation to chaos. Philopator's reign would be chaotic enough, but forasmuch as this King honoured the gods and built them houses, and sent his one hundred pigeons, his fifty geese, his fifty fowls, or whatever it may be, daily to every temple throughout Upper and Lower Egypt, he kept the balance. He would send his offerings of mummified cats for Bastet, mummified ibises and baboons for Thoth, mummified falcons for Horus, and so forth, day by day for six thousand days without fail. He would be a good Egyptian king, the most Egyptian king the House of Ptolemy had produced so far, *netjer nefer* indeed.

The Alexandrians, good at sarcastic nicknames, called him Philopator, *The Father-Loving One,* because they thought he had murdered his father. Perhaps he did. Right or wrong, the nickname would stick to him for all time.

As Pharaoh he was Osiris, and Osiris was Dionysos. *Call me Dionysos,* he said, for he *was* Dionysos, and had a special relationship with the great god of Frenzy, the one that wore the *peplos,* the women's dress. That was the first of reasons for his dressing up, and his heavy drinking: to honour the god of Wine.

As for his throne name, it was longer than that of any other Pharaoh before him: Neterumenxuaenptahsetepenrauserkaamen, requiring your humble servant to write thirty-one separate hieroglyphs, as if this king was more worthy than those who went before him, not less. Seshat will not torment you, Stranger, by trying to make you pronounce it correctly. Philopator was amused by his many titles, by his unpronounceable name. It was his pleasure to be difficult, to do everything different from anybody else. In that, at least, he was a success.

The High Priest of Amun at Thebes thought of this new Ptolemy not as the Horus, the Falcon, but as the Hippopotamus, the beast that was the image of Seth, the bringer of disorder. But Horemakhet, High Priest of Memphis, saw only the Lord of the Two Lands, the King of Upper and Lower Egypt. To him, Philopator was no monster but the Beloved of Ptah.

When Horemakhet gave Philopator even Greek advice, saying, *Wisdom of Khilon of Sparta: Be master in your own house,* it was to warn him of what was to come. But Philopator kept on the road he had chosen, like a deaf man, hearing little of what any man said except for Agathokles of Samos, the man he should beware of most.

From time to time, after his Majesty's dinner, when he wanted to impress ambassadors from abroad, Agathokles and Agathokleia would juggle with firesticks and breathe clouds of flame from their mouths. When Horemakhet saw it he thought of the future: first like a lighted fuse, smouldering, then like a house on fire, the dynasty burning up before his eyes. You might think that Horemakhet would do something to save a man who was trapped in a burning house. But Horemakhet thought, *Not to interfere with a man's fate. Must let the tragedy run its course.*

4.2

Beetles

Aye, danger thickens now about the kingdom of Egypt, both from within and from without, danger, which the first three Ptolemies had kept far off by their energy and wisdom – or, at least, through wise advice. Already in the year of Euergetes' death, Antiokhos Megas, the new King of Syria, successor to Seleukos Kallinikos, thought to stamp Philopator like an insect beneath the heel of his boot, by bringing his army up close to the border forts that were Egypt's great defence in Koile-Syria. Soon he would mobilize all troops.

Philopator's enemies abroad were both young men: Antiokhos Megas was eighteen years old, and the fifth Philippos of Macedon just seventeen. Both kings were full of young men's fire for the conquest of their neighbour, a man who did not sound much like Strong Bull, but was said to be weak, if not mad, a man whose kingdom looked easy to snatch from him.

But in fact at the start of Philopator's reign Egypt was still powerful, with all her great empire intact – Koile-Syria, Kyrene and Cyprus. Egypt's fleet still controlled the Hellespont, parts of Thrace, and many of the islands in the Aegean Sea. All Antiokhos Megas had inherited was a ruined, disintegrating kingdom. In the next twenty years the positions would be changed about: Antiokhos' empire would be secure, strong, powerful, and Egypt would be close to breaking point. But Antiokhos and Philippos were right to think as they did: Ptolemy Philopator cared little for the fire of conquest, nothing for the roaring flame that was battle. The only flame that interested him was the flame of Eros, the fire breathed by Agathokles and Agathokleia, and he had already been scorched by it. Philopator's house would smoulder for sixteen years before the flames finally leapt up. One man only kept the fire under control until then: the treacherous Sosibios, who also harboured thoughts of squashing Ptolemy Philopator under his heel, like a beetle, like the scarab who was Ra and Helios, but also stood for Egypt. Antiokhos was not the only man who wanted Egypt for himself.

Stranger, there can be no doubt that Sosibios was a great man. All might have gone well with his plan for making himself Lord of the Two Lands if he had not been so old when Philopator became king. For Sosibios was beginning to lose his energies, and was happy to let even the young Agathokles of Samos take upon his shoulders some of the burden of governing Egypt – even Agathokles the golden muscleboy, who had plenty of energy left, far too much energy.

Agathokles had always been Philopator's favourite, but now his master was King. Let not Seshat hide the truth of it: Agathokles slept by night in his Majesty's bedchamber, in his Majesty's bed, with the dogs, and the monkeys, and his sister Agathokleia did the same. At least Philopator did not take snakes into his bed. At least there were no crocodiles in his bedchamber. By no means. Just Agathokles and Agathokleia, who might often lie in bed with his Majesty all day, tickling him with an ostrich-feather to keep him laughing, shouting at every official who knocked on the door to go away.

Even now, if Agathokles said to his Majesty, *Ptolemaios, be a chicken,* Philopator would stalk about, clucking, flap the wings, attempt to fly. But he laughed as he did so. Like his grandfather he even had the ability to laugh at himself. He was the Great Laugher, as much as Dionysos. Above all, Agathokles and Agathokleia made him laugh. They laughed not at him but with him, and at the start of the reign it was not sinister, not sinister at all. All the same, they had the ear of the King. They had also other parts of his Majesty under their control. Mostly he did what these two advised; whatever they told him to do.

That Agathokles the favourite should move on to higher things and help govern Egypt was quite natural. Sosibios let him take charge of collecting taxes up-River, army wages, Mouseion accounts. Agathokles had many talents. Between them Sosibios and Agathokles handled palace business, leaving Philopator to his endless dancing.

Now, however, more men disappeared without trace than ever before – men who were the enemies of Sosibios. So many vanished that the people of Alexandria began to say, *The murdered man is fortunate . . . A dead man is a lucky man . . .* Nobody suspected Agathokles of anything ill, just then. By no means. Every man thought that because his face was handsome, his body beautiful, his soul had to be just the same. But what was the truth? His soul was black, like the crow; his soul was ugly.

4.3

Eunuchs

The first thing Ptolemy Euergetes had done every day was to settle down to business with Sosibios, replying to letters from foreign courts, dispatches from the Front, hearing petitions. When he was at Memphis he would perform without fail, in person, the temple ritual. Philopator's days began not with business but pleasure, when the Galloi bounced into his audience hall with their drums and cymbals, to honour Kybele with music and dancing. Aye, Philopator let Sosibios take care of the business.

But you do not know who is Kybele, do you, Stranger? She was the Great Mother of all things, the mother of all life. You should picture a beautiful woman, grotesquely stout in the belly, many-breasted, wearing a crown of turrets – like the city walls of Alexandria – upon her head: the goddess who promoted the fertility of the earth. Her story was as follows: when Attis, her young lover, was unfaithful with a nymph, Kybele took her revenge by driving him into a frenzy, during which he cut off his own testicles with a knife and died, under a pine tree. Kybele brought him back to life as her divine consort, thus ensuring that he would be faithful to her in perpetuity.

Alexander never had much time for this Phrygian cult. Neither did Ptolemy Soter or Ptolemy Philadelphos or Ptolemy Euergetes. These men were not interested in self-harm, not at all keen to chop their own ballocks off. On the contrary, the first two Ptolemies were so amorous they called them *triorkhis*, triple testicle.

The cult of Kybele was a foreign cult, alien to Greeks and Egyptians alike, but Philopator loved it. When he was quite young he had been thrilled by the hypnotic chant of the Galloi, the throbbing drums, the horns and flutes and cymbals, the urgent rhythms, their marvellous cacophony. He saw the band of beggars dancing down Kanopic Street in their saffron-coloured dresses and heavy jewellery, carrying the silver statue of the goddess on their shoulders. He heard them chanting their prophecies of the future. He saw the crowd throwing coins, showering the eunuchs with white roses. He liked to hear the crack of their leather whips, loved to see their great purple bruises, the livid wounds of the half-men as they danced to and from the Metroön, or Temple of the Great Mother, the goddess of nature, of animal life, of life itself. Philopator, like the fish on the line, was hooked, aged only eight or nine. He was still thrilled when he saw the Galloi dancing up Kanopic Street. He still wanted to join them.

In the beginning Philopator had been fascinated because the rites of Kybele were strictly forbidden him. With his parents gone, he could do what he liked. One of the first acts of his reign was to send for the Archigallos, the eunuch High Priest of Kybele and make him his friend. Aye, and he asked to be taught everything that an acolyte of Kybele should know.

For sure, the Archigallos taught him many wonderful things. He had never before had such an eager pupil.

The castration, the Archigallos explained, *is nothing more than the mowing of ears of corn. The arm-slashing is merely the re-enactment of the yearly wounding of the earth by the ploughshare. The ritual bath of Kybele simply means that the earth needs to be watered. There is nothing very strange about the cult of Kybele, nothing sinister about the Galloi.*

I should love to be a Gallos, Philopator said. *I should love to be one of the eunuchs myself.*

Megaleios, the Archigallos murmured, *it would be such an honour for us* . . .

What did the palace think of Philopator's new friends, the transvestites, the wild dancers, the stoneless ones? The cult was nothing new in Alexandria, nothing very outrageous by Alexandrian standards. Sosibios, shocked by nothing, shrugged the shoulder. But Arsinoë Gamma, now eleven years old, felt a strong desire to laugh whenever she saw the men in yellow dresses spinning round in the palace courtyards, men who bleached their hair like the women, and wore ribbons, and painted their faces with white lead – she screamed with laughter to see them.

Aye, indeed, what of the sister, this forgotten sister? She sat in the *gynaikeion* with her waiting-women, waiting: waiting to be old enough to marry, hoping for a husband who was not her own brother. Her days were filled with sewing and horse-riding, for that she was her mother's daughter, and also, from time to time, the weapons practice, because, as she said, *You never know when you might not need to defend yourself, or fight for Egypt.* She preferred tapestry to catapults, weaving purple cloth to hunting oryx, but she rode a horse well enough. She *could* do all those manly things, but she preferred not to. From time to time Arsinoë Gamma would make her prayers even unto Hathor the Golden, the Divine Cow, asking, like the Egyptian girls, for *Happiness and a good husband.* Unlike Nefertiti, wife of Horemakhet, she would get no happiness, none whatever. As for the man who fate had lined up to be her husband – Arsinoë Gamma knew he had already turned out for the bad.

Philopator did say to Sosibios, *Should we not get rid of the sister as well? She serves no useful purpose here, except to remind us of our mother. She says nothing but how she disapproves. Let us murder the sister too.*

But no, Sosibios would not allow it. *The sister,* he said, *is the one you will marry, Megaleios. There is no other female member of your House left living.*

When Horemakhet heard that Philopator wanted to join the Galloi, the castrated ones, he shook the head, folded the hands under his leopardskin mantle, and went to talk him out of his folly. *It has never been the custom for Pharaoh to behave like this,* he said, and he urged his Majesty to see sense, to give up this unseemliness. But Philopator could be just as stubborn as his father and grandfather.

Excellency, he said, *I do not care what anybody thinks. I shall do what I like.*

The dancing was only the beginning of it. As soon as the sun came up, Philopator would knock back his first draught of the powerful wine brewed by the Galloi from pine-nut seeds, and was drunk for the rest of the day. And why not be drunken? To be drunk is to be happy.

Sosibios was untroubled by it, for it meant that his Majesty did not attend to his duty. For Philopator to let go his grip on power meant that Sosibios could have it instead. Sosibios tightened his hold, was very pleased to let Philopator do what he liked.

But what Philopator really wanted was to join in the ecstatic self-laceration, to wield the whip lash knotted with *astragalai,* or sheep's knucklebones. He wanted to carve up his arms and spill his own blood as an offering to the goddess who protected Alexandria in time of war.

To do those things, the Archigallos told him, in the shrill voice of the eunuch, *his Majesty must be an initiate. First, he must learn all about the goddess. First he must learn all the rules. He must be sure that this is what he wants. Once a eunuch,* he said, smiling sadly, *always a eunuch.*

Even when Philopator gave fifty talents for the temple funds, the Archigallos said the same: *His Majesty must wait.*

In the meantime Philopator had to make do with being no more than the patron of the Great Spring Festival of Kybele, when he urged the Alexandrians to follow his example and honour the goddess. On the first day of the festival a pine tree should be cut down, for this tree was a great divinity to the Galloi. Philopator had a pine tree sent from Syria, and stood it in the Metroön. The duty of carrying the tree fell to a Guild of Tree-Bearers, but Philopator was not allowed to help carry, only to watch. They bandaged the tree trunk like a corpse, and decked it with wreaths of violets, the flower that sprang from the blood of Attis.

Even when he gave one hundred talents for the temple he was still allowed only to watch.

On the third day, the Day of Blood, the Archigallos cried out, slashed his wrists and filled a bowl with his blood, which he presented to the goddess as an offering. The Galloi whirled in the dance until they were insensible to pain, when they gashed the face with potsherds, and cut up their arms with knives, and spattered the altar and sacred pine tree with their blood. They, too, presented bowls of their blood to the Great Mother.

On the day when the novices sliced off their testicles with a razor-sharp flint, and dashed the bloody severed meat against the silver statue of Kybele, Philopator saw how the bloody bits were wrapped up and buried in the underground chamber dedicated to the goddess, a ceremony that would recall Attis to life and speed up the resurrection of nature in the spring time.

Philopator took Agathokles and Agathokleia with him and mingled with the crowds as the music of drum and cymbal grew more violent, more barbaric. He watched the madness spread as man after man heard the voice of the goddess inside his head, urging him on. He watched the initiates one by one throw off the clothes, run forward and grab one of the sacred swords, then, with a grand gesture slice off the testicles.

The Galloi, seeing his Majesty, began to chant *Ptolemaios,* urging him to come forward himself. To Philopator it seemed as if the voice of the goddess herself called him by his name, and he felt the passion rising in his breast. He saw man after man pick up the knife, scream the shrill scream of the eunuchs for the first time, then run naked through the streets, clutching his severed parts in his hands. Aye, Philopator watched one of them run up to the house he had chosen to honour, when he hurled his bloody handful of raw meat through an open window. This strange behaviour was a very great honour for the chosen household, which must now provide the stoneless one with his Gallos costume – his yellow dress, his yellow shoes, his golden earrings, his necklaces and heavy jewellery, the uniform of women's clothes that he must wear for the rest of his life in honour of the goddess.

Philopator forgot the petty rules of the Archigallos and sprang forward himself, heart beating hard, urgent to be a eunuch. The crowd roared encouragement.

Let him do it, Agathokles muttered, *may the gods help him to do it.*

Philopator threw off his purple cloak, and hurled it into the air. He ripped off his golden tunic and flung it away.

Agathokles stood there, smiling, watching, willing him not to stop. Agathokleia held her inflammable breath, put her hand over her mouth, for

Philopator was already stark naked, screaming the ritual scream, running forward, hands stretched out to seize the knife.

Agathokles moved not a muscle; never stopped from smiling, enjoying the pleasure of the passing moment, thinking, *If he has no heir, then Agathokles may be king* . . . He let Philopator grab the great bloodstained knife, heard him howl the howl of the eunuchs. But then Agathokles thought of Sosibios' words, Sosibios' dire warning. Agathokles had to do his duty.

He dived into the crowd, pushing his way through, reached the blood-splashed dais, pulled the knife from his Majesty's hand and wrestled him to the ground.

Aye, Philopator screamed, wailed, indeed, then, for Agathokles straddled his chest and held his arms down, and Agathokleia sat upon his legs. The crowd surrounded them, shaking the head, shouting, for shame that he had been prevented from honouring the goddess. As Agathokles led him away to calm him down, Philopator wept.

Into whose house did Ptolemy Philopator plan to hurl his privities? Why, the house of Oinanthe, his nurse, the mother of the beloved Agathokles – a young man who did not, as it happened, plan to seize the knife and become a *hemianthropos,* a half-man himself. By no means. Agathokles of Samos harboured thoughts of founding a great royal dynasty of his own. He was interested in keeping his testicles fixed on, not in throwing them away. Truly, Agathokles was not interested in doing violence to himself, only to others.

And so the moment of crisis passed.

This barbarous worship in honour of Kybele was repulsive to most of the Macedonians, a people widely known for their taste and humanity. Mostly these good people preferred the gentler rites of Adonis. Kybele attracted the rough ones, like the Romans, the barbarians, and the half-crazed, like Philopator himself. No, the rites of Kybele were not repulsive to Pharaoh. By no means. For him, everything the Galloi did was wonderful. He was the keenest of acolytes, but the Archigallos had his orders from Sosibios, what he might and might not do.

However much money he gave to the cult, the Archigallos always said, *His Majesty must undergo the proper making ready before he may be initiated.* He wagged the finger, and said, *He may not cut off the testicle without permission.*

Philopator gave the Archigallos one hundred and fifty talents, a very great sum of money. *Perhaps now you will let me join in the rest of the festival?* he said.

His Majesty may watch, the Archigallos said.

For sure, they could not keep him away. At the end of the Day of Blood the Galloi buried the effigy of Attis in a tomb and fasted, copying Kybele's grief for the death of Attis, and Philopator was allowed to wail and fast with them. Later that night the sadness of the Galloi turned to joy. They lit torches. They opened up the tomb. The dead Attis had come back to life. Now the High Priest of Kybele touched the lips of the faithful with a perfumed ointment, anointed their throats, and whispered: *Take courage . . . the god is saved . . . you too shall be saved* . . . He anointed the throat of Philopator, and the shiver of religious ecstasy surged through his Majesty's body, the shaking of the fanatic, the divine trembling of the convert.

At dawn came the wild outburst of rejoicing, for now every man could do what he liked, and Philopator – minded, of course, by Agathokles and Agathokleia – joined in the revels, dancing down Kanopic Street. No office was too high or too sacred for the humblest citizen to make believe he held it. Agathokles walked about dressed as Pharaoh, wearing even the *khepresh*, or Crown of War, and Horemakhet, hiding his face from all this at Memphis, knew nothing of the ill omen until it was too late. Sosibios did not care that Agathokles got the taste for playing Pharaoh, and cracking the whip. He laughed to see it. As for Philopator, he put on the simple tunic of Agathokles, and got the taste for being a commoner, the proper order of things was turned upside down, and it was the start of the greatest trouble the House of Ptolemy had ever known.

The Festival of Kybele ended on the sixth day, with the ritual bath of the goddess's silver statue, which was drawn in an ox-cart to the beaches east of the palace. In front of it walked Philopator's courtiers, because he said they must, barefoot, and there was loud music, trumpets, pipes, drums and cymbals. The Archigallos, wearing his purple robes, washed the wagon and the statue in the sea, and on the way back to the Metroön the women of Alexandria threw spring flowers. It was a day for laughter, for happiness. The Galloi who had whipped themselves into a frenzy forgot their bruises. The bloodshed was forgotten. Perhaps even the fresh eunuchs forgot their lost testicles, and were pleased with their handiwork. Philopator, the great Laugher, laughed, was happy, despite not being allowed to cut himself up. This time he had remained whole, but he thought it would feel good to be a servant of Kybele, and dedicate his drum and the casket with his testicles in it to the goddess; it would feel so good to join the stoneless ones.

Next time, he said to Agathokles, *I swear I shall do it.*

Philopator could not care less about the succession. He was young. He would not die just yet. His sister, breasts still less than three fingers high, was too young to be his wife. He had Agathokles of Samos and Agathokleia for his *aphrodisia*. He was quite happy to go on dancing with the eunuchs.

No, the Archigallos would not let Philopator injure himself, and it was, of course, because of the strict orders of Sosibios, who said, *Let his Majesty injure his person, and the cult of Kybele will be banned in Egypt for evermore, and the Archigallos will be a dead man.*

To Philopator, then, the Archigallos continued to insist, *Only the initiate may offer his blood to the goddess. Only the initiate may wield the whip and use the knife.* Until he was bathed in the blood of the bull, Philopator was allowed to do nothing more dangerous than bash the cymbals and join the dancing. But his ardour was undiminished. Aye, this King thought a very great deal about the Great Mother, and bloodshed.

4.4

Ghosts

Ptolemy Philopator tried not to think of what had been done, of what *he* had done, to his mother, to Berenike Beta. But he knew, as every Greek knows, that if Athena lets a mother-killer go free, an age of lawlessness must follow, leaving the Furies no choice but to hurry onward the tidal wave of blood that would suck the House of Ptolemy into oblivion.

Some days he would try to wipe out his bad thoughts by thinking about the *Iliad* of Homer. Or he might blot out his mother's face by talking to Aristarkhos of Samos about whether the Earth went round the Sun or the Sun round the Earth. Whatever he did, though, the waves of guilt for his mother, his uncle, his three brothers, even his father, washed over him like a sea of blood. Philopator was the one who slept ill by night for thinking *Guilty, guilty, guilty.* His entire family had gone, and the guilt was Ptolemy's guilt, for not having moved to stop the murders; for having let them happen. Some said it was the Furies, the women with snakes for hair, that drove him into madness, and his frenzied dancing was just the first sign of it.

For sure, some nights Philopator slept easy. He had the hot dark muscled body of Agathokles of Samos, the silky skin of Agathokleia of Samos, for his own possession. Some nights both of them lay in bed with their arms round Philopator's neck, making a twelve-limbed octopus, squeezing him. Mostly he was too drunk to notice the hint of naphtha upon Agathokleia's lips. If he happened to wake up shouting, these two would soothe his nerves, help him to sleep again. But Berenike Beta was coming. Her ghost could not ignore what Philopator had done. He would hear yet the heavy footsteps of the Furies upon his private staircase. The Furies would track him down for this crime, he was sure of it.

In the laws of the Egyptians you will find written down the proper punishment for the son who kills his mother, for to take by violence the life of she who gives a man his life is the greatest crime known to man. The law says that the mother-killer must have pieces of flesh the size of a finger cut out of his living body with a sharp reed. Then he must be laid upon a bed of thorns and burned alive.

Did they carve up Philopator's flesh, throw him upon a bed of thorns and burn him alive? No, of course not, for the laws of Egypt also say: *Pharaoh is outside the law. Pharaoh can do no wrong.* No, they did not cut him up: he would cut himself up.

Aye, they called this King the bad son, worst of his line. What Seshat has told you already, Stranger, might seem bad enough, but even Philopator could not dance all the time. He could not be drunk every day of the year, could he? Seshat says it again: *Philopator was hot to harm only himself, not others.* No Builder can be called bad, and Philopator was not all bad.

He began well, by having his name carved upon the temples even in the deserts of Upper Egypt, at the place the Greeks called Pselkhis, above the First Cataract of the River. He built a temple for Hathor the Golden at Qis, near Lykopolis, where Hathor was made equal to Aphrodite Ourania of the Greeks. Philopator loved Aphrodite, the one who presided over his *aphrodisia,* but he learned also to love Hathor the Cow, the goddess whose udders suckle the Pharaoh. He built a great Temple of Isis and Sarapis at Alexandria, for he was the Beloved of Isis. He spent great sums on temple building. This great King did not neglect the gods of Egypt.

Seshat likes Philopator. Seshat *loves* Philopator, because he was a Builder, like herself. Sosibios would never have built Egyptian temples of his own accord. Nor would the temples have been put up without the will-power of the High Priest of Memphis. Such things would never have been done without Philopator agreed to them in person. He did not surrender up all of his authority.

And do not think of complaining, Stranger, about Seshat's talk of mud bricks, pylons and temple courtyards. The very great interest of Seshat, Lady of the Builders, is the temples of Egypt. If building interests you not at all, Stranger, you may leave us here. Seshat knows, you have better things to do. Go plough your field. Milk your cows. Quit reading now, though, and you will never know what happened to those evil and most evil children of

Oinanthe of Samos, Agathokles and Agathokleia, those now grown-up children who had not learned the difference between right and wrong, who took no notice of the gods of Greece, no, nor the gods of Egypt neither.

Be instructed, Wise One. And save up your tears for later.

No, Philopator did not dance all day and night. By no means. Nor was he drunk all day. He did many other things, such as attending in person to laying the keel of his great ship, the *tesserakonteres*, or forty-er, that outdid in size even the *Alexandris* sent to Egypt by Hieron of Syracuse. The *tesserakonteres* was two-banked, with two hulls lashed together side by side, two hundred and eighty cubits long, fifty-three cubits high, with a total crew of seven thousand eight hundred and fifty. Some said it was an impossibility. Even Seshat, goddess of Arithmetic, says that a ship with so many men on board would have sunk. Some said the *tesserakonteres* – not unlike its owner – was good for nothing but showing off; that it was too big to sail anywhere, nothing but a *party-ship*, for dancing, feasting and drinking to excess. But no, she was a warship, double-prowed, double-sterned, designed for battle at sea, for ramming the enemy. The *tesserakonteres* was indeed a legendary vessel, meant to show the world the greatness of Egypt, and the greatness of his Majesty.

Philopator brought a naval engineer all the way from Phoenicia to make this giant vessel ready for launching, and she was dragged into the sea by the combined traction power of fifty five-banked ships. He did not altogether shirk his military duties, in the beginning, but kept Egypt ready for war.

Such grand projects were good. They gave Philopator something to think of apart from his mother. They took his thoughts away from the murder, until Kleomenes made him think of it again.

You do not need to know much, Stranger, about Kleomenes, sometime King of Sparta, who lived in exile in Alexandria. You may find his story in some other woman's book. But you should know what happened after his death. Kleomenes had tried to stir up revolution at Alexandria, calling on the people to rise up and push the tyrant Philopator off his throne. His efforts failed, quashed upon the instant by Sosibios, who harboured thoughts of having his own revolution, when Kleomenes killed himself. Sosibios strung the body up for a traitor, crucified him, some said, as an example to others who might be pleased to rebel against his Majesty. Kleomenes surely deserved his fate. Observe, however, the behaviour of Philopator when an enormous snake wound itself about Kleomenes' head where he was hung up in public, rotting in the sun, and shielded his face so that the crows could not eat his eyes.

Philopator was told of it, went to look, and was terrified by the sight, shaking in his golden sandals. He thought the snake was a sign of the vengeance of the gods, about to fall on his head for the death of his mother and brothers. He called in Andreas, his excellent and most excellent doctor, to ask for a sleeping potion, said he kept seeing the ghosts, complained of feeling panicky by night.

It was Andreas who urged Philopator to ignore the ghosts, to forget about ghosts. He even wrote a learned treatise, *Against Superstitious Beliefs*, expressly for King Ptolemy, to try and calm his superstitious nature and allay his irrational fears. The treatise was full of wondrous logic, explaining that a ghost is nothing but the embodiment of a man's guilty thoughts. Andreas urged every man of reason to acknowledge the truth: that evil spirits were merely part of his own imagination; that ghosts do not exist.

Philopator read the treatise with interest. He listened to what Andreas said, tried to see the sense of it, but Philopator was really not a rational man. Whether his mother's ghost was real or not, the treatise did not stop Philopator seeing it, and when he saw it, his body trembled, the hair on the back of his neck prickled. He did not imagine those physical signs but swore they were real. Therefore his mother's ghost had to be real.

Arsinoë Gamma, the sister, was also disturbed about this time, upset by her parents' deaths, fearful of the dark, subject to strange visions of the goddesses in her sleep. She saw horrors in her dreams that made her cry out, but nothing that could be called a ghost. Andreas said to Philopator, *It would be good for his Majesty's sister to marry, very good*. But the problem was that Arsinoë Gamma was intended for Philopator himself, who did not want to marry anybody. And she was barely twelve years old, still waiting for her breasts to swell.

Philopator still disliked that sister, who had gotten for herself, even so young, her mother's disdain for his putting on women's clothes, her mother's disapproval of concubines, her distaste for drinking to excess, her displeasure at Philopator's laziness. Arsinoë Gamma hated the grinning Agathokles of Samos, loathed his fat sister Agathokleia, the laughing ones, detested Oinanthe their grossly obese mother, the old nurse, who had her life arranged so that Philopator gave her whatever she asked for – while he made his sister beg for whatever she wanted.

Already Arsinoë Gamma said she had no wish to be married to her brother. She had promised Berenike Beta that she would never be his wife. But even if she was old enough, who could Arsinoë Gamma be married to if not her brother? And who would rule Egypt if Philopator refused to marry, and never fathered a son? Sosibios? Agathokles of Samos? Just then Antiokhos Megas of Syria, who was making ready for the greatest battle ever fought in the history of the world, looked most like to be the next Lord of the Two Lands.

4.5

The Jaws of War

Indeed, Antiokhos Megas was gazing just then with very hungry eyes towards Egypt. He lacked experience of war, but he did not lack fire. He was full of a burning rage, hot to restore to the House of Seleukos its rightful possessions.

Sure, Antiokhos Megas had suffered many blows at the start of his reign. One of his relatives, Akhaios, had jumped up and made himself the ruler of Anatolia. In the eastern satrapies one Molon had risen up in revolt, united the lands east of Syria as far as Babylon and declared himself king of them. Antiokhos had already dispatched his generals east and west to wipe out these usurpers. Now he turned his attention to the man they called the King of the South, Ptolemy Philopator, whom the scouts reported was looking easier to defeat than ever. Antiokhos' spies crept south, seeking intelligence about the best way to overcome the Egyptian intruders who illegally occupied Antiokhos' fortresses in the Bekaa valley.

When Sosibios told Philopator the news of the Syrian activity he laughed. *War is nothing to do with me,* he said. *Sosibios will win Pharaoh's battles for him. Sosibios will repel our enemies.*

But Sosibios thought different. *Ptolemy Philopator will take charge of this war,* he said. *He will be going to Syria himself. He should get himself sober and start to think what he is doing.* Philopator did not like it, of course. He stood up, put his arms out level with his shoulders, and began to turn his body slowly, humming like the Galloi. His feet became a blur. His body whirled. And Sosibios got, as usual, no answer from his Majesty.

Sosibios did handle the war, of course. War was Sosibios' duty. But Philopator would go with him into Syria.

The great peace of Ptolemy Euergetes had lasted twenty years. The Syrian question had slept for seven thousand three hundred days, except in the thoughts of Seshat. Now the question woke up again, demanding an answer.

For twenty years Ptolemy Euergetes had given Syria very good cause for complaint, by stirring up rebellion in Anatolia and Ionia, but Syria had done nothing about it, because of the peace treaty. Now things looked different: Syria had got her strength back. And now Ptolemy Philopator – or Sosibios – more or less invited Antiokhos to attack, by letting Egypt's army fall into habits of laziness, unfitness and disorder. Now Antiokhos accepted this kind invitation, sending his messengers to Ptolemy, saying, *Behold, henceforth we shall treat you as our enemy.*

Hostilities, then, were resumed.

Aye, as early as Year One of the Son of the Sun Ptolemy Philopator, Antiokhos Megas attacked the sea-port of Seleukeia-in-Pieria that had been occupied by Egypt ever since the murder of Berenike Syra, twenty years before. But because the Seleukids were useless at siegecraft, lacking the technology to build the best of engines, and had not one mechanician of the calibre of Ktesibios, Antiokhos put his trust not in artillery but in treachery. He offered bribes of one talent to Ptolemy's officers, who he had heard were restless: men who disliked what they heard of the new king's effeminate dancing, men attracted by the thought of riches.

Philopator's own officers opened the gates of Seleukeia by night, so that Antiokhos' troops could walk inside, and the city fell into the hands of the Seleukids while every man was asleep. Leontios, the garrison-commander, dared not prolong his resistance but surrendered on the spot.

Theodotos the Aetolian, the Satrap of Koile-Syria, led the deserters. He held Philopator in contempt, not only because of the yellow dress, but also because of the sorry business of Magas's murder, during which he almost lost his own life, and for which he had received no reward. The whole trouble was that as Satrap of Koile-Syria Theodotos was dangerous. Sosibios would let no man climb too high up the ladder of promotion. As soon as Theodotos began to look like a threat to Sosibios' power, a man who might lead a rebellion, he had to be gotten rid of. Theodotos mistrusted the courtiers at Alexandria, the men with the knives – Agathokles of Samos, and his friends – the ones who did not always sleep in their beds at night, but roamed about the city, murdering Sosibios' enemies. Theodotos had abandoned Sosibios, Philopator and Egypt before he was murdered himself, before they said even of Theodotos, *He is a dead man, he is lucky.*

Theodotos now made contact with Antiokhos of Syria on his own account, and volunteered to hand over to him the other cities of Koile-Syria, the cities he had charge of himself. Antiokhos was delighted. He welcomed this traitor like an old friend.

That summer Antiokhos turned his fury to Egypt again, force-marching tens of thousands of troops down the coast road to Gaza. He received from Theodotos the keys of Tyros and Ptolemaïs, took those cities without a struggle, and helped himself to forty of Philopator's ships of war that he found in the harbours. Antiokhos found the road empty before him, all the way to Memphis. But he was young, lacking experience of war, and he did not think to take this chance while he could and march straight to Memphis, and it was lucky for Philopator that this young man made the wrong decision. No, Antiokhos did not head for Pelousion but stopped to lay siege to Koile-Syria instead, and his detour used up the whole of the campaigning season for that year. Why did he do this? He had heard of Sosibios' defensive measures, and was afraid of being beaten back. He thought it was more important to gain control of Palestine first. He did not get the support he expected here, but found he must lay siege to Dora, Sidon, and other cities held by Ptolemy, and he had a long wait, for they refused to surrender, holding out for months on end. Antiokhos did not succeed at anything he imagined to do just then. Not one of the cities of Palestine fell into his hands.

Now Antiokhos agreed on a ceasefire of one hundred and twenty days, and wasted the winter locked in peace talks with Sosibios' ambassadors. Then in the spring, when the ceasefire ended, Antiokhos launched himself upon a fresh campaign, beating to a pulp near Berytos the new Egyptian force that Sosibios had shipped to Sidon in order to thrash him. With his rear secure, Antiokhos marched his troops through Galilee and Samaria, across the River Jordan, and snatched back the cities of Philadelphia and Ammonitis from Ptolemy. But Antiokhos still did not succeed in taking the territories that made up Koile-Syria.

The great question – who was to have possession of Phoenicia and Palestine – was not resolved. The battle of all battles was not yet fought, but it drew closer. Seshat, goddess of History, she who counts the years, she who counts the battles, she who keeps the tally of the Egyptian dead, called it the Fourth Syrian War.

As it happened, Antiokhos Megas delayed his attack, did not invade Egypt. All that winter he skulked in winter quarters at Ptolemaïs, master of nothing in Koile-Syria but the waves that crashed upon the beach.

Sosibios began fresh peace talks, trying to forestall Antiokhos' advance. He led the Syrians to believe he was on the point of accepting whatever terms they might care to mention. Antiokhos went back to Seleukeia and the talks lasted all through the winter.

Sosibios showed his very great cleverness now. He sent false intelligence by way of Antiokhos' spies to say that Philopator did nothing, that his troops were on the point of mutiny, lacking vigour, slothful – and very like their master – drunk, fat, sleeping by day, and that no man sharpened his sword in readiness for a fight. The result was that Antiokhos relaxed, allowing his troops to drink double rations of wine for months on end.

However, Sosibios, the master of untruth, had spread nothing but lies. The Egyptian troops were not drunk, fat, idle, or ill-prepared, and Sosibios was busy getting hold of massive reinforcements. He even enrolled native Egyptians as hoplites, putting them through a rigorous training programme. The Egyptian infantry phalanx soon numbered twenty thousand men, farmers and peasants, people famous for their dislike of war. But Sosibios armed them like Macedonians, with sword, short sword, dagger, shield, greaves, breastplate, helmet. He taught them how to wield the *sarissa,* or lance, of Macedon, marching and turning as one, upon the word of command. Hundreds of native Egyptians abandoned their donkeys and camels, enlisted in the cavalry and were trained in horsemanship under Polykrates of Argos, one of the laughing friends of Agathokles.

Sosibios' plan was a fine plan, and would solve the immediate crisis. At Alexandria the winter passed in a fever of military activity. Macedonian officers drilled camps of Egyptian recruits. The weapons factories worked overtime to make ready the gear for a prolonged campaign. The court of Pharaoh took up its usual winter residence at Memphis – through which ran the main highway from Syria to Alexandria – and even his Majesty played his part by entertaining Antiokhos' ambassadors there, putting them off sailing for Alexandria by saying, *Alexandria is so cold in winter . . . There is heavy rain in Alexandria . . . Why not stay in sunny Memphis? . . .* so that they should not see what was going on. Note, Stranger, that Philopator did his duty, up to a point. The streets of Memphis were not loud with the tramp of soldiers' boots. The city betrayed no sign that Egypt was frantic in her making ready for war.

Agathokles was just as clever, cunning, cruel as Sosibios, but he began to drink just as heavy as Philopator. A man who rules a kingdom needs to think clear, not to be drunken. But Agathokles himself now had charge of many important matters, and power made him a little reckless, for he let his mother and sister take care of military appointments, and they gave the highest ranks to their friends and relations. It was Agathokles himself, though, who called up the veterans who had retired to farms in the District of the Lake, men who thought they had hung up their shields and swords for good, and marched them up and down Kanopic Street every morning, ten abreast, as the Phalanx of the Lake. Aye, Agathokles, who had never wielded the sword in battle, rode up and down on his horse, shouting orders as if he had been in the army all his life. Agathokles, good at pretending to be what he was not, had learned fast.

In the spring the peace talks broke down, as Sosibios intended – for he was merely playing for time – and Antiokhos marched south, thinking it would be a simple matter now to prise the valuable territory of Koile-Syria from the feeble grasp of Ptolemy Philopator.

Sosibios was not quite ready to fight, but he laughed even so. *We shall allow Antiokhos to win for a while, let him think he is doing well,* he said, *and then we shall smash him to pieces.* Philotera, Skythopolis, Damaskos, Pella, Dion, Philadelphia – the cities of the Dekapolis – all fell to Antiokhos. The Syrian army stormed Philopator's fortress on Mount Tabor, and took the cities of Philistia, including Gaza, that winter. By the end of the campaign the Egyptian army had been driven out of Palestine, and Antiokhos took up winter quarters in Ptolemaïs again, delighted to think that his campaign was almost over, thinking that victory was in sight, and he let his men drink more, and train for battle less.

In that year Hannibal of Carthage began the Second Punic War by attacking the Romans' city of Saguntum, in Hispania. But in the dispute between Hannibal and Rome, Sosibios and Philopator once again drew attention to Arsinoë Beta's *Amicitia* as the reason why Egypt must stay neutral.

Philopator listened to Sosibios – sometimes – when he lectured him about the war. Some days he made wise judgements and sensible suggestions about what should be done. But he was just as likely to stand up even in the middle of the Council of War, stretch out his arms and start spinning. From time to time, when Philopator spun himself right out of the council chamber, Sosibios would rant about this worthless king, screaming, *How can I run a country with a man like that at the head of it . . . I shall kill him.*

4.6

The Shower of Blood

Although Ptolemy Philopator danced often with the Galloi, and called himself Gallos, he could not yet join in the sacramental meal, for he had still not been allowed to undergo the *taurobolion,* or shower of bull's blood. The

Archigallos would not let Philopator eat out of the drum or drink from the cymbal, because he was not one of the Galloi, not himself one of the *melissai*, the bees, as they were called, because of the way they hummed in the dance.

To sever the testicle, the Archigallos explained, *is not obligatory. His Majesty may dance along Kanopic Street with the beggars of the Mother. But the cutting off is the ultimate sacrifice, not to be undertaken without most careful making ready – for once a man has bade farewell to his privities, he may not fix them back on again. The cutting off must wait.*

But Philopator said, *Really, Archigallos, I am quite sure already.*

It was while Sosibios was busy putting Egypt on a war footing that – without telling Sosibios, or anybody else – Philopator threw a cloak over his head and slipped out of the palace after dark. He had fasted the proper fasts, saying he was not hungry. He made his way through the back streets to the Metroön and got himself ritually purified in the sacred bath. Every Gallos in the city was there to watch the King of Upper and Lower Egypt step into the underground pit and crouch below the grating, breathless for excitement, naked but for a crown of gold oak leaves. For once in his life he was not laughing. He heard the shrill cries of the eunuchs, and the bellowing of the black bull. He looked up to see the garlands of flowers hung round the bull's neck, his gilded horns glittering in the lamplight, the beast who would make him pure of the pollution of his mother's murder.

The priests of Kybele wrestled the bull on to the grating, and held him down with ropes. Philopator felt the bull's breath hot in his face, smelled the sweet smell of the bull, felt the power of the bull, reached his trembling arm up to touch his hoof. He saw the flash of the knife-blade as the Archigallos, intoning the words of the ritual, slit the bull's throat. Then the blood poured in a torrent on to Philopator's upturned face, making his yellow hair red, filling his eager open mouth, splashing over his body, a flood of more than one hundred pints of steaming blood. Philopator shuddered, terrified and ecstatic at the same time. He saw the light shining through the redness, and he saw the face of the goddess, swore he saw her, the saving one, who washed him clean. The hands of the Galloi stretched out to embrace their new companion and lead him from the pit, and Philopator emerged like a blind man, scarlet from head to foot, to their manic applause, their shrill ululation.

You should understand, Stranger, that the *taurobolion,* or bath of blood, was a kind of divine insurance policy against all the bad things that may happen to a man in the way of defeat in battle abroad or revolution at home, or the visitations of ghosts by night. Philopator had risen to a superior state, was reborn to eternal life. His guilty feelings were washed away by the blood of the bull. Now he would forget the murder of his mother, and the other murders, he was sure of it.

The born-again Philopator lived for many days on nothing but milk, like a newborn child. Sober, he was a changed man, talking quite serious to Sosibios about the war, expressing calm thoughts about the pig tax, sensible words about crime and punishment. But the golden vessel containing the testicles of the bull he kept by him day and night as a reminder that he was a true servant of Kybele. Philopator was free, bathed in the strange warm glow that is the holiness of the initiate. He had the tattoo of drums and lilies burned into his flesh with red-hot needles, as proof of membership. His enthusiasm for the Great Mother knew no bounds. Very often, now, he would dress himself up as Attis, in Phrygian cap, tunic and trousers, holding a shepherd's crook. He learned to play the panpipes. And he began to drink again. He could never give up the fine Greek wines of Mareotis altogether, but often he drank nothing but the powerful pine-nut wine of the Galloi. As for eating, nothing but the meat of sacrifice passed his lips, and a little fruit or vegetables. His new friends came daily to recline upon Philopator's couches, where they ate Philopator's meat off a bull's hide table-cloth, and drank Philopator's wine out of golden cups. At his own request they addressed Ptolemy Philopator, the Pharaoh of Egypt, who wore with pride the yellow dress and yellow slippers of the Galloi, as *Sister*.

At the feast, when Ptolemy Philopator danced the ecstatic Gallos dance on his own the applause was warm, and the priests of Kybele screamed for him to dance again. *He is our first and only benefactor*, the Archigallos murmured. *It is wise to tell him that he dances well.*

No, Philopator's body did not present the same picture of Greek perfection as that of Agathokles of Samos. Greek muscles – biceps, triceps, pectorals, iliac curves – Philopator did not have any of them. His belly was not taut and flat like that of Agathokles, but wobbled in the dance. Often he had to stop spinning in order to catch his breath. It was Agathokles that spoke the truth of it, saying to his sister, *His Majesty looks like a chicken dancing.*

Sober, Philopator could play the role of the Lord of the Two Lands, the stern Pharaoh, to perfection. Drunk, he imitated the manners of a madman pretty well. Howling, ecstatic, humming and spinning in the Gallos dance, he could forget that he was a king, throw off all responsibility, and be himself. He flogged his body using the whiplash studded with sheep's knucklebones, and sank his teeth into the flesh of his arms, so that the blood ran down his chin. When the whips cut into his back, drawing blood, he enjoyed the warmth, the thrill of the flesh, so drunk that he hardly felt the pain. Livid weals now covered his back. He spilled his own blood to make up for the death of his mother, blood for her ghost. Guilt for a mother's murder, however, is not so simply purged away.

Sosibios, affecting alarm to see his master's wounds, said to him, *Megaleios, you should remember that if you become a full Gallos, the House of Ptolemy is finished . . .*

Philopator laughed. His voice was still deep, but he longed for the day when it would be shrill, so that he could sing hymns to Kybele in the choir of eunuchs. Perhaps, Sosibios thought, the King did not truly mean to make the final sacrifice but thought only to amuse himself by shocking his guardians. But he ordered Agathokles to keep a closer watch on him, all the same, and report daily whatever Philopator did and said. Somehow Agathokles managed to keep Philopator from picking up the sharp knife and making himself a eunuch. His Majesty remained whole, for the time being. At all events, the escalation of his Syrian War now gave him something other to think about than testicles.

4.7

Raphia

No, Ptolemy Philopator did not notice the pain of his self-inflicted wounds. He loved the sight of blood, so long as he had the blood under his control. The thought of riding into battle appealed to him rather less. Like all the Greeks he was afraid of the darkness of Hades.

Sosibios, however, was firm. *His Majesty's proper place,* he said, *is at the head of his army, sword raised, smiting his enemy, not at home, dancing. You will be riding to war with us, Megaleios . . . Make sure your armour is in good order for battle.* And he added, *You might also have your hair cut – people are saying that the King of Egypt looks like a girl . . .*

Philopator tried to get out of doing his duty, saying, *If Pharaoh leaves Egypt the River will fail to rise, there will be famine and . . .*

Sosibios cut him off. *I will not hear a word,* he said, raising the voice. *You will come with us.*

To Horemakhet, Philopator said, *Really, Excellency, we are not at all interested in war. We really do not want to fight.*

But the High Priest thought the same as Sosibios. *Nobody in Egypt is pleased by the thought of war,* he said. *The Egyptians are a gentle, peace-loving people. But we rely upon King Ptolemy to fight our battles for us. All the priests of Egypt will be pleased if his Majesty rides to war. The troops need to see the figure of Pharaoh on the field of battle, even if he does nothing.*

Arsinoë Gamma did not share her brother's timidity. By no means. She begged to be taken to see the war, after the suggestion of Plato, but Sosibios said to her, *The woman's place is in the house, not in the phalanx.*

And Philopator made sneering remarks: *War's work, my child, is not the province of a young girl. The gods made woman for the spindle and the distaff, not for sword and shield. You are much too young in any case.*

She swept out of the room, then, angry, and in the chaos of the Wall of Metal setting out for Syria she was forgotten. But she said to her waiting-women, *Fourteen years old is not too young to fight. At fourteen my mother did a murder . . .*

In the Spring of Year Four, Sosibios made his heart strong to mobilize the wrath of Egypt and quit Memphis in a cloud of dust, at the head of a great army. Philopator rode beside him, wearing his golden breastplate, golden greaves and golden helmet, so that he shone like the Son of the Sun that he was; so that he might encourage the troops by his presence. He thought not of the words of his beloved Homer, *He rode into battle wearing gold, poor fool, like a girl.* By no means. If Philopator could not do what he liked and stay at home, at least he would wear what he liked. At least the men could see him.

On the highway out of Egypt there were three thousand royal guards, two thousand peltasts, eight thousand Greek hired soldiers, three thousand household cavalry, two thousand hired soldiers on horseback – horse-archers and javelin men – three thousand Cretans, three thousand Libyans in Macedonian armour, and six thousand Gauls and Thracians – that is to say, twenty-five thousand foot and five thousand horse. In Sosibios' second mighty phalanx there were twenty-five thousand Macedonians, and twenty thousand native Egyptians, making a total of seventy thousand foot and five thousand horse. And seventy-three elephants of war.

But there it is, Stranger, the beginning of the last great battle, for in the dust kicked up by one hundred and forty thousand feet, and twenty thousand hoofs, plus the baggage train, horses, mules, donkeys, carts and wagons, the army now marched out of Tjaru that was the real starting place for every Syrian campaign, ninety-six stades' journey west of Raphia, through the waterless desert of Sinai, steering a middle course to avoid the treacherous quicksands.

Every man wore the talismans that bring good luck, and keep away scorpions and serpents. They tramped through the sands to the frontier of Egypt, east of Bethelen and Psinufer, singing the marching songs, every man wearing upon his face the lotion of crushed snails and frankincense against the burning sun, every man ready to lay down his life for King Ptolemy, even the Egyptians. At the front of the column were Sosibios and Agathokles, laughing and making jests. Beside them rode Philopator, wearing the travelling costume of Pharaoh, and the blue leather helmet-crown of war, sober, unjesting. He also wore the best of Greek talismans – the right front foot of a gecko to bring him good luck and a handsome victory. His friend Andreas, the doctor, was with him, to tend to his wounds, if he was hit, because he was afraid of dying. Andreas had no such fear. His horoscope, cast at birth, had said he must die upon the field of battle. It was the reason why he had become a doctor: to cheat his fate. He thought that because he did not fight, he could not die. But Seshat says: *What is written at a man's birth is what must happen. No man may alter his fate.*

Even Horemakhet went to war this time, equipped to defeat the enemy by magic.

At Rhinokolura they pitched the leather tents and lit the fires to cook their porridge, when a defiant figure emerged from the baggage wagons, where she had stowed herself away, travelling among the soldiers' whores, face hidden under a scarlet headdress: the Princess Arsinoë Gamma, dressed in golden armour herself, glittering in the last rays of sunshine.

Philopator screamed abuse, of course, and Arsinoë Gamma screamed back at him, but it was too late to send her home.

I have come to help you, Brother, she said. *Have you forgotten what Plato said? Children should see war.*

Philopator spat his spittle in the sand for contempt, but Arsinoë Gamma now travelled on horseback, astride, like a man, beside her brother, and she demanded a white horse, because white horses are for the gods. Philopator ignored her, saying, *Useless, useless. Whatever use can a girl of fifteen be in battle?* But the first thing to be said about the Royal Sister, no more than fifteen years of age, hardly more than a child, was that she was utterly wonderful.

When they came near to Raphia, Ptolemy – or Sosibios – sent heralds to Antiokhos with word that he meant to do battle near Raphia, in six days' time, at the seventh hour, and he asked Antiokhos to most graciously present himself, accompanied by the dregs of his army, when the Wall of Metal would be pleased to make him do the dog-walk, and rub his face in the dirt. For the rules of war say that no king may make war without he has first declared war, and agreed upon the time and place of the clash. A Greek king must abide by the Greek laws of war, the rules of the contest, just as if battle was no more than a game of draughts, which must be fought fair, the Greek way, with no cheating and no sly tricks, between two perfectly matched sides, when the gods would grant victory to whichever army pleased them best.

Sosibios, Philopator's first minister, had no more experience of organizing a battle with seventy thousand foot soldiers than his master. He had done well, so far, very well, to muster and train so many troops, but here at Raphia even Sosibios faltered a little. He was an athlete by training, not a soldier. His only battlefield had been the running-track. Now he must direct the largest infantry force Egypt had ever put together.

The sight of Antiokhos' sixty-eight thousand troops and one hundred and two elephants of war was enough to give the strongest man pause. For sure, Sosibios had undergone the young men's military training, marching in Euergetes' phalanx for a year or two, but that was during the twenty years' peace: he had never seen actual combat in time of war. After Tjaru, Sosibios and Agathokles stopped making jests, but thought of what lay ahead: blood, and more blood.

Their generals, you might think, must have known what they were doing. Some of them did. The Strategos of Horse, for example, was a man of experience, but as for the others, well, they had not much. And it was because Philopator had given up his authority to Agathokles and Agathokleia, who had played games of dice and drawn straws to assign high military command, even letting their mother, the retired Great Royal Nurse of the King, pick names out of a helmet, as if Tykhe alone, the goddess of Luck, should decide who deserved promotion. Many of the higher ranks had been appointed to their command only a handful of days before. The old generals of Euergetes – who had been victorious in Syria, who had led the army in the Laodikaian War – had long since been retired. The younger ones Agathokles had sent away, murdered, or thrown into prison, laughing, *Old is bad, new is good*.

Who, then, were the new army commanders? Friends of Agathokles, friends of Agathokleia: clowns and jugglers, acrobats and tightrope walkers, palace slaves and catamites, their drinking companions. Aye, and what did they know about war, these jumped-up slaves who took the august military titles once held by Counts and Princes of Egypt? Not much. Worse, they prayed to no god of War, not even Athena, but trusted only Tykhe, Good Luck, and their own foolishness, their ability to make a man laugh. But Seshat says a battle is more serious than making jests, a more difficult business than juggling with four lemons.

Aye, a master's knowledge consists in knowing how to handle slaves, in knowing how to control them, but Ptolemy Philopator had let his slaves control him.

The desert plain of Raphia, upon the borders of Egypt and Palestine, is a hot place in the summer months, mighty hot, and the wind that blows off the sea just here is laden with sand and grit. There was not one tree, not one rock with a shadow to hide behind from the ferocious heat, but there was plenty of sun for the Egyptians to flash the light against their polished shields in order to dazzle the armies of Syria.

Antiokhos was camped at the old Philistine city of Gaza, ten stades from his enemy, and when he heard the news of the coming of King Ptolemy he smiled the grim smile. Now he moved his troops forward to the desert's edge, so that they stood only five stades from the Egyptians, aye, and so that they could roar abuse and dent enemy morale. Minor skirmishes broke out between the men sent to look for water. A few missiles were fired. Rocks were hurled. But the two great armies stood their ground for five sweaty days, waiting, chanting insults, while they made ready for the fight. Aye, and half the vultures in Syria, and all the crows, perched on the baggage wagons, or circled overhead, screaming, impatient to begin feasting.

As darkness fell, Horemakhet prayed the eve of battle prayers to Montu, god of War, Great in Strength, Whose Heart is Glad When He Sees the Conflict, Who is Like a Fire in Straw. He said to his Majesty, *The limbs of the Syrian tremble, the fear of thee is before him. Thy sword will be mighty among the Asiatics; they will be made into fragments.* But he saw that it was Philopator's limbs that trembled.

The captains prayed the proper prayers to Athena to sharpen their wits, suddenly finding the ever-living gods of Greece a comfort, lest they might, after all, help a man to escape death and the horror of war, and going down to Hades fifty years early.

Ptolemy Philopator, Great in Strength, Mighty in Terror, had his sumptuous purple and gold tent pitched upon the plain, but he sat up late, too overwrought to sleep, drinking pine-nut wine with Sosibios and Agathokles, who now laughed and smiled not at all.

And were the fresh generals deep in discussion about strategy, about the terrain, about tactics? No, Stranger, they were deep in wine, getting drunk, out of their very great terror of death. Few of them had been tried in battle before, and however well a man is trained, nothing makes the rivets in his armour shake and rattle like the first time he faces being food for vultures.

No, the generals were drinking. But that was how things were before every battle. They were drinking in the Syrian tents just the same. No man begrudges a soldier a drink or two on the night that might be his last night upon earth. To drink will calm a man's fears. The extra ration of wine on the morning of the battle may have been the only thing that got the phalanx to move forward. No sober man would have anything to do with the madness that is war.

In the camp of Antiokhos one man in particular bore a special grudge against Ptolemy Philopator: Theodotos the Aetolian, now in the pay of Antiokhos. Theodotos was not drinking that night, nor was he sleeping. He was lurking on the Egyptian lines, with his face blacked, dodging the guards, creeping up to the royal tent.

Andreas the doctor retired early, for on the field of battle an army surgeon must pass a busy day. For years and years he had treated his master's insect bites and recurring fevers, his drunkard's tremor of the hands. Every night he had slept in the chamber next to his Majesty, with a rope tied to his wrist, lest the King should have need of his professional attentions. Now Andreas slept in the king's tent, while Philopator sat further off, fingering his good luck talismans, watching the fireflies, listening to the roar of the seventy thousand Macedonians drinking, and to the waves of laughter and abuse floated on the breeze from the Syrian camp.

Aye, it was Andreas who must bind up the sword cuts, stuff the king's guts back in his belly, drill the hole in his head, or saw off his mangled limbs, in the event of his being wounded. Andreas, his nerves were like iron, ready to do whatever a physician must do. He had made his sacrifice to Asklepios and Hygeia. He slept well enough. It was Philopator himself who wanted to run away at Raphia, not the Egyptians, and his physician would help him escape if things went ill for him. A king's doctor was much more than a mere man of medicine: he must taste his master's food for poison; he had his clever tricks for getting the better of the enemy. Andreas could tell from how many squatted with loose bowels, the state of enemy nervousness. The doctor, who does not fight at all, is one of the most useful men on the field of battle. Andreas was, at least, better than Aristarkhos, physician of Berenike Syra. He was a man to be trusted, if a king could trust anybody.

In the dead hours, Theodotos the Aetolian, the turncoat, the untrustworthy one, slipped past the dozing guards into the Egyptian camp. He knew what were Philopator's sleeping habits. He knew that the Son of the Sun woke up with the sun and not before. He made straight for his Majesty's tent, cut a hole in the back wall of it with his knife and stepped inside, listening. He made for the snoring figure upon a folding bed, fitted his knife into his neck just underneath the ear, aye, so that his Majesty's hot blood spurted up into his face. Theodotos fled back to the Syrian lines, unnoticed.

That night Philopator dreamed the dream of drinking blood and woke himself up with his screaming. He pulled on the rope to summon Andreas, but Andreas did not come running, did not shout his usual *One moment, Megaleios* . . . Philopator tugged hard on the rope, and heard some heavy thing fall to the ground in the next chamber of the tent. Angry, Philopator stumbled out of his camp bed in the dark, shouting. He felt his way along the rope, and found Andreas sleeping on the floor. He shook him, saying, *Wake up. Why did you not come?* But he found that his hand was sticky, that Andreas still did not answer, and did not move, and then Philopator screamed for guards and lights.

Aye, when the lights came, Philopator screamed all the more, for his hands were covered in Andreas' blood. It was the doctor that Theodotos had stabbed, not his royal master, on the eve of the battle of Raphia, the night before the clash.

Philopator howled, *Ill omen . . . Terrible omen . . .* and his tears flowed.

Andreas had undertaken important medical researches. His work *On Snakebites* was much valued by the Greeks in Egypt. He was the inventor of a contraption for setting broken arms and legs. He had created an eye-salve that helped when half the desert lodged itself under his Majesty's eyelids. Andreas was the very first of doctors and would be badly missed.

Philopator, his face ran with tears as he paced up and down, saying, *We shall be beaten, beaten,* so that, far from boosting his generals' morale, he made them more nervous.

At dawn Horemakhet came to Ptolemy wearing the leopard-spot mantle, and his arms were wrist to shoulder with every magic charm for victory in battle. Sakhmet and Montu, the gods of War, were with him. He lay on his belly before his Majesty, saying, *Pharaoh will be like a fire sweeping through waterless places. He will remove men's breath from their nostrils. Behold, put your trust in Montu the Warrior, the god whose bread is hearts, whose water is blood, and it will go well with you.*

But Philopator's thoughts were elsewhere. *What about the dream of drinking blood?* he asked. *What does it mean?*

The High Priest reassured him, *Egyptian dream, Majesty, good dream. It means putting an end to your enemies.*

*

Philopator looked out on the troops of Antiokhos Megas, sixty-eight thousand foot, six thousand horse and one hundred and two Indian elephants, lined up, waiting, silent. Antiokhos had called all the military resources of Asia to fight for him: Medes and Kissians, Kadusians and Karmanians. He had mustered ten thousand Nabataians and Arabs. There were Persian and Agrinian archers and slingers. He had Themison, the now ageing Herakles of Antiokhos Theos, as one of his commanders. Theodotos the Aetolian, the deserter, the murderer, had charge of ten thousand men. The sixty-eight thousand stood in the sun, now silent, then, upon the signal, chanting filthy abuse about Ptolemy Philopator, his pretty yellow dress, his lovely catamites, his effeminate soldiers.

Antiokhos galloped up and down before the off, shouting to encourage his troops, with one dozen interpreters shouting the translation of his words. Aye, Antiokhos yelled his message, *Five hundred years ago, in this very place, Sargon, King of Assyria, met Egypt and the allies of the south. He ground their faces in the dust. He defeated them utterly. I believe that Egypt will be defeated again.* And the Syrian host roared against the King of the South, beating sword on shield, rhythmic, urgent, eager for the very last and very final battle in the history of the world to begin.

Hardly three stades away now, Ptolemy Philopator sat upon a white horse with a leopardskin saddlecloth. He wore the lion's-head helmet, gold, with red plumes, just like Alexander's helmet, but he was not Alexander. He was not fearless. He did not quite know what he was doing. His hands shook. Added to the drunkard's tremor was the tremor of fear.

The hot wind blew sand into Philopator's eyes, up his nostrils, into his ears, between his teeth, behind his golden breastplate. The sweat poured into his eyes. There could be no turning back now, no running away, and there was no Andreas to help him escape if everything went wrong. Philopator must go on, and he began to speak into a golden speaking-trumpet so that the seventy-five thousand troops could hear him, his last words of wise advice and earnest encouragement: *Men of Macedon . . . Men of Egypt . . . I beg you . . .* he began, but the hot wind whipped away his whisper. The sand flew down his throat, making him choke. His eyes filled up with water for thinking of Andreas, murdered by mistake for himself. The serpent upon the *khepresh,* the Crown of War, was a living flame which would burn his enemies to a cinder but just then it was as if his Majesty's lips was stitched up with stout thread. He had taken the leather *khepresh* off in favour of gold, had put aside the *ouraios* serpent that was his protection.

Philopator had been given the basic weapons training as a youth – eventually. His father's old generals had tried to teach him the rudiments of strategy and tactics, but he had neither listened hard, nor remembered well. He looked about him, waiting for some other man to shout the orders. Even the Admirable Sosibios seemed not to know what must be done in the waiting for the signal but kept his mouth shut against the flying sand. As for Agathokles, who knew still less, he squatted at the back of the phalanx, shitting himself for terror. The vultures circled above the plain, screaming, and their screams sounded very like laughter.

On her great white horse at Philopator's side sat the sister, Arsinoë Gamma, dressed in full Macedonian cavalry armour, golden breastplate, golden greaves, and the white-plumed helmet, her father's golden helmet. She thought of her brother's sarcastic words: *War's work is not for a mere girl, war is men's business* . . . But in the silence before battle she saw Philopator's trembling, and the anger rose in her breast that was no longer flat, like a boy's. She saw her brother standing beside his horse now, face pressed into the flank. She saw that his body shook; that he had messed his drawers before ever the fight began. The Greeks should have been spurred on, urgent to tear each other's flesh with the pitiless bronze, by the sight of their commanding officer leading from the front, like Alexander. But Philopator said nothing, did nothing but stare at the ground, and the brown liquid trickled down his thighs.

His scornful words stirred up his sister's anger. She would show him that a Macedonian princess did not filthy her legs like a coward. Arsinoë Gamma was a woman, but she had had just the same lessons in how to win a battle as her brother. Unlike him she had remembered what to do. War did not specially excite her; she liked better to think of women's things, and it was the poppies and anemones that she noticed in the quiet before the clash, the scuttling lizards, the circling falcon that was Montu, Egyptian god of War, and Horus, and the blue hills in the distance. But she heard the shuffle of military boots, and the nervous laughter rippling down the Egyptian lines. She saw the vultures perched on every baggage wagon, impatient, heard the vultures cackling above, the raucous laughter of a million crows. She thought of Nekhbet the vulture-goddess, who sat upon Pharaoh's brow, his protector. Unwarlike though she was, Arsinoë Gamma snatched the speaking-trumpet from her brother and began to shout orders.

No, Arsinoë Gamma did not tremble. She thought of the grand example of her Aunt Arsinoë Beta. She remembered the face of her mother, Berenike Beta, fierce, eyes ablaze, teaching her the laws of war. She knew what must be said to the troops in the last moments before the attack. She began to yell –

in Greek. She shouted even some words in the Egyptian tongue. It mattered not whether the men heard or understood: they could all see Arsinoë Gamma proud upon her horse. They could guess, from the way she held her head high, from the way she brandished the sword, what she meant to say. As they stood still, silent, waiting, they saw her throw aside her helmet and gallop along the line of troops to encourage them, her yellow hair floating free, and several miracles took place. The Macedonians saw the Princess Arsinoë Gamma, daughter of the old king, Ptolemy Euergetes, and they thought of Alexander, and famous victories like Issos and Gaugamela. They thought of Olympias, mother of Alexander, and of Arsinoë Beta, and the long tradition of Macedonian queens riding into battle, and they took courage. The unwarlike Egyptians saw the Daughter of Pharaoh, the Royal Princess, and thought of Egypt's great victories at Megiddo and Kadesh. They thought of the native Pharaohs, Nektanebo, Ramesses, Tuthmosis, and they took heart.

Arsinoë Gamma was not downcast by the flying sand or the suffocating heat. She shouted the orders to the generals while her brother was choking, and while Sosibios, the old man, looked about and looked about, wondering how he was going to save his own skin.

It was the sister who worked up the men's fire, Arsinoë Gamma, whose fair eyes, like the eyes of Isis, Lady of Flame, would be upon them to see them fight for her, screaming: *Men of Egypt, dig your heels in the ground, bite your lips with your teeth and stand firm . . . Level them with the dust . . . Make them into mincemeat . . . Aim for the thighs . . . Fear nothing . . . I beseech you by Zeus and Pan and all the gods: hold firm.* The men roared in reply. And when they did not roar as loud as she thought they should, she screamed louder: *I promise to every man two minas of gold if the victory is ours.*

The sandy plain of Raphia was the perfect place for a battle, flat, free of obstacles, the kind of place Epaminondas called the dancing-floor of war. Now Arsinoë Gamma made the trumpets blare. Now she ordered the dreadful slow advance, the creeping forward with measured steps, very like the steps of the dance, stamping the feet down, regular, rhythmic, and the order and discipline of the phalanx was wondrous to behold. Sosibios had trained his army well. Stranger, nothing quite so fine as this had been seen from the Egyptian army in the entire history of the Two Lands. The old Wall of Metal was re-forged, restored, blinding the enemy, dazzling his eyes, and what happened was like some magic of the gods.

Magic was, indeed, at work, for Horemakhet entered the enemy's stomach as a fly. He turned the Syrian's face to the back of his head, and fixed his feet on backwards. He emptied Antiokhos' men of all their strength, aye, and the contents of their bowels. He entered the ears of the Syrian elephants of war as a wasp and stung them to madness. As the cry went up *For Egypt and Victory* . . . *Ptolemaios and Victory, Amun and Victory* . . . Philopator's elephants lumbered forward, trumpeting. In towers, perched on their backs, were archers, javelineers and pikemen, sending out a storm of arrows. The elephants used all their strength, meeting each other forehead to forehead, tusks interlocked, shoving, each one trying to make the other give ground, until the stronger one pushed aside the other's trunk, made him turn, and gored him in the flank. Ptolemy's elephants from Africa, they said, declined the combat, unable to bear the smell and furious trumpeting of Antiokhos' Indian elephants, which were larger, stronger, and many of them turned round and ran away from the fight, driven back into the Egyptian lines, causing chaos. But no, the phalanx was ready for such things. Arsinoë Gamma screamed the order herself, and the phalanx, trained to move as one upon the word of command, stepped aside, and the elephants charged through the gap, harming nobody.

The phalanx lowered the *sarissa*, and began the charge, and the arrows flew like a black rain, and the shining swords turned black with blood.

Then the battle cry went up, the *Alalalalai*, the jaws of war yawned open, screaming. The noise of the Egyptian advance was like wild fowl, like the clamour of startled cranes rising high into the sky, and the charge of horse and elephants was met by the Syrian cavalry led by Antiokhos himself on the right, that broke and routed Ptolemy's cavalry on the left, so that the King of Egypt was swept along in a wild flight to the rear.

Philopator felt in his head a strange dizziness. He was half blinded by kicked-up dust and blown sand. His heart pounded. He was lucky that his horse knew what to do.

Antiokhos of Syria might have won a great victory, but for the streak of rashness in his character, for although he was brave he was young, lacking experience of a great battle such as this: in the excitement of the chase he did not watch the rest of the field, rode too far in pursuit, and disappeared from sight. Aye, the enemy commander-in-chief was made to vanish in a cloud of dust, by Horemakhet's magic.

On the other wing the Ptolemaic horse drove the Syrian horse back. Philopator, with unexpected presence of mind, sprang free from his own phalanx, where he had retreated for safety, and galloped his horse straight into the chaos in the middle of the enemy rank. He showed himself to both armies, directing in person a counter-attack by the heavy infantry in his centre, spreading fear among the enemy and boosting the spirits of his own troops.

Berenike Beta had not allowed her son to grow up without the skill of horse-riding. All the same, his great white war horse knew which way he should gallop, without Ptolemy so much as digging the heel in the flank. He was utterly unafraid in battle, unlike his rider, who was carried away in the surge of horse, waved his sword arm in the air, clung on for life, screaming for help.

Truly, the gods saved this king's reputation by making it look as if he accepted risk and sacrifice, as if he knew what he was doing, leading from the front, like Alexander, and it spurred his men on. But it was the sight of Arsinoë Gamma riding with the cavalry herself, wielding her sword, that really made the Egyptians fight. Aye, Arsinoë Gamma, who had been taught how to thrust the sword up through a man's guts, had no fear of anything. She was the daughter of Berenike Beta, as good as a son, just as her mother had meant her to be. Now she aimed for the face, the throat, the groin. Now she withdrew her sword through the shattered teeth, howling for Egypt and victory, making the blood fly.

The phalanxes in the middle were left to decide the result, two solid bodies of frantic clawing men. Sosibios had carefully placed his Macedonians so that the veterans in the front rows led, and the veterans in the back rows pushed, and so that the Egyptians could not run away even if they tried. The Egyptians fought like Sakhmet the lioness indeed, for when their swords were gone they used their teeth, biting the Syrian to death. And perhaps it was, after all, not just Sosibios' training but the thought of two gold *minas* for every man that made them fight like wild beasts.

The Egyptians, drilled and regimented for eighteen months at Alexandria, held fast, but the Seleukids, battle hardened but battle weary, uttered as one a great groan. Their morale collapsed, the entire army of Antiokhos turned their backs and fled. Where was their King? Dozens of stades away. When at length he realized that the cloud of yellow dust was not kicked up by the phalanxes locked in combat but by his own troops in retreat, he turned himself about, but it was too late: the cry of victory was loud upon the lips of the Egyptians. Antiokhos Megas could do nothing but give the signal acknowledging defeat.

In the time of Ramesses, every Egyptian warrior who killed an enemy cut off his hand, and if the victim were an Asiatic, his *rhombos*. Nothing changes in Egypt: even at the Battle of Raphia, with the latest modern technology in use, these bloody trophies were still presented to the royal heralds to be thrown with the captured weapons into a heap, to be counted by Horemakhet's army of scribes, aided by Seshat, goddess of Arithmetic.

Aye, Seshat is the one who counts, who never stops from counting. Seshat numbered the enemy dead, their severed hands and hacked off *phalloi,* at ten thousand three hundred. Seshat is the one who keeps the Annals of War, who records the storm of spears, the shouting before, and the singing after, the air rank with the stench of rotting flesh, the gorging vultures, the sea of blood-stained sand, the lurid carpet of the mangled dead. Four thousand prisoners they bound and paraded before Pharaoh. The Egyptians and Macedonians stripped the enemy dead of their bright armour, marvelling at the black cloud of flies, the tumultuous buzzing. At dusk the soldiers' fires were lit, and then the song of victory wafted over the plain. From distant villages came the cries of children, barking dogs, and the wail of mourning. The twisted figures of the dead lay in the bloody sand, unattended except by the birds. The stench of death and excrement crept over the field of battle, and the vultures and crows ripped raw flesh.

What of bold Agathokles and warlike Agathokleia in this battle? Killed, fighting honourably for Egypt? Sliced up by Syrian swords? No. These brave soldiers suffered not a scratch. For sure, Agathokles had his swift horses and well-sprung chariots now, but he was a house-boy, just a regular satyr who had made good, not any kind of warrior. Sure, he had wrestled and boxed in the *gymnasion* but he had never undergone the full military training. He was a cupbearer, not even a spear-carrier. He never saw war until the day he was meant to be in charge of it. No, he was paralysed with fear, shiny with the sweat of terror, his legs stained. No man reported witnessing the bravery of Agathokles of Samos in battle. The whisper was that he had hid himself. As for Agathokleia, she crouched under a blanket in the baggage train with the soldiers' whores, unable even to watch.

Philopator gave not much credit for the victory to his sister but boasted rather of his own exploits, saying, *I have made the Asiatics slink away like dogs.*

He said, *It was with the help of the gods that I overcame Antiokhos. It was the gecko talisman that guaranteed our victory.*

He said, *You have made an exhibition of yourself, Sister. You might have been killed riding into battle without a helmet.* And he complained: *We could have won that battle without it costing two gold minas for every soldier. You have given us a most costly war and ruined the finances of Egypt.*

But she said, *The victory was mine. Without me you would have known shameful defeat.*

He had the good grace, then, to say, *Sister, you were tough as ibis-guts.*

But you, she thought, *you were soft as a jellyfish.* She bit her tongue not to say what she was thinking.

It was left to Horemakhet to give this young girl proper praise. *Thy fire raged as a flame behind them,* he said. *I shall cause thy name to be remembered in the future through all eternity.*

Now Horemakhet rode home to Egypt, and Sosibios ordered Arsinoë Gamma to go with him. Philopator would have been pleased to turn back himself. He said, *We have had our bellyful of war. Let us go home.* But Sosibios made him go on, deep into Syria, to inspect the territories that were now his, the rightful property of Egypt.

At the leave-taking Horemakhet said, *Thou art the rampart, protecting Egypt, great is thy might, O victorious king . . .* but his words might just as well have been addressed to the sister. Arsinoë Gamma's courage at Raphia was what you might expect of a *parthenos* about her age. Her boldness was not unlike that of Berenike Beta in murdering Demetrios Kalos. Like mother like daughter, as they say.

Seshat swears: *You need a woman to win a battle.*

4.8

Hierosolyma

Aye, Ptolemy Philopator rode onward, further into Syria, making his tour of triumph. He plundered the cities of Gaza, Askalon, Azotos, Joppa, and when he came to Hierosolyma he delighted the Chief Priest there by making sacrifice to the Most High God of the Hebrews, and admired the beauty and order of their magnificent temple – that is to say, the magnificent outside of it. But then he was seized with a desire and longing to see the inside of the Holy of Holies.

The Chief Priest of the Hebrews showed Philopator the notice on the gate of entry, that said: *No foreigner may enter within the balustrade and embankment around the sanctuary. Whoever is caught will have only himself to blame for his death.*

For sure, Philopator knew that what he wanted to do was not allowed, but he said, *Nobody forbids the Pharaoh of Egypt to do anything.*

The Holy of Holies is a dark chamber, entirely empty, the Chief Priest said. *There is nothing for his Majesty to see.*

I do not believe you, Philopator said. *I think it is full of treasure, and I mean to see it for myself.*

The chief priests of the Hebrews shook the head, wrung the hands, and said, one after another, *It is written: Even the King of Egypt shall not enter here. This place is not to be approached, not to be violated, not to be seen.*

I am the conqueror, Philopator said. *I shall do what I want.* And he stepped forward, showing the teeth, sword in hand, as if he meant to cut down any man who stood in his path. What did he think he would see? Gold that he might take for himself? Jewels that he might wear upon his person? Stranger, the man knew there was nothing inside. He wanted to go into the sanctuary simply because it was forbidden.

He saw the great altar, and the golden trellis with the golden vine growing upon it. He saw the curtain embroidered with an image of the universe that hung across the doorway to the sacred place. But that was all he saw, for though he was no more than one dozen paces away from it he never reached the door.

The Hebrews tell the story that when Philopator was all for forcing his entry the crowd set up a prolonged and vehement howling, for they would rather die than see the Holy of Holies profaned, and it seemed as if even the walls and pavements cried out in anger. And then it was as if the Most High God of the Hebrews laid his mighty hand upon his Majesty, for his legs gave way beneath him, his body arched and shuddered, shaken back and forth like the reed in the wind, his tongue curled itself backwards down his throat, he foamed at the mouth, twitching, speechless – and the howling of the crowd gave place to a storm of cheering.

If, indeed, the Hebrews speak true, we must assume, Stranger, that some kind of epileptic fit came over Ptolemy Philopator, like the fit that struck Philippos Arrhidaios down. Or perhaps Seshat may surmise that this collapse was brought about by an excess of pine-nut wine in the excitement of victory. Andreas might have foreseen such an attack and taken steps to prevent it, but Andreas was dead. Whatever was the reason for his falling down, Philopator did not see inside the Holy of Holies at Hierosolyma that day, or any other day, for Sosibios had him picked up and carried away to his bed, and he never dared to go back for fear of the same thing happening again.

When Philopator recovered his speech and seemed a little better, Sosibios went to talk to him. *His Majesty is twenty-seven years of age,* he said, stern. *He has no wife and no heir. If he had died at Raphia the House of Ptolemy would have been finished. And who would have been Pharaoh of Egypt then? It is time to marry the sister and father some sons.*

Philopator, as famous for stubbornness as his father and grandfather before him, shrugged the shoulder. *We shall marry when we are ready,* he said, sulky, *in our own time, not when Sosibios tells us.*

*

During the rest of his tour Philopator was fit enough to attend to the restoration of Egypt's power in the cities of Syria and Phoenicia. For ninety days Syria huzzaed wherever he drove his chariot, threw flowers at his brave soldiers, and he was not struck down by the hand of any god.

As for Antiokhos Megas, he rallied his men, at length, but he was so downhearted himself, and his troops so broken in spirit, that he offered to negotiate for peace at once. Philopator sent Sosibios to Antiokheia to talk over the details, and set them upon papyrus. Or perhaps it would be truer to say that Sosibios sent himself. Antiokhos, he got off light, not being made even to pay an indemnity. He was ordered to clear out of Koile-Syria as far north as Mount Lebanon. He got to keep the city of Seleukeia-upon-the-Orontes, but was forced to surrender up to Egypt all his other conquests.

The ambassadors sailed from Alexandria to spread the word of the victory of King Ptolemy Philopator to the islands of Greece that were within his power. Throughout the empire there was feasting, rejoicing and processions in the streets, for that the King of Egypt had, in less than one hour's work, got back possession of the whole of Koile-Syria.

Some murmured that it was the only hour's work this king did in all his lifetime.

One hundred and twenty days after Raphia Philopator came home to Egypt covered in glory, his army singing upon the road. He drove into Memphis upon his electrum chariot wearing the *khepresh*, even allowing the sister to ride beside him, the smiling, waving sister.

Philopator celebrated his victory with a parade of the very greatest magnificence at Alexandria, marching his seventy thousand soldiers (less the dead ones) down Kanopic Street in a shower of rose petals, the elephants marching with them; and the veterans and the wounded were wheeled on barrows and carts.

At the end of it he sacrificed four elephants to Helios, the Sun-god, who is equal to Ra. He had bronze statues of the sacrificed elephants put up at Alexandria so that this exceptional offering would be remembered for all time. It was cruelty, Stranger, of which Seshat cannot approve. It was a farewell to four elephants who had done him good service in battle, and might have done so again. His father would not have done such a thing. Nor would Philadelphos or Arsinoë Beta or Ptolemy Soter. Nor even Alexander. The gods were not pleased by this atrocious sacrifice of beautiful beasts. And what did he do with his splendid holocaust? The Alexandrians would not eat roast elephant, which is sickly, sticky meat, though the tongue is something of a delicacy. He burned them up until there was nothing left but the great bones. Seshat weeps to think of it.

A different story says that Philopator planned the massacre of all the Hebrews in Alexandria, in revenge for not being allowed to put his foot inside the Holy of Holies at Hierosolyma. He had arranged for the elephants of war to be his agents of destruction, but with the Hebrews lined up in rows, the elephants turned and attacked the royal troops instead, and the Hebrews celebrated their miraculous deliverance with an annual feast. True or false, perhaps that story is a better reason for the sacrifice of four elephants. Whatever the truth of it, the elephants refused to die without a very great deal of frantic trumpeting, and the foul stink of the sacrifice hung over the city for days on end.

Philopator was not slow to reward his troops, but it was the sister who handed out the two gold *minas* for every man. Aye, and her brother made her pay out of her own funds, saying, *You promised them the two gold minas. You will have to keep your promise.*

If seventy-five thousand men returned from Raphia, how much did that rash promise cost the sister? Seshat, goddess of Arithmetic says seventy thousand foot and five thousand horse at two *minas* a head equals one hundred and fifty thousand *minas*, or thirty million drachmas. Sixty *minas* make one talent. Arsinoë Gamma gave away two thousand five hundred talents, or three hundred thousand gold pieces, a sum that would have built the Pharos three times over. It should be no surprise that Philopator was angry with his sister. But the result of Arsinoë Gamma making every soldier rich for half a year, was to make her popular ever after. Philopator never let her forget her reckless extravagance, but without that bribe of gold for every man Egypt might have been defeated.

Philopator decreed that the anniversary of the battle was to be celebrated every year until there were years no longer, and the five days that followed the anniversary became a festival of wild dancing and drunkenness. The victory at Raphia was meant to mark the start of a glorious new era for Egypt, but the glory would not, in truth, last very long. It was the end of the glory of the Ptolemies rather than the beginning: nothing that came afterwards would quite match it.

Philopator sailed as far as Elephantine in his great barge, to celebrate his victory, taking the sister with him, quarrelling all the way up-River. He performed the ritual in the temples and was welcomed even by the priests and scribes at Thebes. He thought the Two Lands looked happy enough. He showed the teeth himself, and although his – or Sosibios' – taxes upon every essential item from dates to pigs were still high, he saw no sign of unrest.

The war is over, he said to Horemakhet. *We have peace, so much peace that our great ship of war will never be needed.* He looked at his royal barge, thinking it rather small. He thought again of his vow to outdo his father in everything. And so he laid the keel of his Thalamegos, a pleasure boat, or floating palace in the Egyptian style.

The great golden barge of Pharaoh was, of course, nothing new. Snofru had, two thousand years before, his great River barge, *Adoration of the Two Lands,* one hundred cubits long. Amenhotep the Third had had his giant pleasure ship, *Shining in Truth.* The barge of Sesostris, at two hundred and eighty cubits, was just as long as Philopator's great ship of war. Philopator merely copied the idea, made believe he had thought of it himself. Even so, his pleasure boat was two hundred cubits long, thirty cubits wide, and towered forty cubits above the water – as high as ten or twelve men. It had saloons, bedchambers, colonnades. Everything was of precious woods, of ivory, or gilded bronze. The dining-room, in the Egyptian style, had black-and-white banded columns, capitals like rose blossoms, and lotus flower decorations. The Thalamegos was for the River, not for the sea. Lacking the catapults and space for the military, it was meant not for war but for peace: utterly unwarlike, you might say, like Philopator himself.

Philopator thought he had peace, but he was wise not to unstrap the gecko talisman that brought him victory, because, in fact, his war was not over. The Battle of Raphia was just the beginning of Antiokhos Megas his military activities. That king recovered quick from his crushing defeat: Philopator's war with Syria would not be finished for another six years.

Philopator became more difficult, said he felt safe only behind closed doors, when he was with his mistress and his catamite, or with his men of letters, poets, grammarians, philosophers, the ones among whom he spent his more sober hours – the ones who flattered him. He trusted Agathokles of Samos, and Agathokleia, and Oinanthe, and nobody else, and it was, perhaps, because these three exercised their wits to keep his boredom at bay, finding for him ever some exquisite new pleasure, but never losing sight of the fact that his greatest pleasure must be themselves.

Hatred was disguised as love. Already Oinanthe and her children helped themselves to Philopator's golden belongings, and laughed behind his back because he never noticed anything had gone.

Philopator should not have trusted either Agathokles or Agathokleia one fingerbreadth: they were by no means fit to have any kind of authority. They were neither so loyal that he should have blabbed all his secrets in their hearing, nor so very wise that he should have asked for their opinion about affairs of state. They were not so anxious about his well-being that he should have let them taste his food. Agathokles and Agathokleia, egged on by their mother, were thinking of putting poison in his plate themselves; they were the very ones who were plotting to destroy the rule of King Ptolemy Philopator and smash his House to pieces.

4.9

Kakogamia

Sosibios bullied Philopator about marrying the sister as soon as the campaign in Syria was over. He told Philopator blunt, *Megaleios, if you had died in your tent at Raphia instead of Andreas, there would have been no Ptolemy to reign in your place . . . If you were to die tomorrow – there would still be no Ptolemy alive to be king instead of you.*

Never to mention death, Philopator said. *Never to speak of tomorrow.* But he knew what Sosibios would say next.

And what would happen then? Sosibios said. *Egypt would have a native pharaoh, the Greeks would be thrown out. Do you want the High Priest of Thebes to be king in your place? Do you want to see Horemakhet wearing the khepresh?*

Face impassive, Philopator sniffed, shrugged, pushed a heavy vase on to the floor, and began his spinning dance among the wreckage.

You must marry the sister, Sosibios said. *She is a beautiful young woman, a woman of fierce spirit. She will be of the greatest help to his Majesty . . .*

Philopator stopped spinning and put on his face of anger. *I will not marry the sister*, he said. *I would rather marry Agathokleia. I would rather marry old Oinanthe than my sister.*

His Majesty may not marry his own servants, Sosibios said, rather cold.

Philopator spun round, laughing, *I am Pharaoh, I shall do as I please.*

Zeus wooed Hera, Sosibios said, *for three hundred years, but his Majesty will not live quite so long as that . . . We urge him to marry the sister as soon as possible . . . Far better to marry your sister . . . Far better to keep the blood of the Ptolemies pure and undiluted.*

Sosibios was good at talking a man into doing what he did not want to do. And Sosibios kept talking.

Do you not think, Megaleios, he said, *that you owe the sister a debt of gratitude for helping you to win your battle at Raphia?*

Philopator spat on the mosaic for contempt. *I do not,* he said. *The debt is hers, thirty million drachmas of debt.* He started up the humming that went with the Gallos dance, and spun himself out of the audience hall altogether.

For her part, Arsinoë Gamma did not want to marry Philopator either. *I cannot marry a mother-slayer,* she said to herself. *I cannot marry the man who murdered his own father.* Though she did not breathe her thoughts to her brother, for fear of being murdered herself. Such things, such terrible things were never spoken of, but bottled up. She pleaded with Sosibios, *Let me marry some foreign prince, so that I may quit Alexandria, and escape from my brother who is so weird . . .*

But no, Sosibios would not hear of it. *Think, Basilissa, of all the wives and queens murdered at foreign courts,* he crooned. *Remember what happened to your Great Aunt Theoxena in Sicily.*

When Arsinoë Gamma made no reply, he raised his voice. *Have you forgotten what happened to your Great Aunt Ptolemaïs? Do you want to suffer the same fate as Berenike Syra?*

Silence from the Royal Daughter.

All those unhappy women, Sosibios purred. *Far better to stay at home and marry your brother. Better to stay at home and stay alive.*

Would that I had been sent away, she said. *I might have fared better instead of worse. Far better for Arsinoë Gamma if she had never been born . . .*

Then even Horemakhet tried to persuade her, saying, *No other woman in the world, asked to be Lady of the Two Lands, would refuse. Marry the brother, Basilissa, keep the blood of the Ptolemies pure – it will be for the best.*

But she said, in tears, *Excellency, for the Greeks such a marriage is repulsive. Long ago I swore to my mother that I should never marry my own brother.*

Then something made Philopator change his heart, and really, Arsinoë Gamma had no choice once he agreed to marry her. In all things she must do what her brother directed. It was unthinkable for a Greek girl to refuse the bridegroom of her family's choice. To disagree with Pharaoh was treason. If he wanted her to marry him, she needs must do so, whatever her private thoughts. And though her mother had disapproved, the brother–sister marriage was what her father had wanted. *Perhaps, after all,* she thought, *to be Queen of Egypt might not be such a bad thing. At least I shall not be married to one of my brother's enemies . . .*

True, but she happened to be her brother's best enemy herself.

What, though, was it that changed his Majesty's heart? A simple thing, in the end. It was Agathokles of Samos. *Ptolemaios,* he said, *marry the sister. You will not have to give up Agathokleia and me. All four of us will share the same bed* . . . Philopator would do anything this most handsome of men told him. Agathokles had a hold over this king, as if he had him bound by the most powerful magic. Perhaps, indeed, that was the truth of it: that between them, Agathokles and Agathokleia had bewitched him.

The marriage of Ptolemy Philopator to his sister took place not long after the Battle of Raphia. Arsinoë Gamma wore the family jewels: the Greek diadem of gold leaves, the Greek earrings with Eros and Aphrodite, the golden girdle, the snake's head anklets. The snake bracelets went all the way up her thin arms, alternating with just about every good luck talisman in the world. She was now the equal of Agathe Tykhe herself, the goddess of Good Luck, but, for sure, she needed to be. This queen had very great need of good luck, and no, she would have none whatever, none.

Arsinoë Gamma dazzled the company with her beauty, they said, and it was not mere politeness. She jingled as she walked, glittered as she sat, unveiled, smiling a nervous half-smile, dressed in the red *peplos* of a goddess. She was thin, not so thin as Arsinoë Beta, but thin enough, and every man in Alexandria knew that Philopator preferred a fat woman, like Agathokleia.

Philopator himself, utterly hardened, dead to shame, wore the saffron yellow dress of the Galloi for his marriage. He wore his hair long, arranged just like his sister's hair, with scarlet ribbons in it, and every man had to make believe there was nothing out of the ordinary. Aye, then the dancing feet began to pound the mosaic floor. Even on the day of his wedding Philopator threw open the bronze doors of his audience hall with a great cry of joy, and the eunuchs of Kybele bounded in, hundreds of them, with their drums and cymbals, flutes and trumpets, all wearing the saffron-yellow dress.

A near-naked Agathokles of Samos danced the indecent Greek dance that involves kicking the buttocks with the heels. A scantily clad Agathokleia breathed clouds of flame – jealous Agathokleia, who would have liked to be married to his Majesty herself. And Oinanthe of Samos, wearing little more than a yellow veil, danced the violent and indecent Greek dance in which she crossed her feet like tongs, making Philopator scream with delight.

Arsinoë Gamma stared at the ceiling throughout, thinking of the shame brought to her once noble House, thinking of her broken promise to her mother. She trembled to think of what her brother must do to her that night, the crime that was a gross affront to the gods of Hellas, just about the worst thing in the world that any Greek could do, short of murdering his own mother – and Philopator had done that already.

Sophokles the Greek it was that said, *All Girls are afraid of marriage, they are supposed to be.* And so it was in this marriage: Arsinoë Gamma was afraid, very afraid, because she was meant to praise her husband and say, *Everything is good, all is well,* when it so very clearly was not.

Horemakhet said, that day, the customary words to their Majesties, *May the heart of the wife be like the heart of her husband, that they may be free from quarrels* . . . But Horemakhet saw that even on the day of their marriage this husband and wife could hardly bring themselves to look at each other. Their hearts were quite different. They did not think alike upon any matter, and they would quarrel.

May Osiris give you both life, prosperity, health, Horemakhet said, *and a great happy old age,* but he knew there would be no long lifetime, no great happy old age for either of them, any more than there had been for their parents.

No, Arsinoë Gamma was not happily married. She was *dreadfully* married, and all through the wedding ceremonies her thoughts were fixed on one thing: that if she was married to her brother she must bring forth monsters. She vowed the vow in her heart, then and there, *I shall never have any child by my brother.*

Philopator did make the proper move to do what a husband should do on the day of his wedding. He shouted for the music and dancing to stop, and cried, *Now I shall kiss my wife, my lovely lovely wife.* He threw his arms about the sister's neck and thrust his tongue between her lips. But Arsinoë Gamma squealed, *Oh– Oh– Oh– Oh–* and put up her hand to stop him, slapping his face. *Oh, do not, do not, Brother, it is horrible. You stink of wine,* she said, pushing him away from her.

Aye, she said *Do not* . . . *Do not* . . . just like her mother, in her mother's voice. And yes, Philopator turned away from her, as if he had been stung by hornets.

Our sister does not love us, he shrieked, *let us embrace Agathokleia instead.* And then, *Our sister hates us, we shall have to kiss Agathokles,* and then again, *Oinanthe is the only one that loves me, let me kiss her lips* . . . so that Arsinoë Gamma could not but see, and be disgusted all the more.

Agathokleia and Agathokles kissed his Majesty happily enough. But did they love him in return? No, their affection for him was quite false. They loved each other, brother and sister, Egyptian-style, not his Majesty.

Music, Philopator screamed, *dancing, be merry.* And the cacophony started up again, louder than before. And so it would go on: the outrageous behaviour, the wild dancing, everything next to madness, but no sign of true love, for the rest of his reign.

That night, when the drunkenness was more than she could bear, and the dancing disgusted her more than ever, Arsinoë Gamma made her excuses and said to her brother-husband that she must retire to her bed. Sure, now Philopator made as if to embrace his wife, kissing her again on the cheeks and mouth, this time with the lascivious smack of a kiss hitherto reserved for the flaming lips of Agathokleia, the burning hot buttocks of Agathokles of Samos, then trying to kiss her all the way up her arms, but his wife fled from him, wailing, *Oh– Oh– Oh– I cannot bear it, Brother, I do not wish it, please to leave me alone . . .*

Philopator's wild laughter followed her down the corridors.

Husband, he yelled, *call me Husband, not Brother.*

This new husband did not show up for the ploughing that night, but stayed awake, drinking, with Agathokles and Agathokleia sitting in his lap, their arms draped about his neck, and the Galloi and the Geloiastai, the eunuchs and the Laughter-Makers, danced round them until the sun came up orange over Alexandria like a ball of fire breathed from Agathokleia's mouth.

Nor did Philopator show his face for the ploughing the next night or any other night that month, but left his sister-wife alone indeed. Some called it a *kakogamia*, a bad, ill-starred marriage from the very first, for the wife would not go near her husband, and the husband would not go near his wife.

As for Arsinoë Gamma, all the oracles said her marriage should last but twelve years and she found the thought of some comfort. *Twelve days,* she murmured, *married to my monster of a brother would be long enough. In twelve years, with a little help from the gods, perhaps I may be dead, one of the lucky ones.*

Aye, there could only be four thousand three hundred and eighty days until she was free of him, whether by his death or hers, or by divorce, or by whatever horrors the fates had stored up for them both.

We have come a long way, even so, do you not think, Stranger, since the wicked marriage of Ptolemy Philadelphos to Arsinoë Beta? For nobody complained about the marriage of Ptolemy Philopator to Arsinoë Gamma – apart, of course, from the husband and wife themselves.

As for the likelihood of them producing an heir for Egypt, Sosibios laughed for despair, thinking, *How will such a thing ever happen, if the parties refuse to climb into bed with each other?* There would be no heir, Stranger, for years and years. As many as seven years would pass before the belly of this queen began to grow big with the next Horus. Nobody could make Arsinoë Gamma enter her brother's bedchamber. Not even Agathokles could persuade his Majesty to get into bed with the sister. Nor, in truth, did he want him to. Agathokles preferred to be in bed with his Majesty himself, for to be in his bed meant to have access to his riches, to be given everything he asked for, to be in total control of the Lord of the Two Lands.

Aye, Philopator liked to kiss the hot rosebud of Agathokles of Samos better than his sister's cold thin lips. He preferred to squeeze the buxom Agathokleia rather than the scrawny Arsinoë. His distaste for his sister's body was just the same as hers for his.

Horemakhet worried about what would happen to Egypt if Philopator died without leaving an heir: either Sosibios must take the kingship, he thought, or Agathokles; or there would be revolution, followed by a native Egyptian king on the throne of the Two Lands. An Egyptian king might indeed be a goodly thing, but the Macedonians were the ones who knew how to fight off Egypt's enemies. For seven long years Horemakhet regularly urged the king to do his duty as Pharaoh – and give Egypt an heir to the throne.

So very often he asked him, *If his Majesty dies without an heir, who shall be King of Egypt?*

So often Philopator replied, *Excellency, the future may take care of itself.*

One time he even said, *Often in the past the most comely youth in the land has been king . . . Why not let Agathokles of Samos be king? He would make a handsome pharaoh.* And he watched the look of horror spread across the man's face.

Horemakhet, despairing, said, *Wisdom Book of Ankhsheshonq: He who is afraid to sleep with his wife will not have children . . .*

It was a mistake, Philopator said. *Agathokles persuaded me. I did not wish it.*

This miserable girl, Arsinoë Gamma, had been made her brother's wife simply so that a legitimate heir of the blood royal might be bred from her. But Arsinoë Gamma's belly stayed flat. The milk did not rise in her breasts. No happy laughter of children was heard from the women's quarters.

What, then, you may very well ask, was the marriage of Ptolemy Philopator to Arsinoë Gamma good for, if it was not good for the ploughing of legitimate children? It was good for Egypt and the House of Ptolemy, because this brother and sister were associated upon the throne as the *Theoi Philopatores,* the Father-Loving Gods. At the insistence of Horemakhet and Sosibios together, they did perform all the public duties of the King and Queen of Egypt – temple rituals, temple-founding, receiving foreign ambassadors.

They kept up the pretence of good relations between them, smiling the half-smile in public, while in private they hardly spoke, except to exchange some furious insult.

They called Arsinoë Gamma Royal Daughter, Royal Sister, Great Royal Wife, Great Lady of the Two Lands. However much she despised her husband in private for his feminine posing, for his debauched ways, for his neglect of her, in public she did everything that the Queen should do, and Egypt loved her for it. She shared the burden of the kingship, hearing petitions, reading state papers. This was what the king's wife was for: to help his Majesty. She did not hide herself away, sewing and weaving, but looked to the royal stables, the Library, the Mouseion. She had her fleet of merchant ships upon the River. All this she did not for her brother but for her parents' sake. She was as popular as Arsinoë Beta had been. Philopator hardly less so. He was the King who had won at Raphia. Of course he could do no wrong. Nobody hurled rocks at the Greeks just then. Even in Memphis they hurled nothing but flowers at the saviour of Egypt. But in private the brother ignored his sister as much as he could.

The marriage of this brother and sister is a puzzle, is it not? Perhaps we may find a clue to the riddle by looking at what was the gift given by this reluctant husband to his deeply unwanted wife. For he gave her a living gift: the services of Agathokleia his concubine, the one who liked to light fires, to be her part-time *paratiltria,* the woman who plucks hairs from her mistress's body, makes ready her bath, and brushes her hair. Whose idea was it? Not Philopator's. By no means. He liked to have Agathokleia at his side. No, it was the idea of Sosibios and Agathokles together, done for their own wicked purposes.

Agathokleia smiled, and was helpful. She called Arsinoë Gamma *Tati*, like other handmaidens, and made as if to be not only her servant but also her friend. Arsinoë Gamma now saw more of Agathokleia than she did of anybody else. From time to time she would disappear in order to attend to the needs of Pharaoh, but she always returned with some goodly thing for Arsinoë Gamma to eat, some new piece of fine purple cloth. Arsinoë Gamma, then, thought better of Agathokleia of Samos and, unfortunately, began to trust her, and reveal her secret thoughts.

Unfortunately, you ask?

Yes, Stranger, because Agathokleia was the one who would kill her.

4.10

Parasites

Agathokles of Samos and Agathokleia, they kept their place in his Majesty's affections. Sometimes they egged him on to do things he might not otherwise have done – such as handing Agathokleia over to be his wife's waiting-woman; such as marking his initiation into the cult of Dionysos by having his right leg tattooed with an ivy leaf above the ankle. He was proud to be an initiate, proud of his ivy tattoo. Agathokles had suggested it.

Horemakhet disapproved, of course, saying, *Pharaoh does not defile his body with the symbols of foreign gods,* but he might have saved his breath. Philopator respected Horemakhet well enough, but he respected Agathokles more, and as if to show his defiance he made the tattoos spring all the way up his leg.

Agathokles of Samos rose steadily in importance. He was with his master day and night, his helper in everything. He had his own body tattooed with ivy leaves, the same as his master, and in the same places – upon the ankle, upon the thigh, upon his buttocks. Master and servant grew leafier together, the one copying the other: Agathokles the mirror of Philopator, Philopator the mirror of Agathokles. Every day and every night was given up to the worship of Dionysos as god of Wine. Agathokles would drink six, seven, eight bowls. He drank as deep as any Greek ever drank; as much as Herakles. And Philopator kept pace with him, bowl for bowl, trying to outdrink him.

Agathokles had always been among the King's favourites – for there were others – but as the years flew by he became Philopator's only favourite. Agathokles got rid of the rest of them. One was drowned in a swimming accident. Another fell down a marble staircase. A third embarked upon some kitchen carelessness, eating wolfbane instead of horseradish.

Agathokles kept rising, made sure he did. In the year after Raphia he held the eponymous state priesthood, the office given to whatever man his Majesty held in the highest esteem. Aye, it was Agathokles of Samos, he of the glowing olive skin and glistening black eyes, who never stopped smiling, as if he thought there was no limit to what he could do. And then Philopator made him Priest of Alexander. Perhaps Agathokles deserved it. But there were, all the same, men who looked askance at the courtier who had got where he was by being a catamite and a *kinaidos*, a boy who sold his body for men to do what they liked with it. Such a man caused very great concern among the Greeks, for if he thought nothing of selling his body, he would think nothing of selling out the interests of his country. For the nobleman, the *kalokagathos*, virtue of soul and beauty of body go hand in hand: a fair face must mean a noble spirit. But Agathokles was no nobleman. He had physical beauty, but a freed slave could not be expected to behave nobly. Men watched the trouble in the making, for although Agathokles was Priest of Alexander and a minister of the crown, Philopator did not stop treating him like his servant.

Agathokles, he would say, *bring wine,* and Agathokles would bring it.

Agathokles, he would say, *fetch in the flamingo* . . . and the Priest of Alexander would have to wait on his Majesty, and take away his empty plate afterwards.

Agathokles put up with it, because he put up with everything – thinking of what was to come – but he did not like it, of course he did not, even though, in return, he might often make Philopator do exactly what he told him.

So, honours went to Agathokles, and, at the same time, ill-treatment. The same applied to Arsinoë Gamma. Honours did not altogether pass her by. When Philopator put up his famous Homereion, the temple to honour the poet Homer, he showed Time and the World sitting behind the great man, and Time had the face of Philopator, and the World had the face of his sister – granting Homer, as it were, his immortality even above themselves. At least the faces of Agathokles and Agathokleia did not feature on his coins. Philopator was not quite so far gone in madness as to think of allowing that. No, it was Arsinoë Gamma's face that appeared on his tetradrachms and oktodrachms, wearing her hair in corkscrew locks, and the proper Greek veil. On the reverse side was the Horn of Plenty bound with a ribbon, and a star. The sister had her proper share of public glory. The private side of things was not so glorious. She was called Fair of Face, Great in the Palace, the Mistress of Happiness, but it was really Agathokleia of Samos to whom these titles applied. Sure, Arsinoë Gamma wore the queen's headdress of two ostrich plumes with the cow's horns and the solar disk on top; sure they worshipped her as the Tenth Muse, but in the flesh her face was often sad. Even on the coins she looked miserable.

In the great white marble palace of Ptolemy Philopator the chamber still existed, near to the great kitchens, where the cranes and swans were kept in the dark, their eyelids sewn up with papyrus thread, being fattened for the royal table. Arsinoë Gamma was kept in the half-dark of the *gynaikeion* much like this, and her eyelids might just as well have been sewn up for all that she was allowed to see. In truth Philopator treated her not even so well as the chickens, for Arsinoë Gamma was not being fattened up but deliberately made thinner. It was as if somebody wished this wife would go away, as if somebody did not want her, but wished her dead. Indeed, the day was not far distant when Arsinoë Gamma would fly to the sky and become a star herself.

Who, then, wished the charming Arsinoë Gamma ill? Who was her great enemy, if not her husband himself? Agathokleia, the *paratiltria*, was her enemy. She thought that if Arsinoë Gamma could be gotten rid of, Agathokleia might be Mistress of the Two Lands instead.

When she drove out in her wicker carriage Agathokleia waved to the crowds on Kanopic Street as if she were the Queen herself, not just his Majesty's concubine. The palace guards saluted her with respect, knowing that she was the one who could raise them to higher rank, make generals of them yet. Agathokleia already played a great part in ruling Egypt, for she ruled and overruled the Pharaoh.

However grand she became, Agathokleia still liked to amuse herself by lighting fires. From time to time she would scratch the name of Arsinoë Gamma on a strip of papyrus, set fire to it and watch it burn, laughing. She could still breathe fire like the *ouraios* serpent. Once a fire-eater always a fire-eater, as they say. Her kisses were still delivered with the unmistakable hint of naphtha. Agathokleia still breathed fire. Her friendliness was just like her brother's friendship with Philopator, quite false.

Those coins of Philopator were just the same as his father's, with the eagle standing upon the thunderbolt, but the reverse showed him as Dionysos, god of Frenzy, wearing the diadem entwined with an ivy wreath. Upon his shoulder rested the *thyrsos*, or wand, of Dionysos. *Call me Dionysos*, he said. *I am Dionysos, the Thirteenth God.*

Philopator liked to toss these coins of his. On the days when the tetradrachm came down upon the eagle side, he would wear the *pschent* crown, the *chendjyt* kilt, the vulture collar, clutch the crook and flail, and attend to some of Pharaoh's business. On days when the coin came down on the reverse side, he would play at being Dionysos and drink deep. By night he would lead the *komos* of courtiers into the palace gardens, dancing round the palm trees, each man hanging on to the cloaktails of the man in front. Often he fell down, incapable from wine. Sosibios controlled Egypt: Ptolemy Philopator could hardly control himself.

The ivy leaves crept up his arms and legs, slow but sure, then across his body. Just as ivy, the parasite, will creep up a tree and strangle it, Agathokles and Agathokleia twined themselves tighter about the tree that was Ptolemy Philopator.

4.11

The Lightness of Feathers

Nobody ever strangled the High Priest of Ptah at Memphis, not in forty-eight generations. But hardly five years into the new reign Young Anemhor, the old High Priest of Ptah that had retired, the father of Horemakhet, took to his bed and did not get out of it. Nefertiti, his daughter-in-law, was the one who nursed him. She brought him every goodly thing to eat that might help him to recover, but Anemhor refused to eat. On his lips from dawn to dusk was the plea to Ra to make his heart light in the Balance.

Father, your heart will float away, Horemakhet said. *It is already lighter than the feather of Maat.*

Young Anemhor was old, seventy-two years, one month and twenty-three days old. His wife, Herankh, had been six years in the Field of Rushes, waiting for him. Anemhor thought it was time he joined her.

His last words were, *May heaven rain fresh myrrh, may it drip with incense.* Then he closed his eyes and slept the bronze sleep.

Horemakhet embalmed his father after the Egyptian custom. He placed the bandaged body in three gilded wooden coffins, one inside the other, and buried Anemhor with the other High Priests of Ptah, upon the desert plateau opposite Memphis. On the side of the old man's coffin was painted the usual pair of eyes, so that the dead one could see what went on in the world he had left behind.

During the procession to the necropolis it was Horemakhet's wife, Nefertiti, the beautiful one, his daughter-in-law, that wailed for him, tears streaming down her cheeks, rubbing dust into her hair.

The ceremony of Opening the Mouth his son Horemakhet performed, in order to revive the dead man's body so that his spirit might dwell in it again. The coffin was in the upright position, standing upon its feet. Horemakhet burned incense. He chanted the words of the ritual. He poured water over the coffin. He touched the painted eyes, ears, nose and mouth with the adze, so that his father might pass into the next world breathing, hearing, seeing, and the body of the dead man was made anew.

Afterwards, Horemakhet walked with slow steps through the great Ptah Temple. His eyes lingered on the great pylons, their massive cedar doors faced with gold, the forest of bright painted columns, the Temple of Hathor, the Palace of Merneptah. Horemakhet's heart was proud for his father, proud for his long life spent in the service of Ptah, Pharaoh, the Two Lands. Now his father had gone, and Horemakhet was master of the temple himself, without the wisdom of the old man to guide him, but his life was just the same: dedicated to duty. In his rank of Master of Secrets there was nothing this man did not know. He was the Magician, the one who enchants the sky, the earth, the mountains, the waters. He understood the language of birds and snakes, even the roaring of the crocodile. If he said, *Oh, all you gods and goddesses, turn your face towards me* . . . if he spoke the words of power, the gods and goddesses must obey him.

Horemakhet had made rain fall, even so far south as Elephantine. He had been himself the Magician of Imhotep, He Who Comes in Peace, the god who sends sleep, the Interpreter of Dreams. There was nothing he did not know about the world of the sleeping. His gaze was fixed. His eyes were unblinking. He had direct access to the gods. He said of himself, *I mastered every magical art, there was nothing thereof which passed by me,* but it was not boastfulness. Men said of this man, *Even before the tongue has questioned, Horemakhet knows the answer.*

The most important thing he knew about just then was the future: that what lay ahead was serious unrest, violent revolts, bloody revolution. Aye, blood and more blood.

4.12

Strong Bull

Like Horus, Pharaoh had trampled over his enemy. He had ridden into Memphis on horseback wearing full Macedonian battle dress, but with the *khepresh* crown upon his head. His image had been carved in stone, with the King of Syria, Antiokhos Megas, kneeling before him; behind him stood the sister, Arsinoë Gamma, dressed as Isis, with the other great gods of Egypt looking on. Never before had a Macedonian king been shown like this by the priests of Egypt. Philopator was the rightful Pharaoh, and the high priests treated him as Pharaoh, bowing down seven times, kissing the dust before his feet, because he was a god, a living god, and there was none like him in all Egypt. His private life, degraded though it might have been, did not affect his divinity. In public Philopator did whatever was required of Pharaoh, and stopped himself from laughing.

But also because he was Pharaoh, the priests must make their usual demands.

Now Horemakhet said to him, *Might his Majesty be pleased to show, indeed, his gratitude to the gods by making some gift to the temples?*

Philopator agreed to put up the red granite architrave of the east gate of the Temple of Ptah at Memphis, and the masons set to work. It was a fine architrave, but a small thing: not enough, and already too late. The truth was that the revolts began as soon as Philopator came to the throne. Now they started up again, worse, with stone throwing and beatings, and running fights between Macedonians and Egyptians, and any Greek-style house likely to be set on fire. Blood flowed wherever Philopator's soldiers set their boots, a banquet for flies.

Up-River at Thebes the priests rejoiced, for the horoscopists' forecast was for thirty-two years of rebellion, and the feeling in the south country was that Ptolemy Philopator could not survive it, but would soon be calling for his ship to take him away to Macedon. Thebes looked forward to having a dark-faced pharaoh for the first time in over one hundred years.

What, then, had gone wrong? After the Battle of Raphia the twenty thousand native Egyptian soldiers marched home, full of their triumph, but also filled with a strange discontent. They had put to flight the sixty-eight thousand Syrian troops. So far under the Ptolemies the Egyptians had been resigned to their fate, more or less happy so long as they were left alone. Now they began to have hopes of changing everything. Under Philopator the price of every foodstuff soared. The galloping price of grain made even bread expensive. And now Philopator – or Sosibios – raised taxes again, to pay for his Syrian wars. Aye, the natives began to think they could stand up to these Macedonians and do to them what they had just done to Antiokhos of Syria, grind their faces in the dust – and throw them out of Egypt altogether. They had seen how the Macedonians were terrified in the phalanx, how their armour rattled, how they shat their legs like cowards. The Egyptians no longer feared the ones who spoke Greek. Not unlike Agathokles and Agathokleia, they began to think they were better than their masters.

Sosibios heard about it, of course, for Sosibios heard about everything. His spies – the infamous Ears of Sosibios – sat in every village, listening. But now it seemed that everything his government did was designed to enrage the people and make them rise up in protest. It even looked as if the ageing Sosibios was losing his wits, for he seemed to be making all the wrong decisions. Or was it the young Agathokles of Samos, to whom Sosibios had delegated so very much of his business? Aye, Agathokles, his right hand man, who had been given too much power and had let it go to his head.

During the crisis Philopator stopped drinking wine. He even stopped dancing the Gallos dance, for a while – an unheard of thing.

What can we do? the new sober, unlaughing Philopator asked the High Priest of Ptah, worried for the welfare of Egypt.

Wisdom of Merikare, Horemakhet said. *Do not deal evilly with the south country, but be lenient.* He gave Philopator his support. He would not betray this king. With tears in his eyes he said to him, *Behold, I will not leave thee, Megaleios.*

Nor did Horemakhet break off relations with Thebes, but kept searching for the best way to restore the balance of Maat, the balance of order. On Horemakhet's advice, this foreign king tried to attach the Egyptians to his rule by embarking upon a massive programme for building and restoring their temples; by doing everything that a native Egyptian pharaoh would have done in the same circumstances.

He ordered work to continue on the great Temple of Horus at Apollonopolis. He began finishing the temple at Elephantine founded by his father.

It was a brave effort, but a complete new temple did not make much difference in time of revolution. The risings dragged on all the same, without any great battles or prolonged sieges, just fights between groups of rebels and the Macedonian troops and government officers. Bricks were thrown. There was shouting in the streets, angry crowds, much trouble. As the power of Sosibios and Agathokles grew, so Philopator's ability to control weakened. And Sosibios knew nothing of ruling through kindly acts. Philopator did his best, but Sosibios and Agathokles were stronger than he was. His Majesty's lenience was outweighed by his ministers' cruelty. When he suggested following his mother's strategy, saying, *Why not reduce the taxes?*, Sosibios and Agathokles together shouted him down. Aye, and he did what they told him, kept quiet, like a kicked dog.

Horemakhet, speaking with King Ptolemy, did not know what to do or what to say, apart from condemning the violence. *The revolution is nothing to do with me,* he said. When Philopator said to him, *Would you not like to see an*

Egyptian pharaoh upon the throne once again? – as if to test him – the High Priest said, *No, no, I knew nothing of it. We would not dream of supporting Thebes against his Majesty.*

But Sosibios said to Agathokles, *How can Horemakhet not have known? He is the man who knows everything.* He said, *How can the High Priest of Memphis not support an Egyptian revolution?* Aye, and Sosibios did whatever he could, from then on, to smash the power of Memphis, to break the hold the Egyptian priests had over the people. He reduced the government grants to temple funds, withheld all good will, and made every last thing difficult for Horemakhet. It was as if Horemakhet had his two hands tied behind his back, aye, like a prisoner of war.

And yet, Horemakhet stayed loyal to Ptolemy throughout. His firm loyalty to this man who had not chosen to be Pharaoh but had his office thrust upon him, this man who had, at bottom, a great love of the Two Lands, was not false. Horemakhet had come to trust the Laughing One, who could not help himself in his folly, but did not pretend to be what he was not; who did the best he could, even if his best was not so wonderful.

Horemakhet did not trust the unsmiling Sosibios, whose answer to violence was to be violent in return. *Hatred cannot be cured by hatred,* Horemakhet said to him, *only by love.* But Sosibios seemed not to understand such things. He never did stop hating. He sent tens of thousands of troops up-River, and it was like fanning the flames, for they had orders to take no prisoners, but to kill any man who offered violence.

The High Priest did his best for peace. He said even to Sosibios, *Do not do to a man what you dislike, for he will do the same as you.*

Sosibios ignored him. Often he ignored Philopator as well. He was bored by Philopator's drunkenness, his lethargy. *His Majesty will not last long like this,* he said to Agathokles, *he will drink himself to death. And so will you.*

Agathokles smiled, and, as usual, said little. Deeds, not words, for Agathokles. He went on drinking. *Homage to Dionysos,* he laughed, *homage to Hathor.* And Philopator did and said the same, copying Agathokles, obeying Agathokles, the one who led, the one who made the decisions.

Sosibios was not delighted by the orgies in honour of Dionysos, the shouting, singing, dancing and drinking that filled Philopator's days and nights, in which, if he showed his face, Sosibios must join, whether he liked it or not, and dance.

Dancing, Sosibios said, *is not for real men like Sosibios; dancing is for half men.*

Dancing was not for high priests of Egypt either. The Dioiketes was the one who had to dance. He often spent the whole day dancing with his Majesty, trying to get him to write his name at the bottom of a piece of papyrus.

And Ptolemy Philopator, Lord of the Two Lands, lost in his whirling trance, dreaming of the mysteries of Kybele and Attis, cutting his arms and catching his blood in a golden cup for an offering to the goddess, carried on dancing. The royal blood often dripped on to the mosaic floor, followed him in a trail down the marble corridors of his palace. It would not be long before his blood poured out in a flood, like the bull's blood in the *taurobolion*. Strong Bull was weakening. And Antiokhos of Syria was strong again.

4.13

Pleasure

For four years after the battle of Raphia, Antiokhos Megas concentrated his efforts on dealing with internal troubles. Soon he would fix his eye upon Egypt again, everybody knew that, but for the moment he had his hands full. Philopator did not worry. Sosibios would worry for him. But Sosibios thought, *So long as Antiokhos leaves Egypt alone he can do what he pleases.*

Unchecked, Antiokhos grew bolder. He had gained his experience of handling a great army. Now the Mauryan prince Sophagasenos – on the borders of India – recognized the supremacy of the Syrian empire. Even the Parthian king, Arsakes, acknowledged that Antiokhos was *Megas* indeed, Great, the greatest king in the world.

And why was there such indifference in Alexandria to what went on? Sosibios was growing old and delegating more and more of his powers to Agathokles. Sosibios was beginning to be tired of government. What energy he had was used up stamping on revolts at home. Abroad, in such circumstances, might take care of itself.

There had been nine years of war, on and off. But now the war came to a stop. Antiokhos was occupied elsewhere. Horemakhet consulted the Apis Oracle, who promised nine years of peace, that would last – until the next war with Syria. Apis forecast, indeed, that most wonderful thing: three thousand two hundred and eighty-five days of peace. He forecast also that Philopator would not live to see the end of it. This news Horemakhet kept to himself. And so his Majesty gave his days up entirely to pleasure.

The pleasure of Arsinoë Gamma remained, as ever, elusive. *Her* spirits was used up by worry – worry that Egypt had no heir to the throne, worry that it was still her duty to produce him, worry that the House of Ptolemy was heading for extinction.

Night after night, Agathokles and Agathokleia slept in the great gold bed with Ptolemy Philopator: the person who did not lay herself down between the purple and gold sheets was his sister-wife.

Horemakhet, in desperation, begged Philopator to think of Egypt without a pharaoh, saying, *A man to whom no children have been born is like one who has never existed. His name will not be remembered.*

Philopator danced out of the room, laughing.

4.14

The Bull-Calf

Two years, four years, passed since Ptolemy Philopator married his sister, and no child, not even a monster, fell into the hands of old Oinanthe, the Great Royal Midwife, who sat idle in the empty nursery, eating dates, swigging the fine wine of Pharaoh, laughing, growing stouter in the belly herself, instead of her Majesty.

Smile, Oinanthe cried, *you are the Queen of Egypt.* But no, Arsinoë Gamma did not smile. Oinanthe did not amuse her.

Aye, Arsinoë Gamma her belly stayed as flat as ever, and her breasts stayed empty of milk, so that she began to think she might never bring forth the Ptolemy who should be the fresh Lord of the Two Lands. To be childless troubled her, because it must mean the end of the Ptolemies, the absolute end of the line. She began to think that even a monster born out of an incestuous *aphrodisia* would be better than no heir at all.

When Arsinoë Gamma at last spoke of these things to her brother he said only *Euripides says, He that drinks most shall have least sorrow.*

About this time, when she must have been nineteen or twenty years old, the court having travelled to Memphis for the winter, Arsinoë Gamma took herself, out of curiosity, to visit the Apis, thinking to ask him what might be her future, just as bad or worse still, and it was the first time she had come here for the purpose of taking an oracle. She went on foot to the stall, alone, early, as the sun came up, before the crowds came. The slave of the Apis was still asleep, so that she had to wake him up, the boy who guarded the bull by night, sleeping by his side. She followed Horemakhet's instructions, lit the lamps, burned incense. She put her money on the altar to the right of the god's statue. She approached the black-and-white bull and had the slave prod him with a stick to make him move. She stroked his nose, touched his long horns through the window. She stared into the unblinking black eyes of the god. Apis was old, eighteen years old, and could hardly stand, but he was the living image of Ptah, the creator of the world. She whispered her question into his great black ear, then she covered up her own ears with her hands and walked towards the sandy plain outside the precinct of Ptah, where she took her hands down, and listened.

The hour was too early for boys playing. The apes of Thoth did not yet chatter in adoration of Ra. She heard not so much as a donkey braying. Forasmuch as she heard no sound but the wind sighing in the palm trees, she thought that must be the answer to her question. Either her future held nothing, nothing, was empty as a sheet of papyrus, or it would be full of sighs. But then she heard a child crying in the distance, and she knew what the future held for her. Yes, a newborn infant howling, and her spirits lifted.

In Year Eight of Ptolemy Philopator that same Apis bull rolled over and died. The majesty of this noble god, the living Ba of Ptah, calf of the cow Ta-Amen, flew up to heaven. Horemakhet made the usual application for a loan towards meeting the heavy expenses of the embalming. He expected to have difficulty, but Philopator gave the word at once, without complaint, offering double the sum he was asked for.

Horemakhet warned his Majesty, *If you do not go to the funeral, you may expect your trouble to begin before sundown . . .* But Philopator had already made his heart firm to go. He had resisted so many of his parents' orders, but he had not resisted anything to do with the Apis. Like every other member of his family Philopator loved the Apis, who knew the future. The mortal remains of the Apis they dragged to the Sarapieion of Memphis with the proper funeral rites, that lasted fully twenty-nine days. Philopator walked on his own feet behind the mummy of the bull, wearing the costume of Pharaoh, reverent before the great god. The tears rolled down his face.

As soon as the Apis died, he was reborn as a young calf, and the priests, led by the High Priest of Ptah, must ransack every farmyard in Egypt to find him. They cast the eye over every herd of cows, searched every field in the Two Lands for the newborn calf with all twenty-nine identifying marks that proved him to be the new divine bull.

This time they found him without difficulty, when the sadness at the loss of the old bull gave place to rejoicing, and the divine calf was installed at

Memphis, where he lived with his mother, surrounded by his lowing harem of beautiful black-eyed wives with long black eyelashes, whose beautiful flesh Apis sniffed at all day long, smiling the half-smile that was so very like the smile of Pharaoh.

In Egypt the bulls sired calves, the falcon and ibis managed to lay their eggs, the goats gave birth to kids. Every beast brought forth young; every living thing reproduced – except Ptolemy Philopator.

It happened in Year Ten, six years after the Battle of Raphia, that the Romans sent an embassy to Alexandria to ask for corn, saying there was famine in Italia, where the fields had been laid waste by fire, trampled by Hannibal's troops, destroyed by the endless traffic of soldiers' boots.

What Egyptian secrets did the Roman ambassadors tell the Senate on their return? For there is always a hidden purpose behind an embassy beyond the mere getting of grain, or what have you. They told Rome that the rumour was true: King Ptolemy Philopator preferred pleasure to duty, that he liked wine better than war, and that he seemed not to be bothered about the future of his glorious dynasty, for that although he had married a wife – who was his own sister – he had no son to succeed him. He was the king without an heir, the king who wore the yellow dress, the grown man who had a wife but refused to become a father. He was the laughing-stock of the entire Greek world – the king who wanted to chop off his privities and throw them away. Now he was also the laughing-stock of Rome

Sosibios had humoured Philopator's follies for too long. This time, when Philopator ignored what he said and began to spin his body, Sosibios lost his temper.

Stop that foolish dancing, he shouted. *Sit down, and listen to me.*

Philopator pouted, but, shocked to be shouted at, sat on a golden chair.

We have spies in Rome, Sosibios said, *and they tell us what the Romans are saying. Do you want to know what they say?*

Philopator stuck out the bottom lip, shrugged his shoulders.

I am going to tell you, Sosibios said, *whether you want to know or not. The Romans are saying that the King of Egypt could not care less whether his family dies out or not. I have been told that Rome is planning to take Egypt for herself.*

Philopator moved his mouth about, frowning, but he said nothing.

Sosibios' shouting went on for some time, and Philopator did not dance out of the room. It seems that the thought of losing Egypt to the Romans stung him into doing what he might have done six years before, because, as if by some powerful magic, Philopator and Arsinoë Gamma were cured of their distaste for each other's bodies upon the instant.

What, then, were the miraculous words of Sosibios that cured his Majesty of his eight-year phobia for his sister? He said: *When his Majesty stirs himself to father a son, then he may do just what he likes with his secret parts, but he should know that the Archigallos is under threat of execution if he lets the Pharaoh chop his ballocks off before he becomes a father.*

Philopator sat still, sulky, thinking. At length he said, *I may do what I really want to do and become a full Gallos?*

If his Majesty so desires, Sosibios said, very dry.

And cut off the testicle? Philopator said, almost unable to believe what he heard.

Megaleios, Sosibios said, very slow, *you may do what you like with your privities once you have fathered a male heir for the House of Ptolemy upon your sister.*

Whatever were the precise details of Philopator's clambering into his sister's golden bed, or she into his, Seshat knows them not. What she does know is that shortly after the installation of the new Apis bull, and the embassy from Rome, Arsinoë Gamma's famously flat belly began to be flat no more.

4.15

Beloved of Khonsu

Aye, the belly of Arsinoë Gamma swelled like the melon, and it was no phantom pregnancy, but real, and the sister's smiling was real. The father-to-be continued pretty nervous, as he had been, off and on, all these years since his mother's death. Noises after dark still made him tremble so bad that he kept lamps burning all night, for fear of ghosts. By day he watched with furrowed brow the flight of birds, always sending to the bird-diviner to ask the meaning. The ibis standing on his window ledge, a flock of pigeons perched on the top of the Pharos, quails grounded in the palace courtyards – always he asked what was meant. Agathokles bribed the bird-diviner always to tell his Majesty something bad.

At the theatre Philopator had to take care what plays he saw. Sometimes he was caught out, like the night when the actors performed the *Eumenides* of Aiskhylos. And – Oh! – when the Furies, the three women with snakes for hair, real snakes in this theatre, of course, made their howling entrance, threatening to carry Orestes down to the Underworld for the horrid crime of murdering his mother – Oh! – Oh! – Philopator was on the edge of his seat, shaking to hear the words:

There you will see all the other mortals who have sinned against a god, or a guest, or murdered their parents, each one getting the proper reward for his crime . . . Hades beneath the earth is the punisher of men, who oversees everything that happens and forgets nothing . . .

Aye, Philopator collapsed again, and had to be carried to his bed. He continued sick thirty days, when his Greek physicians admitted defeat, and sent for the High Priest of Memphis, saying, *This is no Greek illness, we believe his Majesty is possessed by some Egyptian demon.*

Horemakhet came to Alexandria, wearing the leopard spots and a grave face, and spent hours talking to the sick man, looking into his troubled eyes, thinking, *What god will cure the man who is so sick not in his body but in his soul?*

At length he said, *Khonsu is often called the greatest of all the great gods. His fame as a healer comes from his skill at casting out demons. If any god can help his Majesty, it is Khonsu the Falcon. If he will agree to sleep in the Temple of Khonsu at Thebes he may find a cure for his disorder.*

Philopator did sail up-River to Thebes North, in search of his health. He met the Priest of the Living Baboons, who would look after his needs, for he must pass the night in the Temple of Khonsu, Lord of Truth, the falcon-headed god, who is the maker of destinies, the giver of oracles, the one who breaks spells. Aye, Khonsu, who is one with Thoth, as the master of time, and one of the gods of writing, a moon-god, whose sacred animal is the baboon.

The Priest of the Living Baboons showed Philopator to a small dark chamber beside the sanctuary, like a prison cell, with a bed, but no other object. *All will be well, Megaleios*, he said, *drink the potion to sleep.* At first Philopator lay awake, listening to the distant chanting of priests, breathing the smell of the incense, staring at the dark, thinking he saw things move, hearing mysterious sounds, disturbed by the strangeness of the place.

He drank the potion, for sure, but did he sleep? Was he awake all night? He did not know. All he knew was that in the dead hours he saw the face of the falcon, Khonsu, Lord of Gladness, he who is possessed of absolute power over evil spirits, in his form of a golden hawk: Khonsu, crowned with the solar disk cupped in the lunar crescent, towering over him in the dark. Philopator heard the beat of heavy wings, felt the wingtips brush his face. *I am Khonsu*, he heard, *who burns hearts, who lives on hearts. I am Khonsu, that drives back all who oppose him, the god of Love, the great healer.*

Something happened that night, and Philopator himself did not know what it was. Perhaps he came face to face with his demons. Perhaps, for once, denied his usual seven, eight, nine bowls of wine, he slept well, saw sense, realized that his fears were groundless. Perhaps he saw that Andreas was right – that his mother's ghost was a thing of his own imagining – and found he was at peace.

Whatever happened, Philopator joined the procession of chanting priests at dawn, with the light streaming in through the temple roof, and the smoke of incense up his nose. He performed the ritual for Khonsu in person. Alone in the sanctuary, he broke the clay seal of the gilded wooden shrine. He drew back the bolts. He opened the double doors and came face to face with the god, was fixed by his sparkling eyes of obsidian, gazed upon his jewelled body, felt the shiver down his spine. He embraced the god, dressed him in fresh garments, presented the god with his breakfast, did everything according to the ritual-book, down to the final sweeping away of his own footprints with the broom. Afterwards he emerged with a look of wonder upon his face, and spoke to the High Priest of Khonsu, saying that the hostile spirit had acknowledged Khonsu's supremacy, that he felt well, that his heart was no longer troubled, for that his demons had left him. Philopator shed tears of joy.

Khonsu the Healer, the High Priest of Khonsu said, *who performs miracles and vanquishes the demons of darkness, has saved you.* Perhaps the truth was that for the first time in years he woke up *not* under the influence of pine-nut wine, without the hangover, without seeing hieroglyphics, without the drunkard's tremor and frightful puking.

Thebes made holiday because of it. Amid the jubilation of the priests – for Khonsu's miracle cure of Pharaoh could only bring very great benefits to his temple – Philopator asked, *What may we do for Khonsu to show our thanks?*

And the High Priest said, *It would please the god if his Majesty were to build a fresh chapel for Khonsu-Neferhotep – the noble child who comes forth from the lotus flower.* Philopator agreed to build the chapel, and it would be a fine monument, excellent, beautiful, enduring for ever.

He honoured this great god not only in the south but also in the north, building at Tanis, in the Delta, a temple for Khonsu and his mother, Mut the Vulture, who was also one of Pharaoh's symbolic mothers, the goddess who wore the vulture headdress, just like his real mother. For the rest of his life Philopator called himself not only Dionysos and Gallos, and all those many other titles, but also, now, especially, *Beloved of Khonsu, Who Protects His Majesty and Drives Away Evil Spirits.* He wore on his upper arm the talisman of Khonsu, that guaranteed to keep his demons away for good.

Philopator's troubles came back from time to time, of course. Call it the Furies, call it his conscience, call it his monumental hangover, call it what you will; this king never did rest very easy after the death of his mother. But now that he was Beloved of Khonsu he knew what he must do. When he made offering to Khonsu he felt better, was less troubled. When he drank the potion of Khonsu he slept sound. When he made his prayers to Khonsu the Falcon he was a little less bothered by his mother's ghost.

What was the truth of it? The man suffered from hallucinations, and the cause of it was an excess of wine, the seven or eight bowls of undiluted wine that he drank every night? That he saw things that were not, and all was the result of too much meat, over-eating, everything in excess? The man was tormented by guilt, crazed by guilt? Perhaps the truth was that he could never be fully restored to health. For sure, Sosibios and Agathokles would find it very convenient for him not to be cured at all.

Upper Egypt seemed friendly enough just then, but in the same year, even so, the native revolts broke out again. The poorest people, workmen and peasants, committed many savage cruelties, and the troops sent by Philopator – or by Sosibios and Agathokles in his name – to beat them into obedience committed many cruel acts in return. Neither Sosibios nor Agathokles nor any of their friends who ruled from Alexandria tried to understand the Egyptians. Philopator understood that the Egyptians loathe violence, that they wanted to love the Pharaoh, the father of his people. But Sosibios, it was as if his two ears were so stopped up with sand that he could not hear one word, and so the violence worsened.

Polykrates of Argos, one of the Laughing Ones, a friend of Agathokles of Samos, was the man sent up-River to quash the rebellion. He did his work by means of multiple beatings, by the amputation of thousands of hands, by cutting off hundreds of heads, so that the Egyptians hated the Greeks better than before.

Back in the north, Arsinoë Gamma had Agathokleia fan her with an ostrich-feather fan and felt the gentle kicking of the Infant Horus inside her belly, and the High Priest of Memphis startled himself by thinking the unthinkable thought that a new Horus, a fresh government and fresh ministers might be a goodly thing for Egypt.

Now and at last Arsinoë Gamma found something in her life to love: her son. This girl's parents had held back their love for her, thinking to save their tears if she died young. They thought they had loved Berenike Mikra too much, so much that they had tempted the gods to take her from them. Aye, they had loved Arsinoë Gamma less, holding her, as it were, at arm's length. Perhaps Arsinoë Gamma had not quite loved them in return. At all events, there was an absence of affection in her life so far. She had not loved Philopator. Her three other brothers, she had never got to know them well, and then they were dead, murdered on the same day. Such things this young woman tried not to think about. Perhaps her waiting-women were the only people in the world who loved her. They would have occasion to prove that love later.

But you cannot stop up love, Stranger, can you? Now Arsinoë Gamma had her child in her belly, and she poured out her love upon the unborn Horus, the boy who must be the next Lord of the Two Lands. She would sing songs to him, Greek songs about the hills of Macedon. She would feed and bathe him herself. She swore she would do everything a mother should do for her son. And no, she would not have a nurse, she would not need a nurse. She would be the nurse herself. There could be no repeat of the terrible thing that happened to Berenike Syra's son. Arsinoë Gamma swore never to let her child out of her sight.

At least, she poured out her love upon her son, and did all these things, until it pleased Philopator and Agathokleia to take him away from her.

4.16

Divine Light

That long awaited son of Ptolemy Philopator and Arsinoë Gamma was born on the thirtieth day of Mesori in Year Twelve of his father's reign. He breathed, he howled, and they called him *Ptolemaios,* Ptolemy, of course, and the father did not cast him out, but brought him up, for he was delighted. This boy was Ptolemy son of Ptolemy son of Ptolemy son of Ptolemy son of Ptolemy. For the sake of your health, Stranger, Seshat must call him by his pharaonic title years before he was given it. He was Ptolemy *Epiphanes (uh-PIFF-uh-neez)* a title that meant God Made Manifest, or the Manifestation of the Divine Light. He was the fifth King Ptolemy, and he would be much better than his father.

You might suppose that all that was wrong in the House of Ptolemy would be put right with the birth of this boy. Would that History were so simple, but it is not. No, the trouble got worse, and the children of Oinanthe were the cause of it. For who should be given the job of being the wet nurse of this new Ptolemy – the nurse that Arsinoë Gamma did not need and did not want – but *Agathokleia of Samos.* Aye, Agathokleia of the naphtha-flavoured lips, the one whose pleasure it was to breathe fire, the flaming one, the one that Philopator loved. And it could only be done because Agathokleia by chance, or by design, became about the same time the mother of a daughter. For sure, she would have had a tough time following the trade or profession of wet nurse without she had some child of her own to suckle at the breast. But if you want to know who was the father of Agathokleia's daughter, you will have to do some guessing, Stranger, for Seshat knows it not, and her brother Thoth says there is no point in speculating.

But Seshat always did like to speculate, reading between the fragments to see if she can join them all up. That is what History is all about, do you not think? Aye, about not losing yesterday, but clinging on to it. Could the father have been Philopator himself? If so, no man ever breathed a word of it before, and no woman either. But why not? For sure, it was the Egyptian custom for a woman of the household to bear her master's child if his wife proved barren. Maybe it was the sudden appearance of a bastard that moved Arsinoë Gamma to jump into her brother's arms, so as to produce a legitimate heir – lest the horror of all horrors happened, and the fire-eater's child snatched the kingship.

Could the father have been Agathokles, her own brother? Nobody ever suggested it before, Stranger, for being a filthy, disgusting thought to think, but Seshat thinks it not unlikely. For sure, in Agathokleia's life we hear of no other men but her brother and his Majesty. What was the truth? Did Agathokles fuck his sister too, aping the manners of his master? Did they indulge themselves in an incestuous *aphrodisia* just like Philopator and Arsinoë Gamma? You might have been moved to do the same yourself, Stranger, during pagan times at Alexandria, the city where nothing that a man might imagine to do was forbidden him. Of Agathokleia's daughter, however, Seshat knows nothing more. Perhaps they cast her out, disappointed that she was not a son, after the frequent custom of the Greeks. If she died in infancy, like so many other children of these times, that would have been the best thing to happen to her. Seshat, that knows all of the past, knows also what was to come. It would have been better for that child if she had never been born. And the same words apply to Agathokleia herself, aye, and her brother too.

When Epiphanes was born Philopator was not unkind to his wife. He was pleased to be the father of a son, but the niceness between this brother and sister never did last very many days. Hostilities were soon resumed, and it was, as always, a small thing that set off the fresh war between them. Before Ptolemy Epiphanes was six days old his father proclaimed him co-ruler, and he became urgent to have his son's thigh tattooed with the ivy leaf of Dionysos, wanting to have put some mark of identification upon him, like the Seleukid tattoo, lest he was kidnapped by his enemies, like Berenike Syra's child.

We disapprove, Arsinoë Gamma said, *of tattoos.*

Just one ivy leaf? her brother pleaded. *Just one tiny little leaf?*

I am telling you, Brother, Arsinoë Gamma said, more sure of herself now that she had done her duty by the dynasty, *I disapprove of Dionysos . . . I disapprove of disfiguring a child's body in this manner . . .*

Philopator screamed at her, then, *You disapprove of everything, Sister. You are just as bad as your mother. I care not a fig whether you approve or disapprove. I am the Pharaoh of Egypt and I shall do as I please.*

Arsinoë Gamma screamed back at him. Aye, she gave voice to her horror, saying, *I thoroughly disapprove of my brother's constant homage to Dionysos.*

She had endured many years of provocation. She had suffered much. But she lost control of her good temper, then, forgot herself so far as to hammer her brother with her fists and beat him up. Aye, it was a thing that not even Arsinoë Beta had done to Philadelphos, but Philopator perhaps deserved what he got. Arsinoë Gamma hit out and hit out, until she had her brother cowering in a corner, screaming for her to stop.

While the parents did battle with words and fists, Agathokleia carried Epiphanes away for the tattooing, and his mother did not set eyes on him for months. By no means, for Philopator kept him, as it were, a hostage, in order to make Arsinoë Gamma do what he wanted, and to punish her. Aye, she had made the grave mistake of offering physical violence. Her brother would hardly take any notice of her wishes now.

In truth a tattoo mattered little. The blood of the Ptolemies was the important thing. It mattered not, in the end, whether the heir slipped into the world with club feet, webbed fingers, even a tail; what mattered was the slightly bulging locust eyes, the pale complexion, the sulky pouting lips, the yellow hair. What was important was that the heir looked like a Ptolemy, and Epiphanes did look like a Ptolemy. As it happened, despite having parents who were brother and sister, he showed no visible deformity. There was nothing unusual about this child's physique whatever.

Some saw Agathokleia dandling this fresh prince upon her knee, so happy to put him to her breast and thought she must be his mother herself; that Philopator passed him off as his sister's child; that Agathokleia was the mother not of any daughter, but of this son. But whether it was true or false, even the goddess of History is at a loss to give you the answer. You will have to make do, Stranger, with the question.

At all events, Agathokleia continued to make herself agreeable to Philopator, but Arsinoë Gamma's usefulness now came to a complete stop. She was once more the disapproving one, an obstacle upon her husband's road, the woman who complained, just like Berenike Beta, the Endlessly Complaining One, the sister who had beaten Pharaoh black and blue, and Pharaoh would not forget it, would not forgive. At the best of times the sister had been ignored. Now she would suffer for what she had done. Whatever she wanted – money, allowances for her waiting-women, guards for her door, food and drink – Philopator made her beg for it, saying, *You still owe us from the two minas of gold at Raphia* . . . Aye, Agathokleia of Samos went about dripping with jewels and gold, looking like the Queen of Egypt, but the Great Royal Wife herself seldom set her foot outside the *gynaikeion*, and she dressed in her waiting-women's cast off clothes. When Arsinoë Gamma begged for money, food, and so forth, it very often pleased her brother to give her nothing.

Seshat finds after this point no sign of Arsinoë Gamma's influence in affairs of state. She has nothing in common with the mighty Arsinoë Beta but her name. She was, for sure, a woman of great strength of character, but she could not hope to shift the combined power of Sosibios and Agathokles. Sometimes Agathokleia carried Ptolemy Epiphanes to see his mother; mostly she did not, but kept him at his father's side. Very often they all lay in the one great golden bed together – Philopator, Agathokleia, Agathokles, and Ptolemy Epiphanes. This boy grew up, one year, two years old, and hardly saw his mother's face. Agathokleia was as much as Philopator's queen now, as much as Epiphanes' mother. Arsinoë Gamma had little more to her name than the vulture headdress with the protecting *ouraios* serpent upon her brow. Much good it did her.

They tell just one story about the Queen at this time. She was walking through the palace courtyards with Eratosthenes and her waiting-women when she came upon a man laden with so much green stuff that he could not see where he was going, and bumped into her Majesty. He threw himself to the ground at her feet and apologized, saying that the green stuff was the decorations for the festival.

What festival can that be? Arsinoë Gamma asked.

Why, Megaleia, he said, *the Lagynophoria, the Feast of Flagons, when the King and every man in Alexandria gets drunk out of his head for three days and nights.*

Eratosthenes reported what was said next: *Her Majesty turned her eyes upon us and broke out in bitter words at the shame of her father's house and the abasement of the royal dignity.*

Arsinoë Gamma, the disapproving one, was not a part of that festival, nor of any other festival, neither the Pompe nor the Games, nor the festivals of the gods. The only advantage that woman had was not to be bothered by ghosts. But she lived with far worse than ghosts. She lived in the shadow of the laughing demons who controlled her husband and had spirited away her son. Arsinoë Gamma had small occasion for laughter.

No, Philopator was the one that laughed, the great Laugher. And he laughed longer, better, just now, having found that by honouring Khonsu he could keep his personal demons at bay. He sailed as far as Thebes once more to visit his new temple, dedicated to Hathor, or Aphrodite Ourania, another of the symbolic mothers of Pharaoh – and to Maat, goddess of Truth, the embodiment of cosmic order.

Begun after the Battle of Raphia, this temple stood on the west bank of the River, with its rear wall up against the high brown cliffs there, that turned pink at sunset, not far from the Ramesseion. The main chamber was dedicated to Hathor, the divine cow, who nourishes the dead ones in the Afterlife.

It is all to please the mother of Pharaoh, Philopator said, *the Lady of the Sky, the Lady of the West, the goddess of destruction.*

Philopator had no trouble walking into the holy place here. He looked at the three shrines in the back of the temple, delighted, at first. The shrine upon the right hand was dedicated to the solar god, Amun-Ra-Osiris, the middle shrine to Hathor herself, goddess of Pleasure and Love, and the one upon the left hand to Amun-Sokar-Osiris, representing the underworld. Just here the priests had ordered up the carving of the *psychostasis*, or judgement scene, that showed the Weighing of the Heart against the feather of Maat, the feather of righteousness and truth. Philopator himself appeared in these scenes, together with Arsinoë Gamma, standing before the seated Osiris, all painted in the very brightest colours. Here, too, was the ibis-headed Thoth, scribe of the gods, ready to write down the judgement, while Anubis and Horus weighed the heart of his Majesty in the Balance. In the next scene, the dead Philopator was shown being led to the Hall of Maat to face the Forty-Two Assessors. Waiting to hear the verdict, was Ammut, Eater of the Dead, a female monster, part crocodile, part hippopotamus, part lion, sitting up on her haunches, ready to devour the dead man, even his Majesty, if he failed to satisfy the judges.

Like every other man, Philopator would have to repeat the words:

Hail, thou whose strides are long, who comes forth from Heliopolis, I have not committed iniquity. Hail, thou who art embraced by flame, who comes forth from Kher-aha, I have not robbed with violence. Hail, thou divine nose, who comes forth from Hermopolis, I have not done violence . . .

He would have to say: *I have not slain man or woman. I have not acted deceitfully. I have not uttered falsehood. I have attacked no man. I have not committed any sin against purity. I have not been a man of anger. I have not made myself deaf to words of right and truth.*

The High Priest of Amun at Thebes made sure that Philopator saw the carvings, and understood what they meant. He explained to his Majesty, in most careful Greek, every aspect of the judgement. The day was hot. The scenes swam before Philopator's eyes so that he saw the gods move, nodding the head, Thoth pointing the finger as if to accuse him. Aye, this wretched debauchee, who indulged his vices with male and female favourites, was like to find himself in some trouble in the Afterlife. He trembled to see the writing on the wall, trembled when he was reminded of the judgement. He resolved to mend his ways, to drink less, to take more notice of the gods. He did what he could to ensure his safe passage to the Afterlife – but his shameful treatment of the sister did not change.

In Year Fourteen Philopator paid the bill of very many talents for the decoration of the temple-house of Horus at Apollonopolis, now almost finished. The carvings on the walls showed his Majesty acting as High Priest, opening the door of the shrine, standing reverently before Horus the falcon, offering incense to his deified parents, and before the sacred boat of Hathor, Lady of Drunkenness.

Hathor was shown embracing Ptolemy Philopator. She wore the vulture headdress and cow's horns, and the hieroglyphs carved beside her image said: *King Ptolemy, Beloved of Hathor the Great, Lady of Tentyra.*

Hathor's left arm was draped round the Pharaoh's neck. Her right arm was under his right arm. She clasped both her hands, hand upon wrist together, as the Mother of the Pharaoh, Hathor the cow, who suckles the king, enfolding Philopator in the divine love of the cow.

Ptolemy Philopator, the supposed mother-killer, the suspected father-slayer, he showed himself in these poses of filial piety, loving the divine mother. Did he still feel guilty? Stranger, if you had done what Philopator did, would you not feel the stab of guilt? Do you not think that the heart of a man who has murdered his mother must be heavy in his breast, like a great obelisk of red granite, for the rest of his life?

The final relief carved at Apollonopolis in the reign of Philopator showed him making offerings to Horus, Hathor, and Harsomtous. Behind him stood Ptolemy Euergetes, Ptolemy Philadelphos, Ptolemy Soter – his father, grandfather and great-grandfather, with their queens. All was as it should be, except that Euergetes was paired not with Berenike Beta but with Arsinoë

Beta. Did the carvers make some mistake? Or did Philopator, tired of seeing his mother's face glaring down at him from the temple walls, order it himself? For the Egyptian belief is that the carvings may become real, by magic, that they *can come to life*. If a hieroglyphic owl could be made to fly off the temple wall, so could the image of Berenike Beta come back to life. Had he not given the order, *Show her face no more?*

Philopator had tried hard to pacify his mother's ghost. He had made her a goddess. But his sense of duty fought with his feelings of terror. He knew very well who was the first person he must meet in Hades, and the thought of it still made him break out in a sweat: herself, the Great Disapprover.

4.17

Horwennefer

Later that year a messenger very black of skin brought Ptolemy Philopator the news that Arkamani, King of Meroë, was dead. This was the father of the Arkamani sent to Alexandria in exchange for Ptolemy Euergetes, so that the boy who had the Greek education was now King of Meroë.

What age is the new king? Philopator asked, remembering his father's stories.

Five times ten, the messenger said, showing the fingers.

Send our greetings, Philopator said. *Keep up the peace treaty.*

In the beginning Arkamani was pleased to co operate with Philopator in the building of a Temple of Arensnuphis, the lion-god of Nubia, at Philai, which bore both their names, both their faces. Alexandria and Meroë each agreed to pay half the expense, and it was a good beginning, good for peaceful relations between north and south.

All the same, Arkamani was in no position to make war, just then, on anybody. He had troubles of his own. First he must rid himself of the powerful priests who had ruled his father's court, which he did, by putting all the priests of the Temple of Amun at Meroë to death, beheading them with his own hand. Thereafter he ran his kingdom according to his own wishes. He would be a benefactor of the other temples at Philai. Only when he had put his own kingdom in order would he set about having his revenge upon Egypt.

Philopator need not have bothered to hurry on his public works at Apollonopolis. He need not have troubled to make ready the temple doors of cedar and bronze, for the violent rebellion burst forth before they could be hung up. In Year Fifteen the men of Nubia, under one Horwennefer, seized this very temple, the Ptolemies' mighty fortress against Chaos, marched north and broke off the district round about Thebes to be an independent state, with himself as its ruler. In all that he did Horwennefer was supported by the High Priest of Amun, and even the priests and scribes of Philai joined him. But if you are thinking, Stranger, that Horemakhet must have moved quick to attach himself to this revolution, you are wrong. He stayed loyal to Ptolemy Philopator throughout, and all Memphis with him. Philopator was not half so bad as they painted him. If he was so bad, so wicked, so useless, the High Priest of Ptah would have abandoned him.

The Greeks, unable to pronounce the name of Horwennefer, called him Haronnophris, or Hurgonaphor. For most of posterity he would be known as Harmais, or Horemhab, or Horos-Onnophris. In the middle of his illegal reign Horwennefer himself changed his name to Ankhwennefer, which the Greeks turned into Chaonnophris. Always people would get this man's name wrong. But Seshat assures you, Stranger, all these men were the same man, Horwennefer. Horemakhet called him by yet another name: the Enemy of the Gods.

This Horwennefer now drove the Greeks right out of Thebes and his army of Nubians, black as the soil of Egypt, occupied it in his name, when it pleased the High Priest of Thebes to crown the usurper as Pharaoh even in the great Temple of Amun. Aye, and the Thebans called him *Horwennefer, Living for Ever, Beloved of Isis, Beloved of Amonrasonter the great god*. They did not call Horwennefer *Beloved of Ptah*. By no means. He had nothing to do with Ptah or Memphis.

Now it was Horemakhet's turn to sleep not, for worry that the violence would reach as far north as Memphis. Night and day he worried about the well-being of Egypt, because the revolt meant that there could be no more trade with Nubia, no valuable resources fetched from Upper Egypt or the south lands: no more gold, no more ivory, no more incense, no more ostrich-feathers, no more leopardskins, no more spices. Philopator's Treasury would suffer as a result, and if the Treasury suffered, temple-building would suffer. If temple-building suffered, then the gods would not be happy. If the gods were not happy the River would not rise. Horemakhet knew that if that happened, Lower Egypt would be sure to rise in revolt as well.

Sosibios sent tens of thousands of troops up-River in Philopator's name to put down this Nubian king and squash his revolution. But Horwennefer was ready, having hidden his archers in the reed-beds and cornfields on both banks of the River, so that nobody knew where the next arrow was coming from, and no man dared to step off his ship for fear of being shot down. The

River itself had always been the highway of Egypt, but the Greeks now found it dangerous even to sail upon it, because the oarsmen were sitting targets for Horwennefer's bowmen and slingers. The army of Philopator, that had beaten Antiokhos at Raphia only eleven years previous, was not strong enough to drive Horwennefer out of Upper Egypt. And so Philopator's ships were forced to turn about and sail back to Memphis.

The oracles forecast that the Macedonians would regain control of Thebes, but not until after Philopator was dead. The grim word of Zeus-Ammon was: *Horwennefer will maintain his stranglehold over Upper Egypt for twenty years.*

By reason of this most violent and bloody revolution, all Philopator's temple-building in Upper Egypt came to a stop. *We shall not build temples for rebels,* he said. *We shall not pay for one stone to be set upon another stone.* Even if he had offered to build seventy great new temples in Upper Egypt, Horwennefer would have spat upon his generosity.

Upper Egypt, then, almost the whole of it, was ruled by this Nubian king and there seemed to be nothing that even Horemakhet could do, except to stick nails in wax images of the enemy, and smash pots with the name of Horwennefer scratched upon them, or to make believe that the rising never happened.

The rumours persisted. The Nubian king ruled at Abydos, they said, north of Thebes, and inflicted a humiliating defeat upon Philopator's army. Horwennefer was crowned king, they said, at Lykopolis, Wolftown. Aye, and it seemed like an omen, like an awful warning. It was as if the darkness was falling about Ptolemy Philopator; as if the wolves crept closer: wolves with the faces of Sosibios, Agathokles, Agathokleia, Oinanthe, and now Horwennefer – all of them baring the teeth with intent to rip up his flesh.

Now even the King of Meroë made his move, that second Arkamani, who had been a friend of Philadelphos. Arkamani saw that the influence of King Ptolemy no longer reached the deep south, and he seized the chance to extend his authority into northern Lower Nubia. He added the great border town of Elephantine to his kingdom. He even found the time and money in the midst of bloody revolution to continue Philopator's work on the Temple of Arensnuphis at Philai, and on the Temple of Thoth at Pselkhis, as if he was not waging war but at peace. Wherever he found the thirty-one hiero-glyphs of Philopator's throne name, he scratched the stones clean, and had them carved anew with the name of Arkamani. He put his own image on the walls in place of Philopator, wearing the Double Crown of the Two Lands, the Lady of Spells and the Lady of Dread, and Philopator knew dread to hear of it.

This Nubian king was a builder, like Seshat, a supporter of the Egyptian gods: he did the proper work of Pharaoh. To build temples was what the gods expected in return for granting him a favour. Even the High Priest of Isis at Philai, a place which had welcomed four generations of Macedonian pharaohs, helped the usurper, and spat upon the name of Ptolemy. Aye, Arkamani said to himself, *Perhaps the Greeks in Alexandria should have been more friendly to us when we were young. Perhaps they should have mocked us a little less often for our amazing blackness. Perhaps they should have thought twice before comparing us to the monkeys.*

No, all work upon the Temple of Horus at Apollonopolis stopped, in the last year of Ptolemy Philopator, when the stonemasons threw down their tools and fled. The giant double doors of cedar and bronze that had been made ready for the entrance of the first pylon would lie upon the sand waiting to be hung for seven thousand three hundred and seven days and nights.

What did Horemakhet really think? Did he not, in truth, welcome Horwennefer's excellent and most excellent uprising as a thing that must delight the gods of Egypt, Ptah of Memphis included? Did he not secretly smile upon Arkamani of Meroë, knowing very well that he would make a far better pharaoh than Philopator? Was not Horemakhet working in secret to hand over Lower Egypt to Horwennefer, working for the end of the House of Ptolemy? No, Stranger, it was absolutely not so. Horemakhet was loyal to the anointed one, the Beloved of Ptah and Khonsu. Sure, he read the letters from the High Priest of Thebes, urging him to join the revolution and throw out the foreigners, but his loyalty was like a great stone, like the great unfinished obelisk of Elephantine, unmovable.

Thebes wrote, *Philopator is like Seth, like Typhon, the embodiment of chaos, the hopelessly drunken one. When he makes up his mind to drink wine, nothing can stop him.*

It was true that Philopator was often drunk, but Horemakhet sent back his message: *Hathor herself, the Lady of Drunkenness, is fond of a glass of booza and a cup of wine. To be drunken is no evil. When a man is drunk, his heart is glad.*

Thebes wrote, *Philopator is the foreign one, the Enemy of the Light. Condemn him as an evil force, one who serves no useful purpose whatever. Help us to throw him out of Egypt altogether.*

But Memphis wrote back, *We shall not fight with the High Priest of Amun at Thebes against his Majesty.*

Thebes wrote, *Did not Philopator kill his father, just as Seth killed his father Osiris?*

Memphis wrote, *If Philopator is like Seth some of the time, it is because the gods have made him so, it is for a purpose. Man should not interfere with fate.*

Horemakhet the magician knew the future well enough. No man was more expert at divination in all Egypt. He had seen the future in a bowl of oil. He had stared at the flames, the flying blood, the violent crowd, the young boy on the verge of tears. He had seen the upstart ones brought low. His last message to the High Priest of Amun at Thebes on this subject was short: *You should have patience. The gods will deal with Ptolemy Philopator soon enough.*

Aye, while Horemakhet reasoned with Thebes, and Arkamani and Horwennefer edged north, meaning to take Memphis as well, Philopator went back to his dancing, spinning on the spot, and he began to think once again about singing in the choir of eunuchs.

4.18

Knives

Ptolemy Philopator was thirty-eight years of age. Still he drank wine for his breakfast, wine for his lunch, wine for his dinner, quite possibly far more wine than is good for a man. Perhaps he would, indeed, drink himself to death, but what more wonderful homage to Dionysos could there be? For the moment, though, he lived to drink another day. Still he feasted to excess. Still he dressed himself up as Attis and danced with the eunuch priests, and his agility in the whirling Gallos dance was as much as ever, not specially good, but highly praised even so. Philopator, at least, looked like a happy man.

Arsinoë Gamma began to assert herself about now, taking her son Epiphanes away from his father. She tried to keep him beside her in the *gynaikeion*, away from Philopator and his unsavoury and most unsavoury friends. She prayed to all the gods that the son would not grow up identical to his father (do not worry, Stranger, he did not). But the father took him back again, tried to keep him away from Arsinoë Gamma as much as he could, lest he grow up disapproving, identical to his mother.

Agathokleia was the woman who brought this child up, had her breast in his mouth every day, fed him, carried him about in her arms. But Philopator was no distant uncaring parent. He let Epiphanes ride upon his shoulders, making him shout for delight. He got himself sober enough to tell him the stories about Dionysos, and Kybele. He taught him to trust Agathokles of Samos as his friend, and to cherish fat Agathokleia, his beautiful nurse, as the most marvellous woman in the world. The Admirable Sosibios, now with a white beard, was as much as this boy's grandfather. Obese Oinanthe was as good as his grandmother. These courtiers were Epiphanes' family, and Arsinoë Gamma was not a part of it. She was seldom seen in public, so thin, they laughed, that she had vanished. She had no say in the upbringing of her son. She did not fit into this happy family that worshipped the god of Wine and Frenzy above all others.

From time to time, despite the dangerous situation further up-River, Philopator would have himself carried forth from the palace at Memphis and set sail in the Thalamegos. He would stop by the town of Arsinoë, formerly known as Krokodilopolis, to call upon Sobek, the crocodile god. It amused Philopator to feed the sacred crocodiles there, who were so tame that they would open wide the jaws for the keeper to put in his arm and pick out the bits of flesh that had gotten stuck – or reach inside with a great brush, doing the work of the little bird that cleans the crocodile's teeth, perfuming his mouth, so that the god's breath smelled sweet.

The Egyptians credit the crocodile with the gift of prophecy, and Philopator liked to enquire of Sobek what the future held, whether the end of the southern trouble, or the birth of further sons, or whatever it might be. On the occasion of this visit, in Year Sixteen, Philopator stuck his fingers in his mouth and whistled the crocodiles to him, as usual. But they did not float up to him, glittering-eyed and laughing. Three times Philopator whistled the god of death – that must both be feared and revered – but the crocodiles ignored him. Sobek did not seem to want to eat out of his Majesty's hand that day; did not want to take pig's flesh from the Son of the Sun.

Philopator the great laugher had a desire to giggle. It was unheard of for Hot-Mouth to ignore Pharaoh, and he stood at the edge of the Sacred Lake, with the priests of the crocodile, unsure whether to go on calling, or to quit his overtures to the Face of Fear.

Why will Sobek not come when his Majesty calls? Philopator asked.

The High Priest of Krokodilopolis-Arsinoë spread the hands. *It is a mystery, Megaleios,* he said. *Perhaps he is not hungry today.* But Philopator knew very well that the crocodile is always hungry. And the High Priest of Sobek did know what it meant when the crocodile refused to eat. For the crocodile, out of his great knowledge, knows when Pharaoh's death is near, and that was why he refused to take meat from him. Aye, the crocodile, who must lead Philopator by the hand in the Afterlife, and show him the highways and byways of Heaven, knew that Philopator would soon be a dead man.

4.19

Flying Blood

In what were his last days, when Philopator shouted, *Let us Dance,* the court needs must dance, every man, just the same crazy spinning Gallos dance as his Majesty. Perhaps you would think it no hardship to dance like this yourself, Stranger, but Philopator could keep up his spinning for hours, and no man was allowed to stop before his Majesty stopped. Imagine in your heart the audience hall filled with spinning courtiers dressed as Attis, in the red Phrygian cap and trousers, humouring his Majesty, who shouts the instructions like a dancing-master, spinning all the while himself, like a human spinning-top.

If the whim came upon him Philopator might shout, *Let us all be women.* Aye, and the First Friends of the King, the King's Friends, the Companions of the King, every courtier in Alexandria, would have to put aside his Macedonian *khlamys,* or cloak, and his Greek tunic and put on the saffron-coloured dress of the Gallos, and wear his wife's jewels, and fix his wife's ribbons in his hair, and paint his face with white lead, and rouge his cheeks. Aye, grown men, the Dioiketes, the ministers of finance and war, the generals, admirals and military governors, the Hypomnematographos and Nuktistrategos, must look as if they enjoyed themselves, and spin round like eunuchs.

Pharaoh says smile, smile, smile, shouted Philopator. *Pharaoh says be merry. Pharaoh says dance for Kybele . . .* And they needs must smile, be merry, and dance. Even the bearded scholars from the Mouseion must don the yellow dress and whirl in the Gallos dance.

Arsinoë Gamma saw this disgraceful exhibition once, through the doors of the audience hall, when the Nuktistrategos murmured to her, *Nobody in Egypt has less authority than the king – he has given up all his power to Agathokles and Sosibios, or had it stolen from him.*

Arsinoë Gamma wept. *For shame,* she said, and ran away, sobbing. But what could she do? She had not the power to dismiss a minister of the crown, unless she could become the Regent for the young Epiphanes – and for that to happen Philopator would have to be dead. While her husband lived, she was helpless. Even though her own mother had murdered her first husband, even though her brother had murdered an uncle and three of his own brothers, Arsinoë Gamma could not murder Ptolemy Philopator. *Murder is wickedness,* she said to herself, *quite against my father's principles.*

It suited Agathokles and his laughing friends to rule by themselves, to have the control of Lower Egypt in their own hands. It seemed good to them to let Philopator pursue his pleasures uninterrupted, good for him to be confined to the palace for month after month. The people of Alexandria became used to not seeing Pharaoh go about his business, not receiving ambassadors at the harbour, not inspecting the fleet, not reviewing the troops, not riding up and down Kanopic Street in a shower of flowers, and not throwing back golden tetradrachms. Now Sosibios or Agathokles did these things on his behalf, though they knew better than to throw money.

Towards the end, though, Philopator did not stand up without falling down, and Sosibios and Agathokles had arranged it like this, so as to have him under their complete command. If Philopator's speech was slurred, Sosibios could forbid him to show his face in public. A man who cannot stand on his feet will not be able to walk about the palace seeing what outrages are being committed in his name by his so-called friends.

When Sosibios announced, *The king is drunk,* or, *His Majesty has a hangover,* and presided over the council of state himself, nobody questioned whether he spoke true. They knew what went on. Every minister had been appointed by Sosibios, or was a friend of Agathokles. These two began to keep his Majesty confined to the innermost chamber of his private apartments now, telling him he was ill when he was not, giving him potions that made him feel weak. Thus, at least, they stopped him making the court put on the yellow dress and dance. Now they sent away his army of palace dwarfs and body servants and had him make do with Agathokles and Agathokleia, and his old nurse, Oinanthe. Between them they fed, bathed, nursed, and cared – or did not care – for this phantom monarch. They told him lies about the revolution, saying, *The situation is worse, but Sosibios has everything under control.* Then they began to lock him into his apartments, saying, *For your own safety, Megaleios.*

Arsinoë Gamma knew nothing of it, because Agathokleia treated her just the same, keeping her behind locked doors, saying, *To keep out the revolutionaries, Basilissa.*

From time to time, when she went to brush Arsinoë Gamma's hair, Agathokleia might say, *Her Majesty looks so unwell.*

Arsinoë Gamma would say, *I am not unwell. I have never been ill in my life.* *Her Majesty looks very very ill,* Agathokleia said, showing her her face in a distorting mirror. And she would bring her some filthy remedy to drink, so that she felt ill indeed.

Why should they want to keep the King hidden? So that they might lay their hands on the gold in his treasury, upon the tax revenues of Lower Egypt. Why should they want the Queen to be ill? So that she might keep to her quarters and not see that Agathokles did everything to please himself and nothing to please the people of Alexandria. Aye, so that they might steal from Philopator everything that was his – his power, his wealth, even his kingdom – for themselves.

How, then, did he die, this king that nobody wanted? Always the word was that he died of natural causes, was not murdered, but Seshat herself is not so sure. Was it the surfeit of wine that carried him off at such a young age? Or did they give him poison indeed? Murder came easy, very easy, now to the ever-smiling Agathokles. To do fifty murders in one day did not trouble his heart for one moment. He had charge of every disappearance ordered by Sosibios, hundreds of deaths, and never the smile faded from his lips.

On the day that was the last day of his life Ptolemy Philopator was alone in his apartments with Agathokles of Samos. He danced, as usual, the Gallos dance. He was heavy, unfit for such violent activity. As he spun round, strange visions of the gods flew before his eyes – Kybele on her throne, Attis at her side, Khonsu the Violent, Anubis the great dog, Ptah of the Beautiful Face, Horus the Falcon, Sakhmet the lioness . . . Philopator whirled, fighting for his breath, then fell to the floor. It was how his ecstatic dance always ended, these days, in exhaustion and collapse. *Soon,* Agathokles thought, *he will leap up and spin again.* But Philopator did not get up. He danced himself to death.

Agathokles it was who gave the King the knife and let him do the deed himself. In his last hour, alone in the privacy of his chamber, ecstatic, spinning round, Philopator had, at last, the knife in his hand, and the blade flashed. Out flew the saffron robe of the Gallos as his feet moved faster than ever before. Now he paused. Up swept the shining knife across his loins, up flew his left hand as he spun again: up soared his bloody ballocks out of the spinning blur. Philopator's scream rose up now, high-pitched, the shrill scream of the eunuch, like the ululation of the mourning women, like a dog howling. The blood of the king flew out upon the mosaic of dolphins and sea-monsters. Having sacrificed his manhood, he would put on women's clothes for good, his final homage to the goddess, the Great Mother.

Sosibios had given his permission, but the high priests of Egypt would never tolerate a eunuch pharaoh. Either Philopator must remain whole, or he must make way for another king, a better, more complete king, such as Sosibios; such as Agathokles. Philopator died *because* he sliced off his own privities. He bled to death.

But Thoth says it is pointless to speculate. What we want is the facts. Between us, my husband and I, Thoth and Seshat, we have lost the truth of it. Aye, exactly how this king died, Stranger, is one of the things that the world has quite forgotten. Whether he drank himself to death or was murdered, whether he died of a fever or from poison, or from septic self-inflicted wounds, Seshat knows it not. Philopator died. Is that not enough for you, Stranger? Never mind how he perished. What matters is that the portal was opened for this mighty builder by Seshat, who lets the dead one into the nether world. Fair paths were revealed to him by Wepwawet the jackal, the Opener of the Ways. Sobek led him by the hand along the back roads of the Afterlife, towards the Field of Rushes. Philopator flew to the sky, and those who knew of it carried on sealing his royal seal to every official document as if he was still alive.

We shall keep it quiet, Agathokles told his sister, *tell nobody . . .*

Why should anything change? Agathokleia said. *We might go on pretending to be the King for ever.* They were good at keeping secrets, these three, Agathokles, Agathokleia, Sosibios. They kept the secret of Ptolemy Philopator's death for almost an entire year of days.

Aye, they kept up the pretence that he lived, forging his signature on the papyrus that they took to the Treasury so they might steal his vast riches for themselves, keeping his death a secret even from the Queen. By chance they did just exactly what Laodike did with Antiokhos Theos, just what the waiting-women did with the body of Berenike Syra.

Do you smell a rat, Stranger? Do you think you are being told tall tales? Relax, Wise One, put your whole trust in Seshat the Chronographer, the one who tells the truth.

Agathokles and his sister bought themselves a new house in the city just then, a house as much as a palace, and hired for themselves dozens of Nubian slaves. Now Agathokleia showed herself in public wearing more jewels than her Majesty, and Oinanthe rode about the city in her wicker carriage, smiling, smiling and waving, as if she were Queen herself.

It was not difficult to guess what might be going on, but nobody did guess. No, not even the High Priest of Memphis, that knew everything, guessed that the king was dead. He was busy at Memphis, dealing with the threat of

Horwennefer. He sent his messages to Alexandria concerning the trouble in the south, but it was Sosibios who wrote back to him, not Philopator. No, Horemakhet's days were used up in trying to stop the revolution of Horwennefer from spreading north, in fighting the Enemy of the Sun. Horemakhet was fighting a battle of his own. He did not know the truth, that the Sun was in total eclipse.

Agathokles would be the new sun, shining in glory. He would do well in Philopator's place – for a while – and he and Sosibios begin now the most evil part of their career.

Aye, for they must have cut this dead king up and brought him out in pieces, cooked his flesh on a fire in the courtyard to get rid of the body, in broad daylight. If anybody noticed the stench of human flesh cooking, the odour of the funeral pyre, they were wise enough not to ask questions. Just as four or five vultures may reduce the corpse of a dog to nothing in one quarter of one hour, eating even the bones, so, too, Agathokles made the corpse of the dead Philopator vanish, reducing him to nothing. And then, like the vulture, these two looked out for the next dead man.

For so long as three hundred days Sosibios and Agathokles kept the fact of his Majesty's death quiet. But they could not hope to keep the news from his sister for ever. Somehow Arsinoë Gamma escaped Agathokleia the gaoler, and walked through the palace asking, *What have they done with my son Epiphanes? Where by chance is my idle husband the King?*

Somehow Arsinoë Gamma found out that Ptolemy Philopator had disappeared, was dead. She shed no tears to learn of it. By no means. She felt no untoward feelings. Now, however, the spirit of boldness she had shown at Raphia came back to her. She felt she must take charge of the situation. She was determined to do her best for Egypt one more time. She thought, *There will be an end to chaos, a swift return to order.*

She went to Sosibios and said, *We shall be the Regent and guardian for our young son, until he is old enough to take on the burden of the kingship for himself.* But that was the one thing that Sosibios could not allow. He would not let Arsinoë Gamma govern Egypt. There was no announcement that Philopator was dead, no proclamation of the new King. The secret stayed a secret, and Arsinoë Gamma herself disappeared. Sosibios told her waiting-women that her Majesty had gone to Kos, for her health.

Aye, Sosibios had already made other arrangements for her Majesty.

4.20

Black Smoke

When the deed was accomplished, Agathokleia tried to excuse herself by pointing the finger at Deinon. *It was Deinon that supplied the naphtha, the inflammable liquid,* she said. *Deinon is the man I suspect of setting fire to the fuel. I saw with my own eyes Deinon gathering the ingredients for a fire . . . If only I had stopped him . . . It is not I who am the guilty one. Her Majesty's death is nothing to do with me.*

Agathokleia, Queen of Lies, had been well trained by Oinanthe. Her hands were clean. *I am an innocent woman,* she said. *I saw no smoke, I know nothing of any fire.*

No, Deinon, a servant doing what he was told, would take the blame.

But Philammon was the one who murmured his best wishes into Agathokleia's ear, saying, *A woman's first murder is always the best. You never forget your first murder.*

Philammon did not have ready access to the queen. Of course not. No man could set his foot over the threshold of the women's quarters. If the queen had to die, it had to be at the hand of another woman. Philammon was the man who organized the crime, the man who kept watch, and who would walk free afterwards, or so he thought.

The official story was that Arsinoë Gamma perished in a fire lit on purpose in, or near, her apartments. You would think, Stranger, that if there was a fire fierce enough to fry a woman so that there was nothing left of her, somebody might have seen the flames, smelled the smoke, heard her cries for help; that her death would have been common knowledge. You would think that if there was a fire somebody in that palace might have run to save her. She had guards on her door, day and night. Where were they? You may well ask where was the famous fire-engine of Ktesibios on this occasion. On the other hand, even a fool knows that not only the palace but the entire city of Alexandria was built of Paros marble; that the palace of King Ptolemy was the most fireproof building in the world. For that building to catch fire would have been as much a miracle as the statue that wept tears of blood, or the gods whisking up a woman's hair into the stars – but nobody knew a thing about it.

And yet, the presence of Agathokleia alone meant that some kind of inflammable oil could not be far off. It would have been so easy for Agathokleia the fire-eater to sprinkle the naphtha all over her Majesty's living quarters.

The whisperers said that Arsinoë Gamma returned to her apartments after dark, that she was by no means a prisoner, but free to wander about. She unlocked the double doors. She lit the lamps, as usual, herself, because her waiting-women had been taken away from her, whereupon the whole place, soaked with inflammable oil in her absence, burst into flames. Agathokleia locked the doors behind her mistress, who burned to death.

What was the truth? Did Agathokleia light the fire? Did Arsinoë Gamma burn herself to death? She had good reason to be miserable, good enough reason to kill herself, except that the Greeks think of self-murder as an act of cowardice, and Arsinoë Gamma was among the bravest – remember, if you will be so kind, Stranger, how she acquitted herself at Raphia. Whatever happened, it will have to be enough for you to know that Arsinoë Gamma died, that there were rumours of fire, and that Agathokleia was mixed up in it, but avoided taking any blame – for the moment.

Aye, however it happened, the Queen, Arsinoë Philopator, Beloved of Isis, Great of Happiness, the Lady of the Two Lands, flew to the sky, and there was no Ptolemy left to rule over Egypt but Epiphanes, a five-year-old boy. If his Great Uncle Lysimakhos, or his Uncle Magas, or his Uncle Alexandros, or his Uncle Lagos had been let to live, one of them might have ruled in Philopator's place, but they were long since dead men, murdered by Philopator himself. Now there was no member of the family left who could be Regent for this young boy. Who, then, would govern Egypt until Epiphanes came to man's estate?

Agathokles would be the Regent. That was the great plan. Agathokles would be the ruler of Upper and Lower Egypt. Smiling Agathokles.

Agathokleia the nurse continued to look after the young Ptolemy Epiphanes, as if nothing untoward had happened. Her first murder did not trouble her in the slightest. If there were flames she would have clapped her hands with delight to see them. For Agathokleia, the bigger the fire the better she was pleased. Agathokleia's pyromania was, after all, of long standing.

Agathokles made Philammon the Libyarch, or Governor of Libya, immediately afterwards, but the word spread, later on, that this high office was his handsome reward for making Arsinoë Gamma disappear, aye, for magicking her Majesty away, in a puff of smoke.

Seshat speaks of Agathokles and Agathokleia, but where was Sosibios son of Dioskourides in all this drama? Missing, Stranger, missing. The strangest thing of all the strange things that happened at this time was that between the death of the king and queen and the end of the mourning for them, the Admirable Sosibios himself became one of the Disappeared.

What happened to Sosibios? Rumour said he died, just about now, of natural causes, of a fever. If he did die, his timing was perfect. Had he lived, he must soon have been a dead man anyway.

Other purveyors of rumour said he saw what was coming, grew fresh feet, like the scorpion, and took himself out of Egypt. Sosibios of the winged feet had flown. He had saved Egypt from chaos. A man who can save Egypt may save himself. He would emerge in some other city, under a different name. He was clever enough to slough his skin like the snake, and be reborn.

Further rumours said Agathokles murdered Sosibios before Sosibios could murder Agathokles, so that he could have his power and take all Egypt for himself.

It was a simple thing. As Agathokles said to the sister: *If Agathokles gets rid of Sosibios, Agathokles may do what he likes. If he does not remove Sosibios, he must go on doing what he is told. If we can get rid of Sosibios – we are free.*

Well, then, by Zeus, let us kill him . . . Agathokleia said. And perhaps they did.

Sosibios was old, eighty years old. Old men die, and Sosibios died, but Agathokles may have helped him on his way to the Afterlife. Let us fit words into the old man's mouth. Let his last word of advice to Agathokles be the wise words of Arkhilokhos: *When things go well, rejoice . . . And when things do not, chin up! Observe what pattern governs man.*

Soon, indeed, Agathokles would find out what pattern governs man, and that it is not the lot of any man to prosper for all time.

Sosibios had liked to say, *The hissing of the snake is more effective than the braying of the donkey.* He was the hissing snake himself. Now he left Egypt to the donkeys, and the chief donkey was Agathokles.

Still this man slept well. Still he dreamed of being Pharaoh. But the meat-eater will dream wilder dreams than dreams of glory. When Agathokles dreamed that he had teeth of glass, his interpreter of dreams told him, *It means sudden death, because teeth of glass cannot bite through food.* Agathokles laughed at him. Death was a remote possibility. Impossible. He knew he was the lucky one, soon to be an immortal, the darling of Tykhe. But a man can have too much good luck, is it not so, Stranger?

Then Agathokleia dreamed not that she was eating fire, but that she had teeth like candles, every one of them alight, and it meant the same thing: sudden death.

And so it begins: the beginning of the terrible end. Seshat warns: *You may not be delighted to read what happened, but this is the truth.*

4.21

Spices

With Philopator and Arsinoë Gamma dead, and now even Sosibios very timely dead, or gotten out of his way, Agathokles of Samos takes the government of Alexandria and Lower Egypt into his own really not very capable hands, and for the first time in his life there is nobody to give him orders, nobody. How will he conduct himself now that he is his own man? In fact, Stranger, not very well, for the slave has stepped up into his master's place, and he begins now to show himself in his true colours. He is pretty good at the art of cruelty, pretty sharp, pretty nasty, but it may be that he is not quite good enough at the art of government to last.

Aye, Agathokles had put off and put off the announcement of the King's death, thinking what he should do, helping himself to the money, but he had delayed far longer than was wise. If he announced the news, he must produce the body to prove the truth of it, but the body had stunk so bad that he had gotten rid of it. His first great problem, then, was that he must announce a death but was short of a body; short of two bodies, in fact, and it was his first big mistake.

What would he do? He argued with Agathokleia how to proceed, argued for days on end, but this man without much education, who quite lacked the proper training for either war or government, was at a sudden loss. Somehow he must give out the news that the King and Queen were dead. Somehow he must find the words to declare himself the guardian of the young Ptolemy Epiphanes.

For want of any better idea, Agathokles ordered a raised platform to be put up in the largest courtyard of the palace, and called a meeting of the Macedonian bodyguard and household troops and the senior officers of foot and horse. There was a lot of shouting and jostling among them, but when all the men were gathered together, Agathokles showed himself, looking scrubbed and clean and almost noble, his ivy-leaf tattoos mostly covered up by his long white tunic. He wore his habitual fixed smile, and in his hands he held the royal diadem, the strip of white cloth that he would have liked to tie around his own head, twisting it round his fingers for nervousness. He mounted the platform and made himself ready to speak. On his right stood Sosibios son of Sosibios, looking uneasy, not smiling, for he knew that this crowd would be sure to give Agathokles a rough time. Next to Sosibios stood the young Ptolemy Epiphanes, who had his hair long, Greek-style, and wore the Greek-style tunic. In his arms he held a lion cub, and Sosibios, worried though he was, bent down to encourage the boy with friendly words.

Now you should not make the mistake, Stranger, of thinking that this was Old Sosibios the minister. Old Sosibios has been lucky enough to escape the next part of the history, the bloody part. This man was Sosibios the Younger, his son, the Somatophylarch, or King's Bodyguard, who held the office of Keeper of the King's Seal, though he was not exactly young himself, but must have been at least forty years of age.

Young Sosibios was unlike his father in that he was a good man, honest, worthy, who did not inspire terror. You may very well ask, Stranger, what this paragon of virtue was doing standing next to the dishonourable and disreputable Agathokles, appearing to support and approve of him, and why he had anything to do with Agathokles at all. But the answer is that Agathokles had chosen him, had appointed him to his office, thinking it would look good to have this noble character beside him, and Sosibios the Younger could not refuse such preferment without Agathokles ordering his instant execution for disloyalty. Sosibios the Younger stood there because he had to: his goodness was well known. Never a word was whispered against him. He would survive the dreadful things that were about to happen, with his good reputation intact.

Agathokles held his arm up for silence, still smiling, and the silence was a good while coming, for the troops were not quite Agathokles' friends, but hated his guts pretty well already for such things as wages paid late, food in the barracks not up to standard, and for the way he changed his orders about what they must and must not do, behaving already very like a tyrant. And, of course, Agathokles had risen to these extraordinary heights, this exalted position, simply by being his Majesty's bedfellow. He was handsome, for sure, handsome above all other men in the city, but he was most certainly not popular.

At length Agathokles began speaking. *Macedonians,* he said, *people of Alexandria, I have heard the rumours and have come to set the record straight. I have to tell you,* he said, pausing to dab his eyes, *that the rumour is true. It is not pleasant for me to tell you that his Majesty has passed away.*

For sure, Agathokles had the crowd's attention now, and there was total silence in the courtyard, though not a shocked silence. Philopator himself had been popular enough, for he had been generous regarding the Pompe, generous with extra rations of wine for the soldiery, but in truth the troops had cared not very much for the dancing pharaoh. He was liked well enough, the way people will like a harmless madman who buys them a drink from time to time.

We urge you, Agathokles said, wondering where was the wailing, *to mourn the king in the proper Greek manner*. A few men groaned, two or three serving-women standing by wailed and tore their clothes, making a half-hearted show of grief. Then Agathokles put up his arm again.

I have to tell you that her Majesty has also passed away, he said, managing to make his voice crack with emotion. The crowd murmured. The women set up the proper Greek wailing, this time without being prompted. Somebody shouted, *Where is the body?* Another, *Bring her out here. What have you done with her?*

When the crowd was a little quieter, Agathokles said, *I hereby proclaim the Prince Ptolemy as our new king.* He tied the royal diadem of the Macedonians round Epiphanes' head, so that the crowd had to stop agitating and applaud, and sing the song of acclaiming the King while the Silver Shields hoisted Epiphanes on their shoulders and carried him round the courtyard, cheering, whistling, chanting his name – all according to the time-honoured custom of Macedon. But when that was done, they put Epiphanes down on the platform with Agathokles, and the chanting started up again, rather more hostile: *Where is the Queen? Bring out the body . . .*

Agathokles shouted, *I have here the Last Will and Testament of his late Majesty, and this is what it says.* He unrolled the papyrus, and began to read, a bit slow, as if he was not accustomed to reading, but the very first words of it were:

We hereby appoint Agathokles of Samos to be the guardian of our son . . .

The shouting was at once much worse, but Agathokles read on, regardless:

We beg the officers to remain well disposed and maintain the boy on his throne . . .

But the word was whispered, and then screamed: *The Will is a forgery. Old Sosibios wrote it . . . It is lies . . . The King and Queen are not dead at all . . . Where have you hidden them?*

Believe me, cried Agathokles, *here are the bones.* And he waved his arm, beckoning to his slaves, within, who now carried out two great Greek urns of silver.

In this urn, Agathokles said, pointing, *are the bones of the King . . . In this one . . . the bones of the Queen.*

In fact, one of them did contain Philopator's bones, what was left of them, but when the crowd screamed for him to tip the contents out on to a table, to prove that he was telling the truth, Agathokles shook his head and would not do it. Then one of the guards who stood behind his shoulder stepped smartly forward, took the lid off the urn that held the remains of Arsinoë Gamma and tipped it upside down on the table. What fell out? An avalanche of dry powder of an odd colour, for it was not grey, like ashes, but a brilliant orange. The guard scooped up a handful of this stuff, put it to his nose, sniffing, and then he gave a great roar: *This is not the Queen at all. This is nothing but a jar of spices.* And then the uproar against Agathokles was nothing but hooting, jeering, and chants of, *Yaaah, liar– liar– liar– liar.*

When the women in the crowd kept on screaming, *How did her Majesty die? What have you done with her body?* Agathokles had to say something. He held up the arm. *There was a fire. . .,* he said, vaguely, looking at his sandals, *a fire in the palace . . . Her Majesty perished,* he said. *There was nothing left of her body . . .*

Nobody was much bothered to hear of Philopator's death, but they cared very much to learn of the passing of the beautiful and most beautiful Arsinoë Gamma, who had been very much loved for her kindness to the people of Alexandria. The insults and outrages inflicted on her by her brother throughout her whole life were pretty much common knowledge, however, and when they thought about what sounded like her most unhappy death, the wailing for her spread across the city.

What had really happened to Arsinoë Gamma slowly became clear: Agathokles must have murdered her himself and disposed of the body in some underhand manner. The rumours circulated: he had thrown her body into the sea; he had fed her to the crocodiles. Aye, it was the absence of the body that caused the most anguish, because, if there was nothing left of her to bury or burn, there could be no lavish funeral, and no public feasting at royal expense. It was the thought of every man, woman and child in Alexandria being cheated of the free feast of roast beef that caused the riots that night.

You might think, Stranger, that it should not have been beyond the wit of Agathokles to find a dead body, any old dead body, and say, *Alas, poor Arsinoë Gamma,* in order to make everything all right, but you should not forget that this man was quite unused to being in a position of great authority. He had got where he was by reason of his divine good looks, not by reason of his most excellent cleverness. Agathokles was good at smiling, good at every kind of fleshly pleasure, good at obeying orders, but he was not used to dealing with a crisis, and not used to thinking for himself, and the hostility had unsettled him. Most of his life he had lived in the present moment, just like King Ptolemy, taking not much thought for tomorrow, achieving what he did out of natural cunning. That day his cunning seemed to have deserted him.

Agathokles was, of course, no longer the pretty Ganymede that he had been, but he was still a man in his prime, still so handsome that you would think the Alexandrians might have loved him whatever he did. But no, all Alexandria knew by now how cruel Agathokles of Samos was. He had his flatterers and sycophants, just as he had been a flatterer and a sycophant himself, but even his friends, his so-called friends, were thinking this tyrant could not cling to power for very long, and were already laying their emergency plans, thinking how they would desert him when Agathokles the Regent got his own fingers burned, for that any man could see that he and his sister were playing with fire – far too great a fire for them to keep it under control.

Ptolemy Epiphanes, the boy king, Agathokles now placed in the tender care of Agathokleia and Oinanthe, urging them in a whisper, *Take him away . . . Look after him . . . Do not let him die.*

And then Agathokles got a hold on himself. Wanting to find somebody to punish for the Queen's death, he said, *I now have reliable evidence that when the papyrus from Old Sosibios about the murder of Arsinoë Gamma passed through Deinon's hands, he read it, but did nothing to stop the murder . . .*

Agathokles brushed away his fake tears.

Deinon could have stirred himself to tell somebody in authority what was going on, he said. *He could easily have stopped the conspirators and saved her Majesty's life, but he chose to join in the plot. Deinon must take the blame . . .*

After the death of the Queen, he said, dabbing his eyes, *I heard that Deinon was full of remorse; that he went about saying how ashamed he was for what he had done, shedding tears, saying he was sorry that he let slip the chance to stop the murder. Deinon is the guilty party.*

And so, with the guards sent off to arrest Deinon, the meeting broke up. Although Sosibios and Agathokles had been behind the murder, and then Philammon, and Agathokleia, it was Deinon that took the punishment for this crime. His body was hung up in the Agora, for the crows to dine upon his living flesh.

Next, thinking to gain the favour of the public, and full powers, Agathokles ordered sixty days' wages to be paid at triple the usual rate for the military, soldiers and sailors alike, all eighty thousand of them. A soldier's pay just then was four obols a day. Triple pay was twelve obols. Total ninety-six thousand obols at six obols to the drachma gives sixteen thousand drachmas at sixty days divided by six thousand to give talents . . . Stranger, Agathokles handed out a bribe of one hundred and sixty talents to buy his popularity among the troops. But all the money in Egypt would not have bought Agathokles popularity. They hated him just as before.

Note, though, Stranger, that already Agathokles makes free with the royal purse. There would be no limit to his spending. For the first time in his life there was no man to tell him when to stop. And now he thought to silence all opposition by sending every man of distinction right out of Egypt.

Ptolemaios son of Agesarkhos he sent as his ambassador to Rome.

Tlepolemos he sent away to Pelousion, the frontier fortress in the marsh lands east of the River, to be the Strategos, or military governor, there.

Pelops son of Pelops, sometime Libyarch and Strategos of Cyprus, he sent into Asia, to beg Antiokhos Megas to stick to his peace treaty with the young king's dead father, and stay on friendly terms with Egypt.

Ptolemaios, another son of Old Sosibios, he sent to the fifth King Philip of Macedon, to fix up the marriage Philopator had proposed between Epiphanes and his infant daughter, and to beg for his help. Wisely, Philip played for time, said he would think about it.

Skopas the Aetolian he sent away to Greece with a vast sum of money for the hire of thousands more soldiers. Aye, Agathokles thought to use the fresh troops for any war that might break out, and send the existing force of hired soldiers to the border forts and foreign settlements, as far from Alexandria as possible, and that he would fill up the space in the household troops and palace guards with the new arrivals. The fresh troops, he thought, would know nothing of what had happened in the past and so would be unlikely to take up arms against him. Aye, he was sure they would trust Agathokles as the new beginning, the glorious future, and obey his orders without a murmur of complaint.

At the beginning of his regency, then, Agathokles still showed some signs of efficiency, but these were the last signs of his vigour, not the start of a wonderful new era. The people were encouraged, at first, thinking that things might go better for them with a man like Agathokles in charge, if he could sweep away the old disorder. But Agathokles was not thinking about the welfare of his subjects. He thought only about getting rid of his enemies, the men who hated him for his cruelty in the past. No, he was merely doing what every fresh ruler should do – removing every threat to his stability. He really did not mean to turn himself into a beneficent ruler. Things would not get better under Agathokles, but worse, much worse.

*

Old Sosibios had known this golden youth better than he knew himself. He knew Agathokles would go crazy, just like Philopator, once he got his hands on the Treasury. Agathokles would destroy himself, Sosibios had been sure of it. In Agathokles of Samos you see a ready-made tyrant, Stranger, a man who ordered the whipmakers to work overtime.

When Agathokles felt sure his bribery had taken the edge off the troops' loathing for him, he made them swear the oath that was always taken on the proclamation of a new king, but nobody was asked to swear allegiance to the young Ptolemy Epiphanes. They had to swear loyalty to Agathokles, the Regent, to himself.

And then he went back to his old way of doing things. He gave his friend Nikostratos the august office of Epistolographos, responsible for all official correspondence. Aristomenes the Akarnanian, an able and virtuous man who had considerable political skills, was made a Somatophylarch, or royal bodyguard. He would prove one of the most loyal. For the rest, Agathokles filled up the empty places in the King's Friends with his own friends – butlers and cooks, stable hands and indecent dancers, clowns and tricksters, slaves and palace servants – men who had done him favours in the past, most of them distinguished only for how much money they could spend, and for how much wine they could tip down their throats. He invented fresh court titles, such as Friend of Agathokles, and Companion of Agathokles, and he did not sell them to the highest bidder, but handed them out for free, thinking to get himself faithful supporters as a result. These clowns ate Agathokles' food and drank Agathokles' wine, everything in excess, every man making free with Agathokles' golden palace, making permanent festival.

Agathokles himself, the Regent, if not quite yet the undisputed ruler of Egypt, fixed himself up with his own retinue of bodyguards, his slaves of the body, his palace dwarfs, his fan-bearers on the left and right hand, and his own pair of identical twins to take care of the nails of his fingers and toes, as if he was Pharaoh already. Power went straight to his head and made him drunk, for now he carried himself like a king, and behaved like an identical replica of Ptolemy Philopator – right down to the purple cloak and crown of golden oak leaves.

He had his young parasite, or jest-maker, Philon, who – just like the famous Sotades – never stopped laughing, and whose task was to make sure that Agathokles laughed even when he did not feel like it. He had his own handsome naked cupbearer to pour out his wine. He had his plates and cups and forks of gold, his golden knucklebones, his chamber-pot of gold. Everything that had been Philopator's, and should by rights belong to young Epiphanes, he treated as his own property. He made free with the electrum chariot of Pharaoh, and the white horses of a god, stopping short only of wearing the Double Crown of the Two Lands, thinking he would wait to wear that article, until he was enthroned at Memphis – *an event that he was sure would happen soon.* When he received visitors in the audience hall he made them lie on the belly and kiss the floor at his feet. The only way he did not copy the dead king was in not dancing, not dressing up as a woman, and not trying to chop off his testicles. By no means. Agathokles was very keen to keep himself attached to that part of his anatomy.

And why was it? Because he was thinking of marrying himself to his sister and founding a dynasty that would be Pharaohs of Egypt till the end of time, and because he spent the most of his days and nights whoring. Aye, he made Agathokleia paint his entire body with golden paint, as in the Great Pompe, years ago. No woman was safe from this golden satyr's lustful advances, neither young maidens, nor newly married brides, nor even middle-aged grandmothers long past their bloom. Golden Agathokles, like Priapos made flesh, snapped his fingers and pointed to whomever he wanted next, whatever woman took his fancy. He thought nothing of performing his *aphrodisia* in public, in front of an audience of his ribald, shouting, applauding courtiers. He did not care who watched him play the stallion, but showed off his golden prowess. He drank deep, pretending to be Dionysos, and there was a great deal of cheering and laughing. If things went on the same, this donkey would soon be, like the great Ramesses, literally the father of his nation.

As for Agathokleia, painted gold herself, and dressed in little more than the vulture headdress and golden sandals of Arsinoë Philopator, she joined in, offering her body to all comers. She poured wine down her throat from morning to night, just like her brother. Old Oinanthe did just the same. Ptolemy Epiphanes, the King of Egypt, five years old, wandered about the palace clutching a lion cub, asking, *Do you know where is my mother? What have they done with my father?* But these were questions to which nobody could give him the answer.

Agathokles, then, made holiday, and perhaps it was at last finding that he was free that made him behave as he did, and perhaps it was, as it were, to get his own back for having been so ill-used by Euergetes and his courtiers when he was a young Ganymede, or cupbearer. For if you treat a boy ill when he is young, he will be very like to treat others just the same himself when he grows up. Who, indeed, could blame him for it?

The palace, for the moment, loved the Regency of Agathokles of Samos, loved it, and the music and dancing, drinking and whoring never stopped, day or night, for twelve months. But the city of Alexandria did not love what was going on. By no means. Alexandria already loathed Agathokles. For sure, at first it looked as if he might make himself into some kind of champion of the people, having raised all those low-born friends of his to high office, and that he might even stick up for the rights of the ordinary man. But no, not a bit of it. Agathokles exercised his power just as Sosibios did, without any thought for the common people. He did not learn from Sosibios' mistakes but repeated them. Aye, the slave ever did love to imitate his master. But as for his duty, Agathokles could hardly be bothered to think about it: he was more interested in pleasure. And so the old anger bubbled up, and the Alexandrians began to hate Agathokles still better, like Hades himself.

But what would Alexandria do about all this tyranny? Nobody had forgotten the trouble that Agathokles and Old Sosibios had brought upon Egypt by raising the taxes way beyond what any man could afford to pay, causing much distress and hardship. Everybody remembered the unfairness of calling up the oldest veterans and making them march off to war again at Raphia. But because nobody stepped forward to lead them against this new tyrant, it seemed wise to keep quiet. Aye, the chanting died down, turned into whispering, because Agathokles started to wield the whip – and not, like Philopator, against himself either, but against the people of Alexandria. He flogged offenders in public, in the Agora. He made great use of beatings upon the soles of the feet, stretching upon the rack, and countless other outrages. Meanwhile, Alexandria waited to see what fresh leader might rise up and save them – some tough military genius, they hoped, who would challenge this usurper, who looked far worse than Horwennefer in the south, and stamp upon his handsome face with his soldier's boots.

There was only one man just then who looked capable of getting the better of Agathokles, and that was Tlepolemos, the strong man he had sent away to the borders of Egypt, to get rid of him. It was no secret that Agathokles and Tlepolemos would like to strangle each other. Eventually, after many desperate appeals, this Tlepolemos agreed to become the spearhead of the opposition to Agathokles and his cruel regency.

4.22

Tlepolemos

Tlepolemos was a Persian by origin, whose family had come to Egypt by way of Lykia. He was a fine soldier, good in the heat of battle, though he also liked to show off at shooting arrows, and in the *gymnasion*, at wrestling, or hurling the javelin further than any man could believe it possible, and winning every race he entered. He liked best to spend the morning boxing and swordfighting with the young men. After his exercise he liked to have a drink with these friends of his, and the rest of the day would be lost in drunkenness, if not an alcoholic stupor. Tlepolemos was not perfect, then, but only the gods are perfect. He was better, perhaps, at drinking wine than at governing a citadel, but he had good qualities as well as not so good. He would do Egypt a great service. He was certainly better than Agathokles of Samos.

While Philopator was alive, Tlepolemos had kept his nose out of public affairs, but when the king's death was announced Agathokles sent for him and kept him busy, calming the people down, and he had to do what he was told, of course, or take the whip lash, like everybody else. Then, when he began to look more popular than Agathokles, more efficient, more like one who might oppose him, Agathokles sent him to be military governor of the Pelousion district, where he would not be able to stir up trouble. Tlepolemos did whatever Agathokles asked him, at first, thinking that his Regency was just a temporary thing, that he would soon hand over control to some kind of council charged with the guardianship of the boy and the government of Egypt. But when he realized that Agathokles was fast getting rid of any man who was fit to hold such an office, and that it looked as if he would take the reins of government into his own hands and do everything himself, without any council, like a regular tyrant, Tlepolemos changed his heart quick.

He knew how much danger he was in himself, because of his long-standing feud with Agathokles, and he fully expected the knock on the door in the middle of the night that would mean arrest and imprisonment, if not the knife stuck between his ribs.

Tlepolemos saw that he must move fast, and he gathered his forces around him. Since his own troops as well as those in Alexandria sent him messages of support, urging him to overthrow Agathokles, he still thought it not impossible that he would be named as the guardian of the young King and asked to govern Lower Egypt himself.

Agathokles kept sending orders, trying to make Tlepolemos go even further off, deeper into the desert, or to Cyprus, because he knew he was the one man who might be able to overthrow him. But Tlepolemos said he was quite happy where he was, and refused to budge.

He wrote to Agathokles, *I would rather have my old job back as Nuktistrategos in the city than be stuck on Cyprus.*

And so relations between these two grew worse, because the one thing Agathokles would never do was let Tlepolemos return to Alexandria.

Do what I ask, Agathokles wrote, *and you can stay where you are. But if you come back to Alexandria I shall have you arrested.*

Tlepolemos roared with laughter to read such threats.

So how would Tlepolemos go about restoring order and grinding the face of Agathokles into the dust? First, he had to be sure of his backing, so he set about making sure the commanders, taxiarchs, and inferior officers at Pelousion were firmly on his side, by entertaining them every night with a lavish banquet. When the wine was flowing, Tlepolemos would get to his feet, raise his cup, and say, *Gentlemen, I propose a toast: to the boys who scribble filthy slogans about Agathokles on every wall in Alexandria.*

The troops laughed, shouted, *To the boys . . .* drank, and banged their cups on the tables.

Then Tlepolemos said, *I propose another toast: To Oinanthe the sambuca player, and Agathokleia of Samos, two of the finest whores in the world.*

The troops shouted, *To the finest whores . . .* drained their cups, and cheered.

Then Tlepolemos said, *I should like to propose one more toast. Do you remember the beautiful big boy who walked about naked at Ptolemy Euergetes' feasts, with every man squeezing his bottom, while Euergetes looked on, smiling? Aye, the pretty boy who was so eager to please every man at the drinking bouts when he was the cupbearer . . . Let us drink to Agathokles, the best-fucked catamite in all Egypt, the widest arse in the world.*

The troops roared *Wide-arse,* drank, and went on cheering Tlepolemos, shouting and laughing. And because the men talked about all this to their friends, the spies heard about it, and then word of what was going on reached the ears of Agathokles himself.

He sent Tlepolemos a fresh message, saying, *If you set foot in the city you will be the crows' breakfast.*

Open war was declared when Agathokles publicly accused Tlepolemos of inviting Antiokhos Megas to take over the kingdom of Egypt. It was not true, but Agathokles had always been good at telling untruths. Agathokles thought to work up the Alexandrians' anger against Tlepolemos by saying such things, but he succeeded only in working the Alexandrians into a frenzy against himself. The murmuring against Agathokles grew louder. *Better a soldier like Tlepolemos,* they said, *better a real man in charge of Egypt than a king's kinaidos.* Tlepolemos was the right man to take on Agathokles, the only man, and the Alexandrians were delighted to see the quarrel growing more heated.

4.23

Running Dogs

Things began to grow very ugly when Agathokles called his next meeting with the household troops and appeared on the platform again with Agathokleia and the young Ptolemy Epiphanes. From time to time Agathokles raised a hand to brush away his tears, weeping helplessly, as a woman weeps when she is peeling onions. This was because he held half an onion in the palm of one hand. But, as the Egyptians say, *One eye weeps, the other laughs.*

At first Agathokles made believe that he could not say what he wanted to say because of the tears that choked him, but they might just as easily have been tears of laughter. After wiping his eyes many times on the edge of his cloak he picked Epiphanes up in his arms and made a speech.

Soldiers of Macedon, he said, *on his deathbed Ptolemy Philopator entrusted this boy to my sister Agathokleia, to be looked after by her. But her love on its own cannot guarantee his safety. What happens to him really depends on how brave you are in the coming fight. I want you to help me fight his Majesty's battles for him. Tlepolemos is our new enemy. He would like to be King himself. I always thought Tlepolemos had ideas above his station, but now I have proof that he wants to steal the kingship of Egypt for himself. I hear that he has now fixed the day when he will snatch the diadem from its rightful wearer, King Ptolemy here, and tie it round his own head. But do not rely on my own word about the coronation of Tlepolemos. I have here a reliable eyewitness who has come straight from the camp of the usurper.*

He beckoned a young man to step forward.

Tell the people, Kritolaos, he said, *what you saw at Pelousion.*

I saw with my own eyes the altars being put up, this Kritolaos said, *and the bulls having their horns gilded for the sacrifice. It was all for the king-making of Tlepolemos.*

The Macedonians would not listen to the lies, but hooted, whistled, and jeered so much that afterwards Agathokles said he hardly knew himself how he got away from the meeting without being torn to pieces, because the troops seemed to be on the point of abandoning him for Tlepolemos.

The main thing urging the troops on to change sides and have their revenge on Agathokles was that Tlepolemos had gotten personal control of

the entire food supply that came up-River to Alexandria from the south –
that part of the south, at least, that was not in the hands of Horwennefer.
That is to say, if Tlepolemos did not get the better of Agathokles pretty quick,
there would be nothing to eat in Alexandria but fish.

Agathokles now outraged Alexandria, and Tlepolemos in particular, by
sending his guards to arrest Tlepolemos' mother-in-law, Danaë, in the
Temple of Demeter, where she was living as some kind of part-time priestess.
They dragged her, with her face unveiled and exposed to public view, along
the whole length of Kanopic Street and threw her into the prison. Why did
Agathokles arrest an old woman who had done nothing wrong? To show his
hostility towards Tlepolemos. This act of aggression made the people so
angry that they stopped whispering about the troubles behind closed doors
and came out on to the streets to protest, chanting abuse about Agathokles.
They showed their utter loathing by scribbling obscene slogans all over the
city during the night, so that if Agathokles had not known before how
Alexandria felt about his splendid new disorder it should have been quite
plain to him now.

No, Agathokles could not help but see what was happening and it made
him very nervous. He thought about fleeing the city, but where would he flee
to? Alexandria was his home. He had never set foot on Samos, the Greek
island from which he took his name. Apart from his nightmare excursion to
Raphia he had never been out of Egypt. He was a man who lived one day at
a time, like Ptolemy Philopator. He did not think very far ahead, had laid no
clever plans for a quick escape. He had no swift ship, no fast horses, not so
much as a donkey waiting to carry him to safety if things got too hot for him.
Even if he had, he thought nobody would help him now but his sister. No, he
must stay where he was and fight it out. He recruited extra undercover
agents, and drew up a list of the men who must be murdered, much as every
Ptolemy did at the start of his reign, except that the king's list of victims was
limited to his own family. The great purge of Agathokles' enemies began with
the arrest and imprisonment of anybody even suspected of disloyalty – but
hundreds of men disappeared, and the word went about that Agathokles was
going to kill everybody.

Growing more suspicious by the hour, Agathokles even accused one of his
own personal bodyguards, Moiragenes, of working for Tlepolemos and leak-
ing all his secrets to him. Aye, and how Agathokles treated the man shows just
what Alexandria had to be afraid of, for Nikostratos, the secretary of state,
dragged Moiragenes out of his bed in the middle of the night. He marched
him to a remote part of the palace to be interrogated, and he made use of
squeezing and stretching to make him confess.

However much they squeezed or stretched, though, Moiragenes denied the charges, for he was innocent of the crime. At length Nikostratos handed him over to the soldiers, for more serious torture. Stripped of his cloak, boots, tunic, even his loincloth, he was fixed to a wooden frame, ready for the kind of flogging that left a man dead. He was tied up, naked, while the laughing soldiers cracked their whips and brandished in his face the pincers with which they meant to pull out his fingernails. But in the middle of all this a servant ran up to Nikostratos, whispered something into his ear and ran off again. Nikostratos strode after him without saying a word, striking his thigh with his hand, as if he had been given bad news.

Moiragenes now found himself in a curious situation, ready to be flayed alive, and resigned to eating his dinner in Hades, but without Nikostratos there to give the order his punishment could not begin. The torturers stood looking at each other, wondering what had happened, but fully expecting Nikostratos to come back at any moment. When he did not show his face after an hour or two, they wandered away, one by one, until Moiragenes was left quite on his own, still tied to the wooden frame.

The victim, however, managed to wriggle free, and he ran, still stark naked, through the palace courtyards, out of the gates, past the guards, and kept on running, until he reached the tent where his friends, the Macedonian guards, happened to be eating their breakfast. He burst in and collapsed on the ground, panting. Shaking with emotion, he sobbed, *I beg you to save me. I beg you, save the king from this tyrant, Agathokles . . . but above all I beg you to save yourselves . . . You may be next on the list of men to be tortured, if you do not do something right now, while every man is hot to have his revenge on Agathokles . . . You will soon be dead men yourselves if you do not make a move at once . . .*

The guards did move: their thoughts of revolution had been smouldering for a long time, and they lacked only some man of courage to light the spark. It was Moiragenes who, as it were, supplied the fire. They lent him a cloak and a sword, then set off to visit the other Macedonian tents, then the tents of the hired soldiers, gathering their supporters in a band as they went. Now that the movement had begun it spread, indeed, like wild fire. Aye, the Macedonian troops abandoned Agathokles of Samos by the thousand, that day, and declared for Tlepolemos instead.

It took just four hours for these men of different nationalities, both regular and hired soldiers, to agree to bring down the so-called government of Agathokles. Luck was also on their side, for Tlepolemos himself was reported to be on the road to Alexandria. When the spies reported that Tlepolemos was already in the city, Agathokles so lost his stomach for the fight that he did not bother to issue any emergency orders. Nearly all his men had deserted him. There was little point in giving orders if there was nobody to carry them out. He went off to get drunk, as usual.

Agathokles slumped in his gilded chair and drank the customary five, six, seven bowls of wine, but his manner had changed. The fixed smile had gone. Philon the parasite made his best of jests, as usual, but there was no roar of conversation at the feast, because all Agathokles' friends had left him. There was no proper food to eat, because his cooks had fled. Aye, even the clowns and jugglers had gone over to the camp of Tlepolemos. Only fat Agathokleia remained at Agathokles' side, reclining on a golden couch, fitting figs into her mouth like an automaton, staring ahead, eating, eating, eating, and saying not one word to her brother for worrying about what to do. Agathokles himself kept glancing at the door, as if he thought it was about to fly open, as if he thought he was about to be arrested himself. Philon drank for ten men, and was very drunk indeed, rolling on the floor with laughter at his own jokes, but Agathokles' face was fixed, never to grin again, staring into nothingness. He moved only to fill his cup with wine and drink it down in a great draught. He drank, drank again, belched, fell into a stupor. While he snored the rising spread.

4.24

Oinanthe

In another part of the palace, Old Oinanthe, mother of Agathokles, now some sixty years of age, white-haired, and grotesquely fat, peered out of her windows, shaking with fear. She had passed the day as usual – supposed to be looking after the King, but letting him do what he liked – stuffing her face with grapes and cherries, steadily drinking her way through his late Majesty's wine cellar. She could hear the hostile crowd chanting her son's name. She had heard the rumours, and she saw that the end must be coming upon the House of Agathokles before it had even begun. The situation in Alexandria looked to her beyond any man's control, let alone her son's control. She thought that, even if her son was thrown out and lost his life, she must do something to save herself. She had enjoyed her years of privilege, rubbing shoulders with the living gods. But now that her family seemed to have fallen from favour, she panicked.

Oinanthe gave Epiphanes a message to deliver, and sent him to find Agathokleia. Then she dressed in a slave's clothes and set off through the streets in the dark, on her own feet, running, for she thought to seek sanctuary in the Thesmophoreion, that stood upon the east side of Alexandria, a little outside the city walls, not far from the palace quarter. A Greek woman is not meant to run, ever, and Oinanthe had not run anywhere since she ran in the girls' foot-race on the island of Samos fifty years previous. Since she had been the Great Royal Nurse of Ptolemy Philopator she had hardly so much as walked – except in the Pompe – but had herself carried in a litter. By the time she reached the Thesmophoreion she was soaked with sweat, wheezing fit to die.

The Temple of Demeter Thesmophoros was open for the annual festival of fertility, for it was sowing time. Men were banned from entering here. Oinanthe would be safe. Weeping with relief, she fell upon her knees, and with much waving of the arms, prayed to the goddesses, Demeter, whose hair is like ripe corn, and Kore, her daughter, for help. Then she sat by the altar, trying to get her breath back. The women attendants at the festival were pleased to see the mother of the hated Agathokles in distress, and ignored her, but some of the noblewomen, not yet aware of what was going on in the city, came up to comfort her and ask what was wrong.

Oinanthe was at her most savage, almost growling: *Do not come near me, you beasts. I know how much you hate me. I know you are praying to the goddesses that the very worst may befall my family, but I trust in the will of heaven. I believe I shall yet make you eat your own children's flesh.*

She shouted at the female attendants who kept order at the festival with their rods, *Drive these women away, kick them out . . . Beat them if they will not go . . .* And the attendants had to obey, or face the consequences of angering the Mother of the Regent, and they hit out. The noblewomen ran, then, squealing, indignant, but as they ran they held up their own hands to the goddesses and prayed, *May Oinanthe herself be cursed with the fate that she threatens to bring upon us.* They cried, *May the same thing happen to you, you horrible old woman. May you have to eat your own children's flesh yourself.*

Oinanthe dismissed them with a wave of the hand and a torrent of abuse, then settled down for the night. She dipped her hand in the water of the Nymphs, muttering curses. One drop of water would have been enough to make any righteous woman clean and pure, but, as they say, *Not even the whole ocean can cleanse a wicked woman with its streams.* Fat Oinanthe – the woman who had encouraged her children to take from the late King all his possessions, his gold, his kingdom, even his life, and who had urged on her daughter to murder the Queen – she sat where she was, safe, for the moment.

4.25

The Breasts of Agathokleia

It was the anger of the men of Alexandria that began the revolution, but now the women's fury about the murder of Arsinoë Gamma boiled up as well, hating Agathokles more than ever. That night the trumpet did not sound the hour. For only the second time in seventy-four years, the Pharos was left unlit, because even the men who tended the light had come down to join the protest. The last few remaining supporters of Agathokles scattered, tried to hide themselves, but now the hunt was on, with Alexandria in uproar all night, full of violent shouting, and the noise of hurried footsteps, followed by strange silences, and the distant chanting of the mob.

The open spaces around the palace, the Stadion and the Agora, filled up with crowds of ordinary people – merchants, shop-keepers, sausage-makers, onion-sellers, fishmongers, slave-dealers, slaves, women, even the actors from the great Theatre of Dionysos – all of them shouting, furious, about Agathokles.

When the news of the riots reached Agathokles he was still lying on his couch in a stupor, dreaming the spotted dog dream that meant some terrible thing would happen to him. Philon woke him up, to deliver a message from Agathokleia that said, *Brother, our luck is running out. They will be sure to ransack the palace tonight. We must move to the hiding-place. Time is short. Please to go at once . . .*

Agathokles at last stirred himself, got up, and fell down, too drunk to stand. Groaning, he sent Philon to round up his relatives, the unworthy ones to whom he had handed out lucrative offices, slaves who now lived like royalty. Himself, he put on an old cloak, pulled a wide-brimmed hat over his face, and went off to find Ptolemy Epiphanes, and Agathokleia.

Agathokles was still drunk, still falling about, but he managed to black Epiphanes' face with charcoal from the brazier, and found him a slave's tunic and an old cloak. And since Epiphanes would not leave his lion cub behind, the lion cub went too.

Hide him under your cloak, Agathokles said, slurring his words, *cover him up.*

And so, holding the young King by the hand he set off with him, on foot, followed by his ragged retinue – Agathokleia, his other sisters, his relatives, their children, and a handful of bodyguards, the last of the faithful.

What is happening? Epiphanes asked. *Why must I wear these horrible old clothes?*

It is just a game, Agathokles said. *We are playing a game.*

Aye, he thought, *a game like life, that you may win or lose, and Agathokles looks like losing.*

Why may we not ride? Epiphanes said.

Agathokles made no answer, thinking what to do, walking fast, and not too straight either, so that Epiphanes had to run to keep up with him.

Where are we going? Epiphanes asked.

To the theatre, Agathokles said.

What play is it? Epiphanes asked.

You will see, Agathokles said, *when we get there.*

Aye, he thought, *the Tragic Death of Agathokles, most likely.* But they were going to the theatre, the great Theatre of Dionysos that overlooked the Great Harbour, just by the palace. When Epiphanes complained that he could not walk any further Agathokles picked him up and carried him on his back. This man was not wholly lacking in kindness, Stranger, not altogether so wicked as Seshat may have made you think. He carried the young King up to the Syrinx, or covered gallery, that stood between the ornamental garden called the Maeander and the Palaistra, or wrestling-school, that joined the palace to the Theatre. The reason for going there was that this was a good hiding-place, for it had a secret exit, through which they might all escape, if escape became necessary, or, indeed, possible. Arsinoë Beta had built it, years ago, and it was built strong, with stout doors, so that her family might take refuge there in the event of civil unrest or other troubles. Now the time of trouble had indeed arrived.

Agathokleia had the key and let them in, when Agathokles slid the heavy metal bolts across and barred the first two doors. Then they barricaded themselves behind the third door. Agathokles, that lived in the passing moment, and had drunk too much, had not laid very good plans. He had brought no lights, there was nothing for the King or anybody else to eat or drink, no chair to sit down on, and the night was cold. They sat on the bare stones, in silence, shivering. Then Agathokles was sick all over the floor.

Epiphanes said, *I want to go home. I do not like this game. I am hungry. Take me back to the palace at once. This place smells.*

Agathokles and Agathokleia took no notice.

I can have you executed for this, Epiphanes said.

Agathokles said nothing, thinking, *No doubt I shall be executed anyway.*

The gallery was, all the same, a specially good place to take cover, for the doors of it were heavy, with open lattice-work through which Agathokles might perhaps negotiate the release of his royal hostage – and nobody else could get in without wielding the axe.

Agathokles had at least remembered to bring with him the materials for writing, so that he might send out a message. He sat in the half dark, listening to the distant shouting, and the sea pounding the harbour walls, and scribbled a letter:

I hereby renounce the office of Regent, he wrote. *I hereby abandon all my powers and dignities and all my revenues. I beg simply for my poor life and for enough food to eat, so that I may go back to my original obscurity, where I can not in future do anybody harm, even if I want to. . .*

Meanwhile the Alexandrians poured out of their houses by the thousand, so that not only Kanopic Street itself but every adjoining roof and flight of steps was crowded with people, as many as on the day of the Pompe – men, women, and even children, because it was already the custom for the children to play just as great a part in a riot as the adults, having been trained from a young age to chuck rocks and roof tiles – and the confused hubbub and clamour went on all night.

At dawn Oinanthe was still sitting in the Thesmophoreion. Agathokles, Agathokleia and Ptolemy Epiphanes and the relatives were still shivering in the gallery. It was difficult to make out what the crowds were shouting, but *Bring out the King* seemed to be what they wanted. By now Tlepolemos' troops were ready to make a move. First they seized the Gate of Audience, then they burst into the palace itself, not looting or burning, not touching a thing, in fact, but looking for the Regent. Their quarrel was not with the monarchy – Ptolemy Philopator had been good to the city – but with Agathokles. Agathokles had not been good to Alexandria. Aye, and it did not take the troops long to work out where he was hidden, for they went round to the gallery and ripped the first of the doors off its hinges almost at once. Then they stood in front of the second door and yelled for Epiphanes to be brought out to them.

Agathokles now thought less about hanging on to power than of how to save his own bacon. He asked one of his bodyguards to take his letter to the Macedonians, his admission of defeat. The man refused. All Agathokles' bodyguards, to a man, refused to carry it, saying, *I dare not . . . They will kill me on the spot . . . No, master, it is more than my life is worth.* However many times Agathokles said through his teeth, *You will do as I say . . . I order you to take this message . . . If you do not obey, you shall die at once . . .* they all shook their heads and looked at the floor. Agathokles was losing not only Alexandria but also his authority.

In the end Aristomenes volunteered to take the letter. This man had been very quick to honour Agathokles in the hour of his success. He was the first man in Alexandria to present him with a crown of gold oak leaves, a great honour among the Greeks, usually paid only to the king. He was also the first man who dared to wear a ring with Agathokles' portrait engraved on it. When his wife gave birth to a daughter he had even called her Agathokleia. Aristomenes, then, was a loyal – if misguided – supporter, and maybe, after all, the truth of it was that if he inspired such loyalty Agathokles cannot have been half so evil as Seshat has said he was. No man, perhaps, is wholly bad. There is some good in everybody, Stranger, even the man who commits murder and cannot stop himself from smiling afterwards. The mob of Alexandria, however, had decided that Agathokles was wholly bad, thoroughly bad, and that they must get rid of him just as quick as they could.

Aristomenes slipped out by the wicket gate to the Macedonian troops with the letter and explained what were his master's demands in return for handing over his hostage. The Macedonians, of course, drew the sword and made to run Aristomenes through, shouting, *This is Agathokles' man, give him the death he deserves.* But several of the men held their hands over him, shouting, *Leave him alone, he has done nothing wrong. Let him live. Let him speak.*

Aristomenes said what he had to say, and he took the Macedonians' message back to Agathokles in the gallery. The Macedonians' orders were simple: *Come back with the child . . . If you dare to come back here without him, you will sleep tonight in Hades.*

Aristomenes set off, taking a roundabout route, glancing often over his shoulder, trying to make sure he was not followed, but of course they did follow him. The Macedonians slunk up to the gallery behind him and began to smash up the second door. Agathokles and his people, alarmed by the soldiers' violent mood, jumped up, pleading with them, *We beg you to spare our lives . . . Really, we have done nothing wrong . . .* and the women began to wail, as if somebody was already dead.

All this time Ptolemy Epiphanes sat in a corner, on the floor, clutching his lion cub. From time to time he set this beast down and put his hands over his face, or over his ears, wanting neither to see nor hear, and certainly unable to understand what was going on.

I am hungry, he said. *The gallery stinks. Take me away from here.*

Nobody took any notice of him.

Then Agathokles pushed his hands through the lattice of the door, pleading for mercy, saying, *We were only doing what Old Sosibios told us to do. I was only obeying orders. Old Sosibios is the guilty one. I am an innocent man. You should let us go in peace* . . . He was lucky he did not have his hands cut off there and then, for it was all lies. Agathokles had known well enough what he was doing. He was not innocent but guilty of multiple atrocities.

If you happen to be a woman yourself, Stranger, you will know there are times when your breasts get in the way, are a wretched nuisance unto you. Sometimes, like Seshat herself, you may have wished to be rid of them, to cut them off, and be breast-free, like the Amazons, all the better to draw back the bow in battle. That night Agathokleia had reason to be thankful that she was a woman and had given suck. For just then, at a loss whatever else to do, she pulled open her *peplos*, and stuffed the tools of her trade through the door so that they stuck out through the lattice-work. She hammered upon the wood with her fists, shrieking and sobbing, *These are the breasts that gave suck to his Majesty. I am the Great Royal Nurse of the King. I have done nothing wrong. I beg you to let me go free.*

She knew very well, of course, the famous story of Phryne and Hypereides, in which Phryne, accused of some monstrous crime, ripped open her dress before the judges and laid bare the gleaming charms of her bosom, and how they refused to condemn her to death because of her surpassing beauty.

Agathokleia knew how Menelaos forgave Helen of Troy and forgot her adultery, at the sight of her bare breasts, the rosy apples of her bosom.

Now, in her turn, fat Agathokleia wailed, desperate, exposing her breasts. *I beg you not to harm the Great Royal Nurse of Pharaoh,* she sobbed. *I beg you to let us all go free.* It was a fine piece of acting, and it worked.

Aye, Agathokleia thought her breasts had saved her life. But the truth was that the Macedonians went further off, distracted by the execution of one of Agathokles' henchmen nearby, wanting to join in bludgeoning the man to death, cutting off his head, and so forth, and for some reason they did not come back.

All that day Agathokles and Agathokleia quarrelled violent, very violent, about what they should do.

Sister, Agathokles said, *we are finished. We shall have to surrender . . . Our luck is quite used up.*

No, Brother, Agathokleia said, *let us wait. The gods will be sure to send us a miracle.*

Agathokles laughed bitter. *Sister,* he said, *the gods have long since abandoned us. The gods exist only in your woman's mad imagination.*

But at last they agreed that to fight on and on was pointless, and they decided to send out the boy king to the Macedonian troops of Tlepolemos. When nobody was in sight, and without saying a word of why, nor a word of farewell, they shoved Epiphanes through the wicket gate. Two of the body-guards they pushed out as well, to look after him, then they slammed the gate shut and locked it behind them.

Epiphanes said, *What is happening? Where are we going now?* But the bodyguards did not have the answer to such questions.

Agathokles and Agathokleia strained their ears, listening for the tramp of soldiers' boots, but they could hear only the slap of the water in the harbour, the waves washing on to the beach. They slipped out through the secret back door of the gallery themselves, with the relatives still tagging along behind. (And yes, it would have been better for them if they had jumped into the sea and drowned themselves then and there.) As they emerged at the outer wall of the palace, on Cape Lokhias, right by the seashore, they saw Ptolemy Epiphanes in the distance, walking along, a small boy wearing a filthy cloak, who might have been anybody. As the sun went down they watched the two bodyguards lead him away, each holding one of his hands. The sky over Alexandria was red, like blood, as if in warning.

4.26

The Stadion

The Macedonians lifted Ptolemy Epiphanes on to the back of a great white horse and led him along Kanopic Street in the gathering dark, quite bewildered. He was in no danger. Every man in Alexandria knew that pale triangular face, those slightly bulging eyes, the unmistakable yellow curls of a Ptolemy, and in spite of his father's often strange behaviour, the royal family remained in high favour with the Alexandrians. Again, you see, Stranger, Ptolemy Philopator was not bad through and through. Seshat defends his blackened reputation. Everywhere the crowd stopped their furious chanting against Agathokles and his sister, parted to let his Majesty through, and broke into warm applause.

The horse turned south, into the native quarter, Rhakotis, past the great Temple of Sarapis on its artificial hill, and out through the city gate to the Stadion. Epiphanes' entry there was greeted with tumultuous cheering, the frenzied clapping of hands, and the chanting of *Pto-le-mai-os, Pto-le-mai-os, Pto-le-mai-os, mai-os, mai-os*. The soldiers lifted him down from the horse, and Sosibios son of Sosibios – the good Sosibios – the Keeper of the King's Seal, who was devoted to the King – sat him down in the royal seat. From the start it looked as if this Ptolemy was going to be *popular*.

Epiphanes looked about him. The Stadion was jammed full, and it held twenty thousand persons. Torches flickered everywhere. A bonfire had been lit in the middle of the racing-track. He was unafraid of crowds – he had been in the Stadion before – but he had never seen such fury, and he would never forget the half-demented howling of his subjects. The people of Alexandria were beside themselves with anger that those guilty of murdering Epiphanes' mother had not been brought to justice. They continued to scream *Agathokles ... Agathokleia* in strophe and antistrophe, and, *Bring them to us . . . We shall punish them*. But they had used up the whole day shouting in vain.

Sosibios the Younger, seeing that there was not a hope in Hades of calming the people down, and that the boy was beginning to look frightened and like to weep, for that he found himself among strangers, lifted up a speaking-trumpet and asked for silence. Then he said, *Men and women of Alexandria, I am going to ask the King a question, and the question is this: Will his Majesty punish the guilty ones, the people who did bad things to his mother?*

The crowd roared, *Agathokles . . . Agathokleia . . . Agathokles . . . Agathokleia . . .*

Sosibios held up his arm for silence, and the *Ssssshhhh . . . Ssssssshhhh . . .* echoed round the Stadion.

Ptolemy Epiphanes sniffed. His lip quivered. The people were silent, listening now. No, he would not weep. Herakles never wept. Epiphanes yawned. Then he nodded his head.

There was a deafening outburst of roaring, then the chanting began all over again. Most of the crowd sat in the seats, waiting for the spectacle. Others stood up, the better to see what was going on. Wherever there was wooden planking, they drubbed their feet on it. Any man with a stick or a weapon bashed it on something that made a good noise.

Men and women of Alexandria, Sosibios son of Sosibios said into the speaking-trumpet, *the King is tired . . . It is past his Majesty's bedtime . . . If it is agreeable to you I shall take him to a place of safety for the night. Then we shall bring Agathokles and his sister here.* The crowd screamed approval, louder than ever. And so Sosibios son of Sosibios led Ptolemy Epiphanes gently away from the uproar and the scene of what could only be grave trouble, the scene of the horror that was about to happen.

The mob of Alexandria had always been pretty volatile, often getting so worked up by the chariot race that they tore off their clothes and hurled them at the competitors. The Stadion was by tradition the place where the Alexandrians showed anger. Now their anger was boiling over.

But where were Agathokles and Agathokleia? By some miracle, indeed, they had escaped from the gallery without being spotted. Then they had walked calmly through the crowds, faces blacked, unrecognized, heading for their house in the city – in itself the stupidest thing they could have done. If only they had the wit to head straight for the ships, and get out of Egypt altogether, because very soon a great number of soldiers – some acting on their own, without orders from Tlepolemos, others forced to go by the crowd – set off to hunt them down. Aye, the famous mob of Alexandria began to take the law into their own hands.

What, then, did Agathokles and Agathokleia think they were doing? They remembered the story, how Arsinoë Beta managed to keep her treasure in the midst of the crisis at Kassandreia, and they thought to do the same. However, they had not quite the same organizational skills as that Great Lady. They were frantically packing their belongings into boxes, thinking – too late – to flee the city. They had not the sense to leave behind their wealth and save themselves. Of course not. Without riches they would be nothing again. They would rather die than lose the jewels, the gold, the finery, every august costly stone. They must take all this stuff with them, wherever they meant to go, and it was the possessions, the paraphernalia of royalty that weighed them down, used up their precious time, and led to their capture. Aye, for the door of Agathokles and Agathokleia their house was soon knocked flat, amid tumultuous roaring, and they were thrown on to the street, stark naked, with their arms bound behind their backs like prisoners of war, and iron chains hanging round their necks and ankles.

4.27

Sparagmos

While the crowd in the Stadion screamed for Agathokles and his sister, and waited, patient and impatient, for them to be brought, Philon, Agathokles' young parasite, or jester, who had been at his master's last feast, staggered into the arena, far too drunk to think what danger he might be in, or even what he was saying. When he saw how agitated the people were, he began to scream with laughter, saying, *What's eating them then?* He pushed the man standing next to him, and said, *If Agathokles comes out here you will be sorry.*

The man pushed him back, saying, *They will eat YOU,* and he began to shout: *This is Agathokles' man . . . He deserves to have his guts pulled out of him . . . Here is one of Agathokles' lovers . . . would you not love to see him die?* Others jostled this Philon and knocked him over, and when he tried to stand up and defend himself the man beside him tore the cloak off his back. Others pushed him down again, shouting, *This is one of Agathokles' friends, he deserves death,* and they jabbed their spears into his body, jabbed him over and over again. Philon was still breathing, still laughing, as they hauled him into the middle of the Stadion and flung him down in the sand. Philon had lived by laughing, and he died laughing. That was the Alexandrians' first taste of blood that night, and it gave them the taste for more.

The crowd who saw Agathokles of Samos dragged in chains down Kanopic Street on the end of a rope, stumbling, scrambling to his feet, falling down, then getting up again, were mostly silent: some hissed him, some threw stones. Agathokles wore nothing but the ivy-leaf tattoos that covered his body. In this last procession he was not painted with gold paint, nor wearing golden wings. He wore no great grin upon his face, and they made him walk. As he passed through the native quarter, the people flung the contents of their dung carts, all manner of filth, chanting abuse, baying for his blood.

Agathokles entered the Stadion hissed and jeered on all sides. Then the roaring and whistling started up again. But Agathokles was a lucky man. As soon as he appeared, some of Tlepolemos' men ran up to him and plunged their daggers into his belly. It was more an act of kindness than of hatred, saving him from the worse fate that was coming to his sister. Agathokles fell to his knees, clutching his belly as the black lifeblood poured out of him.

Next came Agathokleia, riding on the back of a horse, because her legs had given way. She was followed by her relatives, all chained together, the unworthy ones she had turned into generals, admirals, and ladies-in-waiting, and the cry was, *Kill her, kill all of them . . . Kill, kill, kill . . .*

While Agathokleia's captors argued about what manner of death she deserved, the crowd shouted, *Poke her eyes out . . . Cut her tongue out . . . Hang her on a rope . . .* and *Carve her up.* As they pulled Agathokleia down from her horse, she recovered her strength, broke free, and knelt in the sand beside her brother, with the tears falling down her cheeks. She must hear his dying words and receive his last breath, the brother who had been as much as her husband, and the crowd held back, straining to hear what words their brave tyrant might speak in his dying moments.

Agathokles' eyes were already misting over, but Agathokleia kissed his perfect chiselled lips. She kissed his bleeding forehead. She kissed his bloody wounds.

We shall fly . . . to the sky . . . upon the wing of Thoth . . . Agathokleia, he said.

We are done for, Brother, she sobbed, squeezing his bloody hand.

We shall . . . meet . . . in the Field . . . of Rushes . . . after all, he said.

Agathokleia stroked his bloody cheek.

I . . . beseech you . . . Sister, he began.

Do not try to speak, Brother, Agathokleia said.

Do not . . . I beg you, do not . . . let . . . the dogs . . . and . . . birds . . . eat . . . but then Tlepolemos himself came up, his eyes angry, pushed Agathokleia aside, and stuck his knife in Agathokles' throat, up to the hilt. Aye, the blood poured out of his mouth, then, and his eyes stared, unseeing, and his body went limp.

Last came Oinanthe. They did not dare to slice up the old woman in the Thesmophoreion, fearing that any such act would make the gods send down a scourge upon the city, in punishment for the violation of the sacred place. No, they would deal with her properly, in the Stadion, in public, make her wait, make her suffer. They dragged her from her place of sanctuary, ripped her clothes off and led her away on horseback, and the crowds of people she passed through roared for her blood indeed. Oinanthe herself shrieked the prayers of the desperate, to Artemis, to Demeter, to Apollo, to Zeus the Saviour. But Zeus seemed to be in no hurry to rescue her. He left Horrible Oinanthe to her horrible fate. She screamed like some great scavenging bird, at first, then sat silent, shaking with terror, sure, now, that the gods had stopped listening to her.

Some said Agathokleia and Oinanthe were crucified for the murder of Arsinoë Gamma, but no, the fate of those women was worse than crucifixion, much worse. Aye, for the good people of Alexandria began to beat Agathokleia with their fists, and bite her with their teeth, and stab her with their kitchen knives, and cut out strips of her flesh, and gouge out her eyes with their fingers, and they set about pulling her body apart, tearing her limb from limb, as a child might pull the wings off a moth. Aye, like the moth, it is a good comparison. Agathokles and Agathokleia, had flown too close to the flame.

Think, Stranger, if you will be so kind, of a time when you have eaten a cooked chicken with your bare hands. You must pull the leg from the body. You must detach the wing from the breast. The succulent flesh resists, then it lets go of its moorings with a sucking sound, does it not? That is what the good people of Alexandria did with Agathokleia and Oinanthe her mother, and their relations. They pulled them apart, pulled their legs and arms off, uncooked, still alive.

The last words of beautiful Agathokleia were nothing but screaming, nothing but screaming. Neither her divine good looks nor her beautiful breasts would save her this time. The young Ptolemy Epiphanes would never reward this Great Royal Nurse of his for her good milk. She would not have his thanks for her lovely breasts. He would not care for Agathokleia in her old age with every goodly thing, or set up a worthy tomb for her. The famous breasts of Agathokleia were meat for hungry dogs.

Such was the end of the woman who was pleased to murder the Queen of Egypt, the Lady of the Two Lands, the Mistress of Happiness.

For all Oinanthe's screeching that her breast was in the old king's mouth for one thousand days and nights, they still tried to pull the old woman's legs off, much as a child might pull the legs off some fat and nasty insect, but Oinanthe was tough, all gristle, not so easy to take to pieces. Aye, now they were obliged to have the tug of war with her body, for they fixed ropes to her arms and legs and literally tore her body apart. Then they set upon her with their teeth, *as if old Oinanthe were a rare steak*. These one-time servants, who had robbed their masters down to the last jar of pickled olives, they learned how terrible is the cruelty of the Alexandrians when their anger is roused.

Seshat assures you, Stranger, every word is the truth. But LOOK! How very like it was to the *sparagmos*, the frenzied rite called *Tearing Apart*, in which the devotees of Dionysos rip up raw meat and devour it, with the hot blood trickling down their chins. And did the Alexandrians *eat* the flesh of Agathokles and Agathokleia, their raw flesh, after the custom of the Dionysiac *sparagmos*? Had not Old Oinanthe hoped to make the women in the Thesmophoreion *taste the flesh of their own children?* How could these women fail to oblige her by turning her evil wishes upon herself? Aye, now her own children's flesh was, indeed, stuffed in her mouth, and her own flesh was in the mouths of those very women, who ate her raw, yes, indeed, as if her too rash words had prophesied her fate. Above the tumultuous shouting of the crowd that night rose the wail of the dying Oinanthe, the great mother who saw her own children butchered before her eyes, and was made to eat their flesh, her terrible terrible wailing, soaring high above every other noise in the Stadion, like the best of singers at the Theatre of Dionysos, more shrill, indeed, than the highest note of her own sambuca, until it was stopped short by Tlepolemos himself, by the final thrust of his knife in her throat, so that the rest was nothing but gurgling.

Aye, we should not forget, Stranger, that Dionysos was not only the Bestower of Bliss, the god of Wine and Joy, but also the god of Frenzy. He was also the persecuted god, who suffers and dies, just as Ptolemy Philopator was persecuted, suffered and died, Philopator who was himself Dionysos. All whom Dionysos loves, all who attend him, must share his tragic fate, his dramatic death. Agathokles had played Dionysos himself, naked but for a pair of hunting boots. Agathokles and Agathokleia, who had been part of Dionysos's drunken retinue, must die too.

The hair of a man who has died by violence is an ingredient of many of the magic spells of the Greeks.

The dog-teeth from an unburied corpse will make a useful talisman against the toothache.

The back of a dead man's left hand will heal every affection of the throat, and all manner of scrofulous sores.

Sure, they threw the torn-out genitals of Agathokles, castrator of horses and throttler of dogs, to the dogs to gorge upon, and you may choose, Stranger, to see it as the revenge of Anubis, if you wish, but there was not much of Agathokles of Samos left for the dogs when the people of Alexandria had finished with him.

In this unpleasant manner, the charming Agathokles, sometime Dioiketes, or first minister of Egypt, sometime Ganymede, or Cupbearer of Pharaoh, met his death. He was a little older than the late King Ptolemy Philopator, perhaps thirty-nine years of age, and left no known progeny.

4.28

The Libyarch

As for Philammon the Libyarch, the man who had charge of the Queen's murder, he should have stayed where he was, in Libya. Perhaps he thought to join Tlepolemos and help topple Agathokles. Perhaps he simply found Libya too hot. Whatever was the reason for it, he returned to Alexandria just about this time, and it was a grave mistake, for the one dozen beautiful young wait-ing-women of Arsinoë Gamma, her sometime close companions, got to hear of it, and gathered together, saying: *How can we let her Majesty's murderer go unpunished? How can we sit here sewing while the man who killed beautiful Arsinoë still lives and breathes?*

In the dead hours of the night these high-born waiting gentlewomen went to Philammon's house with axes and smashed down his door. These noble-women, well trained in the art of self-defence, pulled Philammon out of his bed and threw him down into the street, where they set about cutting him to pieces, turning him into dog-food. His young son they strangled with their bare hands. These beautiful and most beautiful Macedonian ladies, whose lives had been devoted to nothing more violent than playing the lyre and weaving cloth of purple, now dragged Philammon's wife naked and scream-ing into the Agora, where they clubbed her to death.

4.29

Harpokrates

Out of the chaos there emerged a new kind of order. At length Horemakhet, High Priest of Ptah, arrived in Alexandria to do his duty by the King, sorrow-ing over the violence and bloodshed.

Why did you not come before? Epiphanes asked him. *Where have you been, Excellency?*

But Horemakhet said only, *I am here now, Megaleios, all will be well now with your Majesty.* Though all was not quite well, for Upper Egypt was still under the sway of Horwennefer.

This Ptolemy was the fifth Ptolemy. Horemakhet saw to it that he was given a Greek title, *Epiphanes,* meaning God Manifest. It referred to two stars, or comets, that appeared about this time. Epiphanes was the new comet, who would leave a fresh trail of sparks across the heavens. Horemakhet gave him a second title for good measure: *Eucharistos*, meaning Blessed. These titles, that slipped so easy off the Greek tongue, were good Greek renderings of the hieroglyphs, for the Egyptian equivalent of Epiphanes is *He Who Comes Forth*, and Eucharistos signifies *One of Goodness*, and *Lord of Beauties*, or *One Whose Favour is Beautiful*. Epiphanes' titles sounded just fine to Egyptian ears. They were fine to the Greeks too, because

Dionysos, by chance, happened also to be the god of Epiphany, the god of showing forth. Such was the excellent and most excellent work of Horemakhet.

As for that crazy Dionysos, you might think that the Macedonians would have had the sense to quit their worship of this god forthwith, in view of the recent wild events in the Stadion. But no, they did not, of course. Man cannot simply decide to abolish a god, just because he dislikes his character. The worship of Dionysos was not a thing that might be given up upon a whim. By no means. Even at the very end of the line of Ptolemies, *six generations later,* Dionysos would still be enjoying their zealous worship, for they did enjoy worshipping him: they loved Dionysos more than any god – he was the god of *Drinking*. The Macedonians could no more give him up than they could give up wine. Stranger, the world will still be worshipping this charming and delightful god in your own day, tearing the world apart under his violent influence, though, for sure, by then they will have quite forgotten his name, just as surely as they have forgotten the name of Seshat.

Horemakhet had hopes for Ptolemy Epiphanes, great hopes. He was the first Ptolemy to be born of a marriage between full brother and sister, and it made the Macedonian royal family look more like the mirror image of the Egyptian gods, Isis and Osiris, the brother and sister whose child was Horus. Epiphanes *was* the Horus, and it was good.

The young Ptolemy Epiphanes walked in his father's funeral procession. He carried the Greek urn of silver that had in it his father's ashes. He did not stumble. He did not drop it. Nor did he weep. Horemakhet had taught him to bite the lip, how not to think of what was happening. It was not difficult. Epiphanes did not, just then, have much understanding of death. But Epiphanes it was, even so, that ate the pease pudding, the funeral dish of the Greeks, for his dead father. Thus, at least – and at last – the Alexandrians got to eat their funeral feast of roast beef, and were a little happier than before. As for Arsinoë Gamma, Epiphanes carried her empty silver urn to the Tomb of Alexander, with her name upon it, against the day when what was left of her might come to light.

The Egyptians proclaimed Epiphanes King of Upper and Lower Egypt at Memphis and in Alexandria, at the age of five, but they would not crown him until his Coming of Age ceremony, some nine years later, when he would be fourteen.

When it came to finding him a wife, there would be no sister for him to marry, and perhaps it was just as well. Already Horemakhet planned for him a foreign marriage, to the Kleopatra who was the daughter of Antiokhos Megas of Syria, and she would be the first of seven Kleopatras in the House of Ptolemy. Perhaps you will have come across the name before, Stranger.

Horemakhet thought of the day when he should crown Ptolemy Epiphanes with the Double Crown of Egypt. He would hold the falcon's wing over his head. He would dangle the vulture wing over his brow. As if in anticipation he talked Epiphanes into having his head shaved right now, leaving only the Horus sidelock hanging there, like a native Egyptian pharaoh indeed.

For the time being the now six-year-old Ptolemy Epiphanes *was* Harpokrates, the Infant Horus, with his finger still stuck in his mouth, and it was fitting, most fitting. Perhaps, Horemakhet thought, Egypt might find it in her to *love* this Pharaoh who was a child, as they had not quite come to love his father.

Just then, far from the House of Ptolemy enjoying a shower of gold from Zeus, it looked as if Zeus had *pissed* upon the descendants of Ptolemy Soter. Now, though, they had the golden opportunity of a fresh beginning. Aye, Horemakhet, the great one, who knew the mysteries, who proclaimed what was forgotten, who remembered both the fleeting moment and the very end of time, and could report on what happens even during the hours of darkness, he had very great hopes for this fledgeling falcon.

4.30

Lady of Hieroglyphs

Seshat would like to put the Romans just here. It would give balance to her book if there were Romans in the middle, Romans at the end. For either Agathokles of Samos or the people of Alexandria had sent a delegation to Rome to request that they protect the orphaned Ptolemy Epiphanes and safeguard his kingdom. The reason for it was to counter the pact already made between the fifth King Philip of Macedon and Antiokhos Megas, King of Syria, who had agreed to carve up the kingdom of Egypt between them.

The Romans welcomed the delegation. They looked forward to making war on King Philip. And they very much looked forward to taking Egypt for themselves. Ambassadors were duly sent off to Syria and Macedon to tell Antiokhos and Philip to keep their evil hands off the Two Lands, and Marcus

Aemilius Lepidus was duly sent to administer Alexandria and all Egypt as Ptolemy Epiphanes his guardian.

We know a good deal about this Marcus Aemilius Lepidus, Stranger, the youngest of the three *legati*. He was about twenty-nine years of age when he set his boots upon Egyptian soil, full of a proud self-assurance, the most handsome Roman of his day. He was already a Senator, at the beginning of a brilliant career that would make him twice Consul of Rome, Censor, *Pontifex Maximus*, and *Princeps Senatus*. He was the man who would build the famous Via Aemilia, that stretched from Placentia to Ariminum. The official line was that he was sent to inform Ptolemy Epiphanes of Rome's victory over Carthage, and to offer him Rome's thanks for staying loyal at a time when the situation was difficult, for all Rome's other allies were deserting her cause.

We know just who came to Egypt with Marcus Aemilius Lepidus: Gaius Claudius Nero, and Publius Sempronius Tuditanus, two distinguished senators, good at showing the teeth, hard men, with the handshake like the iron wrench, but not so good at smiling with the eyes.

We know also that Marcus Aemilius Lepidus was appointed *Tutor Regis*, or Guardian of the King. Some even said that it was Ptolemy Philopator himself who with his last breath put his son under the guardianship of Rome and Marcus Aemilius Lepidus, as a far far better thing than letting his disapproving and most disapproving sister get her hands on the Regency.

There is just one thing wrong with this neat ending to Seshat's book, Stranger, and that is this: a Roman delegation may have visited Egypt about this time, but you will find no honest man who will agree that Marcus Aemilius Lepidus was either Ptolemy Epiphanes' guardian or his tutor. It simply did not happen. All scholars of chronology agree that Egypt did not come under the protection of Rome at this time, but remained independent. Seshat, the divine chronologer and chronographer, agrees with them. This is one of those manifestly false idle foolish stories that should have been scratched out from the pages of History. You should not think of believing it.

Aye, you can never be too careful with the Past, Stranger. But you may be assured that Seshat is the careful one, who counts the days, who swears to tell the truth. You have no idea how difficult it is to be the goddess of History, always to get your story right with hardly a shred of evidence to go on; never to show ill temper, always having to look beautiful, *always having to tell the truth*. It is like being dead, only you never die, but live for ever. Seshat has no truck with lies. Even for the Greeks, to tell lies about the dead is one of the very gravest crimes.

In Egypt men will appear out of the storm of sand and say to you nonsensical things, such as, *Man fears Time, but Time fears the Pyramids*. But I say to you, *Time should fear Seshat, the Original One, who was ancient herself aeons before Khufu – or Cheops – dreamed of building his absurd pyramid.* You should realize, Stranger, that it was Seshat herself that marked out the ground plan of that mighty monument. That is why you may still marvel in your own day, Stranger, at the accuracy of pyramidal orientation: it is the gift of the goddess, Seshat, Lady of the Builders, who was there at the Stretching of the Cord, when there was nothing at the place you persist in calling Giza but blown sand.

The pyramids are not the only thing to be seen in Egypt, Stranger. When the storm of sand passes away, look about you. Do not omit to visit the temples that Ptolemy built. Speak his name, if you please, that he may, indeed, be Ptolemy *Living for Ever.* But think also of the gods that inspired the work, such as Thoth; such as Seshat. Man should fear THOTH, who writes down the judgement, not Time. Man should fear Seshat, Lady of Hieroglyphs, who is older than Time, Seshat, who controls the day of his death. Aye, fear Seshat, who was there at the beginning; who will be there at the very end, still counting, still writing everything down for you. On that you may depend, my friend.

Glossary

Agathos Daimon: Gk., the Good Spirit; the divinized lucky house snake of Alexandria; sometimes personified as Thermouthis.

agora: Gk., market place.

Amicitia: Lat., friendship, alliance.

Ammut: Eg., a composite beast, part hippopotamus, part crocodile, part lion; devourer of the dead.

Amonrasonter: Gk. name for Amun (as King of the Gods), who by Ptolemaic times was directly equated with Zeus.

Amun: Lord of the Thrones of the Two Lands; supreme god of the Egyptians.

Anubis: Eg., god of the Dead, shown as a jackal, or jackal-headed man.

Aphrodite: Gk. goddess of Love, Beauty, Fertility. The Greeks made her equal to the Egyptian Hathor; at Rome she was assimilated as Venus.

Apis: Eg., the sacred bull of Memphis; the Living Image of Ptah; known to the Greeks as Apis, or Epaphos, and to the Egyptians as Hap.

Apollo: Gk. god of Music, Prophecy, Healing and Medicine, and Archery.

Apollonopolis: town between Luxor and Aswan, still dominated by its temple; the modern Edfu.

Archigallos: Gk., chief priest of Kybele.

Arensnuphis: Meroitic god, shown in human form with a feathered crown.

Ares: Gk. god of War; the Mars of the Romans.

Artemis: Gk. goddess of Fertility and protector of women in childbirth; the maiden huntress; daughter of Zeus.

Asklepios: Gk. god of Health; Eg. Imhotep; Lat. Aesculapius.

ataraxia: Gk., calmness, impassiveness, balance of soul.

Athena, Athene: Gk., the maiden goddess of War, and patroness of arts and crafts; the personification of wisdom; Lat. Athena or Minerva.

Attis: a Phrygian deity, the youthful lover of Kybele, and prototype of her eunuch devotees, the Galloi.

Atum: Eg. Sun god and creator of the Universe; Lord of Heliopolis.

Ba: Eg., the spiritual part of a person that survives after his death, preserves his individuality and is able to wander at will. The Ba is often shown as a bird with a human head.

Basileus, Basilissa: Gk. titles, roughly equivalent to king and queen.

chendjyt: Eg., the pleated loincloth, or kilt, of Pharaoh.
cubit: Gk. measure equal to 18 or 20 fingerbreadths (about 18–20 inches).

dekadrachm: Gk. ten-drachma coin.
Demeter: Gk. goddess of corn; mother, by Zeus, of Persephone. These two were
  known as 'the Two Goddesses'. Their most important festival was the
  Thesmophoria.
dexiosis: Gk., handshaking.
Dioiketes: Gk., Chief Administrator of Ptolemy in Egypt; First Minister, Vizier and
  Minister of Finance.
Dionysos (Dionysus): Gk. god of the Vine and Wine; god of Frenzy; Lat. Bacchus.
dodekadrachm: Gk., twelve-drachma coin.
drachma: Greek coin equal to six obols; 6,000 drachmas make one talent. Also a
  measure of weight: one drachma = 4.36 grams.

Epiphanes: Gk. title meaning God Made Manifest, or Manifestation of the Divine
  Light.
Eros: Gk. god of Love and Fertility; the son of Aphrodite.
Euergetes: Gk. title meaning Benefactor.

Fates: Gk., a trio of goddesses (Klotho, Lakhesis, Atropos) that ruled people's destinies.
Furies, or Erinyes: Gk., also known as Eumenides, 'the Kindly Ones'; avengers of
  crime, especially against the ties of kinship. They are represented as winged
  women, sometimes with snakes about them.

Gallos, Galloi: Gk., eunuch priests of Kybele.
Geb: Eg., the earth god; son of Shu and Tefnut; father of Isis, Seth and Nephthys.
Geloiastai: Gk., the Laughter-Makers, members of a drinking-club founded by
  Ptolemy IV.
gymnasion: Gk., place of exercise for males, designed to make the youths of the city
  fit for military service.
gynaikeion: Gk., women's quarters of a house, where males were forbidden access
  after the age of seven years.

Hades: brother of Zeus; Gk. god of the Underworld, who ruled over the dead with
  his wife Persephone; also known as Pluto.
Hapi: Eg. god of the Nile.
Harpies: Gk. 'snatchers', personifying the demonic force of storms; represented as
  birds with women's faces.

Harpokrates: Eg., the Infant Horus, or Horus-the-Child; often depicted wearing the sidelock of youth, and sucking his fingers.

Harsomtous: Eg., a form of Horus-the-Child as sistrum-player; also called Ihy.

Hathor: cow goddess of the Egyptians, symbolic mother of the Pharaoh.

Heb-Sed: *see* Sed festival.

Helios: the Sun god of the Greeks.

hemiobol: Gk., half-obol coin.

Heptastadion: Gk., the seven-*stade*-long bridge linking the city of Alexandria to Pharos island.

Hera: Gk. wife of Zeus; queen of the gods; goddess of marriage. Lat. Juno.

Hermes: Gk. god of Fertility and Good Luck. The Greeks made him equal to Thoth.

Hierosolyma: Gk. name for Jerusalem.

Hippodrome: Gk., horse-racing track.

hoplite: Gk., heavy-armed soldier.

Horus: Eg. the falcon god, Lord of the Sky; the symbol of divine kingship in Egypt. The Pharaoh is the Living Horus.

Hygeia: Gk., personification of Health; daughter of Asklepios.

hypokephalos (Lat. hypocephalus): Egyptian amulet in the form of a disk of painted stuccoed papyrus, intended to warm the head of the dead in the Afterlife.

Hypomnematographos: Gk., writer of memoranda.

Imhotep: Eg. deified architect of the first pyramid, considered to be a god of wisdom, writing and medicine linked with the cult of Ptah. The Greeks made him equal to Asklepios.

Isis: Eg. goddess, More Clever than a Million Gods. She is a goddess of immense magic power, the symbolic mother of the Pharaoh, and mother also of Horus and wife of Osiris. She is called Clever of Tongue, Great of Magic, the Lady of Many Names.

Ka: Eg., the life-force, or 'double', of each individual that continues to live after death; the essential ingredient that makes a living person differ from a dead one.

kalokagathos: Gk., a perfect gentleman, or a perfect character.

kanephoros: Gk., basket-bearer.

khepresh: Eg., the blue leather helmet-crown of War.

khlamys: Gk., the military cloak of the Macedonians.

Khnum: Eg. ram-god, who created life on the potter's wheel.

Khonsu: Eg. moon-god, linked with Thebes; son of Amun and Mut; shown as a mummified human figure, often falcon-headed.

kinaidos: Gk., catamite.

klepsydra: Gk., water-clock.

Koile-Syria (Coele-Syria): region of Syria-Palestine – Hollow Syria, thus called to distinguish it from Syria between the Rivers (Mesopotamia).

Kybele: Phrygian goddess of fertility, the 'Great Mother'; associated with her lover, Attis.

Maat: Eg. goddess, the personification of all the elements of cosmic harmony as laid down by the creator god at the beginning of time – Truth, Justice, Moral Integrity. She is shown as a woman wearing one ostrich feather standing upright on her head – the Feather of Righteousness and Truth.

maenad: Gk. word meaning 'madwoman' – the votary of Dionysos.

Megaleios, Megaleia: Gk., Majesty.

Memphis: Eg. city, formerly called Ineb-Hedj, or Mennufer, the city of Menes, the first Pharaoh; sometimes also called White Walls. The Greeks called this place Memphis.

Meroë: capital of Kush, or Nubia, situated on the east bank of the Nile between the Fifth and Sixth Cataracts.

Metroön: Gk., sanctuary of the goddess Kybele, the 'Great Mother'.

Mikros: Gk., Small One.

Min: the Egyptian fertility god of Koptos; equated by the Greeks with Pan.

mina, minas: Gk. measure, equal to one pound weight of silver, or 100 drachmas.

Montu: Eg., the falcon-headed god of War.

Mouseion: Gk. Temple of the Muses, founded at Alexandria by Ptolemy I Soter.

Muses: Gk., the nine daughters of Zeus and Mnemosyne, usually named thus: Kalliope (epic poetry), Klio (history), Euterpe (flute-playing), Melpomene (tragedy), Terpsikhore (dancing), Erato (the lyre), Polyhymnia (sacred song), Ourania (astronomy) and Thalia (comedy). Isis was leader of the Muses.

Mut: Eg. Theban vulture-goddess, wife of Amun and mother of Khonsu; usually shown as a woman wearing a red, feather-patterned dress, and a vulture head-dress; also shown as a lioness.

nauarkhos: Gk., fleet-commander, admiral.

Nekhbet: the vulture-goddess of Upper Egypt.

Nike: Gk. goddess, the personification of Victory.

nome: Gk. term used to refer to the forty-two traditional provinces of Egypt.

nuktistrategos: Gk., captain of the night-watch.

obol: Gk. coin; one-sixth of a drachma.

oktodrachm: Gk., eight-drachma coin.

oneiroscopist: Gk. interpreter of dreams.

Osiris: Eg. god of the Dead; husband of Isis, the Great God, the Mighty One.

ouraios: Gk. form of the Latin uraeus; *see* Wadjet.

Pan: Gk. god of Flocks and Herds and Fertility; patron of shepherds and herdsmen; the Min of the Egyptians.

Panacea: Gk., the 'All-Healer', daughter of Asklepios.

paratiltria: Gk., female slave who plucked the hairs from her mistress's body.

parthenos: Gk., maiden.

peltast: Gk., light-armed soldier.

penteres, pentereis: Gk., oared galley, a 'five'; the equivalent of the quinquereme.

peplos: Gk., woman's dress.

phalanx: Gk., the formation of the heavy-armed foot soldiers in battle, consisting of 4,096 men.

Pharos: Gk., the Great Lighthouse of Alexandria, begun by Ptolemy Soter.

Philadelphos: Gk. title meaning Brother-Loving, Sister-Loving.

Philopator: Gk. title meaning Father-Loving.

Pnephoros: Eg., a crocodile god.

Pompe: Gk., the grand procession founded by Ptolemy Philadelphos.

Poseidon: Gk. god of Earthquakes and Water, later a god of the Sea and associated with horses; brother of Zeus and Hades; Lat. Neptune.

Priapos: Gk. god of fertility, said to be the son of Aphrodite and Dionysos.

pronaos: Gk., columned hall with open or half-open façade at the front of a temple.

propylon: Gk., temple gateway.

prostagma: Gk., order, decree.

pschent: the double crown of Upper Egypt (white) and Lower Egypt (red).

psittakos: Gk., parrot.

Ptah: the Egyptian creator god of Memphis; Gk. Hephaistos; Lat. Vulcan.

Punt: the South Country, perhaps the modern Somalia.

pylon: Gk., gateway of the Egyptian temple.

Ra (Re): the creator Sun god of the Egyptians at Heliopolis; shown as a falcon with the Sun disk on his head. The Greeks made him the equal of Helios.

rhombos: Gk., magic wheel; *phallos*.

Sakhmet (Sekhmet): Eg., lioness-headed consort of Ptah of Memphis.

sambuca: a triangular stringed instrument with sharp shrill tone.

sappheiros: Gk., the costly blue stone known as lapis lazuli.

Sarapis, Serapis: god with both Egyptian and Greek characteristics. From Zeus and Helios he draws his aspects of kingship and Sun god; from Dionysos, fertility in nature; from Hades and Asklepios his connection with the Afterlife and Healing.

sarissa: Gk., the lance of the Macedonians, 12 or 14 or 16 cubits in length.

satrap: old Persian word meaning provincial governor, or governor of a province.

Satyr: Gk., a half-bestial spirit of the woods and hills, attendant upon Dionysos.

Sed festival (or Heb-Sed): Eg. ritual of renewal and regeneration celebrated by Pharaoh after thirty years on the throne.

seistron: Gk., sacred rattle used in Egyptian temples to ward off evil; Lat. *sistrum*.

Seshat: Eg. goddess of writing and measurement; wife and/or sister of Thoth.

Seth: Eg. god of the desert; the embodiment of disorder; brother of Isis. Sometimes shown as a hippopotamus, pig or donkey.

skollopendra: Gk. (lit. millipede), the carrying-chair of Pharaoh, borne upon the shoulders of twenty men, with one man in front, leading – thus forty-two legs, equal to the number of *nomes*, or districts of Egypt.

smaragdos: Gk., emerald.

Sobek: the Egyptian crocodile god. The Greeks identified him with their own god Helios.

Soter: Gk., Saviour, or Deliverer from Danger; a title of Zeus, also bestowed on Ptolemy I.

sparagmos: Gk. rite of tearing apart, performed as part of the worship of Dionysos.

stade, Stadion: Gk. measure, equal to 600 feet; also the name for the Greek running track, and for the foot race that was one length of the Stadion.

Strategos: Gk., general; also military governor.

strophion: Gk., band worn round the breast by women.

Symposion: Gk., drinking-party; Lat. *symposium.*

talent: Gk. unit of weight and money, equal to sixty minas or 6,000 drachmas, or 36,000 obols.

taurobolion: Gk., bull-sacrifice in honour of Kybele.

taxiarch: Gk., commander of a *taxis* – a corps, or squadron, of 128 men.

Tefnut: Eg. goddess, personification of moisture; daughter of Ra; often shown in leonine form.

Thalamegos: Gk., state barge.

Thebes, Egypt: to the Egyptians this city was Waset, or the Southern City; to the Greeks it was Diospolis – City of the Gods – or 'Hundred-Gated Thebes'. The modern Luxor, or Karnak.

Thesmophoria: Gk. women's festival in honour of Demeter.

Thesmophoreion: Gk., the Temple of Demeter Thesmophoros.

Thoth: Eg. god of wisdom, learning and writing, portrayed as an ibis-headed man or a baboon; husband and/or brother of Seshat.

trieres, triereis: Gk. war-galley with three banks of oars, equal to the Roman *trireme.*

Tykhe: Gk. goddess of Chance, or Luck. Lat. Fortuna.

Wadjet: The cobra goddess of Egypt. The *ouraios* or *uraeus* cobra is the symbol of sovereignty the Pharaoh wears on his forehead – it is Wadjet rising up in her anger to spit flames in defence of the monarch. Wadjet, or Udjat, is the tutelary goddess of Lower Egypt. Her southern counterpart is Nekhbet the Vulture.

Zeus: Gk., King of the Gods, the father of gods and men. He is the supreme ruler, who controls thunder, lightning and rain, and who upholds justice, law and morals.

Zeus-Ammon: Gk., renowned oracle in the desert of Libya; the modern Siwa.